Books By The Author

Dorothea Orleen Grant, Dorothea O. Grant, or D. O. Grant are: -

Chakras Introduction To The Seven Major Energy Centers.
Enchantment Is Yours – A Journey Of Spirit,
Pathways – Tales For Everyone.
Lily-Butterfly – And The Path Of Life's Experiences – Part 1
Lily-Butterfly – And The Path Of Life's Experiences – Part 2
Lily-Butterfly Journal – Personal Life Story Review
Universal Wellness – A Shaman's View – **Coming in 2021**

CDs are: -
Deep Relaxation
Sacred Activation

LILY-BUTTERFLY

AND THE PATH OF LIFE'S EXPERIENCES PART TWO

D. O. GRANT

BALBOA.PRESS

A DIVISION OF HAY HOUSE

Balboa Press books may be ordered through booksellers or by contacting:

Balboa Press
A Division of Hay House
1663 Liberty Drive
Bloomington, IN 47403
www.balboapress.com
1 (877) 407-4847

Print information available on the last page.

ISBN: 978-1-9822-4994-6 (sc)
ISBN: 978-1-9822-4996-0 (hc)
ISBN: 978-1-9822-4995-3 (e)

Library of Congress Control Number: 2020911273

Balboa Press rev. date: 06/25/2020

This book is recommended for men, women, and teenagers 18 years and older.
Below 18 years old parental supervision is recommended.
I thank you for purchasing this book. Below is my signature of gratitude. I choose to pre-sign this book so that everyone who purchases this book can have a signed copy. May you enjoy, find positive assistance, helpfulness, and awakening from reading this fiction story. Many blessings, love, and peace. D. O. Grant.

Acknowledgement

Much gratitude to Pia G. Pessoa for her line editing
contribution to the creation of this book.

This book is dedicated to every human.
All energies can be useful.
Most things are not like they seem on the surface.
Be aware that with the right view, sometimes
the wrong road and people;
can lead you to the right road and people.
Amin.

Awareness

Fiction Alleged perception.

There is a Creator Force that creates all things, positive or negative. Everything returns to this Creator Force.

Some people might say prove that this Creator Force exist. I will say prove to me that it does not.

Every human is entitled to their opinion and perception.

Positive and negative people have the same original power and will of choice. The sacred process that creates everything gives the same options to everything.

Positive energy frequencies create a certain result. Negative energy frequencies create a certain result. All energies can be useful depending on the intention and perception of the person.

The process of creating something is choice, responsibility, action, practice, many infinite repeat practices, transformation, and then change can occur.

Jealousy can be a deadly weapon. Jealousy can be in connection to seeing someone with something that is desired. The person does not realize that all they must do is, perform the work to have that same thing, or even create something improved.

Sometimes the person you help the most, is the person who has the most potential to hurt you.

Creating love, which includes care and respect, can help you to improve in positive ways. Creating fear, which include not caring and disrespect, can help you to deteriorate in negative ways. Choice is the first step in positive or negative creations. The choices are yours to make.

Introduction

In my style of writing sometimes things might be repetitive or seem repetitive. This is intentional. Also, it gives every character, and the story teller, the freedom of their personal talking expression. Why? Because I classify my stories' purpose as teaching stories, and to assist people by choice in reconnecting to their authentic humanity. Through repeated practice people can improve, learn, and grow, by choice. Plus, different people process in different ways. My story expressions are not Grammarly modern language and speaking perfect. Thank you for choosing to read my stories.

Below is the introduction for LILY-BUTERFLY – And The Path Of Life's Experiences - Part Two, and below part two's introduction is the introduction from part one. This previous introduction can help to refresh your memory as you immerse yourself into the reading of part two. The only additional awareness I will add is that I recommend that part one of this story is read before part two. This way you will get the complete story in continued sequence, from beginning to end. In this part two, Lily-Butterfly moves with her daughter Rebornstar from the island of Kawomaya to the United States of America. Lily-Butterfly continues to follow her internal guided path to find and discover her chosen destiny and life's purpose career. Step by step Lily-Butterfly's talents continue to reveal themselves, and she continued to work on her own personal healing and transformation. As the story unfolds Lily-Butterfly gave birth to another daughter. She was guided in a dream to name this daughter, Holly – like the holly tree. Lily-Butterfly choose not to marry Holly's father. Lily-Butterfly continued her journey onward with two daughters. Later on, in life Lily-Butterfly's Manana Leila (who was her earth mother, grandmother, healer, spirit guide, teacher, and sacred ancestry representative) dies at 99 years old. Guided by a dream and other situations, Lily-Butterfly remarries for the second time, soon after her Manana Leila dies. In the dream Lily-Butterfly was told that this marriage would last about seven years, and it did. Lily-Butterfly's second husband was Greek, and his name was Theo. This was a great, loving, compassionate, caring, rewarding, complete, and fulfilling experience for both Theo and Lily-Butterfly. The separation and divorce between Theo and Lily-Butterfly was created by Theo having to return to Greece to fulfill his karma and destiny. It was a very difficult decision for both of them to end the relationship. This separation and divorce was a test for Theo and Lily-Butterfly. Lily-Butterfly chose not to give up her life's purpose destiny and go with Theo to Greece. Theo decided to stop trying to escape his destiny and return to Greece. This separation and divorce occurred after Lily-Butterfly was deeply rooted in her chosen destiny life's purpose career practice. Ms. Gina, Lily-Butterfly's birth mother died December 24, 2018, the day when D. O. Grant had finish writing part one of LILY-BUTTERFLY – And The Path Of Life's Experiences. You must read this fascinating part two of LILY-BUTTERFLY – And The Path Of Life's Experiences, to see the very interesting things and events, that happened after part one.

A summary of other things that Lily-Butterfly decided to add to her authentic spirit and soul, talents, and skills were: - returning to the University two more times. One time for a Master of Science degree in Hospitality and Tourism Management. The second time Holistic Theology Institute to be certified as a Metaphysician. She entered a monastery for monastic training. Learned how to professionally practice and teach the healing art of Universal Life Force Energy, creating sacred space the ancient way of her ancestors and the disciplined art of Feng Shui, learned the ancient healing art of the Inca Shamans, received certification in the art of a Birth Doula, and also became a non-denominational ordained minister. Lily-Butterfly created a very successful Holistic health care healing arts center. She chooses how she would like to use her awakened talents to continue to help herself and other humans, who choose to be on a spiritual path. It was clear to Lily-Butterfly as she lived her life's experiences that she could not give what she did not have. So, Lily-Butterfly's quest to discover her chosen destiny and life's purpose, she had to first discover and heal herself as much as it was possible, plus learn tools to express herself and her talents from the inside to the outside.

This is a story of a woman's focus, motivation, inspiration, determination, hope, love, compassion, respect, care, and honor. Getting to her spirit and soul chosen life's purpose career took all that Lily-Butterfly had learned along the pathways of her journey. The complete journey, and to maintain the process of spiritual growth to the current day, was accomplished by practicing the following practices of – choice, responsibility, action, practice, infinite continuous and consistent repeat practice, transformation, change, right view, right action, right mindfulness, right speech, right aspiration, right effort, right concentration, diligence, patience, wisdom, generosity, meditation, prayer, morality, trusting herself and others to be who they really are – and not projecting on other people who she wanted them to be, awareness of her boundaries in relationship to other people's boundaries, and consistent right livelihood. This might seem like a very difficult path to choose as a spirit, soul, and human. But, because this was Lily-Butterfly chosen destiny life's purpose and focus, she was completely committed to her spiritual path. This might not be a path for everyone, but useful awareness can be discovered by reading this story that has a wide range of multi-faceted views, awareness, and lessons. Take what you choose to find useful and leave the rest in its sacred place and space. Like a drum's beats the vibrations of the **story** in - **LILY-BUTTERFLY – And The Path Of Life's Experiences – Part One and Two;** can be available each time you choose to read these books. These books give **a summary** of Lily-Butterfly's life experiences and not a complete version of her life.

Lily-Butterfly's professional life's purpose experiences will continue in another book titled *UNIVERSAL WELLNESS – A SHAMAN'S VIEW BY D. O. GRANT.* With the Creator's help and will, this book will be published in 2021. Stay tuned to read and discover more of Lily-Butterfly life's experiences; from A Shaman's view.

INTRODUCTION FROM - LILY-BUTTERFLY – And The Path Of Life's Experiences - Part One.
Is the foundation of everything sexual? Sex is an action and connection between different objects that transforms the past into the present in many ways. Sex can be a symbol of new life, renewed life force energy, and to categorize gender. Without proof, it is said that it takes a sexual connection, a yoking, a joining, an interconnection, an interdependent, and a relationship to create, and destroy everything. And that human's foundation is constructed positive or negative on a platform of sexual creative energies.

Inside the womb, and, or, once humans are born, at least one negative thing is experienced. This experience can be conscious or unconscious. With positive transformation and practicing what is desired, these imprints can be improved. With time the person can experience a rights-of- passage to rebirth and a renewed life. Some people call this "being born again."

Lily-Butterfly's life began from a cocoon of deception. With luck, recognizing, awakening, choices, prayer, responsibility, taking-action attitude, transformation, and purification, Lily-Butterfly walked the path of her life. From a disguised sexual encounter, Lily-Butterfly's mother Gina conceived her. She was the secret her birth mother kept buried deep within her inner being and womb. Lily-Butterfly and Gina were the only ones that carried the secret like a seed carry Universal intelligence. Gina never said a word to anyone about her wordless secret; not even the owner of the sperm that helped to create the chrysalis that lie within the natural protective casing of creation and her womb. From day to day Lily-Butterfly grew within Gina's perception of shame, deception, and denial.

Gina's French stepfather Ivan would be very surprised if he knew what awaits him in the future. Through one act of secret, illicit sexual encounter between himself and his stepdaughter Gina, a girl child was conceived. Gina's mother Nana Leila, love and compassion, will be tested. Will Nana Leila's love and compassion be enough to lighten the burden of the secret within her daughter Gina's womb? Only the Divine Creator knows.

After nine months inside Gina's womb, Lily-Butterfly was born seemingly dead. Dead to Birth. Birth to death. Birth to no one. Lily-Butterfly was abandoned from conception and as she embraced the process of birth, she was also between the wrestling of the process of birth and death. Even within this wall of her mother's disconnection, she hung on to the creation of life. Under the big circle light of a full moon the night had arrived. The pain had arrived as well. Gina's pain was knocking at the door of her nerves and she moaned in secret. The baby had begun the journey of descending and staying connected to life, even when death was lurking close by.

Lily-Butterfly was born by giving birth to herself. Gina wanted Lily-Butterfly out of her body and at the same time did not, because of her perception of shame coming out into revelation. Lily-Butterfly was born of weak bones, physical structure, organs, spine, and no rib cage. The strongest thing she had was her spirit, soul, and light.

At birth Lily-Butterfly heartbeat was silent, no heartbeat. Silent to everyone in the room, except for herself. Everything about Lily-Butterfly was rubbery and weak. Her head had many lumps and bumps from consistently banging her head against the unopened exit from Gina's womb. Her face was deformed, and her two eyes shine out like two bright stars shining through. In addition, Lily-Butterfly had no outer structure of a nose, only two holes on her face where her nose should have been. Abundant rays of light streamed through her blood, spirit, soul, and flesh that kept her alive like a Universal incubator.

Even though Lily-Butterfly was born hanging in between birth and death, she was brought back to life and sculptured into complete form, from head to feet, by her Nana Leila's two hands, love, healing talents, herbs, ancient healing prayer techniques, and a cradle created into the mother earth. Nana Leila saw this almost dead child, looking deeply at her, and the child intuitively told Nana Leila the unspoken secret between her daughter Gina and her husband.

Against all odds Lily-Butterfly survived in her birth mother's womb journey. Nana Leila and the process of life helped her to grown strong and healthy. Gina gave Lily-Butterfly to her mother Nana Leila when she was born. Gina left her mother's home completely when Lily-Butterfly was four months old. Surrounded by nature and love, Lily-Butterfly grew from birth to about four years old living with her grandmother thinking it was her mother. At about four years old Gina brought another daughter she had name Lucy to her mother Nana Leila to keep. When Gina came with Lucy Nana Leila told Lily-Butterfly that Gina was her birth mother, and that she was her earth mother, guardian, guide, and caretaker.

At 6 years old Lily-Butterfly was re-united to live with her birth mother Gina. Lily-Butterfly lived with her birth mother Gina until she graduated college. Lily-Butterfly's physical presence was a constant reminder to Gina of the secret she worked very hard to keep buried. With Gina's efforts to deal with her perceived secret, she tried to destroy Lily-Butterfly spiritually, mentally, emotionally, physically, her health, well-being, and in every way. Lily-Butterfly's strength of spirit and soul kept her in harmony and balance. Lily-Butterfly confronted her birth mother to completely stop the abuse at eighteen years old. She learned and awaken the skills and tools from within herself to make choices, take responsibility, be wise, stay in positive harmony and balance, be self-reliant and inspired, motivated, and to ask for help when it was necessary.

As Lily-Butterfly grew she cultivated and nurtured the passion for learning, reading, and writing. This gave her a positive outlet from her negative experiences. Some of the tools Lily-Butterfly discovered that helped her were:- asking the Creator for help, doing self-treatments of positive Universal life force energy, praying, practicing peace mindfulness kindness meditation, focus on education, reading, journaling, writing, learning, facing her negative experiences and emotions instead of trying to hide and disconnect from them, working out her problems as soon as possible instead of hiding from them or filing them away inside her to create an endless pit of darkness, facing her fears, knowing that trust was about her trusting herself, taking, responsibility, and time to get to know people, that people will always be who they are, not make people out to be what she wanted them to be, wait and with time people will show the other sides of them self, that people have many faces, that there are positive and kind people, that there are negative and mean people, there are people that can be positive and negative at the same time, stay connected to joy, peace, and love. She learned that there was beauty and confidence in simplicity, learned self-reliance, help herself as much as possible and when in need ask for help, and that all energies can be useful.

Read this novel to see Lily-Butterfly's experiences. Learn about all the alternative solution she created for emancipating, surviving, transforming, and transcending all her negative life's experiences.

Lily-Butterfly – And the Path of Life's Experiences can provide awareness insights for, healing, empowerment, unconditional love, compassion, inspiration, motivation, awaken, evolving, courage, kindness, and optimism.

No part or character in this story is more important than the other. Take from this story what you like and leave the rest undisturbed. Awareness, while reading all of D. O. Grant's books, to get the most out of the information shared, try to: - keep an open mind, step beyond your modern rational people thinking views and ego, read with renewed eyes and views, transcend people created alphabet and *grammar rules, and that the messages in the story is the bottom-line view. Awaken to realize that the stories and information shared by D. O. Grant is a work of rare elegance, artistic creation, a form and style of ancient story telling that emanate rich detail, feeling, and imagination. A style and form that might have become extinct, because of many modern human created reasons. With respect, come to realize that some artistic creations are just the way they are, and that they do not have to be like the way you think they should be. Remember this is a work of fiction and a work of art.*

*Artistic creations must be free to **Be Artistic Creations**.* ***Thank you.***

Step outside your normal human perception. Respect and Enjoy!

1

There are no accidents. Everything is for a positive, and, or, negative reason. The awakening of a human's spirit and soul is a very gradual process of growth through; choice, responsibility, action, practice, infinite repeat practice, transformation, and change. This process can be like when an oak tree seed is planted. An oak tree must wait approximately fifty years or more before it grows acorns consistently. And each acorn can take up to eighteen months to mature. Everything in human life is a process and journey; as well. Some books and stories can be like Universal drum beats.

Lily-Butterfly life's journey took her from the small remote village of Yaj, in a valley on the island of Kawomaya to Somerville, Massachusetts, in the United States of America. Rebornstar, Lily-Butterfly's daughter was with her as consistent company, student, and teacher. Both Rebornstar and Lily-Butterfly was in Manana Leila's living room sleeping on her couch, resting, and transitioning from their life changing journey from the island. Lily-Butterfly still had her open palms on her face. Before falling into a deep intoxicating sleep Lily-Butterfly prayed, expressed gratitude, and appreciation for everything.

At 7:00 PM Lily-Butterfly woke up. She telephones her Manana Leila and told her that she had arrived. After talking on the telephone, she brought all the suitcases into the bedroom. Ten minutes later Rebornstar woke up. They made dinner together and ate. When dinner was completed, they cleaned up the kitchen and dining room, organized their clothes in the closet and drawers, and took showers. Before Rebornstar went to sleep Lily-Butterfly told her a bed-time story. A re-cycled story that was repeatedly told to Lily-Butterfly by Manana Leila when she was a child. Rebornstar went to sleep in Manana Leila's bed. Lily-Butterfly chose the pull-out couch in the living room as her bed. She dressed up the pull-out couch and pillow, with clean sheets and pillowcase. Lily-Butterfly wrote in her journal and laid down. Tiredness from the day's journey and her current life's experiences percolated within her whole body. Lily-Butterfly prayed and reflected on her life's story. Gradually sleep arrived and transported her to dream land.

Lily-Butterfly had a dream in which a five feet cricket with a lamp came up to her, while she slept. The cricket said, "well done. Stay strong and aware. Stay free and be wise. You have transitioned to the next level and foundation of awakening to remember, your chosen destiny. You are not alone." As if awake in her dream Lilly-Butterfly smiled at what the cricket said.

The next morning Rebornstar and Lily-Butterfly woke up feeling more refreshed from their night's sleep. They had breakfast, cleaned up the kitchen, and the rest of the apartment. When this was completed Lily-Butterfly wrote her dream in her journal. They both got dressed and left the apartment. Lily-Butterfly took Rebornstar to the park. Next, they visited some stores and had lunch at a restaurant. Before Lily-Butterfly returned to the apartment she bought a newspaper. Arriving back at the apartment Lily-Butterfly looked through the classified section for a job, and Rebornstar took a nap. This day continued with Lily-Butterfly usual activities, including dinner, showers, story time, journal, prayer, reflecting, contemplating, going to sleep, and waking up to a new sunrise and day.

The first thing Lily-Butterfly did after breakfast and clean up, was to telephone the Immigration Lawyer to schedule an appointment to file for her and Rebornstar permanent resident visa application. For the rest of this day and week, Lily-Butterfly and Rebornstar visited in the town of Somerville, parks, shopping plazas, and restaurants. They also took the bus and train to downtown Boston and Harvard Square. On Saturday morning Manana Leila came home to her apartment. They went with Manana clothes and food shopping, attended church, went to the park, and visited Manana's half-brother and his family, who lived about three miles away in the same town. At 6:00 AM on Monday morning Manana Leila traveled back to her full-time work. At 9:30 AM on this Monday morning Lily-Butterfly took Rebornstar with her to go to the Immigration Lawyer. Lily-Butterfly got all the information and documents she needed to file for her permanent resident visa application process.

Lily-Butterfly completed all the visa application. The following weekend when Manana Leila came home, Lily-Butterfly asked her to fill out the section that she was responsible for and sign the documents. Manana Leila gave Lily-Butterfly all the relevant documents that she needed to accompany the visa application. The following Monday

Lily-Butterfly returned to the Lawyer with everything she needed for the visa application process. The Lawyer took the application and documents and did the visa filing process. Within one month the Lawyer contacted Lily-Butterfly to tell her that the permanent resident visa application was accepted by the Immigration and Naturalization Services, and she would be receiving a work permit within two months.

While Lily-Butterfly waited for the work permit she continued to look for a job in the classified section of the newspaper, do research on all her options for work, and reflected on how Rebornstar would fit into her work plans. Rebornstar was four and a half years old. She did not have the money to send her to preschool, and she might be working away from the town where she lived. During this time Lily-Butterfly also thought of returning to college or university to further her education.

Lily-Butterfly waited for the work permit, researched all her options, searched for work, research about further educational studies, prayed to be guided to the best choices and action, and reflected on her life from birth to the present time. Lily-Butterfly decided that until Rebornstar became of age to attend public school, taking a full-time live-in nanny childcare job that she could have Rebornstar live with her, was the best option. From Lily-Butterfly's research she found out that she could not work in an office administrating job, because she did not have advance computer skills.

Lily-Butterfly focused her prayer on being guided to finding the best opportunity for a full-time live-in nanny childcare job opportunity. In addition to Lily-Butterfly's everyday activities, she surrendered into every moment of her intention and heart's desires, prayed, weeded through all the nanny childcare job advertisements, took action, prepared, and read books. With contentment Lily-Butterfly grounded into the perception of her intention and new life's journey.

2

There is no secret in this Universe. The spirit of every human, records ***everything*** *known and unknown. The spirit's records as a program and system is called the soul records, and, or Akashic records. The mind is the container of the spirit's information and navigational system. The body is the home of the spirit. Everything is energy and energy is everything. The spirit is like an individual intelligent energy computer or machine. The spirit of every human is interconnected to every other spirit in its energy level vibration. Every human is responsible for the role they perform in all their experiences. Lily-Butterfly knows this and chooses to communicate in a direct, focused, and compassionate manner, that some people might find abrupt. Lily-Butterfly chooses mindfully how she participate in the things and people she attracts. She looks below the surface of things, because most things are not like they seem. Lily-Butterfly knows that not everything she attracts is necessarily positive, useful, and that everything is for a positive and, or negative reason. Based on the karma guidelines of free will, it is the individual's responsibility to release things perceived not for their greater good. Choice is one of the powers of every human creation. When choice is not used by an individual, they resort to complain, victim, and blaming.*

The second week in August the work permit arrived for Lily-Butterfly. The first week in September Lily-Butterfly saw a job for live-in nanny childcare that appealed to her intention. The job was for taking care of two children. Lily-Butterfly called the telephone number in the newspaper. She talked to the woman Susan who answered the telephone. Lily-Butterfly informed Susan that she had a four and a half years old daughter that would attend the interview with her, if they gave her the job her daughter would have to live with her as well, and be a part of the job agreement and arrangement. Susan informed Lily-Butterfly that she and her husband were both Lawyers, and that her husband Jeff would be present at the interview. The telephone call was like a mini interview where things that they both needed to consider was expressed. Susan promised to take Lily-Butterfly's daughter living with her into consideration.

The appointment was scheduled for an interview. Susan gave Lily-Butterfly her home address.

Lily-Butterfly researched how she would get to Susan's home which was in Newton, Massachusetts. Her journey to Susan was, taking the bus from Manana Leila's apartment to the nearest train station. This train would take her to downtown Boston where she would change trains to go to Newton Center. From Newton Center she would take a taxi to Susan and Jeff's home. Manana Leila worked in Newton as well.

Until the day of the appointment arrive Lily-Butterfly prayed to the Creator for a positive outcome of the nanny childcare job, guidance into making the best decision about this job opportunity, create a home school program for teaching Rebornstar until she was ready to attend kindergarten in public school, how she would manage taking care of Rebornstar at work without conflict of interest, and writing about all of these plans and awareness in her journal.

Monday, the day of the interview arrived Lily-Butterfly and Rebornstar got dressed and left Manana Leila's apartment, for the unknown journey to the interview. They took the bus to the train, changed trains in downtown Boston, and arrived at Newton Center. They took the taxi from Newton Center to the address given to her by Susan. As the taxi drove along Lily-Butterfly was amazed at the vastness of the homes. They look like castles. Lily-Butterfly arrived at Jeff and Susan's home fifteen minutes early. Lily-Butterfly paid the taxi driver, got out of the car, and rang the house doorbell.

"This is the biggest house I have seen so far. I look like a large castle," mumbled Lily-Butterfly.

The door opened and Susan and Jeff were standing inside the doorway. They greeted one another.

"Welcome Lily-Butterfly and Rebornstar. It is nice to see you," said Susan. "Come in."

Lily-Butterfly and Rebornstar entered the home. The first room they entered was the kitchen.

"Come this way. Over here. We are going to the office. The children are in the playroom next to the office. Follow me," instructed Susan.

Lily-Butterfly, Rebornstar, and Jeff, followed Susan. They arrived at the large office. There was a large table with eight chairs. They each sat down on the chairs where there were four empty glasses, and a large jug of water.

Jeff spoke first. "The children are next door in the playroom. Josh is three years old and Sue is two months old. We are Lawyers and we work together. We have a law firm just the two of us and an Office Manager. Sometimes we work from home. We do not have the best parent skills. We would like to hire someone that can take complete responsibility for taking care of the children Mondays to Saturdays – 8:00 AM to 7:00 PM, off every Sunday, and off every other Saturday as well. So, two complete weekends off per month and every Sunday off per month. You would receive ten vacation days off per year. Do you have a permanent resident visa or work permit? Here is an application for you to fill out. Is it okay for me to take your daughter to the nursery to play with Josh? She does not need to be a part of this interview."

"Yes. Rebornstar can go play with Josh. Thank you. I have a work permit, and I have filed my application for a permanent resident visa."

"Okay. Please fill out this application I will be back. I am going to check on the children," said Jeff.

Jeff left the room. Susan sat looking at Lily-Butterfly. Lily-Butterfly filled out the application. When she was finish, she gave the application to Susan. Jeff returned.

"The baby is sleeping, Josh, and Rebornstar are playing with toys while they watch cartoons," said Jeff.

Susan read the application and gave it to Jeff.

With a twinkle in her eyes Susan said, "Lily-Butterfly you are overqualified for his job, and you will not stay. You can find a job in an office as an Administrative Assistant or Office Manager. Do you have any professional childcare and housekeeping experiences?"

"I have housekeeping and child care experiences working on a small family farm until six years old, working in a housekeeping capacity for a lady on the island of Kawomaya, from a young age taking care of one sister, and two brothers, and my personal experiences taking care of my own home and daughter. I think I am overqualified in childcare and housekeeping experiences as well. Currently, I choose this kind of job, because of the well-being of my daughter and not having advance computer skills. If I decide to take this job and you choose to hire me, you will both see the exceptional quality of my work."

Jeff remained silent and observant.

"As Jeff said the workdays are long, 8:00 AM to 7:00 PM. You will have Sue two months old, Josh three years old, and your daughter four and a half years old to manage and take care of. Do you think that you can really manage all these children, cook, for them, light housekeeping, and everything else? Light housekeeping means do everything for the children from 8:00 AM to 7:00 PM, cook, laundry, tidy their rooms, clean up after them, and organize all their rooms – nursery - playrooms. Plus, take them to the park, read them stories, play with them, give them each a bath before bed, and so forth. Basically, you are being hired as a paid parent. We come home from work at about 7:00 to 7:30 PM. At least one of us will be home by 7:00 PM. When we get home the children should be in their rooms and prepared for sleep. We will spend time with the children before work and when you are off from work. Unless we choose to do otherwise. We are asking you to commit to staying at least two years minimum. The pay for living here and taking care of two children is $800 per week. But because you are going to bring your daughter to live here, we are going to subtract from this $800, rent and food for her. We will pay you only $350 per week. Daily you and your daughter can eat all you like, and make our house your home. Lily-Butterfly do you understand?" said Susan.

"Yes, I understand. Yes, I can manage the three children and everything the job requires, and more. I would like to be paid $450 per week. This is a big job and very large house to navigate. The quality of the job I am going to have to perform is worth the $800 per week even with having my daughter being with me. I can see and sense the stress of this job, being here, and taking care of the two children. My daughter Rebornstar will not be an issue. She is already trained, I will create a plan to manage her outside my time with your children, and I will spend quality time with her before and after work; just like going to regular job. I think my biggest issue will be both of you. I do not know directly how or why. But my intuition is telling me this. I am not afraid of work. Do you both understand me?"

"I see. We must think about the counteroffer of $450 per week. Five people from a cleaning company come in twice per week to get the complete house clean. They clean half on Wednesdays and return to do the other half on Fridays. We do all the food shopping. Susan's parents own a chain of department stores. Sometimes they come to spend the weekend and vacation here. If they are here during the time they are here, you will have to work around them. We truly suck as being parents. You will see. Therefore, having the right person for this job is important. We love our children, but are not equipped with parental skills. Okay?" said Jeff.

Lily-Butterfly said, "I hear what you are both saying. There must be a second interview. There will be a lot for me to process before saying yes to taking this job."

"I agree," replied Susan. "Same for us."

Lily-Butterfly replied, "where is the current Nanny? What date would I start working? Can I have a tour of the house before I leave today? I need to take this into consideration as well. Are there any food restriction for the children? What is the living accommodation for Rebornstar and I?"

Susan replied, "the last Nanny quit without notice. She was overwhelmed by everything. This is a very responsible job. It can be difficult and requires a lot of patience and compassion; I mean understanding. Yes, we will give you a quick tour of the house. The children do not have any food allergies or restrictions. At your second interview you can take another look at the complete house. It is getting late and the baby might wake up. You and Rebornstar will live in a two bedroom apartment on the other side of the house. This section of the house has a two bedroom, living room, dining room, kitchen, and bathroom. This apartment is completely furnished with everything you will need, everything. You would start working next week Monday to Saturday. Have Sunday off. We need a break. Since the last Nanny quit, we have been taking care of the children ourselves. We have no patience for parenthood and children stuff. We really suck in every way at parenting our children. We love our children and want to have them. But we are not interested in the messy parts of parenting. We are not born for parenting detail activities. We say this to give you the right view on how responsible this job will be. Lily-Butterfly do you have any further comments or questions? I must go make lunch for the children, before Sue wakes up and starts screaming. She is a screamer. Her screaming makes me feel crazy. My husband will take you on the house tour. Come back on Thursday of this week for the second interview, 10:00 AM should be good. Okay."

"Okay. There will be a lot for me to think about and digest. Mr. Jeff let us go on the tour."

"Okay Lily-Butterfly let us go," said Jeff.

"Thank you. I will be in the kitchen. Lily-Butterfly I will see you before you leave," said Susan.

Two and a half hours had gone by and the glasses and jug were empty of water.

With Jeff leading the way, the house tour began downstairs in the pool room on the right side of the house. This room was the full length of this side of the house. A large rectangular pool was in the center of the room, lounge chairs, kitchen, a bar, and three bathrooms with tubs, two toilet rooms, and showers. This section of the house also had a steam room, gym, sauna, game room, theatre, pool table, and slot machines. In this section all the entrance doors were always locked, and the keys kept in a box high up on the wall. Next, they went to the guest room area. There was a completely furnished guest two bedroom apartment, which included a kitchen, dining room, living room, and large bathroom. The large office with a nursery inside Lily-Butterfly had already seen. It was the room they had the meeting in. Next to this office was the large nursery and playroom. Next there was a large formal dining room with a large dining table with twelve chairs. Beside this room was a small kitchen, a living room, and a half bathroom, with toilet and hand washing sink. There was a 1,200 square feet kitchen with a dining area within. This was at the back entrance of the house. A mud room was outside the kitchen entrance. On entering the house from the outside the mudroom was the first room. This entrance was used as the main entrance by everyone daily. In a large circular driveway, two luxury cars were parked outside this entrance and exit. There was also a five-car garage, standalone building on the opposite side of the circular driveway. A children's playground equipped with a jungle gym, two slides, three swings, and a tree house. This playground was on the right side of the garage.

In the basement was a very large laundry room with three washers and three dryers, a large food pantry, a room with two extra freezers and two extra refrigerators, a storage room for household equipment, wine cellar, and a large two bedroom apartment with no furniture. Last, they went to the third floor of the house where their bedrooms and the nanny's living quarters were. Going up two flight of stairs the first section on the left, was a door. Beyond the door was a hallway to the nanny's apartment. To the right was a hallway that lead to five bedrooms. The first two bedrooms were for Sue and Josh. Inside their bedrooms were bathrooms and large closets. Across the hallway from the children's room was a large playroom with toys and a linen closet. Next, the hallway continued, and at the end was a large wooden door that separated the children's area from the rest of the floor. Opening this door and entering this area was three bedrooms. The largest room was the master bedroom. It was in the very extreme end of this section. Inside the master bedroom were two large bathrooms with tubs, and two walk-in closets. On each side of the master bedroom was two other bedrooms and a furnished living room, with leather couches and other furniture. One bedroom was used as an extra closet. The other bedroom was filled with clothes from the floor to almost the ceiling. Lily-Butterfly inquired about the room filled with clothes from floor to ceiling. Jeff told her that they were dirty clothes they did not have time to wash, they were good clothes, they did not want to throw such good clothes away, over the many years the dirty clothes pile up, when they ran out of clothes they would just go buy more clothes, and they did not want to pay someone to wash so much dirty clothes. The cleaning company that cleans the house does not have a laundry service.

After seeing Jeff and Susan's bedroom section of the house Lily-Butterfly felt totally drained and exhausted. They went back downstairs to the kitchen.

"Please, can I have a glass of water and a lemon?" asked Lily-Butterfly.

"Sure. Help yourself," replied Susan.

Susan was feeding the baby milk from a bottle and Josh was eating his lunch. Lily-Butterfly made some lemon with water. She drank some and gave some to Rebornstar.

Lily-Butterfly said, "Susan and Jeff I am leaving now. I will process this interview. If I choose to not return for the second interview on Thursday, I will telephone you."

"We will process this interview. If we change our minds about you coming to work for us, we will call you to cancel the appointment, and inform you about our decision," said Jeff.

"Yes," said Susan.

"Thank you for today's interview. Can I use your telephone to call the taxi?"

"Yes. Sure," replied Susan.

Lily-Butterfly called the taxi.

"Bye and thanks again," said Lily-Butterfly.

"Thank you. You are welcome. Bye," said Jeff and Susan.

Lily-Butterfly and Rebornstar went outside to wait for the taxi. The taxi came and took them to Newton Center train station. They had lunch at a restaurant before taking the train. After lunch Lily-Butterfly and Rebornstar journeyed back to Manana Leila's apartment in Somerville. By the time they had arrived home it was 5:00 PM.

Monday night, Tuesday, and Wednesday Lily-Butterfly processed her interview experiences, telephoned Manana Leila to seek guidance and second opinion about the job, journaled, prayed, wrote down the positives and negatives about the job, and the possible consequences of this nanny childcare job. The processing made her feel extra drained and thirsty. By Wednesday night Lily-Butterfly had decided to return for the second interview on Thursday.

Lily-Butterfly's last thought before she fell asleep on Wednesday night was, I need to work, this seems like the path I must take for whatever reason, the job will not be easy at first, sink or swim, this is the way, and the way will show the way. This job also supports the wellbeing of Rebornstar. This is the most important reason to take this job.

Lost in her contemplation Lily-Butterfly drifted off to sleep, like a dry leaf on a slanted river.

3

One road lead to another. Most times the destination cannot be visible until you get to it. Sometimes when things do not seem to make sense is when it makes the most sense. Seeing beyond the surface takes courage, choice, responsibility, action, readiness, and so on.

On Thursday morning Lily-Butterfly and Rebornstar returned to Jeff and Susan's house. Jeff, Susan, and Lily-Butterfly sat in the same room as before. Rebornstar went to play with Josh, and Sue was sleeping in her crib.

Jeff spoke first, "Lily-Butterfly we have decided to give you the job if you choose to take it."

"Yeah. Lily-Butterfly, what have you decided?" said Susan.

"I have decided to take the job. Thank you."

"You will start working on Monday. We have decided to pay you $500 instead of the $450 you requested per week. I suggest that you come back here on Saturday at 3:00 PM to move in, clean the apartment how you would like it, organize your things, and yourselves into your apartment. This way you are ready to start work on Monday morning at 8:00 AM. Bring all your clothes and things that you will both need for next week. Gradually you can bring more of your things here, and so, on and so, forth. We would really like to have you come take care of our children. I called all your references and the Personnel Director of your last job on the island of Kawomaya. They said great things about you. We are lucky to have you work for us. Have you decided to commit to minimum two years working here?" said Susan.

"Yes. I will commit to only two years. After two years I will be returning to the University and my daughter will be going to kindergarten in public school. Thank you for deciding to pay me $500 per week. As time goes on you will see that my efficiency and the quality of my work is worth over $800 per week. Anyway, please explain to me again my work responsibilities, time of work, living in arrangements for my daughter and myself, food situation, and all the other things I should be aware of," said Lily-Butterfly.

Jeff and Susan explained everything as Lily-Butterfly requested.

After this conversation and everyone was satisfied Lily-Butterfly was given tax information to fill out.

"Please fill out this tax and paycheck information. You will receive your paycheck every Friday, starting next week Friday. On Saturday mornings you can go to Newton Center to cash your check. The account connected to your paycheck is at this bank. You can also open an account at this bank, or whatever bank you like," said Jeff.

"Thank you for the bank information. Here are the forms I have filled out. Can I meet the children today?" said Lily-Butterfly.

"Sure. Sue is sleeping. Come into the playroom next door. You can look at her and see Josh," said Jeff.

Jeff, Susan, and Lily-Butterfly went to see the children. Jeff and Susan talked to Rebornstar. When the adults were finished with the children introduction, they all went back to the meeting room.

"Lily-Butterfly, what do you think so far? Do you have any more questions or comments?" asked Jeff.

"Jeff and Susan, this job will take lots of love, kindness, care, and passion about taking care of children, multitasking, patience, managerial skills, and dedication. Plus, every skill you can think of, and not think of, is needed for this job. I will also let you know that things here are more than they seem on the surface. As time goes on the things will reveal themselves to me. I will work with these things as they reveal themselves. I will try my best to keep my two years promise and commitment no matter what happens. Thank you very much for agreeing to have my daughter come live here with me as a part of this arrangement. I really appreciate this. Thank you very much for everything else. I will surely learn to practice all my talents from working here. I will do my best," said Lily-Butterfly.

"Thank you too. You are welcome. You come highly recommended, as a professional, trustworthy, dependable, self-motivated, integrity, direct, focus, organized, and everything else that is positive. You are more than nanny qualified and we are lucky to have you. Our only concern is that because you are overqualified for this job, you might not stay when you experience all the difficulties of this job. Working here can be overwhelming and exhausting. This is our home and children and we feel crazy from being here. You will see what I am talking about," said Susan.

"I already have a sense of what you are talking about. My experiences will give me the reality of this job and living here. I promise to stay here for maximum two years. My words and promise are my bond of commitment. We have met for many reasons. As time goes on and to the end of two years, we will see the benefits and reasons of this connection. Okay. Time will tell. Until then let us have positive faith and hope for the best," said Lily-Butterfly.

"Lily-Butterfly, you seem spiritual," said Susan.

"Yes, I am spiritual. And the Creator is my shepherd, guardian, guide, and teacher. Okay."

"I see," replied Susan.

"I noticed a very stinky smell upstairs by the children's room, in your section of the upstairs, and when I opened the refrigerator to get a lemon. Where are these smells coming from?" said Lily-Butterfly.

"I think it is the dirty diapers in the garbage can. We do not empty the diaper garbage can until it cannot fit anymore diapers. Plus, the room of dirty clothes smells. We are like slobs and we do not mind stank, musty, and stinky smells. You can fix the stinky smells if you do not like them. Do whatever you like within this house to feel comfortable and at home. We also welcome positive changes. This is good for the children. The refrigerator has left over food from only God he knows when. The fridge has not been cleaned since we bought it ten years ago. The cleaning company does not do laundry, clean inside refrigerators, and empty garbage cans. And like I said we do not mind the mess, stinky smells, dirt, and so forth," said Susan.

"Okay. I see. Same situation with your luxury cars. There is milk stains, ketchup, mustard, other dirt, and food on the glass. Plus, garbage and clutter piled up inside. I do not have to be nosey to see this situation. Why do I mention these things? I am going to be here as you have said as a paid parent for the children, everything both of you do, and do not do, affects the children. So, I recommend that you both consider taking your cars to the car detailed place to get cleaned inside and outside. One thing can affect the other thing. Everything is connected. Your actions as parents affects your children's psychological health, mental health, well-being, stability, contentment, happiness, and so on. Mr. Jeff and Mrs. Susan, do you understand what I am trying to say? The things that you might find negative about me is my directness, no-nonsense attitude – which might make me seem abrupt, and my awareness on Holistic views. Everything is connected. And one thing affects the other things, and so forth," said Lily-Butterfly.

"We understand. Therefore, we choose you. We and our children need straightening out. We will try our best to transform our negative ways, attitude, and actions. On Saturday we will take both cars to the car cleaners and take out all the clutter out of the car, put the things in garbage bags, and put them in the basement. Thank you for everything," said Jeff.

"I agree with everything you say Lilly-Butterfly. I will do my best with maintaining the positive vibes that you bring here to share with us. We will try to appreciate and maintain what we can," said Susan.

"Thank you for your support and permission to do whatever it will take to get my job done, and to feel comfortable living here. This way my commitment of working here for two years is more possible. Is there anything else I should know?" said Lily-Butterfly.

"Sue fusses a lot and she likes to scream. She seems miserable if she is awake. Josh has gotten use to us over the years and he is nervous. Josh plays alone a lot. We do not like to entertain our children in any way or play with them. We love to entertain ourselves with food, wine, and other things. We are not the skinny and eat healthy type. Please leave me a grocery shopping list every Friday of foods you would like us to buy for you, and the children. If there is anything else to tell one another we can do so as the days go on. Hmm. Um. Is there anything else? I must go prepare the children's lunch. If I do not give Sue her bottle the minute, she opens her eyes she will scream until I do. Her screaming drives me crazy," said Susan.

"No, for now, I do not have anything else to say," reply Lily-Butterfly. "Oh, I almost forgot to ask both of you to open all the windows in this house between now and Saturday, to let in fresh air. The oxygen in this house is nonexistent and stagnant. I can hardly breathe. I am used to breathing fresh air and this is good for the children's health and well-being. I do not like stressful environment. I think that is it for now. Okay."

"Thank you. We will open all the windows on one floor, each day. You are right. We need this straightening out. All the things you have said and not said is part of why Nannies get overwhelmed and quit. In three years, we have had seven Nannies quit without notice. Oh my. They did not have what it takes to show us what was needed. Thanks very much. Keep being direct with us, some things we just do not know. We look forward to seeing you return on Saturday," said Jeff.

"Yes. I cannot wait. I feel so stressed and overwhelmed. This is our life and children and we cannot quit and run away. We cannot wait for you to take over the responsibility of the children; more for their sake. See you and your daughter on Saturday at 3:00 PM," said Susan.

"Okay. Jeff and Susan, I understand. Can I use the telephone to call the taxi?"

"Sure. Use the telephone whenever you like. Our home is now your home, for as long as you are here, and choose to stay. We welcome you and your daughter with open arms," said Susan.

Lily-Butterfly used the telephone to call the taxi.

"Bye Jeff and Susan. Rebornstar and I are going outside to wait for the taxi. We will see you on Saturday at 3:00 PM. Hang in there," said Lily-Butterfly.

"Bye. And thanks again. See you both soon," replied Jeff and Susan.

When Lily-Butterfly got back to the apartment she telephoned Manana Leila to tell her about taking the job, that she would be leaving on Saturday to go back to the house, and all the other details. They planned about seeing each other on the weekends. Manana Leila also told Lily-Butterfly that her pay arrangement was great, because she is getting fifty dollars per week from 1972 to the present time. For this pay Manana Leila lived in the house, took care of six children over the years, and did housekeeping as well. No pay raise since 1972. She makes fifty cents per hour and sometimes less depending on how many hours she worked per day. And Manana Leila always had money to share with Lily-Butterfly, Ms. Gina, and the other people. Manana Leila never said no to financially helping when asked or not. Her Social Security payments subsidize her pay. This for Manana Leila was like working for free with an allowance. And Manana Leila was grateful for everything.

Thursday night before Lily-Butterfly went to sleep she wrote in her journal the story of her job interview experience and she prayed as usual.

Lily-Butterfly prayed, "Creator thank you for everything that was done to assist with my job searching and finding the job situation that is best for me at this time. I can already see that this is another school experience on my spirit and soul journey to awaken and practice my talents. How exactly are my experiences going to show up? As usual, only time will tell. I must continue to remind myself that, by choice, what does not kill me can possibly make me stronger. The way will show the way. One road leads to another. This spirit and soul journey of awakening and growth is not an easy quest. Please

16

continue to remember me in your busy and multidimensional infinite work schedule. Amin."

That weekend Manana Leila came home to her apartment. Saturday, they had a great time enjoying breakfast and lunch together. All the things Lily-Butterfly had decided to take with her was gathered by the front door of the apartment. They said goodbye to Manana Leila and left. At 1:35 PM Lily-Butterfly and Rebornstar took a taxi from Manana Leila's apartment straight to Jeff and Susan's home.

4

Stepping into the unknown can be uneasy. Surrendering and taking a leap of faith can be a very uneasy feeling as well. Why do I write in detailed fashion? My writing style can assist with expressing imagination, visualization, exercise the human – mind, emotions, improve brain function, and thinking abilities, take people to places out of their normal human perception, create a visual of the events in the story, teach patience, and this is the way my ancient ancestors told stories in the valley and village of Yaj, on the island of Kawomaya. At the time of my ancestors' ancient story telling days, oral tradition was the way people teach and learn. My ancient ancestors had no books, television, electricity, radios, and so forth. So, the more expressive the story, the more the person could visualize the events of the story and bring things alive to every person's visual perception and projection. Plus, storytelling and listening could be used as a healing tool. The tempo of the story can be like a dance, tango, rattle, drum beat, and, or any other primal tempo. Decide how this style may work for you or not.

At 3:15 PM Lily-Butterfly and Rebornstar arrived at Jeff and Susan's house. Lily-Butterfly paid the taxi driver. He helped her to bring all the things to the door. She presses the doorbell. Susan came to unlock and open the door.

"Hi Lily-Butterfly and Rebornstar. How are you doing? Welcome," said Susan.

"We are doing great. Thank you for having us," replied Lily-Butterfly.

Lily-Butterfly and Rebornstar entered the room carrying their things and pulling their suitcases. Jeff came over to Lily-Butterfly.

"Hi, do you need help?" said Jeff.

"No, thank you. We can manage," replied Lily-Butterfly.

"Here is a set of keys for the house. On top of the counter by the telephone is a large notebook. I have written some things in it that can be useful to help you with your job responsibilities. There are directions to the park, library, and other places in walking distance. In this notebook you can write notes to us and use it however way you choose. I forgot to tell you that at 10:00 PM each night we set the security alarm. This alarm is connected to all the windows and doors, so be mindful to not open them after 10:00 PM. If you plan to be out later than 10:00 PM let us know and we will set the alarm after you come in. You are welcome to take any food that you like for you and your daughter. You can even cook upstairs in your apartment. You have a full equipped kitchen and apartment. Okay that is it for now. Let us know if you need help with anything. Go set up yourselves in the apartment. Thank you for coming. Come and go as you wish. Rebornstar is free to use the playground outside and so forth. We are very happy that both of you are here. Thanks. We might sound over appreciative and thankful. It is because we are truly happy, feel lucky, and blessed that you choose to come and work with us. Okay," said Susan.

"Okay Susan. Thank you for everything. We are also completely appreciative for the opportunity to be here. We will go up to the apartment now."

Lily-Butterfly and Rebornstar went up to the apartment. They organized and set up everything. At 5:00 PM Lily-Butterfly went down to the kitchen to see what was available for her to cook for dinner. She found some food items for dinner and breakfast and brought them upstairs to the apartment kitchen and made dinner for herself and Rebornstar. After dinner, cleaning up the kitchen and dining room, they took showers. Lily-Butterfly read a book for Rebornstar, and at the same time showed her how to read and pronounce words for herself. After story time Rebornstar had a choice of another activity she wanted to do for an hour before she went to sleep.

"Rebornstar every morning I will set the alarm for you to get up at 8:00 AM. Turn off the alarm, get dress, and brush your teeth. I will return to let you know when it is time to come downstairs for breakfast. You will eat breakfast with Josh. Come over here I will show you how to turn off the clock alarm."

"Okay mama."

"Sunday after breakfast we will leave and go look for the park and visit other places in walking distance. We will have time to walk to Newton Center and have lunch there. We need the exercise. Walking is good for us. When it is time to go back to Manama's apartment, we can walk to the train station in Newton Center instead of taking the taxi. Okay."

"Yes mama. Okay. Being here is like a new story and adventure."

"Exactly Rebornstar. We will experience and see the adventure of being here and how this story ends. Good night."

"Good night mama. Sweet dreams."

Lily-Butterfly finish talking to Rebornstar and went to her bedroom.

Lily-Butterfly stood in her bedroom by the window and looked outside into the flower garden. She thought, my life is like a garden and I am the gardener. Being here in this house and job is like new seeds I choose to plant in the garden of my life. I must be mindful and choose skillfully how I manage my experiences, in this renewed garden of life's experiences. At the end of this part of my journey, I will see all the reasons for choosing to be here. Life is primarily a classroom of swimming or sinking in the ocean of life. I am tired. It is time for me to write in my journal to empty my thoughts and talk to the Creator in prayer before I go to sleep.

Lily-Butterfly fell asleep as soon as her head rested on the bed. She decided to not use the pillow that everyone used in the past. Next time she went home she would buy a new pillow and bring it with her. At 10:30 PM Lily-Butterfly and Rebornstar were asleep. At 4:30 AM Lily-Butterfly was awakened by the crying and screaming of Josh and Sue. She looked at the clock and decided to ignore the situation. There was a sound of someone banging on a door. The screaming and crying continued as well. At 5:00 AM the children were still screaming and crying. The banging of the door continued as well. Lily-Butterfly thought, what is going on. My work does not start until Monday. If I were not here the situation would be as it is. But I cannot hear the screaming and crying of these children and not go to see what is happening. Here is part of the real situation of this job and children.

Lily-Butterfly got out of bed, put on her robe, and went outside her apartment. In the dark she walked the six steps up to the upper floor hallway, to Jeff, Susan, and the children's rooms. Their son, Josh was standing at the large door to his parent's section of the house banging on the door alternately with his two fists. Lily-Butterfly walked away from Josh and went into two months old Sue's room. Sue was still scream-crying. Lily-Butterfly turned on the light. She walked to the crib and look at Sue. Sue was laying on her back. Poop and pee covered the spot where she laid, her legs, hands, the bottom of her shirt, and the diaper as well. The room smelled stinky. Lily-Butterfly got clean sheets from Sue's linen closet and put them on the rocking chair. Next, she took off all Sue's clothes and the diaper, gave Sue a bath, dressed her, and put on a new diaper. Lily-Butterfly applied lots of diaper rash ointment on to Sue's bottom, sides, between her legs, and front. Sue had so much advance diaper rash that were now like sores. Josh noticed that Lily-Butterfly was in Sue's room. He stopped, banging on the door, crying, and came into Sue's room. Josh watched as Lily-Butterfly changed all the sheets in Sue's crib and put the dirty sheets in a garbage bag. Next Lily-Butterfly changed the garbage bag of the over full garbage can and washed her hands. Josh sat beside Sue who was laying on a blanket on the carpeted floor. After the bath Sue had stopped cry-screaming. Next Lily-Butterfly got a diaper from Josh's room and changed his diaper and applied diaper rash ointment as well. She washed her hands again. Josh also had diaper rash, but it was not as advanced as Sue's. Lily-Butterfly had not said one word since waking up to investigate the situation. In silence she chose to do what she did. After changing Josh's diaper and washing her hands, Lily-Butterfly picked up Sue, and left her room. Josh followed Lily-Butterfly carrying Sue in her arms. Lily-Butterfly thought, I think Sue is hungry. I am going to give her a bottle of warm milk, burp her, and put her back in her crib.

The first words Lily-Butterfly spoke were, "Josh would you like some warm milk and cookies?"

"Yes, ma'am. Thank you," replied Josh.

Lily-Butterfly warmed milk and gave it to Josh, with three cookies. Josh ate in silence. The bottle with warm baby formula milk was ready for Sue. Lily-Butterfly fed Sue as she sang to her. Sue drank seven ounces of milk. Lily-Butterfly burped Sue, kept singing, and gently patting her back she fell asleep. Josh finished eating his cookies and drank all the milk.

"Josh, listen, I am going to put your sister in her crib. She is sleeping. Now you are going to go back to your room, get into your bed and go back to sleep, or play quietly in your room until your parents wake up. Do not bang on your parent's door and no more crying. Banging on the door and crying can wake up your sister. Okay?" said Lily-Butterfly.

"Okay ma'am. Thank you."

"All right let us go back upstairs. Come."

Josh walked in front of Lily-Butterfly as she carried sleeping baby Sue. It was now 6:50 AM. Sleeping Sue was placed in her crib.

Lily-Butterfly brought Josh to his room, he got into his bed, laid on his stomach, and Lily-Butterfly covered him. Lily-Butterfly closed both the children's doors half way. She took the full garbage bag with dirty diapers downstairs to the garbage room in the basement. Lily-Butterfly found a night light and brought it up to the hallway where the children's rooms were. She plugged the night light into the plug across from Josh's room. Lily-Butterfly thought, at night this will help light the hallway so that it is not dark anymore. Oh, my Creator this journey has already began. Please continue to help me as I journey on this path.

Lily-Butterfly went back to her room and laid in her bed. She contemplated what she had just experienced with the children. Some of her thoughts were, the areas of Sue's body enclosed by the diaper have such deep wound sores, raw diaper rash. Oh my. How could this be? What did I choose to get myself into taking this job? I must really help these children. How? I promise to stay two years. I cannot ignore the diaper rash-sores. This job situation is multi-layered, deep, and wide. On Monday I will have to say something to Jeff and Susan. Lily-Butterfly sighed. At 8:30 AM she got up and got dressed, washed her face, brushed her teeth, and made breakfast. When Lily-Butterfly had finished making breakfast, she set the table, and woke up Rebornstar. Rebornstar got out of bed, dressed, washed her face, and brushed her teeth. They had breakfast. They tidied up the apartment and washed all the dirty dishes. Lily-Butterfly ignored what was going on with Jeff, Susan, and their children. She heard them and knew that they had gotten up. At 10:40 AM Lily-Butterfly and Rebornstar left the apartment. They got outside by walking down a hallway, going down two flight of steps, and then through a door on the side of the building where they lived. This Lily-Butterfly chose as her entrance and exit to the house, when she was not working, going home to Manana Leila's apartment, and returning for work. The key to use this door was on the set of keys she was given. Lily-Butterfly thought, I am so thankful that I do not have to go through their kitchen to leave the house.

Rebornstar and Lily-Butterfly spend their Sunday at the park where Rebornstar played, going to a restaurant for lunch, returning to the park to read and Rebornstar played some more, visiting shops in Newton Center, doing some food shopping, and returning home to make dinner, and eat. By 10:00 PM both Rebornstar and Lily-Butterfly were asleep after their end of the day routines. As usual every night Lily-Butterfly's going to sleep routine stayed the same. She would write in her journal to process her experiences and clear her thoughts, prayer, meditation, deep breathing, and continue to process and reflect on her day. During the reflections and deep breathing, she would drift off into sleep.

Monday morning at 4:45 AM Lily-Butterfly was awakened again by the same banging on the door, Josh crying, and Sue cry-screaming. She put on her robe again and went to investigate. Josh was again doing the banging. Josh saw Lily-Butterfly and stopped banging the door to his parent section of the house. He followed Lily-Butterfly into Sue's room. When Sue cried her face became flushed, her face was bright pink. Lily-Butterfly removed her soaking wet diapers and wet crib sheets. It was obvious to Lily-Butterfly that Sue could be affected by the pain from the diaper sores soaked with pee. She gave Sue a bath, put on a pink tee shirt dress, and put diaper rash ointment on all the diaper sore areas. Lily-Butterfly changed Sue's crib sheet, put a plastic sheet protector on top of the sheet, fold a white twin bed flat sheet, and place it on top of the plastic protector. Next, she placed Sue on top of this sheet to lay down. She did not put a diaper on Sue. Sue had stopped crying. Next, she took off Josh diapers, gave him a bath, put on diaper rash ointment, and put on a boy's brief instead of a diaper. This was the first day Josh had stopped wearing diapers during the day, and his first day of potty training. Lily-Butterfly brought Josh to his room and helped him to climb into his bed. She covered him and told him that she would come back to get him when it was time to go downstairs. Lily-Butterfly took two king size bed flat sheets and cut them into diaper size portions. She made thirty-six cloth diapers for Sue.

As Lily-Butterfly created the cloth diapers from the sheet for Sue she mumbled, "the children seem to not be given daily baths and regular change of diapers. This is one reason why the diaper rash has become sores; especially for Sue. Wearing these cloth diapers can help Sue diaper sores to heal, and air can get to the area to aid in the healing process. I guess my workday starts whenever I choose to get up and attend to these children, and not at 8 AM. Another issue is these children are being neglected. I will tell Susan to take Sue to the doctor to get a prescribed antibiotic medication ointment. Maybe I will only put a diaper on Sue at night when she goes to bed, or on a need to do so basis. I will go get dress for work after making these diapers. Lily-Butterfly, welcome to your new training and adventure of practicing unconditional love, compassion, care, giving, patience, and so forth. Creator, you sure give me great opportunities to awaken, practice, and improve my talents."

Lily-Butterfly put on one of the homemade cloth diapers on Sue and went to get dressed for work. When she returned to the children it was 7:00 AM. Josh was awake and playing with some toys in his room.

"Hi Josh. Come let us go downstairs. First, I will get Sue. Okay," said Lily-Butterfly

"Yes, ma'am."

"Josh, another thing, today is the first day of learning to use the toilet for pee and poop. You will wear diaper only when you take a nap and go to sleep at night. When you feel you would like to pee, or poop let me know and I will help you to use the toilet. Plus, at different times during the day I will take you to use the toilet just to check if you need to, and practice using the toilet. This will also give your diaper rash more opportunity to heal. Do you understand?"

"Yes ma'am I understand. Good. Now I am going to learn to be a big boy."

"Yes. Exactly. Good. You are a smart boy. Come with me. I am here to help you."

Lily-Butterfly took Sue downstairs in her arms and Josh walking ahead of her. In the nursery she placed Sue in the play pen. She went back upstairs to get a new plastic protector for the crib mattress, a clean white full-size flat sheet, and twelve cloth diapers. Lily-Butterfly put the plastic crib protector in the crib over the mattress and fold the sheet into a small size to fit over the plastic protector. Next, she placed Sue into the crib. Sue was still sleeping. Lily-Butterfly prepared a five-ounce bottle of warm baby formula. She woke Sue and gave her the bottle with baby milk formula. After Sue was finished drinking the milk Lily-Butterfly burped her and placed her back into her crib.

"Josh are you hungry and ready for breakfast?" asked Lily-Butterfly.

"Yes ma'am. Very hungry."

"What would you like for breakfast?"

"Pancakes, eggs, bacon, and orange juice."

"Wow. You are a hearty eater. Okay, I will make this for you. Go to the table and color in your coloring book, while I make your breakfast. I will let you know when the breakfast is ready."

Jeff and Susan came downstairs into the kitchen while Lily-Butterfly made Josh's breakfast.

"Good morning Lily-Butterfly. We saw that you started your job early Sunday morning. We are so happy that you are here, and the children too. I see what you did upstairs for Sue. We know that you are going to be great for this job. Welcome. Thank you," said Jeff.

Lily-Butterfly gave Josh his breakfast.

"Yes. I am so relieved. Sorry about the children's diaper rashes. We did the best we could. Thank you for all that you have done and for choosing to be here. God will bless you. What a relief I feel, and it is not even one week yet since you are here. Really, thanks," said Susan.

"Thank you for your kind words and compliments. But this is not enough. I need your actions as well. As you already know that the children are being neglected. I need your co-operation to continue the transformation and changes even when I am not at work, and especially when I am off on weekends. Remember, I will be here only for two years. I will try my best to keep this promise and commitment. Did you hear the children crying, screaming, and Josh banging on the door?"

"No. We lock the hall door to the children' room and the other door to our section, and our bedroom door. We cannot hear them through so many doors. This is one of the reasons we lock these three doors," replied Susan.

"Well. This is not a good idea, because what if the children are in danger. Hello, power can be selfish, and selfishness can be dangerous, especially as parents. You have three years old and a two-month-old. They cannot take care of themselves. They might need your attention during the night. One of you should check on the children during the night at about 10:00 PM before you go to sleep, and again at 2:00 AM or 3:00 AM. I am serious," said Lily-Butterfly.

"Well, I mean. We hope for the best when we put them in their rooms at 7:00 PM for the night. Hmm...," said Susan.

Lily-Butterfly interrupted Susan.

"You are telling me when Sue, a two months old baby is put in her crib at 7:00 PM no one goes back to check on her until both of you choose to wake up the next morning?" said Lily-Butterfly.

Jeff tried to leave the kitchen.

"Mr. Jeff this conversation is important so please stay and participate, even if it is only listening and hearing. Thank you," said Lily-Butterfly.

Susan continued to talk, "Josh and Sue are supposed to sleep through the night. The only way for them to practice sleeping through the night is to not go to check on them, and when they cry surrender to their crying, by going to cuddle them. So far, they have been okay. They are alive. No kid dies from crying. From crying they get to exercise their lungs. Eventually they get tired from crying and go back to sleep. This way they learn that we are not going to be controlled and manipulated by their crying and fussing, and learn how to be independent. We need time for us to rest and sleep," said Susan.

"A two months old will need to be fed and diaper change about every three to four hours, and not every thirteen hours. If she naturally sleeps for thirteen hours without waking up, you would still need to check on her to see if she is okay. Both of you told me that I am hired to be a paid parent. I am here for the children's positive greater good and well-being. This is part of my chosen intention and perception to be here. No child gets damaged on my watch, or while I am working here. Understand my style of childcare, learn, and practice. If the children continue to be neglected and abuse. I will leave before the two years. I cannot be an accomplice to negative childcare, and I cannot pretend and avoid the situations. What if Josh goes into the bathroom and turns on the pipe, fills the bathtub, and gets into it, or does something else dangerous. Please get child safety locks and put on every bathroom door with a shower and tub inside. Do this today."

"Okay if you say so," replied Jeff.

Josh had finish eating and left the dining table. He went to the nursery to play. Sue still slept.

"These are your children. I am here to work. I hear your views. Both of you might think that I am just the childcare help. I am going to do the best job possible. Fire me if you do not like my attitude and the quality of child care services I provide. I will not support child neglect or child abuse. Today I am starting to potty train Josh on the adult toilet using the child adjustable toilet seat that is in his room closet. I will only put diaper on him when he goes to sleep at night, nap time, and on a need to do so basis. This should have started already. Plus, this will give his diaper rash an opportunity to heal," said Lily-Butterfly.

"Sure. Great. When you are not here, if this toilet training is hard for us for whatever reason, we will put on a diaper. Okay. Toilet training for Josh is wonderful. This toilet training stuff takes patience, dedication, and attention. We do not have these parental skills. Sorry, but we will do our best. You are the woman of mothering. Good that you are fearless about telling us what to do and how to act. We surely need awareness about childcare. Thank you," said Susan.

"Thank you, Lily-Butterfly. I understand that you would like to do the job we hired you to perform. You can let them cry at night. They usually get tired of crying and go back to sleep. Josh usually falls asleep laying on the carpet by the closed door. This is all right. I, we, love our children, although we are not the best parent," said Jeff.

"I am going to change the subject. I hear all that you have said. I am going to feed Sue. We will talk more after I feed Sue. Enjoy your breakfast," said Lily-Butterfly.

"Wait one minute. You are the best. Can we call you Lily? Your name Lily-Butterfly is long," said Susan.

"No. Call me by my complete name Lily-Butterfly, or do not say my name at all, just talk to me without saying my name. My name is as it is for a reason. When I am called by my complete name, I remember my complete self all the time. A human's complete first name is their first ritual of transmission and grounding instrument into human life, like a key to life. Thank you. My ways might seem old fashion and antique, but they work in a complete way. The ancient pathways work fool proof all the time," replied Lily-Butterfly.

"Okay. We understand," replied Susan.

Lily-Butterfly prepared Sue's milk and went to the nursery to feed her and change her cloth diaper to a dry one. As Lily-Butterfly fed Sue she thought, I feel exhausted already and it is not afternoon yet. After I am finished feeding Sue, I will take Rebornstar breakfast upstairs to the apartment to give her. I had prepared breakfast for myself and Rebornstar when I made Josh's breakfast. I think that she is up and dressed but is not coming downstairs, because she heard us talking. There is a lot of things to straighten out in this home, with these parents, and children. I must pace myself and remember to take care of myself and Rebornstar, as well. It is almost 10:00 AM. I will burp Sue and bring her to her parents.

"Here is Sue. I just fed Sue. I will put her in this bassinet by the dining table. Enjoy Sue's wonderful presence while you both eat breakfast. I am going upstairs to eat breakfast in the apartment with Rebornstar. I will be back in thirty minutes. It is now 10:15 AM. See you by 10:45 AM. I have something more to say to both of you."

"Okay," replied Jeff and Susan.

Lily-Butterfly returned to the kitchen after eating breakfast with Rebornstar and setting her up with activities to do in the apartment.

Susan said, "Lily-Butterfly please call us plain Jeff and Susan. No, Mr. or Mrs."

"Okay. If I have to say things, I will, but I do not like to talk too much, or complain. Everything I will do and say is for this childcare job, for the greater good of the children, and to keep my two years promise to stay here. Susan, today make an appointment for both children to see the doctor. The children's diaper rashes have become sores, especially the baby. Some of Sue's diaper sores are showing signs of infection. I think that they need prescribed antibiotic medication ointment. Plus, I think that Sue has a bladder infection for whatever reason. I notice that when her stomach is touched below her belly button she seems in pain. I am not a doctor or diagnosing anything, this is my opinion and observation. The last request I have for today is, can I clean the refrigerator?"

Susan replied, "Sure you can clean the refrigerator whenever you like. You are right about everything you have told us about the children. Today I will schedule doctor's appointment for Josh and Sue. Josh also had advance diaper rash and I had to take him to the doctor. I feel embarrass to return with Sue. You are right her diaper rashes are now sores, and infected. Plus, like you have said she might have a bladder infection. I am acknowledging everything. Good that you have the strength, integrity, and courage to confront us. We try to be honest. We told you that we are slobs and lack parenting skills, even after over three years of being parents. We love our children and want the best for them. Thank you for caring and choosing to be here. Keep being direct and giving us direction and awareness. We will use your guidance in whatever ways we choose. Thank you for everything. All the nannies that quit before you had a good reason. Thank you for shedding light on our childcare and parent situations."

Jeff was listening to the conversation while he read the newspaper.

"Thank you," said Jeff.

"You are welcome. Thank you for hearing and listening. Please let me know the time and date of the children's doctor appointment so that I can plan it in my schedule. Have a great rest of the day. I am going to go on with my workday schedule."

"I will let you know about the appointment. Thank you. We are leaving for work at 12:00 PM." said Susan.

Lily-Butterfly went to check on Josh and Sue and continued with her plans for the day.

5

When power comes easy, the person can act immature and irresponsible. Power earned is power respected. The energy of fear subtracts.

At 12:30 PM Josh, Sue, Rebornstar, and Lily-Butterfly had lunch. After lunch Lily-Butterfly combed through the refrigerator and threw out all the expired and rotten food and products. What was left she put in the refrigerator in the basement. Next, she used soapy water with some bleach to soak inside the fridge. Before taking the children to the park she gathered all the dirty clothes in the children's room and took them to the basement laundry room. She separated the dirty clothes into piles and put two loads into the washing machine to wash. The dirty clothes in the children's room was making the room smell stagnant. All morning Lily-Butterfly was monitoring Josh's potty training and Sue's cloth diaper change. Before going to the park Josh used the toilet. Lily-Butterfly put a disposable diaper on Sue until she got back home. When all of this was set up Lily-Butterfly thought, we all needed the fresh air, spending time in nature, and walk. She took Rebornstar, Josh and Sue in the double stroller, to the community park playground. At the park the children had a great time playing. Lily-Butterfly read to all the children before they left the park.

At 3:30 PM Lily-Butterfly and the children had returned home. She fed Sue and burped her. Lily-Butterfly helped Josh with his toilet training, and he laid down in the nursery for a nap, or quiet time. Sue went to sleep. Rebornstar went upstairs to the apartment to take a nap or do a chosen quiet activity. At this time Lily-Butterfly cleaned the fridge and replaced the items she had taken downstairs to the basement fridge, attend to the laundry, and set up dinner for the children and herself. By 6:30 PM Lily-Butterfly and the children had eaten dinner and Sue had drank her milk. All day Sue did not cry once because Lily-Butterfly had given her the attention she needed at the right time. She also went downstairs to the laundry room to remove the dried clothes from the dryer and add more clothes to the washing machine and dryer. By 6:45 PM Lily-Butterfly had completely cleaned and tidied the kitchen, and loaded all the dirty dishes in the dish washer. Jeff and Susan arrived home at 6:55 PM. Lily-Butterfly and all the children were in the kitchen. She was ready to take the children upstairs to give them baths and get them ready for bed. Lily-Butterfly's official work schedule was 8:00 AM to 7:00 PM. She woke up at 4:45 AM and has been working since then. It was now 7:00 PM and she had not given both children baths, or get them into bed. Lily-Butterfly thought, I am so tired. When am I going to finish working today? I must adjust my working schedule starting tomorrow.

"Hi Lily-Butterfly. How was your day?" said Susan.

"My day was good. It has been a long day. Thanks to all my work experiences, organizational skills, calm personality, and the children cooperating with my guidance I am not stressed, but I am tired. I woke up this morning at 4:45 AM from the crying and banging, worked all day, and now it is beyond 7:00 PM and the children still needs to be given baths and put to bed."

"I see. I made the doctor's appointment for Josh and Sue. The appointment is for 10:30 AM tomorrow morning. Have both of them ready at 10:00 AM to go with me," said Susan.

"Okay Susan. I am going to take Sue upstairs to prepare her for bed. Josh can stay down here to spend some time with you. When I am ready for Josh, I will return to get him. You can visit with Sue in her room if you like."

"Yes. Sure. We will go with your flow. We see that you can manage well. Thank you. Really. We appreciate very much that you are here. I am sure that the children notice the difference between your loving care and what we could do. God bless your heart. Thanks," said Susan.

"Thank you very much as well. I feel so relieved knowing that you are here," said Jeff.

"You are welcome. Come Rebornstar let us go upstairs. It is time for a shower and preparing to go to bed. Say thank you to Jeff and Susan and come upstairs."

"Okay mama. I am coming. Mr. Jeff and Mrs. Susan thank you very much for everything," said Rebornstar.

"You are more than welcome. You are lucky that you have a blessed mom. Have a good night," said Susan.

"Bye," said Jeff.

"Yes, thank you, good night," replied Rebornstar.

Rebornstar went upstairs to the apartment to take her shower and prepare for bed. Before going to sleep Rebornstar watched television for an hour and read a book.

Lily-Butterfly prepared Sue for bed and read her a bedtime story. Sue for the first time made cooing sounds and smiled, it was as if she was talking to Lily-Butterfly.

"You are welcome Sue. I will see you in the morning. Have a great night sleep," said Lily-Butterfly.

Sue was placed in her crib, she did not fuss, or cry. She seemed content. Lily-Butterfly closed Sue's bedroom door halfway and went downstairs to get Josh.

"Jeff and Susan, would you like Josh to return to spend time with you after he is prepared for bed?" asked Lily-Butterfly.

"No. We are tired. You put them to bed. It seems like they listen to you more than us," replied Jeff.

Josh kissed his parent's good night and went upstairs with Lily-Butterfly. Lily-Butterfly prepared Josh for bed and read him a bedtime story while he laid in bed. During the story Josh fell asleep. Lily-Butterfly covered Josh, closed his door halfway, and left his room.

It was 8:45 PM when Lily-Butterfly went to the apartment.

"Hi Rebornstar. Thank you for being a good listener today and following my instructions. You were very helpful. I will read you a story. Mama loves you."

"Okay mama. I read a story already. Thank you. Mama, you need to rest. Take a shower and relax. I am fine."

"Okay my star. Sweet dreams. See you in the morning."

After a long consistent sixteen-hour day of work Lily-Butterfly took an hour sea salt tub soak and bath. During the salt soak she meditated, reflected, process her day, said prayers of gratitude for everything, and surrendered some more to her chosen commitment of working in this job for two years. By the time the salt soak and bath were completed Lily-Butterfly was more relaxed. She wrote in her journal and wrote a renewed workday schedule for finishing work closer to 7 PM. As Lily-Butterfly wrote her work schedule she thought, tomorrow is another day to experience similar and additional events of working for Jeff and Susan. I instinctively feel that the experiences living in this house could get worse, before things get better. I must prepare myself for whatever happens by staying connected to acceptance and being neutral. Life's journey can be interesting and mysterious. I must stay optimistic and positive. Amin. Lily-Butterfly got in the bed and covered herself. Within five minutes she was asleep. Sleep had arrived and turned the pages of her day to a renewed cycle.

The next morning Lily-Butterfly was awakened again by Josh's crying and banging on his parent's hall way door. Sue was also scream-crying. She looked at the clock. It was 4:10 AM. She did not get up immediately and decided to give the situation about fifteen minutes to see if Jeff or Susan would hear them and come to fix the situation. This did not happen. Lily-Butterfly got up and put her robe on. She went to check on the children. Josh was now laying on the carpet by the door crying. He had stopped banging on the door. Lily-Butterfly held Josh's hand and helped him to stand up. In silence she guided him back to his bed. Josh got in his bed and she covered him.

"Josh lay in your bed. I will be back. I am going to check on your sister."

"All right. Can I have some water?"

"Sure. Your water is right here. Drink what you like, put the glass back on the nightstand, and lay back down."

"Okay."

Lily-Butterfly went to Sue's room. She changed Sue's diaper, went downstairs to get five ounces of warm baby formula for Sue, sang to her while she fed and burp her, and replaced her in her crib. Sue went back to sleep again within ten minutes. Lily-Butterfly returned to Josh's room. He was lying awake in his bed.

Lily-Butterfly said, "Josh, you wake up each morning about the same time, crying, and banging on the hallway door to your parent's room. Why?"

"Ha. There is a little boy scaring me. He pushes me out of bed, shakes me by my shoulders, grabs my legs, and bothers me all night. He tells me get out of his bed."

"Are you sure? How is this possible?"

"I do not know. I am scared, so I get up to call mommy and daddy and they do not hear me."

"How long have this been happening. Have you told your parents?"

"Yes, I told my parents. They say it is my imagination and try to not pay attention to what is happening. I notice him a while now. He is mean and angry. I am scared. It feels real to me."

"I understand. Okay. What does this little boy look like?"

"He has brown hair and naked."

"I will talk to your parents about your experience. Maybe I can help this little boy to not bother you. Try not to be scared. I will try to talk to him. Do you like this little boy?"

"No. He is mean and angry."

"Is he here now?"

"Yes, standing by the door."

Lily-Butterfly looked in the direction of the door.

"Little boy. Do not bother Josh. If you do you will have to deal with me. This is Josh's bed now. You can go be with your parents in their room. Or, you can go to one of the other bedrooms. I am here now. Leave Josh alone. Do not ever think of bothering Sue. Sue is definitely a no, no. Little boy if you can hear me, move the curtain," said Lily-Butterfly.

Suddenly, the curtains moved as if someone went behind them.

"Amin. I see you. Stay away from Josh. Little boy for now, you can lay on the floor, go be with your parents, or go into another bedroom. These are your only choices," said Lily-Butterfly.

The curtain moved again, and the cold chill of a little boy's spirit left the room.

"Josh I will help you and this little boy. I will speak to your parents. I think that the spirit of this little boy will not bother you again. Do not worry I will try and help to fix the situation long term. Cover up, close your eyes, breathe, and relax. I will return to check on you. Do you understand?"

"Yes ma'am. I understand. Thank you. I hope he does not come back. It is scary, because he looks like white lines and puffy clouds. He does not have a body like me. So scary."

"I understand I am here to help you. Relax. I will take care of this situation. I do not think that he will bother you again. I am going back to my room to prepare for work."

"Okay. Mmm. Thanks."

Lily-Butterfly left Josh's room door open and walked back to her apartment.

"I think that Jeff and Susan had another son before Josh. The bedroom Josh is using now was his room. He died, and never crossed over. He is here haunting his brother and sister. And maybe if this situation is not addressed it could long term affect Josh in negative ways. Oh, my Creator this job gets more and more interesting each day. I will talk to Jeff and Susan at the right time. I will give my attention to this spirit-ghost-haunting situation. I think the child died in the bedroom. I think he died from drowning. Mr. Jeff and Mrs. Susan will be very surprised when I ask them about this dead son spirit-ghost-haunting. Let me get dressed for work. A new day in this wonderful job. Hahaha. This is not funny," mumbled Lily-Butterfly

6

The secrets people keep and hide from themselves and others, can keep them stuck and hold them hostage. You cannot hide from your secrets. You cannot hide or run from yourself. Conscious or unconscious these secrets are stored within you. They become a part of your life, foundation, intention, perception, and the people, places, and things that you attract; and everything you choose to do and create. All the things that people do not resolve is waiting to be resolve. So, the saying of 'leave the past in the past' is not possible, because your past, present, and future are within you.

Returning from Josh's room to her apartment, Lily-Butterfly went into Rebornstar's room to check on her. Rebornstar was sleeping like a baby bear during hibernation season. At 6:30 AM Lily-Butterfly got dressed for work and went back to check on Josh. Josh was awake and playing with his toys. Sue was still sleeping.

"Josh, put your clothes on and come with me downstairs. I am going to fold laundry. You can help me bring your clothes to your room."

"Yes ma'am."

Josh got dressed and went with Lily-Butterfly to the basement laundry room. Going down the stairs Lily-Butterfly thought, forget about the time work starts, instead I will try to leave work close to 7:00 PM. Being here seems to be the gate I must go through to move forward. With how busy I am going to be, working here two years will arrive like a breeze. She arrived in the laundry room with Josh by her side. She removed the dry clothes from the dryer, add the washed clothes to the dryer, and added more of the children's dirty clothes with soap to the washing machine. The amount of dirty clothes that the children had will take Lily-Butterfly about one month to wash, dry, and fold. Josh helped Lily-Butterfly to sort out his clothes from the dry clothes. Josh folded his clothes and Lily-Butterfly folded the other clothes. When they were finished, they brought all the clothes to the children's rooms. Lily-Butterfly took off Josh's diaper and put on a boy's brief. Josh's participation in his potty training continued with great success. Sue was still asleep. Josh and Lily-Butterfly went back downstairs to the kitchen. Lily-Butterfly made tea for herself and gave some apple juice to Josh. After sitting with Josh to drink her tea she made breakfast for the children and herself, and got Sue's milk bottle ready. During all these morning activities Lily-Butterfly reflected on, her life from birth to the present moment. The journey of her life merging like an awake and sleep dream, and its continuation to where she was sitting in Jeff and Susan's kitchen. In these reflections the journey seemed like a life's story writing itself, and she was a willing participant. Lily-Butterfly was brought out of her daydream and reflections by Susan entering the kitchen.

"Good morning Lily-Butterfly. It seems as if you had an early start this morning as well," said Susan.

"Yes, very early start. I cannot feel comfortable hearing Josh and Sue cry, bang, and scream-cry. No matter what, it is not normal to me to just ignore the situation. I cannot assume that they are okay. I must check on them. This is my choice."

"I thank you for all that you do for my children. The children look as good as new and today is only your second day working. They are sleeping like two little angels. I have not heard Sue scream-cry since you have been here."

"You are welcome. Josh, go play in the nursery. Susan, can I talk to you about something?"

Josh went to the nursery.

"Sure. What is it?" replied Susan.

"Susan, this conversation might seem strange, but I am going to ask you some questions, and so forth. Did you have another son before Josh was born? He was about five or six years old when he died from drowning in the bathroom in Josh's room. The room that Josh has, was it his room?"

"Why do you ask?"

"Susan you are answering my question with a question. Anyway, Josh told me that a little boy pushes him out of his bed at night, pulls him, and says 'get out of my bed.' I see the spirit-ghost, and it looks like the child died between five and six years old. This spirit-ghost and situation seems to be disturbing Josh a lot. This is part of the reason that between 3:00 AM and 4:30 AM he is up banging on the door to your section of the house and crying very loud. You and Jeff do not seem to hear Josh or Sue. I suggested that you get up at night and check the children. You have not chosen to follow my guidance. Are you going to wait for another disaster to feel sorry about? Denial and avoidance can be a very powerful river that can create destruction. Ha."

"Lily-Butterfly you can see spirit-ghost? Oh wow? How do you know that he drowned?"

"I am very intuitive, and I can see into the invisible realm, and much, much more. When I am in Josh's bathroom, I sense the story and let it go, thinking it was just my imagination. I thought nothing of what I was experiencing. So, when I talk to Josh about what was happening, why he would wake up, cry, bang on the door with such urgency, he told me about his experience. He also told me that he talked to you and his father about his experiences. Hello Susan, what is the story? If I can help this situation, and the children, it will help you, Jeff, and me as well. I would not have to wake up so early every morning to attend to the children. This situation and spirit-ghost is affecting the baby as well. It is time to resolve this situation. Hiding, denial, and avoidance does not help to resolve secrets and negative experiences."

"Yes, I had another son. His name was Dan. He was my first child. He drowned in the bathtub when he was six years old. He was born one year after we moved here. We do not hear the children crying."

"Okay. This is the boy Josh see in his room. Maybe he does other things to Josh. Like try to go inside his body, and Sue as well. So, what happened to Dan?"

"Dan drown in his bathtub in his bedroom. One-night Dan woke up, I think he tried to get into our side of the house and could not, because we always lock this door to prevent the children from waking us up at night. The next morning Jeff and I did not hear or see him. We went into his room and he was not in bed. We went into the bathroom and he was in a full tub of water. He was dead. It seems as if he closed the tub drain, filled the bathtub with water, took off his clothes, got into the tub of water, and fell back to sleep. During his sleep he sank down under the water and drown. It was the most horrible situation for us. Really. We try to forget this experience."

"And you still do not choose to get up and check on the children at night. Before I knew this story, I had a strange feeling. I asked you to buy child proof doorknobs and put on every bathroom door with tub and showers. This has not been done. This is your home, children, and choice. I am only the nanny. I think Sue is awake I am going to her room to change her diaper and feed her. It is breakfast time for the other children as well. We will have breakfast in the guest dining room. You and Jeff can use the kitchen dining room. We will continue this conversation at another time."

"Yes. Whenever you are ready, we will talk," said Susan.

"I will have the children ready at 10:00 AM for their doctor's appointment."

"Okay thank you," said Susan.

Josh, Rebornstar, Sue, and Lily-Butterfly had breakfast together.

During breakfast Susan told Jeff about the conversation she had with Lily-Butterfly about Dan. At 9:00 AM Jeff left for work. Josh and Rebornstar went to the nursery to play, and Lily-Butterfly put Sue in her crib. Lily-Butterfly returned to the kitchen to clean up and load the dishwasher. Susan came to talk to her in the kitchen.

"Lily-Butterfly, are you saying that Dan is a ghost in the house?"

"It seems so. I saw him. Josh told me he sees him at night. To not increase Josh's fears, I did not make a big deal about the situation with him. I talked to Dan's spirit-ghost so that Josh would feel more safe and re-assured. Susan, what do you think that you should do?"

"Lily-Butterfly I do not know. First of all, we do not believe in ghost. So, I do not know what to do. When Josh told us that he saw an invisible boy, we thought that it could be Dan, but we did not acknowledge to Josh or ourselves that he saw Dan as a ghost. We told Josh that ghosts are not real, and that it was his imagination."

"First thing get child safety locks installed on all the bathroom doors. Every single one of them. I do not care how you choose to do this. The history and stress imprints of a tragic incident and accident can repeat itself. As long as I am working here no child will get killed or damage under my watch. If you do not choose to listen and hear me this will cancel my commitment of staying here to work for the two years promise. So, make sure that you fix the bathroom door situation, today. Did you mourn, make closure, and say goodbye to Dan when he died?"

"No. Other than the funeral, I think we pushed this experience in a closet and lock the door. We pretend that the experience did not happen. We thought that his energy; I mean spirit went to where dead people spirit goes. I do not know what else to do."

"Well, Mrs. Susan, the complete energy system of a human is called spirit. When the body dies this complete spirit energy system called spirit is supposed to go through a momentum tunnel, cross over to be reset, and filed in a realm based on the spirit's energy system vibration. Sometimes for many reasons the spirit of a dead person does not go where it is supposed to go. The spirit of a dead person is called a ghost. In my opinion spirit-ghost is a very simple ideology and perception. Anyway, if you are interested to know what else you can do ask me when you are ready. Think about if you really want Dan to leave the house and cross over to where people's spirit goes after death. Another thing get two sacred protection symbols of your religious belief system and put one on each on Josh and Sue's bedroom door. Until you decide to take further sacred spiritual action, can I put inside the room something to discourage Dan's spirit from haunting Josh and try to get into bed with him?"

"Oh yes Lily-Butterfly. You have both our permission to improve this situation. Like I keep saying we love our children, but we are dumb when it comes to other parent-hood stuff. Especially this supposedly ghost situation. I will get the hardware store to send someone to put safety lock devises on all the bathroom doors. Oh my. You are here for many reasons."

"I can see very clearly that I am here for many reasons. But, remember that I am leaving after my two years commitment. Plus, if you and Mr. Jeff do not support in action, words, and deeds, the safety and care of these children, I am leaving before the two years. I cannot be a part of child abuse and accidental death situations. This is my opinion, intention, perception, and choice. If things do not shape up, I am shipping myself out of here. Okay."

"I understand. What more can Jeff and I do?"

"See if the hardware store can put safety devices on the tub water turn on fixture. A bathtub can become a mini pool and dangerous for children. This drowning that happen with Dan in his bathroom can happen again. I might seem dramatic but maybe my expression is what is needed to get you to see the seriousness of this situation. I am going to help like I say. In addition, Mr. Jeff or you should get up at 3:00 AM every morning and check on both your children. Even if it is just going to make sure that they are sleeping and not in danger. Safety is important where children are concerned. Process this conversation, talk to your husband, and let me know if you want Dan to cross over to the 'other side' and stop being a spirit-ghost."

"Alright Lily-Butterfly. I will do as you guide me. You are a very interesting woman. Thanks. Do whatever you like to protect Josh and Sue. I will do what you say about child proofing all the bathroom doors, pipes, and protection symbols from our religious belief for the children's doors. Oh my. You are God sent. Life can be an un-known dilemma."

"I hear you Mrs. Susan. Human life can be a multitasking

adventure. I am going to get the children ready to go to the doctor it is 9:55 AM."

"Okay. We will talk more about this later. You do not have to call me Mrs."

Lily-Butterfly went to get the children ready for the doctor. When the children were ready, she brought them to Susan.

"The children are ready. Would you like me to help you put them in the car?"

"No. Thank you for asking. I should be back by 12:00 PM. See you then. You can prepare lunch. Wish me luck. Bye."

"Okay all the best with everything. See you when you return."

"Yes. Listen out for the man from the hardware store. I called them. He should be here by 10:45 AM."

"Okay I will."

When Susan left, Lily-Butterfly instructed Rebornstar to go to the apartment to do some writing of the alphabet and mathematics assignments, color in her coloring book, and learn how to read. Lily-Butterfly went to the laundry room to attend to the laundry. The man from the hardware store came and installed the child safety equipment on the bathroom doors and pipe turn on valves. After attending to the laundry Lily-Butterfly took six clear large bowls from the pantry in the basement and six boxes of one pounds of salt. She poured one box of salt into each clear bowl. Next, she brought all the bowl of salt upstairs to Josh's room. Lily-Butterfly change the bed location in the room, and put the night stands one on each side. On each night stand she put a bowl of salt. She put two bowls of salt on the carpet midway down the length of the bed, halfway under the bed. The other two bowls of salt she placed one on each side at the foot of the bed. Lily-Butterfly saw Dan's spirit-ghost standing at the open bathroom door. Dan was looking at her. Lily-Butterfly said a prayer of protection in the room standing by Josh's bed.

Lily-Butterfly said to Dan's spirit-ghost, "Dan, hear and listen. This room and bed belong to Josh. You are no longer in human form. Your body has died. You are your spirit's energy system. Leave this room and find another room to be in until it is time for you to transition to the other side of this realm where dead people should go. I will help you to transition to the other side when I receive your parent's and your permission. This room is now too warm for you.

Go now. Leave. Choose another room over by your parent's section of the house or downstairs. Go now. Leave. If you hear and understand me walk out of this room. Amin. Amin. Amin."

After saying the second amen, Dan looked at Lily-Butterfly, the bed with the six bowl of salt surrounding it and floated out of the room through the bedroom door.

"Amin and Amin. People do not realize that spirit-ghost can hear, listen, and understand, if they want to," said Lily-Butterfly.

The spirit-ghost entity left the room without looking back. Who knows where it chose to go? I guess the future and time will tell. Lily-Butterfly never focused her attention on Dan's spirit-ghost even if she saw it in the house. Lily-Butterfly tidied up Josh and Sue's room, cleaned their bathtubs and sinks, opened their bedroom windows, changed their garbage can trash liner, and left their room. She went to her apartment to check on Rebornstar and opened her apartment windows for fresh air to come in.

Lily-Butterfly went back to the basement to attend to the children's laundry. Lily-Butterfly folded the laundry and added more clothes to the washer and dryer. She thought, I will see if this salt protection and sacred prayer vibration really discourage Dan from haunting Josh; and being in his room. Thank you, Divine Creator God, for everything. With your help and assistance everything is possible, if it is meant to be. Continue to help with Dan's spirit-ghost situation. Amin.

7

Sometimes, taking responsibility can be difficult. The longer someone waits to take responsibility, the more it will cost them in the present and future. The future is made up of the past and present experiences and situations.

At 12:00 PM Lily-Butterfly made fresh home-made egg, cheese, and vegetable salad for the children's and herself, for lunch. Susan returned with the children at 12:46 PM. She brought the children into the kitchen.

"Lily-Butterfly, you were right. Both children have bladder infection. This could have contributed to how often they pee. I was not aware of how often they pee, because I hardly changed their diapers. And even if I noticed they were peeing often, it would not make a difference, because my parental awareness is very lacking. Here I received antibiotic medicine and diaper rash ointment. Thank you very much for your direct communication style. Oh wow. You might seem abrupt and dramatic, but you are on the right positive focus awareness and expression," said Susan.

"You are welcome. Good for the children that you heard and listened. Teamwork can go a long way in creating the right outcome. It is never too late to fix a problem or situation. I will not choose to be a part of child abuse and trauma. Child neglect is child abuse, and this can create needless negative emotional stress and suffering. Children depend on their parent or childcare giver for assistance, safety, protection, and help. Children are born physically helpless and this is why they have parents or care giver of some kind. I will go and put on some of the ointment on both of them and give them some medicine. I will remove their diapers. Josh will wear his boy's brief and Sue will wear the home-made cloth diapers until the diaper rash-sores heal," replied Lily-Butterfly.

"Yes. The medicine is given orally after every meal, three times per day. The medicated diaper rash ointment is used three times per day as well. I suggest putting on the medicated ointment when they wake up, after lunch, and after their nightly bath at the end of the day."

"Okay sure this is a good plan. So, I will do the medication and ointment after lunch. Good. Susan you are very polite and show your appreciation for everything I do. Thank you for your acknowledgement. You can have some of our lunch. It is egg, cheese, and vegetable salad with bread; apple juice to drink."

Lily-Butterfly set up the lunch for everyone on the table in the kitchen. The children and Susan sat down at the kitchen dining table. Lily-Butterfly fed Sue with baby formula from her bottle.

"Thank you, Lily-Butterfly. I spoke to Jeff about Dan's ghost. We decide to do as you suggested about helping Dan's spirit energy system to transition to the other side, and for us to make closure with his death. What should we do?"

"Please listen to my sacred guidance without negative fears and judgements. Okay. Buy some sacred herbs of myrrh, frankincense, dry white sage incense leaves, lavender, juniper berries, and sweet grass. I will need these to cleanse and purify both children's room. Please let me know when you have these sacred herbs. Plus, I have moved Josh's bed to another position in the room, say a sacred prayer of protection, and put six bowls of kosher salt around it to create a protective circle. The salt and prayer can help with purification, protection, and safety symbolic vibes. Let us see if this works. I hope that it was okay with you for me to do this. When the situation is resolved and Josh feels safe, I will remove the bowls of salt. Remember to buy the two sacred symbols from your religious belief system, to put on the children's door."

"Lily-Butterfly all the things you do to solve this problem, help the children, and help us, is more than okay. Where do I buy these sacred herbs?"

"Research to find a place that sells dried herbs, telephone these places, if it is not the right place ask the person who answers the phone where you can buy them. Figure this out, you might learn new things along the way."

"All right, I will ask one of my friends, she is always talking about this stuff. Tomorrow Wednesday the house cleaners come to clean half of the house. On Friday they will return to clean the other half. They have a key to come and go as they need to. When I have the sacred herbs, I will let you know. I am going to work. I will see you later."

"Bye. Oh, by the way the man from the hardware store came. Have a great day. After lunch is medication time, cleaning up the kitchen, and going to the playground outside. At 3:00 PM Josh and

Sue will take a short nap. Sleeping and naps are good for growing children, it can help them to relax and reset their nerves."

"Good that the hardware store sent the person to fix the door and pipe situation. I will see you later. Bye," said Susan as she left for work.

At 3:00 PM the children took naps, Rebornstar went upstairs to the apartment to do an activity by herself, and Lily-Butterfly attended to the children's laundry. After the laundry Lily-Butterfly sat on a blanket outside under a tree in the flowers garden to write in her journal and rest. She did this while enjoying the birds chirping, and the wind caressed her whole body. At 4:10 PM Lily-Butterfly set up a small chicken to bake in the oven for dinner. The children woke up. Josh and Rebornstar went outside to play in the playground. At 5:30 PM Lily-Butterfly gave Josh, Sue, Rebornstar, and herself dinner. Dinner and cleaning up the kitchen were completed by 6:30 PM. At 6:37 PM Lily-Butterfly went upstairs with the children to give them baths, their medicine, put on the diaper ointment, read them stories, and put Sue to bed. Lily-Butterfly explained in a simple way the story of the salt bowls around Josh's bed to him and the Dan's spirit-ghost situation. Josh seemed to understand and looked more at ease about Dan's spirit-ghost situation. Josh was instructed to play in his room and when he was ready to sleep to go into his bed.

Rebornstar went to the apartment to shower and get ready for bed as well. Lily-Butterfly went downstairs to fold some laundry, put some more clothes into the dryer, and added another three loads of the children's clothes to wash. Lily-Butterfly left the laundry room and went back upstairs. Jeff and Susan had come home and was preparing dinner in the kitchen for themselves.

"Good night Jeff and Susan. The children are in their rooms and ready for bed. Josh is playing and will go to sleep when he is ready. Would you like me to bring them downstairs to spend time with the both of you?"

"No. Leave them in their rooms. Good. We are tired and feeling stressed out. We will check on them before we go to sleep, and we will see them in the morning. Thank you for everything," said Jeff.

"You are welcome. I am finished working for the day, it is 8:00 PM. I will see you in the morning. Have a good night."

"Good night," said Jeff and Susan.

Lily-Butterfly went to the apartment. Rebornstar was finished with her shower. Lily-Butterfly told her a story about life on the island of Kawomaya living in the valley and village of Yaj. When the story was finished Lily-Butterfly decided to go for a walk outside.

"Rebornstar I will be back in thirty minutes. I am going for a walk outside in the garden. I will use the entrance and exit door on this side of the house. I will be back. Go to sleep when you are ready. I will see you in the morning my star."

"Okay mama. See you in the morning."

"Yes. Sweet dreams my star."

Lily-Butterfly went for a walk outside, came back, took a shower, wrote again in her journal, prayed, and went to sleep. Her last thought before she fell asleep was, today was an improved day. It is not even one week since I have been working here and it feels like one year. Two years might feel like forever. I give thanks for everything, the sweet and the bitter. Amin.

8

Patience is an internally created and awakened talent. Karma means action. The system of karma is consistently recording the thoughts, words, and actions of every person and returning the same action to the person in a random fashion. Whether someone believes in karma or not, karma still works in performing its responsibility and duties. Hence the saying 'what goes around, comes around.'

The next morning arrived with the sun peeking through the bedroom window in Lily-Butterfly's room. She opened her eyes, stretched, and looked at the clock. It was 6:10 AM. It was quiet.

"Amin. It seems as if Josh slept through the night. Let me prepare myself for work," mumbled Lily-Butterfly.

At 6:35 AM Lily-Butterfly went to Josh's room he was still asleep in his bed. Sue was awake, moving her arms and legs, but not crying. Lily-Butterfly took off Sue's diaper, washed her bottom, put on the medicated ointment, and put on a home-made cloth diaper. She replaced Sue in her crib and went downstairs to get a warm bottle of milk. Lily-Butterfly returned to Sue's room with the warm milk and fed her sitting in the rocking chair. Lily-Butterfly sang to Sue as she fed her. Sue kept looking up at Lily-Butterfly with a smile. When Sue was finished drinking her milk Lily-Butterfly burped her and brought her downstairs to lay in the bassinet in the kitchen. Lily-Butterfly gave Sue her medicine and checked on the laundry situation and set up a new batch of clothes to wash and dry. She plans to fold the clothes later. Returning to the kitchen Lily-Butterfly made breakfast of oatmeal with raisins, prunes, and cranberries for Josh, Rebornstar, and herself. Next, she went back upstairs to wake up Rebornstar to get dressed and went to attend to Josh. When Josh was dressed and ready, they went downstairs to the kitchen for breakfast. Before sitting down to eat breakfast, Lily-Butterfly moved the bassinet with Sue inside to her side of the table. Josh, Rebornstar and Lily-Butterfly had breakfast in the guest dining room. Sue was content laying in her bassinet and eventually she fell asleep.

Jeff and Susan came down for breakfast they ate in the kitchen dining room. When Lily-Butterfly and the children had finished

46

eating their breakfast, the children went into the nursery playroom to play. Lily-Butterfly put Sue into her crib to sleep and gave Josh his antibiotic medicine. Lily-Butterfly went to the kitchen to clean up and load the dishwasher.

"Good morning Jeff and Susan. Did you check on the children last night?"

"Yes. We both checked on them before we went to sleep. They looked like sleeping angels. And I checked on them at 3:15 AM. They were fine and sleeping. Lily-Butterfly whatever you did seems to have worked. Thank you for bringing peace, wisdom, and serenity to our children, our lives, and home," said Susan.

"Yes, thank you," said Jeff.

"You are all welcome. I am going downstairs to attend to the laundry. Sue is sleeping and Josh is in the nursery playing with Rebornstar. You can go visit with them if you like. Have a great day."

"Yes, thank you. You too. When you do not see us, we are gone to work. My children are in great hands. See you later," said Susan.

"Okay. Bye. We will have a great day. Thank you for your support and participation. Bye," said Lily-Butterfly.

At 10:00 AM the house cleaners arrived. Sue woke up and Lily-Butterfly fed and burped her. Lily-Butterfly decided to go to the community park and playground with Josh, Sue, and Rebornstar They left for the park and returned at 1:00 PM. When Lily-Butterfly returned to the house, the cleaners had left. They had lunch. After lunch Lily-Butterfly gave Josh and Sue their medicine and applied the medicated diaper rash ointment. This medication and medicated diaper rash ointment process went on for two weeks. Josh and Sue took an hour nap after lunch and Rebornstar went to the apartment to do her learning activities and spend quiet time alone. Lily-Butterfly decided to take a break from the laundry and went outside to the flower garden to read a book for an hour and write in her journal.

Wednesday ended for Lily-Butterfly, Josh, and Sue as it usually did; dinner, feeding Sue her milk formula, baths, dressing the children for bed, Susan and Jeff coming home, story time, singing to Josh and Sue, and bedtime. Plus, now the new addition of antibiotic medicine, and medicated diaper rash ointment. Within fourteen days the diaper rash and the bladder infection got better, and the children became pain free.

Rebornstar and Lily-Butterfly days also ended the usual way of, going to their apartment, showers or baths, Rebornstar television time for one hour, read a story or being told a story by her mother, and or quiet time before falling asleep. For Lily-Butterfly a walk outside, journal, read, prayer, meditation, and sleep. A current thought for Lily-Butterfly was, start talking even less, conserve her energy, and figure out how to resolve on her own within herself anything she found irritating.

Thursday morning Josh stayed asleep until Lily-Butterfly woke him up after attending to Sue diaper situation, feeding, and burp. After making breakfast she went upstairs to wake up Rebornstar and attend to Josh. Josh and Rebornstar came downstairs for breakfast. They ate in the guest dining room to leave the kitchen dining room for Jeff and Susan. Sue laid in her bassinet by Lily-Butterfly and eventually Sue fell back to sleep. When breakfast was over Sue was placed in her crib, Josh, and Rebornstar played in the nursery. Lily-Butterfly continued with her morning chores of loading the dishwasher, cleaning up the kitchen, going downstairs to the laundry room to attend to the laundry, tidying up the children's room, and opening the windows for fresh air in the children's room and her apartment. Lily-Butterfly never goes over to Jeff and Susan's bedroom section of the house. She had enough to take care of and wanted to mind her own business by not seeing any possible disconcerting things. Except for saying good morning Lily-Butterfly did not talk to Susan or Jeff and they did not try to talk to her as well. After opening the windows, Lily-Butterfly went back downstairs to the kitchen.

"Lily-Butterfly, wait, I would like to say thank you again for whatever you did so far for the children. I checked in on Sue and Josh before I went to sleep and again at 3:00 AM. They were fine and asleep," said Susan.

"Me too. Thank you," said Jeff.

"You are both welcome. Good. Congratulations for all your parental improvements," replied Lily-Butterfly.

"I left you $100 on the kitchen counter by the telephone. You can take the children and yourself to lunch at Newton Center. Take a taxi to the center and back. It is about a mile and a half walk one way. Your choice to take the taxi or walk. A change of scenery can be refreshing," said Susan.

"Thank you, Susan. I will take them."

Lily-Butterfly proceed to plan dinner for her and the children. Jeff and Susan left for work. Before Lily-Butterfly left to go to Newton Center she telephoned Manana Leila, fed and burp Sue, changed her diaper and applied the medicated diaper rash ointment, and gave her the antibiotic. For Josh she applied the diaper rash ointment and put a diaper on him. Lily-Butterfly took the antibiotic medicine with her to give to Josh after he ate lunch. At 12:00 PM Lily-Butterfly telephoned the taxi. The taxi came and she took the children to Newton Center for lunch. She also did some window shopping. At 2:30 PM Lily-Butterfly took the taxi back home. As usual Josh and Sue took naps. Rebornstar went outside to the playground to do some learning activities sitting at the picnic table. Lily-Butterfly rest for one hour in the flowers garden. She read a book and wrote in her journal. For Lily-Butterfly at 4:30 PM she prepared dinner. By 6:30 PM Rebornstar was in the apartment doing her nightly preparation for bed activities, and Lily-Butterfly was getting Josh and Sue ready for bed; by performing all their end of day bed-time activities. By the time Jeff and Susan came home at 7:45 PM Lily-Butterfly was in her apartment and the house was quiet. This day was the first day of many days she left work close to the end of work day time, and talking less to Jeff and Susan. Each day Lily-Butterfly would write daily summery of the day's activities, and anything else she needed to say to Jeff and Susan, in the large black notebook by the telephone. It was up to Jeff and Susan if they visited with their children at the end of the day in their rooms, and check up on them at 3:00 AM the following morning. Josh and Sue were now content and sleeping through the night. The children's health and well-being were Lily-Butterfly's main intention and focus.

Friday came with the same routines for Lily-Butterfly. The house cleaners came, and Lily-Butterfly left the house with the children and went to the community park until lunch time. When she returned from the park the house cleaners had left. The day continued with taking care of all the children's needs, laundry, dinner, bedtime care, story time, and going to sleep. Rebornstar and her mother did some game activities together and story time. Lily-Butterfly did not like to watch television she preferred writing in her journal and reading. Rebornstar was asleep at 9:45 PM.

Lily-Butterfly had finish with her end of day routines and prayer. This was Lily-Butterfly's first Friday night living in Jeff and Susan's house. She laid in bed meditating, and she smelled smoke. The smoke smell was familiar to Lily-Butterfly. It was the smell of marijuana-ganja. She wrinkled her brow and decided to ignore the smell. Ten minutes went by. And suddenly there was very loud rock and roll music. The music was so loud that the walls of Lily-Butterfly's room was vibrating.

"What is going on? How can we sleep with this loud music?" grumbled Lily-Butterfly.

She decided to wait before she did anything about the situation. For about fifteen minutes Lily-Butterfly try to sleep, ignored the loud music, and marijuana smell. She could not sleep, and she was also concerned that Josh and Sue would wake up. Lily-Butterfly got up, left her bedroom, and walked to the door that separated her apartment from the rest of the floor. She opened the door. A rush of marijuana smell, smoke, and rock and roll music embraced and surrounded Lily-Butterfly. She turned, closed the door, closed Rebornstar's bedroom door, put on her robe, reopened the apartment door, and went to check on Josh and Sue. They were still sleeping. Lily-Butterfly closed the children's bedroom door, took towels from the linen closet, roll the towels, and laid them across the bottom of the children's bedroom door.

The music was louder, and the marijuana smell and smoke were even stronger. Lily-Butterfly walked over to the locked door that separated the parent's bedroom and knock about six times. No one came to open the door. Lily-Butterfly went down to the kitchen and got a hammer. She walked back up to the same door, and used the hammer to repeatedly bang on the door. After seven bangs Jeff came to open the door. He was totally naked and holding a whisky bottle in his hand. Marijuana smoke and rock and roll music bellowed out through the door. Lily-Butterfly stepped back. She was surprised.

"PLEASE. TURN DOWN THE MUSIC AND COME BACK!" yelled Lily-Butterfly.

"Okay. Do you want to join us? Ha. Come in," said Jeff.

"NO! TURN DOWN THE MUSIC AND COME BACK! I WOULD LIKE TO TALK TO YOU!"

"Okay. I will be right back," replied Jeff.

Lily-Butterfly went to get a towel from the linen closet and covered her nose. Jeff turned down the music and returned. Susan staggered to the door. She was also totally naked. Susan had a bong smoking apparatus in her hand. Lily-Butterfly gathered her senses. She thought, I need to act quickly. I am breathing in this marijuana and whatever else is in this herb drug mixture.

"Please keep the music volume down. Lock the room door that you are smoking in. Keep the marijuana and drug smoke to a minimum. I do not want the children to wake up by this loud music or breathe in this drug smell and smoke. I do not want to breathe in this drug smell. I cannot sleep with the music so loud. The music is vibrating the walls. It is almost 11:00 PM. Please be aware that you are negatively affecting everyone else that is present on this floor. Thank you."

"Do you want to come in and party with us?" asked Susan.

"No. This is your house. Your children are next door sleeping. I am your employee. My daughter is sleeping in the apartment. I can smell the drugs and feel the music vibrating the walls from my bedroom. We are all being negatively affected by what you are doing. Also roll towels and put across the bottom of this door when you close it. If this is going to be a every Friday experience for me; I do not want to be here. I do not choose to be a part of this situation. Next time do not ask me to be a part of your negative crap. Do you hear and understand me? Let this Friday night be the first and last night that this happen while I work here. The things you choose to do in your home is your personal business. Please conduct yourselves in a manner that keeps these things private. Do not let this stuff invade the children and my space. Thank you very much. Do you agree? If you do not agree I have no choice but to call a taxi and leave immediately with my daughter."

"Sorry Lily-Butterfly. We will immediately do as you request. We will not make this happen again," said Susan.

"Make sure this does not happen again. I have choices. I can leave. After tonight's experiences the only reason that I am staying is for the children. I am trying to honor my two years promise. Remember this. Choose to tone down your crap."

Jeff took the bong from Susan and walked away.

"Susan another thing, I work tomorrow Saturday until 7:00 PM. I am off Sunday. I had plan to stay here on Sunday instead of going back to Somerville. After this experience I have change my mind. Every Saturday night after I finish work, and I am off on Sunday, I am leaving this house on Saturday night to go to my Manana Leila apartment in Somerville. Plus, every Friday night after I finish work, and I am off Saturday and Sunday I am leaving on Friday night. I will return every Sunday night by 9:00 PM. Every Friday night please leave my paycheck on the kitchen counter by the telephone. Tomorrow morning, I will remind you and write this in the black notebook by the telephone. I no longer want to be here if I do not have to. Enough is enough. I suggest that you and Jeff choose to take a break from all the negativity, before the negative history of Dan's death repeats itself. Maybe that is what is needed at this time, and one of the reasons I am here. Okay. You guys are intelligent and wise people. Good night."

"Wait Lily-Butterfly. We are sorry. You are right. This will not happen again. We are used to doing this every Friday night as a part of relaxing and shaking off our stress. You are right the children are affected by this behavior as well. Sorry about your paycheck I will leave it for you on Friday morning, instead of the night," said Susan.

"Good for both of you. I am speculating that all the negative crap on top of everything else has been causing all the other nannies to quit without notice. What else is going to reveal itself? Oh wow. Know that whatever it is, I am not going to choose to live with it. So, if both of you know about any other crap, that might be performed by both of you, choose to think twice, three times, and not do whatever it is. Try your best. Good night."

"Good night Lily-Butterfly. Thank you. We understand."

"I hope so, for all your greater good."

After saying this Lily-Butterfly walked away from Susan standing naked at the open door. The children did not wake up.

Some of Lily-Butterfly's thoughts as she laid in bed were, if Jeff and Susan do not choose to minimize their personal negativity, I cannot stay for two years. Many things are the cause as to why in three years all the other seven nannies quit without notice. Josh and Sue were stressed from all their parent's negative action, non-action, un-mindful behavior, Dan's spirit-ghost haunting, child neglect, stressful environment, and so on and so forth. Creator keep guiding me to the most productive views and actions. My intention, perception, and experiences to live a spiritual life of purpose, is like a never-ending revolving door of stuff and adventure. At about 11:55 PM Lily-Butterfly drifted off to sleep, during processing her thoughts.

9

Respect is important.

The next morning Lily-Butterfly got up at 6:00 AM. She got dressed and went upstairs to attend to Josh and Sue. She told them that she was going home and will be back on Monday. Although Sue was two going on three months, Lily-Butterfly felt that Sue understood her when she talked. Breakfast and lunch came and went, mixed in with the usual activities that were done daily. Every day working for Jeff and Susan was a process of similar routines. One week of Lily-Butterfly's experience working for Jeff and Susan and taking care of their children had come to an end. As the weeks went by Lily-Butterfly took action to improve her work experiences and master her daily experiences.

At 1:00 PM Jeff and Susan came downstairs. Lily-Butterfly had finished lunch and cleaned up the kitchen. She took all the children outside to the playground to play and read to Sue. At 3:00 PM Lily-Butterfly went back inside to feed Sue her formula and burp her, next she put Sue in her crib to take a nap. Josh had the choice of being with his parents, taking a nap, or spending quiet time resting.

"Here is your check Lily-Butterfly," said Jeff.

"Thank you. Remember that I am leaving tonight after I do everything to get the children ready for bed. I am leaving by 7:30 PM and I will return on Sunday night by 9:00 PM. I will leave and enter the house using the door on the apartment side of the house. See you on Monday morning. Remember to be home tonight by 7:30 PM. Do you remember what I said to both of you last night?"

"I think so. We will be here. We understand. Please do not quit. We will try our best to be mindful. Sorry about last night," said Susan.

"Yes sorry," said Jeff.

"I hear both of you. Would you like to spend time with Josh now? During this time, he usually takes a nap or spend quiet time resting. I am going upstairs now to pack our bags to go home later. Enjoy your afternoon."

53

"Let Josh do his usual routine by taking a nap or quiet time. We are going to the supermarket and should be back by 7:00 PM. Before you go home do everything you usually do for the children. Also put them to sleep before you leave tonight," said Susan.

"Okay."

"Would you like us to give you a ride to the train station in Newton Center tonight?"

"No thank you. We will take a taxi from here to our home in Somerville and return by taxi. I will not be taking the train this late. It would take me a long time to get home. Thanks."

"Okay. We understand."

"I am very concerned about my experience last night and wonder what would have happened if I did not come to ask you to stop what was happening. I might sound dramatic, direct, and seem like I talk too much. But I would like both of you to take everything I said last night very seriously. I am grateful for this job and the opportunity to have my daughter living with me at work. But I will not choose to suffer to keep this job. I have suffered enough to get to this place in my life. Suffering can be a part of growth, awakening, and transformation. Currently I choose to grow without needless suffering. So, choose to curb the negativity in your house and home, or you are going to end up taking care of your own children. In these current so-called modern times, I do not want to breathe in drugs, and I must sleep to be rested for work. The marijuana smoke last night did not smell like only marijuana there was some other drug mixed in. Please keep your personal private life, discrete and private. The stuff both of you do over your section of the house needs to stay within that section. I am here in a professional employee capacity. I like clear lines and boundaries, and business to be business. I do not want to be an accomplice to corrupt actions and these negative things affecting the children. Thank you for your consideration. Oh, on Sunday remember the children's medicine and diaper rash ointment, three times per day."

"Yes, regarding Josh and Sue's medicine and ointment. We understand. We are embarrassed now that you have confronted us about our behavior. Maybe we needed exactly what you did and said, for us to change our actions and attitude. Okay, we cannot be sorrier for our actions. We both stood naked in front of you, using drugs, smoking down the place, music vibrating the walls, our two children are right next door, and as two Business Lawyers asked you to come join us. This was very irresponsible behavior. Yes, we should keep our personal private life, discrete and private. You are right. Good that you are a strong person in your sense of self and confidence. We understand, and we hear you. We are leaving now for lunch and food shopping. We will be back by the time you leave to go home. See you on Monday. Bye," said Susan.

"Bye. After 7:30 PM you know that we have left. I will not be coming to say goodbye to both of you. I will make sure that you are here before I leave. Thank you," said Lily-Butterfly.

"Okay we understand. Bye," replied Jeff.

Lily-Butterfly and Rebornstar took the taxi and arrived home in Somerville at 9:30 PM on Saturday night. Manana Leila was home for the weekend. Lily-Butterfly unlocked the apartment door and walked in. Manana Leila was surprised. They were all happy to see one another.

"What made you come home? Coming home for one day is a short time. Anyway, I am happy to see both of you," said Manana Leila.

"A short time of de-stressing, rest from the everyday situations, and feeling free of certain situations, is precious, and priceless. I guess therefore you have this apartment and your own personal home. This helps you to have a sense of self, and a place to seek refuge from your everyday work experiences. With a weekly pay of fifty dollars you could have chosen to not rent an apartment."

"I hear you my child and I understand. We give thanks for everything, even one drop of opportunity is better than nothing. I am thankful for my job. What happened at work?" said Manana Leila.

"I am grateful for my job. I am getting acclimated to everything and all my experiences. Living and working in someone else's house is a multidimensional adventure. I do not want to complain. So, I will just say that I need a break from the whole situation to process and decompress. I am used to going to work and coming home daily. As you know having to live at work, work long hours, and constantly being and living in someone else life can be challenging. I do not want to talk about my employee's personal business and life. Plus, it stresses your nerves, and will have you worry about how I am doing. I have daily conversations with the Creator, myself, and my journal, to process my feelings. So how are you doing? Seeing you renews my spirit and soul."

"As usual I am doing well. As long as my spirit, soul, mind, emotions, and body is doing great, then my life will be great as well.

My outer life reflects my inner life. My body mirrors what is going on with my spirit, soul, mind, and emotions. I try my best to not make my outer life's experiences corrupt my inner self. Thanks to the Creator's will, so far so good. You are right about what you said about me having my own apartment, and home to come to when I feel like it. It is not easy to help manage, direct, and care for people's lives, children, home, and everything else. And I do not think our employers really realize the amount of work and care we perform. Our kind of work is a labor of love. I took care of six children and two parents. Imagine this, and at the same time take care of myself, health, and well-being. I am old now and time to simmer away from this human nature life. You are younger than me and have stronger nerves. You will be fine. There is a lot of human nature experiences and modern life's stress to encounter as you journey to discover and awaken your talents and find your authentic life's purpose and chosen destiny. From January 1972 to now I get paid fifty dollars per week and I pay my taxes. My social security payment and benefits helps me. Plus, my employees give me an extra $3,000 at Christmas as a bonus. You are lucky in these modern times to get paid as much as you do. With my pay I still feel very prosperous. Prosperity comes from within your spirit and soul, and not from physical things. Physical things are tools that help you to live and have resources to have more choices and opportunity. I am content with the simplest things and choices. Sometimes too many choices can create confusion, corruption, and becoming a lost spirit and soul. This is what I am used to growing up in the village bushes, with beautiful mother and father nature, and as a country bumpkin. Some people think this is a poor life have less money and so forth. I say they do not understand. My child, authentic simplicity and humility is the deepest ocean of grace, wisdom intelligence, unconditional love, care, respect, and compassion for yourself and everything else; to the point that there is no need to make waves. There is a letter here for you from the Lawyer. It is on the center table. Check it out. Rebornstar come over here and give your Manana a hug."

"Yes, my Manana," replied Rebornstar.

"Yes, Manana I am sitting here soaking in your words of purity and wisdom. Your words are exactly the additional medicine I need to enrich my spirit and soul. I am so happy that I am here even if it is for one day. I understand everything you say. The words you speak are also my priceless philosophy. Thanks be to the Creator for everything," said Lily-Butterfly.

Rebornstar hugged her great grandmother Manana, went to shower, and get ready for bed. It was past her bedtime. Lily-Butterfly read the letter from the Lawyer.

"Manana, the Lawyer's letter says my permanent visa application is accepted."

"Good. After your visa is approved, I will file for Gina's permanent resident visa to come and live in this country. She can add Henry and Dean to the application. Lucy is over twenty-one, married, and has a child. When Gina becomes a citizen, she can file for Lucy and her family."

"Manana, I hear you. I mostly forgot about Ms. Gina until you mentioned her name. Ha. Life is very interesting when I can see and understand what is happening."

"Tomorrow after breakfast we can all go to church. The idea of church supports the awareness of a Creator. Do you want to go to church?" said Manana.

"Yes. Let us go to church. The church inside us helps us to find something to enjoy with the modern way of churching. Hahaha. Amin. I can be funny."

"Yes, indeed, you can be funny. Serious, neutral, and funny can keep things in harmony and balance. It is late. I am going to sleep. Sweet dreams," said Manana Leila.

"Yes. Good night. Sweet dreams to you as well. I am happy to be here. Thank you for sharing your home with us."

"You are both welcome."

On Sunday after breakfast Manana Leila, Lily-Butterfly, and Rebornstar went to church, the nature park, had lunch at a restaurant, and went home for a nap. All three ladies prepare dinner together, and they ate. At 7:30 PM Lily-Butterfly and Rebornstar said goodbye to Manana Leila and took the taxi back to Jeff and Susan's home. They entered the home through the door on the apartment side of the building. After preparing for work they went to sleep. On Monday Lily-Butterfly woke at 6 AM and got dressed for work. When she went to Josh's room, he was still asleep. Sue was awake and quiet. When Sue saw Lily-Butterfly she smiled and kicked her legs.

"Hi Sue. I am back. How are you doing?"

Sue smiled again.

Lily-Butterfly bathed Sue, put on the diaper ointment and a cloth diaper, got her dressed, placed her in her crib, and tidied her room.

Next Lily-Butterfly took Sue downstairs to feed her. The kitchen looked like a disaster. There were toys, books, and food scattered on the floor. And dirty dishes, pots, cups, glasses, and utensils all over the table and tops of cupboards. Lily-Butterfly fed Sue, burped her, gave her the medicine, and put her in the bassinet. Next, she cleaned up the whole kitchen, load the dishwasher and turned it on. After the kitchen she checked the laundry and loaded two loads of dirty clothes for the children to wash.

It was time to wake up Josh. Lily-Butterfly went upstairs, she checked to see if Rebornstar had gotten up. It was 8 AM and the alarm had gone off. Rebornstar was getting dressed. Lily-Butterfly went to Josh's room. She woke him up and helped him to get dressed. Josh and Lily-Butterfly cleaned up his room and took all the dirty clothes downstairs to the laundry room. Rebornstar came downstairs. She helped with folding the children's clothes while Lily-Butterfly made breakfast of pancakes with strawberry toppings drizzled with honey, and orange juice. She also made tea for herself as she usually does. Lily-Butterfly said the prayer to bless the food, and they ate in the guest dining room. Sue laid relaxed in her bassinet beside Lily-Butterfly. Susan came into the kitchen when they were almost finished eating.

"Hi Lily-Butterfly. We are happy that you are back to start your second week with us. Thank God that you are here. Welcome back," said Susan.

"Okay Susan. The diaper rash is almost healed, Josh is more content and sleeps now through the night, Sue is more peaceful and has not scream-cried. The children's care is my priority. Cooking for the children, laundry, and light housekeeping are my secondary priority. If I choose to stay, I will always do my best. Please remember that I am leaving on Friday night at 7:30 PM. I will take a taxi."

"You do not want to leave on Saturday morning?"

"No. I want as much time as possible in my own environment. When I go home, I reset, refresh, digest, process, regroup, and rebalance to come back here to work as renewed as possible. I must take care of my health and well-being as well. When I am not here, I recommend that you are mindful of the smoking, drinking, and the loud music in relationship to the children."

"Alright. Yes, we will be mindful. I understand."

"Good for both of you."

Jeff came downstairs and he had breakfast with Susan.

Lily-Butterfly guided Josh and Rebornstar to go play in the nursery. She put Sue in her crib. In ten minutes, Sue fell asleep. Lily-Butterfly went downstairs to attend to the laundry. Jeff and Susan left for work.

Life for the next two years followed the same routine with regards to Lily-Butterfly and work. She planed her workdays with the intention of seeing Jeff and Susan as little as possible. Sometimes she only sees Jeff and Susan about thirty minutes in the morning, a casual here and there talk in the evening, and if she or they had some specific situation that they needed to talk about. On the weekends when Lily-Butterfly had Saturday and Sunday off when she went home Manana was there. They have lots of fun spending time together; going shopping, restaurants, church, parks, resting, relaxing, and going to museums.

The seasons came and went. Lily-Butterfly and Rebornstar experienced the colorful expressions of the spring, summer, fall and winter. And they got used to the cold and snow. December of 1983 Lily-Butterfly became twenty-six years old and Rebornstar was five years old. They had a great holiday, birthday, and New Year's Eve celebrations. At the end of December 1983 Lily-Butterfly had been working for Jeff and Susan for four months and one week.

In Lily-Butterfly's care and unconditional love Josh, and Sue had grown, and thrived. Josh was completely potty trained during the day, and almost during the night. Jeff and Susan expressed their daily gratitude for everything Lily-Butterfly did for them, the children, and their home.

10

Unconditional love and compassion mean love without expecting something in return. Love is not about trading something for another thing. Compassion means deep understanding.

Monday January 9, 1984 Lily-Butterfly had done all the morning preparation she usually does for Josh and Sue. It was now breakfast time and Lily-Butterfly said the prayer to bless the food and they ate. Sue was in her bassinet on the floor by Lily-Butterfly. Susan came downstairs into the kitchen. She walked over to the dining table in the guest room where Lily-Butterfly was sitting with the children.

"Lily-Butterfly I have all the purification herbs that you asked me to get for the sacred transition ceremony to clear Dan's ghost."

"Would you and Jeff like to do the ceremony on a morning or afternoon? Night is not a good time."

"We can do it tomorrow morning. I will tell Jeff."

"Okay. Be ready at 9:00 AM. Today I will purify and cleanse both children bedroom and bathrooms, to prepare for tomorrow morning closure and Dan's transition ceremony. In the morning I will cleanse the rooms again, create a sacred space with prayers and blessings, and call the momentum tunnel of light and angels, for Dan to use to cross over to the other side. After breakfast with the children I will be ready to tell both of you what to do. Is this okay with you so far."

"Tell me now our parts and what we have to do, so that I can process and prepare today. I will tell Jeff the process. Tomorrow morning when it is time if we need to refresh our memory you can tell us again. This is a great and priceless opportunity."

"I will cleanse the outside of your body by smudging both Jeff and you with the sacred herbs smoke. Smudging is like being surrounded by the smoke from your marijuana bong pipe. After I smudge, both of you will enter the restroom where Dan drowned. Both of you will do the same things. Sit on the floor by the tub. I will get the spirit-ghost of Dan to go into the bathroom. Jeff and you will close your eyes and visualize Dan as you are comfortable. Focus in your heart space and connect to Dan in your awareness, like a dream. Place both hands on your chest and sincerely express with words out loud or silent how you feel and think about Dan, his death, any expression of love, regret, and so forth. Say naturally and sincerely everything that comes to your awareness to say. At the end say goodbye to Dan. Tell him to go through the tunnel and follow the light, and that he is not alone the angels will accompany him to the other side. Say what else comes naturally for you to say to guide him through the tunnel and to follow the light and angels. Both of you might express emotions like crying, heat, cold, shiver, and shaking. Let this happen, this is the body's way of shaking off and releasing stress. When you are finished come and let me know. I will close the sacred space and the momentum tunnel of light. Do you hear and understand?"

"Yes. Tell me one more time. Please. Oh wow. Lily-Butterfly you can do these things. This is like a Priest or Rabbi work. Do you think that we can do all of this by ourselves, only the two of us?"

"Yes, you will do great. After the process is completed say a thank you prayer from your religious belief system. When this is completed come to let me know you are finished with the process. Remember that the angels that are guardians of the sacred momentum tunnel and the Creator God will be in the room. You will do it, trust. Jeff will follow your example if he forgets. I will talk to the spirit-ghost of Dan and explain everything and give him the awareness to go through the momentum tunnel of light. When you are finished you will see how it works."

"Lily-Butterfly, really, this is a big deal. Are you sure that we can do this?"

"Yes Susan. Yes. Your sincerity of heart will create the way for the process to be accomplished. Dan might reveal himself to you. Do not be afraid. Let yourself experience all the emotions that come up. I will create a safe and protective sacred space after I take Josh and Sue downstairs before breakfast. I will close the sacred space when both of you have completed the process. You seem to have a good memory, go write down everything I told you. Bring the paper to me and I will see if you wrote everything correctly. Give this paper to Jeff for him to read and know what to do."

"Good idea. I will go write down everything you told me. The process you have told me sounds and feel good to me. I will guide Jeff in what to do. You are very interesting Lily-Butterfly. It is a blessing to have you work for us. We are lucky."

"Amin," replied Lily-Butterfly.

Susan wrote down the instructions and returned with the paper. Lily-Butterfly checked what she wrote.

"Yes, this is correct. I know you could do this. Or else I would not be here guiding you to do this."

"Where did you learn how to do these sacred and spiritual things?"

"From my ancestors, and my spirit and soul. I come from a long lineage of talented spiritual ancestors and healers, and so it is wired in my blood and DNA."

"Oh, wow I feel excited to do this process. Finally, we get to make closure with Dan's death and so forth. Maybe this will motivate us to transform our negative addictions and patterns, and help us to practice being improved positive parents."

"Maybe. Sometimes the Creator God works in mysterious way. Remember to thank your representation of God in your own way for this complete process and opportunity. Without the Creator God's help none of this can be possible. It is my pleasure to assist you and your family with this process. I must go take care of some other work stuff before Sue wakes up. Susan enjoy your day."

"You too."

The next morning Lily-Butterfly usual routine preparing Josh and Sue for the day. She brought the children downstairs. Sue was fed, burped, and placed in her bassinet. The medicine and medicated diaper rash ointment was always done on the right schedule. Josh played with some toys in the kitchen. Lily-Butterfly returned to open the windows in the children's room, covered all smoke alarms in that area with foil so that they would not go off, and with sacred herbs smudged both rooms. Jeff usually gets up and turn off the security alarm at 5:00 AM. There was no need to be concerned that the alarm would go off from opening the windows. After smudging Lily-Butterfly opened sacred space and the momentum tunnel of light for Dan's spirit-ghost to cross over to the other side. On completing this she located the spirit-ghost of Dan and talked to him about the process his parents would perform. Part of the conversation Lily-Butterfly had with Dan was that he had the free-will to cross over or not. But it would be for his greater good that he did choose to cross over, and she explained to him the benefits of crossing over to the other side. Lily-Butterfly completely prepared the sacred ceremony process for Jeff, Susan, and Dan. The sacred process knows the way and what to do. Lily-Butterfly went back downstairs to the kitchen. Rebornstar and Josh were sitting at the guest dining room table. For breakfast Lily-Butterfly made scrambled eggs with English muffins, blueberries, orange juice, and some tea for herself. They were finished with breakfast at 8:50 AM. Sue was placed in her crib. Josh and Rebornstar played in the nursery playroom. Susan came downstairs at 9 AM and Lily-Butterfly guided her and Jeff how to perform the sacred process ceremony.

Jeff and Susan finished the sacred process ceremony, and everything went well. Lily-Butterfly did her part in ensuring that the process was successful and complete. Jeff and Susan were very emotionally expressive during the ceremony. They got the opportunity to release all the negative stress emotions they were carrying for over four years, and make closure with the death of their son Dan. After Jeff and Susan were finished in Josh's room and went back to their bedroom section of the house Lily-Butterfly went to Josh's room smudged the room again with sacred herbs, closed sacred space, and closed the momentum tunnel of light. The process felt complete to Lily-Butterfly. She left all the windows open and went back downstairs to continue with her day and duties.

Jeff and Susan went back to bed, I guess to talk and continue to process their experiences. When the laundry process was set up Lily-Butterfly fed and burped Sue. The other children used the restroom, and they all went to the community park. When they returned from the park at 12:30 PM Jeff and Susan were in the kitchen eating.

"We thank you again very much. This experience is speechless. You know everything already. We will remain in as much silence as possible and continue to simmer and process. Dan said good-bye to us. We saw him. He listened to us and went into the tunnel of light. As Dan walked away and into the tunnel, we saw two white cloudy figures beside him one on each side. You are the only one we could tell this to, because you know everything about this stuff already. If we tell anyone else, they would think that we are totally crazy. Words, money, or diamonds could not pay you for what you did for us. This is a priceless opportunity. We thank God for everything, including you. Amin," said Susan.

"Susan speaks for both of us. I do not even feel like talking. I did not think what I experienced was possible, and stuff like this was real, or could be real. After this experience I know better. Oh wow. Once you know something it is difficult to go back to the unknown. Respect to the process and to you and all you did to help us. Really," whispered Jeff.

"You are all welcome regarding everything you have said. It was a pleasure to assist you and Dan. Enjoy your processing, and day. I am going to give the children lunch. Take care," said Lily-Butterfly.

Jeff and Susan left for work at 2:00 PM. Lily-Butterfly and the children continued with their routine and the rest of the day.

After that day Lily-Butterfly did not see Dan's spirit-ghost around the house anymore. Josh and Sue did not have any more disturbances from Dan's spirit-ghost, because Dan crossed over to the other side. At this time, I will summarize the rest of Lily-Butterfly's time working for Jeff and Susan. Every day was like how it was described in the past story expression; except for some long-term changes that Lily-Butterfly did to support the family long term, as she got closer to leaving at the end of her two years commitment. During this time Lily-Butterfly turned more within the vortex of her spirit and soul, contemplating, reflecting, meditation, and consistent prayer and creating mode. She communicated with the children as much as she should, but spoke to Jeff and Susan when she needed to, or when they wanted to. This kind of mood Lily-Butterfly knew very well. It was something that happened automatic when she was about to shift into another level of her spiritual growth ascension, and life changing events were going to appear, and be created by choice, in her life. And she would have to mindfully manage and direct all her chosen evolutions, while journeying and caring for her daughter Rebornstar.

For the remainder of the time Lily-Butterfly worked at Jeff and Susan's house, Josh and Sue's diaper rash and bladder infection healed and never re-occurred. Both children grew, thrived, slept through the night, became content, and peaceful. For using the toilet both day and night, Josh was completely toilet trained. At two years and two months old, Sue was toilet trained for using the toilet during the daytime, and almost for the nighttime; most mornings she would wake up with a dry diaper. Jeff and Susan over the rest of the time became more attentive to their children. Lily-Butterfly taught Jeff and Susan, when they ask, how to take improved care of their children, themselves, their home, and environment. They also learned from just watching how Lily-Butterfly did things. Lily-Butterfly over time, washed all the dirty clothes Susan and Jeff had in their section of the house. She also washed all the dirty clothes the children had over three years. When all the clothes were washed Jeff and Susan donated all the clothes that they no longer choose to have, and clothes that did not fit the children at this time. Jeff and Susan improved their mindfulness and awareness.

Lily-Butterfly created a main organized room, for clean and folded clothing, sheets, towels, and other garments. She sorted through and de-cluttered all the children's toys, clothing, shoes, books, and organized the children's rooms and drawers. All the things that were no longer needed were donated. Jeff and Susan improved very much with donating everything they no longer need, use, and did not love or like. Lily-Butterfly guided them to find a new house cleaning service that emptied the house garbage cans, clean refrigerators, did all their laundry, and add another day for this cleaning service to accomplish these duties. So, they hired a company that provided all these services, and they were employed to work three days. Two days the cleaning company cleaned the house. One day someone came in to wash, fold all the laundry for everyone, and clean the refrigerator. Close to the time for Lily-Butterfly to leave Jeff and Susan asked her to interview potential nannies to make sure that they had the right person for the job. They knew that although Lily-Butterfly was leaving she naturally cared that someone with the right potential would be hired for their continued success; especially for the children's greater good. Lily-Butterfly organized everything so that the new nanny had an easier time doing her work responsibilities.

Lily-Butterfly hired a nanny with experience, someone who chose to, and was comfortable living in the home fulltime, a widow in her fifties and still single, kind, caring, flexible, nurturing, and seemed to love children. Lily-Butterfly worked with this woman for two weeks to train her and observe her natural childcare talents and offered her a weekly salary of $500 per week to care mostly for Sue. Josh went to kindergarten September 1985 just before his sixth birthday; and when Lily-Butterfly left. At four plus years old Josh started pre-school. Lily-Butterfly home schooled Rebornstar all along so when she went to kindergarten, she would be okay. Lily-Butterfly noticed that Rebornstar was a slow learner, so she did not mind delaying formal school for another year. Lily-Butterfly left Jeff and Susan Saturday August 30, 1985. Rebornstar went to kindergarten in Somerville where Manana Leila lived September 1985. December of 1985 Rebornstar became seven years old and Lily-Butterfly became twenty eight years old.

In July 1985 Lily-Butterfly received a letter from the Immigration Lawyer that the permanent visa application was complete, and that she and Rebornstar needed to return to the island of Kawomaya, Capital City Embassy to be interviewed for the final visa approval process. This appointment was for August 12, 1985. Lily-Butterfly arranged with Jeff and Susan to take five vacation days off with pay. Lily-Butterfly had not taken any of her annual five vacation days since she was working with them. Susan took five days off from work to take care of the children while Lily-Butterfly was gone. Lily-Butterfly plan to be off from work August 12 to 18, 1985.

Saturday August 10, 1985 Lily-Butterfly and Rebornstar took the plane from Boston Logan International Airport to the Capital City on the island of Kawomaya. They stayed at a hotel close to the embassy. The embassy interview was successful and Lily-Butterfly and Rebornstar received their permanent resident visa. On Wednesday August 14, 1985 they took the plane back to Boston Logan International Airport, and a taxi back to Manana Leila's apartment in Somerville. The rest of the week Lily-Butterfly went to local places with Rebornstar, register Rebornstar for kindergarten in Somerville public school, and visiting Harvard Square with Rebornstar to show her the Harvard University Campus. Lily-Butterfly told Rebornstar the story of when she first came to visit Manana in the United States, visiting Harvard Square, and discovering the Harvard University Campus. Revisiting this place was also a symbolic reference of what Lily-Butterfly had decided to do when she left Jeff and Susan's employment.

Sunday August 18, 1985 Lily-Butterfly and Rebornstar returned to work, for the last two weeks of working at Jeff and Susan's home. Monday the children were happy to see her. At breakfast time Susan came downstairs when they were almost finished eating. Josh was ready for Susan to take him to pre-school. Susan came to the dining room that they were eating in.

"Good morning Lily-Butterfly and children. It is great to see you Lily-Butterfly. In two weeks, you will be gone forever from our life. How sad. We would like to offer you $800 per week to stay. This is the pay we should have paid you from the beginning. All the work, and genuine effort that you performed was more than worth $800 per week. We would like to offer you this pay for you to stay. Think about our offer," said Susan.

"No. I will not stay. Thank you for your offer. I plan to go back to the University to improve my education. For one thing I must learn how to work with computers, plus other things. In the future I must discover my life's purpose and chosen destiny. This job is not it. There are more things that are more important than money and material possessions. I know that in my heart I was born for using all my spirit and soul talents as tools to help humanity. I must keep doing what must be done to get to this discovery and destination. I am a spirit and soul traveler coming from a faraway realm to perform what I promised. I must discover what I promised to do and get what I promised done. With the Creator as my spirit and soul guide I trust that I will eventually fulfill my commitment and promise. This is all spiritual talk I hope that you understand me, and do not ask me to stay again. You should have paid me the $800 from the beginning, and do not try to insult my intelligence and wisdom, by offering me $800 per week to bribe me now to stay. Do you understand what I am saying Mrs. Susan? I would like to leave here in respect and peace. I have done more than enough while I was here, in making sure that you and the children will be okay after I have left, and so on and so forth. I have selected the best nanny to continue to help both of you and the children. Enough is enough. Thank you and Mr. Jeff for everything. Excuse me, I have things to do."

"I am sorry if you feel insulted by my offer. I am very sorry. It is normal for us to want you to stay. Our offer was not meant to be an insult."

"Well I guess that it is normal for you to be selfish. This is all a selfish offer. And to me selfishness always smells like rotten fish. I came here and shared with you and your family unconditionally and unselfish for all your greater good, regardless of the pay. I did this because I want to and could. Now I would like for you to respect the two years that we agreed to and that I must leave now. I will miss you, your husband, and most of all the children. I will really miss the children. For two years I took care of these children, as I would take care of my own children; and not because of a job and pay. I must go on to what is next for me and my daughter; just like you, your husband, and your children will go on with what is next. This is life. I cannot be a permanent fixture in your lives. This is not my chosen destiny. Mrs. Susan do you understand."

"Yes, I understand you, loud and clear. Sorry. I see. Thank you for enlightening me again. Thank you for everything. You are right. We wish for you all the best of everything. You seem upset. Sorry."

Susan and Lily-Butterfly carried on with their day.

The rest of the two weeks Lily-Butterfly spent getting the children and herself emotionally ready for her exit. She performed her exit strategies. Lily-Butterfly knew to follow her internal guidance navigational system and heart, even when it seemed to not make sense to other people, and their human nature.

On Friday morning August 30, 1985 Jeff and Susan came downstairs to the kitchen and spoke to Lily-Butterfly.

"Thank you is never enough to express my gratitude for all the things you have done for us. But I will forever say thank you anyway. I, we, the children appreciate very much all that you have done for us for the last two years," said Susan.

"I say the same thing. In addition, I would like to take this opportunity to say we will surely miss you. I think there is only one of your spirit in the Universe. My perception is that your spirit is like mother-nature. We see it as a blessing, and an answer to our unconscious prayers that you came to help us. And, just like you came to help us, you must go on now to what is next. We understand. We will miss you. We should have found it in our hearts to pay you at least the $800 per week. We did not do the right thing, so with this awareness we would like to give you the extra $300 per week that we did not give you over the approximately last 105 weeks. This total amount is $300 times 105 equals $31,500. After we deduct taxes the total is $25,200. When you file your tax returns you will get whatever refund, if we took too much for tax. The tax deducted is on the pay stub. In addition, here is your paycheck for this week and the five vacation days that you did not take. We would like you to leave here in balance and harmony. We cannot take so much of everything you gave and not balance it with giving you this money that you are rightfully entitled to. We grew up religious and spiritual and we know about karma and balance. Thank you for reminding us and helping us to get back on the right path. Here, all the best with everything you choose to do and become. Goodbye. Blessings and Amin," said Jeff.

"Amin and thank you for everything and this money. I see. You both come to understand me and where I am coming from. You are welcome. Blessings to all of you as well. I was not born for any one person, I cannot be owned by any people, I am a Universal spirit, and soul on a mission of discovering my authentic purpose and chosen destiny. One road will lead to another. And the way will show the way. Thanks again. I accept this money as an equal exchange for all my practices and performances here. Blessings. At 7:30 PM tonight we will be gone. We will take the taxi home with all our things. As usual I will get the children ready for bed before I leave. Your new nanny will be here tomorrow, Saturday. She starts work on Monday. All the information about her is in the black notebook. Now that everything is in harmony and positive balance you and the children should be fine. Take care of yourselves, the children, and the next nanny. Learn from your past and mistakes. Thanks again for the money. I will use it to pay for my advance university certification, and other expenses. Thanks for everything else as well. Okay," said Lily-Butterfly.

"Okay we feel closure and peace. And our conscience and heart feels resolved and at peace. Goodbye Lily-Butterfly. Your name suits you," said Susan.

All three of them take turns hugging one another. They all cried.

"Goodbye and thank you Mr. Jeff and Mrs. Susan," said Rebornstar.

That night Lily-Butterfly told Josh and Sue her final goodbye. Josh cried, hugged her, and he seems to accept and understand the situation.

Sue smiled and hugged Lily-Butterfly and said in her two years old voice, "bye L-B."

"Bye Sue,"

Lily-Butterfly and Rebornstar brought all their things that they had in the house outside. The taxi came. They got inside the taxi. The taxi drove away from Jeff and Susan's house. The revolving door of Lily-Butterfly turned completely to what was next.

11

Rebornstar was in kindergarten. School was going great for her and she like being in school. Lily-Butterfly had done research, visited two universities, and chosen her course of studies. She registered for a Boston university after passing the entrance exams. Lily-Butterfly started her course of study in October 1985 before her twenty-eighth birthday. The extra money Lily-Butterfly got from Jeff and Susan was used to help pay for the Master of Science Degree in Hospitality and Tourism Management certification. Lily-Butterfly took the bus to school five days per week after taking Rebornstar to school. Her courses were from 9:30 AM to 1:30 PM. At the university, in her classes Lily-Butterfly was the oldest one. She was friendly with her classmates but did not seem to have anything in common with them except for her class studies. Being focused on schoolwork, a confident introvert, speaking when needed or necessary, not a complainer, taking time to contemplate decisions, taking wise actions, no time for gossip, no nonsense attitude, direct communication style; did not make Lily-Butterfly a popular classmate. She liked this, it makes her unnoticeable, sort of like invisible, and this way her class time was spent productively, she came and went with ease, had less static, and felt stress free. Most time she enjoyed her quiet and peaceful internal process of meditation and prayer.

As the months go by Lily-Butterfly integrated the wild mother-nature world within her with the wild mother-nature outside her. She spent as much time as possible jogging for exercise, writing in her journal, reading, schoolwork, taking care of Rebornstar, going on local trips, and other activities that support her health, well-being, and positive stress-free living. School became easy for Lily-Butterfly after three months, because she started to do subjects that she had learned already in college on the island of Kawomaya. To help classmates that needed extra help, Lily-Butterfly would tutor them for a donation.

Twenty months into her university certification Lily-Butterfly started to research finding employment in the hotel and restaurant food service industry. She found an ideal job in a hotel. An entry level Hotel Management position, with good pay, and benefits. Her Master of Science Degree in Hospitality and Tourism Management certification was going to be completed on August 7, 1987. After Lily-Butterfly graduated, September of the same year Rebornstar would be going to second grade. Things seem to have lined up to take this job. She had to contemplate if she wanted the job, to decide to schedule an interview. Why? Because she would have to move to another state, change Rebornstar's school location, move away from Somerville and Manana Leila, and this decision would take her on a long leap into the future. The job would be in New York City. Moving to New York City would be going way out of Lily-Butterfly's comfort zone and into the opposite unknown.

Lily-Butterfly had a very short time to decide. She researched the hotel and the hotel company, called the hotel to speak to the Personnel Manager and the General Manager. After learning more about the job and processing all the information, Lily-Butterfly scheduled an interview for the job. At the end of July Lily-Butterfly asked Manana Leila to take seven days off from work to take care of Rebornstar, so that she could visit New York City for the interview. Manana Leila told Lily-Butterfly yes, about taking care of Rebornstar. Manana Leila also told Lily-Butterfly that if the job was meant to be, she would get it, and she should move and take the job. Lily-Butterfly made a reservation for three nights at the same hotel that she was having an interview to work. The interview was on the second day of her arrival on August 11th. She decided that staying in the same hotel would give her a close-up view of her future work environment if she got the job and decided to take it. The inner guidance to take the job was very strong and hard to ignore. She decided to use public bus transportation to travel to New York City. The day before departing to New York City, Lily-Butterfly packed her bags and left them by the front door.

On the morning of Lily-Butterfly's departure to New York City she got up at 5 AM, got dressed, and took a taxi to the bus station in downtown Boston. The bus ride from Boston to New York City was about four and a half hours. Lily-Butterfly got on the bus, put her bags in the over-head compartment, sat in her seat, and prayed. Thirty minutes after the bus left the Boston bus station, she took out her book and started to read. In-between reading, she looked with curiosity out the bus window at the different scenery. Lily-Butterfly was most amazed at the tall apartment buildings that people lived in. She taught that tall buildings were only for hotels and offices. At one point in her observation, Lily-Butterfly thought, I would not live in such tall buildings. How would I get out in emergency situations? Living in an elevator building would not be the choice for me. I hope this hotel I am going to does not have over seven floors. If I get this job, I wish I work mainly on the first floor. Me and my old fashion country bumpkin style and views, as I evolve to accept the modern views and ways. Amin. Creator you are funny and work in mysterious ways.

The bus arrived in New York City Port Authority bus terminal. Without getting off the bus Lily-Butterfly could sense the hustle and bustle. To her it was as if she was transported to a whole new world and out of her comfort zone. The feeling reminded her of the experience of getting on the bus the first time with Manana Leila to go live with Ms. Gina. And when she permanently moved out of the valley, and village of Yaj, to live in a more modern place name Mansa Town; on the island of Kawomaya.

Waiting for her turn to be able to get off the bus, Lily-Butterfly mumbled, "oh Creator here we go again. More growing and awakening pains and training opportunity. This environment is stressful and will be difficult for me. I guess it is time for me to get back on the tread mill of deeper awakening, choice, action, improved responsibility, practice, transformation, change, improving my modern life experiences. Four years of some sort of rest I guess is enough. Here we go again. I know that if I do not choose to go forward and embrace what is next, my destiny will find me on the path I took to escape it. So, as usual I will surrender and voluntary leap forward into the unpredictable unknown. Amin."

Lily-Butterfly got up and took her bags. She was the last one to walk off the bus. She took a taxi to the hotel.
"I feel claustrophobic. Tall buildings on both sides, noise of many description, crowds, lots of traffic, people look like they are in a blank trance, and an atmosphere of not a care about anything. This is my opinion and perception," whispered Lily-Butterfly, sitting in the back of the taxi.
The taxi arrived at the hotel. Lily-Butterfly paid the taxi driver, got out of the car, and walked into the hotel with her bags. Inside the hotel things were quieter. Lily-Butterfly checked in at the receptionist

desk. She received her room key. She talked to man that attended to her at the receptionist desk.

"Sir, where is the management office?"

"Walk to your right and turn right. You will see a sign that says Management Office."

"Okay, thank you."

Lily-Butterfly picked up her bags and walked up the steps to the second floor. She chooses to not use the elevator. Lily-Butterfly did not mind what people think or perceive regarding her spiritual, country bumpkin, and ancient ways of expression. In the hotel room Lily-Butterfly washed her face and called Manana Leila and Rebornstar to tell them at she arrived safely at her destination. After the phone call she laid down on the bed looking up at the ceiling.

"I am in the city that never sleeps. Whatever that means. How could people live in an environment that never sleeps and rest? I guess it is time to practice an amplified version of being in a place opposite to my comfort zone and being comfortable. Oh, here come Ms. Gina's vibes training again. Nothing or no one is going to take away my authentic essence, positive vibes, and fearlessness. Love and peace are the way for me, as I function on this revolving door that never takes a break. Whatever this means I must wait and see. Ms. Gina is my first and last shadow boxing teacher of overcoming fear, trauma, suffering, corruption, and negative energies. All energies can be useful. I do not have to choose to be stuck in negativity if these energies come knocking at the door of my experiences. I know this is easier said than done. We will see. Let me go downstairs to the restaurant to have an early dinner. When I return, I will journal all my experiences so far, meditate to calm my nerves, shower, pray, and go to sleep early. This way I will be rested and ready for the interview tomorrow at 10:00 AM. Life is as easy as I perceive it to be. Why am I in this stressful place? Okay. Calm down. It is the way to the way. My life's purpose and destiny are beyond this location. This is a gate I have attracted to get to the next gate. One step at a time, conscious, and steady, I journey on the path of my chosen destiny. Stop. Enough. I do this endless chatter to process my resistance to what I know I am going to end up choosing to do. Mm. Hum. This is too much expression of continuous chatter, although I am just processing my discernment," Lily-Butterfly mumbled on and on, like a rambling and babbling brook.

At 6:30 PM Lily-Butterfly got out of the bed, walked out of the door, and locked it. She walked down the stairs to main floor and chose a restaurant in the lobby for dinner. She ate dinner and refused to continue the inner chatter and repeated contemplation regarding taking the job and moving to New York. During dinner Lily-Butterfly focused on meditation.

Will Lily-Butterfly be offered the job? Will she choose to take the job? Only the Creator knows for sure. We will see, the will of the Creator, her spirit, soul, and her chosen destiny.

12

The next morning Lily-Butterfly woke up at 5:00 AM. At 8:00 AM she was dressed and left the room to go to breakfast. When Lily-Butterfly finished breakfast, she returned to the hotel room to complete her final preparations to attend the interview. She arrived at the interview fifteen minutes early. At this time only the hotel General Manager was in the room, she entered and introduced herself. The interview began. Some of the things that happened were, giving her previous work reference letters, and college and university certifications. The General Manager gave Lily-Butterfly a five-page form with many questions to fill out. One section of the form was a psychological review, without Lily-Butterfly knowing it. During the time she filled out the form, four more interviewer executives joined the General Manager for the interview. Lily-Butterfly completed the form to the best of her ability. She had no intention to get the job if it was not right for her. And wanted the job only it was in her destiny for her greater good. On the form she wrote that she would relocate if they decided to give her the job, and that she would need about a month to relocate. The interview lasted approximately two hours. At the end of the interview the General Manager told Lily-Butterfly that she would contact her if they had decided to give her the job, after interviewing all the other applicants. Lily-Butterfly gracefully left the conference room after the interview and went to lunch. She had a lunch of chicken vegetable soup, fish sandwich, and drank water with lemon. During lunch she processed her interview and other experiences.

"There is so much noise in this city. Wow. Maybe the noise seems overwhelming to me, because I am used to and like more of a quieter space. I do not know if I can acclimate to so much perceived noise and instability. Oh, my Creator I only want this hotel job if it is for my greater good, the best interest of my unknown chosen destiny, and discovering my life's purpose," whispered Lily-Butterfly.

Completing lunch Lily-Butterfly got up and left the restaurant. She went window shopping. There were many stores on both sides of the street, crowds of people walking back and forth, and so many different motor vehicles.

"Wow, this place seems interesting," grumbled Lily-Butterfly.

A light blue jaguar motor car pulled up at the sidewalk, to park. This car parked on the same side of the street that Lily-Butterfly was looking in a jewelry store's display window. A man got out of the car. He walked towards the jewelry store and opened the door. He paused and looked at Lily-Butterfly.

"Hey beautiful. You can come in and look. No charge for looking. Come in. This is my store. My name is Croco. What is your name?" said the man.

Croco opened the door wider. Lily-Butterfly entered.

"Are you new in New York City? You have the cautious and quiet vibes. You seem like a country girl type. What brought you to the city, beautiful?" said Croco.

Still Lily-Butterfly kept silent. She looked at the different jewelry and continue to ignore Croco.

Croco stopped talking to Lily-Butterfly. He went into a room at the back of the store. Lily-Butterfly looked as much as she liked and left the store. Croco noticed that she had left. He hurried out of the office and store to catch up with Lily-Butterfly.

"Hey. Miss. Wait. Why did you leave?" said Croco.

Lily-Butterfly ignored Croco. She did not look back. Croco walked briskly and caught up to Lily-Butterfly.

"Hi beautiful. Are you deaf, dumb, or just do not like me?" said Croco.

Lily-Butterfly stopped walking. Now they are looking at each other, face to face, and eye to eye.

"What do you want?" asked Lily-Butterfly.

"You seem like an interesting country girl. I like your outfit and how you look. What is your name? Can I give you a ride somewhere? Ha."

"My country girl vibe is so obvious? I do not need a ride. I am staying in this hotel right here."

"Yes, you seem like a country quiet type girl. Okay. This is very rare around here in the city. Are you from the island of Kawomaya? Your accent sounds like it. Hahaha. Plus, I know a thing or two."

"Yes, I was born in deep country, on the island of Kawomaya."

"I am from Kawomaya too. I am a city boy. Interesting. What brought you to the big city?"

"I came for a job interview. Too many questions. I do not know you. I must go. Bye."

"All right miss beautiful. Questions helps me to get to know you. Getting to know you must start somewhere. I hope that you get the job. If you do, maybe I will see you again, and you will tell me your name then. Bye. Take care miss beautiful."

"Bye Mr. Croco."

Lily-Butterfly stepped away and around Croco. He stepped aside and watched her enter the hotel lobby. She walked up the steps to her room on the second floor. Arriving in the room Lily-Butterfly washed her face, picked up her journal, and sat at the table in the room to write. Next, she wrote in her journal all her day's experiences. As she wrote in her journal the things that agitated her the most were about meeting Croco. Some of the things she wrote about meeting Croco were: - Croco seems to be a Capital City kind of a guy. He seems confident, street smart, and the slick type. He has eyes that change color. Croco eyes are sometimes light green, light blue, light brown, and sometimes different shades of light yellow. He looks about six feet four inches, strong, athletic build, light brown skin, and of mixed ancestry. In my opinion, Croco is the type I should stay away from. Oh well. Currently, I have no time to waste on men's nonsense and games. But Creator what I want, think, and what is your will for my destiny, is three different things. Anyway, I am expressing my opinion. Creator you know everything best. Amin. After rambling in her journal, she closed the book, took off her shoes, and laid in the bed to take a nap.

During Lily-Butterfly's nap she had a lucid dream. In the dream she was dressed in a mother and father nature brown cloak with a hood attached. The hood was up and over her head. Lily-Butterfly was walking on a path up ahead the one path divided into three paths before her. At the point where the path divided into three paths there was a five feet high and four feet wide bolder. At the bolder a man appeared. He was dressed in a long golden robe. He told Lily-Butterfly to choose one of the paths. She looked at the left, center, and right pathways. She chose the center path. The man told her good choice. This is the most advance and difficult path. The center path is made up of the left and right path combined. In addition, the man told her, since you chose the center path, your quest is to master all three pathways, and at the same time, do not get stuck in any. This center path practice is to create and master a complete authentic neutral path. Lily-Butterfly continued to stand in silence and the man continued to speak. There are two paths to the dimension of spiritual wakening and growth. A mountain path that leads up and a low-level earth-bound path. In these modern times they are called the pathways of love and fear. To master love, you must master fear as well. To master fear, you do not have to master love. So, the path of fear which most people choose can be an easier path. Choosing the left path would take you up to the path of love. Choosing the right path would lead you down to the path of fear. Choosing the center path, you will be weaving both pathways together as one as you walk this path, like the sacred creative law of tantra, weaving, unweaving, reweaving, repeatedly, and so forth. The path of love creates light and the path of fear creates darkness. The path of love will be alchemizing the path of fear as you walk, weave, unweave, and reweave all pathways. This will be difficult for you. You will experience both positive and negative experiences. All energies and experiences can be useful depending on your intention and perception. Your most difficult quest is to not get stuck in either as you journey to awaken, develop, and practice your talents. Your chosen destiny, and life purpose practice will need the skills that you will un-knowingly create.

The dream continued. The oracle in the dream asked Lily-Butterfly, "are you sure that you want to choose the center path?" She told the golden cloak man, "yes." He replied, "know and let it be recorded that you chose this path. This was what you also choose before birth. This is the reason why your life's experiences are as it is so far. Good that you have not changed your mind. You can un-choose this path at any time. Know that no matter what happens this is the way of the path. Stay awake, stay connected to the upper realms, and stay grounded in the lower earth realms. Which means the light is light and the shadow is light. Be of both and do not get stuck in either. This is the sacred awareness of what authentic balance means. Stay awake and stay aware. This path you have chosen will not be an easy one. Call and pray 'help' whenever you need to. Lily-Butterfly thought, this is a sacred spirit guide oracle and angel.

The golden cloak oracle continued to speak. Whenever fear filled negative energy experiences comes into your life choose to create what you feel is right from the experience. In doing this you will unblock and clear your path. Unblocking and clearing your path, the way will consistently reveal itself to you. The pathway will show you the way. The way will show the way. This path will help you to awaken the gates you need to transition through and awaken your talents. When you are ready, your chosen life's purpose will reveal itself to you, in the form of a prayer master and a way maker. You will decide what human perceptive tools to use to express your talents. "Do you understand?" said the golden cloak oracle. "Yes," replied Lily-Butterfly. "Okay. Let us proceed to walk together," said the golden cloak oracle.

The golden cloak oracle continued to talk as they walk. "Listen and hear. Soon one of your spirit soul sisters, and guardian angels will show up to help you, and accompany you on your journey. You will know her when she arrives. When she arrives from the sacred un-known her head will be totally bald. She will not have one single hair on her head. The only thing she will have on her scalp is a blue mark in the shape of a small map. A map that she must follow to return home to the sacred unknown realm that she came from. Help her to follow this map as she accompanies you on your journey. This blue map will be on the upper left side of her head close to her crown. Remember that she will help you and you help her. Take care of each other until this is no longer necessary. Do you understand? "Yes, I understand? Where is she coming from?" replied Lily-Butterfly. "You will see when the time comes. You will surely see." replied the golden cloak oracle. He continued, "do not let the form of your female embodiment limit your way and your views. Be and keep on being who you are meant to be."

They arrived at a river filled with green water. "Come, Lily-Butterfly, kneel down. Use both hands to drink from this river. This is the river of life, like the tree of life. After drinking step into the river. Refresh yourself. Hold your breath, lay down on your back, and sink down under the water until it covers your entire body and face. Count to nine and then bring yourself above the water. Swim to the other side of this river and get out of the water. Walk forward without looking back. Keep walking. Trust. You are never alone. Your next guardian angel will join you and will be with you until it is time to change again. I will disappear at some point. When you do not hear my voice, I am gone. Do not look back. Continue to take care of yourself, because you cannot give what you do not have. Continue to follow your inner guidance and the Creator's will, they are one and the same. Keep walking until you walk out of this dream.

When you do not hear me, I am gone. Remember do not look back." This was the last words of the golden cloak oracle. "Thank you very much oh great golden cloak oracle angel. Bye for now. Amin," said Lily-Butterfly.*

Lily-Butterfly heard and listened to the mysterious guidance of the golden cloak oracle angel.

This was one of Lily-Butterfly first balanced dream in the most unbalanced city that never sleeps. She woke up when a door slammed in the hallway close to her room. Lily-Butterfly sat up and looked at the clock. It was 5:30 PM. Lily-Butterfly had slept for almost two hours. She got up, took her journal and wrote down all the parts of the dream she could remember.

"Hu. Mm. This is a divine dream in such an unbalanced, noisy, crowded environment. The dream is also recorded in my spirit and soul. This dream is very interesting. Here we go again. Creator and guardian angels, please remember me in your busy schedule. Amin. It is dinner time. I will eat in the hotel restaurant. This will be my second night here. Oh, the story of my life's experiences is so dramatic, and can be bewildering," mumbled Lily-Butterfly

From 7:00 to 9:00 PM Lily-Butterfly had dinner. She returned to her room. After a long warm shower, she read, watched a movie for the first time in a long time, prayed, and went to sleep at 11:45 PM. Lily-Butterfly had a good night sleep filled with more lucid dreams.

13

The next morning Lily-Butterfly woke up and decided that she wanted her last day in New York City to be one of accepting all the vibes and new sensations of the city as it was.

On the way to breakfast Lily-Butterfly muttered, "I dreamt many enjoyable dreams even being in New York City. My strong connection to dream-land stays with me wherever I go. If I get the job I must acclimate to this city and new environment. Amin."

The event of breakfast went by and the next thing on Lily-Butterfly's agenda was to visit all the boutiques and shops on the main floor of the hotel. There were boutiques and shops that sold clothes, shoes, jewelry, flowers, accessories, food, and a book – magazine – newspaper shop. She also decided to practice transforming her perception about using an elevator. So, she used the elevator to visit all twenty-three floors of the hotel. This was her way of exploring her possible new work environment. When this exploration ended, she went to the park across the street to enjoy some mother and father nature fresh air, write in her journal, and start reading a book that she had bought.

At 12:30 PM Lily-Butterfly went to lunch. She chose a French restaurant about five blocks from the hotel. Lily-Butterfly entered the busy restaurant and she waited in line to be seated. There were five people ahead of her online. In ten minutes, she was seated at a table close to the entrance, but off to the right side. Lily-Butterfly looked through the menu. The waiter came and she ordered soup, cheese and vegetable sandwich, fruit, and water with lemon to drink. Lily-Butterfly continue to look through the menu.

"Hi beautiful," said a voice.

When Lily-Butterfly looked, standing in front of her was Croco. She was surprised by Croco's physical presence standing right in front of her view. She ignored him, stayed silent, and looked back at the menu.

"Can I sit with you earth angel," asked Croco.

"If you would like to. Just do not block my view by sitting right in front of me. Thank you."

"Ha. She speaks. Okay. I can see that you are very direct, know what you want, mysterious, and not as shy and demure as you look. Hahaha."

Croco sat down at the table to Lily-Butterfly's left side. The waiter came and took his order.

"Beautiful angel are you trying to memorize the menu, or trying to ignore me?"

The waiter came and Croco ordered his food.

"Ignoring you. Are you stalking me?"

"No. I come here regularly for lunch. Here we are together for the first time. There are no accidents. We keep meeting by coincidence. Everything is for a reason. Ha. I am happy to see you. To me, it is very refreshing to meet a country girl. Something different. Country girls can be very earthly and mother-nature like. What is your name? Where do you live?"

"I live in Somerville, Massachusetts."

"And you have no name, right?"

"I like your green shirt. Now your eyes color match your shirt color and with shades of brown. Very interesting. From observation your eye color changes with your mood and energy."

"Thank you for your compliments. About my eye color, I do not know if the color changes with my mood. I never pay attention to my eye color. These are the eyes God gave me. Personally, I have no complaints about my eye color. People seem to like them, because they always say something about them. Ha. Do you like my eyes? I like you and your eyes. Your eyes and yourself, carries a sense of no-nonsense mystery. Any way let us eat the food is here. I have to go in thirty minutes."

"Okay. I do not like or dislike your eye color. My observation is that people with hazel eyes their moods are reflected in their eyes, the more-hot tempered the more the hazel."

Now both were silent. They ate. Lily-Butterfly looked up from her food intermittently to look at Croco. He pretended to not notice and smiled. They finished eating and Croco ordered desert for the two of them.

"I already ordered my dessert. A serving of strawberries," said Lily-Butterfly.

"Okay. No problem. I can share my chocolate cake with you, and you can share your strawberries with me. Is this okay with you?"

"Okay. Sure."

Lily-Butterfly was intuitively reading Croco's surface vibes. She pondered on her awareness.

"I see that you can talk without using your speech and mouth. You are checking out my vibes. I am sort of intuitive as well. Ha. Um. What is your name? Give me your phone number. When are you leaving New York?"

"I leave tomorrow. I do not have a phone number."

"And you seem to have no name. Okay. I think that we were destined to meet for whatever reason. And you know this too. So, I will wait until our faiths bring us together again, and maybe then, you will surrender to what is. What do you think?"

"Faith will find me no matter what I think or choose to do. So, we will see. Maybe I choose to delay faith, so that I can exercise my free will to choose what I think is right for me. I do not tend to rush into things. I have a cautious, aware, and steady personality. This way I take responsibility for my choices, experiences, and actions. I do not blame others and become a victim to people, places, and things. Being a victim is a strong wound trauma imprint. What is your ancestry?"

"So, I choose to answer all your questions and you choose to answer what you like. Interesting."

"Your choices are your own responsibility. So, you can choose to answer my questions or not."

"Okay confident angel. Ha. Hmm. My ancestry is mixed. Portuguese, Scottish, Irish, African, and other European mix. Let me guess, you will not tell me your ancestry until you feel like it."

They continue to eat desert.

"I am very mixed ancestry like you, very similar."

Croco finished eating his desert. He asked for the check.

"I have to go. I am late for a meeting. I hope that you get the job. This is the only way I will see you again. Have a safe journey home angel. We will leave things your way, that is, let us leave our meeting again to faith and another chance encounter. Bye beautiful."

"Bye Sir Croco. Thank you for your company and conversation."

They shook hands and Croco left to talk to the waiter.

Unbeknownst to Lily-Butterfly, Croco paid the bill for the two of them and left. Lily-Butterfly finished her desert and asked for her bill. The waiter told her that Croco paid the complete bill. Lily-Butterfly paid the tip and left the restaurant. She returned to the park across the street from the hotel. She sat read her new book and wrote in her journal. At 3:30 PM Lily-Butterfly returned to her hotel room to take a nap. As she lay in bed, she pondered on the golden cloak oracle angel dream. Some of her thoughts were, I wonder who this spirit and soul sister is, where will she come from and when. I will know who she is by the small blue map at the back-left side of her bald head close to her crown. How strange? My life is filled with strange events and things to ponder about. This has become normal to me. I have become more and more accepting of my strange life's experiences. There is no use in trying to escape the will of the Creator and my chosen un-known destiny. Creator your will is my will. Everything belongs to you and will always go back to you. Creator I guess by your will, when the time is right, I will see how Mr. Croco fits into this part of my journey. In the realm of pondering Lily-Butterfly fell into a deep sleep.

At 5:30 PM Lily-Butterfly woke up and packed her bags. This was her last night staying in the hotel. Tomorrow morning after breakfast she will take the long bus ride back to Manana Leila's apartment in Somerville. After packing her bags Lily-Butterfly went downstairs to the hotel restaurant for dinner. It was 7:00 PM. She ordered her dinner and some tea. As Lily-Butterfly drank her tea she reflected on the hotel. She thought, so far, I like this hotel. It is in the heart of the city with many businesses and different choices of transportation. The hotel was built in 1924 and an historical building with twenty-three floors. It is a strong building made from stone and bricks. The architecture is magnificent and a work of art. I will like coming to work here. I could learn a lot from this job. I surrender to this job if it is meant to be. The Creator knows best. For empowerment I still need to choose all my will to be done here in my life and living. I have come a far way and still a lot farther to go. I cannot help but wonder what exactly is next. After dinner I will go telephone Manana and Rebornstar. She sighed. The dinner came and she was already halfway finished eating during her pondering. As Lily-Butterfly continued to eat she choose to stop the pondering thoughts and change her mood to meditation and silence. When dinner was over, she returned to her hotel room.

Telephoning Manana and Rebornstar, Lily-Butterfly told them about her experiences and confirmed with them her date and time of arrival home. She told them nothing about meeting Croco. With contentment in her heart Lily-Butterfly prepared to go to sleep. Looking out her hotel window she saw the hustle and bustle of the people, the crowded traffic, and the park across the street. The few stars that peppered the sky amongst the tall buildings seem like light houses on a dark night out at sea. The last thing she did before laying down was to say her prayers. In prayer she gave gratitude for all her experiences and asked for support to have a safe and enjoyable bus ride home. Lily-Butterfly sighed, climbed into bed, and hugged the pillow that she had brought with her. Her head relaxed on to the pillow and she fell asleep.

Life, living, and the city percolated around Lily-Butterfly as she slept. Another one of her big discoveries on her life's journey was, New York City; a city with a continuous heartbeat. She slept as undisturbed as she would have, while living in the valley and village of Yaj, on the island of Kawomaya. From the visit to New York City part of the ongoing lesson for Lily-Butterfly is that; a part of life is about perception projected from within. The city is as it is, and her projection is as it is.

14

It was Thursday morning. Lily-Butterfly woke up, got dressed, completely packed her bags, and went downstairs to eat breakfast. At 11:00 AM she checked out of the hotel. A taxi was waiting at the front door of the hotel and she got into it. Within forty minutes she had arrived at the Port Authority Bus Terminal. Lily-Butterfly bought her bus ticket, found the departing gate, and got on the bus. At 1:05 PM the bus departed from the bus station. The bus drove further and further away from the majestic, modern, very busy, inviting, crowded, embracing, and fantastic city.

At 7:30 PM Lily-Butterfly arrived back at Manana Leila's apartment. It was August 13, 1987. Manana Leila and Rebornstar greeted Lily-Butterfly in the living room.

"Hi Lily-Butterfly we are happy to see you," said Manana Leila.

"Yes mama. I am glad that you are here. I had a great time with Manana," said Rebornstar.

"I am happy to be back. I enjoyed my trip. The bus ride was like a picturesque adventure and an opportunity to rest. New York City is nothing like I have seen before. It seems always alive, busy, crowded, rumbustious, and very interesting. You would have to experience this city to know what I am talking about. Some buildings seem to touch the sky. The hotel I stayed in was twenty-three floors. It is an historical building. I think that I am going to get the job. If they offer it to me, I will take it. We will see. If this is meant to be, it will be. I even had an incredible dream when I was in New York City. Oh wow. I am going to put my bags in the bedroom. Thank you Manana for taking time away from work to take care of Rebornstar. Thanks to the Creator and myself I return home safely. Really."

"Dreams can be an, oh wow, moment. Dreams are like telephone calls from the Creator to your spirit, soul, mind, and body, when you are most quiet. This time is usually when you are asleep. The people in the dreams are messengers, guides, and helping to dramatize the messages. Your dinner is in the oven. We ate already," said Manana Leila.

"Yes, thank you. I must take a shower before I eat. I feel very sticky."

Rebornstar went with her mother to the bedroom. Lily-Butterfly opened her suitcase and gave Rebornstar a tee shirt that said, 'I Love New York.'

"Thank you, mama. I like the tee shirt. Are we going to move to New York City?"

"Yes, my child or somewhere in New York. We will wait and see if I get the job. Living outside the busyness of the city would work best for me. The Creator willing, we will be as fine as possible. Life is what I choose it to be."

"Okay mama. We are travel companion in this journey of life. I am a young spirit and soul, learning so many things from journeying with you."

Lily-Butterfly took a shower and ate. After eating she gave Manana Leila a tee shirt like the one, she gave Rebornstar.

"So, Lily-Butterfly, if you get the job when would you leave here?" asked Manana Leila.

"The move would be a quick decision. By the end of this month. Rebornstar starts second grade the first week in September. I would have to move, find a place to live, and register her for school before I start working. This will be a short time to accomplish many things. If all this job and relocating is meant to be, everything will work out. All I know for sure at this point is, I have decided to take the job if they offer it to me. The present moment will take care of the future. Now, I would have to go off into the wilderness of an improved modern world by myself with Rebornstar. We are going to the total opposite city of my comfort zone. The wheels and revolving doors of my life are always turning. I am thankful that I do not choose to stay stuck. As I grow, awaken to my talents, and purge this life's experiences new things show up, and new revelations unfold. Manana, my life is surely interesting to say the least."

"My child you are born brave, a spirit, and soul survivor. You will surely not live a boring and normal life. You have chosen to have Rebornstar as a long-term companion to practice life, unconditional love, and compassion with. Plus, beyond this you are never alone. You have guardian angels and spirit guides that changes when it is time. I will keep you in my prayers. For sure what is to be will be. I will miss you and Rebornstar, but what is to be will be, and we must let it become a reality. Whatever this means. In scary times remember that you are truly blessed and lucky. Really, truly blessed."

"I am mama's companion?" asked Rebornstar.

"Yes, my child. Your mother really chooses to have you. She fought repeatedly through the doors of life and death, and back to life to have you and her stay alive, and for you to be born. Both of you have mastered the doors of death to be alive and here today. Plus, your mother has done this many times before you were born. Your mother survived being in Gina's womb, and being born. Gina consistently trying to demolish your mother during her complete birth journey, and when your mother lived with Gina. When a human has done this, they become fearless and not afraid of death. Lily-Butterfly, I wonder what lays at the end of this path for you. This is surely a big mystery," said Manana Leila.

"I wonder many times myself. Currently only the Creator knows everything. We will have to wait and see how things unfold. Life can be like a seed that is planted and unfolds itself over time. The way will show the way. We will see. Keep praying for me. Sometimes my life's experiences can be overwhelming, disconcerting, and a powerfully responsible. But I have seemed to have what it takes to work through it all and get beyond perceived difficulties. Manana keep praying for me. Thank you for everything. I have to go face the big wide modern world without you."

"Sure, my child. Prayer is my best companion. Keep me informed of things as they unfold. We will see. I will go back to work on Monday morning. Call me at work if you are leaving."

"Yes, Manana, I will."

"I am going to bed now. Sleep has arrived in my eyes. Good night angels. Sweet dreams," said Manana.

"Good night. I am tired too. I am going to bed after washing the dishes. Rebornstar you can go to sleep. Sweet dreams my star. I will see you in the morning."

"Good night mama. See you," replied Rebornstar.

Friday morning Lily-Butterfly woke up first and made breakfast. The three of them ate. At 10:00 AM Lily-Butterfly and Rebornstar went to the library. Rebornstar went to the children section of the library and Lily-Butterfly went to research in books and on the computer about possible towns on the outskirts of New York City to live. She chooses White Plains Road in the Bronx. Who knows why this appealed to her? Maybe the word 'White Plains Road' gave her some internal reference. Lily-Butterfly also chose Real Estate Agents, Apartment Managers, and their contact information. This information gave Lily-Butterfly the security of having help to find an apartment just in case she got the job and had to relocate. Lily-Butterfly had learned from her past experiences that she had to take action to be a success, in this perceived so-called modern created human world of materialism, knowledge, education, and wisdom were great tools. And that positive intended prayers can amplify and give support no matter the frequency of prayer vibration. A Universal truth was that both positive and negative people prayed. Lily-Butterfly wrote all her collected information in her journal, took Rebornstar with her, and left the library.

Manana Leila met Lily-Butterfly and Rebornstar at the town square and they went to lunch at a restaurant. When they were finished with lunch, they took the bus to Harvard Square. Here they visited the park and some stores. On Saturday they took the train to downtown Boston to go clothes and shoes shopping. On Sunday after breakfast they went to church, the park, and stayed at home for lunch and dinner. Monday morning August 17th Manana Leila went back to work and she planned to return to her apartment on Saturday August 22nd.

For the week Lily-Butterfly plan to continue her preparations to relocate to the state of New York. Along with this preparation came more pondering, reflections, and organizing things in her mind and decluttering her current physical possessions. Lily-Butterfly had a strong feeling that she was going to be offered the job. With all the relocation preparation she went along with enjoying all the other activities that Rebornstar and her shared. On Wednesday August 19th the telephone rang. Lily-Butterfly picked up the telephone.

"Hi good morning. This is Lily-Butterfly may I help you?"

"Good morning Lily-Butterfly, this is Betty Butler the General Manager at the hotel. I am calling to offer you the job as hotel Assistant Manager in training. You would work with me as my Assistant for one year to train and to get to know the job. Your work schedule would be my schedule, Monday to Friday 9:00 AM to 5:00 PM. If you would like the job you need to return for a second interview this week Friday August 21st at 9:00 AM. During this interview you will fill out all the other necessary employment paperwork. Hi are you there. You are so quiet," said Mrs. Butler.

"Yes, I am here. I am hearing and listening to what you are saying. Mm. Thank you, Mrs. Butler. Yes. Sure. I would love to accept this job opportunity. I am a little flustered about your call and offer. Thanks again. I will be there. Is there anything else?"

"Yes. Please remember to bring your identification and social security card. All your college, university, work references, and personal references has checked out to be authentic and positive, going all the way back to the island of Kawomaya. We are looking for someone with a new set of views, perception, and eyes. Plus, you have all the qualifications. It is easier for me to teach someone with no preconceived idea about the hotel industry, self-motivated, and all the other qualities that you seem to have. We can use all your other training, experiences, talents, and skills as an asset to our small and solid hotel company. Good for you. My opinion is that you have earned this opportunity. We will see how you perform. Do you have any questions?"

"No Mrs. Butler. I will see you on Friday August 21st at 9:00 AM. Thanks again. Bye."

"You are welcome. See you then. Bye."

Lily-Butterfly hung up the telephone and sat down on the couch in a reclined position looking up at the ceiling. Oh wow, she thought. Nothing else came to her mind it was as if her brain was frozen.

15

When Lily-Butterfly recovered ten minutes later from the news of the job offer she telephoned Manana Leila at her job.

"Manana guess what? I got the job. I must return for a second interview. I must be at the interview this Friday morning August 21st at 9:00 AM. Can you come home tonight or very early tomorrow morning to take care of Rebornstar until I return? This would be from August 20th to 24th. You can return to work Tuesday August 25th. I would really appreciate this very much. Ha. Oh my."

"Yes. Sure, I can. I will be there in a taxi at 9:00 AM Thursday morning. Be ready and take the same taxi I arrive in back to the bus or train station in downtown Boston. I guess this is it. The ship of yourself will sail off into the wide ocean of life. You are young, fearless, strong, wise, and brave. You will manage as the captain of your ship, the Creator willing. Yes, my child. You have my blessing. You were born for this."

"I hear you Manana. You are my earthly mother-nature, guide, and human angel. I could not be anything without all your help and assistance. To me all that you have been to and for me is wordless. Infinite thanks."

"You are welcome. It is a pleasure to help and assist you. When I do all I do, I am doing everything to help and assist the Creator. Bye my child. Take care. You have some quick planning to accomplish. Seek with sincerity and you will find what you are looking for. Bye now."

"Bye. Thanks."

Manana Leila hung up the telephone, and so did Lily-Butterfly. Lily-Butterfly telephone the bus station for the bus schedule. She telephoned the same hotel to make reservation for four nights stay. Last but not least she telephoned a Relator and made an appointment to show her two apartments on White Plains Road. The Relator appointment was for Saturday August 22nd. After hanging up the phone from the Realtor Lily-Butterfly informed Rebornstar about everything. Next Lily-Butterfly researched how to take the New York local train system and how to get from the hotel in New York City to the Realtor White Plains Road, in the Bronx. She thought that this would be a good first practice for her to learn how to take the train back and forth to work, the environment, and become acclimated to her new environment. And as usual Lily-Butterfly went into her pondering and reflections to process the situation, her thoughts, and everything she had to do to organize and accomplish.

"This whole situation is a whole new level of testing me and everything I have learned and practiced so far in my life. I will see what happens as all of these situations evolve. Oh, mighty Creator you sure know how to give me a complete spirit, soul, mind, emotion, body, and life work out. Here we go again," mumbled Lily-Butterfly.

Within courage and meditation Lily-Butterfly continue to make her plans. She drew a vision board map of the whole situation in her journal. For the day Lily-Butterfly processed the vision board map. She tracked and made sure that the train routes were correct to get to and from her destinations and called the Realtor to help her confirm the train transportation routes. With this job a whole new world opened up for Lily-Butterfly. Now she would have to learn how to travel underground in the New York train system. Having to do this in Boston was a warmup to taking the trains in New York. Lily-Butterfly checked her pocketbook to make sure that she had her check book, cash, bank card, identification, social security card, old journal with the vision board map, and a new journal, because there were no pages left in the previous journal. Next, she packed her suitcase for four nights. When everything was ready for her journey, she left the apartment and took Rebornstar to the community park. As Lily-Butterfly walked with Rebornstar to the park they talked about her going back on Thursday morning to Monday for a second interview, changing school, moving, her new job, creating a renewed life, and so forth.

Thursday morning came and Manana Leila arrived at her apartment in the taxi. She came inside to let Lily-Butterfly know that the taxi was waiting.

"Bye Manana and Rebornstar. I am leaving to see what is next on the path of my chosen destiny. Life is life. I shall return more aware and wiser than I leave here today. I have to take another leap into the unknown. See you next Monday. Bye."

"Go my daughter. Blessings, love, and peace to you and your journey. May everything work out as effortless as possible. The

Creator is with you. I will see you on Monday. Bye," said Manana Leila.

"Bye mama. Take care of yourself, as you always do. See you on Monday."

"Thanks for everything Manana. Bye."

Manana Leila and Rebornstar hugged and kissed Lily-Butterfly. Manana Leila opened the front door of her apartment. With a little reluctance Lily-Butterfly stepped through the portal of the front door carrying her pocketbook and pulling her suitcase beside her. With tears trickling down from her eyes to her cheeks she open the taxi door, got in, and sat down. The taxi driver put her suitcase into the car trunk.

"I am off for another adventure into the unknown," whispered Lily-Butterfly.

Lily-Butterfly arrived at the bus station, bought her ticket, and found the bus departing gate. She got on the bus, found her seat by the window, and put her suitcase in the overhead compartment. She closed her eyes and prayed. Thirty minutes after the bus left the station, she fell asleep. After a two-hour nap Lily-Butterfly woke up and read her book while looking through the window at the outside scenery. At 4:30 PM the bus arrived at the Port Authority Bus Terminal. Lily-Butterfly took a taxi to the hotel. On checking in she requested the room that she had before. The room was available, and she took the elevator to the room on the second floor. Entering the room, she placed her suitcase on a chair and unzipped it. She hung all he clothes in the closet and called Manana Leila and Rebornstar to let them know that she had arrived safely. Next Lily-Butterfly went downstairs to eat dinner. After dinner she returned to the hotel room to prepare everything for the interview. At the end of the day and a long bus ride she was tired and sleepy. After a shower and prayer Lily-Butterfly went to sleep.

The next morning Lily-Butterfly woke up at 6:10 AM, got dress, and went to eat breakfast. She arrived at the conference room at 8:45 AM for the interview. Mrs. Betty Butler the General Manager was seated around the conference table. She gave Lily-Butterfly some payroll forms to fill out, sign, and date. When Lily-Butterfly finished filling out the forms they talked about her job responsibility and training.

"Lily-Butterfly, some of your job responsibilities and training will be managing the employees, marketing programs, general daily planning, coordinating and administering hotel services, planning and managing budget, sales, maintaining financial records, customer service and complaints, ensuring compliance with health and safety legislation, learn licensing laws, manage spontaneous daily occurrence, and everything else to do with the hotel's function and success. This job is a lot of work and multitasking, and can be stressful, but I think that you have the nerves and patience to be successful. This job is a lot of responsibility. Do you agree with me that you can manage this job?" said Mrs. Butler.

"Yes, I agree that I can manage this job. I am good at learning, self-motivated, like to learn new things, follow instructions, manage my stressful experiences, and complete my work timely and efficient. At this time, I can only work the day shift. I have a daughter who is eight years old and I need to be home by 6:30 PM."

"You will work with me as my assistant until I am ready to change your schedule. Your schedule and my schedule are the same, Monday to Friday 9:00 AM to 5:00 PM. There are three regular shifts, 7:00 AM to 3:00 PM, 3:00 PM to 11:00 PM, and 11:00 PM to 7:00 AM. Your salary will be $41,600 per year, medical and dental insurance, five sick days off, and fourteen vacation days off after one year. You can eat at fifty percent discount in all the hotel restaurants. Do you have any questions?"

"What is the dress code? When do I start working?"

"Here, take this paper with the information about the dress code. You will start working on Monday September 21, 1987. This should give you enough time to relocate, register your daughter in school, and organize whatever else you need. Is there anything else? I am here if you ever need help or guidance about performing your work. Plus, I will train you how to do everything. You seem like a slow processor of information, because you use your whole brain, and at the same time a quick learner. Once you learn something it becomes like a well-oiled machine. Not too many people use their brain in this manner. If you have any questions or concerns, you can telephone me. Here is my business card."

"Yes Mrs. Butler. I process slow because I am using my complete brain. This is an old fashion way and system of using the human brain. In these modern times people do not have to use their whole brain, but I still do. I use the old ways and the modern new ways. No further questions at this time. Thank you for choosing to give me this job. I really appreciate this opportunity. I will be here for work on September 21ˢᵗ. See you then. Bye."

"You are welcome. Bye Lily-Butterfly. See you then."

Lily-Butterfly left the hotel conference room. She thought, in the village of Yaj there is a saying 'if someone talks less, they can see and hear more. Plus, complaint and defense seems like static annoyance, irritation, and justifications.' Starting today I am going to start talking even less, become more observant, and continue to process my feelings and emotions within and in my journal. This part of the journey is like climbing another mountain. I wonder what is at the top of this mountain. The way will show the way. The things I need will manifest when it is time.

For the rest of the day Lily-Butterfly had a pleasant time going to the French restaurant for lunch, going to the park, writing in her journal, processing, pondering, dinner, watching a movie on the television, shower, relaxation, praying, and going to sleep.

Saturday morning came and Lily-Butterfly had an appointment at 10:00 AM to meet the Realtor at his White Planes Road office. At 9:30 AM she had navigated the complex and noisy train system and was standing on White Planes Road in the Bronx. Lily-Butterfly asked for direction to get to the Realtor's office. When she arrived at the office, he was waiting for her. They went to look at two apartments. One was a two-bedroom apartment at the back of a three-family house, with its own entrance. The other was a two-bedroom in a five-story brick building. Lily-Butterfly chose the two-bedroom apartment in the three-family house. This apartment was on White Planes Road, close to the train station, many offices, public elementary school, library, laundry facilities, a community park, grocery shops, stores, and restaurants. Everything she needed was close by where she would live.

The Realtor and Lily-Butterfly returned to his office to fill out the forms for renting the apartment. The cost per month for renting the apartment was $1,200. This rent included heat, hot water, and regular water. Lily-Butterfly gave the Realtor a check for $4,560 for one-and-a-half-month security, the first month rent for September, nine days rent August 23 to 31ˢᵗ, and one month rent Realtor fee. The Realtor accepted her proof of employment as income, because she did not have pay stubs. He rented Lily-Butterfly the apartment in good faith. He gave her the keys to the apartment the same day. Lily-Butterfly could move in after this day any time she liked. Effective immediately Lily-Butterfly had a place to live.

Lily-Butterfly asked the Realtor, "can I change the lock on the entrance door?"

"Yes. Sure. Give me a copy of the key when you change the lock. Good, for security reasons this is recommended."

"Okay. I am going back to the apartment now to look at the space again in more detail."

"Okay. Do you need me to give you a ride there?"

"No. Thank you for asking. I will walk. Exercise is good for me. Plus, I get to see more of the neighborhood and stores. This is a busy and convenient neighborhood."

"Yes, be aware of safety. New York City and the Bronx is a place of many ethnic people and ancestry in one community. And like living anywhere else stay aware, and blend in. Here are copies of your lease, the landlords contact information, and my business card. Please let me know if you need anything repaired. Thank you. Enjoy. Have a nice day."

"Thank you, sir, for everything. Bye."

Lily-Butterfly left the Realtor office and arrived outside into the hustle and bustle of the Saturday White Planes Road crowd. She walked to the nearest furniture store. The furniture Lily-Butterfly purchased was one twin bed, one full bed, two chest of drawers, one dresser, four nightstands, one dining room table, four chairs, a center table, a large radio with CD player, a couch, a television, a telephone, a bookshelf, curtains, curtain rods, and an entertainment center to put the television on. Lily-Butterfly spoke to the furniture store Manager and asked him if he could deliver all the things that she purchased within one hour. He told her yes and she paid the extra fee for the delivery. She went to a store to purchase kitchen utensils, pots, pans, plates, cups, glasses, and all the things she needed in her kitchen. They also had a delivery service and she paid the extra fee to have these things delivered within one hour. Next Lily-Butterfly went to the hardware store to request the service of a lock technician to come change the lock on the apartment door. She paid for the lock and service fee and requested that the person come to the house within one hour to change the lock. The last place she went was the grocery store to purchase cleaning supplies, broom, disposable cleaning gloves, mop, bucket, and food for her lunch. These things she carried back to the apartment herself. When Lily-Butterfly returned to the apartment the first thing she did was eat her lunch. After lunch she put up the curtain rods using tools from a toolbox in the utility closet. Put up the curtains. Next Lily-Butterfly cleaned the bathroom, everything in the kitchen, windows, sweep the complete apartment, and mopped all the floors. After all the floors were mopped and dry all the items that she had purchased came. The two furniture delivery men assembled all the furniture and placed everything in each room as instructed by Lily-Butterfly. The lock technician came and changed the lock on the door and gave her two keys. Lily-Butterfly gave each person who came to deliver all the items and change the lock on the door a very generous tip. She expressed her appreciation to each person before they left. She was very grateful for all the help she received, to accomplish all the things she had planned on her written vision board map.

Lily-Butterfly was satisfied that the apartment was ready for Rebornstar and her to move in. Before leaving she said two prayers a sacred prayer to bless the apartment environment and a prayer of gratitude for the things, she was able to accomplish.

Lily-Butterfly' gratitude prayer, "thank you Creator for everything. Thank you to the spirit guides, guardian angels, Mrs. Butler, the Realtor, all the delivery men and lock technician. You have all helped me very much in accomplishing everything I need and want in this current time and situations. Creator I surrender to the way forward with continued guidance, good fortune, blessings, safety, effortlessness, positive health, and well-being. Continue to assist me with the courage, strength, and fearlessness that I need to accomplish the known and the unknown. Amin."

When these prayers were completed Lily-Butterfly smiled, closed and locked all the windows, locked the apartment door, and left. She took the train back to the hotel. When Lily-Butterfly got off the train at 6:30 PM she was two blocks from the hotel. She walked from where she got off the train to the hotel. When Lily-Butterfly entered the hotel lobby it was 6:45 PM. She went straight to one of the hotel's restaurant and had dinner.

Saturday night was her third night at the hotel.

16

When dinner was complete Lily-Butterfly took the elevator to her room. She wrote in her journal notes about the trains to take, the routes, and where to get on and off the trains. She wrote down the story of her day and checked off her to-do list all she had accomplished. Taking a warm shower was a welcoming experience to cleanse the stress of the day and simmer into a relaxed mood. Getting into bed Lily-Butterfly snuggled up to her pillow and said her prayers laying on her side. Within five minutes of completing her prayers sleep arrived and captivated Lily-Butterfly to dreamland.

The next morning Lily-Butterfly woke up. Before opening her eyes, she reflected on how she felt in the moment.

"Today, Sunday is another day in this cosmic stew of my human life. I guess I can look forward to more experiences in this more advanced modern nature of things. As my life's experiences continue to unfold, I give thanks for everything, Oh well. Mm. Today is a whole new day to enjoy everything," muttered Lily-Butterfly

When Lily-Butterfly got out of bed it was 9:00 AM. She felt like having a slow day being tired from all the things she had accomplished the day before. By the time Lily-Butterfly got dressed and went downstairs the hotel it was 11:00 AM. She decided to have brunch in the hotel restaurant. Finishing brunch Lily-Butterfly visited the park across the street from the hotel. Sunday at this park there were many vendors with displays of artwork, food, clothing, and books, for sale. She browsed the stalls and bought some items.

Later that night after dinner Lily-Butterfly packed her suitcase for her return to Manana Leila's apartment. This was her last night sleeping at the hotel. Monday morning at 11:00 AM after breakfast Lily-Butterfly checked out of the hotel. The taxi arrived to take her to the Port Authority Bus Terminal. As soon as Lily-Butterfly walked outside and on to the sidewalk she saw Croco standing in front of her.

"Hi beautiful. Are you leaving?"

"Hi. Yes."

"Did you get the job?"

"Yes."

"Okay. Great. When do you start working?"

"Next month. I have to go. The taxi is waiting."

"Okay. Have a safe journey. See you soon. Stay beautiful. Bye."

"Okay. Bye."

Lily-Butterfly got into the taxi. The taxi drove off into the thick blanketed traffic. Lily-Butterfly observed the people, places, and things around her as the taxi journey to the bus terminal. She sighed.

As the taxi drove Lily-Butterfly automatically went into prayer mode. She whispered, "dear Creator as you can see, I have not pondered too much about Mr. Croco. I know that it is not an accident he keeps showing up. I find Croco appearing a little irritating. Without fear and a lot of trust I keep moving forward with thy will and my chosen unknown destiny. Part of being human is curiosity. Where does Croco fit into the puzzle of the next part of my current life's experiences? Just asking, although I know that I have to wait and see what happens. Oh well. I could not help asking anyway. The way will show the way." Lily-Butterfly sighed again.

The taxi arrived at the bus terminal. Lily-Butterfly paid the taxi driver and got out of the car. She entered the bus terminal, bought her ticket, and found the bus. Lily-Butterfly got on the bus, placed her suitcase in the overhead compartment, and sat in the seat by the window. Passengers kept coming on the bus. Twenty-five minutes later the bus drove off. Within an hour New York City was left behind. At 2:45 PM Lily-Butterfly ate a sandwich she had brought with her. At 3:30 PM she closed her eyes in silent reflections of all the things she had accomplished and remembering that she had an apartment in New York. Within this silent reflection and processing Lily-Butterfly fell asleep.

While asleep Lily-Butterfly had a dream. In the dream, Lily-Butterfly was sitting on the ground in the middle of a field of pink, yellow, red, white, and reddish-purple rose plants. She sat in silence observing the many different rose plants.

When Lily-Butterfly woke up she wrote down the dream in her journal. She was aware that sometimes the simplest dream can have strong; medicine, message, and power. Lily-Butterfly pondered on the dream. She thought, rose plant is symbolic of sweet and bitter, positive and negative, and light and dark. The flowers are beautiful and sweet smelling. The green of the plant represents nourishment, part of mother-nature, and nurturing. The thorns can represent something negative, hurt, wounds, caution, new beginnings, and mindfulness. A sweet-smelling flower evolving out of a place of thorn bush plant. The rose was one of her favorite flowers. To me sitting up in the field of rose plants can symbolize staying cautious, experiencing very positive and very negative experiences, balance, restarting life, neutral, and being aware, within the next part of my life's experiences. I wonder what will happen? All I can do is wonder. Things are not revealed to me until it is time. I will try my best to not worry. Worrying is useless. Oh well. Things will surely reveal themselves when it is time. Lily-Butterfly knew that repeat practice of something can create improvement, transformation, and change. This simple dream was processed and digested over and over through Lily-Butterfly until the bus arrived at the bus terminal in Boston. The bus parked in its station. It was time for the passengers to get off.

When it was her turn Lily-Butterfly got up, took her suitcase, and walked off the bus. She took a taxi to her Manana Leila's home. When she arrived, she paid the taxi driver and got out of the car. She went inside the apartment. Manana was busy preparing dinner.

"Hi mama. You are back. I miss you mama," said Rebornstar.

"Yes, I am back. I miss you and Manana. I have good news and accomplishments."

"How was your trip?" asked Manana Leila.

"My trip was successful. I have accomplished all that I needed and wanted. Officially I got the job. My supervisor the General Manager of the hotel seems kind and understanding. I learn to take the trains. I took the train to the place I wanted to live. I found the Realtor. I rented a two bed room apartment on the third floor of a three-family house. I have my own outside entrance. I cleaned the whole apartment and put up curtains I purchased. I purchased all the furniture I currently need and they were delivered. A hardware store lock technician came and changed the lock on the front entrance door. I know how to get to and from work from the apartment. My opinion is that everything worked out effortlessly. Thanks be to the Creator. My new job pay is enough to pay all my monthly expenses and save. The only bill I will have is rent, utilities, food, clothing, child care, transportation, plus if other things come up. My new jobs gives me health and dental insurance for Rebornstar and myself. This is a lot of accomplishment that I am very grateful for."

"So, when are you leaving?" said Manana Leila.

"This is the sad news, Manana we have to leave your nest and under your wings. We will miss you. I guess it is time for me to fly and practice using my own wings to navigate the bewildering modern world. I am concerned and at the same time trying my best to not worry. We are leaving next week Monday August 31st. I will be living on White Planes Road Bronx, New York. I have to go register Rebornstar in second grade in public school. School starts the first week in September. I have to move to my new home and figure out everything. Plus find a child care person to take care of Rebornstar after school, until I get home from work. Manana we are going to go live in a very busy neighborhood compared to here. Clearly, I feel another adventure in my life has begun."

"Good. So far you seem to be staying positive, confident, and you are in the best of health. Um. I was wondering if the Lawyer that filed your permanent resident visa can do the same thing for Gina. Remember I told you that I wanted to do this for her."

"Yes. I remember. Are you sure that you want Ms. Gina to come live with you here?"

"Yes, I am sure. This is the best and maybe last thing I can do for Gina and her two sons before I die. Do you realize that I am over eight years old? I am strong and healthy for my age, but nothing last forever. Currently I can still take the train to and from work. My mother Katherine died at one hundred and five years old without one sickness. Our ancestors, and so far, myself as well, never get sick. Knock on wood. I wonder what will happen to me. Gina can automatically bring Henry and Dean with her if they are twenty-one years and younger. Lucy is over twenty-one, plus she have a husband and children. Maybe Gina will file Lucy's immigration papers when she becomes a citizen."

"Okay Manana. I will get the Lawyer to start the filing of Ms. Gina's immigration paper work this week before I leave. I will leave all his contact information on the dining table. Leave on the dining table all the documents that I will need to fill out the forms. I will help in every way I can before I leave. When you return home on Saturday morning, we will go over all the forms together. Monday morning August 31st we will return the forms to the lawyer before I leave for New York City. When you go to work tomorrow write to Ms. Gina to tell her your intentions."

"I already ask Gina. She said yes. I have her new address. I write to her sometimes. Lily-Butterfly please wash your hands and set the table; it is past dinner time."

While Lily-Butterfly continue to talk she set the dining table. The three of them sat down to eat dinner. The conversation continued.

"All right Manana I will. You are the kindest and most considerate human I have met so far in my life. Plus, a pinnacle of unconditional love, care, and compassion. Really. Do you want to come and live with us in New York? I feel sad leaving you here."

"No, my child. My place and life is here in Massachusetts. Maybe when Gina comes, she will live here and help me in my old age. Who knows what Gina will say and do when the time comes? She chose to become a lost and stuck spirit and soul. Maybe she will choose to heal herself and transform whatever she chooses. I wish for her all the best of everything. While there is life there are opportunities. Everything is her choice. I like living here. The owner of this house is my friend and she lives downstairs. I do not want to have to get used to living somewhere else at my age. At my age familiarity is comforting. Over eighty years old is time to stay with what is familiar and get ready to die. There is a time for everything. I give thanks for everything. Do you understand? I will miss both of you. With the Creator's help and will, things usually work out as good as possible."

"I understand. My destiny is calling me in a different direction. Sometimes if someone is looking for a perfect life, they could miss their authentic life's purpose and chosen destiny. Oh well. Different situations for different people. The thought of Ms. Gina coming to the United States is interesting to me. Oh my."

"Yes, very interesting. I can only give Gina the opportunity and see what she chooses to do. We will wait and see. Today is another day for us to be grateful for everything."

"Yes Manana. I learn from you and myself. Gratitude is one of my consistent prayer and mantras."

After dinner Lily-Butterfly cleaned up the kitchen, Manana Leila and Rebornstar watched television. The last thing Lily-Butterfly did before she went to sleep was prayed. After her prayer she drifted off to sleep like a tired log on the ocean of life.

17

On Tuesday Lily-Butterfly took Manana Leila's documents to the Lawyer to fill out the permanent resident visa application for Ms. Gina, Henry, and Dean. She gave the Lawyer a check deposit. She took the prepared forms back home for Manana to sign when she came home on Saturday morning. This Saturday was the last Saturday Manana Leila would see Lily-Butterfly and Rebornstar until the following year August 1988.

Wednesday and Thursday Lily-Butterfly and Rebornstar packed all their personal things in ten boxes. She took all these boxes to the post office in a taxi and mailed them to her new address in New York. She planed that Rebornstar and herself will take one suitcase each with their other personal items. Friday Lily-Butterfly was still busy mentally, emotionally, and physically with her final moving preparation. Saturday seemed to arrive again like a surprising lightning and thunder. Manana Leila came home for their last weekend together. Manana walked home from the bus stop at the town square and she came into the apartment like a quiet new born mouse.

Lily-Butterfly did not hear Manana Leila enter the apartment until she said, "hi girls. I am home. I have a gift for you Lily-Butterfly. You have to accept my gift gracefully without saying no. Here is some emergency money. $3,000 cash and a check for $2,500."

"No Manana this is too much. You are getting older and you need money too."

"I am going home to the end of this life. You are coming along the first part of the beginning of your life. You need more money than me. Call it an investment from the Creator through me to you. We are human guardian angels from lifetime to lifetime. Maybe I am repaying you for previous karma action for something you did for me in another lifetime. I also think that you would do the same for me as well. One positive deed deserves another. Here, I have put it in your pocketbook. The situation is closed. Amin."

"I graciously say thank you very much. You are speechless."

"Sit down Lily-Butterfly. Hear and listen to me," said Manana Leila. Lily-Butterfly sat down.

"The Creator provides. I am sure that I want to give this money to you. I am also guided to give this money to you. I get social security payment every month, plus a bonus of $3,000 every Christmas holiday. The money I am giving you is part of the cash bonus I receive over eighteen years. You are young and going off into the unpredictable unknown with a child. You are the first one in our ancestry linage that will do what you are going to do. I do not think you realize that you are carrying and taking the ancient ways of the ancestors from the valley and village of Yaj, in the bay town, on the island of Kawomaya, to the United States of America to find some way to use your talents for an unknown destiny and life's purpose of service to humanity. Look at what you have gone through so far. And you are traveling on this perilous journey with one child and maybe another one is lined up to come in through you for whatever reason. This is incredible. In the end of your life's experiences and journey, if you told anyone your life story, they would think it is fictitious. Starting with me, the ancestors bless, and thank you. You are creating a path for the spirit and soul in our ancestral linage to use in the present and future. This is a path where the ancient ways is woven with the modern ways without one disadvantage and infinite advantages, for the positive energy good of all living things. It is like upgrading and reweaving the positive energy of the ancient pathways. You will see completely what I am saying when you get to the end of the mission. Until then you will be where you will be. And maybe one day you can choose to do something priceless to help me before I die and after I die. You never know, life is full of pleasant and unpleasant surprises. Money has no value if it is not spent as a wise investment. See all that I have done for you and given you as a wise investment. Save up what I give you as an emergency fund. I will miss you and Rebornstar very much. But I know that you have to go. Great spirits and great soul do not hang around staying in one spot gathering dust. You have a life's purpose and mission to accomplish. So far you are doing great. Keep following how you are being guided while awake and, in your dreams, until you awaken to everything. Blessings my child and all the best with everything. Keep taking good care of yourself and your children. I have said everything. Amin."

"I am speechless. When you talk like this it is as if I am in a dream. Thank you for everything. I was born to find you and I did at the first opportunity. My real father and Ms. Gina choose to take action that aligned with my conception and birth and here I am, thanks be to their illicit affair. I have accepted and understand the actions that created my birth opportunity. It is sad and unfortunate that Ms. Gina's spirit and soul could not handle the experience and chose to stay stuck in fear and shame. We have tried our best to help her to choose to be unstuck and she still chose to be where she is. On top of everything Ms. Gina chose to create many negative karmas connected to my birth situation and me. I have forgiven her, I understand, and I am working on dissolving the last drop of hate that I still feel towards some of the things she did to me. With time I know that I will do a complete job dissolving the hate. We are spirit and soul travelers showing up when it is necessary to help each other for a higher purpose and greater good of humanity. Things are not as personal as people seem to take things. Sometimes things are just things, loyalty, and opportunity. I am very grateful for you, Ms. Gina, my birth father, and everything else. Without Ms. Gina's eggs and my birth father eggs, I could not have been here to find you, and I could not be where I am today. Words is not enough to express all my gratitude. I will try my best with everything. My birth opportunity and journey will not be a wasted one. I will start working on September 21st. Plus, I have $2,000 left from my savings. We thank you for everything. We really do."

"I know my child. I feel your gratitude without saying one word. Let me go put my things in my room. After let us go to the park to take in some of mother-nature's positive energies. Rebornstar could play, and we can continue to talk or meditate in silence. After the park we can go have lunch at our favorite restaurant in the town square. Tomorrow we can go to church together for the last time."

"Sound good. Manana right now, my eyes are filled with frozen tears. My tears are so much that they cannot flow. My heart is heavy with sincere gratitude. Thanks again for being my first expression of sincere unconditional love, compassion, and care. Manana I love you so much. I really do. To me love is a positive nurturing energy I choose to absorb and digest, or not. Manana I choose to receive your positive energy of unconditional love to nurture my spirit, soul, mind, emotions, body, and life. I am going to stop talking for now. If I continue to talk, I would be repeating myself again and again. Oh wow. Life can be interesting. I need to process our conversation. Let me know when you are ready."

Later all three of them went to the park.

That weekend was the last time they saw one another until August the following year in 1988. After that about nine years would pass before they saw one another again. Manana Leila and Lily-Butterfly kept in touch through phone calls and letters. No matter how things got bad in Lily-Butterfly's life in the present and future she never troubled her Manana Leila with troublesome news. She felt one priceless gift she could give her Manana Leila was an opportunity to enjoy peace.

Over the many years in Lily-Butterfly's future she dealt with all her negative experiences on her own and with the Creator's help. The pathways of life can be filled with many pot holes. If Lily-Butterfly fell into a pot hole she would get up, climb out, and get out of the pot hole. After getting out of the pot hole she would take care of all her emotional wounds, stress, trauma, suffering, and keep love and fearlessness, alive within her and outside of her in her life. Lily-Butterfly did the same thing with and for her children. A few of Lily-Butterfly's awareness were to learn from mistakes and falling down, take leaps when they come, and to not make the same mistake twice.

On Monday August 31, 1987 Lily-Butterfly took Gina's immigration forms to the Lawyer with Manana Leila. After they took the taxi together to the train station. Manana Leila got out of the taxi at the train station after she said good bye to Lily-Butterfly and Rebornstar. This was the day Lily-Butterfly said good bye to Manana Leila and Somerville, Massachusetts. The taxi left the train station and arrived at the Boston bus station. Lily-Butterfly paid the taxi driver and got out of the taxi with Rebornstar. She went to the bus ticket counter and bought bus tickets for Rebornstar and herself. They found the gate for the bus to New York City, got on, and found their seats. They had entered the transportation that would drive them effortlessly into the open arms of New York City, their future, and the next part of their destiny. Lily-Butterfly gave Rebornstar the window seat. She put the suitcases into the overhead compartment. The bus was cold from the air conditioner. Lily-Butterfly put a large green shawl around Rebornstar's shoulders and she put on her pink sweater. Lily-Butterfly sat down. She sighed. With curiosity Rebornstar looked through the bus window. The bus drove off within twenty minutes. Gradually the bus, Lily-Butterfly, and Rebornstar left Manana Leila and Massachusetts behind.

"This reminds me of the bus ride journey from the valley and village of Yaj with my Manana. Now I am taking this bus out of

Massachusetts to New York City. I wonder what exactly awaits us. I really wonder. But, as usual only the Creator and the future knows this answer. I will just have to wait within each present moment until the future arrives. The future is made up of each step and the present moment. The way will show the way. Sigh. The infinite kaleidoscope wheel and doors of my life continues to turn. I go by my choice and will. Amin and Amin," whispered Lily-Butterfly.

18

Lily-Butterfly and Rebornstar arrived at the Port Authority Bus Station in New York City. They got off the bus and took a taxi to their new home on White Planes Road in the Bronx. In ninety minutes, they arrived at their new home. Lily-Butterfly paid the taxi driver and they got out of the taxi. There was a coincidental surprise waiting for Lily-Butterfly.

"Hi beautiful. What are you doing here? Is this your daughter? Do you need help to carry your bags?" said Croco.

Immediately Lily-Butterfly thought, Creator are you serious. Immediately I have to deal with Croco. Gosh. Lily-Butterfly stood as if frozen with surprise. She saw across the street from her apartment Croco sitting in a light blue Jaguar car.

With a smile and smirk on his face, Croco again said, "hahaha. There you are. I see you. You cannot hide anymore."

Lily-Butterfly did not respond to Croco. She tried to ignore him.

"Come Rebornstar this is our apartment. Let us go inside. Come," said Lily-Butterfly.

Croco parked his car in a parking spot across the street and got out of the car. He crossed the street and approached Lily-Butterfly.

"You live here?" asked Croco.

"Yes. I am busy and tired. Go."

"Nice to see you too, Miss No-Name. Is this your daughter?"

"Yes."

"Oh okay. I am trying to be a gentleman and help you. Do you need help with these suitcases?"

"No. Thank you for asking. I am tired. Bye. I have to go."

"Okay. If you insist. I will leave. I am just trying to be helpful. I like your stand-off-ish attitude. It is very refreshing to me. Usually women chase me. I live up the street about a mile and a half. What a coincidence. I was surprised to see you here. Anyway. No problem. I will leave. Bye. Take care of yourself beautiful."

Croco crossed the street and got into his car. He drove off.

Lily-Butterfly held Rebornstar's hand and they entered the yard. They took the steps up to the front door. She took the apartment key out of her pocketbook and opened the door. They went inside. The boxes she had mailed had not arrived. They went from room to room to look around. The place was secure and as she had left it. The home atmosphere felt peaceful. Both of them brought their suitcases to their room and emptied the contents into the chest of drawers and dresser. Lily-Butterfly realized that she had forgotten to buy sheet sets for the beds.

"Come Rebornstar. Mama has to go buy sheets for the beds before the store closes. I also need to buy some groceries. Come. Hurry."

"Okay mama. I am coming. Who was that man?" said Rebornstar.

"I met him by the hotel that I will be working in. He owns a jewelry store close to the hotel."

"Oh. Let us go. We have to cook dinner. I am hungry. I will help you."

Lily-Butterfly and Rebornstar left the apartment. They bought the sheets and groceries and returned home. When they got home, they made their own beds. Next Lily-Butterfly opened all the windows and smudged the complete apartment to cleanse the energies and refresh the environment. As Lily-Butterfly did the smudging she added more prayers and blessings to her new home. At 7:00 PM Lily-Butterfly and Rebornstar made dinner together and ate. When dinner was over, they both cleaned up the kitchen and dining area and washed the dishes. Next, they both took turns having showers. Lily-Butterfly told Rebornstar one of the ancient stories her Manana had told her. When story time was over Lily-Butterfly kissed Rebornstar on her forehead, covered, her, turned off her room light, turned on the night light, closed the door half way, and left her room. Lily-Butterfly thought, Rebornstar is a good student for me to practice unconditional love and compassion with. At her birth and after I had to save both our lives. I learned so much from this experience. Rebornstar is a young spirit and soul who chose to learn about love, compassion, survival, trust, diligence, and so on and so forth. She is my first student after myself. Hu. Mm. Life can be interesting when I can see the signs. The signs are always all around me. And sometimes the signs and assignments arrive when I am not ready, like Mr. Croco. Creator you are very funny and interesting. The last things Lily-Butterfly did before she got into her bed was check to make sure that she had locked all the windows and door, write in her journal, and prayed.

The next day after breakfast Lily-Butterfly took Rebornstar with her to the public elementary school to register her for second grade.

The office was open. They got a tour of the school. Rebornstar got her school supply list. They left the school and went to purchase school supply for Rebornstar. After shopping for school supplies Lily-Butterfly used a public telephone to call Manana Leila to say that she had arrived safely, and they talked for about ten minutes. Next, she used the same telephone to call the electric and gas company to transfer the account into her name, and telephone company to request telephone service for her home. Food shopping was next on her list. They bought the groceries and returned home to make and eat lunch. They enjoyed eating lunch together and talking. The house chores were done and dinner was set up. Rebornstar had packed her book bag for school the next day. The next thing on their plans for the day was to locate the community park.

When they found the park, it was about half a mile from the elementary school. The children park equipment looked well worn, but functioning. There was a basketball court, swings, slides, jungle gym, benches, picnic tables with benches, and a section like a garden with grass. Rebornstar played while her mother supervised her safety. During this time at the park Lily-Butterfly sat down, meditated, and relaxed. After fifteen minutes of meditation and relaxation her mind naturally flowed to reflecting on the first time, she met Croco to the current time. Lily-Butterfly did not entertain the thoughts about Croco for more than ten minutes. She diverted her mind to focusing on her list of priorities. After an hour at the park they returned home to continue on with their day.

When Lily-Butterfly arrived home from the park all the boxes she had mailed from Somerville had arrive. They were by her front door on the steps. Rebornstar helped her to unpack all the boxes and put everything in its correct place. During this organizing process Lily-Butterfly thought, I must find childcare service to take care of Rebornstar after school until I return home from work.

"Having a child or children can give parents a great opportunity to practice being unselfish, unconditional love, multitasking, care, sharing, and so many other things. If I fail this child can fail as well. Oh my. Um. Uh. Naturally failing is not an option and choice for me. Tomorrow I will investigate if there is a childcare after school program at the elementary school. I really pray that they do. Or I guess something else will show up to help me with this after school childcare situation. Hi Creator, I need help with this childcare situation," mumbled Lily-Butterfly.

The next morning when Lily-Butterfly took Rebornstar to school for her first day of school she inquired about after school childcare program. They had a childcare after school program Monday to Friday from school is dismissed to 7:00 PM. This program was exactly what Lily-Butterfly had wished for. The payment for the program was based on the parent income. Lily-Butterfly filled out the form and signed up for the program for Rebornstar. On Monday Lily-Butterfly planned to start Rebornstar's first day staying at this program. She had nineteen more days at home before her first day going to work at the hotel. Lily-Butterfly had this time at home to help Rebornstar adjust to her new home and school environment.

Walking back home from the school Lily-Butterfly whispered, "the revolving and evolving doors of my life keeps turning. I am traveling through theses doors and my life with one child. I have to make sure that we stay positively balanced within this system. Oh my. The more ancient the spirit and soul, the more advanced the chosen destiny and life's purpose. Also, the more difficult the life's experiences and journey can be. I wonder what my unbeknown chosen mission is. Again, the answer to this question is, only the Creator knows. If I knew ahead of time, maybe the journey would be premature and possibly not work out authentic. This spiritual stuff can really be very weird. I guess myself and everyone just has to follow the path, wait, and see what happens. Amin."

Lily-Butterfly got home and continued on with her day.

19

Monday came. A new week had begun. Lily-Butterfly took Rebornstar to school. Today was her first day at after school childcare program. Before Rebornstar went into the school building her mother informed her about staying for after school program.

"Rebornstar remember where to go after school for the childcare after school program. Today is your first day. Today is the start of a long day at school. At this after school program you will have supervision, time to do your homework, study, have snack, play, and meet other children. I will be back to get you at 6:30 PM. You will be going to this program until you are old enough to go home by yourself. Have a great day my star. Mama loves you. See you later and take care of yourself."

Lily-Butterfly gave Rebornstar a hug and a kiss.

"Okay mama. I understand. I love you, bye."

On leaving the school one of the parents whose son goes to the same school gave Lily-Butterfly a flyer advertising childcare and hair dressing services. She took the flyer and put it in her handbag.

"Maybe I will try her hair services. In my whole life I have been to the hairdresser only three times. This is also a way for me to get to know her and her home regarding possible childcare services. I will need childcare services for holidays off from school and so forth. Interesting how my wishes are coming to reality," said Lily-Butterfly.

As time went on school in general and after school program for Rebornstar was a success. She likes going to school. After two weeks of school Rebornstar was classified to be in special education for extra help with mathematics and language. By the time Lily-Butterfly was ready to go to work she was sure that Rebornstar would be okay, acclimated to school, her environment, and the neighborhood.

Monday September 21, 1987 came and Lily-Butterfly started her first day of working at the hotel. On the first day of work she could tell even more that she liked her supervisor the General Manager Betty Butler. They worked together like a team. Betty Butler knew Croco. He came into the hotel lobby for business purposes. Croco sold jewelry to the hotel's jewelry store located in the hotel's lobby. Lily-Butterfly saw Croco at least once per week and she tried to ignore him. When Croco asked Lily-Butterfly out to breakfast, lunch, or dinner, she would tell him she was busy.

Inside Lily-Butterfly's spirit, soul, mind, and body she knew she met Croco for a reason. Although she wanted to know the reason, she was also delaying the reason to come into reality. For one thing she saw that Croco was dangerously physically handsome, and he acted like he know it. Lily-Butterfly was dangerously beautiful inside and outside. These things could be a hot fire pit for one, or both of them getting roasted. Currently unbeknownst to Lily-Butterfly Croco was a water sign. And Lily-Butterfly was a very earth sign. Between Croco and Lily-Butterfly there was much magnetism, fire, and passion. She felt this. And like touching fire or a hot surface she chose to not engage in encouraging Croco. For as long as possible she was focused on delaying the reason why they met. The more she avoided Croco's invitations for a date, the more her inner guidance brought Croco to her awareness.

After seven weeks of saying no to Croco's invitation Lily-Butterfly accepted his invitation for a date into the future. She told him she would meet him for lunch on a Saturday at a restaurant in walking distance from her home. Lily-Butterfly choose not to get into Croco's car until she knew him more. She knew that she could be seen as a country girl with all her actions, but she did not care. To Lily-Butterfly country girl meant smart girl.

One day Croco said to Lily-Butterfly in the hotel lobby, "you are really a country girl at heart. I like that. You are refreshing, mysterious, and interesting."

"Good for you," replied Lily-Butterfly.

Lily-Butterfly scheduled an appointment at the hair dresser and childcare provider. Her name was Mrs. Beech. The appointment was on a Saturday two weeks before her date with Croco. She took Rebornstar with her to the hair appointment. For her first hair appointment she had one inch of hair trimmed, wash, condition, and blow dried her hair straight. At this appointment Lily-Butterfly made another appointment to return in two weeks for childcare services for three hours. Mrs. Beech would provide childcare services for Rebornstar so that Lily-Butterfly could go on the lunch date with

Croco. Lily-Butterfly's delay tactics were coming to an end with regards to surrendering to the reason for this Croco guy being in her life. Follow along you will see the reason when Lily-Butterfly discovers the reality of the Croco manifestation.

On the day of the date, Lily-Butterfly took Rebornstar to the childcare provider Mrs. Beech at 11:15 AM. From Mrs. Beech's house she walked to the restaurant. The lunch date was for 12:00 PM. When Lily-Butterfly arrived at the restaurant at 12:00 PM, Croco was already there. He was sitting at a table off to the right side of the dining room. He walked over to her and smiled.

"Hi Miss beautiful. Until you choose to tell me your name, beautiful is what I will call you."

Croco reached out and shook Lily-Butterfly's hand.

"Hi," replied Lily-Butterfly.

"It is nice to see you today. I have tried for over four months to get your name and a date. Congratulations to me today. Hahaha. Come sit over here with me. Where would you like to sit?"

"I would like to sit on the left side of the table and not across from you."

"Good for you. That says you are being feminine, cautious, and wanting to observe me and your experiences from the side line. A wise decision. Go ahead."

Lily-Butterfly did not reply. Croco pulled out the chair and she sat down. The waitress came over to take their orders. The restaurant sold food from the island of Kawomaya.

"Would you like a beer or some wine?" asked Croco.

"No. I do not drink alcohol."

Croco laughed and smirked.

"That is interesting. I have never met a woman who does not drink alcohol. Seriously. You have never drank alcohol?"

"No. Never. I would like a bottle of water. I would like it in the bottle. Thank you."

"Hahaha. Why in the bottle? You do not trust that their glasses are clean enough."

"Yes exactly. I do not stay as beautiful as I am from being reckless with my health."

Lily-Butterfly was quiet again.

"I find you interesting and different. Please tell me your name. I have waited long enough."

"Lily-Butterfly."

"What? Are you serious? Hahaha. Lily-Butterfly?"

"Yes. Plain and simple."

"This name is not simple. This name is saying that your beauty can be poisonous. You are complicated. Your purity can be dangerous. Butterfly symbolize transformation. You are patient and wise, and so on and so forth. Think about it, Lily and Butterfly. Ha," responded Croco.

"Exactly. Now you see what I was protecting you from. Good for you that you can see this with your worldly, city boy intelligence, and street-smart views."

The waitress brought the food, water, and Croco's fruit punch. They ate. Croco was the first one to talk.

"So, finally you told me your name. Lily-Butterfly. Are your married? Do you have a boyfriend?"

"No and no. If I did, I would have told you, and I would not be here having lunch with you. I like a simple life without complication. Do you have a wife or girlfriend?"

"Maybe. I am trying to be mysterious like you. Maybe and maybe not. I will tell you later, and, or you will find out. Ha."

"How convenient? Okay. This is a good conversation."

"What is your job at the hotel?"

"I am being trained in business administration, hotel-tourism-restaurant management. Currently this is the work I am certified to perform. I am working as an assistant to the General Manager Mrs. Butler, and she is training me to work in this hotel."

"Oh. So, you are a woman who loves to read, study, and learn. Did you study at college or university?"

"Both. Yes, you are correct I love to read, study, and learn. Plus, I love to write."

"How about you?"

"Well. I went to technical school. My training was in air-condition and refrigeration technician. Later on, in life I met some men who introduced me to the buying and selling of precious stone, semi-precious stones, jewelry, gold, silver, and so forth. After three years I became a wholesaler and retailer of these things. I travel a lot to many different countries to buy and sell. Plus, I have my own jewelry store close to the hotel; as you know. Usually I am a busy guy."

"Croco, how old are you?"

"Thirty-nine. Why?"

"Just wondering. You seem confident."

"How old are you?"

"I will be thirty in December. You are about nine years older than me."

"Lily-Butterfly you act more mature than your age. Were you married before?"

"Yes. I was married before. I have always lived a responsible life. This makes me responsible, and live a life being aware of consequences to my choices and actions. I try not to make choices that could damage the health and well-being of my daughter and myself. But at the same time, I do not think I am perfect. My opinion is there is no state of perfection, only states of completion. Have you been married before?"

"No. I have not found the right woman as yet. Maybe you are the one. Ha. What do you think?"

"Mr. Croco are you asking me to marry you; on the first date? I do not think that I am the wife for you. I am allergic to negative people and energy. Plus, my life's purpose and destiny is not to be only a wife. My spirit and soul cannot be owned by any human. I cannot be trapped or stuck in a humanistic box. This I know for sure. You seem like a possessive man who likes to own things as private and precious possessions. I am not the one for this kind of relationship. I know that I met you for a reason. This is one of the reasons that I chose to accept your invitation. We will see where this connection goes. I have a direct communication style and I talk and see things from a deep perspective. Try not to take personal my conversations style. My spirit and soul functions on a Universal love and compassion vibration. I am not only a country girl. I am also like a jungle, an authentic diamond in the rough, and an untamed Universe. You might not understand what this means. Anyway, what else would you like to know about me?"

"These are the things I sense why I like you so much. I might want to marry you. But I have not completely decided as yet. I find you fascinating. Yes, you are like a diamond before it is refined. You have mastered the art of keeping your precious self, disguised and invisible. But I can see under your disguises."

"Thank you for your compliments, conversation, and lunch. I have to go. It is getting late to pick up my daughter from childcare. Two hours went so fast. It is said, time seem to travel fast when having fun. Interesting."

"Okay. I will give you a ride home."

"No. But thank you for your offer. I will walk. I like to walk. Exercise is good for me."

"Alright. When can I see you again? Next week I will be in Africa. From Africa I go straight to London. I will return home in two weeks."

"When you return, I will see you. At that time, we can decide if we want to go on another date. At this time let us enjoy today and leave the future date to, if it is meant to be, it will become reality. After processing today's date and conversation, I will get a better view on how I really feel about another date. Is this okay with you? I like to look before I leap and feel comfortable with my decisions and choices. I know that there are no perfect situation. This is just part of my personality."

"I understand. Thank you for being direct and honest. Yes. No rush. I will see you when I return. No worries. No problem. Stay, smart, wise, and beautiful. I will pay the restaurant bill. You can go. Thank you for today. Bye."

"Croco thank you for lunch and everything else. I will see you when you return. Have a safe and successful trip."

"Good Lily-Butterfly. I will see you when I see you. Bye."

"Okay. Bye."

Croco and Lily-Butterfly shook hands. She smiled at him and he smiled back at her. Lily-Butterfly walked away from Croco and left the restaurant.

20

Lily-Butterfly walked to Mrs. Beech's house to get Rebornstar. Mrs. Beech lived ten minutes from Lily-Butterfly's home. Rebornstar expressed that she enjoyed playing with Mrs. Beech's son who is in third grade. Lily-Butterfly paid Mrs. Beech, thanked her and left. When Lily-Butterfly got home she did her chores. During her chores she reflected on the lunch date with Croco. Lily-Butterfly's journal entry at the end of the day was writing about her lunch date with Croco, and all her intuitive awareness about her experiences for the date. The last thing she did before going to sleep was pray about her awareness.

Lily-Butterfly prayed, "dear Creator once upon a time when I was born, almost thirty years ago my life was simple and peaceful living in the valley village of Yaj, on the island of Kawomaya. From about six years to now my life is the opposite. As you already know and see, I am living in this modern, complicated, crowded, busy, stressful environment, and sink or swim situation, of consistently managing my life. On top of everything I met Croco. Whether I like it or not, I feel Croco is here for a reason, only known by you. Please guide my choices, actions, mind, body, and heart in the right direction regarding this Croco situation. I feel as if I am going to sabotage the Croco connection. Continue to protect Manana Leila, Rebornstar, and myself. This prayer is to express how I feel. I know that you know everything already. Good night. Thank you for everything."

Two months into Lily-Butterfly's job she had learned so much from Mrs. Butler. Her job got easier and easier. Thanksgiving had gone by and the busy season of the holiday had taken on new vitality. It was very busy everywhere and it took more time to get to and from work. Lily-Butterfly used Mrs. Beech childcare services as a backup plan if she was going to be late to pick up Rebornstar from her after school program.

One day the second Wednesday in December Lily-Butterfly was eating lunch in the hotel's restaurant, Croco walked into the restaurant. Lily-Butterfly saw him and thought, I cannot hide, avoid, and run from Croco forever.

"Hi. I came here specially to see you, beautiful. Calling you beautiful is like saying your name Lily-Butterfly," said Croco.

"Okay. But beautiful is not my name."

"I know. Anyway, I have been looking for you since I returned from London. Finally, here you are. I would like to invite you for dinner at my home this Saturday at 8:00 PM. Can you come?"

"No, I cannot come."

"Why?"

"I do not eat dinner at 8:00 PM. Plus, I would have to make arrangements for the childcare provider to keep her until I return. I have to be at the childcare provider's home by the latest 10:30 PM to pick up my daughter. I do not live a single care free lifestyle."

"I see. Okay. Hahaha. All right how about lunch?"

"Are you going to be the one cooking?"

"No. I cannot cook. I have a cook that comes to cook for me part time every week when I am in New York. Are you coming or not?"

"Okay I will come. What is your address and telephone number?"

"I will come and pick you up."

"No. I will take a taxi to your home. I do not want to be captivated and hypnotize by your charms, intention, and energy. My spirit and soul want to consciously choose what I become involved in. This way I am not a victim of anything. I also know even with my cautious style and attitude I can have negative experiences. But at least I will know I chose my experience."

"Okay. You are not an easy woman."

"No, I am not."

Croco went over to the waitress and got a piece of paper from her. He wrote down his address and telephone number.

"As you requested, here is my address and phone number. Here is fifty dollars to pay the taxi."

"I do not need the fifty dollars for taxi. Keep your money. I will pay the taxi to and from your home. Thank you for offering to pay the taxi. I will see you on Saturday at 12:30 PM. My lunch break is over. I have to go back to work now. Enjoy your day."

"All right see you on Saturday. Enjoy your day as well."

Croco left the restaurant. Lily-Butterfly paid the waitress and went back to work. Lily-Butterfly made an appointment for Saturday at 11:00 AM with Mrs. Beech for five hours child care services for Rebornstar. She also made a hair appointment for 10:00 AM. The morning of the date Lily-Butterfly took Rebornstar with her to Mrs.

Beech for the hair appointment. When Lily-Butterfly left Mrs. Beech at 11:00 AM Rebornstar stayed and had lunch at Mrs. Beach's home. Lily-Butterfly went home got dressed and called the taxi. The taxi came. At 12:20 PM Lily-Butterfly was at Croco's home. The house was a one family brown brick building on a quiet street. The taxi stopped at the address. Lily-Butterfly paid the taxi driver and got out of the car.

Lily-Butterfly walked up to the large brown wooden door of Croco's house. She rang the doorbell. A man in a large white chef's hat and white shirt opened the door.

"Come in. Nice to see you. Croco is in the shower. Come this way. Have a seat on the couch in the living room. Croco will be with you soon. Would you like something to drink?"

"No thank you. I am okay."

"All right let me get back to the kitchen."

The chef went back to the kitchen. Another man was sitting at a desk in a room close to the front door. From her seat on the couch Lily-Butterfly observed the things in the room. Croco walked into the room.

"Hi beautiful. You look even more beautiful today. Your beauty keeps improving every time I see you. Give me a hug, you beautiful thing."

Croco walked over to hug Lily-Butterfly. She stood up and reached out her hand for a hand shake. Croco stepped back. He shook her hand.

"Come this way to the dining room. I think lunch is ready. Do you like fish, lobster, chicken, vegetables, fried plantains, rice and peas, carrot juice, and sweet potatoes island style pudding?"

"Yes, I like all these foods. Thank you. It sounds like a feast. What are we celebrating?"

"We are celebrating our meeting each other. Relax Lily-Butterfly. Everything is going to be all right."

"I am relaxed. I also practice trusting my instincts and senses. We will both be seeing where this path leads us. Time will tell everything."

"Are you afraid of being here with three men?"

"No. I do not practice fear. I stay conscious and awake to my experiences. I trust me and how I feel. So far, I have not felt danger, but I feel caution."

"I see. Come. Sit here," said Croco.

He pulled out the chair for Lily-Butterfly to sit. She sat down.

"You are in safe hands with us. The man in the room close to the front door is one of my security guards. The chef has been working for me for five years, and I am just a handsome jewel merchant. I love beautiful things."

"I know that you love and like to possess beautiful things. This is why I am being cautious that I do not end up being one of your beautiful possessions. You need to learn that you cannot possess, buy, and own me. Plus, do you know that a person's first name can say a lot about the person?"

"Yes. So.?"

"So, your name is Croco. Croco could mean that a part of you can be like a crocodile. This crocodile shadow part of you can show up at any time. People can have many masks. They usually show the one that they are most comfortable showing. When people get used to someone, they show a fuller range of them self. We will see when your crocodile face is going to appear and how it acts."

"Could be. Good for you that you know all of this. The crocodile side of me you never want to see, if, and when it shows its face. We will see. Time will tell, like you say beautiful. Right now, let us eat and enjoy this wonderful feast. We can talk and eat in the comfort of my cozy dining room. Ha. This is good. I am so happy that you are here. I feel like a lucky guy now that you are here by my side. Ha. Hahaha."

Lily-Butterfly was silent. She was observing Croco and processing her experience.

The chef brought in the soup, appetizer, and carrot juice for both of them. They eat, talk, and drink.

"Why do you have a security guard?"

"I have three security guards. One works in the house to protect me and the contents of the house, one is at the jewelry store, and one travels with me when I go away on business trips. I have very valuable things in the house, sometimes on me, and so forth. People know me and know that precious stone, metal, and jewelry merchant. Understand?"

"I think I understand. Basically, you and your life are in danger all the time. And you want me to come share this dangerous life with you. Jewelry, precious stones and so forth is the only thing you sell?"

"Yes, my life is dangerous. Every human will die from one thing or the other. What else do you think I sell? What I say I sell is dangerous enough. I am an easy-going guy. I am also a complicated guy."

"I see Mr. Croco. Do you live here alone?"

"Yes, I live here alone. I own this house and the one my mother lives in. I also have a house that is rented out. Would you like to come live here with me; and your daughter as well?"

"No. For now, I am fine where I live. Currently my focus is work, taking care of myself and my daughter; and eventually creating my life's purpose career."

"I understand. I am working in my chosen destiny and life's purpose career. I have a perfect and fortunate life. Christmas will be here soon. What are your plans?"

"I have no extravagant plan. I will have a quiet, simple, and enjoyable holiday celebration with my daughter."

"I would like to invite you and your daughter to my mother's house on Christmas day for dinner."

"No thank you. I would rather stay home and keep things simple and quiet. I am comfortable with my own company."

"Okay. After we are finished eating, we will go outside in the beautiful flowers garden. Nature is great. Are you okay with this?"

"Yes. I love nature."

"Okay good. Chef will clean up everything before he leaves. No worries. No problem. I have something that I brought back from Africa for you. I am going to get it. I will be right back."

Croco got up and left the dining table. He came back with a black pouch. Croco took out of the black pouch a black stone with sparkle diamond fragments embedded within the stone.

"Look this is a black onyx semi-precious stone with diamond fragments within it. I think this is so unique. Here. This is for you. A unique stone for a unique person."

"I like this. Thank you," said Lily-Butterfly as she took the stone and the pouch.

"I am happy that you like it. Enjoy. Nature is magnificent. Very magical. The Creator of everything is great."

"I agree with everything you just said. The Creator of all things is truly very creative. I will keep this stone under my pillow. Thanks again for the stone and a very great lunch."

"You are welcome. I had chef put some of the lunch in containers for you to take home. I have to leave here at 4:00 PM to go to the jewelry store in the city. I will give you a ride home."

"Thank you for the offer. But I already told the taxi to return to pick me up at 3:30 PM. What time is it?"

"It is 3:15 PM. The taxi will be here soon or maybe it is already waiting at the gate. I can see that you like to be independent. Good for you."

"Yes, I like to be independent. But I also like to be taken care of in a mutual committed relationship. I do not know you and I have not committed myself to any relationship with you. Right now, I am just doing what feels right for me and what is right for me. I cannot assume that we are in a committed relationship, when we are not. I think that the taxi is here. I have to go pick up my daughter. I will see you again. Thanks again for everything."

"Good. When can I see you again? Maybe New Year's eve or day?"

"New Year's day is good for me. You can have chef prepare lunch again. I will come over for lunch and bring my daughter. We can be here at 12:30 PM. We will take the taxi here. Is this okay with you?"

"Yes Lily-Butterfly. Perfect. Thank you. Let us go. It is getting late. Thank you for coming. When you are with me, I feel peaceful and re-energized. See you on January 1st."

"Okay."

Lily-Butterfly got her pocket book. They walk to the front door together. The taxi was waiting. Lily-Butterfly and Croco hugged. Croco kissed her on her cheek. He laughed. She smiled.

"Bye beautiful."

"Bye Croco."

Lily-Butterfly walked out the door to the waiting taxi. Croco watched her walk away until she got into the taxi. The taxi drove away. Lily-Butterfly took the taxi to Mrs. Beech's home. She got out of the taxi and got Rebornstar. Lily-Butterfly got into the taxi with Rebornstar and the taxi driver took them home.

21

After the lunch date at Croco's house Lily-Butterfly's inner self was never the same anymore. She had more to contemplate, talk to the Creator about, and write in her journal. Thinking about Croco added more inner work to Lily-Butterfly's daily reflections and pondering. Some of the things she reflected on and pondered about was; Croco's home life, his career, his security guards, his energy, their dates, his business trips around the world, his possible crocodile shadow side, the black onyx embedded with diamond chips, and the possible reasons for him in her life. Lily-Butterfly spoke to the Creator in prayer about, Croco, her concerns, and experiences. Lily-Butterfly had awareness of the Creator saying that; life can be like the black onyx stone embedded with the diamond chips, things are never only like they seem, there are no random events, and that everything is for a reason. Lily-Butterfly had soaked the onyx stone in some salt water to cleanse and purify it. Currently it is now under her pillow.

Lily-Butterfly made an appointment at the Gynecologist with the intention of getting a checkup and birth control pills. The doctor's assessment of her health was good. She got the birth control pills and started to take them immediately. By the time Lily-Butterfly saw Croco again on January 1st she was already taking the birth control pills for one week.

"Prevention is better than cure. I do not want to get pregnant. As far as I know I am very fertile. If I choose to have sex with Croco at least I am taking responsibility to not get pregnant. Should I just rely on Croco to use a condom? I do not think so. I have to face the facts that if Croco and I continue to date we will eventually end up having sex. Reality and awareness can be wise," mumbled Lily-Butterfly.

Rebornstar and Lily-Butterfly had an enjoyable holiday and birthday celebrations by themselves. Rebornstar became nine years old and Lily-Butterfly became thirty years old. During the holiday Lily-Butterfly telephoned Manana Leila and told her about their life living in the Bronx, and working in New York City. Lily-Butterfly said nothing to Manana Leila about Croco, or anything that would cause her to worry.

New Year's eve Lily-Butterfly telephoned Croco to confirm their lunch date for January 1st. Friday January 1st the taxi brought Lily-Butterfly and Rebornstar to Croco's house. It was 12:25 PM. They walked up to the front door and rang the doorbell. Croco came to the door he had a big smile on his face.

"Hi Lily-Butterfly it is nice to see you. You look more beautiful than the last time I saw you."

"Thank you. Happy new year to you."

"Same to you. What is your name little lady?" said Croco.

"Oh. Hi. My name is Rebornstar."

"Welcome to my home both of you. Come in. It is cold outside."

"Thank you, sir," replied Rebornstar.

They went inside and took off their coats.

"Put your coats over here on this coat rack. Lunch is on the table. Come on. Let us eat," said Croco.

"Okay. Good. We are coming," said Lily-Butterfly.

They went into the dining room and sat at the table.

"Hi chef. Thank you for lunch. Happy New Year," said Lily-Butterfly.

"Happy New Year to you. You are welcome," replied the chef.

"So, did you girls have an enjoyable Christmas day?" asked Croco.

"Yes, we did. Plus, December 15th and December 27th are our birth dates. We had a great time celebrating in a quiet way. How was your Christmas day?" said Lily-Butterfly.

"Lily-Butterfly you should have told me about your birthday. I had a great holiday with friends, my mother, and my son. He is three years old," said Croco.

Lily-Butterfly thought, here comes the secrets and shadows out of the closet.

"You have a son?" asked Lily-Butterfly.

"Yes, I have a son. I know his mother for five years. We fight like cats and dogs. So, the relationship never became long term. We are too much alike in some ways and she acts just like my mother. She is very miserable, spiteful, unstable, jealous, suspicious, lies, materialistic, angry, mean, and selfish. Lily-Butterfly she is not peaceful and positive energy like you," responded Croco.

"Are you saying that your son's mother has the negative ways you and your mother has? A chip never fall far from the piece of wood when you chop it."

"I did not look at myself this way. So. I would say no. I am my own person," replied Croco.

"Mmm. Hu. Uh. We will see. It takes two to tango. I cannot choose to live within friction, negativity, and instability. This is not my choice of living. I am cautious about human nature. I have to live in a peaceful environment for my positive health and well-being. My birth mother is my first negative influence in my personal life. I have decided that this is enough. I will not personally choose crap," said Lily-Butterfly.

"I understand. Good for you," replied Croco.

"I know that people can have many faces and masks. Depending on how long I am around someone I will see different sides to them. Anyway, time tells everything. Good for you that you have a son," said Lily-Butterfly.

"Thank you."

Rebornstar was happily eating.

"Chef is a great cook. This food is delicious. Does he have a restaurant?" said Lily-Butterfly.

"No. He has a private by appointment only business, cooking, and doing grocery shopping for people. He is from the island of Kawomaya as well. Today we have Christmas fruit cake and ice cream for dessert."

"Sounds yummy," said Lily-Butterfly.

Dinner was a successful feast. Croco and Lily-Butterfly had orange blossom tea sitting outside in the garden. Rebornstar took her bag of toys, dolls, coloring book, crayons, and story book with her to play. She sat around one of the picnic tables under the shady trees in the back of the yard.

"Croco what is on the first floor of your house? It looks like a garage," said Lily-Butterfly.

"Yes, it is a garage. I love luxury cars. I do not have time to drive them as often as I would like."

"Oh yes. What kind of cars do you have in there?"

"Well. I have a blue Jaguar as you know. A BMW convertible, a BMW motor bike, an antique Mustang, a Honda Accord, a Porsche convertible sports car, and a Mercedes Benz SUV. That is, it."

"Wow. You ride a bike?"

"Yes. I love riding my bike."

"Can I see your motor vehicles?"

"Okay. Sure. Let me go turn off the security alarm system to the garage and get the key. My security guard is off today."

"Okay Croco. You are interesting."

Croco got the key and returned. He showed Lily-Butterfly all his motor vehicles.

"You can drive them if you like Lily-Butterfly. Do you have a driver's license?"

"Who? Me? No. I am not interested in driving any of your cars. I have no driver's license. I was just curious and wanted to see them. The country girl in me is not yet interested in driving a motor car. I know how to ride a horse and donkey. That is, it. Using my legs, taking public transportation, and taxi is my current personal daily choice of transportation. Maybe one day in the future I will learn how to drive and get a driver's license. I am not ashamed of my country bumpkin ways and ideas, and old fashion wisdom. To me this is a part of my beautiful preservation and uniqueness. I am an old fashion country girl at heart, spirit, and soul. Modern ideology is also a great resource in this current way of life and living."

"No problem. I understand. How you are is refreshing to me. You are confident and comfortable in what matters most to you. Lily-Butterfly you have an unapologetic strong self-worth and know what you want. Good for you. And could be intimidating for others."

"Thank you. The wealth that I create within my spirit, soul, mind, body, and life is enough for me. I like all your motor vehicles. They are very beautiful and shiny."

"Yes, they are beautiful. Thank you. I love them. Anyway, I am going to lock up the garage. We will go back outside in the garden to drink some more tea. I will go inside to get some more tea."

"Thank you, Croco."

Croco returned with the hot tea. He sat down across from Lily-Butterfly. Lily-Butterfly continued to take mental notes from their conversations and questions.

"So, where does your mother live?" asked Lily-Butterfly.

"My mother lives close by, about a mile away."

"Oh. Okay. What age did you come to live in the United States?" said Lily-Butterfly.

"I left Capital City of the island of Kawomaya to live in the United States at twenty-five years old. My mother left my two brother and I on the island. I was five years old when she left me with her sister. I did not see her again until I was twenty- five years old. To my awareness she never even sent us money or anything. I think that I have a lot of stored up resentments towards her. To me she acts unstable and dysfunctional. I try to care about her well-being and quality of life in materialistic ways. But, to me we do not have a mother and son bond. The issues we have is a daily struggle. I call her auntie Gene. At this time, I do not want to talk about my mother any more. One day you will meet her and you will see what I mean," said Croco.

"I understand. It seems like every human life has at least one difficult passage, bridge to cross, and mean dark energy human experience to overcome. It depends on many things how the person and their life's journey will turn out. Life can be a mysterious wheel that seems to never stop turning. Really, my opinion is that every human must do the work to earn their life, place, and energy balance on this planet. The worse human imbalance is mental health issues. The mind is like the navigational system of the spirit, body, and the person's life. Mental health issues can result in inner conflicts, torment, instability, stuckness, and the person becomes lost to themselves and their life. Human life can be a dilemma. There is an old country bumpkin saying from the valley and village of Yaj, where I am from. The saying is 'as humans we all have to chop our own wood and carry our own water.' Time will reveal everything. I think I have met you for a reason. This is why I am choosing to get to know you. Until the reason shows itself, I am here. After the reason shows itself, we will also see how things evolve. I will keep reminding you that you cannot own and possess me, like your cars locked up in the garage. What time is it?"

"Why? It is 5:30 PM."

"Rebornstar and I will leave now. I am going home to telephone my Manana Leila to wish her happy New Year and so forth. Can I use your telephone to call the taxi?"

"I will take you home."

"No. Rest easy. You are busy most of the time. Stay home and relax. Maybe next time you can drive me home. We will take the taxi. Thank you very much for having us over to share your wonderful food with us and everything else. I enjoyed our conversations as well. You were a great host. Chef is the best. I will see you again?"

"When?"

"Give me pen and paper I will write down my telephone number. You can call me at home. Stop in at the hotel one day, we can have lunch, and plan our next time together. We are both very busy people. Thanks again for everything."

"Lily-Butterfly you are very welcome. Beautiful, I will call the taxi for you. Thank you for coming and your caring thoughts. You really bring out the best in me. When I am with you, I can see my better side. Your energy relaxes me. You have my telephone number. You can call me too. Thanks again for coming."

"You are welcome."

Lily-Butterfly went inside the house to thank the chef and use the rest room. Rebornstar packed up her toys and waited by the gate for her mother. Croco telephoned for the taxi service. Croco and Lily-Butterfly hugged. They kissed each other on the cheeks. The taxi came. Lily-Butterfly and Rebornstar got into the taxi, and went home.

22

Lily-Butterfly got home and she telephone Manana Leila. They talked. Next, she wrote the events of her day and how she felt about Croco in her journal. At 7:00 PM Lily-Butterfly made dinner for Rebornstar and herself. Before going to sleep that night Lily-Butterfly talked to the Creator in prayer about her summary of Croco and his life's perceptions.

It was another new year since she left the island of Kawomaya. At work Mrs. Butler was a great teacher and guide to Lily-Butterfly. Mrs. Butler mentioned to Lily-Butterfly that she was going to retire soon. She was sixty-seven years old and felt burned out from working in the hotel industry for over forty-five years. Taking the train was never an easy exercise for Lily-Butterfly, but she got acclimated to the public train system and accepted the experience. The exercise of running or walking fast to catch the train and get to work on time was good exercise for her health and body. In addition to the public transportation system exercise her work in the hotel kept her walking around for most of the work schedule.

Thursday night of the second week in January 1988 Croco telephoned Lily-Butterfly at home. She picked up the telephone after it rang twice. Her telephone had not rang so late at night before.

"Hello. Hello," said Lily-Butterfly.

"Hi. It is me Croco. How are you?"

"Hi there. I am doing great. Sleepy. I was just about to fall asleep."

"Oh. Okay. Early to bed early to rise, makes a girl like you healthy and wise. Ha, beautiful."

"Yes. Plus get up on time to take my daughter to school and getting to work on time. How are you doing?"

"I am doing great. My only problem is, I cannot stop thinking about you. Even when I am sleeping, I think about you."

"Good for you. At least you have something positive to think about."

"Yeah. Real good. I am calling to see how you are doing and invite you on Saturday at 6:00 PM to my mother's home for dinner. I will come and get you at your home no taxi."

"Okay. You can pick me up only if you promise to take me home by 9:30 PM. I have to pick up my daughter from the childcare person before 10:00 PM."

"I promise, beautiful. I will see you on Saturday at 5:30 PM. I will come to your house to get you and go with you to drop off Rebornstar at childcare. Go get your beauty sleep. Sweet dreams. See you on Saturday."

"Bye Croco. See you on Saturday. Good night. Sweet dreams handsome."

They hang up the telephone.

The next morning Lily-Butterfly telephoned Mrs. Beech to schedule a hair care appointment for 10:00 AM and childcare services for Saturday at 5:45 PM. At different times during the day she thought about Croco and going to his mother's home for dinner, what his mother was like, and so forth. When Saturday morning came Lily-Butterfly had surrendered to visiting Croco's mother's home. Saturday morning after the hair dresser appointment Rebornstar and Lily-Butterfly went out to a restaurant for lunch. When they got home Lily-Butterfly took a nap until 4:30 PM. Rebornstar was going to eat dinner with Mrs. Beech and her family. Lily-Butterfly woke up from her nap, took a shower, and got dressed. Getting dressed for Lily-Butterfly was simple and elegant. At this age she still wore no makeup on her face except for very light coconut or sesame oil for moisturizer and lip gloss. She was ready. Croco arrived. Lily-Butterfly and Rebornstar got in his BMW SUV. They drove to Mrs. Beech's house.

"Hello girls," said Croco.

"Hi Croco," replied Rebornstar and Lily-Butterfly.

"Okay. Tell me the direction to the childcare person's house."

"Turn left at the next corner and go straight. I will tell you when to stop," said Lily-Butterfly.

"Okay."

They got to Mrs. Beech's house.

"Stop at the white and yellow house, on the right side of the street," said Lily-Butterfly.

"Yeah. Here. What is the childcare person's name?" asked Croco.

"Mrs. Maxine Beech."

"Interesting. This is my mother's cousin. Small world."

"Yes. Small modern concrete world. I will be back. Come Rebornstar."

"Yes mama. Bye Mr. Croco."

"Good bye Rebornstar enjoy yourself."

Mrs. Beech came to the front door after Lily-Butterfly rang the doorbell. She opened the door and looked at the BMW SUV parked in front of her house. She waved to Croco sitting in the car.

"Good bye mama," said Rebornstar. She ran into the house.

"Lily-Butterfly are you dating Croco?" asked Mrs. Beech.

"Yes. Why?"

"His mother is my cousin. Be careful. In his career he is involved with shady people. About five times people tried to rob him and his jewelry store. One time he got shot. His mother acts possessive and crazy. Plus, he might have enemies trying to kill him. Lily-Butterfly as you know all that glitters is not gold or diamonds. Things might not be as they seem beyond the glitter and surface appearance. Keep your eyes open. Do not get swept away by his handsome looks, riches, and material possessions. Make up your own mind using your instincts and wisdom. Anyway go. Do not tell him that I told you anything. I will see you at 10:00 PM."

"Okay. Thank you for the awareness. I will keep my eyes open and stay grounded. I will not say you told me anything. Thanks for everything. See you later."

Lily-Butterfly got back into Croco's SUV. They talked until the car arrived at a brick and stone house. Croco drove into the driveway and parked.

"We are here. I think my older brother and his wife are here as well. Come beautiful."

Croco got out of the motor vehicle and opened Lily-Butterfly's door. She got out. Croco used a key to unlock the front door of the house. They went inside. Croco's mother greeted them in the living room. She was cooking in the kitchen.

"Hi. Croco told me about you. My name is Gene. Good finally I get to meet you. What is your name? Is it Green or Lemon-Butterfly?"

Lily-Butterfly was silent. She reached out her hand and shook Ms. Gene's hand.

"Hi Ms. Gene. My name is LILY-BUTTERFLY! Did you hear me?"

"Yes. I am not deaf. My older son and his wife is in the dining room. You can join them. Croco you can go introduce your friend to them and come back here to help me carry these foods to the dining table."

"Yes Ms. Gene. I will be right back," said Croco to his mother.

Lily-Butterfly thought, here comes the shadow boxing, shade, and unmasking. If Croco's mother think my simplicity is a symbol for stupidity she is wrong. Oh, Creator and guardian angels stay by my side.

Croco guided Lily-Butterfly to the dining room. He introduced her to his brother and sister in-law. They introduced themselves. Croco turned and walked back to the kitchen. Unbeknownst to Croco Lily-Butterfly turned and walked behind him. She did not sit at the dining table like Croco thought she would. She had a feeling that his mother was going to say something about her. Before Lily-Butterfly reached the kitchen door she heard Ms. Gene talking to Croco.

"Croco, what a weird name you friend has. Lily-Butterfly. Ha. Um. You sure know how to choose them. She looks smart and beautiful. But watch it. She might be after your riches. Watch it my son. You work hard for your stuff for some gravalicious wise snake to come and claim it all. I like your son's mother better. This Miss. Lily-Butterfly looks too good to be true. Anyway, take this chicken and potatoes to the dining table."

"Watch your mouth Ms. Gene. Lily-Butterfly is a good woman inside and out. Mind your business. I think that you are jealous. Any time you think a girlfriend has my undivided attention you start your poison talk about her. The reason you like my son's mother better is, because we fight a lot and are like oil and water. You know that we bring out the worst in each other. Ms. Gene start acting like my mother instead of a jealous girlfriend. Maybe if you do, I can feel like calling you mom instead of Ms. Gene. Watch yourself. Do not say anything to upset Lily-Butterfly. Do you hear me?"

"Yes, son dear. If you say so."

When Ms. Gene and Croco turned around. They saw Lily-Butterfly standing inside the kitchen by the door. She had heard everything they were talking about.

"Where can I hang my coat? May I help you Ms. Gene?"

"Come over here my beautiful. I will show you where to hang your coat."

Ms. Gene looked at both of them and smiled. Lily-Butterfly followed Croco. She hung up her coat.

"Tonight, I must remember that if I do not have something positive to say to stay quiet. There is an old time saying in the valley and village of Yaj, 'get to know the tribe before you put yourself into it. The person is a mirror of their ancestors and their tribe.' This is a true saying. It is like modern days saying 'the chip does not fall far from the block, and an apple does not fall far from the tree. Croco calls his mother Ms. Gene. It seems like a hot and cold mother and son relationship. Thanks to the Creator for my Manana Leila and my other ancestors, before Ms. Gina. I must stay aware tonight. This experience should be very peculiar," mumbled Lili-Butterfly.

Lily-Butterfly went to the kitchen. She approached Ms. Gene.

"Ms. Gene I would like to help you and Croco to bring the food to the table. What can I take to the table? You look very tired and drained. Please relax and let me help you."

"Ha. Hm. Mmm. Okay. If you insist. Take the bowls over by the stove. Be careful not to get burned. Thanks."

"You are welcome. You do not have to worry about me with hot stove and getting burn. I am a country bumpkin, who grew up using wood fire stove on the earth, or a cast iron stove to cook. From about three years old I am used to fire, bon fires, flames, hot stove, and helping with cooking. Plus, from about three years old walking about thirty miles per day carrying buckets of water on my head from a community pipe, being a shepherd for the goats and sheep, and so forth. Try to not take my simplicity for stupidity. My beauty is beyond skin deep. I am like a wild untamed jungle."

Ms. Gene coughed, and coughed, and did not reply to what Lily-Butterfly had said. She felt dizzy from what Lily-Butterfly had said, and what she had been drinking in the cup disguised as tea.

Lily-Butterfly helped Croco to bring all the food to the table. When this was completed the five of them sat at the table to eat. Croco, his brother, Gene, and brother's wife started to eat.

"Stop eating everyone. Let us bless the food before we eat. I hope this is okay with all of you. I will say the food blessing," said Lily-Butterfly.

Everyone looked at Lily-Butterfly with a surprised look on their face.

"Yes. Sure. Blessings the food is good," replied Croco's brother.

"Okay. Dear Creator of everything thank you for this food, the cook, and all the things that created this opportunity for us to get together tonight. Please continue to help us to improve our negative ways, health, well-being, and life. Amin," said Lily-Butterfly.

Everyone said, "Amin."

Croco's mother looked at Lily-Butterfly with her eyes turned to the side without turning her head. They ate. They talked together, except for Lily-Butterfly who was silent. She observed and listened to their conversations and interactions. The night continued on. For two hours they ate and talked.

"Lily-Butterfly would you like some wine or other alcoholic beverage," asked Croco's brother.

"No. I do not drink alcoholic drinks," replied Lily-Butterfly.

"Are you a Puritan?" asked Ms. Gene.

"I do not know what this word means. I am Lily-Butterfly."

It was now 9:10 PM. Lily-Butterfly stood up.

"Please excuse me. It is almost time for me to leave. Croco and I will wash the first set of dirty dishes and start to clean up the kitchen," said Lily-Butterfly.

"My son does not clean kitchen and wash dishes. I will do it. I do not know where you come from acting like a peasant and servant. I will do the cleaning of my dishes and kitchen," protested Ms. Gene.

"Yes, peasant and servant I am; and my ancestors before me. Peasants and servants of our own lives and the Creator of all things. Come Croco let us help to clean up before we leave. To me this is an expression of gratitude for giving back for what I have received. Ignorant people can say and think whatever they like. Ms. Gene you look very tired, tipsy, and drained. Relax. Rest. We will help to clean up before we leave. No worries. No problem. This is an expression of our gift to you before we leave. Thank you for this food, all the work you put into preparing everything, and so forth. Come Croco. Take your mother and everyone else's plate."

"Okay. Yes. Sure," replied Croco.

"Okay. Go ahead Lily-Butterfly. I will finish cleaning up. Let me know when you are finished with what you choose to do," said Ms. Gene.

Croco and Lily-Butterfly took all the dirty dishes from the table to the kitchen.

"Lily-Butterfly are you okay? You seem upset."

"I feel drained and tired. I do not like the negative energy of this house environment. I heard everything that you mother said to you about me when we first arrived. I want you to know that I do not pretend, act pretentious, and fake. I would like to show appreciation for Ms. Gene efforts and being here for dinner. Let us help with the dishes. After I would like to leave and go to my home. Anyway, it is almost 9:30 PM now. Is this okay with you?"

"Sure. I understand. We help and after we leave. I find Ms. Gene irritating as well. She is the gold digger. Any girlfriend I have that she feels is good for me she gets jealous. Ms. Gene acts like the more I give to my girlfriend the less she will get. Oh, my she needs help. Ms. Gene acts more like my wife instead of my mother and parent. It is interesting that you pick up this vibe meeting her for the first time. She does not know how to act. Sorry about what you heard. I am really sorry. We will help and leave like you suggested," said Croco.

Croco and Lily-Butterfly helped with the dishes and cleaning of the kitchen.

"We are leaving now Ms. Gene. Lily-Butterfly has to go pick up her daughter from childcare. Bye everyone. See you next time," said Croco.

"She has a daughter? Oh Lord," said Ms. Gene.

Before Ms. Gene could say another word Croco screamed, "STOP MS. GENE. ENOUGH!"

Croco walked away towards the coat rack. He got his coat and put it on. Lily-Butterfly was already standing at the front door with her coat on. They left Ms. Gene's home. Lily-Butterfly was silent. Croco talked but she did not respond. They arrived at Mrs. Beech's home.

"Croco thank you for taking me to your mother's home for dinner, introducing me to your mother, brother, and his wife. Do not feel bad for what happened. You know your mother already and what she is capable of. Her actions are not your fault. You do not have to apologize for her. I like you. We can continue to date and see what happens. There is a reason why we met. I do not think the things I experienced tonight is the reason. If I leave you before the reason is experienced, I would be missing the reason, although I do not know what the reason is. At this time, I feel very tired and need to go to sleep. I am going inside to get my daughter and you can take us home."

"Okay. I like you as well. Sorry anyway."

Lily-Butterfly went inside Mrs. Beech's house. She came back out in five minutes with Rebornstar. Croco took them home.

"Good night Croco. Thanks again. Call me or I might see you at my job."

"I will see you soon. Bye."

Rebornstar was already dressed for bed. She went into her room, got in her bed, and went to sleep. Lily-Butterfly took a shower and wrote in her journal. She emptied all her emotions about the situation at Croco's mother's home. She knew that the connection with Croco was far from over. Usually she would just stop a relationship with many red flags. This red flag relationship continued as Lily-Butterfly was guided to do. Her continued question was why did they meet? I guess we will all wait and see what happens.

Interestingly Lily-Butterfly prayer this night was simple.

Lily-Butterfly prayed in a whisper, "Divine Creator of all things you know everything already. I will wait until your will regarding Croco is manifested. Until then I will continue on this path with Croco in my life. Thank you for everything. Amin."

Lily-Butterfly got in her bed, closed her eyes, and fell asleep.

23

Sunday Lily-Butterfly spent the day doing all their chores, preparing for school and work for the coming week, going to the park, reading, and resting. Monday morning, they both woke up rested and refreshed. Lily-Butterfly and Rebornstar got dressed for school and work. As they were eating their breakfast the telephone rang. Lily-Butterfly picked up the telephone.

"Hi this is Lily-Butterfly. May I help you?"

"Hi, it is me, Croco."

"Hi. Oh. I am surprised. You never call me in the morning before."

"Yes. I want to say sorry again for my mother's actions towards you on Saturday night. Really I hope that you will continue to see me."

"Yes, I will continue to get to know you and your life. From my experiences with you I will decide if I stay in your life or not. I cannot choose to have a permanent long-term relationship with you if it is going to be abusive, traumatic, and damage my health, well-being, and personal life. I have a child and I have to live a life for her greater good as well. We will talk more the next time we see each other. Right now, I have to finish my breakfast, take my daughter to school, and get on the train, so that I can be at work on time. Have a great day. We can talk at a more convenient time."

"Okay beautiful. Have a nice day."

"Thank you. You too. Bye."

The more time Lily-Butterfly spends with Croco, the more they got to know each other and the interactions of the relationship dynamics. Some of the negative expression from Croco were: -talking to Lily-Butterfly about his mother Ms. Gene. If Croco was upset, seemed irritable, and stressed, she would guide his on how to process his negative emotions. This would help to diffuse Croco's anger and irritations. This she thought helped her as well and prevented a buildup of Croco's toxic negative emotions, and stress. After Lily-Butterfly's experiences with Ms. Gina she promised herself to never be a part of any relationship that would create trauma, suffering, and abuse. Plus, damage her life, health, and well-being. Sometimes Lily-Butterfly thought, how much could she really help Croco to really manage his mood swings? Sometimes Croco would be the nicest, kindest, and loving person. Other times, depending on the severity of something he perceives is negative, Croco's mood would go to the other extreme. He would immediately switch into being someone mean, angry, impatient, negative, breaking things, and destructive. Currently, these expressions were not towards her. They were just towards people, places, and things. It was as if he would lose total control and then switch back. Sometimes he would seem like he forgot what happened. Lily-Butterfly often wondered when he was going to feel comfortable enough to also express these negative emotions towards her and on her. To her it was obvious that Croco had some mood disorder and mental health issues. One of the things that would set off Croco's mental explosion was Ms. Gene, his mother. It was as if he wished that she was someone else. It was obvious that there was some kind of dysfunctional psychological issue between both of them, that needs to be resolved, or improved in some way. This issue Lily-Butterfly never tried to help Croco with. If she was around, she might choose to listen to Croco tell her about the problem or choose to go home. If they were talking on the phone, she would tell him that she had to go. Lily-Butterfly would tell Croco every time that she did not want to digest the angry energy expressions.

One-night Croco telephoned Lily-Butterfly at her home. It was 9:00 PM. At this time of the day she was preparing to go to sleep. Rebornstar was already asleep. She answered the telephone.

Croco said, "I do not know what to do with my mother. I try to help her, but she acts entitled and is stuck in destructive behaviors. I received an eviction notice from the bank that gave me the mortgage for the house she lives in. It is my house. I give her money each month to pay the mortgage. This way she is aware, and takes some responsibility about having the house as her home. She has not paid the mortgage in five months. The bank kept sending letters to the house regarding the mortgage situation. She ignores the letters and does not open them. I went to the house today. By accident I saw all the unopened bank letters and read them. This is one of the ways Ms. Gene expresses her denial and avoidance behavior. I went to the bank and fixed the situation by paying the five months mortgage. Ms. Gene is at work. I telephoned her at work and she hang up the phone on me. I do not know what else to do. I talk nice, yell, and scream. Everything I do does not seem to make a difference in her choices and behavior. Sorry to be venting my negative emotions on you again."

"I hear you Croco. Next time do not call me at home at this time to tell me any negative stories or venting your negative emotions. I am getting ready to go to sleep. I do not want to come between you and your mother. I cannot help you to solve your mother and parent personal issues. Maybe there are other issues that adds up to creating the problems and issues that you are having with her."

"What do you mean?"

"Well the time when I went to her home for dinner, to me she seemed drunk. When I was cleaning up the kitchen, I found five different mugs and one glass with alcohol mixed in with coffee and tea. The glass had only alcohol. The mugs had coffee and tea mixed with alcohol. I emptied the cups and glass and put them in the dish washer. When I emptied the mugs and glass into the kitchen sink is when I smelled the alcohol. To me it seems as if while drinking she forgets where she puts her drink. Or is not sure if she drank it all. So, she makes another drink. I did not say anything to you. It is your mother and you must know that she has an alcohol problem, and maybe drugs too. Maybe she uses the money for the mortgage payment to support her addictions. The alcohol she seems to drink is clear, it could be vodka or gin. I am suspecting that you know about her addictions. Talking to me about this situation just before I go to sleep is not helping you or me."

"Ha. Mmm. Um. I know that Ms. Gene, my mother, likes to drink vodka and gin. Yes. So."

"Listen this is your issue. After tonight I do not want to help you with Ms. Gene's issues because her problems are not my business. By the statement you just made my perception is, you are in denial of whatever it is about Ms. Gene you are avoiding. Well, maybe she is always drunk and this is her normal state, and I think that you are aware of this. This state could be called an alcoholic. It is not for me to diagnose your mother's issues. Ms. Gene being drunk could also contribute to her forgetfulness and other mental, emotional, physical, and life issues. Maybe she is seeing a mental health doctor and is on prescribed antidepressants and at the same time drinking alcohol. The money she works, mortgage money, and all her other money could be going towards supporting her addictions. Ms. Gene also gets concerned when someone you care about comes into your life, because legally she is your next of kin and certified beneficiary of everything that you own. If you get married your wife legally becomes your beneficiary and next of kin. The last thing Ms. Gene would encourage is you getting married. Now I am tired of hearing you talk about issues between you and your mother, using my time, and energy uselessly. After tonight I choose to not participate in any conversation about her with you. Talk to Ms. Gene yourself about the root of her issues. Both of you get therapy about your issues. I am not a mental health doctor. Last but not least I will not let her practice her demons and shadow negative energy on me. Croco do you understand all that I have just said?"

"Yes, on some level I do hear and understand you. I am sitting here listening to you and I am lost for words. You hit the nail on the head. Yes, I am aware of her alcohol drinking. I think her alcohol drinking was normal, because I have always seen her drink alcohol in here tea and coffee, and by itself. I am seeing now that this could be contributing to her personality, attitude, and disguising her mental health issues. I am being aware from what you just said that she could always be tipsy or drunk, and maybe high on some kind of drugs. Oh, my Lord. Wow. Like you say the issues are deeper than the surface. I am going to talk to her if she will choose to listen to what I have to say. Ms. Gene likes to wear masks, avoid, and be in denial of the root of her issues. Maybe I am like her in some ways and use materialistic things, money, and traveling for work, and being busy to avoid fixing my real issues. The chip does not fly too far from the block. I see. Thank you for opening my eyes a little wider. After tonight I can see things with new eyes about our situation. Maybe your life's purpose destiny career is helping people with their issues."

"Maybe. Croco addiction and mental health issues are serious diseases. Plus, your mother works in a nursing home where prescribed medication for the residence can be easily accessible to her. Okay, I have said more than enough. Try to understand why she is how she seem. Look at her situation with compassion. I have to go to sleep now. It is 10:30 PM. I have to get up on time to take care of my daughter and my life. Choice, action, responsibility, consequence, and mindfulness are some of the important practices in living a successful balanced life. Everything good comes with lots of effort and repeat positive practices. Anything free is worthless and cannot have value to the human mind and human nature. Amin. Good night. Call me tomorrow night by 8:00 PM. The next time you call me at 9:00 PM or after I will not be answering the telephone, because I would have gone to sleep. Bye."

"Okay thank you. I will talk to Ms. Gene about her possible addiction and everything else. I know that she will not listen to me and be in denial. But I will try my best. I do not have the knowledge and patience to handle Ms. Gene. Good night my beautiful angel. Bye."

"I am not any human (my- anything). I am myself and the Creator is my shepherd. Bye."

Lily-Butterfly did not wait for Croco to respond to her last sentences. She hung up the telephone. After Lily-Butterfly got off the telephone she prayed.

"Dear Creator. What now? To me this Croco situation vibes seem like sitting in a den of scorpions waiting for them to sting me or not. I know that my views of myself, my life, people, and everything is a direct and no-nonsense approach. Croco seems to be at the root of his spirit a positive lost soul. We both know that I cannot change him. He seems to have an issue managing his moods and other imbalances. I like his positive sides, but his negative sides can be too much for me to digest. I feel like I know Croco from another life time. I cannot remember the direct story of knowing him. I trust you and your guidance. This is why I choose to still have Croco in my life. I am ready for the reason why karma and destiny have brought us together. Please let this Croco karma and destiny that brought us together be revealed and manifested as soon as possible. Dear Creator although I am saying this to you, I also know that you know best. Let your will be done. I am ready to take the leap. Amin," whispered Lily-Butterfly.

After praying Lily-Butterfly went to sleep. Her sleep took her deep into dream land. She had a dream that she was fighting in a war. In the dream she was a man and the lead warrior and commander of an army. They were fighting with swords, bow and arrow, and daggers, in a bloody battle. In the dream Croco was one of the warriors fighting in the same group as the lead warrior of the army – who was Lily-Butterfly at the time. This lead warrior of the army saved Croco's life. The dream revealed to Lily-Butterfly where she knew Croco from, and the karma that brought them together.

The next morning Lily-Butterfly got up at 4:30 AM. She took her journal and wrote down the dream. She processed the dream.

"Ha. Hu. Wow. Now I see. It is simple and complicated at the same time. Croco's spirit and soul is in my life to repay the karma of saving his life in that lifetime. This is fascinating. A life for a life. But how is this karma repayment going to happen is the disguised revelation waiting to happen. How is Croco going to give me a life? I am already alive and here. I guess we will see. The Creator works in mysterious ways. At least I am aware of something more than before. I need to wait and give Croco the opportunity of repaying the karma of saving his life. The rest is just static of this karma repayment matrix. I see. Give Croco the opportunity to repay the karma without me getting woven and stuck in his other personal karma drama matrix. This will not be easy. It will be like walking on hot stones in a scorpion's den. I do not know for sure how this karma repayment is supposed to manifest. I have to use trust and wait. The way will show the way. Croco seems to have a sensible side and a reckless side. I guess when the karma is repaid, I will know what action to take next. Oh, my Creator. My life is like a circus and chess game. I can see how easy it is for people to get lost and become losers. This dream was short, but very profound and enlightening. Thank you dream realm and the angels of the dream realm. Life is life," mumbled Lily-Butterfly.

After this dream Lily-Butterfly looked at Croco and everything in his life with renewed-eyes, intuition, perception, and understanding. She just had to wait and see what will happen. To know ahead of the karma repayment would disturb the authenticity of the complete process. The process had to be genuine, pure, unconditional, and neutral on both sides. Lily-Butterfly got a bird's eye view into the karma repayment plan so that she would be still and not end the connection between Croco and herself before the karma repayment. The Creator know very well that Lily-Butterfly's spirit and soul will do everything to protect itself from damage.

Time went on and the connection between Croco and Lily-Butterfly got closer. But as usual Lily-Butterfly was mindful and cautious to not weave her spirit and soul into Croco's spirit and soul. She also protected her spirit and soul from Croco weaving his spirit and soul into her spirit and soul. Lily-Butterfly was a master of being grounded and positively maintaining with confidence and balance her individual spirit and soul boundaries. People would need her permission to cross her boundaries. Lily-Butterfly's spirit and soul personality was to remain wild and free, like father and mother-nature; for the purposes of her life's purpose. Lily-Butterfly knew in her heart that she was destined to travel with humility; light, grounded, clear, and unclaimed by all humans. She knew that damage to her spirit, soul, mind, emotion, body, health, well-being, and life would take a lot of time and energy to repair, plus she could become derailed and get lost. Her first and last dark arts shadow teacher birth mother Ms. Gina, together they had done a magnificent job. Lily-Butterfly chose to not go down this trauma drama path again. Lily-Butterfly never told Croco about the karma dream she had, that revealed why they were in each other's life.

Croco and Lily-Butterfly had added sexual physical intimacy to their sharing of intimate interactions. She was still taking the birth control pills and she insisted that Croco used a condom as well. Croco resisted using the condom and Lily-Butterfly insisted. On Saturdays she choose to spend more time at Croco's home and from Monday to Friday, plus Sundays she was at her home with Rebornstar. Most times during the week Croco was away travelling for work and so forth. Summer of 1988 Lily-Butterfly put Rebornstar in summer camp five days per week. She would take Rebornstar to Mrs. Beech's home before work. Mrs. Beech would take Rebornstar to camp, pick her up at 3:30 PM, and Lily-Butterfly would get Rebornstar on her way home from work.

Croco repeatedly encouraged Lily-Butterfly to give up her apartment and move in with Rebornstar into his house. Her consistent reply was no. She also told him that she will not live with a man unless she choose to marry him. Lily-Butterfly's perception about marriage was that it is a sacred union and yoking together of two spirits and souls as one. Most time people do not see the sacred and binding energy commitment of the marriage ritual. That people connect to marriage on a superficial, entertaining, and physical level. To her marriage was a sacred, serious, binding spell ritual, and long-term permanent contract. Sometimes this serious contract is easy to dissolve and sometimes it is not; especially when children are involved.

Taking into consideration Croco's mood swings, lack of anger management skills, frequent business travels, his mother issues, and everything else she experienced; every time Croco brought up the subject of marriage Lily-Butterfly would tell him that she was not ready to marry him and why. Croco does not like to take no for an answer. Anyway, with understanding Lily-Butterfly managed the relationship between her and Croco. And time went on.

24

The third week in August 1988 Lily-Butterfly took one week vacation off from work. She went with Rebornstar to visit Manana Leila at her home in Somerville, Massachusetts. Manana Leila was very happy to see them in person and hear their stories of life living in New York. Manana Leila had never been to New York City. All three of them took the ferry to Martha's Vineyard for two nights and three days. They stayed in a small bed and breakfast hotel.

While on Martha's Vineyard Manana Leila informed Lily-Butterfly that Ms. Gina's permanent resident visa was progressing and maybe in one year the visa would be approved. Manana Leila told Lily-Butterfly that Lucy could not come with Ms. Gina because of all the reasons they had speculated before. Lily-Butterfly listened throughout the Martha Vineyard trip as Manana talked to her about Ms. Gina's visa situation without giving her complete opinion. She just let Manana Leila talk and kept what she knew about Ms. Gina and Lucy to herself. Lily-Butterfly choose to hear and listen to everything that Manana wanted to speak. Maybe talking to Lily-Butterfly was Manana Leila's way of processing her negative emotions, worry, and concerns about the visa process. Manana seemed overwhelmed by the reality of the complete Ms. Gina visa process, and having Ms. Gina come to live with her. The time was getting closer for the visa approval and Ms. Gina moving to live with her.

As Lily-Butterfly listened to Manana Leila she thought, Lucy would not choose to come currently to the United States. Lucy would not choose to leave Kawomaya and her husband's family, because she worked very hard to weasel her way into his family, and orchestrated a firm hold. Lucy's psychological health and well-being seem to need her husband's family map for survival and her sense of self. Lucy did not graduate high school and wondered if she had gotten her GED certification. Lucy is baptized as a Christian, I am not. Christians do not usually socialize with non-Christians. Lucy had married the son of a pastor much older than herself. She knew him from a very young teenager. They met going to spend time with a second cousin who attended the church his father was a pastor.

This family is considered an aristocratic upper-class family. Lucy adopted her husband's parent as her fantasy father and mother. She even called them dad and mom, devaluing her connection to Ms. Gina and her original real home life situation. Lucy and I never had a close relationship, sister relationship, or any real relationship. I was more of a parent figure in Lucy's life. After Lucy married into this supposedly upper-class family, she saw me even more as a lower class and servant person, especially because she saw how Ms. Gina treated me. I invited Lucy to my wedding when I got married at twenty-one years old, and she came. That was the only time I saw Lucy to date. Lucy never invited Ms. Gina, me, and her two half-brothers to her house, or anything to do with her, and her new found family. Ms. Gina, Henry, and Dean attended Lucy's wedding when she got married at twenty-three years old. She invited me but I chose not to go, because of something shitty that Lucy did to me close to her wedding date. I am peculiar and could be seen as strange. I would get a big zero if I had to pretend and stuff down how I really felt about a perceived negative action towards me. People are created for their own spirit and soul's journey and purpose. Lucy could be in love with her husband, infatuated, or look up to him as the father she never had. In marrying him she could also have his father as another father as well. Does all of this matter? Maybe and maybe not. People usually have their own perceived value for things. Lucy was not going to divorce her husband. I think that she will stay married for ever to this man. If he is not choosing to move to the United States, Lucy would not choose to come, and leave him on the island. He was her psychological mental comfort cushion. Her husband would not choose to leave his original father and mother family. Lucy would not leave this family unless she saw that the opportunity and value was greater than the family, she had penetrated herself into. Lucy's technique to value herself is associating with other people she perceive has social statue. Her husband might not choose to come to the United States and leave his successful career, aristocratic family map, and comfort cushions to start over. I have never told Manana about everything Ms. Gina did to me. I am not going to gossip to her about Lucy either. All these thoughts, speculation from past experiences percolated within Lily-Butterfly's mind as she heard Manana Leila talk. She kept her opinions, judgments, and negative real perception, about Ms. Gina's visa situation and Lucy to herself. Talking her thoughts out to Manana was useless complaint. Lily-Butterfly was also processing many ideas about how she could help

Manana Leila with Ms. Gina, Henry, and Dean when they move to the United States. These thoughts seem to also help Lily-Butterfly process more of her personal negative emotional pandora box energy regarding past Ms. Gina and Lucy experiences. 'Facing the truth can set someone free,' was one of Lily-Butterfly beliefs.

After returning from Martha's Vineyard one day they visited Manana Leila's half-brother and his family. They lived in Somerville about six miles from Manana Leila's home. They enjoyed spending time with one another talking about the year's events, and visiting Martha's Vineyard. Lily-Butterfly did not tell Manana Leila about Croco. On the sixth day of visiting Manana Rebornstar and Lily-Butterfly to the bus back to New York City. They were happy to have visited Manana Leila.

School for Rebornstar would start again in three days. Everything was prepared for school before they went on vacation. Rebornstar would be going to third grade. Croco was away in Brazil on a business trip. When he returned, he telephoned Lily-Butterfly one night after work.

"Hi beautiful. How was your vacation?"

"It was good. We visited with my Manana, went to Martha's Vineyard, visit her half-brother, and did other local activities. My Manana is doing well. We are fine and Rebornstar is back in school. How was your trip?"

"My trip was great. I got to sell most of the jewelry and precious stones I bought. Business is always good for me. I miss you. When can we see each other? Is this Saturday okay?"

"Can you come over to my home on Saturday morning at 9:00 AM for breakfast? All three of us can have breakfast together. Ha?" said Lily-Butterfly.

"All right. Sounds good. This is a surprise. You finally made the decision to invite me into your home. Thank you."

"Yes. Good for you. What did your mother say about the addiction and not paying the mortgage? I said I did not want to talk about her, but I am curious."

"I think that you know already what she would say. She told me that she was not an alcoholic or drug addict. She admitted liking to drink vodka, gin, and taking pills for pain and stress."

"What did she say about her memory?"

"She admit that sometimes she forgets things, and said that people naturally forget things sometimes."

"I see. Croco Ms. Gene is your issue. Do as you like. I have another surprise for you. I took off the last week of October to spend some time with you during the day when Rebornstar is in school. After I take Rebornstar to school I will come over to your house at about 9:00 AM. You can take me home at 5:00 PM. Is this okay with you?"

"Yes sure. I will take you with me everywhere I have to go. We can have lunch together every day. Good. I am going to go now. Sweet dreams. I will see you on Saturday morning and maybe bump into you while you are at work. Bye."

"Bye."

Lily-Butterfly hung up the telephone. At the mention of sweet dreams again Lily-Butterfly remembered the Croco karma repayment dream. She did her nightly routine, journal writing, prayer, and went to sleep.

Saturday morning came. Lily-Butterfly made breakfast. Croco arrived at 9:00 AM. He knocked on the door.

"Come in. The door is unlocked," said Lily-Butterfly.

Croco turned the door knob and came in. Rebornstar was seated at the table.

"Welcome to my simple and humble home," said Lily-Butterfly.

"Yes, thank you for inviting me"

"I am the cook. I hope that you like my food."

"It smells good. Where should I sit?"

"Sit where you would like."

Croco sat down. Lily-Butterfly put all the food on the table. She sat down and blessed the food. They ate.

"The food tastes very good, better than chef's cooking," said Croco.

"Hahaha. Funny. You think so? Croco I think that you are right. A little extra woman's touch could have amplified the spices and so forth. I love chef's food very much as well."

"Yes. Seriously."

Rebornstar smiled.

"I love eating at your house. I just sit back, relax, and enjoy the food. When chef does not come to cook do you eat in restaurants?"

"Yes. I cannot cook. The only thing I can cook is eggs, toast bread, and make coffee and tea. This is as far as my cooking skills

148

go. I travel a lot. I eat in restaurants about seventy percent of the year. I do not mind. I really love your cooking. It is very tasty. Your spice blending is very creative. Good. Thank you for inviting me."

"You are welcome."

Rebornstar watch, listen, and sometimes smirked.

"People from the island of Kawomaya cook island food most of the time. I love this kind of food; it can make me strong and healthy. So Croco what are you going to do for the rest of the day?" said Lily-Butterfly.

"After I leave here, I will go to work at the jewelry store. I have inventory and paper work to do. Maybe one day you will quit the hotel work and come manage my businesses."

"I do not think so. Absence makes the heart grow fonder. We would get on each other's nerves. I usually see and sense things beyond the surface and so forth. It would be hard for me to mind my own business. You need your space to do as you like and so do I."

"I see. I see. What are you going to do after I leave?"

"I am going food shopping, laundry, take Rebornstar out to lunch and to the park."

"I see. I will telephone you tonight before you go to sleep. Or you can call me."

"I will call you at home 8:30 PM."

Rebornstar had finished eating.

"May I leave the table mama?"

"Yes Rebornstar. Go finish cleaning up your room and make your bed. After Croco leave we will go food shopping, do the laundry, go to lunch, and to the park. Fresh air and exercise is healthy for us."

"Yes mama. Let me know when you are ready. Bye Mr. Croco."

"Bye Rebornstar," replied Croco.

Rebornstar went to her bedroom. Croco helped Lily-Butterfly to wash the dirty dishes and clean up the kitchen and dining room.

"So Croco do you go to night clubs and bars?"

"No. I do not like drinking. Maybe a glass of wine or scotch on special occasion. I love to watch television. I do not like clubs and bars. I have everything I need to my comfort at my home. I do like to go to restaurants to eat."

"I never see you drink alcohol; this is why I ask. I understand."

They finished with the dishes and cleaning.

"Lily-Butterfly I am leaving now. I will talk to you tonight."

"Okay Croco. Enjoy your day."

Croco and Lily-Butterfly hugged, kissed, and said goodbye to each other. Croco left. Lily-Butterfly and Rebornstar continued on with their day.

The last week of October came and Lily-Butterfly was on vacation again. She had plan to spend Monday to Friday from 9:00 AM to 5:00 PM with Croco, walk to his house in the morning after taking Rebornstar to school, and Croco was supposed to take her home at 5:00 PM. The first morning on Monday she walked to Croco's house.

"I can come and pick you up at your home. You do not have to walk here," said Croco.

"I like to walk for the exercise. You might think that I keep insisting on staying country and independent. Maybe, but walking also gives me exercise. As a young girl I walked a lot. Why do you think I am so athletic and strong? Inside and outside beauty comes with work. Nothing is really free. Thank you for your offer."

"You are right. Nothing is free. So true."

"Yes. What are we going to do today?"

"First come with me over to my mother's home. I am going to see if she paid the mortgage for October. I called the bank and they told me that they did not receive the payment. I gave her the money in cash last week."

"I do not understand. Why not pay the mortgage yourself with a check?"

"Why? A stupid reason. I want her to take complete responsibility for something. To me Ms. Gene acts irresponsible."

"Croco you cannot use control and manipulation to force Ms. Gene to change. You cannot get blood out of steel no matter how hard you use a hammer to bang on the steel. This gives both of you more stress. Now on our first day together you are asking me to go with you over to her home. I do not think this is a good idea. I smell trouble."

"Come with me, please. Come on. Let us go now. Ms. Gene is at home. At 2 PM she goes to work."

"When I was born my grandmother became my mother. My birth mother gave me to her mother. This is a long story. Anyway, I called her mama and then Manana, because she was my grandmother and mother. Sometimes I used to not call my birth mother by any name at all or titles. Maybe once in a while I would think mama. I used to also call her mama, even when she was very mean and abusive to me. I was confused as to how to address her. To me she was my birth mother, and I needed to find a way to respect her no matter what she did to me. So, currently most times I called her Ms. Gina. It is interesting that you mother is Gene and my birth mother is Gina. Thanks to the Creator I had a great mother-earth and mother-nature replacement mother. My Manana took the very best care of me to this day. She is an angel. If not my life and myself would have been totally dismembered. (Lily-Butterfly sighed). Okay come I will go with you. Remember compassion when you go there to talk to her."

"I will try. I cannot promise that I am going to be cool, calm, and compassionate. I will try my best. Let us go."

Croco and Lily-Butterfly arrived at Ms. Gene's home. Croco rang the doorbell and he used his key to unlock the door and enter the house.

"Hi Ms. Green-Butterfly how are you," said Ms. Gene.

Immediately Croco said, "her name is not Green-Butterfly. It is Lily-Butterfly."

"Ooops. Sorry," replied Ms. Gene.

Lily-Butterfly stood by the living room door which was close to the front door. The energy inside the house was like a dark cloud, smelled like cigarette smoke, alcohol, and cloudy vibes. Ms. Gene was smoking a cigarette, watching television, and drinking something from a mug.

"I can smell the alcohol, stress, and cigarette. Oh wow," mumbled Lily-Butterfly.

Croco looked through all the mail on the kitchen cupboard.

"Did you pay the mortgage?" asked Croco.

"What mortgage are you talking about?"

"What do you mean? This house mortgage. Do not act like you do not know what I am talking about."

"Oh yeah. This house mortgage? I forgot to pay it. Sorry."

"Where is the money?"

"I spent it."

"What? Forgot? Spend the money? Sorry. I am tired of your absent-minded crap. What are you drinking?"

"Coffee. What do you think?"

"Let me see the mug. Give me the mug."

"No. Why? Do I need a supervisor for what I choose to drink? No. I will not give you the mug."

Croco took the mug from Ms. Gene and smelled what was inside.

"Yep. You are drinking vodka and coffee."

Croco threw the mug across the room. The mug hit a glass mirror and broke it. Ms. Gene walked towards Croco. He avoided her and walked into the dining room. Croco returned with a dining room chair. He used the chair to crash down and break everything breakable in the living room. Everything was broken including the thirty-six inches television, book shelves, cabinets, entertainment center, glass figurines, and center table. When he was finished the chair was broken as well. Croco turned to grab another chair. This was when Lily-Butterfly intervened.

"Oh no. Stop. Stop Croco stop. Pull yourself back from the anger. Come over here to me."

Lily-Butterfly went to the kitchen and got some cool water from the refrigerator and poured some in a glass. Croco had stopped what he was doing and turned toward Lily-Butterfly. Ms. Gene sat on the couch and seemed in a bewildered drunken daze.

"Here Croco drink this. Calm down. You have exploded like dynamite. I do not want to digest any more of this experience and energy. I am going to call the police if you do not stop. Manage your temper. I am going outside to wait on you. Give me the car key."

"Lily-Butterfly, I am leaving with you. Ms. Gene maybe now you can remember things. Take a good look around you. I am taking the mortgage payment booklet. From now on I will pay the mortgage. I am not giving you any more money to pay this bill. Now you can figure out what you are going to do without this money. Whatever you use the money to do, you will not have this money to use any more. Bye."

Croco took the mortgage payment booklet and walked out of the house. He slammed the door shut. Lily-Butterfly was already standing by the car. Croco unlocked the car.

"Wait. No. Do not get into this car with me with all that negative anger vibes and adrenaline. I am allergic to this vibes and fear hormones chemical. Go for a walk down to the end of the street and come back. Please," said Lily-Butterfly.

"You are right. I will go for a walk. Sorry. Her non-sense brings out the worst in me. I will be back."

"Take your time. Give me the car key and mortgage payment booklet. I will wait here for you."

"Here," replied Croco.

Lily-Butterfly took the car key and booklet. She put the booklet in the car and went for a walk in the opposite direction to process her thoughts. She had confirmed all things that she was thinking and speculating about Croco and his mental health. At the first shop she came to she stopped and bought two large bottles of water. One for her and one for Croco. She drank her bottle of water before she returned to the car. When she returned to the car Croco was waiting for her by the car.

"Here drink this water."

Croco took the bottle of water and drank some of it.

"Thank you. I feel better now," said Croco.

"I think you know that what you did just now is wrong and very horrible. This is your mother no matter what she does. Throwing the cup across the room into the mirror was enough in my opinion. After that you crossed the line of no return. Maybe this is how you used to communicating with Ms. Gene. But, I never want to experience this again. I cannot imagine what you would do to me if I did something you perceive wrong. You have an anger management problem plus other mental health issues. Ms. Gene does too. Two wrongs does not make something right. Let us go eat lunch now. It is after 12:00 PM. After lunch take me home. Today I do not want to go back to your house."

"Sorry. I could not help myself. I got so angry."

"This is the point. Getting so angry is not normal. You were beyond anger and into rage mode. At some point I would have experienced this side of you. Violence is never a positive thing."

"Sorry I will try next time to manage my mood. These emotions just come up from within me without notice."

"I have to process today's experience regarding you and your mother. You have a problem. You go from one pole to the next instantly. You need to figure out your mental and emotional issues. You need a mental health specialist to help you. I will let you know right now that I will not live with you. Now I see very clearly why you and your son's mother fight a lot. You both might have the same issues. No human is going to damage me. Know this."

"No one is perfect. I will try to fix my issues."

Croco stopped the car at a restaurant on White Planes Road close to Lily-Butterfly's home. They went inside and have lunch. They kept silent for most of the time. After lunch Croco took Lily-Butterfly home. Before she got out of the car, she talk to Croco some more about her experience.

"Croco no one is perfect. But I have to choose what is right for me. A person with mental health issues that you seem to have, can be unpredictable, unable to manage their mind, emotions, and actions. I understand what is going on with you. But, I cannot and will not choose to be damaged by how you can function. Sorry Mr. Croco. The truth is that you are mentally damaged and also have a lot of unresolved mother, father, parent, and so forth issues. Choose to seek the help and support of a mental health Psychologist and or Psychiatrist."

"I am not going to see a broken mind doctor. I am not crazy."

"Your mother would say the same thing. Figure out your situation. You are currently way beyond just depending on yourself for help to fix these issues. I surely know better than to think I can fix you, and make you improve your mental health. I also do not do co-dependency by pretending that you do not have mental health issue. Know that you will not hold me hostage in an abusive relationship. Bye."

"Okay Lily-Butterfly. Sorry again. I will see you tomorrow morning at 9:00 AM. Are you coming to my house?"

"Yes. Tomorrow is a new day for improvements. Think about seeing a mental health doctor."

"I will think about this suggestion. See you tomorrow. Bye."

Lily-Butterfly got out of Croco's car. Croco drove away. She went inside her home and lit a candle that was on her dining table. Lily-Butterfly wrote everything she felt in her journal and process all the experiences to cleanse her nervous system.

Lily-Butterfly prayed, "Creator today you see what happened with Croco and his mother Ms. Gene. Thank you for giving me the opportunity to see this situation to confirm what I was sensing, speculating, and perceiving. I know that my life's purpose destiny is not about living in a war zone relationship environment with any human. Give me a signal when this Croco karma repayment is complete. I will try to wait on this to be completed. I choose living in peace within myself and in my life. You know everything already. I will wait to hear from you regarding this Croco karma repayment situation. Thank you for everything. Amin."

The praying and processing was finished and Lily-Butterfly laid in her bed and took a nap.

25

Tuesday was a more positive experience for Lily-Butterfly spending time with Croco. They went on errands, to his office at the jewelry store, met his employees, had lunch, walked in the park, and then went back to his office. At 4:10 PM Croco took Lily-Butterfly home.

"Bye. See you tomorrow. We have three more days together and then you are back to being without me," said Lily-Butterfly.

"I love being with you. I feel peaceful and positive. I miss you when you leave. Time will go fast today and after tonight you will be with me again. Bye. See you soon beautiful."

"Bye Croco, Have a positive rest of your day."

Lily-Butterfly gave Croco a hug and left the car. He drove away. Lily-Butterfly went to get Rebornstar from the after school program, made dinner, ate, and continued on with the rest of their day.

Wednesday came. Lily-Butterfly went to Croco's house. The security guard opened the door. The chef was there. Croco was eating his breakfast. The house cleaner was there cleaning and doing the laundry.

"Lily-Butterfly good morning. It is great to see you. Come have breakfast with me. Sit. Today is a great day," said Croco.

"Okay. I had breakfast with Rebornstar already. I will have some tea."

"Okay. We are going to have a lazy day. Chef will make lunch for us today. I will go to my office at the jewelry store when you go home. Today is a great day to relax. Your kind of day."

"Great. Good for you. Relax. How was your sleep?"

"My sleep was good. I dreamt that we were laying on a beach snuggled up together. So, I decided to stay home today and snuggle up with you. We are two hard working people. We deserve a lazy do-nothing day. My nerves need a break. Lily-Butterfly I have been thinking about everything you said yesterday. I am looking for a Psychotherapist. A good one. But, with my travelling and work schedule it will be difficult going consistently. Ha. What do you think? You are quiet and listening to me."

"I am listening to you. Whatever you value and want to work, you will choose to make it work. Your life and yourself is your choice and responsibility to take care of. Your health is your responsibility as well."

"Thank you for showing me and being positive. My negative way of being was so normal to me. I did not realize that some of my normal negative ways, anger, and stress was an issue. Thank you for coming into my life, beautiful."

"You are welcome. Enjoy the beauty of the relationship while it last. Just so you know. My opinion is that living in New York is not my chosen destiny. You love the city. I am not a city person. I love the peace and quiet of the country atmosphere. I am in New York for as long it is meant to be. My destiny and life's purpose is my ultimate long-term destination. When and where this destination will be? I do not know. Do you understand?"

"No, I do not understand everything you say. But I hear you and I am listening. All the things you say sure sounds positive and good. I wish I could be like you, even for one day."

"All you have to do is decide what you want for your health and take action to achieve your intentions."

"Sounds good. Hi chef, I am going back to bed. Call me at 1:00 PM when lunch is ready."

"Okay boss," replied chef.

"Come Lily-Butterfly. Come cuddle and snuggle up with me. Plus, we can......"

"Plus, we can, what?" replied Lily-Butterfly.

"We can see where the cuddling and snuggling goes. Hahaha."

"Okay. Let us go. Passionate and un-managed boy," said Lily-Butterfly.

"Yeah. I will show you more of my passion and untamed self."

Croco picked up Lily-Butterfly and took her to his bed room. Wink-wink. He put her in the bed. At this time some of you readers are feeling irritated by what is currently happening between these two, and maybe not. Unbeknownst to everyone including Croco and Lily-Butterfly this is the most special sacred time they will ever have together. Anyway, keep reading.

"Let us make love-sex-passion come alive through our passionate union and yoking, my beautiful queen."

"I do not belong to you and I am not your queen. You are lucky. Every time I have sex with you, I absorb like a sponge your stress, toxins, and negative energy. When I go home, I have to process and clean these energies out of me by having a salt soak bath, smudge with sacred herbs, and use fire to cleanse as well. Today before I leave let us light a fire in your fire place and cleanse. I will show you how to do this. On your own you can perform the fire cleansing as well."

"All right sounds good," replied Croco.

Croco took off all his clothes and got into the bed naked and hot. He undressed Lily-Butterfly.

"Hey Croco. Where is the condom? Do you think it is time to possess me by getting me pregnant?"

"Why not? You can get pregnant. I do not have a condom today. Something has to tame your wild untamed jungle and independent spirit. If you get pregnant you can move in with me and stop working. You would have no bills to pay and so forth. Be my wife and mother to my children. Surrender and be mine."

"You wish. Listen Croco I cannot be owned by a human. I have been married before. I know that this human marriage creation works for some people. So, far I have not been impressed in a positive way about people's commitment to marriage. I see that people use marriage as a physical possession and to me it is not. I see marriage benefits men the most. Marriage can be like an insane asylum I do not want to be in. Positive health works best for me. It is not in my destiny to be damaged by anyone, including me. No condom, no problem. I have been on birth control pills since before our first date. My menstrual cycle starts again next week. I will have sex with you for the first and last time without the condom. Today is your lucky day. Next time make sure that you have one. Men will be men. You might be having sex with other people. I know that I am not the only beautiful woman on this planet. A man like you traveling around the world is not going to be a saint where sex is concerned? I am humble, peaceful, and country girl vibes. But remember that I am not stupid. I am even more street smart than you. It is called universal intelligence."

"I am laying here and listening to you talk. Beautiful I love to listen to you talk but enough talking. Let us get the love making sex performance activated. Ha. Come over here my beautiful queen. Be a silent lioness."

"Let women be women," replied Lily-Butterfly.

Croco and Lily-Butterfly had sex, made love, yoked, cuddled, and snuggled. Within the cocoon of this vortex they both fell asleep in each other's arms. They were not aware that that a spirit had arrived from the invisible realm of the unknown. A rare opportunity created by Croco's selfish possessive intention. Stay tuned.

At 12:45 PM Chef knocked on the bedroom door to announce that lunch was ready. They got up, took a shower, and got dressed. Chef had made another delicious lunch of barbeque chicken, corn, sweet potato, and spinach. Some cool lemonade refreshed the complete meal. They ate lunch in a cool and mellow mood, contemplating, and inner reflections. When they were finish eating lunch Croco got up and left the dining table. He returned with a jewelry box in his hand.

"Lily-Butterfly I have a surprise for you."

"What? Your beautiful eyes that change color without notice, depending on your mood, is enough surprise for me. I never know what color will show up next. Your eyes are very mysterious, unmanageable, and have an unpredictable mind of its own."

"Silence please."

"Okay. As you request. Silence I will become."

"The last time I went to Africa, I saw this very rare eighteen carat diamond, like my eyes it changes color when it wants to. An unpredictable diamond. I think that you will enjoy it and find it interesting. It was made into a ring. Will you accept this diamond ring as a promise to marry me? Lily-Butterfly will you marry me?"

Lily-Butterfly was silent. Croco took her hand and put the ring on her married finger. It fit. Words could not do justice to describe the diamond stone. The diamond change color from clear to yellow, black, blue, red, and pink. Lily-Butterfly was still silent and seem to be looking at the ring. She saw the physical beauty of the ring, but she was really looking within herself and the crystal ball of her spirit, soul, and consciousness. Croco was silent as well. He waited with his fingers crossed for her response to his marriage proposal. Lily-Butterfly smiled and with mindfulness words disturbed the unstable silence between them. She spoke.

"Dear Croco thank you for giving me the best ring in this whole Universe. It is magnificent. I appreciate your proposal. I will keep your proposal as a treasured request to consider. Do not become disappointed by me not jumping with joy and saying yes. Currently I am committed since I met you, to dating only you. If I decide to end this relationship, I will let you know. Engagement therapy is not going to guarantee that I will stay with you. This engagement intention will not fix your mental health issues and encourage me to stay with you regardless of my experiences with you; and that I am yours. I do not think that you are giving me this ring unconditionally if I choose to end the relationship after accepting this ring and your proposal, I am sure that you will take this magnificent ring back. So, because of this I will not take this ring. I am not sure that I will stay forever with you. Why take a ring that I might end up having to give back? Me, this ring, engagement, marriage, material possessions, and money cannot and will not on its own fix your mental imbalances. Know this. Realistically I cannot wear an eighteen-carat diamond ring on my finger every day; plus, I take public transportation. Someone might cut off my hand trying to steal the ring. It is beautiful beyond words. Thank you. You can keep it in your safe. If the relationship lasts long term, and I decide to marry you, on the wedding day you can put it on my finger with the wedding band. I love you without conditions and also without this magnificent unimaginable diamond ring. Keep it in your safe. Thank you very much for your thoughtfulness. Amin."

After this ring response Lily-Butterfly drank some water.

"I need to pee," said Lily-Butterfly.

Without waiting for a response from Croco she got up and went to the rest room. When Lily-Butterfly was finished using the rest room she returned to sit at the dining table with Croco.

"Wow. Lily-Butterfly you are really direct and unpretentious. I hear everything you have said. I do not agree with your decision. But I will not force you to wear the ring or accept my marriage proposal. When you are ready let me know. I like you and I love you. The beauty I see in you is the beauty I see in this diamond. I will put it in my safe. Ask me for it when you are ready. Okay."

"My opinion is the beauty I see in myself is infinite and cannot be expressed in this diamond. I am me; and the ring is itself. To me there is no comparison. These are two different spectrums of beauty. Wearing and totally accepting such a ring is a big responsibility that I am not sure aligns with me, my life's purpose and destiny, and taking care of my daughter. I keep saying that my spirit and soul cannot be owned and possessed by any human. I have to remain free and unclaimed. I am not sure you totally understand what this means. The infinite Universe, sun, moon, and stars realistically cannot be bought or sold. I do not feel that you have the maturity, unconditional love, and compassion ability to take care of yourself much less me. You cannot give what you do not have. If I took this ring and lost it your response would be worse than what I saw you do at your mother's house the other day. I feel danger revolving around this magnificent diamond ring. I must also tell you that the spirit of this diamond stone cannot be owned. Anyone who wears this ring will lose their spirit and soul to the spirit and soul of this diamond. As you know there is a price for everything. I cannot give my spirit and soul to this diamond, or to you Mr. Croco. Know that I am very impressed by your action of generosity to captivate my spirit, soul, mind, body, and life. But again, I will say, nothing is free and there is a price for everything. I cannot sell my spirit and soul to you or any human. Sorry. I am sorry that I cannot. Please do not ask me again. If I change my mind, I will let you know. This engagement situation got me infinitely deep within my spirit and soul. I am tired. I do not want to say anything more about this ring proposal situation. I would like to go home now."

"I am very surprised and lost for words about your response. How could you refuse this magnificent ring and my proposal? Maybe you are the crazy one to turn down such a magnificent ring and my proposal. I do not understand. I sit and listen. I hear you. I will wait."

"Maybe I am the crazy one like you say. We will see. The proof is in the pudding. Time will tell everything. I choose to be your girlfriend because I do believe that we were brought together for a reason. After this reason is fulfilled and based on my experiences with you, these things will help decide how long this relationship is meant to last. I am allergic to abuse and suffering. I was not created for abuse and suffering. Abuse and suffering might be tools for transformation for me, but I have passed this part of my journey. Time will tell everything Mr. Croco. Give thanks for everything."

"Yes, we will see Lily-Butterfly. I am going to put your ring in my safe as you suggested. I will be back."

"I am going to get ready for you to take me home. I do not want to stay until 5 PM."

"Okay you are the boss of yourself."

By now chef had cleaned up all the dishes and kitchen. He was now cooking food for Croco for the next two days. Croco came back to the dining room. He was dressed to take Lily-Butterfly home.

"Come. I will take you home now as you requested. I am very sad that you did not accept my ring and proposal. I will recover from my sadness. Thank you for coming into my life. Let us go."

"I will come back tomorrow morning and make breakfast for both of us. Is this okay with you?"

"Yes. Sure," replied Croco.

Croco took Lily-Butterfly home. They hugged and she got out of his car. Croco drove off. Lily-Butterfly went into her home and got her journal. She went to the park in her community to write in her journal all the experiences of the day. She wrote, digested, processed everything, and took a two miles walk. Lily-Butterfly left the park and went home to take a nap. When she woke up she went to get Rebornstar from after school program and prepared dinner.

26

Thursday morning when Lily-Butterfly arrived at Croco's house she made breakfast. Chef was not coming back to cook until Saturday. During breakfast the conversation was light. When breakfast was over, they each put their dirty dishes into the dish washer and cleaned up the kitchen. Croco disconnected the smoke detectors and made a fire in the fire place. As the fire flames dance and expressed itself they talked. As they sat by the fire the heat percolated in and around them, creating a purifying effect. Lily-Butterfly showed Croco how to use his hands to take the flames and cleanse his body. When the flames died down and finally dissipated Lily-Butterfly added some sacred purifying herbs of sage, frankincense, myrrh, juniper berries, dried lavender, and sweet grass. The smoke from the herbs further cleansed them and the home. Lily-Butterfly opened the windows to let the smoke outside.

Croco and Lily-Butterfly sat by the fireplace on the floor enjoying the warmth of the fire.

"I am thinking about buying an eight-floor apartment building. What do you think about this?" said Croco.

"I am the last person you want to ask about this idea," replied Lily-Butterfly.

"Why?"

"I have no interest in owning buildings, home, property, and anything like this. So, I have no idea what to tell you. I do not want to say something just to talk. The words I speak has to have purpose and meaning. Buying property is a serious and big decision. You know more than I do, because you own several properties already. My ancestors and I believe that humans are stewards of the earth, planet, and that too much ownership of anything ends up owning us. Old time sayings and beliefs might sound stupid and crazy to modern materialistic people. But in the end if you think about what is said it makes sense. Maybe we would own the property we live on, but that would be it. We do not think of it as possession. You have five properties already. Why do you need more? Too much of anything is good for nothing. You can do whatever you like. What I say is my own opinion and thinking."

"Lily-Butterfly with this thinking you will never be rich."

"You are right. People material wealth is physical. Being rich in spirit and soul is my life's purpose and what I love and like. This is the only thing I can take with me when I die. Everything else is temporary value and resource. You never know, maybe when it is time, I will buy a house if it is meant to be. Until them here I am with my stupid, crazy, and no rich views. You own five properties, a jewelry store filled with jewelry, many luxury motor vehicles, lots of cash, and money in the bank and you are still not satisfied, plus you are so stressed out and mentally unbalanced. I am the opposite of you. I have education and credentials, very creative, talented, I take care of myself and my daughter, and have a little savings for emergency. But I feel great, peaceful, healthy, content, balanced, and best of all my spirit and soul is fantastic. Please remember that I am not for sale, rent, or to be your personal possession. Ha. Do whatever you like, because you will."

"I hear you. You are right. We have opposite views on material and physical wealth. Plus, I am surface, egotistic, and materialistic. You are deep, spiritual, and independent. These qualities will not get you far in the normal people realm. Really, believe me. Choose to change if you ever want to marry again and be a wealthy successful person. Men feel useless with independent thinking woman."

"I do not agree with what you said about woman and so forth. Not every man is like you say. I do believe that there are confident and spiritual men who are comfortable being with confident and spiritual women. Croco my chosen destiny in this life and living is not a normal one. I think and feel I am learning more and more every day about you, people, the modern people created physical realm, and the spiritual realm. The spiritual realm is more my natural place to be. I am not going to become a lost spirit and soul. Do what you like. How come you did not say to me that you found professional help to improve your mental and emotional health? Do you think buying an eight-floor apartment building as a rental investment is going to be mental health therapy and an upgraded self-worth investment? Ha."

"Yes. To fix my mental health will cost me lots of money. To buy the building will give me money."

"Plus make you more stressed out. I have a feeling that you should not buy this building. In some way I think buying this building will minus some vitality from your health, well-being, and life. Take my words into consideration. I am not being just a big mouth, talking a lot of crap. Wise words to wise people is sufficient. Anyway, I have said enough. What are we going to do for the rest of the day?"

"Come with me to look at the apartment building that I am talking about."

"I cannot believe after saying all that I have told you, that you would say this. I have no more opinion on this apartment buying situation. If I come with you, I will wait in the car. This apartment building is cursed. Do not buy it."

"Okay come with me and wait in the car."

"You are so interesting. Okay," replied Lily-Butterfly.

Croco drove to the eight-story apartment building with Lily-Butterfly in the car. When he arrived at the building, he stopped the car and got out."

"Are you coming to look at the apartment with me?"

"No. I told you no before. I will wait in the car for you."

"What? Come in with me."

"No. I can see everything from outside."

"What do you see?"

"For whatever reason this building has a negative curse. There is a lot of dark energies internally as well as surrounding this building. Buying this building will increase and amplify all your negative health issues. The tenants do not pay their rent. Buying this building will be a liability and not an asset for profit and success. This building will drain away all your money with maintenance and repairs. This building will be a money and health sucker and not a money maker. Once you connect your name to this property you will be dizzy from the stress it is going to give you. Most people usually do not value and respect free advice and recommendation. You might even be thinking that I am saying these words, because I do not want you to buy the building. Please realize that I am giving you a spiritual reading about this situation. Try to respect what I am saying. This apartment will cost you big time. Listen and hear me."

"Okay. Hahaha. You are talking crazy. I am going inside to look at the building. I will be back in about twenty minutes."

Croco left and went inside the apartment building. Lily-Butterfly sat in the car with the windows open. She pondered about the situation, Croco's attitude and personality, and his views about life. Lily-Butterfly also thought about, her life and herself. She was getting to know Croco and herself more and more. Twenty-five minutes went by and Croco returned to the car.

"I am going to think about the apartment building and what I saw for two more days. After two days if I choose to proceed with the purchase, I will submit an offer. We will see what happens," said Croco.

"There is no we with the purchase of this building and anything to do with you and your life. So, use the word I when you talk about this situation and everything else. Do not use identifying with me in your choices and everything to do with you and your life. Thank you very much. I do not like the vibes around you today. I would like to go home."

"Stop taking life so serious. No lunch today. You want to go home already. Let us go to lunch and then the park for a walk. At 3:00 PM I will take you home. I like spending time with you. When I am with you, I feel energized and peaceful."

"You mean taking my energy. After I leave you, I feel drained and tired. I have to spend time in nature and take a nap to recover. I do not think that this relationship is going to last much longer. We are opposites and as much as we like and enjoy some things, we are very opposite. I am spiritual and you are not. You love and like material possessions, and I do not. I see the material and physical things as resources. These great differences for both of us will create daily irritation, friction, and conflicts for both of us. I will not live in a conflict, suffering, and war zone with you. We both need to find someone that naturally loves and likes what is important for each of us. Seriously. The more time I spend with you the more I can see the reality of our relationship situation. I do not do things for convenience sake and lie to myself. I will come with you for lunch. At 3:00 PM take me home. It is not good for you to want a girlfriend and wife that do not want what you want, and you do not want what she wants."

"Oh, so you want me to become a monk, priest, and spiritual. We will learn how to work together and compromise to make the relationship work. This is what we will do. Do you understand? Plus, you are the woman which means, wife, mother; and care taker of me, my children, and our life. Practice this now. A woman with too much independent attitude is a trouble maker in a man's life."

"I am feeling irritated processing your energy and your words. My focus is not laboring on you, this relationship, and to improve you and your life. I am not going to work on changing you or improving you. You and your health and well-being is your responsibility. I will not make apologies about being who and what I am; and you the same. I have to accept you as you are, or not; and you the same. Currently I do not want to marry you."

"You know that you love and like me. We are going to lunch. I hear everything you have said. Your words are woman talk. You will come around to see things my way. Until them, enjoy everything I share with you. This is supposed to be a courting period, and not a lecturing women views and non-sense talking. Let us go into this restaurant. Tomorrow, Friday is our last day of this week to be together. We will go to together to my office at the jewelry store, lunch, and the museum. Everything will be okay in the end."

"We will both see what happens in the end of this journey together. I know what is really going to happen. You can tell yourself whatever you like. When is your next business trip?"

"I am going away the second Monday in November. I am going to Australia for seven days. Why?"

"Nothing. I was just wondering."

Croco and Lily-Butterfly had lunch. She made herself calm down and did not speak too much. After lunch they went to the park close to Lily-Butterfly's apartment. At 3:20 PM Croco took Lily-Butterfly home. She took her journal and walked back to the park to write and process her emotions. At 4:30 PM Lily-Butterfly went home to take a nap before she got Rebornstar from after school program. Over the weekend Lily-Butterfly chose not to spend time with Croco. She and Rebornstar spent time doing chores, going to places, and preparing for the following week of work and school.

Monday morning came, Lily-Butterfly and Rebornstar went back to their regular schedule of home life, school, and work. Croco and Lily-Butterfly spoke on the phone at night before her bed time. As usual Lily-Butterfly never forget to write in her journal and pray at the end of every day.

Wednesday of this new week came and Lily-Butterfly became more concerned that her menstrual cycle did not start for the month. Before she worried in silence not even her journal was aware of this situation. She waited and prayed. Only the Creator knew of this perceived perilous situation. Her menstrual cycles was supposed to start on Monday. Now it was Wednesday, she was hoping and praying that it would arrive. On her way to work she stopped at the pharmacy to buy a pregnancy test. Thursday morning Lily-Butterfly got up and did the pregnancy test using the first urine of the day. The test result said loud and clear, 'PREGNANT!' Lily-Butterfly had bought two tests. She did the test again. The result was the same.

"Oh sxxt. Oh no. This is not good. Creator is this a joke. Hello. I do not know what else to say. Really. Ha. Hu. Mmm. Maybe the test is not working right. I will buy another test today. Tomorrow morning, I will do the test again. Now I must get prepared for work, have breakfast, and take Rebornstar to school."

On the way to work Lily-Butterfly bought another pregnancy test. Friday morning, she did another pregnancy test. The result came out the same; pregnant. Naturally her heart sank with sadness. She decided to talk to the Creator in prayer.

"Dear Creator you know everything already. What now? I am pregnant. I get pregnant even with birth control. Maybe I was born to never have sex. What should I do now? I never wanted to have another baby after my experiences with having Rebornstar. I am taking this pregnancy situation very personal, because it is. These seeds that are fertilized within my reproductive system and womb is only one week old. What do I do? Should I terminate and abort these seed plantation, or not? You always tell me that I have the free will to do things, although there are karma consequences to my actions. I have to decide on a termination of the pregnancy before the seeds take root within me. I never thought I would ever say no to a spirit and soul who chose to be planted within my womb as a baby. Oh, Creator guide me and my bewildering thoughts and feelings. How can I be pregnant and having to take two trains to get to work, work in the city, and stay a single parent with two children. I guess the same way other women do this, is how I will do. I will not marry Croco. Is this situation a trick and test of my faith? I know that marrying Croco is not my final destination on this journey of manifesting my chosen destiny life's purpose. I will keep my perception as clear and optimistic as possible. Deep down I feel this is another difficult test of everything about me. Thank you for listening. I know that you do not give me more than I can handle. So, therefore deep within me I have to awaken the tools and talents that I need to handle this situation. First, I have to accept and surrender to this situation. Last but not least, make a decision to stay pregnant or terminate the pregnancy. Oh, Creator sometimes this human life can be beyond my imagination. Thank you for everything. Amin."

Lily-Butterfly did her morning activities and took Rebornstar to school. On the train to work, talking to herself started again. In perceived difficult and negative situations, Lily-Butterfly naturally goes into a processing of her emotion's mode. She feels that is it helpful to talk to herself and process her perceived negative emotions about her experiences. She really takes advantage of the old fashion saying that 'talking to one-self is good for the spirit and soul.' So here she goes during this pregnancy dilemma talking to herself again and again.

"Another spirit and soul have arrived inside my womb and oven of creation. Hello spirit and soul within me. Why are you here? I am no longer alone as I personally perform my daily tasks. Oh my. Oh, what a situation. Now I sound crazy. Maybe I am crazy. A crazy person does not know that they are crazy. Oh Lily-Butterfly, stop the thinking. Okay, let me meditate. I am great at meditating. Maybe this will calm my over active thoughts and imagination," whispered Lily-Butterfly.

Lily-Butterfly got off the train at her stop. She walked the fifteen minutes in the crowded pedestrians and traffic all around her. At the end of the day Lily-Butterfly arrived back home to her personal life and daily routine. At the end of her day before she went to sleep, she telephoned Croco. Croco answered the telephone. Without hesitation she told Croco her pregnancy situation.

"Croco I am pregnant," announced Lily-Butterfly.

"What? Pregnant? Good. Now you will marry me. Your independence goose is cooked. Let me see what you will do now Miss. Independence. This is great news."

"We will see Mr. Crocodile. Maybe this pregnancy will help us see ourselves and each other more clearly. Just so you know, I am thinking of terminating the pregnancy. So, if you think that I am going to marry you out of convenience, you are wrong. I will keep this pregnancy if it really meant to be, and it is proven to be so."

"What do you mean? What do you mean by termination?"

"Hello have an abortion, this is the term you are familiar with. I will not marry you because I am pregnant or what people will say. I will only marry you if it is for the greater good of both of us. In this case I do not think so."

"I do not think that you should have an abortion. Marry me, this is the solution to all your problems."

"See. You call me being pregnant a problem and marriage the solution. Currently I see being pregnant a problem. If I decide to not terminate the pregnancy, I would have accepted the situation, and stop seeing it as a problem. I do not think that marriage is the only solution to this pregnancy. I can have my baby and still remain single. I will let you know if I decide to have this baby, or not. This is my body, and my choice."

"I do not agree with an abortion. But like you say, it is your body. If we were married, I would legally have a choice in this pregnancy situation. Let me know your decision."

"Okay. I have a very difficult decision to make that I never thought I would ever have. I will make a decision from a place of conscious mindfulness, taking into consideration the spirit and soul inside me, and how I am being guided. The Creator has the last work. I will let you know my decision. I am going to sleep. Good night. Bye."

"Good night beautiful. Sorry to end your independence. Sweet dreams. Bye."

"End of my independence. Ha really. You do not have the power to end my independence Mr. Croco. One day you will end your own independence with your greed for materialistic things."

"Lily-Butterfly, whatever. We will see. Time will tell mama times two."

"You are trying to make me upset. Time will tell. Know that hard is easy and easy is easy for me. This baby might be here for me to even improve who and what I am. I am sure that whatever my decision is, things will eventually work out for the greater good. I am a spirit and soul survivor. I can choose this pregnancy situation as another opportunity to learn and grow. I will not give fear permission to take up residence within me, and permanently control me and my life. Bye. Good night."

"Wait remember I will be in Australia next Monday for seven days. I will call you every night. Bye my beautiful wife."

"Good night Croco."

They both hung up the telephones. Lily-Butterfly fell asleep that night. The concerns about her pregnancy weighed heavy on her brain and heart. That night as she drifted further and further into sleep, she sunk down beyond dream land, like an anchor under a ship in a harbor at sea. For the first time when Lily-Butterfly woke up the next morning with no recollection of her dreams.

27

Up to five weeks of pregnancy Lily-Butterfly was still undecided about her pregnancy situation. She gradually distanced herself a little from Croco. She had grown more irritated by his actions and what he said. With Lily-Butterfly's direct style of communication, she was having to energetically tape her mouth a lot, by ignoring most of what Croco said and did. Lily-Butterfly thought of many things for example, was she being like Ms. Gina. Could she have the nerves to have the child and give it away for adoption? Could she have the child and manage taking care of two children as a single parent. Marrying Croco she did not give herself this option. Every time she tried to visualize herself as Croco's wife she felt stuck and stressed. What if Croco's karma repayment was offering her the eighteen-carat diamond ring? This would mean Croco's karma repayment was complete, even if she refused the proposal and ring. Daily Lily-Butterfly was in a bewildered mood. At work she would set aside her thoughts until work was over. So far, the option that felt most positive within Lily-Butterfly was, having the baby, and taking action to work on each situation as they arise. But her second option to terminate the pregnancy hung like a carrot in front of her face.

At the end of the fifth week Lily-Butterfly telephoned Croco before she went to sleep.

"Hi Croco currently I feel like I am going to decide to have the baby. But maybe I will change my mind."

"Marry me. Move into my house at the end of December or January, quit your job, and your problems are solved. Why be a single mother with two children? Do not let your independence, strength, stubbornness, spiritual righteousness, and so forth make you choose the path of difficulties. Really. Beautiful, listen and hear me. Ha."

"Croco I will only marry you if the Creator wills it, and I feel that this will be positive for my health, life, my children, and well-being. I will not marry you for financial and material purposes. I love you without conditions just like I love everything else. I cannot choose a life of danger for my children and myself."

"Whatever. I cannot make you marry me. You are being ridiculous and making a big mistake. With time you will see that I am right.

Anyway, I want to change the subject. I bought the eight- floor apartment building. If you marry me, what is mine will become yours. No worries and no problems."

"I am not interested in the things you own. What good is physical material wealth when you do not have positive health and unconditional love for yourself? Buying yourself things is not love."

"Lily-Butterfly what is done is done. You will wake up to realize that the things that matters most is money. Money talks and is the real power. Until then I will leave you with your unrealistic views. Keep doing what you do best; talk and more talk. Talking cannot buy anything. In this modern world money is king, and some people see money as their God. Okay beautiful. What do you want for your Christmas and birthday?"

"Nothing. I have everything I want and need. I do not want to go to your mother's home for holiday celebration. You can go by yourself. I am going to sleep. Good night. Bye."

"Good night beautiful. From the first day I saw you I knew that you were going to be mine. All you have to do is surrender to this reality. I will talk to you tomorrow. Have a good night sleep. Bye."

Lily-Butterfly hung up the telephone without saying one more word.

At work on the third week before Christmas day The hotel General Manager Betty Butler sent out a memo to all the managerial staff telling them that she would be retiring February 27, 1989. Lily-Butterfly was very sad about Mrs. Butler's retirement, because she would miss her. The new General Manager was being promoted and transferred from the State of Washington, D.C. The new General Manager worked for the same company for many years. In November 1988 Lily-Butterfly was promoted to Hotel Manager and no longer a trainee. She was still working with Mrs. Butler and had the work schedule that supported her well-being and life. Lily-Butterfly was concerned that when the new General Manager came her schedule would change. If she chose to have the baby, she would be obviously pregnant in March when the new General Manager comes. After processing all her thoughts and concerns, Lily-Butterfly decided to accept Mrs. Butler's resignation, and all the changes that would come with the new General Manager.

With a baby in Lily-Butterfly's belly, she took each day, one day at a time. The thought of terminating the pregnancy still lingered in the back of her mind especially when Croco got into one of his mental health imbalances about one thing or the other. Croco now felt comfortable showing his true colors, many faces, and masks. Christmas day 1988 Croco had a dinner party at his house. Chef and one of his assistants did all the cooking and preparations for the dinner. Lily-Butterfly and Rebornstar were invited. When Lily-Butterfly arrived at the dinner, Croco told her that his mother Ms. Gene would be attending the dinner party. Croco's brother, his wife, his son, and some friends would be at the party as well. When Lily-Butterfly was told at the party that Ms. Gene was attending she was upset.

"Croco, you should have told me that your mother would be here today when you invited me."

"If I did, you would not have come."

"You are surely right. I am not in the mood for her non-sense."

After saying this Ms. Gene walked into the house. She had brought Croco's son with her. Croco's brother and his wife came into the house as well. Ms. Gene looked at Lily-Butterfly and laughed. Croco said hi to everyone and excused himself to take a shower.

"Lily-Butterfly I can see that you have a bun in your oven," said Ms. Gene.

Lily-Butterfly ignored her.

"Hello Lily-Butterfly I am talking to you. Are you pregnant to seal the captivation of my son?"

Lily-Butterfly walked away to the living room. Ms. Gene followed her.

"Hi Lily-Butterfly I am talking to you. Is your mouth glued shut? Listen and hear me miss whatever your name is. You are last in line and will forever be last in line where my son is concerned. After Croco there is me, his son, and his two brothers. You and the child in your belly, if it lives, will come last in Croco's life. Mark my words as true. Make sure that you do not marry him to skip the line to become number one. I know you, innocent snake in the grass type. If you marry my son, I will be a constant knife in your side. Remember this. This conversation is a warning between you and I. If you tell Croco what I say, you will be sorry."

Lily-Butterfly was silent. She thought, if I have nothing good to say to someone it is best that I remain silent. I think that she is drunk.

Ms. Gene looked around the house for Croco.

"Hello my son. Where are you? The queen, your mother is here. Hello dear son," said Ms. Gene.

Croco was in the bathroom taking a shower. Lily-Butterfly went to sit outside where Rebornstar and the other children were playing in the backyard. When the food was ready Croco came outside to get Lily-Butterfly and Rebornstar.

"Come inside my beautiful. Dinner is ready. Try not to let my crazy mother irritate your peace and stability. Come inside. Ms. Gene is just jealous."

"Jealousy is a dangerous negative energy mixed in with instability. After dinner take me home. You can come back and enjoy your family and friends. I need peace, positive energy, and not being drained by negativity."

"Okay I will take you home after dinner. Or, I could take my mother home, so that she does not cause problems. Come inside."

Lily-Butterfly sat beside Croco with Ms. Gene on her other side. Croco sat with his son on his other side. Croco got up and decided to make a surprise announcement.

"Hi everyone may I have your attention. My queen Lily-Butterfly is pregnant and I might be getting married soon. Let us give a toast to new life, renewed life, both of us, marriage, and my continued success. Also, I just bought another property, an eight-floor tenant apartment building. Life is great."

Everyone gave the usual symbolic cheers clanking glasses together. Lily-Butterfly was not impressed. She knew that she was not going to marry Croco, and she was still not one hundred percent feeling comfortable about having the baby. She took deep breaths and sighed.

"I will cheer to the new property. That is, it. Baby and marriage is a lost cause. You know that once you live with a woman your demons start to show their faces. We will see Mr. Son. We will see. Ha," said Ms. Gene.

"Mother be quiet or I am taking you home right now. Stop. Shut up. Now," replied Croco.

Everyone sitting at the table became quiet.

"Croco I feel like I want to throw up. Please take me home. I would like to leave now. Have chef pack some food for Rebornstar and I. We will eat at my home. If I stay, I might vomit on the table having to hear your mother talk; or you might have to be mean to your mother to defend me. No one should have to digest this crap at a holiday dinner. You might lose your mind, get angry, and crash down the dinner table and food. I am volunteering to leave. I will be outside waiting with Rebornstar. Bring the food to me outside and take us home. Please."

"Okay. I will see you by the car."

Croco took Lily-Butterfly and Rebornstar home. They hugged and said good bye to each other. Lily-Butterfly had a peaceful dinner with Rebornstar. Lily-Butterfly explained to Rebornstar her perception of what Ms. Gene was saying and doing. For the complete holiday season Lily-Butterfly was in a melancholy mood. She lifted up her spirit and mood by praying and having positive conversations with herself. Lily-Butterfly decided to distance herself some more from Croco. She told him that at this time she could only talk to him on the telephone. Rebornstar and Lily-Butterfly celebrated their birthdays as usual by themselves. Lily-Butterfly became thirty-one and Rebornstar ten years old. New Year's eve and day Lily-Butterfly also choose to stay home with Rebornstar. Part of the distancing reason for the decision was that every time after the Christmas day dinner, she saw Croco and remembered his mother, she felt like vomiting, and a fainting sinking feeling in her whole body.

In January of 1989 at Lily-Butterfly's third Gynecologist checkup she asked the Doctor to recommend a Doctor to terminate the pregnancy. She was three months pregnant. As strong as Lily-Butterfly was, sadness had captured her spirit, soul, mind, emotions, and body. She felt like she was caught between three main portals. Choosing what was right for her, what was right for the baby, and choosing what was morally, spiritually, creationally the right thing to do. The three main portal urges were stronger than listening to how she was being guided by her usual instincts, her morality, and what the Creator was saying.

The Doctor responded to Lily-Butterfly's request for a referral Doctor to terminate the pregnancy.

"You are three months pregnant. It is too late to do a regular abortion. You would have to go to a surgical center. Try to get over how you feel. The feelings will pass. This is just a rough spot. In your fourth month you might feel better. I know that you do not really want to terminate this pregnancy. Stay away from stressful situations. Okay."

"Do you do pregnancy terminations?"

"Yes, in the early stages maximum six weeks. Not at this late stage. At three months you need a surgical procedure. At this stage there is an alive baby inside you. You are at the end of the first trimester. Take some time to rethink your decision," replied the Doctor.

"No. Even the strongest thing has a weak point. I would like you to give me the contact information and address of a Doctor you can recommend for this pregnancy termination, abortion, surgery, or whatever it is called. Please."

"Okay I will give you the information of a Doctor I know. If you are going to do this do not wait any longer than next week Saturday. Here. Doing this will not make you feel better. You will actually feel worse. All the best with everything. My next patient is waiting. Bye."

"Thank you very much Doctor. Have a nice day. Bye."

Lily-Butterfly left the Doctor's office. She went home and called the Doctor to terminate the pregnancy. She made an appointment for next week Saturday. After Lily-Butterfly made the appointment she telephoned Croco.

"I have decided to terminate the pregnancy at a surgical center. The appointment is for next week Saturday. I choose to go by myself. I will leave Rebornstar at Mrs. Beech."

"I do not want you to have an abortion. It is your body and it is our baby. I know that you will say it is your choice. You are choosing to kill a baby. Killing a baby is between you and God. You have me and my mother as support system. I will talk to my mother to stop her mean crap. You do not have to do this."

"You do not understand. I know that this choice is ultimately between the Creator and I. At this time for many reasons I do not feel like I can have this baby. Maybe at the last minute the Creator, my spirit guides, and guardian angels might intervene, and prevent my decision. My bottom line is, I will leave this decision of mine to faith, destiny, and the Creator's will. Maybe a miracle will happen and wake me up from my bewildered decisions and action. I will be at the Doctor on Saturday into the hands of the sacred I place myself. Bye."

Lily-Butterfly did not wait for Croco to say something; she hung up the telephone.

After Lily-Butterfly got off the telephone she prayed.

"Divine Creator of all things known and unknown. You know everything already. You know all my spirit, soul, and life's experiences. If this situation I am in is a test of my faith, honesty, and strength you need to intervene. If I am not supposed to terminate this pregnancy and kill this baby, please do something to stop me. I am taking this leap of my own decision and honoring how I feel. My spirit and soul is very low and sad. Please help me. I do not want to commit this sin of not giving a spirit and soul a chance to live. Look how hard I worked to save the life of Rebornstar and myself when I was giving birth to her. Currently I feel this overwhelming negative emotion. I am very stuck in my perception of all the reasons to not have this baby. I am being honest. I am on the cliff' edge of being trapped and stuck in fear for the first time in this human life. Maybe I have digested too much of Croco's negative energies and fears. This intrusive energy of fear is trying to completely capture me. Help. The complete picture and reality of Croco, his mother, having another child, my past experiences giving birth to Rebornstar, and everything else in my past life's experiences are activated in my memory. Help me. Stop me if I am not meant to go through with committing this sin of killing this baby growing inside me. I am being honest. Maybe this situation is testing my honesty. Give me a sign. Create an intervention. Creator you already know that I trust you the most. Please forgive me and do not abandon me if I go through with this decision. Do something to help this situation if my destiny is to have this baby. Help me, please. Currently I feel stuck. Creator let your will be done. You always say that honesty is the best decision. Here I am on my knees being really, really, honest with you and myself. Show me the way out of where I am currently stuck. Into your sacred hands I deliver myself, this baby as a spirit and soul, and my decisions. Being human is not an easy process. Your faithful servant Lily-Butterfly. Amin."

Rebornstar was at Mrs. Beech the childcare provider. Lily-Butterfly had left her there to go to the Doctor. After the prayer Lily-Butterfly's face was covered in a river of tears. She climbed into her bed and pulled the cover up over her head. She cried herself into a very much needed sleep. When she woke up it was 4:30 PM. Lily-Butterfly took another shower and got dressed. She went grocery shopping. On her way home from the supermarket she stopped at Mrs. Beech's home to get Rebornstar. They went home put the groceries away and made dinner together. At the end of this day was another interesting day in the life of Lily-Butterfly. Before she went to sleep that night, she wrote everything about her day in her journal.

The following week Lily-Butterfly remained in the same tormented stuck dark cloud cocoon vortex. Saturday came Lily-Butterfly got dress and gave Rebornstar breakfast. For the surgery she could not eat anything after mid night Friday night. Lily-Butterfly took Rebornstar to Mrs. Beech's home. At 9:45 AM she arrived at the Doctor's office. Her appointment at the Doctor was for 10:00 AM. Lily-Butterfly signed in and talked to the Receptionist. The Receptionist told Lily-Butterfly to have a seat. She would let her know when it was her turn. Lily-Butterfly felt frozen. She sat and prayed. At 11:00 AM Lily-Butterfly was still sitting. Other patients that came after her went in and they were attended to and left. At 12:00 PM the Receptionist did not call Lily-Butterfly for her 10:00 AM appointment. Lily-Butterfly got up and ask the Receptionist the reason she was still waiting. The Receptionist told her to wait until she called her. Lily-Butterfly sat down again. She did some reflections and contemplated on her prayer to the Creator for help about her situation. She left the Doctor's office and walked down the block. Lily-Butterfly returned to the Doctor's office. She sat down. She saw patients come and go. At 1:00 PM the Receptionist still did not call Lily-Butterfly. Lily-Butterfly decided to pray again.

"Creator is this your way of showing me not to do the pregnancy termination surgery? If the Receptionist does not call me to go in next, I will cross my name off the list and leave. I will have this baby and trust that as usual things will work out. After the walk down the block my dark cloud emotions seems lighter. This life of human is not easy, to me sometimes it can be like a puzzle, circus, revolving door, leap of faith, and so forth. Anyway, Creator the Receptionist called another woman to go inside. It is now 1:35 PM. I am hungry and tired. My last meal was dinner on Friday. The baby must be hungry as well. I am crossing out my name. I am leaving quietly. Thank you for everything. I have received your guidance. Amin."

Lily-Butterfly crossed her name off the sign in sheet and walked out of the Doctor's office. She walked to Mrs. Beech to get Rebornstar.

"Oh wow. I feel the baby kick and move for the first time. Interesting. The baby has spoken. Thanks be to the Creator. Amin. It is my destiny to have this baby for whatever reason. I must work through my negative emotions and surrender completely to having this baby. My priorities are taking care of myself, this baby inside me, and Rebornstar. Let the negative vibes of Croco and his mother go. If being around them is stressful and toxic I should choose not to be around his mother and limit my contact with Croco for my greater good, health, and well-being. I guess I will always be in training to keep me sharp," whispered Lily-Butterfly.

Lily-Butterfly got Rebornstar and went home. She took a nap while Rebornstar watched a program on the television.

28

Saturday night at 8:00 PM Lily-Butterfly telephoned Croco. He answered the telephone.

"Hi Croco."

"Hello Lily-Butterfly. How was your Doctor's visit?"

"You mean my pregnancy termination appointment? Well. I have firmly decided not to do it. I am now convinced without a doubt that I should not do it. I arrived at the Doctor 9:45 AM. The appointment was for 10:00 AM. At 1:35 the Receptionist did not call me inside to do the procedure. All the other patients came after me went in and left. I prayed to the Creator for a sign if it was not destined for me to terminate the pregnancy. I think that the sign was not being called in to do the procedure. After I left the Doctor while walking home, I felt the baby kicked and moved for the first time. So, here we are."

"Great news. Good for you that you choose to leave. Accept the engagement ring. Marry me. Move into my house. This is what this means."

"I will not live with or move into a man's house unless I choose to accept a marriage proposal with the commitment to marry him. So far from getting to know and experience you and your mother, I have decided to not accept your proposal and marry you. Even when my decisions seem wrong, I choose to respect, accept, and honor them. Why? In the future my decisions turn out in some way to be right. Unless the Creator shows me otherwise, I am sticking to my decision about marrying you. I am going to follow my instinct, how I feel, and how I am being guided. I know that we met for a reason. I do not think marrying you is the reason. Until the real reason shows I will wait for it. Pregnancy termination, abortions, marriage, politics, and religion are personal choice and personal decisions. Do you understand Croco?"

"I do not understand all your opinions. I do not agree with all your decisions. You are the one that has to live with them. You are not a monk, nun, and priest. Your decisions, choices, and outlook about life does not have to be so spiritual. Anyway, I have to go. Thank you for your call. I will call you tomorrow."

"I can understand why you are upset. Sorry, you seem so out of control not having the ability to control me. You are so used to getting and buying what you want; not this time. I have to be true to myself and my positive and negative feelings. If my instincts say no it is for a positive reason. This is how I learn to trust me, know the energy vibration of trust and safety, respect myself, and give the same to other people. When I can trust me, then I can trust other people. Bye."

Lily-Butterfly hung up the telephone. Ten minutes later Croco telephone Lily-Butterfly.

"Hi beautiful. It is me again. Would you like to come over to my house and sleep over here tonight?"

"No thank you. I am tired and I am already in my bed. Plus, Rebornstar is asleep. I do not want to absorb your stress vibes. I am still digesting my own emotional stress about today's experiences. I feel sleepy, tired, and my own bed is the best medicine for me at this time. Okay."

"I think that for whatever reason you are distancing yourself from me and taking me for granted. But, anyway bye. I will telephone you tomorrow. Sweet dreams. Bye."

"Good night. Bye."

Lily-Butterfly hung up the telephone. She said a very short prayer, laid down, and covered herself. Immediately she sunk into a deep sleep and dream land.

At 2:30 AM Lily-Butterfly had a dream. There was a distinct voice. The voice was not connected to a physical presence.

The voice in dream said, "follow, hear, and listen to my words. Today you have entered another new phase of your life's journey, chosen destiny, and life's purpose. This new phase will be a cycle of seven years. Stay grounded and cautious. Keep following your instincts and how you are being guided. Good that today you passed the test of choosing the right action. Follow me."

After the voice told Lily-Butterfly to 'follow me.' The voice was silent. In the dream Lily-Butterfly followed the voice down a grassy path to a field of large holly trees. All the holly trees were in full bloom with very red berries. The very bright green leaves mixed in with the very red berries made the field of holly trees look magical, majestic, and un-real. Lily-Butterfly looked at the holly trees in full bloom. She thought, oh wow. What now? Holly trees are similar to rose bushes and roses. Rose bushes have thorns and beautiful flowers, like holly trees have prickly thorns on each leaf and beautiful red berries. Another bitter-sweet rite of passage. Lily-Butterfly was alerted back to the distinct voice by the distinct voice's request.

"Hello Lily-Butterfly hear and listen to me."

"Sorry dream voice. I was admiring these holly trees and berries, and processing my thoughts. I am hearing and listening," replied Lily-Butterfly.

"Oh. Okay. Have a deep look at these trees."

"Yes, I see them. This is what I was doing before."

"Hear and listen to me. Do not say one word until I am finished telling you the story of these holly tree. You and the baby within your cradle of life is going to receive the holly tree transmission and rite of passage. Do you understand?"

"Yes. I understand dream weaver. I am ready."

"These holy trees are a symbol of the next maximum seven years of your life. Good that you listened to the guidance presentation at the Doctor's office and chose not to terminate the life of the child within you. Good performance in honoring your feelings and at the same time following your intuition and perception. The answers to the journey's quest is always within the steps. The message again at this level is to honor thy self. Honor and respect thy self, so that you can honor and respect others. You cannot give what you do not have. The holly tree's message and symbology is to continue to cultivate integrity, honesty, and truth. Truth is the focused tool of creation. Other symbology of the holly tree's message are, cultivate deeper unconditional love, death, rebirth, reincarnation, renewal, unselfishness, love peace, good fortune, and continue to transform and heal all your toxic experiences, as you journey. The red berries is a symbology to remember your essential self, staying grounded in your spirit's blood and roots. Your blood is the elixir of your body. Ground the roots of your spirit and soul like these holly trees. It is time to receive more ingredients to grow, awaken your talents, and spread the branches, leaves, and blossoms of yourself. The prickly thorns of the holly tree leaves will remind you of protection, safety, balance, that things are not like they seem, unseen surprises can appear, show your true colors, difficulties, and to remain in positive harmony and balance through sweet or sour times, and no matter what happens. Last but most important. Hear and listen. The child in your womb will be a girl. Her name is Holly. When she is born and both of you grow and awaken, you will see the reasons you were brought together. Fear not. You are never alone and are always being watched, and is protected beyond the veil. Do you understand everything that I have told you? You may speak."

"Yes, I understand. Is the Croco karma repayment complete?

My human life is like an infinite roller coaster, fairies' wheel, and revolving door, with no beginning or end. I surrender to welcoming Holly into my life."

"When this child is born, after seeing her, you will see very clearly if the Croco karma has been paid. The child Holly will bring a certain un-spoken language. Read all the messages the child Holly will bring. Put all the dream guidance and the un-spoken messages from the baby Holly together. The final answer to the Croco karma repayment certification will come from you choosing that the Croco karma is complete. Yes, your life is infinite and without a speculated destination. I will go in another minute or two. Continue to take care of yourself. Come over to me. I will tap you on both shoulders with this holly tree limb and blossoms. This will be my final act in the holly tree rite of passage for you and baby Holly within your womb," said the voice of the dream weaver.

"Here I am," replied Lily-Butterfly.

Lily-Butterfly knelt down, placed her hands in prayer at her heart, and closed her eyes. She felt nine taps on each shoulder and the dream weaver said a prayer while this was being done. During the performance Lily-Butterfly smelled very strong fragrance of holly tree and blossom. There was silence. A silence like a void and gap in-between time. The dream weaver distinct voice disappeared. Lily-Butterfly was left in the field of holly trees. She opened her eyes and saw the holly trees and herself. Lily-Butterfly said a prayer to thank the dream weaver and the holly trees. After the prayer she turned and walked down the grassy path out of the dream and back into her bed, the room, and her home.

Becoming conscious that the dream was complete. Lily-Butterfly sat up and took her journal. She wrote down all about the dream. After writing she read what she had written twice. She processed and digested the complete dream.

"Wow what an interesting dream. If I had chosen to go to Croco's house I might not have had this dream. I have these strong sensations on both shoulders. I can smell the fragrance of the holly tree leaves and blossom. The baby's name is Holly. It is a girl baby. Wow. Another girl. This is another powerful dream. Oh, my. It is 6:00 AM. Almost time to wake up. Hello Creator I hope that Holly's birth is nothing like Rebornstar's birth journey. I can see that I am being tested all the way. As you would say, the way will show the way. Thank you very much for everything," mumbled Lily-Butterfly.

Lily-Butterfly closed her journal. She went to use the restroom. Next, she prepared a teapot of relaxing tea. As she drank the complete teapot of tea, the holly blossoming tree, complete rite of passage, and the baby Holly dream, continued to digest, process, and percolate within Lily-Butterfly. The weekend seemed like a long decision-making adventure for Lily-Butterfly. This dream continued to percolate within Lily-Butterfly even after the birth of baby Holly.

Stay tuned. This adventure of Lily-Butterfly and her life's experiences continues on-ward.

29

January 1989 came to an end. February began and rolled along with Lily-Butterfly's life being filled with the similar things of her life. She had settled and surrendered into all the facts of her life situation. She had taken the leap and crossed the threshold of the next seven year phase of her life. On February 24, 1989 her mentor Mrs. Betty Butler the General Manager of the hotel retired. Lily-Butterfly gave her a gift and a handwritten thank you card for all she had done for her. Mrs. Butler wished Lily-Butterfly good luck with her life and the birth of her child. Lily-Butterfly was sad for an entire week about Mrs. Butler not being around anymore. The new General Manager started to work on February 27th. She had an unpleasant dry personality that lacked team work, understanding, and flexibility. It was like trying to work with a storm.

"It seem as if this new General Manager has a wall installed in front of her like a battle shield. I do not think we are going to work well together. If she thinks that she is going to exercise her demons on me; she is wrong. I think I am in for my next challenge and making a life changing decision. Everything is for a positive or negative reason. Oh, my Creator, where are you? Here I go again," grumbled Lily-Butterfly.

March 6th came and the new General Manager called Lily-Butterfly into her office at 10:00 AM.

The new General Manager said to Lily-Butterfly, "you are a good Manager with exceptional quality work and qualifications. I know this."

Lily-Butterfly interrupted and said, "And. So. I already sense that you do not like me. I will also let you know that I do not like your Managerial style. To me your style is un-professional. Professional business is not personal. So, what have you planned for me to make my working here difficult? I already feel that you are up to no good when it comes to me. Ha."

"Let me finish what I was going to say. I know of your great work. Mrs. Butler highly recommended you. The reason for this meeting is to let you know that I do not want you as my Manager to work with me in accomplishing my responsibility as a General Manager.

While you might have been great for Mrs. Butler, I choose to work with someone else. So, as of next week I am changing your schedule to working Wednesday to Sunday 3:00 PM to 11:00 PM. You would be off on Monday and Tuesday. Here is what I have said in writing. There is no law that says that I cannot change your schedule. Do you understand?" said the new General Manager.

"Yes, I do understand perfectly. I was right about what I sensed about you."

Lily-Butterfly took the letter and read it.

"The schedule I am currently working is the only one that I can work. This was the agreement when I took this job."

"Well Mrs. Butler is no longer here. I am the General Manager now. As your boss and supervisor, I can do what I like and want. This previous schedule arrangement with Mrs. Butler is cancelled. This is the new schedule. Work this schedule or do whatever you like."

"Please reconsider this new schedule decision. I take the train from White Planes Road in the Bronx to get to work. I am pregnant as you can see. Working a 3:00 PM to 11:00 PM schedule is not safe for me. I would be on the train after midnight and would not get home until 12:30 AM or later. I have a daughter who is ten years old that I have to pick up from school at 6:30 PM. Plus be home on the weekend to take care of her. You know that giving me this schedule you are technically forcing me to quit or make my life difficult. You know that you do not have a reason to fire me. Please I am asking you to reconsider your decision. Let me work my current schedule."

"Hello Lily-Butterfly business is business; like you say. This is not a personal decision. This is what I need to perform my work as a General Manager. You cannot keep your previous schedule. Your only option is to work the new schedule, Wednesday to Sunday from 3:00 PM to 11:00 PM. Got it. This is what it will be for as long as I am the General Manager and your boss. I am finished with this conversation. Is there anything else? Your replacement will be here in two weeks."

"I will call the Personnel Manager."

"Go ahead. Call him. I have already talked to him and all the relevant people. I have gotten their approval to change your schedule. So, what now?"

"I see and understand. You feel threatened by me. I am more qualified than you to have this General Manager job. So, you feel threatened by me. You have only hotel working experiences and no other qualification. While I have university certifications, office administrative work experience and qualification, and was mentored by a great hotel General Manager Mrs. Betty Butler. I do not want your job. If I did you would not have gotten it. I would have asked Mrs. Butler to recommend me when she told me she was retiring. Please let me keep my current schedule."

"No. I have things to do. This meeting is over. Are we done here?"

"Okay. Yes, we are done here. I do not feel comfortable working with you, not even one more minute. I quit effective immediately. You can work alone and do both your job and mine. Jealousy is a serious weapon and poisonous toxic energy. I can sense that you are a ruthless person. I am going to trust my instincts to leave immediately. If I stay in this job no matter what my schedule is you are going to try and make working here for me difficult. I am leaving. Here is your letter. I am leaving it right here on your desk. I will call the Personnel Department to mail me my last pay check. There is no law on quitting a job, just like you say there is no law in changing an employee schedule. Here are the keys. On a daily basis may your time working here be a reflection of your attitude, spirit, and soul. Bye."

Lily-Butterfly got up from sitting in front of the new General Manager, picked up her pocket book, and walked out of the General Manager's office without looking back. She walked to the train station and took the train home.

On the way home Lily-Butterfly thought many things. She thought, there are good humans on this planet. One of them will help me with a job. I do not have to be at the mercy of negative people. Ms. Gina is the first and last human to exercise their demon on me. I will use my savings until I find another job. Maybe my time in this State of New York City is coming to an end. Now Croco will be happy I quit my job. He might think now I am more desperate and will choose to marry him. He is wrong about this. Every time he speaks to me about marriage, I get this trapped danger feeling. Stress and fear is not my friend. I will find a job when and if I choose to. What is this General Manager woman thinking changing my schedule? I am not in the mood for fighting with anyone or anything. Oh well, nothing last forever in this material realm. Now I do not have medical insurance. But I will figure things out. I will not sell my soul and suffer. Oh, Creator keep helping to guide me and light my way.

When Lily-Butterfly got home she was drained and tired. She got something to eat and went to sleep. When it was time to get

Rebornstar from school Lily-Butterfly went to get her. They came back home and prepared dinner. During dinner Lily-Butterfly talked to Rebornstar about having another baby, leaving her job, looking for another job until it was time to have the baby, and possibly moving after the baby is born. Lily-Butterfly also told Mrs. Beech the basics of everything that was going on, and that she will be home until she found another job.

Croco telephoned Lily-Butterfly the same night that she quit her job. She answered the telephone. Her mood seem damp and no-nonsense.

"Hi Croco. How are you doing?"

"I am doing great. Today I went to the new building I bought to look at it with a building inspector. Things are looking good. I am going to proceed with purchasing the property. The major repairs is replacing the complete roof. Oh well. I have to spend money to make money. How are you doing?"

"I quit my job today."

"What? You quit your job?"

"Yes. The short story of this situation is, the new General Manager changed my schedule to Wednesday to Sunday 3:00 PM to 11:00 PM, and off Monday and Tuesday. I cannot work this schedule for many reasons. I told her that I cannot work this schedule. She told me that I had no choice. So, I quit. I am going to look for a new job working part-time. Maybe a childcare job. No career professional job will hire me at almost five months pregnant. I will be fine."

"Yes, you will be fine. You have me. Do not find another job. Move into my house and marry me. If you do this all your problems are solved. Also, now you have no health insurance, bills, rent, and two children. Wake up and act smart. Being so spiritual is not going to help you financially."

"Croco, I am already wide awake. The more I get to know you; I see you very wide and deep. This is why I know that marrying you is not my solution. Every time you tell me about moving in with you and marrying you, I feel danger, doomed, and trapped. For whatever reason I know that your perception and intention is not the solution to my life. My instinct says no and no. So far in my life my instinct is never wrong."

"I see. Let me know if you change your mind. I know that you will change your mind."

"I am going to change my Doctor and go to the midwife maternity department at the hospital close by where I live. This is where I will have my baby as well. The hospital prenatal fee is affordable. Tomorrow I am going to look into the newspaper for a childcare job opportunity."

"What? Look for a childcare job. A woman like you with so much qualifications is going to work in someone house as childcare and housekeeper? Find a job with health insurance. I hope that you know I am not going to pay the many thousands of hospital bill for you to have this baby. Hello Lily-Butterfly I work very hard for my money. I will not be paying your over $25,000 maternity care hospital bill. This is what the cost was for my son's mother to have him. It was a good thing that she was on welfare and Medicaid. If you choose to not come live with me, get a job with insurance, apply for Medicaid; you are on your own with all the bills. Why are you silent?"

"I am silent so that you can express your true nature and feelings. I am also thinking that every day you prove me right about my decision to not move into your house, take your engagement ring, and marry you. I can sense and see your true nature of meanness, anger, self-serving personality, and conditional kindness. I will not become another possession of yours and hostage. Do you hear me? I will figure out my situations as positively as I can. Bye."

Lily-Butterfly hung up the telephone before Croco could say anything more. Croco telephoned her immediately after she hung up the telephone. Lily-Butterfly did not answer the telephone. After getting off the telephone Lily-Butterfly wrote in her journal all her experiences for the day. She also wrote an action plan to find a temporary job until it was time for her to have the baby.

The next morning after taking Rebornstar to school Lily-Butterfly bought a newspaper and returned home. She called Manana Leila.

"Hi Manana. How are you doing?"

"I am doing great, as usual. As long as I am healthy, I have no complaint. How are you doing?"

"I am almost five months pregnant. I quit the hotel job, because the General Manager I used to work with retired. The new one changed my schedule to Wednesday to Sunday, 3:00 PM to 11:00 PM. For the reasons of safety traveling on the train after midnight, having to be home for Rebornstar, and being pregnant this schedule is not good for me. She refuse to let me keep my original schedule, so I quit. I am going to find a part time childcare job until it is time to have the baby. I did not tell you that I was pregnant, because I did not want you to worry. When I get off a positive vibe track, I make myself get back on the right path. That is everything in a nut shell."

"Oh, wow. Are you going to get married? Do you have money?"

"No, I am not getting married. I do not feel that I should for many reasons. I know now that I should have this baby. I have some very good reasons for my decision. The rest about the baby will be revealed upon her birthday. Her name is Holly. Sometimes the crooked road leads to the straight road. As you know everything happens for a positive or negative reason and there are no accidents. I will always have to figure out the solutions to my perceived situations and problems. How is the Ms. Gina immigration visa process going?"

"How do you know that it is a girl? I think Gina's visa process will be complete by one year. I have to figure out a place for Ms. Gina and her two sons to live when they arrive here. My apartment is not big enough. I love my apartment and living with my friend downstairs. I do not want to move in my old age. We will see what happens when the time comes."

"I am guided by the Creator, my guardian angels, and different dream weaver oracles show up in my dreams to give me messages. This is how I get to know things, confirm things, and so forth. I have some savings. Even being pregnant I will find a job. Good spirits and soul always show up to help me when I need help. I will help you with Ms. Gina, Henry, and Dean living accommodations. They can live with me for maximum one year. I will buy them winter clothes, feed them, and they do not have to pay me any rent. I will help them to find work. Show them how to take public transportation. When they have money for an apartment, I will help them to rent an apartment. The three of them can live together in one apartment until they decide their individual personal choice. This is my intention I have been thinking about helping you and them this way for a while now. This will help you to take a break from having to help so much. Let Ms. Gina know this for immigration and buying her plane ticket purposes. You have helped me so much all my life. I would like to do this to help you, and also to help Ms. Gina and her sons. Although she treated me very bad, my deep understanding of things helps me to know better; so, I do better. You know that we have to respect the pathway and ancestors that bring us into this realm. Respect, unconditional love, and deep understanding is my chosen way to help Ms. Gina, in exchange for my birth passage. I have to work some more on erasing my dislike for what she did to me. After everything, here I am rolling along with the evolution of my life's journey. When it is closer to the time for the visa to be approved, I will give you my address and phone number for them. I think that I will be moving after I have the baby. Where am I going to move to? This is the big question. The next location for me to live will show up soon. I feel this in my heart. With the Creator's help everything will work out one way or the other."

"I hear you my child. You have come a long way. You still have a long way to go. You are going to do what none of the ancestors have done so far. You will pave the way for us when we return in the future to perform the Creator's will and work. Thank you so much for the help with Gina and her sons. Even in the midst of all your situations and uncertainties you are offering me this priceless help. Do you realize that six of you will be living in a small apartment? Plus, you will have a young baby."

"Yes. You have helped me through many impossible situations to get this far in my life. This is one very big gift and sacrifice for you, Ms. Gina, Henry, and Dean. I will make sure that I do my best with and for them. Do not worry I will not let them take disadvantage of me in any way. It is time for me to practice my grown-up self with them. Ms. Gina might be in for a big surprise. I am just going with how I am being guided. After I get off the telephone with you, I am going to look in the newspaper for a job. I will find one. When one door closes another one opens. I just have to do the work to find the open door for the present time. Money is a great resource in this so-called modern realm and time. But what good is money when everything else sucks? Do not worry. I will be fine. I am watching my stress and how much negative energy I soak in, although there is no perfect situation. I am going to check the newspaper. Take care of yourself."

"Okay I will. You do the same for yourself and the children. Now the Creator is giving you one more company. I am going to send you some money for emergency. What use is the money just sitting here when you need it? My child take it."

"I have money saved and I will find a job. You do not have to give me money."

"I want to give you the money. This will set my heart at ease knowing that you have extra money resources. It is a gift from the Creator, me, and the ancestors as well. Take it. I will send you a check for $3,000. It is from my work bonus from last Christmas holiday. I have more money as well. Thank you for being considerate. Stay healthy, wise, strong, flexible, and confident. Savor yourself for the long journey ahead of you. Plus, you will be traveling with two children, one on each side. Now you will have double company and students of the way. Blessings to you. Our ancestors are very proud of you. Make good positive use of the pathways and opportunities given to you. Let me know when the baby is born and when you move. Bye my blessed child. Bye."

"Bye my blessed Manana. Without you I would not be here and where I am in this life. This current human life is not easy. I will do my best. I accept the money. Thank you for your motivational and up-lifting words. I will keep doing my positive best and net get lost and tangled up into negative people, places, and things. Take care of yourself my beloved Manana, spirit guide, and teacher of the path of unconditional love, peace, and deep understanding."

"Thank you, my child, for giving me the opportunity to help you. Take care. Bye."

Lily-Butterfly got off the telephone. She looked in the newspaper and found a Childcare Employment Agency. The office was located in New Jersey the state next to New York. Lily-Butterfly felt in her heart this was the door to what was next for her. She called the agency. They had work like she was looking for. Getting a job in New Jersey seemed to be a leap out of where she was currently. She never heard of New Jersey before, but she choose to take the leap. Her instinct was telling her that this was the way to go. The Childcare Employment Agency Director scheduled an appointment for Lily-Butterfly to come to the office in New Jersey for an interview. The Director guided her that New Jersey was the state next to New York and what to do to find her office. Lily-Butterfly told the Director that she was pregnant. The Director told her being pregnant was fine as long as she could perform the job she was hired to do, and the employer agreed to take her as an employee. After Lily-Butterfly got off the telephone she started her plan and research how to get to the Childcare Employment Agency.

Lily-Butterfly went to the library to do research on the state of New Jersey and to find the location of the office on a New Jersey map. Next, she went back home to telephone the bus and train station to inquire about what trains to get to the George Washington Bridge. She also called the New Jersey Transit bus company to find out what bus would take her from the George Washington Bridge bus terminal to The Childcare Employment Agency in Tenafly, New Jersey. When Lily-Butterfly was finished with her transportation research she found out that she had to take three separate trains, changing trains at certain points, to get to the George Washington Bridge bus terminal. It was lots of up and down flights of steps at each train and bus stop. From this terminal she would take one bus to Tenafly, New Jersey. The Child Care Employment Agency was on the main street of the bus route. This was her route to New Jersey and back home to the Bronx. Especially being almost five months pregnant his traveling seemed like a lot of work, but this was what she was being guided to do, so she just did it. Plus, if she got a job in New Jersey she would have to do this traveling back and forth daily to get to and from work. Lily-Butterfly's spiritual training and discovering her talents for her chosen destiny and life's purpose career was very hands on, began before birth, challenging, and might seem crazy.

When Lily-Butterfly finished her research about getting to the Childcare Employment Agency in Tenafly, New Jersey she got information on the trains, bus schedule, distance, time the journey would take her each way, cost, and effort. The total time one way she estimated to be two hours. The appointment was for 11:00 AM on Thursday. She planned to leave home at 8:30 AM to have enough time to get to the appointment by 11:00 AM. When all this research was completed and digested Lily-Butterfly felt drained and tired. She had something to eat and laid down to take a nap. As she laid there in further contemplation she decided to pray.

"Creator why am I going to this place so far away from my home to apply for a part time job? It will be minimum two hours to get to the employment agency and the same amount of time to return home. The job I might get might even be further away from the employment agency office. This will be another journey of focus, more exercise, endurance, faith, and trust; especially carrying a baby within my womb. I know that I have free will to choose. I am choosing to do all that I am doing; and have done. I do not feel like I am a victim to this situation. My instinct tells me this is the door and way to go; so onward I choose to go. Creator only you know everything. I am the last one to know things. Here I sit behind the veil of mystery and revelation. I am traveling with my two constant companions my two children, students, and teachers; one known and one un-known. Forward I surrender to the leap of this faith. Creator there are many weeds to pull from the garden of my life's journey, many seeds to plant, and many things to give birth to. One step at a time I will get to the destination of my destiny. The island of Kawomaya and the valley village of Yaj is becoming further and further in the past. My human life is beyond interesting. To get to my destination is a lot of work to prepare myself for what I am going to perform when I arrive. I am grateful for everything. Amin," whispered Lily-Butterfly.

Her eyes were closed and she fell asleep within the experience of processing her day.

30

Thursday morning came. Lily-Butterfly took Rebornstar to school and went to the train station. She got on the trains and got to the George Washington Bridge bus terminal. Along this whole journey she asked questions to strangers to make sure she was taking the right trains and going in the right direction. She found the bus ticket counter and purchased her bus ticket. At 10:05 AM she was sitting on the bus as it drove across the George Washington Bridge into the State of New Jersey. As the bus drove down the highway and through the different towns, Lily-Butterfly paid attention to the bus route, scenery, and the less busy environment.

"I think that I am going to like this New Jersey the garden state. The first State over the George Washington Bridge. Let me pay attention to the name of the towns and streets the bus passes through. I do not want to pass my stop. This is the right street. Let me look at the numbers. Here is the agency's office. It is time for me to ring the bell," whispered Lily-Butterfly.

She rang the bell and the bus stopped at the next stop which was close to the office. She walked back to the office building. Entering the building Lily-Butterfly took the elevator to the second floor. She located the office and entered through the open door. The Receptionist greeted her. Lily-Butterfly was given an application to fill out. She put Jeff and Susan as one of her reference. When the form was completely filled out the Director of the agency interviewed her. The interview went well. The Director had a part time job available to take care of a recently born baby girl and a two years old boy. The Director gave Lily-Butterfly the job description to read and asked her if she could perform all the duties that the mother would request. Lily-Butterfly told her yes. The job was working with a mother and her two children, plus light housekeeping. Her work schedule would be Monday to Friday 9:30 AM to 3:30 PM. The pay was $300 per week. The home was in Demarest the next town. The travelling time to get to work would almost be the same. Lily-Butterfly accepted the job opportunity and the Director scheduled an interview for the job. The Director gave Lily-Butterfly the home address phone number of the parent, and directions to get to the house from the Employment Agency. The interview with the parent was scheduled for next week

Wednesday at 10:00 AM. When the interview was completed Lily-Butterfly thanked the Director and left the office. The bus stop to take the bus back to the George Washington Bridge bus terminal was directly across the street from the Agency's office.

The bus came after Lily-Butterfly waited fifteen minutes. Lily-Butterfly arrive back home at 3:30 PM. She ate a bowl of steamed vegetables, boiled eggs, and drank tea. Both Lily-Butterfly and the baby were hungry. All they had eaten after breakfast were healthy snacks, an apple, and drank water. As Lily-Butterfly ate she talked to herself.

"I think today was an enlightening and successful journey. I like very much New Jersey, Bergen County, the Garden State vibes. I can see now why I was guided to go to this place. Currently I think and feel that I will move to this state after I have Holly. The Creator surly works in mysterious ways. Tomorrow Friday I will visit the hospital Midwife maternity department that I will have Holly. I will fill out the application forms for my prenatal visits and schedule my first appointment. I am thankful for everything. Now I will go get Rebornstar from school. Next dinner, prepare for bed, journal, and prayer. Prayer to me is great. Maybe Croco will telephone me tonight. If he does not call me, I will not be calling him. I am tired and need to rest, process, and digest my day. Amin," whispered Lily-Butterfly.

By 10:00 PM Lily-Butterfly was in her bed and asleep. The telephone rang and woke her up. Lily-Butterfly did not get out of bed to answer the phone. She went back to sleep. The next morning Lily-Butterfly took the bus to the local hospital. She located the Midwife maternity department, registered for prenatal visits, scheduled her first appointment, and met with the Midwife assigned to her. The Midwife gave Lily-Butterfly the form to apply for Medicaid to help her with the hospital bills and delivery of baby Holly. When she was complete with the hospital process she went back home. Lily-Butterfly telephoned the Gynecologist to cancel the appointment that she had scheduled with him. At 4:30 PM after lunch and a nap Lily-Butterfly telephoned Croco. He answered the call.

"Hi Croco. I think that you called me last night. I heard the phone ring after 10:00 PM. I was already in bed and sleeping. The ringing of the phone woke me up. How are you?"

"My nerves needed a break from you and my mother's crappy attitude. I am as good as possible. I know from your actions that you are avoiding me. I have not seen you since the Christmas dinner situation with my mother. How was your job interview?"

"The interview was great. I have an interview for a job next week Wednesday. If I get the job, I will be working part time helping a mother to take care of her new born baby and her two year old son, plus light housekeeping. I would have to travel about two and a half hours each way to get to and from the job. Also, three trains and one bus each way. This might sound like a crazy decision to you, but this is the truth I choose. This is what my instinct tell me to do. Okay. I know that you are happy that I am pregnant and quit my job. This way you think I am trapped and will surrender to your mercy and your conditional offers disguised as generosity. This is not going to happen. I will not set myself up to be damaged by your unpredictable mental health imbalances."

"Okay there is many ways to get something done miss independence. Did you go to the hospital?"

"Yes. I registered and schedule my first prenatal appointment. The Midwife gave me the form to apply for Medicaid."

"Good for you this is why you pay tax. When you refuse to marry me, and you need financial help to pay the hospital bills you apply to the government for help. Maybe you are going to choose other public assistance as well."

"No, I will never go on Welfare. I am qualified to do so many jobs. I do not need Welfare and public housing. You think that if I do not marry you, I will be doomed? Ha. You are wrong. You seem to also be the type that to find a way to punish me, you would not pay child support either. What is the point of you having so much so-called wealth, material possession, and money, when you are poor in your spirit, soul, mind, and body?"

"Maybe I am the type to do whatever I like. Ms. Beautiful wait and see the facts of what happen. You and your spiritual talk."

"Croco thank you for all your genuine unconditional kindness. When I first met you and up to me refusing the engagement ring and marriage proposal you were Mr. Great. Now your fake mask has been removed and little by little the other real Crocodiles are showing their faces."

"Hahaha. You are funny. You are great with words. I think that you are a great poet and writer. You are great with words and wisdom. Come over to my house I have not seen you in a long time my beautiful queen. Tomorrow Saturday come over to my house and bring Rebornstar. Chef will cook for us. You and Rebornstar can sleep over if you like. Next week Monday I am gone traveling for ten days. Are you coming?"

"Yes, I will be at your home at 1:00 PM. We will not be sleeping over. Croco life is life. People will be the people they choose to be. See you tomorrow. We will walk there. To me walking is good exercise. Bye."

"Okay beautiful. Bye."

Croco hung up the telephone. Lily-Butterfly continued on with her day. Saturday when she visited Croco she hardly talked and was being observant. There was no triggering incidents because Lily-Butterfly was in a 'I do not care' mood. She ignored most of what Croco said and did. The spent most of the time outside lounging under the large trees. Lily-Butterfly and Rebornstar stayed at Croco's house for lunch and dinner. After dinner she asked Croco to take them home. Sunday at Lily-Butterfly was the same as usual preparing meals, laundry, cleaning the home, preparing for the following week, taking Rebornstar to the park, reading, journaling, meditation, prayers, and food shopping.

Wednesday morning came and Lily-Butterfly took the three trains and was on the bus at 9:00 AM going over the George Washington Bridge and going into New Jersey.

"I feel like I am crossing another big bridge in my life's journey and destiny. Where will this bridge lead me? I do not know for sure. All I know for sure is that it is wise to follow the path and do not get lost," mumbled Lily-Butterfly.

Thirty-five minutes passed since the bus crossed the bridge. Lily-Butterfly looked at her written directions, she had passed the Childcare Employment Agency's office. Lily-Butterfly was close to her stop. She closed the book she was reading. She ask the bus driver to stop at the closest bus stop to the cross street to get to the house. In five minutes, the bus driver stopped the bus and Lily-Butterfly got off. She turned right and walked towards the address written on the paper. Lily-Butterfly walked about one and a half mile to get to the house. She arrived at the house 10:05 AM and rang the doorbell. A pleasant looking woman came to open the door.

"Hi, I am Mrs. Charm. Are you Lily-Butterfly?"

"Yes I am. Good morning Mrs. Charm."

"Good morning. Come inside. You have a very interesting name."

"Thank you. I love my name."

"You traveled all the way from New York to come here?"

"Yes Mrs. Charm. I did."

"Are you sure that you want to travel all this distance Monday to Friday to work here? It is a far distance for a part-time job."

"Yes, I agree that it is far. I know that I would like to work for you. It is strange coming from so far, but maybe the reasons for me coming here to work is priceless. Mrs. Charm do you believe in the Creator?"

"Do you mean God?"

"Yes."

"Yes, I believe in God. Actually, I prayed for God to send me the best person to help me with my children. After having my daughter, I was diagnosed with post-partum depression. I have fallen into a deep black hole and need someone nurturing to help me and my children."

"Well, maybe I am here to answer your prayer. Only you and time can tell if this is true. I am committed to doing my best if you give me a chance by hiring me."

"Okay. I am concerned about you being pregnant. Will you be able to do the duties I am hiring you to perform? You would have to take care of a six weeks old baby and a two years old active toddler, plus light housekeeping. How many months pregnant are you?"

"I am five months pregnant. I can work until July. Maybe by July you will feel better. Yes, I can manage the job. I need to work until I have my baby, to have money to help me with my rent, and other bills. I have a daughter who is ten years old. I need to be home to get her from her after school program at 6:30 PM. Try me for two weeks. If you are not satisfied with my work you can fire me."

"Where did you work before? What happened to your previous job?"

"I will tell you the short version of this answer. I have a Bachelors in Business Administration and a Masters in Tourism and Hospitality. My last job I worked as a Hotel Manager. The General Manager I worked with retired. The new General Manager changed my schedule from Monday to Friday 9:00 AM to 5:00 PM to Wednesday to Sunday 3:00 PM to 11:00 PM. Currently my choice of transportation is the train and bus. For safety and having to take care of my daughter reasons I quit. I like to earn my money. So, I would rather work than seek free money from public assistance, and so forth. I can be the greatest help and I will be here on time. I can work until the day I give birth. If you do not see me show up for work one day, then you know that I went to have my baby. You are the answer to my prayer and I am the answer to your prayer. Would you like me to work for you or not? I do not want to waste our time continuing this interview if you do not want me to work for you."

"I feel I should let you stay. You seem so brave, confident, and strong. All your references and the one from Jeff and Susan in Massachusetts are fantastic. Plus, I know a good thing when I see it. I choose for you to stay. Like you say, if one morning you do not show up you have given birth. Maybe I can learn courage, strength, and bravery from you. Come let me introduce you to the children."

"Thank you very much Mrs. Charm. I am committed to doing my best work. I do not think that you will regret hiring me. Really. Time will confirm my abilities and talents. With me here Monday to Friday you can take a break from your life and recuperate your mental and emotional health. If I do not like working here, I will let you know."

"All right, good. Come meet the children."

Lily-Butterfly drank some of the water from her water bottle. She always traveled with her reusable water bottle with water in it.

Mrs. Charm took Lily-Butterfly to meet the two children, show her the home environment, and the back yard. After they went back to sit at the dining table.

"Lily-Butterfly would you still like the job?"

"Yes Mrs. Charm, I do. To me this is much more than a job. It is a symbol of transcendence to where I do not even know. Mrs. Charm I am very spiritual. Do not mind my poetic and spiritual style of talking. I meant to say I value this job opportunity more than you could ever know."

"Okay. I understand. I am spiritual in my own ways as well. You are a wise woman. The job will be primarily taking care of my six weeks old daughter and two years old son. When they take naps, you can do as much house work as possible. I have a cleaning service come in once per week to clean the house. I will do all the cooking. You will take care of snacks and lunch for my son and feed the baby with milk from a bottle. I do not breast feed my baby. By the time you arrive here in the morning we would have already had breakfast. Your work schedule is Monday to Friday 9:30 AM to 3:30 PM. The pay is $300 per week. My son is not fussy and a normal toddler. My baby is fussy and colicky. After my daughter's birth I fell into a black hole of postpartum depression. I go to Psychotherapy and take medication. Maybe by the time you stop working here my health will improve. I prayed for help and the right person. And here you are. Lily-Butterfly thank you for coming and from so far away."

"You are welcome Mrs. Charm. Both our prayers fulfill each other's request. I hope this opportunity works out for both of us. Relax, rest, and restore your health. I will do the best job possible. Your children will be in safe and good hands. Do not worry about me being pregnant. My baby is deeply rooted within me. She will stay that way until she is ready to come out. I forget to tell you that I need one day off per month to go for check up at the hospital Midwifery department."

"You are having a girl? Yes, you can have one day off per month."

"Yes, it is a girl. Her name is Holly, like the holly tree. I sing to her and she listens. From the island of Kawomaya where I was born the regular village custom is that the baby is not celebrated before birth. In this case, in a dream, an oracle came and told me it is a girl. Her name was chosen in the dream. I did not do an ultrasound to confirm if it is really a girl. I do not want to do an ultrasound. I trust the visions and the oracle in the dream. Children are great. They can give us reasons to want to do our best. Anyway, enough of my spiritual talk. Is there anything else you need to tell me? When do you want me to start working?"

"I like your spiritual talk and words of wisdom. You seem wise beyond your years. I find it refreshing. I would like you to start on Monday. Is this okay?"

"Yes. Great. Monday is good."

"Do you have any more questions or concerns? The baby woke up. It is time for me to feed her."

"No. I have no questions or concerns. I will figure out things as I go along. You take care of yourself. I will be here on Monday. Hard is easy and easy is easy for me. Plus, I am an optimistic person. Coming here, getting back home, and working here will be one long exercise. I will manage, moderate exercise is good for having an easy labor, and the birthing process. I am used to walking a lot from a child. I will see you on Monday at 9:30 AM. Thanks again for this opportunity. Good bye Mrs. Charm. Oh, can I use your restroom?"

"Sure, there is a restroom close to the front door. When you are finished you can go out the front door and pull it close. I am going to feed the baby. Good bye Lily-Butterfly. Thank you very much for coming to work with us. Bye."

"You are welcome. Bye."

Lily-Butterfly picked up her pocket book used the restroom, and left Mrs. Charm's house. She walked back to the bus stop on the main road. Lily-Butterfly crossed the main road and sat down inside the bus stop. She drank some water and ate an apple, crackers, and some peanuts that she had brought in her pocket book. After eating she read a book that she had brought with her. The bus came in twenty minutes. When the bus came, she went onto the bus and sat at a window seat. She continued to read her book. Periodically Lily-Butterfly looked out the bus window. She liked the many beautiful gardens that she saw in people's yard.

"Today is a great day. I like this New Jersey state. Today I give thanks for my many blessings," whispered Lily-Butterfly.

Lily-Butterfly went back to reading her book. The journey of the bus and three trains took her back to her current neighborhood on White Planes Road in the Bronx. She entered her cozy home sweet home.

"I am very grateful for the state of New York, the greatest diverse city, and my home as well. Amin," said Lily-Butterfly.

31

Lily-Butterfly telephoned Croco to tell him that she got the job. She made plans with Croco to go to his house the next morning after taking Rebornstar to school. Lily-Butterfly offered to make breakfast for both of them. Thursday morning Lily-Butterfly arrived at Croco's home. She made breakfast and they ate. The conversation between them was light. She did not encourage any possessive attitude from Croco. When she did not want to talk about certain things, she would let him know. After breakfast they cleaned up the kitchen and dining room. At 11:00 AM the security guard in the first room by the door came and called Croco to the office and they talked. Croco returned to the living room where Lily-Butterfly was seated.

"Lily-Butterfly I will be back by 12:00 PM. Stay here. I have to go take care of some business for a little while. As usual the security guard is in the first room. Read your book or watch television."

"Okay. You seem in a serious mood. What is going on?"

"Nothing. I will be back by 12:00 PM lunch time."

"Okay."

Thirty minutes went by. The house front doorbell rang. The security man went to the door to see who it was. He opened the door. It seem to be someone he knew. A man and a woman came into the house. The security guard spoke to them. He told the man and woman that he was going to telephone Croco. The lady asked for some water. The security guard postponed calling Croco and he went to the kitchen to get her a glass of water. The man and woman followed the security guard towards the kitchen. When the security turned his back to them to get the water the man shot the security guard in his leg. The glass of water crashed to the floor. When Lily-Butterfly heard the gun shot and the glass of water crash to the floor she quietly rushed to the master bedroom. She entered the bathroom and pushed a chest of drawer against the closed bathroom door. The bathroom door did not have a lock on the door knob. Lily-Butterfly sat with her back against the chest of drawer. The security guard pulled his gun and shot the man and woman. All three of them were wrestling out in the hallway adjoining the kitchen.

"Holy smokes. It seems like a robbery," grumbled Lily-Butterfly.

Lily-Butterfly remembered that there was a clear sack with diamonds on Croco's dresser in the bedroom. She pushed away the chest of drawer from the door, peeked through the slightly opened bathroom door, rushed over to the dresser, and grabbed the sack of diamonds. Lily-Butterfly ran back to the bathroom, closed the door, and pushed the chest of drawer back against the closed door. She placed the sack of diamond inside the toilet bowl, took some blue cleaning product and poured it in the toilet bowl, and closed the toilet lid. The cleaning product was to disguise the sack of diamond. She sat with her back against the chest of drawer and prayed.

"Creator please protect Holly and I in this dangerous situation. Is today going to be our last day living on this planet? Are we going to die? I do not think so. Wrap your warm coils of light around us and make us invisible. I am shaking and I feel cold. Protect the security guard and help him to get the robbers to flee. Amin."

After the prayer Lily-Butterfly's attention was brought back to furniture crashing down, and more gun shots. Lastly there were people running towards the front door. A door slammed. Then there was silence. Lily-Butterfly sat frozen, folded within herself, and focused on connecting to her baby within her. The baby lay still, no movement, she might be asleep. Not sure what was going on Lily-Butterfly still sat on the floor with her back against the chest of drawer.

"I hope that the robbers left and the security guard is okay. If he was dead then the robbers might not have run out of the house. They would be searching the house for whatever they came to take. The robbers might have seen me. Holly are you okay. I hope so. I feel that we will be fine," whispered Lily-Butterfly.

At the end of Lily-Butterfly talking to herself the baby kicked and turned.

"Holly thank you for letting me know that you are alive and okay. *I will sing your song to us. Blessings Holly my complete bridge to help me cross the waters of my past life. Welcome to mama's life. We will discover our chosen life purpose destiny, moving forward into the unknown. Mama help you. You help mama. Moving forward into the unknown, we go. Forward into the unknown we go, with love, peace, and understanding. Forward we go with, love, peace, and understanding. Forward we go. Forward we go. Forward we go. Amin.*"

Lily-Butterfly was about to start the song over again when she heard the security guard calling her name.

"Lily-Butterfly. Lily-Butterfly where are you? It is me the security guard. Come out from where you are hiding. The robbers have left. Come."

Lily-Butterfly got up and pushed the chest of drawer back to where it was. She opened the bathroom door and went to the living room.

"Thank God that you are okay. I was looking for you. I called Croco on the telephone. He is on his way back to the house. The people he was supposed to meet seemed to have arranged a robbery. They created a diversion by arranging for Croco to meet them somewhere. When Croco got to the place and waited no one showed up. These two clowns came here to rob Croco. My God. When I thought about you being in the house, I could not let them kill me. If they killed me, they could have killed you as well. You are too beautiful of a lady to die like this. Come here. Here. Drink this lemonade it will calm your nerves and remove the bitter vibes from your nervous system. Sit at the dining table. How is the baby doing?"

"The baby seems fine. Why did you open the door and let in the robbers?"

"We know them. They are customers of Croco. The always come here or at the jewelry store to pick up precious stones for their boss. Now this is a big problem. Be careful coming back here. Coming here is dangerous for you and your children. Croco can be a charming person, but he is dangerous to be around for many different reasons. I recommend that you stay away from this house and Croco. Saying this is my gift to you. Do not say one word that I told you these things. Please do not breathe one word to Croco about what I just said. Okay. Promise me that you will not."

"I promise you I will not say anything about what you told me. You are the second one that told me a similar danger warning about Croco. I can see and sense the danger as well. This is why I do not come here too much. Plus, Croco has a lot of stress vibes that keeps his mental health unbalanced. I became aware of the danger vibes. This is why when he asked me to marry him and move here, I told him no. As time goes by, I get to know Croco more and more. I am aware. Thank you for everything. I think that because of you we are alive today. Thanks very much. When Croco gets here, I am going home. You will not see me again. Thank you."

"Okay good. Take care of yourself and your children. God has other plans for you than to be Croco's wife living in danger. I think he is here. Drink all the lemonade. I have to go to the office. Bye."

"I will. Bye and thanks again."

The security guard was shot in his leg. It was only surface wound. He wrapped the leg using a clean towel. Croco and the security guard talked. Lily-Butterfly went into the bathroom to pee. She had forgotten that she had put the sack of diamonds into the toilet bowl. She sat peeing and thinking about what the security guard had told her. Croco rushed into the bathroom.

"Lily-Butterfly there was a clear sack of diamonds on my dresser. Did you see it?"

"Yes. Oh wow. Yes, I forgot that I hid them in the toilet bowl. I just peed on them. Sorry."

"What? Put them in toilet bowl. Why? Peed on them. Get up."

Croco pulled Lily-Butterfly off the toilet bowl and punched her on her shoulder. Suddenly she stood up. Croco pushed her out of the way to get to look inside the toilet bowl.

"Are you crazy? These are diamonds. You do not know the value of things. Why did you put them in the toilet bowl?"

Lily-Butterfly recovered from her surprise regarding Croco's actions. She had regained her balance, pulled up her underwear, and pulled down her dress. She was still silent. Croco used his hand to take the sack of diamonds out of the toilet bowl. He emptied them in the sink and counted them. Then he proceeded to wash them with liquid soap.

"They are all here. You are lucky. What were you thinking throwing them in the toilet bowl?"

"You are the one in luck regarding the diamonds. I am lucky that I am alive. I had forgotten that I had hidden them in the toilet bowl to look out for your best interest. I could have flushed the toilet. You came in at the right time. I put them into the toilet, because I thought this would be safe. This was the last place the robbers would look for them. So, even if they killed me your diamonds would be safe. I am looking out for the diamonds, you, the baby, and myself. It is interesting to me that you are concerned first about the diamonds and then yourself. I see the deeper side of you very clearly. I perceive today's dangerous experience as a warning and blessing in disguise. Negative energy and situations can be helpful and give powerful caution messages. I am good at learning, and I do not make the same mistake twice."

"What are you talking about? Ha. Hey. I have no time for your spiritual talk and perceptions. There are no comparison. The diamonds are the diamonds. And you are you."

"Would you do to the sack of diamonds what you just did to me?"

"What are you talking about? I do not have time for this conversation. I have to go take care of some jungle justice. Come let me take you home. Come now. Hurry."

"What does jungle justice mean? Did you call the police?"

"Shut up. I do not need to call the police. No one died. Nothing was stolen. The security guard took care of his surface leg wound. Come on. I will take you home. You do not need to know what the words jungle justice mean. Hurry I have to go take care of some business."

"You have a personality of a crocodile, wasp, and dove. Do you realize that you just pulled, pushed, and punched me on my shoulder? Abuse is not a light situation. You might think that what you did is normal and okay. Do not do this to me again. Be aware of karma. Any negative action you do to me will be returned to you. Do you understand?"

"Beautiful I do not have time for this conversation. What I did is nothing. You are lucky. Sorry. But, what can you do to me if I did what I just did again? Nothing. You are funny. Just make sure that you stay on the right track to not trigger my demons. Get up. Stop sitting down. Come on. I will drive you home."

"I might not do something to you. Karma will return to you ten-fold anything negative you do to me. Take my words as a warning to you. What happened to you today could be because of karma. What happened to me today could be positive karma caution and warning message. You go take care of your business. I will walk home. Walking is good for me. I do not want to be in your predatory negative energy vibes. You look like a great and handsome man. But physical looks can be deceiving. What is essential is invisible to your two eyes. I do not think that I will be coming back to your house and home. Bye. Go take care of yourself and business."

"Okay. The security guard and I have to go somewhere. I have to lock the door. Come."

"I will be at the door in one minute. Let me go get my hand bag."

"Yeah. Hey. Hurry."

Lily-Butterfly got her hand bag. They left the house. Lily-Butterfly walked home.

As Lily-Butterfly walked home she processed her thoughts and feelings. Some things she thought were: - with time people will show beyond their surface face. Nothing or no one will rob me of my authentic spirit, soul, mind, and body. Abuse, suffering, and trauma is very damaging to a human. Croco's dove nature is not going to fool me into a relationship with him, and then his crocodile and wasp nature personality capsize me into becoming stuck in hell, and damnation. Looks and surface treatment can be deceiving. I have to trust my instincts. It is a good thing that I was not glamorized by Croco's engagement proposal, the engagement ring, and his invitation to move into his house of danger. Creator you told me that I met Croco for karma repayment. The dream oracle told me that by the day Holly is born, I am the one to certify that the Croco karma has been repaid. I am telling you right now at this moment that I choose that the Croco karma has been repaid. I am not waiting until Holly's birthday to prove that it has been repaid. Creator I hope that you are hearing and listening to me. Today's experience is the last straw. I do not choose any more of Croco's crap. Maybe the sperm he gave to create Holly is karma repayment. A life for saving his life in whatever life time you showed me. Maybe and maybe not. Either way I accept all my experiences with Croco as his karma repayment. We are free as of today to move on with our life. Croco is free from his karma repayment to me. Creator keep protecting and helping me as I continue on and also going to this long transportation job adventure starting on Monday. Thank you for everything. Holly I think that you are strong and flexible like the holly tree, branch, leaves, and blossom. Hang in there, mama is here. We will work together with this growth within my womb, birth journey, and delivery. Do not give mama any trouble. Be safe and be well. I will sing you your Holly song. Amin.

Lily-Butterfly sang repeatedly to Holly until she got home.

"Blessings Holly my complete bridge to help me cross the waters of my past life. Welcome to mama's life. We will discover our chosen life purpose destiny, moving forward into the unknown. Mama help you. You help mama. Moving forward into the unknown, we go. Forward into the unknown we go, with love, peace, and understanding. Forward we go with, love, peace, and understanding. Forward we go. Forward we go. Forward we go. Amin," sang Lily-Butterfly.

"Hello Holly, we are home. We will eat lunch and take a nap."

Lily-Butterfly had lunch and took a nap. When she woke up,

she prepared dinner and went to get Rebornstar from after school program. That night Croco did not telephone Lily-Butterfly. She was happy about this. The next night was Friday, Croco called to talk to Lily-Butterfly. She answered the telephone. They talked for a short time, because Lily-Butterfly told Croco that she was tired and wanted to go to sleep. She also told Croco that her main priority was her health, and taking care of her children and herself. Croco say goodbye to Lily-Butterfly before he went on his two weeks business trip.

32

Monday arrived. The first day of Lily-Butterfly's new part time and short-term job. She enjoyed the exercise and adventure of getting to view a new State and Town, changing trains three times, going up and down steps to get on the trains, going on the bus, crossing the George Washington Bridge, meeting and seeing different people, walking almost one and a half mile to Mrs. Charm's house, and working with Mrs. Charm and her children. This new job experience helped Lily-Butterfly expand her views and awareness of people, places, and things. Lily-Butterfly over seven weeks got used to her traveling back and forth to work in New Jersey.

Lily-Butterfly often talked to Holly. They were together all the time. Within Lily-Butterfly's cradle of life and womb, Holly listened to her mother talk and sing her the song she had created for her. Sometimes Lily-Butterfly told Holly that from all the exercise she would be strong, slender, and athletic. Daily Lily-Butterfly got home from work by 5:45 PM. She got Rebornstar from the after school program, after setting up dinner. When she returned from the school, she would cook the dinner. At the end of each day Lily-Butterfly was very tired. Before going to sleep she would shower, write in her journal, process her day, pray, and meditate. Meditation and focusing on her breathing would help her to drift away into sleep and dream land. Lily-Butterfly was asleep by 10:00 PM every night, so that she could be up by 5:30 AM, the latest 6:00 AM.

If Croco telephoned Lily-Butterfly after 9:30 PM she did not answer the telephone. After the robbery incident, Croco's mean treatment towards her, and the security guard and Mrs. Beech warnings, Lily-Butterfly did not go back to Croco's house. Sometimes she invited Croco to her house. It was Croco's choice to accept the invitation or not. Croco did not like to go to Lily-Butterfly's house. To him this was an inconvenience and another rejection of his perceived wonderful and luxurious home. Plus, he was annoyed about Lily-Butterfly spiritual expressions and wise talk. Croco was outside of his element at Lily-Butterfly's home environment. Lily-Butterfly refusing to go to Croco's house put more space between them, and Croco complained about this. Lily-Butterfly ignored Croco's complaints and saw them as his way to get more control over her and her life. Lily-Butterfly was not intimidated with Croco's ignorant attitude, negative emotional expressions, and complaints. He even started to threaten her that if she did not listen to him, he was not going to help her financially with the baby food, shelter, and clothing. To Lily-Butterfly this behavior proved more and more to her that living with Croco was not a positive choice for her. Lily-Butterfly desires to move to New Jersey grew. This desire even played out in her day and sleep dream.

One day Lily-Butterfly asked Mrs. Charm for a New Jersey telephone directory. Mrs. Charm gave her a New Jersey telephone directory she could keep and take home. Lily-Butterfly looked through the telephone directory yellow pages and maps. Lily-Butterfly wrote an action plan in her journal to move to New Jersey. Before going to sleep that night Lily-Butterfly prayed.

"Dear Creator I feel that I should move to New Jersey. How is the plan I have created going to work out? I am not sure. Being a single parent with two children will not be easy. I will have to, as usual, figure out my way as I go along. Please continue to help me with everything. I know that I have to choose, ask for help, take action, take responsibility for the things I choose, and practice, to create what I desire. The inner call to move to New Jersey is getting louder and louder. Moving to New Jersey will take miracles and every inner talent I have to make this a reality. Currently, I can see for sure that my life's purpose destiny is in service to you. Show me the way how to use my inner talents in service of assisting you with humanity. Let thy will be done in my life, as my chosen destiny wills it. Amin," said Lily-Butterfly.

Eight weeks had gone by since Lily-Butterfly started to work at Mrs. Charm. She took care of both children and light housekeeping like a mother and manager. The baby was no longer colic and restless, and she slept through the night. Mrs. Charm postpartum depression had improved tremendously, and she still visited a Psychologist for her personal issues. The house was more organized and there was improved harmony and peace within Mrs. Charm, her children, her husband, and her home environment. With Mrs. Charm mental, emotional, well-being, and health improvements, she took her son out for enrichment learning programs until lunch time.

At thirty weeks pregnant, Lily-Butterfly packed her bag for the hospital. She asked Mrs. Beech to provide childcare services for Rebornstar when she goes to the hospital until she came home. Rebornstar would go live at Mrs. Beech's home until Lily-Butterfly came home from the hospital. When it was time to go to the hospital Lily-Butterfly would take Rebornstar to Mrs. Beech's house. Mrs. Beech agreed to provide childcare services for Rebornstar and told Lily-Butterfly the daily cost. Next, Lily-Butterfly told Rebornstar about her going to live with Mrs. Beech when she was at the hospital to have the baby.

"Rebornstar mama will go to the hospital within the next eight weeks to have your sister Holly. You will stay with Mrs. Beech until I return. I think that we will be moving by the time Holly is six months old. We will be moving to the State next to New York next year January 1990. The name of the place is New Jersey, the garden state. The next big news is I have promised Manana Leila that I will have Ms. Gina, Henry, and Dean come to live with us for one year or less when they move to the United States. We will all be living in a small apartment. Get yourself used to this idea. This is a very courageous, kind, and generous offer that I choose to do to help Manana, Ms. Gina, and her sons. I have a sense that this experience will not be easy. But I think I can manage the situations as they arise. It would take me my current life time, to tell you how good Manana has been to me from birth. This story is a very long one my child. To me Manana and I story is un-speakable. I have to help, and I choose to help them. With the Creator's continued help and assistance, we will be fine."

"Okay mama. I understand. If you are fine mama, then we will be fine. No worries. Things will work out. You always seem to make things work out in a positive way. Please give me some money to buy some books at the school's book fair tomorrow."

"Okay I will. Thank you for being my company, student, and teacher over the past ten years."

"Thank you too mama."

"You are welcome my child."

When dinner was completed Rebornstar and Lily-Butterfly cleaned up the kitchen and dining room.

Before going to sleep Lily-Butterfly took a large piece of white construction paper and created a collage of her plans to move to New Jersey in January of 1990. Some of her plans on the collage was to look for another childcare job when Holly was three months old. Ask Mrs. Beech to provide childcare services for Holly and Rebornstar until she moved. Look in the New Jersey newspaper for childcare jobs. Ask the Childcare Employment Agency for a job. Decide what town to move to in New Jersey. Look in New Jersey newspaper for an apartment. Pray for help with everything she needed to accomplish. Find a childcare job that will accommodate the salary needed to pay the bills. Find a compassionate landlord who will choose to rent her an apartment with the salary she will be making. Find a childcare employer who is open for her to bring Holly with her to work if necessary.

Some of her thoughts after she did the collage were, good humans always show up to help me when I need help and assistance. I hope Croco's karma is paid by the time I am ready to move. I do not think that I want to be around Croco anymore. Croco is getting more and more irritable, because I am not going to his house anymore. My greatest wish is that I can work and live in the same town. This would be easy for me, because I do not have a driver's license and car. I hope that Croco does not become physically violent with me. I need to go to sleep. It is pass my bed time. I have to get up early to get to work on time. Creator all the things I have put on my collage and all my thoughts, are my prayers for tonight. If the direction of moving to New Jersey is the right path, please help me to effortlessly manifest everything I choose, want, and need for this desire and dream. Amin. Lily-Butterfly folded the collage to the size of her pillow and place the folded collage paper under her pillow. Saturday morning, she plan to telephone Manana Leila to give her an update on her current life's plan situations.

Going into the eight month of Lily-Butterfly's pregnancy she moved a little slower and she was more tired at the end of the day. She was not sick during the pregnancy and the baby felt firmly rooted within her. Croco telephoned Lily-Butterfly and asked her to go to dinner with him at a restaurant on a Saturday evening. She chose to go. Lily-Butterfly wanted to listen to the Creator about Croco karma. She also wanted to also listen to how she felt. She often wondered if the Croco karma had been repaid. She felt it was, but was not sure. At this Saturday night dinner, Croco threatened Lily-Butterfly that if she did not move to his home, he would not be giving her money to help pay her rent, utilities, and other expenses during the time she could not work after having the baby. He told her that all her problems would be solved when she moved into his house and marry him.

Lily-Butterfly did not agree with the things Croco told her. During the dinner she had heard enough and felt stressed. She got up, said good night to Croco, and walked out of the restaurant. From the restaurant she walked to Mrs. Beech's home to get Rebornstar. The restaurant was on the same road Mrs. Beech lived on. Lily-Butterfly got home and prepared Rebornstar and herself for bed.

"Every time Croco presents his wonderful plans in having me move into his house and getting married, I feel doomed and trapped. The thought of having to experience his mother Ms. Gene was another stressful view. Croco tries to make me look crazy for refusing all his offers. Maybe I am crazy. But the proof is in the situation, how I feel, and my perceived experiences with Croco. All my life I have been listening to my instincts and inner voice, so far this has never been wrong. Another child without a father being around is an important awareness. But living in violence, suffering, abuse, and damaging my health and the children is not an option. Maybe a personal intimate relationship is not meant to be a priority for me at this time. Maybe currently relationships are only meant to be karma bridges for me to cross to get where I am supposed to be going. Whatever will be, will be. I am not going to choose pride, fall down in a black hole that keeps me stuck, and I cannot get out. I choose to follow the path of the purpose I was born in this bewildering planet, in this so-called modern time of fear. Holly is an interesting spirit and soul growing inside me. This baby seems like an extra energy battery amplifying all my spirit's energy and soul. I am sharper and clearer since I became pregnant. Croco's karma repayment had better be confirmed soon. If Croco thinks I am getting weaker, because I am pregnant; he is wrong. Dear Creator know that whatever I am saying to myself I am saying to you as well. Creator all this talking, thinking, and contemplation tonight is my prayer. I know that you know everything already, but I am still choosing to talk to you about everything. Creator you are my everything. You are the very best Creator I have to talk to on this mysterious and complex human life's journey. Thank you for my Manana, she is priceless. Thank you for my children and all the humans I have met so far. As usual I thank you for everything. It is time for me to go to sleep to face what is instore for me when the sun rises again tomorrow. Amin," whispered Lily-Butterfly.

After this long contemplation, thinking, awareness, in prayer Lily-Butterfly went to sleep.

Everything at Mrs. Charm home continued to improve. The baby was now almost six months old. At the start of Lily-Butterfly's ninth months of pregnancy her belly started to drop down low, like it should. This made it more difficult to move with her usual speed. She felt more tired and sleepy, even with her best intentions to function as usual. One morning the second Tuesday into July Lily-Butterfly fell asleep on the bus, on her way to work. This was her ninth month of pregnancy, when nature usually takes it normal course of action. Lily-Butterfly was on the bus sleeping when it got to the main bus terminal at the end of the route. The bus driver woke her up. Lily-Butterfly took the same bus back to her stop and got off to go to work. This was the first morning she was late for work. When she arrived at work, she was ninety minutes late. Lily-Butterfly rang the doorbell. Mrs. Charm came to open the door.

"I am sorry. I fell asleep on the bus. When the bus got to the station the bus driver woke me up. Here I am, sorry."

"Oh wow. I thought you went to have the baby. You had told me any morning you do not show up this is what has happened. Do you want to stop? Make this Friday your last day. Ha. You look like you are going to have the baby very soon. Really. You can stop. You do not have to keep the commitment you made."

"Commitment is important to me, as well as my health and well-being. If I feel that I should stop I will. Know this. I will not choose to put myself in harm's way. The money I get paid helps my children and myself. When I feel like it is time to stop I will. I think I have two more weeks left working here. I fell asleep just this one time and this is my first time being late; but I still feel bad. Sorry. I know myself. I am going to have this baby in the hospital. Not on the train, bus, and so forth. This baby is wise. She is going to come at the right time and in the right place. You have my address and phone number. You can telephone me and mail me my last pay check, if I leave before you give it to me."

"All right Lily-Butterfly. Thank you for everything. You have helped me, and my children, home, and family. You have helped us more than you can ever imagine. I really appreciate all your care and love. Your spirit and personality is like mother-nature. Thanks. Really."

"You are welcome Mrs. Charm. It is my pleasure. We both helped each other. I really appreciate very much you hiring me being pregnant and living so far away. Thank you for giving me this opportunity and trusting me. Many blessings to you and your family. Based on karma both our prayers helped each other. None of our actions are more important than the other. This is why it is important to me to honor my original commitment as to how long I stay here. Some things are priceless even when they might seem simple. Your payment in exchange for my work is going to help me move, and relocate my children and myself out of New York. I am planning to move to New Jersey. With the Creator's help I will be fine. When I pray the Creator helps me. I have to take action for the prayer to work completely. Being pregnant or not, my life has to go on constructively. Coming to help you and work for you is worth every energy and effort. I am on a sacred and so far, unknown, destiny life purpose mission. When I leave continue to love and take care of yourself and the children. I will be leaving soon, but not today. Maybe in two weeks the baby will come. At this moment I am giving you two weeks to prepare for me to leave. At the end of the next two weeks my original commitment is complete. Thanks again for this opportunity. Okay?"

"Okay I will prepare myself and the children. Lily-Butterfly you are very spiritual, inspirational, and have an optimistic attitude."

"I try my best to do the right thing and be positive. I will do everything to protect myself and my children if I have to, as well. Sometimes niceness does not work for some people and some things. Most people see simplicity, humility, and niceness as stupidity. In my case if this happens, I usually let people know that I am not stupid. All energies can be useful. Anyway, let me go get some work done."

"Okay Lily-Butterfly. You are interesting. Thank you for everything."

From the day Lily-Butterfly fell asleep on the bus unbeknownst to her she had started the journey of having the baby. Baby Holly mindfully and smoothly was on her journey of birth. She did not give her mother one second of pain or discomfort, at least not until the night of her birth. Lily-Butterfly felt slow, calm, and sleepy. But she made sure that she did not fall asleep on the train or bus. On the last Friday of the two week notice Lily-Butterfly acknowledged to Mrs. Charm that she was in the early stages of giving birth. There was a lot of pressure on her pelvis.

"Mrs. Charm I feel like I am ready to give birth soon. Today is my last day. I am ready. Thank you for everything. It was nice meeting you. You are a great spirit, compassionate, and kind. Maybe we will meet again. We have served each other well. Good bye."

"Oh my. Lily-Butterfly will you be okay? Will you make it home safe? Do you want to take a taxi home?"

"No. Thank you. I think I will make it home okay. By Sunday night early Monday morning Holly will complete her journey out of my womb. We will be fine. No worries. I feel content and at peace."

"How do you know all of this for sure?"

"I have clear instincts, perception, and intuition. So far, all my life all of this has proven itself to be correct. So, I trust my faith and internal spirit's guidance. Do you understand? I am going to go. The bus is coming soon. Okay. Good bye Mrs. Charm."

"I think I understand. Here is your check for this week. I gave you an extra $1,000 as a bonus. Your work and being here was priceless. Thank you very much for everything. Many blessings to you, your children, and your birth journey. Okay. Bye."

"Oh wow. Thank you very much for the extra money. Money is always a great resource."

"You are more than welcome. I wish you a safe journey home. All the best with your dreams and everything else in your life. May all the good that you do multiply and be returned to you. Go, I do not want you to miss the bus. Bye."

"Good bye Mrs. Charm. Take care of yourself and the children. Thank you for all your good wishes. I will be fine. Do not worry. The Creator is always checking in on me. Bye."

Lily-Butterfly left Mrs. Charm home. The bus came in ten minutes. When she arrived at a restaurant close to her home, she bought some food for her and Rebornstar. Inside the restaurant a man told her that she looked like she was about to give birth. She agreed with him. Lily-Butterfly was not having pain, only lots of pressure on her pelvis. After the restaurant she went to Rebornstar's school to get her from after school program. She telephoned Mrs. Beech to tell her about her giving birth situation. Rebornstar and Lily-Butterfly enjoyed dinner. Lily-Butterfly told Rebornstar that she was going to have the baby within the next three days. Lily-Butterfly helped Rebornstar to pack her bags to go stay at Mrs. Beech's home until she returned from the hospital. Lily-Butterfly's labor progressed smoothly and painlessly. On Sunday evening after Rebornstar and Lily-Butterfly had dinner she took Rebornstar to Mrs. Beech's home. Previously Mrs. Beech and Lily-Butterfly had gone over the birth plan regarding Rebornstar staying with her until she returned from the hospital. Lily-Butterfly was not in a talkative mood. She had turned within herself and the cocoon of the birthing experiences and conserving energy. When Lily-Butterfly returned home she put her hospital bag by the front door of her home.

Lily-Butterfly telephoned Croco. He answered the telephone.

"Hi Croco. It is time for me to give birth to the baby. I think that I am in the last stage of the birth journey. But I am going to wait until the sack of fluid break before I go to the hospital."

"Oh. Hi. Wow. I will come and take you to the hospital. The time for having the baby came so silent and quick. You have not complained about anything about your pregnancy journey so I was not even aware that the time went by so quick. You seem so peaceful and calm."

"I could take the taxi to the hospital. If you come, I would like to not be irritated by the crap that you talk about. I know that I am responsible for my own perception and feeling of annoyance, but still I do not need these vibes. Please do not say anything about engagement, hospital bill, marriage, and moving into your house, or any of your usual idea and complaint to control me. Just stay as quiet as possible. Or I would rather take the taxi."

"I will be there by 11:00 PM. Call me if you need to go to the hospital before I arrive there. I will try to be quiet and on my best behavior."

"Okay thank you. I am going to lay down now. I will see you later."

At 11:00 PM Croco came to Lily-Butterfly's home. He rang the doorbell. Lily-Butterfly got up and unlock the door. Croco came inside.

"Hi beautiful."

"Stop. My name is not beautiful. Do not talk. Lay on the couch, watch television, or do whatever you like. I am going back to lay in my bed. When it is time to go to the hospital, I will let you know."

"Okay. No worries. You seem calm for a woman that is about to give birth. Anyway, let me shut up. Let me know when you are ready to go."

"Okay. Thank you. Calm and peace are energies of positive vibrations. This is the energy I currently need."

"Okay. It is 11:35 PM now."

Lily-Butterfly went back to lay down in her bed. She fell asleep.

33

Monday morning July 31, 1989 at 1:26 AM, Lily-Butterfly woke up. She felt like she needed to pee. She sat up and slowly stood up to go use the rest room. She could hardly move her legs, because there was so much pressure and slight pain. As soon as she stood up a very warm liquid ran down her legs and on to the floor. Lily-Butterfly used the rest room to pee, changed her under wear, put on a sanitary feminine pad, wiped the amniotic fluid from the floor, changed her night gown, and put on a robe. The pain was currently getting worse with breaks in between. When all of this was done, she picked up her pocket book and turned off all the lights except for the lamp in the living room. She woke up Croco.

"I am ready to go to the hospital. The amniotic sack of fluid broke and now I am having increased pain."

"I am coming. Let me wash my face and put on my shoes."

Lily-Butterfly did not reply. She picked up her suitcase and went outside. She stood on the steps outside. Croco came outside. Lily-Butterfly locked the front door. They walked to the car. Croco took the suitcase and put on the backseat of the car.

Croco and Lily-Butterfly arrived at the hospital emergency room. It was 2:10 AM. Lily-Butterfly filled out the admittance forms. She was admitted into the hospital. The Midwife examined her. She was eight centimeters dilated. The process was good to go and almost over. An IV with saline solution was connected to Lily-Butterfly's left arm. She was taken to the delivery room. Croco stayed at the Midwife's Reception area to give the forms in and wait for the forms to be processed. During all the experiences of birth journey, admittance, examination, IV process, and being transported to the delivery room Lily-Butterfly was calm. When there was pain, she breathed. Lily-Butterfly was also observing internally what the baby was doing.

"This baby's birthing style is interesting. It is as if the baby is meticulously and mindfully charting its course of birth. She is swimming, pushing, and like a drill and well-oiled machine making a smooth entrance. Oh wow. I have hardly any pain and when there is pain it is bearable. This is the complete opposite experience from giving birth to Rebornstar. Thanks be to everything for this. I can feel everything the baby is doing and being. I can also hear her crying like a chant. A baby cannot cry until it is born. How does she do this? Anyway, I have enough to handle so I am so grateful for this positive energy birthing situation," whispered Lily-Butterfly.

The Midwife arrived at the birthing room with Lily-Butterfly. There were three other Midwives and the senior Midwife waiting in the room. The bed with Lily-Butterfly was arranged in the room amongst all the medical equipment. Lily-Butterfly looked at everyone. She liked the positive vibes of everyone in the room. The Midwives talked to Lily-Butterfly and gave her instructions. She followed the instructions and went back to her breathing. Occasionally she looked at each person in the room. The pain was moving quickly without a break.

"This is the strongest pain so far. Holly we are almost at the end of this birth journey. I think Holly is working on getting her shoulders out," whispered Lily-Butterfly.

No one heard Lily-Butterfly's whisper except for Holly.

Quietly Lily-Butterfly processed the pain and sang to Holly.

"Blessed Holly my complete bridge to help me cross the waters of my past life. Welcome to mama's life. We will discover our chosen life purpose destiny, moving forward into the unknown. Mana help you. You help mama. Moving forward into the unknown, we go. Forward into the unknown we go, with love, peace, and understanding. Forward we go with, love, peace, and understanding. Forward we go. Forward we go. Forward we go. Keep coming forward to mama. You are almost here. Almost here in mama's arms. In mama's arms. In mama's arms. Amin," sang Lily-Butterfly.

Lily-Butterfly kept repeating the song. She could feel Holly's swimming out into the un-known human life and into the room, and hear her crying power chant. It was like a miraculous experience to Lily-Butterfly. Lily-Butterfly seemed to be the only one that could hear Holly crying from inside her. Unbeknownst to Lily-Butterfly she had another great surprise coming in five minutes. The pain was now at an unbearable level. Lily-Butterfly breathed in-between grunts. She looked around the room and she saw two angels of birth one on each side of her. They were standing behind the Midwives.

"Almost there. Do not push. The head and shoulders are out," said the Senior Midwife.

The Senior Midwife and another Midwife each held one of Lily-Butterfly's foot. Each foot was trembling. Holly paused her crying. She was regrouping. The pain paused. Holly rested her chin on her neck. She prepared for the last big push by activating her legs and trapped arms.

Lily-Butterfly sang internally to Holly. *"Blessed, Holly my complete bridge to help me cross the waters of my past life, welcome to mama's life. We will discover our chosen life purpose destiny, moving forward into the unknown. Mama help you. You help mana. Moving forward into the unknown, we go. Forward into the unknown we go, with love, peace, and understanding. Forward we go with, love, peace, and understanding. Forward we go. Forward we go. Forward we go. Keep coming forward to mama. You are almost here. Almost here in mana's arms. In mama's arms. In mama's arms. I wonder what you look like. Amin."*

As soon as Lily-Butterfly said Amin at the end of the song the Midwife said, "push. Push. Take a deep breath and push as hard as possible. Again. Push. Take deep breaths. One last push. Good."

Holly also was moving her legs and arms helping with the push. Holly was crying all the way. Holly gave a very loud cry when the Senior Mid-wife held her up in the air for Lily-Butterfly to see her.

"It is a girl. Born on Monday July 31, 1989 at 3:33 AM. Congratulations Lily-Butterfly," announced the Senior Midwife.

In-between crying Lily-Butterfly said, "thank you Creator. Thank you everyone."

The Midwives looked at one another and at Holly. Lily-Butterfly had stopped crying and was looking at Holly as well. Holly was bright yellow. She looked like a human sun. Holly did not have one single hair on her head. She had long legs and arms. And most remarkable observation for Lily-Butterfly was that Holly had a blue map on the upper left side of her head close to her crown. When Lily-Butterfly saw this, she closed her eyes and reflected on the dream she had when she had gone to New York City for the job interview. The golden cloak oracle dream weaver's dream. See the complete dream below from chapter twelve of this story.

During Lily-Butterfly's nap she had a lucid dream. In the dream she was dressed in a mother and father nature brown cloak with a hood attached. The hood was up and over her head. Lily-Butterfly was walking on a path up ahead the one path divided into three paths before her. At the point where the path divided into three paths there was five feet high and four feet wide bolder. At the bolder a man appeared. He was dressed in a long golden robe. He told Lily-Butterfly to choose one of the paths. She looked at the left, center, and right pathways. She chose the center path. The man told her good choice. This is the most advance and difficult path. The center path is made up of the left and right path combined. In addition, the man told her, since you chose the center path, your quest is to master all three pathways, and at the same time, do not get stuck in any. This center path practice is to create and master a complete authentic neutral path. Lily-Butterfly continued to stand in silence and the man continued to speak. There are two paths to the dimension of spiritual awakening and growth. A mountain path that leads up and a low-level earth-bound path. In these modern times they are called the pathways of love and fear. To master love, you must master fear as well. To master fear, you do not have to master love. So, the path of fear which most people choose can be an easier path. Choosing the left path would take you up to the path of love. Choosing the right path would lead you down to the path of fear. Choosing the center path, you will be weaving both pathways together as one as you walk this path, like the sacred creative law of tantra, weaving, unweaving, reweaving, repeatedly, and so forth. The path of love creates light and the path of fear creates darkness. The path of love will be alchemizing the path of fear as you walk, weave, unweave, and reweave all pathways. This will be difficult for you. You will experience both positive and negative experiences. All energies and experiences can be useful depending on your intention and perception. Your most difficult quest is to not get stuck in either as you journey to awaken, develop, and practice your talents. Your chosen destiny, and life purpose practice will need the skills that you will un-knowingly create.

The dream continued. The oracle in the dream asked Lily-Butterfly, "are you sure that you want to choose the center path?" She told the golden cloak man, "yes." He replied, "know and let it be recorded that you chose this path. This was what you also choose before birth. This is the reason why your life's experiences are as it is so far. Good you have not changed your mind. You can un-choose this path at any time. Know that no matter what happens this is the way of the path. Stay awake, stay connected to the upper realms, and stay grounded in the lower earth realms. Which means the light is light and the shadow is light. Be of both and do not get stuck in either. This is the sacred awareness of what authentic balance means. Stay awake and stay aware. This path you have chosen will not be an *easy one. Call and pray 'help' whenever you need to. Lily-Butterfly thought, this is a sacred spirit guide oracle and angel.*

The golden cloak oracle continued to speak. Whenever fear filled negative energy experiences comes into your life, choose to create what you feel is right from the experience. In doing this you will unblock and clear your path. From doing this the way will consistently reveal itself to you. The pathway will show you the way. This path will help you to awaken the gates you need to transition through and awaken your talents. When you are ready, your chosen life's purpose will reveal itself to you, in the form of a prayer master and a way maker. You will decide what human perceptive tools to use to express your talents. "Do you understand?" said the golden cloak oracle. "Yes," replied Lily-Butterfly. "Okay. Let us proceed to walk together," said the golden cloak oracle.

The golden cloak oracle continued to talk as they walked. "Listen and hear. Soon one of your spirit soul sisters, and guardian angels will show up to help you, and accompany you on your journey. You will know her when she arrives. When she arrives from the sacred unknown her head will be totally bald. She will not have one single hair on her head. The only thing she will have on her scalp is a blue mark in the shape of a small map. A map that she must follow to return home to the sacred unknown realm that she came from. Help her to follow this map as she accompanies you on your journey. This blue map will be on the upper left side of her head close to her crown. Remember that she will help you and you help her. Take care of each other until this is no longer necessary. Do you understand? "Yes, I understand? Where is she coming from?" replied Lily-Butterfly. "You will see when the time comes. You will surely see." replied the golden cloak oracle. He continued, "do not let the form of your female embodiment limit your way and your views. Be and keep on being who you are meant to be."

They arrived at a river filled with green water. "Come, Lily-Butterfly, kneel down. Use both hands to drink from this river. This is the river of life, like the tree of life. After drinking step into the river. Refresh yourself. Hold your breath, lay down on your back, and sink down under the water until it covers your entire body and face. Count to nine and then bring yourself above the water. Swim to the other side of this river and get out of the water. Walk forward without looking back. Keep walking. Trust. You are never alone. Your next guardian angel will join you and will be with you until it is time to change again. I will disappear at some point. When you do not hear my voice, I am gone. Do not look back. Continue to take care of yourself, because you cannot give what you do not have. Continue to follow your inner guidance and the Creator's will, they are one and the same. Keep walking until you walk out of this dream. When you do not hear me, I am gone. Remember do not look back." This was the last words of the golden cloak oracle.

"Thank you very much oh great golden cloak oracle angel. Bye for now," said Lily-Butterfly.

Lily-Butterfly heard and listened to the mysterious guidance of the golden cloak oracle angel.

Back to the delivery room at the hospital, on Monday July 31, 1989. In about five minutes one of the Midwife wrapped up Holly in a cloth blanket and gave her to Lily-Butterfly to breast feed. Holly looked up at her mother with eyes opened wide and stared at her face.

"It is me, your mama. We have been together for nine months already. Welcome spirit and soul sister Holly. Thank you for coming," whispered Lily-Butterfly.

"What is the baby's name?" said one of the Midwife.

"Holly," replied Lily-Butterfly.

"Great. We are going to take Holly and wash her off, give her the required immunization shots, and check if she has jaundice, because she is very yellow," said the Midwife.

The Midwife took Holly and gave her a bath in a sink in the room. The Midwife did everything they needed to do in the same room. They dressed Holly and returned her to her mother. Lily-Butterfly breast fed Holly. She was quiet the whole time. She looked at her mother with her bright eyes wide open. The Midwife informed Lily-Butterfly that Holly did not have jaundice and she was in complete health. By now the other Midwives had cleaned up Lily-Butterfly and she was dressed in a clean hospital gown.

The Midwives continue to prepare Lily-Butterfly charts and everything to transport her and the baby to a room.

"Welcome Holly. Welcome my new student and teacher. You have come a long way. We will help each other. In a dream the golden cloak oracle told me someone like you would show up. I was waiting for you without knowing how, when, and where you would show up. You were growing inside me all along. The Croco karma was repaid on the day I conceived you. A life for a life. Equal exchange. Today I am very sure that the Croco karma is completely repaid. The Creator sure works in mysterious ways. Thank you, Creator, spirit guides, guardian angel, and birthing angels. Thanks again to all these wonderful Midwives," whispered Lily-Butterfly.

After saying this affirmation there was a knock on the door. It was Croco. They let him in. Croco came over and looked at Lily-Butterfly and Holly. All the Midwives left the room to carry on with their work. One went to locate the room that they were going to transport Lily-Butterfly to.

"What is her name?" asked Croco.

"Holly," replied Lily-Butterfly.

"Holly? Holly like the holly tree?"

"Yes."

"Why did you choose this name?"

"She came with her name. You would not understand. Okay. Please. No nonsense talk. I am tired."

"Ha. Good the baby is born. This was quick. She looks like me," said Croco.

"She looks like herself. Thank you for providing the egg to create her. Our karma cross roads together is complete. Thanks be to the Creator. In another life time I saved your life. To repay me for saving your life in that life time you provided the seed to assist with the creation of this baby. Thank you. Our karma together is complete. We are now free to move on with what is next in our lives. Amin. Thank you very much," announced Lily-Butterfly.

"What are you talking about? Are you okay? You are the one that is always talking crazy. Maybe giving birth has made you crazier with your mumbo-jumbo spiritual talk. Ha."

"Whatever you say Croco. You do not understand. I am very okay. Anyway. Thank you for helping with the creation of Holly."

"Lily-Butterfly giving birth can be a very traumatic experience. After and during birth, women can say strange things. Anyway, can I hold Holly?"

"When she is finish feeding."

The Senior Midwife had returned to the room when Croco was talking about women and what they say.

"Mister. Can you please leave the room? You can see Lily-Butterfly after she is transported to the room that she will be staying in. Thank you very much," said the Senior Midwife.

Croco looked at the Midwife and was about to say something to her. Lily-Butterfly intervened.

"Go Mr. Croco. I will see you outside. When I am taken to the room come with me. Thank you," said Lily-Butterfly.

Croco left the room. The Senior Midwife removed the blanket from Holly's head and put on a hat.

"Holly sounds like Holey. A great name. This name is on her chart and every relevant thing in the hospital nursery. You can take Holly with you to your room. A nurse will come to get her later to take to the nursery. Can we give Holly bottle formula?"

"Yes. I also want to breast feed her."

"Okay. This way you can get some rest as well. During the night 10:00 PM to 7:00 AM Holly will stay in the nursery. We will feed her if she wakes up during the night. Holly will be brought to you at about 8:00 AM. You can keep her with you in the bassinet by your bed. Never fall asleep with Holly on the bed. You and the baby do not need any medicine or medical procedure. You will go home in two days. Wednesday August 2nd by 6:00 PM you will be discharged from the hospital," said the Senior Midwife.

"Okay. Thank you."

"You are welcome. You had a problem free labor and delivery. Well done. Continue to take care of yourself. Two Midwives will come to take you and the baby to your room. Please let us know if you need anything."

"Okay. Usually I am concerned about my baby being mis-placed in the hospital nursery. I will know if I get the right baby each time, she comes from the nursery by seeing the blue mark on the top left side of her head. Plus, everything else about her stands out as radiant and unusual."

"Oh, yes. You need not be worried about getting the wrong baby. Holly has a distinct physical appearance. She has a special birth mark on her head, no hair, long arms and legs, a bright yellow color, and glowing complexion. Holly is unique. May God bless her. Amin."

"Amin and thanks again for everything. Have a great day. Bye."

"Bye Lily-Butterfly."

The Senior Midwife left the room. Two Midwives came, prepared Lily-Butterfly and Holly to go to a private room, and brought her to the room she was going to stay in. Croco was waiting outside the delivery room. He came along with Lily-Butterfly and Holly to the room. After the Midwives set up Lily-Butterfly and Holly in the room they left.

"Thank you for my baby girl," said Croco. "She looks like me. She has my long arms, body, and legs. Hahaha."

"Stop. Do you have a bald head and blue birth mark? Holly has her own appearance, spirit, mind, and body. Let her looks be her looks. Yes, you both have long arms and legs. Please calm down your vibes," said Lily-Butterfly.

"Can I hold her?" asked Croco.

"Yes. Not for too long, because she needs to relax and acclimate to this environment, and being born," replied Lily-Butterfly.

"Okay I will not be here for long. I am leaving after I hold her. I have to go. It is 7:30 AM. I am tired. I want to go home, take a nap, eat, and shower, before I go to work. I am so tired," said Croco.

"Seriously. Tired? All you did was sit and wait. How about the baby and I who did all the work? Do you think that we are tired? Enjoy your material fixation day. I will see you when you choose to visit. Wednesday we are going home. Can you take us home on Wednesday at 6:00 PM? Thank you for everything you did."

"You are welcome. Yes, I will take you home on Wednesday at 6:00 PM. By the way, did you fill out the Medicaid form to get the medical bills paid? Ha. Did you?"

"Yes. Do not worry. All you contributed so far to creating this baby is your sperm. Do not worry about spending your precious money on paying our medical bills. Your money is for your precious material possessions. I have learned that you are conditionally kind and clueless about real love and care. Whatever you choose to contribute to our existence and survival is your choice. Remember this. Bye Mr. Croco."

"Good. See you later beautiful. Now I have two beauties. Bye."

"Whatever. We have ourselves. You never had us and you never will. Bye. I leave everything to your karma."

Croco left the hospital. Lily-Butterfly breast fed Holly. Holly fell asleep. Lily-Butterfly ate her breakfast. The nurse from the hospital nursery came to check in on Lily-Butterfly. The nurse suggested that she could take Holly to the nursery so that Lily-Butterfly could sleep, rest, and recuperate. Lily-Butterfly agreed to send Holly to the nursery. Holly was still sleeping when the nurse took her. After eating breakfast Lily-Butterfly slept until 12:30 PM.

34

Croco returned to the hospital on Tuesday at 12:00 PM. Lily-Butterfly was eating lunch. Holly was in the nursery. Croco brought some flower in a small pink shoe vase.

"Here Lily-Butterfly. Thank you for my daughter," said Croco.

"Thank you for the flowers and the priceless seed that you provided to create Holly."

"What happened? You seem to have a negative attitude."

"I am fine. I did not say anything negative. I really meant the things I said. All I did was say the truth. Maybe you are being defensive because of your conscience. What else? Do you realize that Holly needs medical bills paid, food, shelter, and clothing? Not just your lip service and one small vase of flowers. I am just stating gratitude for what you have really given. I am still tired and need to rest. Bickering is not a positive vibe for recuperating, resting, and healing. I do not think you understand about pregnancy, giving birth, and how a woman can feel after birth. I do not need to feel negative attitudes, more tired, drained, and negative energy. I am not responsible for your moods and you are not responsible for mine."

"What? I did not do anything wrong."

"Me neither. I need to finish eating lunch."

"Let us start this visit again. Here I brought you some flowers."

"Thank you. Please put it on the night stand on the other side of the bed."

Lily-Butterfly returned to eating her lunch. She was silent. Croco sat looking at Lily-Butterfly. After ten minutes he talked.

"Can I see and hold the baby," said Croco.

"Yes, the nurse will bring Holly after I am finish eating lunch."

"What time?"

"By 1:30 PM."

"This is at the time when I plan to leave."

"You can change the time you plan to leave, or do as you planned."

"I am going to the nursery to ask the nurse to bring the baby to the room."

"The nurse is not going to bring Holly, because you tell her. She does not know you. I have already pre-scheduled when to bring Holly and when to come back to get her. Sorry. I did not know when you would be visiting. At 1:30 PM the nurse will bring Holly. Wait or not. Also, you must know that when a woman gives birth they are naturally in a seemingly irritated mood until the birthing energies calm down. Your selfish unawareness and negative emotional energy is not helping my emotional situation."

"Lily-Butterfly are you trying to be spiteful?"

"Ha. No. Only I can go or telephone to request the baby. I am eating. I do not want to talk about this anymore."

"So, there is no respect and right for the father? Ha."

"You see what I mean. As a human I respect you in every way. You are taking what I say personal. Please do not. I am tired. Let me eat in peace. Leave. Come back later."

"I would like to see Holly before I leave."

"Father does not mean sperm contributor. What else have you done other than wanting to see her?"

"When you accept my engagement ring and proposal. Agree to marry me, move into my home, and get a DNA test to prove that Holly is mine; you will receive everything. You can take me to court for child support if you want child support. As long as you keep resisting my proposals, and keep living in your own apartment, you will only have what you have, and what I choose to give you. Understand this. Being stupid, spiritual, and independent will not get you further than you are. At some point you are going to surrender and do as I say and want. Until then you are where you are. This is a man's world. You as woman, do not get to do as you choose, and want. Do you understand me Ms. Lily-Butterfly?"

"Yes, I understand everything very clearly. In your mind you think that you are God because you have money. Let me tell you the Creator is my God and not money or material possessions. You just expressed all the reason why my answer to everything you offer is no and no. I will not do anything you say or propose. Trying to control and manipulate me is useless. The right thing to do without conditions, is contribute money towards health care, food, shelter, and clothing for me and Holly. This is the law."

"Accept my proposals and all of this is included. Except, first get the Medicaid to pay the hospital bills."

"This conversation should not be happening at this time and in the hospital. Leave."

The nurse brought Holly. Croco and Lily-Butterfly remained silent. The nurse placed Holly in the bassinet.

"Lily-Butterfly a nurse will return at 9:00 PM to get Holly. She was just fed. Would you like a bottle of milk at 5:00 PM? You can breast feed her before the nurse comes to get her at 9:00 PM. Do you need help with anything? Tomorrow morning the Doctor and Senior Midwife will visit you at 11:00 AM for a checkup before you are certified to go home. Do you have any questions?"

"Thank you for everything. Yes, bring the milk at 5:00 PM. I am okay. Currently I do not need anything. Thanks."

"Okay. Take care of yourself. Bye."

The nurse left the room. Croco picked up Holly. Holly started to fuss and cry.

"Here put this blanket on your shoulder and in your lap. Please do not kiss Holly on her lips. You can kiss her on her forehead or cheeks. And do not ask me why?"

"Okay mother bear. I do not want to waste money paying for two homes. Move in with me all bills and expenses will be paid."

"You seems so fixated on this engagement, marriage, moving into your house ideas. To me it is as if you feel out of control if I do not do these things. I smell danger. This dangerous energy I sense is not good for the children and my health, well-being, and life. My senses says this and I am going to listen. You are supposed to pay child support whether I do what you say or not. I will not take you to court. I will leave you to karma. I will not apply for welfare government financial support. If you do not give me financial support, I will go to work. You do not get to hold me hostage."

"Ha. With two children and yourself to support how are you going to manage. You would have to pay for childcare for two children and all the other expenses. Do not let your independence block reality."

"I guess that your life's experiences regarding women gives you the views that you have about women. You have not met a real woman before. I understand. I will figure things out. I am tired. I am giving you ten more minutes and then you are leaving. The baby and I need to rest. Are you coming Wednesday at 6:00 PM to take us home? I can take the taxi."

"Yes, I will come. You are strong and tough."

"Good for you that you can see this. This is a part of growing up in a valley and village in the deep jungle of Kawomaya. I am solid and have animal instincts. So far, my instincts are right. I trust myself and I trust you to be exactly whom and what you are. So, do not try to push me around. It is not going to work. Real power is silent and invisible. Be very mindful of not abusing us in any way."

"Or, what? What can you do?"

"I do not personally have to do anything to you. Your karma will take care of you. Be aware. You have been warned."

"We will see," said Croco.

"I guess we will all see. Time will always tell everything."

"I am going to leave now. See you tomorrow at 6:00 PM. Bye."

Croco kissed Holly on her forehead. He put her in the bassinet. He tried to hug Lily-Butterfly. She pushed him away.

"Keep your negative stress energies to yourself. Have a great day within your perfect material world. See you tomorrow."

"Bye Lily-Butterfly. Sweet dreams."

Croco left the room. Lily-Butterfly breast fed Holly and she fell asleep. Lily-Butterfly telephoned Mrs. Beech to tell her about Holly and the birth, that she would be home by 7:00 PM tomorrow, to give Rebornstar dinner, to bring her dinner at 7:30 PM when she brought Rebornstar to her home, and to talk to Rebornstar. After talking to Rebornstar Lily-Butterfly went over the plan with Mrs. Beech to cook dinner for her and Rebornstar for two weeks, take Rebornstar to school and from school, washing her and Rebornstar's laundry, and doing food shopping. Lily-Butterfly asked Mrs. Beech to give her an itemized bill for everything. Mrs. Beech agree to everything Lily-Butterfly asked her to do. Lily-Butterfly would hand wash Holly's clothes in her kitchen sink. Mrs. Beech's priceless help would give Lily-Butterfly the ability to heal, rest, and recuperate for the next two weeks. When both Mrs. Beech and Lily-Butterfly felt confident that they understood everything about the plans for the next two weeks, they hung up the telephone.

Wednesday morning the Gynecologist Doctor and Senior Midwife came to certify Lily-Butterfly and Holly's medical condition for them to leave the hospital. They were approved to check out of the hospital by 6:00 PM Wednesday August 2, 1989. Lily-Butterfly received from the hospital a supply of plant-based milk for Holly, disposable diapers, and other baby supplies. Lily-Butterfly planned to use mostly cloth diapers for Holly and keep the disposable diapers for on a need to use basis. At 5:30 PM Croco arrived to take Holly and Lily-Butterfly home. Croco carried all the bags. Lily-Butterfly carried Holly, they sat in a wheel chair and the nurse pushed the wheel chair to the door of the hospital. Lily-Butterfly got out of the wheel chair carrying Holly, thanked the nurse, and went to sit in the back seat of Croco's Jaguar car. Lily-Butterfly was silent. She was waiting to see what Croco was going to do and say.

Out of the silence Croco said, "beautiful would you like to come over to my house tonight? You can stay with me as long as you like. Chef will do all the grocery shopping and cook for us, there is a house cleaner, and you would not have to do anything except be there and take care of the baby. Oh, and of course Rebornstar can come too. You can have anything you like, wish, and want if you come. All your problems and concerns will be over. Be wise."

"Thank you for asking. No, thank you for your offer. It is easier for me to stay at my home. I already have everything I need there. My home supports the health and well-being of my children and myself. I need to rest and not be stressed. I had already done grocery shopping. I made arrangements with Mrs. Beech to provide all the help I will need for the next two weeks. Would you like to pay half the bill for these services?"

"No. Oh no. I am giving you a free service option of coming to my house and home. You are impossible."

"Nothing is free. I am preventing my children and I from being damaged. I seek and have the most nourishing help and support I need for my continued birth recovery, health, and well-being. After my experience with you and the robbery situation I have decided not to go back to your house. Apart from child support and financial help with Holly I do not need anything from you. I do not feel safe within your seemingly conditional generosity, stress energy, negative attitude, and chevalier charades. Take me to my peaceful, safe, and sacred space home environment. I thank you very much for whatever you offered. I am not interested in accepting any offer to captivate my spirit, soul, mind, emotions, body, health, well-being, and life. Abuse, suffering, and trauma will negatively affect my children as well."

"Come only for tonight and the rest of the week until Sunday. I will have Chef cook for us."

"You are not hearing, listening, and respecting what I have said. No thank you. I have already made plans with Mrs. Beech to help me. I am finished having this conversation. Take me to my home. Thank you for picking us up and taking us home. Keep thing simple and positively balanced. Take us to my home. Croco I keep repeating myself and you are still not listening. This conversation is over. Thanks again."

All right. I tried to help you. Do not say that I never tried to help you. Have it your way."

"Thank you. My children and my health and well-being is the foundation of my wealth and success. I would like to keep it that way."

"Whatever miss independence."

"I am one of the Creator's precious creature and something that you cannot buy. I am priceless. I am not for sale."

"Whatever. I am not giving any financial support for you to live in your home. If you come to my home you will naturally benefit from whatever I have. Know this. Here we are. You have arrived at you precious home."

"Thank you for everything that you did so far. I will be fine no matter what you do. I choose to have this wonderful baby, I carried her for nine months in my body, and I choose to give her a safe passage to be born for her life's purpose. I also choose to do the very best to make sure that she is given the best care and opportunities as a human. Have a great day and life. Amin."

Croco arrived at Lily-Butterfly's home. He stopped the car and brought all the bags to the apartment steps. Lily-Butterfly opened the car door and got out of the car carrying Holly. She closed the car door and walked towards her home. Croco walked pass Lily-Butterfly without saying one word. He got in his car, slam the car door close, and speed off down the street. Lily-Butterfly unlocked the apartment door and brought Holly inside. Lily-Butterfly placed Holly in a bassinet at the side of her bed. She went back outside to bring in all the bags. Lily-Butterfly put away the things in the bags she had brought home, went to lie down in her bed, and closed her eyes. Holly was asleep.

35

At 8:00 PM Mrs. Beech arrived at Lily-Butterfly' home with Rebornstar. Rebornstar had already eaten dinner. Mrs. Beech had brought dinner for Lily-Butterfly. She had eaten the hospital dinner at 5:00 PM before she left the hospital. But she welcomed Mrs. Beech home cooked meal as a welcoming treat.

"Here you go Lily-Butterfly. We cannot wait to see you and your angel Holly," said Mrs. Beech.

Rebornstar and Mrs. Beech ran to Lily-Butterfly's bedroom.

"Oh wow. Mama are you sure you have the right baby. She is so yellow and has no hair," said Rebornstar.

"Holly looks interesting and divine. Very strange, unique, and beautiful. She has thick skin, her mother's shape face, her father's long limbs, her own spirit, soul, and unique appearance. Look she has a special blue birth mark on the left side of her head. She is heavy and looks strong and healthy. Congratulations. Well done," said Mrs. Beech.

"Rebornstar, yes I have the right baby. She looks exactly like how she came out of me. This is our new companion on our life's journey. All three of us will keep journeying forward. This child is the Creator's messenger, student, and teacher. We are all born for a purpose. We will see where all three of us end up. I think that Holly is a spirit and soul sister from the beginning of creation. Anyway, here we are and our life must go on as well as possible."

As Lily-Butterfly talked Rebornstar and Mrs. Beech looked at Holly with curiosity. Holly looked at everyone with seemingly wonderment.

"Very good Ms. Lily-Butterfly now you have two company to take care of, practice unconditional love with, and everything else. So special. I am happy both of you are okay. Stay blessed, healthy, and no heavy work, or lifting. You do not want to hemorrhage or get sick and have to go back to the hospital," said Mrs. Beech.

"I love her mama. She is very cute and beautiful. Now I am a big sister. Oh wow," said Rebornstar.

"Rebornstar her name is Holly, like the holly good luck tree. Your name is Rebornstar like a star that keeps renewing itself. We are all born for a purpose and here we are," said Lily-Butterfly.

"Yes mama. The tree with prickly leaves and red berries," said Rebornstar.

"Do not try to pick up Holly. She is fragile and you have to be very careful. If you want to hold her let me know. You have to sit down and I will put her in your lap. You cannot pick Holly up without my supervision. Okay."

"Okay mama. I will only look at her and touch her. She seems quiet and nice. I love her."

"Yes, Holly is quiet and calm like you were when you were a baby. I have two calm beautiful babies. Rebornstar you were beautiful and unique as well when you were born and also now. You are a good mama helper as well. We will continue to work together as a team, even if it is just listening to mama. Thanks be to the Creator I have no negative complaints about my children. I choose very consciously to have both of you. I feel that it is my responsibility to make sure that I am the best mother and parent possible. I love both of you very much. Okay."

"Yes. Okay mama. Thanks, you are the best mama."

Mrs. Beech was holding Holly. She put Holly back into the bassinet.

"Ms. Lily-Butterfly it is getting late. Do you still want to eat the food I brought or should I put it into the fridge?"

"Please leave the food on the dining table. I will eat it after you leave. Maybe I will leave some for lunch tomorrow. I will eat before I breast feed Holly. Thank you very much. Now I have two children to take care of and myself. Oh my."

"You will do just fine. God does not give more than you can handle. I only have one ten year old son. This is all I could handle. Anyway, we all have what is meant to be," said Mrs. Beech.

"I hear you Mrs. Beech. After Holly I do not think I want to have any more children. Two children is enough for me. My life's purpose is my next focus creation. Anyway, where is my bill? Did you bring it?"

"Yes, here it is $1,310 for everything. This includes taking care of Rebornstar from Sunday night to tonight."

"Okay thank you. Here is $1,676. It includes a tip and all the extra things that you might choose to do and so forth. I really appreciate everything that you do to help me. Your help is priceless to me. We appreciate you. I am meant to meet you. Meeting you is not an accident. Do you understand what I mean?"

"Yes, I understand. Thank you very much for respecting me and my help. I will keep doing my best. You are very considerate and generous. I am leaving I will see you in the morning when I come to take Rebornstar to school. On my way back from taking the children to school I will take all the dirty laundry that you have and wash them. Get the dirty clothes ready in a laundry bag. Okay."

"Okay. Good bye Mrs. Beech. I will see you in the morning. Thanks again."

"You are welcome. Bye."

Mrs. Beech left. Rebornstar sat looking at her sleeping sister. Lily-Butterfly went to eat some of the dinner Mrs. Beech brought.

"Rebornstar take a shower and get ready for bed. Remember that you have school in the morning. It is late."

"Okay mama. I will go now."

After finishing all the things Lily-Butterfly had to do, she went to sleep at midnight. Croco did not telephone that night. Thursday and Friday went by filled with peace and happiness. Croco still did not telephone Lily-Butterfly. On Saturday morning after eating breakfast Lily-Butterfly telephoned Manana Leila to tell her everything about the birth of Holly. Manana was happy to hear Lily-Butterfly's good news about the birth of Holly. Manana told Lily-Butterfly about Ms. Gina's visa process, and that Ms. Gina might be getting her visa in about seven months. Manana also told Lily-Butterfly that she gave Ms. Gina her current telephone number. Lily-Butterfly got from Manana, Ms. Gina's current contact telephone number at her job. Lily-Butterfly informed Manana that she was moving out of New York when Holly was about six months. Lily-Butterfly's conversation with Manana was very uplifting. When Lily-Butterfly got off the telephone she breast fed Holly.

Saturday at 12:00 PM Croco telephoned Lily-Butterfly and she answered the telephone.

"Lily-Butterfly would you like to come to my home with the children? My mother is here and she would like to see Holly."

"No. I would not like to come to your house. I do not want your mother to put her evil eyes on my daughter. I do not want to see your mother. You can come here by yourself to see Holly. Please telephone me first before you come, to let me know that you would like to visit."

"You want to be selfish with Holly? Ha?"

"Call what I say whatever you like. I told you more than once that

I will not be coming back to your house. I have no reason or desire to want to see your mother. Stop harassing me. I must be mindful of my stress. I just had a baby five days ago I have to be mindful of my health, well-being, and stress. Now I have to go. It is lunch time. It is time to feed Holly, Rebornstar, and eat my lunch. Have a nice day. Bye."

"Okay be that way. Bye."

Croco hung up the telephone. Lily-Butterfly and Rebornstar had lunch. After having lunch Lily-Butterfly fed Holly. And they both took a nap. Rebornstar played by herself and watched cartoons on the television.

Sunday morning at 11:16 AM there was a knock at Lily-Butterfly's front door. Rebornstar and Holly were in their mother's bedroom. Lily-Butterfly had left her bedroom to see who was knocking at the door. When she looked out the window, she saw Croco standing at the door. She unlocked the door and opened it. Croco pushed her inside and came inside. He was carrying a large box. He put the box down by the bedroom door.

"Why did it take you so long to open the door?" said Croco.

Lily-Butterfly saw that Croco was in an angry temper tantrum mood. She did not reply to his question, and walked back into her bedroom.

"Hey. Yeah. Lily-Butterfly I am talking to you."

Lily-Butterfly remained silent. Croco grabbed a clothes hanger from the closet. He pushed Lily-Butterfly and hit her repeatedly on different parts of her body. Rebornstar jumped up from where she was sitting and rushed over to Croco and pushed him and tried to grab the hanger away from Croco. Croco pushed Rebornstar very hard and she flew into the opposite corner of the room. Rebornstar peed herself. Lily-Butterfly hurried over to Holly and picked her up. Croco rushed over to Lily-Butterfly and grabbed her by her arm. Holly dropped out of Lily-Butterfly arms and fell on the bed. Holly had a very small scratch on her nose from when Croco grabbed Lily-Butterfly's arm. Croco's finger nail seemed to have grazed Holly's nose. Lily-Butterfly turned simultaneously when Holly fell and picked her up, turn her over, and put her in her bassinet. Rebornstar was crying. Holly was silent.

"STOP! STOP! LEAVE! GET OUT! NOW!" screamed Lily-Butterfly.

Croco stood looking at Lily-Butterfly.

"Leave now. Do not ever come back here. Now you have totally crossed the line of no return. Get out. Go. This is another reason I choose to not accept your engagement proposal, marrying you, and come to live in your house. I was not born to be damaged by any human. Leave. I will not fight with you, your mental health issues, and demons. All your negative demons are disguised under the mask of being handsome, conditionally kind, wealthy, and every material possession. Do not stand there. Go. I will call the police or the neighbor will. I will scream so loud your heart and brain will rattle and become useless. Do not show your face to me ever again and never telephone my home. Stay away. All your negative karma has just been activated. You need mental health help. Go now."

Croco stood speechless looking at Lily-Butterfly, Holly, and Rebornstar.

"Sorry. My temper got the best of me. Sorry beautiful."

"Do not say another word from your lips inside my home. Get out."

Lily-Butterfly walked pass Croco and open her front door as wide as possible.

"Go now. Get out. Go."

Croco walked out. Lily-Butterfly locked the door.

Later on, that evening when Mrs. Beach came to deliver the dinner Lily-Butterfly opened the door and there were a large box on the doorstep. Croco had left it there. It was a baby stroller. Earlier when Croco had first come into Lily-Butterfly's home he had brought inside the other box a crib with a chest of drawers attached. This crib could also be converted into a twin bed. Mrs. Beech brought the box into the apartment and put it in the living room. Lily-Butterfly pulled the box with the crib and left it beside the other box with the stroller.

"Did Croco bring these things? Why he did not assembly them?" asked Mrs. Beech.

"Croco came in to my home with his anger and terrible temper tantrum. He is trying very hard to make me accept his engagement proposal, marriage, and move into his home. Since I told him no, he resorted to physical and emotional abuse. He came here this morning pushed Rebornstar and me, then hit me repeatedly with a clothes hanger, and grabbed my arm while I was holding Holly. Holly flipped out of my arm and onto the bed. I am not open to be abused. Once a person hit me once I know that next time the abuse will be worse. No way am I going to let him or any human damage me. I told Croco to leave and never return here. It is a long story. Anyway, thanks for all your positive help. I leave Croco to his karma and the Creator. So, this is a short version of the Croco dilemma."

"Do you think that he is not going to come back here and telephone you? You wish. People who think they have power do not respect anything. They only care about themselves and what they choose to do. I told you. Lily-Butterfly be careful. Croco is one good example of the saying, 'not all that glitters is gold.' You are wise I know that you will find a way out of this negative Croco situation."

"Mrs. Beech as of today I leave Croco to the manifestation of all his karma and the Creator. Okay. I am not afraid of Croco. Maybe this experience confirms that I should move out of New York. Today this violence from Croco is the icing on the cake. Today is the last time he is going to do what he did to us. Thank you for the dinner. We surely appreciate your dinners and all your other help."

"You are welcome. Live your truth and whatever you think is right for you and your children. I am happy to be of service to you. Good help is very hard to find. Croco does not know any better. He does not understand. He never grew up with anyone showing him real love and care. He also seems to think that more and more money and material things will make him feel loved and secure. But it is obvious that this is not true for him. He thinks that material possession is going to cure his mental health issues and give him love and care. Good for you that you are strong and know better than to accept his trauma, abuse, and negative treatment as normal. Enjoy your dinner, cool down your nerves, relax, and keep praying. Prayer works if you believe in a higher power, Creator, God, and whatever. I will see you tomorrow. Have a good night. Bye. Let me look at Miss. Holly and then I am leaving," said Mrs. Beech.

"Okay Mrs. Beech. Thank you for everything. Good night."

Mrs. Beech looked at Holly and left.

Rebornstar and Lily-Butterfly ate dinner. During dinner Lily-Butterfly talked to Rebornstar about the violent situation with Croco. After eating dinner Lily-Butterfly fed Holly. They continued to process and recover from Croco's violent experiences. At the end of the night Lily-Butterfly's journal helped her to continue processing her day's experiences and her plans to move. The last thing she did before going to sleep is pray.

"Dear Creator as you know it is not easy being human, and you know everything else. I talk to you often because I feel this is a positive action and the right thing to do. I can see that Croco's karma has been repaid to me. Our reason for meeting is over. I am choosing this Croco meeting to be complete. I have learned that there can be collateral damaging situations in the repayment of karma. It is my choice to transcend these situations with Croco without creating negative karma. Currently I am completely ready to go on to what is next in discovering my chosen destiny life's purpose creation. With two children, one in my arms and one walking along beside me, I am ready for what is next for us. Please continue to help me, check in with what is going on with us, and give me insight, instructions, and guidance. Your loyal, faithful, and loving spirit and soul. Thank you for everything," prayed Lily-Butterfly.

36

Holly and her mother continued to get more and more improved with their health and recovery. The next time Croco telephoned Lily-Butterfly Holly was three weeks old. He informed Lily-Butterfly that he was going away for three weeks. She listened to what he said, and did not comment, except to tell him good bye. In conversations with Croco and what Lily-Butterfly repeatedly told him, it felt as if she was listening to a broken record on repetitious repeat. The three weeks Croco was away seems to go by fast. On the third day of returning he telephoned Lily-Butterfly.

"Come over to my house. I would like to talk to you about something," said Croco.

"No. I cannot come I have to take care of Holly, make breakfast for Rebornstar to go to school, and walk her to school. I am busy. You are not hearing and listening to what I am telling you. I do not want to come to your house."

"Did you take some money from my room when I was away travelling?"

"No. How would I get into your house? You have security. I do not have a key to get into your house, and you have a security system with cameras. Why would you think I took your money?"

"I do not know? I have some money missing and I am checking around with the people I know that could have taken it."

"I have to go take care of the children, like I said before. Bye."

Lily-Butterfly hung up the telephone. She did not wait to hear if Croco was saying anything else. When Lily-Butterfly returned from taking Rebornstar to school there was a knock her apartment door. Holly was asleep in her bassinet. Lily-Butterfly went to see who was at the door. It was Croco. She unlocked the door and opened it. Croco pushed the door and rushed inside. He grabbed Lily-Butterfly's blouse and pulled her towards him.

"Where is my money? I put this money in my second chest of drawer before I left. Where is it?"

"I think that you are looking for a reason to be violent with me. Let go my blouse. I have not been to your house since the attempted robbery. Let go my blouse. Leave my home."

"You took the money. My mother told me that she did not take it and you must have been the one that took it. Give it to me."

"I do not want to say and do anything to amplify the negative emotional state you are in. But if you keep pushing me beyond my boundary of coping with your violence, I will do something or something will be done to you. Hear and listen, stop creating negative karma towards me. Stop."

"What are you going to do to me? You cannot and would not hurt not even a fly."

"Leave. Let go my blouse. I have not been to your house. I would not take one penny of your money. I think that you know this already. You are just using negative actions to get attention from me. Stop. I do not have a key to your house. You have a security guard. Outside and inside your home there is security alarm with camera. I do not have the code to turn off the security alarm. I think that you know who really stole your money. You are afraid to confirm who it is. Go home look at your security camera video and you will see who took your money. Your mother has a key to your house. Except for you and your security guard your mother is the only person that knows the security code, and so forth. Go home the evidence of who stole your money is there. Why are you really here? To terrorize me and break me down. This will not happen. Let go my blouse. Leave. I am not afraid of you. Go."

Croco let go Lily-Butterfly's blouse. He stared in her face. She stared back at him.

"We will see who has power. We will see," said Croco.

"You are right. I guess we will wait and see what happens."

Croco pushed Lily-Butterfly and slapped her face. He slapped her on her hand, punched her on her shoulder, and pushed her so hard she fell down. Croco kicked Lily-Butterfly's legs and walked out the door. Lily-Butterfly got up. She went to lay down in her bed and cried.

"Croco's violence towards me is getting worse. I have to get my plans into action. This is my chosen way out of this very negative violent situation," grumbled Lily-Butterfly.

Lily-Butterfly picked up her journal and read the last plan of action that she had written.

The action plan said, "telephone Childcare Agency to get a long-term job. When Holly is three months old, I will go to work. It must be a job where I can take Holly with me. When Holly is six months old, I will move. Find an apartment in New Jersey to move to."

After writing in her journal Lily-Butterfly prayed, "Creator I need help and I am asking for help with this Croco violent situation. I do not want to telephone the police to arrest him, but if he returns again I will. Please keep Croco away from me. His karma is already repaid to me. As you are aware Croco is now creating negative karma with me. My previous karma with Croco is over. I choose to not fight with him. I now choose an effortless path out of Croco's life and out of New York. Thanks again for sending Holly. Now I have to climb this spiritual mountain with two children. Keep assisting me with everything I need to awaken all my talents, manifest my chosen destiny, and life's purpose career. If there is something more, I need to see in this negative violent Croco experience, help me to see whatever this is. Please help me find a job that I can take Holly to work with me. Thank you for everything especially our health and well-being. Amin."

That same night, Croco telephone Lily-Butterfly's home. Lily-Butterfly's phones at that time did not have a caller identification feature. She picked up the phone and answered.

"Hi. May I help you?"

"Hello Lily-Butterfly. I looked at the security camera video. I saw on the camera that my mother went to the draw and took all the money. Before I told her that I saw her on the camera she was insisting that you had taken the money."

Before Croco could say another word Lily-Butterfly hung up the telephone. She did not wait for him to say another word.

The next morning Lily-Butterfly telephoned the Childcare Agency. She requested a childcare job that she could take Holly to work with her. The Director of the Agency told Lily-Butterfly that to find a childcare job that she could take her three months old daughter with her was very rare. The Director ended the conversation by promising to let Lily-Butterfly know when a job opportunity was available. Lily-Butterfly thanked the Director and hung up the telephone. She thought, if this job is meant to be, as rare as the opportunity is, this job will show up. The way will show the way.

Lily-Butterfly continued on with her daily activities. She went for a walk in the park with Holly laying in her baby over the shoulder baby holder, on the front of her chest. Holly lay asleep in the cocoon of her mother's warm love vibrations, and listening to her mother's heartbeat. When Lily-Butterfly arrived at the park she sat at a table to read her book and meditate. Holly was now Lily-Butterfly's constant companion. Holly grew very much, was very active, and alert. At two months old she still did not have one fuzz of hair. Holly looked like a monk or nun with a bald head and a unique blue birth mark on her bald head. In the dream Lily-Butterfly always remembered that the dream oracle told her that the blue mark on Holly's head was a spiritual map. Where was this map going to take Holly? Currently, only the Creator and the map knows the secrets it holds.

This night like all nights Lily-Butterfly completed her daily activities. This included feeding Holly and putting her into her bassinet to sleep. Rebornstar was already asleep. Lily-Butterfly hardly watch television, especially the news. This night she had a guided awareness to watch the news. So, she turned on the television and watched the news.

The man reading the news said, "this evening a man fell off the roof of an eight-floor building in the Bronx. He is in very critical condition and in a coma. As soon as we get further information on this situation, we will give you an update."

The television showed the man lying on a gurney being wheeled to an ambulance.

"It is Croco. Oh wow. I will see if more update news come on before I go to sleep," said Lily-Butterfly.

Before the news program ended there was an update about the man that fell off the eight-floor roof of an apartment building in the Bronx.

The news man said, "from further investigation and identification the man in the Bronx that fell off the roof is Croco. He is still in a coma. He fell while inspecting some work done on the roof of the eight-floor apartment building. It was raining and windy when Mr. Croco was on the roof. A woman passing by the building saw when Mr. Croco fell and ran to the nearest home to called 911. He is in the hospital. More updates will be given as soon as it is received."

Lily-Butterfly felt like telephoning Croco's home, the hospital, and his mother. After pondering about the current and past situation regarding Croco she decided not to telephone anyone. Lily-Butterfly decided that going to sleep was the best thing to do. She wrote in her journal and prayed. In prayer Lily-Butterfly did not say anything to the Creator about Croco's accident. She was still processing the sudden news. After twenty minutes Lily-Butterfly fell asleep while meditating.

The next morning Lily-Butterfly could not resist her desire to telephone Croco's house. She dialed his phone number and his mother Ms. Gene answered the telephone.

"Hello, who is this?"

"It is me, Lily-Butterfly. I am calling to see how Croco is doing."

"Well, whatever your name is. He is not doing anything. Croco is in a coma, brain dead, spine broken in five parts, neck broken, both hips dislocated, both arms and legs broken, cuts, battered and bruised all over. It is as if every bone is broken. The doctor is not sure that he will come out of the coma. All night and now Croco is still in surgery. I came here to get some things for him."

"Oh, wow. This is bad. Very bad."

"Listen to me Miss. Butterfly."

"This is not my name," said Lily-Butterfly interrupting Ms. Gene.

"I do not care what your name is. You had better fly away. Stay the fxxk away from my son. I am so happy that you decided not to marry him. So now I am the next of kin, responsible for all his money, property, businesses, and every material possession. Stay away, do not come to this house, and do not come to the hospital, or anything else. Croco's life will never be the same again if he lives. Everything is in my control. You had better not try to get child support. If you try you will have to deal with me. You would get a big zero. Who knows if it is Croco's child anyway? Move on. Take my good advice. Never call again," said Ms. Gene.

Ms. Gene hung up the phone. She did not wait to hear another word from Lily-Butterfly. In a state of surprise, Lily-Butterfly hung up the telephone.

Lily-Butterfly went to sit on her couch. Holly was sleeping and Rebornstar was at school.

"Ms. Gene is a mean-spirited woman. I am thankful for her showing me her true nature. This also helped me to decide to distance myself from Croco. It is a good thing that I did not let her evil eyes see Holly. Croco has become a broken up and squished vegetable. Oh wow. I told him not to buy this building. I saw a dark cloud around the building. I told him to be mindful of his negative actions and karma. Maybe this destiny would find Croco no matter what. Tomorrow is not promised to anyone. Karma finds people whether they believe in karma or not. Every human karma and choices manages their life and destiny. Karma destiny will find people no matter where they are. So sad. I wish for Croco the best regards. Such a waste of life. Croco spend over twenty-five years of his life accumulating so much material possession, money, and everything else and look what happened. He never thought he would be like this at forty-eight years old. So sad. I have to feed Holly and go for a walk. I will go to the park, process, ponder, meditate, and pray. Oh, Creator you know everything best. Now I am very sure that my plans to move out of New York is meant to be. Creator thanks for everything, especially our health, success, well-being, and the ability to be mindful of karma, love, care, understanding, and everything else," mumbled Lily-Butterfly.

With Holly on her chest in the baby holder Lily-Butterfly walked to the park. Her pondering took her beyond New York back to her roots in the valley and village of Yaj, on the island of Kawomaya. Lily-Butterfly and Holly arrived at the park, where the pondering, processing, and reflecting continued. Lily-Butterfly knew that she had a lot to be grateful for in the past and present.

37

Two weeks went by since Croco was taken to the hospital. Lily-Butterfly's unconditional love, empathy, and curiosity captured her decision. She decided to telephone the hospital to inquire about Croco. The telephone operator answered the phone and transferred the call to the intensive care department. A Nurse answered the telephone and told Lily-Butterfly that she could only give her general information. The Nurse informed Lily-Butterfly that Croco was still in a coma, he might never wake up out of the coma, he is recovering from a two days surgery, and that Croco had a lot of irreversible injuries to his body. Lily-Butterfly asked the Nurse if Croco's mother Ms. Gene was there. The Nurse told Lily-Butterfly no. Lily-Butterfly thanked the nurse, said good bye, and hung up the telephone.

"Croco's injuries are very bad. Everything I told Croco about spirituality and karma he say was mumbo-jumbo. Some things, whether people believe them are not, it is just what it is. Not believing in unproven things does not make them unreal. Anyway, I sent Croco some love, light, blessings, and positive energies. He really needs some positive vibes. Every tub has to sit on its own bottom and in its own created karma drama. Oh wow. Sad," mumbled Lily-Butterfly.

Two more weeks went by and Lily-Butterfly talked to Rebornstar about moving to New Jersey, Croco's accident, his current health situation, and that he was in the hospital.

"Mama this news is sad. I feel sorry and sad for Mr. Croco. But I also feel relieved that he is gone and not coming around anymore. He is angry, mean, and scary. Now I feel safer. Mama I am ready to move to New Jersey."

"I am ready to move myself, although I will miss Mrs. Beech and you will miss your friends as well. We will meet good and positive people where ever we move to. There are good-positive people and bad-negative people everywhere. Really genuine, diligent, loyal, moral, loving, caring, kind, wise, and respectful people are human treasures. Living a positive human life is the most responsible job as a human. It is not easy. Rebornstar it is a complicated set of emotions to process feeling sorry and sad; yet relieved. Life is very interesting. Very soon, I am going to start packing for us to move.

I am going to start working again as well. I will take Holly to work with me. Mrs. Beech will pick you up from school and take you to her home if I am coming home late. I will be traveling back and forth on three trains and one bus carrying your sister with me to work. I will cultivate improved inner and outer: - effort, concentration, strength, patience, positive views-action-and speech, flexibility, mindfulness, and aspiration to move forward in my life. With every step, choice, action, responsibility, practice, and repeat practices; one day I will get to the chosen destiny and life purpose career I was born to serve in. Rebornstar you might not understand everything I am saying. Take what you can understand and file away the rest. When it is time you can source from everything. Okay. My experience with some people is that they think I am weird and too spiritual. To me the Creator, created the spiritual realm. To me the unseen things is more real than the seen things. Everything in the material and physical world was created by people; even fear. Thank you Rebornstar for listening to my deep spiritual talking. Mama loves you and Holly very much. With you girls by my side I cannot fail. If I fail, I fail both of you, and the Creator. Anyway. We have to live life and not let life live us. Holly traveling with me back and forth on a daily basis from New York to New Jersey she will get accustomed to the train, people, bus, and other things. Oh my. Mama's life journey is a work out and deep spiritual training of awakening all my talents. My star, with my life's experiences so far, I have really earned being me. I could talk on and on. Let us go for a walk to the park with Holly. Rebornstar get your shoe and put them on. Let me know when you are ready."

"Okay mama I like your talking. It makes me feel warm and safe inside. Yeah. You are the best mama."

They all left to go to the park.

One-week later Lily-Butterfly started gathering empty boxes for packing to move. Daily she went to the business on White Planes Road to get empty boxes. She started packing things she would not need until February of 1990. Rebornstar who was almost eleven years old helped her mother pack for moving. On October 16, 1989 the Director from the Childcare Agency telephoned Lily-Butterfly to inform her about a full-time nanny job. The employer is open for her to take her baby with her to work. Lily-Butterfly immediately replied that she would like to attend the interview. The interview was scheduled for 11:00 AM on Wednesday October 18th. The address was the first town over the George Washington Bridge. Lily-Butterfly wrote down the name of the mother and child, and their address and telephone number. She telephoned Mrs. Beech to arrange an appointment for her to baby sit Holly so that she could attend the interview. They also talked about Croco's accident and his current medical conditions.

"This address could not be any easier to find. I get off the bus at the first stop over the George Washington Bride. Lily-Butterfly read the directions, I go up the steps to the main road, turn right at Main Street turn right again, and the building is the last building on the second block. Amazing when things are meant to be. Thanks be to everything this job journey is as easy as it could be. I have to carry Holly in the over the shoulder baby holder. I do not like strollers because of the opening and closing, going up and down stairs, hustling to catch the train and bus on time. And it is more nourishing for Holly if I carry her. Here I go again. The next phase of my spiritual training. I am going to telephone Manana to tell her about my current life situations. Thanks be to the Creator for my Manana. I till telephone Manana this afternoon," whispered Lily-Butterfly.

Lily-Butterfly by now had mastered the art of talking to herself. She knew from her experiences that talking to herself was productive for her spirit, soul, health, well-being, success, life, and transformation.

Lily-Butterfly telephoned Manana. They talked about Ms. Gina's visa situation, having Ms. Gina, Henry, and Deans stay with her, moving, her new job interview, Holly's father accident and medical situation, taking Holly to work with her, and everything that was currently happening. Lily-Butterfly find talking to her Manana Leila a sacred uplifting exchange. Lily-Butterfly adored and valued every word her Manana Leila told her. She perceived her Manana as the first and most sacred healer, teacher, and guide of the path of love, peace, and understanding, from the sacred tabernacle of the Creator.

Wednesday morning Mrs. Beech picked up Holly on the way back from taking her son and Rebornstar to school. At 8:30 AM Lily-Butterfly left home for the interview. It was the same trains and bus she took when she worked for Mrs. Charm. The journey was easy and effortless. She arrived at the address forty-five minutes early. After locating the address Lily-Butterfly walked back to a Café down the street to enjoy a cup of tea and a scone, while she waited for 10:40 AM to arrive. The walk back to the address was about ten minutes and the interview was for 11:00 AM. At 10:50 AM Lily-Butterfly was standing in the lobby of the luxury building waiting for the Concierge to telephone to announce her arrival to Mrs. Diana. Lily-Butterfly was given permission to go upstairs using the elevator to get to Mrs. Diana's apartment.

Lily-Butterfly arrived at the apartment and rang the doorbell. Mrs. Diana opened the door and invited Lily-Butterfly to come in.

"Hi Lily-Butterfly, my name is Diana Speech. It is nice to see you, come in. As you can see my two hands are full and my nerves need a break. (Sigh) Please close the door behind you. Thank you."

Mrs. Speech was holding her three week old daughter Ana. Ana was crying and she was looking very pink.

"Okay Mrs. Speech. I will close the door. I am grateful to be here for this interview," replied Lily-Butterfly.

"You do not have to call me Mrs. Speech. Please call me Diana."

"Okay Mrs. Diana. Thank you."

"Please have a seat on the love seat couch. I will sit on the bigger couch where I can put Ana beside me. I am so tired and stressed. My daughter was born three weeks ago. I had two baby nurses taking care of her the first two weeks of her birth. My husband and I have been taking care of her from last week. Only one week and we are already a nervous wreck. My husband helps with Ana when he comes home from work. As you can see, we are not having the easiest experience. Ana hardly sleep during the night and day. Plus, she is colicky. She cries so much her face turns pink most of the time. I cannot seem to calm her down. Oh my. How are we going to do this interview, with Ana crying so loud?"

"Can I hold Ana?" asked Lily-Butterfly.

"Sure. Take her."

"Okay give me the blanket first and then give Ana to me."

Mrs. Diana gave Lily-Butterfly the blanket and then Ana. She observed with curiosity what Lily-Butterfly was doing. Lily-Butterfly talked to Ana.

"Ana my name is Lily-Butterfly. You have a strong lung. Rest, peace, calm. It is okay. Your mama and I are here. Calm, rest easy. No worries. Peace, calm, be still."

Lily-Butterfly kept repeating what she was saying to Ana. Ana gradually stopped crying. Lily-Butterfly sang a song and hummed a tune to Ana. Ana stopped crying. She looked at Lily-Butterfly's face.

She took deep breaths. Lily-Butterfly put the blanket on her shoulder and put Ana up to her shoulder, sang to Ana, and gently pat her back. Ana burped three times. Gradually Ana fell into a deep sleep. Lily-Butterfly removed the blanket from her shoulder and placed it across her lap. She placed Ana on her stomach on her lap with Ana's face turned to the side. Ana continued to sleep. Mrs. Diana watched Lily-Butterfly with amazement and relief.

"Okay. Now we can do the interview. You take a break from feeling overwhelmed and enjoy the interview process," said Lily-Butterfly.

"How did you do that?" asked Mrs. Diana.

"Ana just chose to follow my peaceful vibes. I have a lot of practice taking care of babies and children. My mother and father-nature vibes. I am not her mother so Ana connects to my neutral vibes. She is very tired, the soothing song, and gently patting her back can help to calm her nervous system. I have a peaceful nature so she vibes with this, and many more things. Your baby resonates and is very connected to you and your emotional vibration. Ana will mirror how you are feeling. No worries and no problem. Let us have the interview now."

"Thank you. Now I feel relieved. After I gave birth to Ana, I have been feeling very stressed, overwhelmed, tired, sad, and frustrated. I cannot wait to get back to work. I am supposed to return to work in two weeks."

"Okay. Can I have a glass of water?" asked Lily-Butterfly.

"Sure. I should have offered you something to drink. I forgot. Let me go get water for both of us."

Mrs. Diana went to get the water. She returned.

"Here is the water Lily-Butterfly. You seem to have the magic touch on how to take care of babies and children."

"Everyone I have worked for with taking care of their children, says this. Thank you for your compliments. I love to help children. My Manana Leila is great with children as well. It is part of my personality to do my best. What would my job responsibility be?"

"I have no specific clue what to tell you. Except to say take the very best care of Ana. Do everything that needs to be done to accomplish the greatest care. I myself do not even know how to boil water, much less an egg. My husband does all the cooking or we eat out. I am an expert in ordering food from a restaurant menu. That is, it. I am being honest."

"Do you breast feed Ana?"

"Breast feed? No. I feed her cold milk from a bottle. My husband

and I pre fill the milk bottles. We make about twelve at a time and put them in the refrigerator. I just grab one and feed her. Very easy. I am scared of making the milk too hot and end up burning Ana. Plus, this is how I see my mother and everyone I know do it. Cold milk is danger free."

"Okay. What would my work schedule be?"

"I am a Lawyer and my husband is an Investment Banker. We have to be at work at 9:00 AM. He works in town, about fifteen-minute walk from here. It takes me twenty minutes to drive to work. So, the short of the long answer is we must both leave for work by 8:40 AM. Your schedule would be 8:30 AM to 5:30 PM. Whichever one of us get home first you can leave. The pay is $350 per week Monday to Friday. Your job responsibility is to only take care of Ana. When she sleeps you can do her laundry, clean her room, and prep her milk bottles. My husband and I will keep our home clean. It is a three bed room apartment. One master bed room and two smaller bed rooms. Our living and dining room is in one large room. A small kitchen and two bath rooms. The starting pay for this job is $350. Is $350 okay?"

"Like you say $350 for the starting pay for someone with no experience. This is a Monday to Friday, 8:30 AM to 5:30 PM. A nine-hour work day. Correct?"

"Yes. Long term means that we hope someone will stay to take care of Ana for five years."

"I am a professional childcare person. Did the Agency tell you that I would like to take my daughter with me to work?"

"Yes, they did."

"Okay. I would like to make a proposal. The proposal is this job is worth $450 per week to start. If I can bring my three months old daughter with me to work you pay me $350. In addition to this I will offer you the extra work of daily cleaning one room, when I have free time, and doing as much laundry as I can. When my daughter is two years old, I will put her in a day care nursery. This way she can be with other children and for her personal development. At this time Ana can go to school enrichment programs and so forth. When I put my daughter in nursery school at two years old you pay me $450. I will use the $100 towards paying for day care. I am also guaranteeing that I will stay for five years. When my daughter is five years she will be going to kindergarten. I will be going to work in my other trained professional career. Is this proposal okay with you?"

"I would have to think about all you have said and talk to my husband. My concern is, can you take care of two young babies. My daughter and your daughter is about nine weeks apart in age. Are you going to favor your daughter over Ana? You working without your daughter, I feel totally comfortable with this. You seem like a natural, but I am just saying something that could happen. I would not want Ana to be neglected."

"Do as you like in discussing my proposal with your husband. I know that I would not neglect Ana. You have to feel comfortable with the idea. It is your choice to agree with my proposal or not. I could wait for the next interested childcare employer. I know me and the quality of my work. You have to decide if you want to trust me or not. I am planning to move from New York within three months. If I get this job living close by would be very good for me. Mrs. Diana what would you like to do?"

"Lily-Butterfly I will talk to my husband, think about this interview and your proposal, and interview two more women. If I choose to have you, I will telephone you on Friday afternoon to return for a second interview next week Monday October 23rd at 11:00 AM. You would start working Monday October 30th. Is this okay with you?"

"Yes. What you just said is okay with me. If you choose to have me, I will try my best to be here rain, snow, or sunny weather. If I have an issue and cannot come to work, I will let you know as soon as possible. Nothing is perfect, but I always try my best. Can I put Ana in her crib?"

"Yes. Come. Here is her room. Please put Ana in her crib. I will call you on Friday afternoon if I choose you. Okay. I like you Lily-Butterfly."

"I like you too Mrs. Diana. I hope that you will feel comfortable choosing me and my proposal."

Lily-Butterfly placed Ana in her crib. She was still sleeping like a log.

"Okay Lily-Butterfly it was nice and peaceful meeting you," said Mrs. Diana.

"Yes, thank you. It is nice meeting you as well. Ana might sleep for another two hours. She was very tired. I suggest that you get something to eat and take a nap yourself."

"Good suggestion Lily-Butterfly. I am going to take a shower, eat, and take a nap. You are like a child whisperer. It was amazing to me how you got Ana to calm down and fall asleep. Lily-Butterfly Ana seems to like you. Thank you for coming to the interview and for what you did for Ana."

"You are welcome Mrs. Diana. I am more like a human spirit whisperer. Take care of yourself and Ana. Bye."

"Bye Lily-Butterfly. Thanks again."

"You are welcome. I look forward to the opportunity of being chosen for this job. I will also respect your choice if for whatever reason you do not choose me. Bye."

Lily-Butterfly left Mrs. Diana's home. She walked to the bus stop, took the bus over the bridge, changed trains three times at the correct station, went to Mrs. Beech's home to get Holly, and walked home carrying her bundle of Holly.

38

When Lily-Butterfly got home she fed Holly and they both took a nap. During this nap Lily-Butterfly had a short dream.

The dream revealed a large invisible face. Only a face outlined in white, with white beard, eye brows, eye lashes, and lips. The face had large bright purple eyes. This face said, "Lily-Butterfly. Lily-Butterfly. So far. So good. You are on the right path. You are going in the right direction. Do not regret. Do not look backwards. Keep moving forward. Go forth manage your precious cargo; yourself, Rebornstar, and Holly. Be very aware that you are never alone."

In the twinkle of an eye the dream face oracle disappeared.

Lily-Butterfly got up and wrote down this reassuring and conformational dream in her journal. To her it was also a confirmation that Mrs. Diana would give her the job. After writing everything about the dream, Lily-Butterfly's last sentence was I am very grateful for everything.

Friday afternoon, Mrs. Diana telephoned Lily-Butterfly.

"Hello Lily-Butterfly."

"Yes Mrs. Diana, this is me."

"Yes, the reason for my call is to tell you that we have decided to give you the job to take care of our Ana."

"Oh wow. Thank you very much. I really appreciate the opportunity. I will do my very best."

"Well Lily-Butterfly with the other two women I interviewed I decided to do the baby crying test. Ana was crying when both women arrived. I gave each of them Ana to hold. Both times Ana screamed much louder than she screams when I am holding her. She screamed very loud and would not calm down until I took her from them. The women got overwhelmed and showed signs of frustration and clueless about what to do. I took Ana fed and burped her and put her in the crib. She cried and eventually fell asleep. This is how I was able to complete both interviews. Believe it or not these women made me look like an expert. So, you are chosen by your talents and Ana for the job. I could not imagine Ana crying and neglected all day while

I am at work. When you get here on Monday we will talk more about your proposal. Okay."

"Okay, and thanks again. I will see you on Monday at 11:00 AM. Bye."

Lily-Butterfly telephoned Mrs. Beech to make an appointment to take care of Holly so that she can attend the interview on Monday. When Rebornstar got home from school, Lily-Butterfly told her when they were eating dinner about: - Getting the new job. As well as her plans to move to the town she was going to work as soon as she found an apartment. Her changing school in the middle of the school year. Holly would go to day care nursery when she was two years old, to learn, and interact with other children. She would work in this childcare job until Holly was five years old and can attend kindergarten. Ms. Gina and her sons would arrive early in the New Year to live with them until they got their own place to live. Holly was always around the dining table laying in her bassinet or in her mother's arms when they ate. At the age of three months old Lily-Butterfly would feed Holly with some of her food from her plate. She would squish the food or chew it before she gave it to Holly. Lily-Butterfly only cooked nourishing and healthy meals of mostly vegetable, grains, fruits, poultry-goat-lamb as meat, and sea creatures. Holly drank milk made from vegetables and breast milk. At almost three months Holly was sitting up, active, seems to understand when her mother talked to her, and was big for her age. At three months Holly still had no hair on her head.

Monday at 11:00 AM Lily-Butterfly arrived at Mrs. Diana home. She rang the doorbell. Mrs. Diana opened the door. Ana was in her arms crying. Lily-Butterfly smiled.

"Hi Ana. Should your mother change your name to cry? How are you doing? Lily-Butterfly is here. No more anxiety and crying. Let peace be your new reference point. No worries. No problem."

Ana heard Lily-Butterfly's voice. She stopped crying. Ana looked at Lily-Butterfly and smiled.

"Here take her. She likes you more than me. I am not offended. I am actually relieved. Ana is now your student from now on. Teach her how to be. She is in your training from now on. Good. I am so happy. Here."

Lily-Butterfly put her pocket book down on the dining table and took Ana. It was as if Ana knew Lily-Butterfly. Ana observed Lily-Butterfly's face.

"Is Ana hungry?" asked Lily-Butterfly.

"Maybe. The last time I fed her was 7:00 AM."

"Okay. I think that she is hungry. Where is the milk?"

"In the fridge. I have to sterilize the dirty bottles and make some more milk bottles."

"Mrs. Diana, I recommend that you start to warm her milk to even room temperature before you give it to Ana to drink. Warm milk and burping her can help with digestion and colic. We have to work on the same vibes as close as possible for Ana to be positively trained. I will show you a very simple way to warm Ana's milk."

"Okay great. Everything that is good and positive for Ana's health and well-being we endorse completely. I am here, show me."

Ana was still quiet and looking in Lily-Butterfly's face.

"Hi Ana. Thank you for choosing me. We will be working together for five years. We are here to help each other. Welcome."

"Amin. Just to let you know, Ana had a mild case has translocation down syndrome. Maybe with your magic touch healing vibes she will improve this syndrome. Okay, show me how to warm the milk."

"Give me a bowl or small pot," said Lily-Butterfly.

"Look in the cupboard below the sink you will see pots. Choose the one you like."

"Okay. Look. Put the closed bottle with milk in the pot. Put the pot with the bottle in the kitchen sink. Turn on the kitchen sink pipe to hot. Let the hot water continuously fill the pot. Turn off the pipe when the pot is full with hot water. Let the milk bottle stay in the pot for about five minutes. Check the warmth of the milk by draining a little in the palm of your hands. Room temperature or a little warmer is good. It is not warm to room temperature, replace the bottle in the pot with hot water and wait another five minutes. If you think the milk is too warm. Empty the hot water out of the pot and fill it with cold water. Replace the bottle in the pot with cold water, for about three minutes. Come let us try this together."

"Sounds simple, great. Show me," said Mrs. Diana.

Lily-Butterfly demonstrated what she had just told Mrs. Diana. The milk after the first five minutes was at room temperature. Lily-Butterfly let Mrs. Diana feel the milk in the palm of her hand.

"One question. Can I taste the milk to check the temperature?"

"Yes. You can pour a little of the milk in a cup and taste it. For hygiene and health reasons I do not recommend that you taste the milk from the nipple of the bottle. Sometimes babies can be vulnerable to certain adult viruses."

"Great. I understand. Sick baby is not good. Prevention is better than cure."

"Exactly."

"Okay. We can sit down to do the interview. I will feed Ana. Can I have a bib?"

"Yes. There is one on the couch."

They sat down and Lily-Butterfly fed Ana. Ana drank the bottle of milk. Lily-Butterfly burped her. Ten minutes later Ana fell asleep and Lily-Butterfly placed her in her crib. The interview continued.

"Lily-Butterfly you are so confident with this childcare stuff."

"Yes, I have a lot of experience. I took care of my half-sister and two half-brothers before I was a teenager. I have two children. The first one was born just before I was twenty-one years. I have worked in two other professional childcare jobs before this one. I will be thirty-two years old in December this year. I have had negative and positive life's experiences. These experiences have taught me many things, and awakened some spirit and soul talents. I am spiritual, I love children and all humans. I might not like some humans and the things they choose to do and be. I have learned lots of human created education. I love and like to learn. My nature is inquisitive, human created knowledge is power. I love and like to learn human created knowledge. I have a bachelor's degree in Business Management and Master's degree in Hospitality and Tourism Management. My communication style is direct. I have a no-nonsense attitude, and a cautious, slow, and steady personality. I was born in a small valley village called Yaj, deep in country jungle of the island of Kawomaya. I am the first one of my ancestors that have done so much so called modern human created knowledge. I mix all that I have learned so far with my spirit, soul, and Universal intelligence. I have two daughters. Rebornstar will be eleven years old in December and Holly is almost three months old. I was married once and currently divorced. I chose not to marry Holly's father. I respect all my choices and life's experiences. This job is my bridge to move out of New York and journey into the next phase of my life. This is me in a nutshell. What else would you like to know about me?"

"Oh wow. You have said it all. Good for us that you are here. We are lucky and happy to have you. We will work with you as a team.

I am comfortable with you bringing your daughter Holly with you to work, as you requested."

"You are welcome. Thanks to you, Ana, and your husband for this very precious and valuable opportunity. Although I am so over qualified for this job I am still simple, humble, basic, and grateful for this job. This job is very important and valuable to me. What have you decided about my complete proposal?"

"We have decided to pay you the complete $450 as you suggested, with no conditions. If you are sick or need days off, and for public holidays off, you will receive the complete pay. You will get one week off with pay every year for the five years you promise to work here. With the $450 weekly pay you can also save in-advance towards Holly's day care nursery payment when she becomes two years old. We see this as an investment in encouraging you to want to work here. We care about you and choose to support your well-being because you will be left with the responsibility to take care of our precious daughter Ana. You can bring your daughter Holly to work with you whenever you like. Your work schedule is Monday to Friday 8:30 AM to 5:30 PM. Your starting date is next week Monday October 30th. You committed to stay for at least five years. You can use my name as reference to rent an apartment. Let me know if you need help with anything else. We appreciate very much your priceless time, skills, talents, and energy. We grew up spiritual and religious as well, although we do not currently practice our religious faith. We understand your sense of spirituality. Do you have any questions?"

"No, I have no questions. Again, thank you very much for this opportunity and generosity. I promise to do the best quality care for Ana and everything else. My instincts tells me that we will work successfully together."

"Great. I think so too. There is a book on the kitchen cupboard by the refrigerator with all the telephone numbers for my husband, my work, the Pediatrician Doctor, downstairs at the Concierge desk, my parents, and sisters, and so forth. There is a playground at the back of this building that you can take Ana and Holly. There is a nature park across the street that you can go to as well. The library is three minute walk down the street. The post office is five minute walk down the street. There is money in an envelope in the drawer by the fridge, just in case you need money for taxi or other emergencies. If there is anything else that we need to discuss we could do so as time goes on. Come let me show you the apartment. There is not much else to see except my bedroom and the bathrooms. Our home is simple, easy to take care of, and maintain. Come."

Lily-Butterfly went with Mrs. Diana to look at the rest of the apartment. When the tour of the apartment was over it was time to leave.

"Thanks again Mrs. Diana. Do you have Sunday's newspaper? I would like the classified section to look for an apartment."

"Sure, yes, it is right here in the garbage can. Look through the garbage can and take the sections you want."

"Thank you. I would like to find an apartment in this town. Is the interview over?"

"Yes, the interview is over. Lily-Butterfly we are going to miss you. But Monday is only six days away. Thank you very much for choosing to work with us. We really appreciate everything that you will do for us. Bye. Have a safe journey home."

"You are welcome. Say bye to Ana for me. I will see you on Monday at 8:30 AM. Thank your husband for me as well. Bye."

Lily-Butterfly took the bus over the George Washington Bridge. For the complete journey on the bus and trains, Lily-Butterfly combed through the apartment section of the classified section of the newspaper for her next home. Lily-Butterfly knew that with the Creator's help, her choice, and action that she would find the apartment that was meant to be the next home for her and her children.

39

When Lily-Butterfly arrived at Mrs. Beech's home to get Holly. Lily-Butterfly told Mrs. Beech that she had gotten the childcare job, her work schedule was 8:30 AM to 5:30 PM Monday to Friday, taking Holly to work with her, because it saved money that she needed to move, moving as soon as she found a place to live, and wanting to live in the town that she worked in. Also, Lily-Butterfly asked Mrs. Beech to provide childcare services to take Rebornstar to school and pick her up after school. Last thing they talked about was Croco's health and accident situation. When they were finished talking, it was time for Lily-Butterfly to pick up Rebornstar from school.

Tuesday morning Lily-Butterfly telephoned the Medicaid office to discontinue her Medicaid benefits at the end of November 1989. She sent a letter to her current landlord to discontinue her month to month lease at the end of November 1989. She telephoned Mrs. Diana to request arriving to work two hours late on the morning that she needed to register Rebornstar in school. Mrs. Diana agreed and requested that Lily-Butterfly let her know the exact date in advance. Lily-Butterfly finished talking to Mrs. Diana and reflected on talking to herself.

"How do I know that I will find an apartment in New Jersey by the end of November? I hope I will. This will be good. Winter is coming. Traveling back and forth to the Bronx and carrying Holly will be difficult in the cold and snow. Creator do not forget about me and all my situations. I know that you are very busy. By the end of November this year, please help me to find an apartment in the town that I will be working in. Let my new home be in the best location as possible, the cost per month be affordable based on my pay, a safe and healthy place for my children and I, and a playground for my children to play. Please guide my new landlord's spirit, mind, and body to assist in every way with this manifestation of our new home relocation. I am grateful for everything you do for my children and I," prayed Lily-Butterfly.

The rest of the week Lily-Butterfly spent preparing for starting her new job on Monday, packing for moving, and telephoning people who had apartments for rent. Monday morning came, Lily-Butterfly woke up at 4:30 AM. She dressed herself and Holly. Lily-Butterfly woke up Rebornstar for her to put her clothes on for school. They all had breakfast. Lily-Butterfly put two thirty two ounce can of milk for Holly into her backpack diaper bag, and made sure that the diaper bag had all the things that she needed for the day. Rebornstar got her book bag, put on her shoes, and turned off all the lights. Lily-Butterfly put on her shoes. Next, she put on the over the shoulder baby holder and put Holly into the baby holder in front of her chest. After Lily-Butterfly picked up the back pack diaper bag and put it on. Out the door they all went. Lily-Butterfly locked the door. At 6:15 AM they all arrived at Mrs. Beech's home. Rebornstar rang the doorbell and Mrs. Beech came to open the door. Rebornstar went into Mrs. Beech's home. Lily-Butterfly walked to the train station. By 6:45 AM Lily-Butterfly and Holly were on their first train and on their way to New Jersey to work. Lily-Butterfly arrived at work at 8:20 AM. This was her routine every work morning from Monday to Friday. She was on time every morning. It was as if some Divine force was assisting Lily-Butterfly with synchronicity in creating an easy and effortless path, for her journey to and from work.

On the first morning when she arrived at work the door man sent Lily-Butterfly upstairs. Her name was placed on the visitor's list at the receptionist desk by Mrs. Diana. Lily-Butterfly arrived at Mrs. Diana's door and rang the doorbell. Mrs. Diana's husband opened the door.

"Hello Lily-Butterfly. I am Ted, Diana's husband. Come in. It is nice to meet you. Is this your daughter Holly?" said Mr. Ted.

"Yes, this is my daughter Holly. It is good to meet you Mr. Ted."

"Holly looks so big and alert. You carry her in a sling? She looks heavy. You are strong to carry her all this way from New York in the Bronx like this," said Mr. Ted.

"Once I get into the first train station and get on the train I sit down. I change trains three times. There is not that much walking. It is getting up and down the stairs to get to the next train. The longest walk is from the 'A' train, going up the two-long flights of stairs to get to the bus, and then walking here. The sling is the best way to carry Holly for many reasons. Yes, I am strong. I have been walking a lot all my life. It takes inner and outer strength, endurance, trust, courage, and faith. Soon, I wish to find an apartment in this town to live in. As good as I am with this situation and traveling, easy is good as well. Good morning. I am happy to be here. Where is Ana and Mrs. Diana?"

Mrs. Diana came into the kitchen with a towel around her hair.

"Hi Lily-Butterfly, good morning. We are happy to see you. Ana is in her room. She fell back to sleep after I fed her at 7:00 AM. I think she is rest assured that you were coming. Let me see your Holly."

"Good bye everyone. I am leaving for work," said Mr. Ted.

"Bye Ted dear. See you later," replied Mrs. Diana.

Lily-Butterfly took off the diaper bag back pack and put it on the kitchen counter. Next, she took Holly out of the over the shoulder baby holder. Holly was awake. She looked at Mrs. Diana.

"Oh wow. Holly is big and alert. She has no hair and a blue birth mark on the left back side of her head. Very interesting and unique. Is her father from the same island that you are from? Holly skin is very yellow."

"Yes, her father is from the same island. He has brown skin color like me. We both are very mixed ancestry. The lighter skin ancestors are in our gene pool. All the ancestor's DNA can show up at any time and create many shades of skin color and so forth. Do you have an old comforter I can use on the floor to create a bed for Holly?"

"Look in the closet in the hallway across from Ana's room you will see comforters and sheets. Take what you need to use. I understand about mixed ancestry. Let me go finish blow drying my hair. You can set up Holly and get organized. Plan your work day as you like. Call me at work if you need anything. Enjoy your day. When I am finished with my hair I am leaving."

"Have a great day Mrs. Diana. See you later."

Lily-Butterfly folded the thick comforter and made a bed for Holly to sleep, play, and lay on. She placed Holly on the folded comforter. Next, she gave Holly some water in her bottle to drink. After Lily-Butterfly took the large note book with the phone numbers and wrote down a work plan that she would use every day for working at Mrs. Diana's home. The planned schedule was, time each baby was to be fed, Ana's daily bath times, gathering laundry, washing-drying- folding laundry, both babies nap times, eating lunch, clean both restroom, clean master bedroom and Ana's room, take children to park for fresh air, clean living and dining room, clean kitchen, vacuum each room, and mop kitchen once per week.

When Lily-Butterfly had finished creating the schedule it was

9:20 AM. Ana woke up and Lily-Butterfly fed her with warm milk. Holly lay on the comforter playing with a rattle and intermittently glancing over at her mother. After feeding Ana, Lily-Butterfly burped her, changed her diaper, and placed her in a bassinet in the living room. From the bassinet Ana could see Holly and Lily-Butterfly. Next Lily-Butterfly prepared milk for Holly, fed and burped her, and changed her diaper. In feeding both babies Lily-Butterfly sang to them songs she randomly made up and she read them stories. The children seemed interested in the lullaby songs and stories, they listened, and did not cry. Holly did not usually cry she was a trained and content baby. Immediately Ana was acclimated to the peace and contentment vibes that was a part of Lily-Butterfly's aura. Part of Lily-Butterfly's plan to train Ana was to get her to trust that she would always be there for her, and there was no need to use crying to control and manipulate having her attention. Holly was already trained in this way. Lily-Butterfly placed Ana in her crib and turned on her musical carousel over her crib. Ana watched the carousel and when it stopped playing Lily-Butterfly returned to turn it back on. Ana did not cry. She seemed to trust in Lily-Butterfly returning to turn it back on. Gradually Ana and Holly fell back to sleep. During the time the babies slept Lily-Butterfly cleaned the master bedroom and bathroom, tidy the kitchen, load the dishwasher and turn it on to wash what was inside, ate her lunch., and loaded Ana's laundry to wash. Holly woke up before Ana. Lily-Butterfly fed her lunch and loaded Ana's clothes in the dryer to dry. Lily-Butterfly loaded another load of clothes to wash. Ana woke up and she was fed a warm bottle of milk. At 2:00 PM Lily-Butterfly took both babies out to the park in the back of the apartment building. Lily-Butterfly pushed Ana in her stroller and carried Holly in the over the shoulder baby holder. She sat with them, sang, and read them stories. At 3:20 PM Lily-Butterfly went back upstairs and fed both babies again. After both babies were fed and burped, Lily-Butterfly changed Holly's diaper, and gave Ana a bath. At 4:10 PM both babies fell asleep. Lily-Butterfly placed Ana in her crib and covered her. Holly was placed on her created bed on the floor and Lily-Butterfly covered her. Next Lily-Butterfly folded laundry, put in another load of laundry to wash and dry. The dishwasher was finished washing and drying the dishes. Lily-Butterfly put all the dishes away. Next, she made up twelve - six ounce bottles of milk for Ana and put them in the fridge.

Lily-Butterfly got the Sunday's newspaper and took out the

classified section with the apartment advertisements, and put it into her back pack diaper bag. At 5:10 PM Ana woke up and Lily-Butterfly fed and burped her. Holly woke up while Lily-Butterfly was feeding Ana. She was quiet and played with her rattle as she looked at her mother. Lily-Butterfly changed Ana's diaper and placed her in the bassinet. Next Lily-Butterfly fed, burped, and changed Holly's diaper. Lily-Butterfly got her back pack diaper bag ready to leave. Mrs. Diana came home from work.

"Hello Lily-Butterfly. I am home. Are you alive?" The place is peaceful and quiet," said Mrs. Diana.

"Yes, we are all alive and well. Come look around and check everything. In one day, your wonderful daughter Ana has become a saint. I hope that she is the same way with you and her father. Like a miracle Ana personal journey of calm, peace, trust, reassurance, and confidence has begun and seems to be taking root. Let us keep our fingers crossed that she continues on this path. Holly was already trained. Look she is laying in the bassinet awake and not one crying or fuss. In the book with the telephone numbers by the telephone you will find the daily work schedule that I created. When you look in this book you will see what I do every day. This book will have a daily report of everything I plan to do for my schedule, what I actually did, and reports about Ana. If there is anything to tell you I will write it in this book as well. Plus, you can look around and see what I did every day. Look around your home it is tidied up, laundry is done, bottles are set up, and dishes are washed and put away. We went outside to the park in the back. Check everything out and let me know if there is something you wanted me to do that I have not done. Like I told you before I will always do my best. I am a self-motivated person."

"Wow Lily-Butterfly this is a miracle. Look at Ana she is so calm, laying down by herself, and not crying. You are really an expert. You seem calm and peaceful as well and Holly too. You are definitely a baby whisperer. They look like two angels."

"Do you think so? Good. The way I take care of them, they should feel like baby angels. You are funny Mrs. Diana."

They both laugh.

"Lily-Butterfly the book idea with your daily schedule plan and so forth is a good idea. This is so thoughtful of you. You are going to end up spoiling all of us. I usually clean this apartment and do the laundry, on a need to do so basis. Now that you are here, we have to get used to such a neat, clean, organized home, clean laundry, and a peaceful and quiet Ana. Now things are too good. We are going to feel bored. Just kidding. I really appreciate all you did and are going to do for us. Paying you is money well spent. You deserve every penny and more."

"You are welcome. The last time I fed Ana was 5:15 PM. I also changed her diaper after I fed her. Feed her again between 7:30 PM and 8:00 PM. She should sleep through the most of the night. I had a talk with Ana. I told her not to give you and Mr. Ted any trouble and to sleep through the night. Let us see if she listens."

"Really. Ana sleeping through the night? Are you kidding or dreaming?"

"I am serious. I hope for the best and stay positive. This can happen. We will see what happens. I have to go, it is 5:51 PM. I am late for the bus. Good night Mrs. Diana. Let me go tell Ana good bye and get Holly."

Lily-Butterfly went to say good bye to Ana, get Holly, and the back pack diaper bag. Mrs. Diana looked around the apartment.

"Okay, Lily-Butterfly everything looks great. I read the reports. Wow, you get all this done and took care of two babies. I could not ask for more. This is so wonderful. Good job. Go. You must be very tired. I will see you in the morning. Have a safe journey home. Good by Holly. I will see both of you in the morning. Go it is now a little after 6:00 PM. Go. Bye."

"Okay bye. See you in the morning."

Lily-Butterfly left Mrs. Diana's home in fifteen minutes she had walked the one-mile distance to the bus stop. She got on the first bus that came that was going across the George Washington Bridge. At 6:43 PM Lily-Butterfly and Holly was on the first train. As Lily-Butterfly traveled on the train she thought, I am tired. Holly is fine. I willingly do what I have to do, or things will end up doing me. My life's path is one of conscious practice. One pathway seems to lead to the next pathway. With the Creator's help I seem to manage and create my life. I am grateful for everything. Holly had closed her eyes and seems to be sleeping.

When Lily-Butterfly got to Mrs. Beech's home it was 7:46 PM. She rang the doorbell and Mrs. Beech opened the door.

"It is nice to see you and Holly. You must be tired. I gave Rebornstar dinner already. I will give her dinner every night for an extra cost. Is this okay with you? This is one more thing that you would not have to worry about and have to do. I will only charge you $20 per day to bring her to school, pick her up, and give her dinner. This is my contribution to this part of your journey. You are something else. I wish that I had your everlasting spirit and soul. Many blessings to you Lily-Butterfly. You are a blessed woman. Ha?"

Tears was flowing down Lily-Butterfly's cheeks. She was overcome with Mrs. Beech's kindness and care, and her heart that expanded with infinite gratitude.

"I am so grateful for everything you have done in the past and present to help me and my children. The Creator has created you to be here to help us at this part of our journey. You are doing an incredible complete job. I always know that good humans are on my path. I will never forget you. Many blessings and gratitude for all your help. Yes, I am tired. Everything you have done in the past and present have helped me to feel less tired. Mrs. Beech you are like a cool spring of water at the end of a hot and thirsty journey. Infinite thanks. I am going home to give Holly a bath, feed her, put her to sleep, and get something to eat. I should be finished with this by 9:00 PM. For the whole day this is the first time I will get to relax and rest. After about six hours sleep it will be time again to repeat all the things I have done today. The repetitive action practice can seem to make thing easier and effortless. I give thanks for everything. Have a great night's sleep. Bye. Come Rebornstar let us go."

"Bye Lily-Butterfly. I will see you and the children in the morning. Take care of yourself."

"Yes. Thank you. Bye."

Lily-Butterfly and her two children entered the bosom of the dark night outside. They walked home in silence. When they arrived home Lily-Butterfly gave Holly a bath and prepared her for bed. Rebornstar took a shower, prepared herself for bed, and went to sleep. At 9:11 PM Lily-Butterfly ate her dinner of chicken and vegetable soup. Next, she set up breakfast for the next morning, packed Holly's diaper back pack for the next day, took a shower, and brushed her teeth. The children were already asleep. Lily-Butterfly wrote all the day's events and experiences in her journal and prayed. At 10:25 PM Lily-Butterfly laid in her bed, covered herself, and closed her eyes. With gratitude in her heart for everything, Lily-Butterfly drifted off to sleep. The last thing she remembered before falling asleep was her breathing.

40

Tuesday, Lily-Butterfly planned to look through the classified section of the past Sunday newspaper for an apartment while she ate her lunch. Her ability and choice to see beyond the surface of people and things improved.

Tuesday, the second day of work Lily-Butterfly arrived with her baby Holly at Mrs. Diana's home. They did the usual greeting and then Lily-Butterfly continued on with her busy day. Lily-Butterfly followed the same scheduled plan as Monday and at the end of the day she had another successful experience. Both children were taken care of and the home environment as well. During Lily-Butterfly's lunch break both babies were sleeping. As Lily-Butterfly ate she combed through the apartment section of the classified newspaper. With destiny, faith, intention, prayer, optimism, and action combined Lily-Butterfly saw a one-bedroom apartment for rent in a condominium apartment complex. It was located about one mile away from Mrs. Diana's home. The cost was $700 per month. This would fit into her financial budget. Lily-Butterfly telephoned the person who was listed in the newspaper. The Realtor that answered the phone scheduled an appointment for Lily-Butterfly to see the apartment on Saturday November 4th at 11:00 AM. Lily-Butterfly would meet the Realtor at the address listed in the newspaper. When Lily-Butterfly hung up the telephone she started pondering and talking to herself.

"I think this is the apartment for my children and I. I have the money saved up, plus the money Manana gave me, and I have a job. Everything is set for me to have this apartment. With $700 per month rent I will have about $1,100 left per month for utilities, food, clothing, and other expenses. I will just have to live within my budget. I do not use credit cards and I have no debt. I have a little savings I just have to choose to spend it wisely until my financial situation improves. Creator if this apartment is for our greater good please assist in creating this opportunity," mumbled Lily-Butterfly.

At the end of the day Mrs. Diana came home from work.
"I am happy to be home. How was your day Lily-Butterfly?"
"My day was great. I think that I found an apartment. Ana did

excellent as usual. I gave her a bath. She is over by Holly in the living room by the couch. I am going to meet the Realtor at the address of the condominium apartment complex on Saturday. Please give me a letter of employment and reference, with my salary included in the information."

"Okay. Sure. Where is the apartment?"

"It is about one mile from here, in this town. A one bed room apartment for $700 per month for rent. Here is the address on this paper. Look, maybe you know where this place is located. I am so happy. I think that I will get it. Winter is coming. It will be so great to not have to travel every day back and forth to New York carrying Holly."

Mrs. Diana read the address on the paper.

"Yes, I know this place. It is a three-building structure condominium complex on a quiet street about one mile from here. I hope that you get it. I will write the letter tonight and leave it on the dining table for you. You are lucky. Positive energy can create luck. Lily-Butterfly you have a lot of positive energy. I can feel it and Ana too. The house looks great, actually perfect. Thank you for today. Hurry and go it is getting late. You have to go all the way to the Bronx. I do not know how you do all you do. Hurry and be safe. Go."

"Thank you very much for everything Mrs. Diana. I always make sure that my children and I are safe. Luck is my wealth created by my positive energy and karma. I take nothing and no one for granted. Material wealth is one wealth and finite resource. Positive energy and karma is another kind of infinite wealth and resource. Anyway, let me get my Holly and go. Read the report in the book everything about our day is written down. You can see that your wonderful Ana is becoming improved with her calm, peace, confidence, and self-reliance. Bye. See you tomorrow morning."

"Good night Lily-Butterfly. Take care of yourself. Bye."

Lily-Butterfly left Mrs. Diana's home it was 5:40 PM. Her precious bundle of Holly was laying on her chest in the over the shoulder baby holder. They merge as one force as Lily-Butterfly hustle towards the bus stop at the George Washington Bridge on the New Jersey side of the border, about a mile away. Getting on each transportation successfully they arrived at Mrs. Beech's home, picked up Rebornstar, and walked home. When Lily-Butterfly and her children got home they continued on with all their activities, until everything was completed, and everyone was nestled in their bed fast asleep.

Every day Lily-Butterfly and the babies worked together like a great team and a well-oiled machine, supporting one another. They got more and more acclimated to the daily routines of the day's events. Lily-Butterfly first week of journeying back and forth from New York to New Jersey got easier and more accepting to her. Although by choice this journey might be coming to an end, Lily-Butterfly was still appreciative that she made it through one complete week. Lily-Butterfly got the employment and reference letter from Mrs. Diana. She put the letter, her check book, the directions to the apartment, and everything that she needed for Saturday's interview with the Realtor inside her pocket book. Lily-Butterfly made an appointment for Saturday November 4th with Mrs. Beech for childcare services for Rebornstar and Holly.

Friday night after writing in her journal and prayer she laid down on her back. The pondering, processing, and reflecting continued.

"I have nine months' rent money saved up. I get $450 per week for my pay. I get my security deposit back from my current landlord. In addition, I have enough money to pay the first month's rent, one and a half month's security, Realtor fees, and moving truck expenses. Here goes the wheel and revolving doors of my life moving again. I surrender and go with the flow into the unknown with my two children," whispered Lily-Butterfly.

She turned on her side and went to sleep.

Saturday morning at 8:30 AM Lily-Butterfly got on the first train and journeyed to the bus terminal in New York to go over the George Washington Bridge. She took the bus and got off at the first bus stop in New Jersey. The same bus stop she gets off to go to work at Mrs. Diana. Walking up the stairs to the main street she turned left and walked towards the taxi terminal. Lily-Butterfly selected a taxi. She gave the driver the address. In ten minutes, the taxi arrived at the address. It was 10:35 AM. Getting to the location was easy. The taxi left the terminal and turned left at the light. The taxi driver drove pass a shopping plaza, a supermarket, the high school about three quarter miles from the taxi terminal the driver turned right at the light. Drove less than a quarter mile to the end of the street and turned right. Then turn right again into the condominium complex. The first building in this complex was right on the corner. Lily-Butterfly paid the taxi driver and got out of the car.

The condominium complex had three buildings. One on the corner on the right side, one building in the center, and one building on the left side. The driveway into this complex was a horse shoe shape two lane drive way. The buildings were made from brown bricks and each building had three floors. Beautiful flowers were planted at the front of each building and at the front of the horse shoe shaped driveway to enter the complex. Immediately Lily-Butterfly felt this was really the next place for her and her children to call home. Lily-Butterfly refocused her awareness on locating the Realtor waiting for her. She saw a woman standing at the entrance door of the building on the right side and on the corner of the block. She speculated that this was the Realtor and walked over to talk to her.

"Hi my name is Lily-Butterfly. Are you the Realtor waiting to rent me an apartment?"

"Yes," replied the woman.

"Thank you," replied Lily-Butterfly.

They shook hands.

"Come this way. We are going into this building. This is building one. The apartment is on the third floor. Let us use the elevator this is the first floor. The basement is below this floor."

"Okay."

The Realtor and Lily-Butterfly took the elevator to the third floor. The Relator arrived at the apartment and unlocked the door. Lily-Butterfly walked inside behind the Realtor. They look at the apartment together. The apartment was completely carpeted except for the kitchen. It had one large bedroom on the far end of the space with a closet. Walking down a short hallway, next to the bedroom was a bathroom with a tub. Closets were across from the bathroom. Leaving the hallway there was a large living room. To the right and end of the living room was a kitchen and dining area. On entering the apartment, the kitchen was to the left and the living room was to the right side. The apartment had five windows that looked out to a flower garden and the street. Everything about the apartment was great, except that it was one bedroom now for her and her two children. Plus remember that Lily-Butterfly had offered Manana Leila the commitment of hosting Ms. Gina, Henry, and Dean inside her home for maximum one year. Lily-Butterfly promised herself to cross the Ms. Gina bridge when the time comes. She was going to keep her promise to Manana Leila no matter what happens. She was not afraid of Ms. Gina and her crap. Now her focus was first finding a place as a home for her children and herself. Lily-Butterfly and the Realtor toured the apartment in silence. Out of the silence Lily-Butterfly was the first one that spoke.

"This apartment is great. I love and like everything about it. I would really appreciate it if you choose to let me rent it," said Lily-Butterfly.

"Okay. Let us go outside and do a tour of the property, to see if you like the environment. If you have children this can be a great living community for them. This is a middle-income family apartment complex, with children of various ages. The elementary school is less than a quarter of a mile up the street, turn left and cross the main road by the traffic light. There is always a crossing guard at the traffic light that helps the children that walk to school, to cross the street. Come, let us go look outside. You will see what I mean."

"Okay. Thank you."

The Realtor and Lily-Butterfly left the apartment, took the elevator, and went outside.

"There are landscape of trees, flowers, plants, a circular two-lane entrance and exit driveway. Another garden in front of the driveway. In front of the building are tenant's parking spots. In the back of the buildings are parking spots as well. Each one bedroom has one assigned parking spot, and two to three bedrooms have two parking spots. Beyond the large back parking area is a large playground that covers the whole length of the property. They are two tennis courts, a young children's playground, and an older children's playground, picnic area, benches for sitting, and a children pool. Next door to this property is a small environmental center park. The community is quiet and the streets back here are not busy. Across the street from the park as you can see is another apartment building and homes. Let us go back inside the building. I will show you the laundry facilities inside the basement. There are coin operated washers and dryers," said the Realtor.

"Okay. Thank you," replied Lily-Butterfly.

Lily-Butterfly was silent, listening, and hearing, as the Realtor gave her the tour. Finding this apartment rental opportunity has surpassed her dreams and prayer for help to the Creator. She listened in silent amazement. To her the complete experience was like being in an awake dream. At this time tears had dampened her two eyes. She used her blouse sleeves to wipe the tears from her eyes as she walked alongside the Realtor.

"Hello Lily-Butterfly. Are you okay? Why are you crying?" said the Realtor.

"I am just so happy and grateful for this rental apartment opportunity."

"Okay. Do not worry. I already felt guided to rent you this apartment. So, if you want the apartment. I will rent it to you. You got it. Your parking spot is number twenty seven."

"Thank you so much. I really appreciate you giving me the opportunity to rent this apartment."

"Alright. Here is the laundry room. Look around. Do you like it?"

"Yes, I love and like everything."

"Let us walk back to the apartment. Here, fill out this application. Do you have a pay stub or letter of employment?"

"Yes, I have a letter of employment and reference letter."

"Okay. Give me the letter. During the week I will telephone your work and personal references. After, I will let the owner know that I have found a tenant."

"Thank you. Here is my job and reference letter. I will write my other references on the application. Do I give you the check payment today?"

"Yes, I will take all the payment today."

"How much money should I write the check for? What name should I put on the check?"

"Write the check for December 1, 1989. The amount is $1,400, for the first month's rent and one-month security deposit."

"Wow. That is, it? There is no Realtor fee and one and a half months security deposit?"

"No, plain and simple. The first month's rent and one-month security deposit. The landlord will pay me."

"Oh wow. Thanks. When can I get the key?"

"Monday I will check out all your references, telephone your employer, and deposit your check. If everything goes well meet me here at the front entrance of the building on November 18th at 11:00 AM. I will give you the keys. You can prepare the apartment how you like and start moving in. If there is a problem, I will telephone you. If you do not hear from me, meet me here as I told you."

"Great. Why have you decided to rent me the apartment, before checking my references and employer?"

"My instincts and feeling vibes tell me to give it to you for whatever reason. I know this is business, but sometimes in professional business I also use my instincts. I want a long-term tenant, and I feel that you are the one to give the opportunity. Some things and decisions are priceless. Do you understand?"

"Yes, I understand perfectly."

"Okay. Finish filing out the application and write the check. I will be right back. I am going to get my business card and the contact information for the landlord to give to you. Congratulations. Welcome to this neighborhood and your new home. I will be right back."

The Realtor returned. She gave Lily-Butterfly all the landlord's contact information and her business card. Lily-Butterfly gave her the application form and check payment.

"Thank you, Lily-Butterfly. Would you like me to give you a car ride?"

"No. Thank you for asking. I am going to have a second look around the property, walk to the school to see where it is, and walk to the bus stop. I will see you on Saturday November 18th at 11:00 AM. Thanks again for everything."

"You are welcome. Enjoy."

"Okay bye."

Lily-Butterfly toured the condominium apartment complex property, walked to the school, and to a plaza shopping center across from the bus stop. She went into a restaurant inside the plaza and had lunch. After lunch she took the bus to her first train ride home. When Lily-Butterfly arrived at Mrs. Beech's home it was 4:30 PM. She told Mrs. Beech that she had gotten the apartment and everything about the complete experience.

"Mrs. Beech I am moving Saturday November 25th. This gives me three weeks to complete my preparations to move. I have to find moving truck services. I am going to get the apartment keys on Saturday November 18th. Can you please provide childcare services for the children again? Everything about the apartment is great. More than I imagined it to be."

"Yes, I will take care of the children when you go to get the keys."

"Thank you, Mrs. Beech for everything. You might sometimes ask yourself why I say thank you so many times. This is my way to acknowledge how much I appreciate all you do for us. The Creator chose you to help me. Without you, my children and I would have things more difficult and less secure. Thanks a million."

"Thanks to you as well. I have learned so much from you and everything that you do. You are welcome regarding everything I do for you and the children. You deserve my help. Continue to take care of yourself and your precious children. I will see you on Monday morning when you drop off Rebornstar. Go home now and get some rest. Have a good night."

"You too. Bye."

Lily-Butterfly took her children and left Mrs. Beech's home. She carried Holly and Rebornstar walked alongside her holding her hand. Unknown to Lily-Butterfly conscious confirmation awareness, everything was in destined alignment. All she had to do was continue to follow the inner guidance, guided pathways, surrender, and leap into the unknown with her children.

41

Lily-Butterfly got home, she did the chores with Rebornstar's help, and made dinner. Before going to sleep she wrote in her journal the events of the day, plan of action to get the moving service, completed the packing, and all the other moving assignments. The last thing she did before going to sleep that night was pray to the Creator. Lily-Butterfly thanked the Creator for her and the children's health, Mrs. Beech, Mrs. Diana and her husband, her new home in New Jersey, the Realtor, and everything else. Lily-Butterfly cried tears of joy during the prayer. Even when she closed her eyes and entered dreamland the tears continued. Holly was sound asleep beside her mother's bed. Rebornstar was asleep as well in her room next door. They all slept in contentment.

On Monday when Lily-Butterfly went to work she told Mrs. Diana that she got the apartment. Mrs. Diana expressed her happiness about Lily-Butterfly's apartment accomplishments. During lunch time on Monday Lily-Butterfly found a moving service company in the newspaper. She telephoned them and scheduling moving service. Tuesday night when Lily-Butterfly came home from work she telephoned Manana Leila. She told Manana Leila the complete stories about all her accomplishment and gave her the new address in New Jersey. Manana Leila told Lily-Butterfly that she would give Ms. Gina the new address. The conversations they had that night was with mixed emotions.

"Lily-Butterfly I am happy for you and the children that life is improving. Good for you that you are finding your way in the perilous ocean of human life."

"Thank you Manana for your inspirational words. With the Creator's help and guidance, I am finding my way. One road lead to another, the way shows me the way, and people, places, and things shows up to help and assist me with everything. I am grateful for everything."

"I hear you my child. You are lucky and blessed. I have some news that might dampen your attitude. Gina, Henry, and Dean got their permanent resident visa approved. I will give Gina your new address. She will buy their plane tickets to arrive at Newark, New

Jersey Airport. When you give me your new telephone number, I will give it to her. Gina is planning to arrive on Saturday January 20, 1990. Gina telephoned your home but you were not available. Do you want her work telephone number to call her?"

"No, you tell Ms. Gina to call me any night at 9:00 PM my time. Any news regarding Ms. Gina makes me feel apprehensive. But I have to accept this news. I will prepare my spirit, soul, mind, emotions, body, and life to accommodate what I promised you I would do to help. There seems to never be a dull moment in my life. After sixteen years of being with corrupt Winston she has chosen to take a break and move to the United States. Let me see how Ms. Gina is going to get Winston's visa to come live with her. Or maybe she is planning to live in both places. Anyway, I am just expressing my opinion. Ms. Gina will always choose to do what Ms. Gina wants. I have to go. I am tired. Manana take care of yourself. Thank you for everything."

"You are welcome my child. I am so thankful to you for providing a place for Gina, Henry, and Dean to live until they can rent their own apartment. Good night. Take care of yourself and the children. Bye."

"Yes, Manana. Good night and bye."

That night Lily-Butterfly's prayer conversation with the Creator was, "Creator when am I going to get a break from my life's training? Hu? In eleven weeks, Ms. Gina my wonderful dark arts shadow teacher will be here to live with me. I know that this is not an accident and the interesting thing is I consciously chose this commitment. I committed to this arrangement to help Manana Leila, but I can also see how it will also help me. This experience living with Ms. Gina, Henry, and Dean in such a small apartment is going to be a test of everything I have accomplished so far within me. This experience will test my unconditional love, diligence, patience, unconditional generosity, forgiveness, care, confidence, peace, mental and emotional health, understanding, and so on and so forth. Most of all I think this is to repay Ms. Gina the karma of using her womb to create me. Nothing is free. I surrender to everything that involves the current Ms. Gina karma repayment situation. I am grateful to repay Ms. Gina now, so that I do not have to meet her in another lifetime. You are the Divine Creator God and knows best about everything. Continue to let thy will be done in my life as it is meant to be, and as I choose it to be. Good night. Amin."

When the prayer was completed Lily-Butterfly continued on with processing and pondering. She thought, the most important thing for me is to stay positive. Currently my children and I are healthy. My opinion is health is wealth. We will continue to eat healthy. My New Jersey rent will be less than my current New York rent. Maybe food is more expensive in New Jersey. Soon I have to live with Ms. Gina, Henry, and Dean in a one bed room apartment. What is my daily life going to be like with this new Ms. Gina situation? I do not think that I can do this for more than one year. This is my commitment and promise. I want to help Ms. Gina and Manana, but at the same time I feel disconcerting. Hello self, Lily-Butterfly stop this pondering. It is almost 11:00 PM. Go to sleep. Talking to myself is good for my spirit and soul, but enough is enough. Too much of one thing is good for nothing. The last sentence was the last words that Lily-Butterfly said to herself. She focused on her breathing, went into meditation, and her mind stopped the contemplating and pondering. Within ten minutes she was asleep.

Thursday night at 9:00 PM Lily-Butterfly telephone rang. She picked up the telephone.

"Hi. This is Lily-Butterfly."

"Hello. Hello. This is me, Gina. I am calling you to let you know that we are coming Saturday January 20th next year. Are you coming to the airport to get us?"

"Hi Ms. Gina. No. I do not have a driver's license or a car. I will pay for a taxi to bring you, Henry, and Dean to my home. This cost less money than to pay for a taxi to take me to the airport, and then for the taxi to take us back to my home. After you collect your luggage go outside, you will see taxis. Choose one and give the driver my address. He will take you to my home. I will be here waiting for you. If you need help with directions to go outside to find the taxi, ask an airport attendant. Did Manana Leila give you my new address?"

"Yes, mama gave me your new address."

"Okay. When the taxi arrives come inside and get me. I will come outside and pay the taxi. Be aware that I will be living in a one-bedroom apartment with my two children. I am going to be sharing this apartment with you, Henry, and Dean. If any of you have a problem with this, feel free at any time to go rent your own apartment. You and your sons can live with me for maximum one year. I will loan the three of you my living room. This is the largest room in the apartment. My children and I will sleep and live in the smallest room, which is the bedroom. I will help all of you to get jobs. After saving enough money to get an apartment, I recommend that this is done. I am willing to share everything I have to help you and your sons. I do not live a life of luxury. I live a very simple and mindful life. Ms. Gina do you understand me?"

"Yes, I hear you. When I arrive there, we will talk more. You have another child? I never know this. Oh wow. Thank you for your offers. We will be getting everything free from you to start our life in the United States of America. I do not think that we are going to be picky and critical of what you have to offer us. We will see you soon. Bye."

"Yes, I have another daughter. She is almost four months old. Her name is Holly. I will see you January 20. Good bye."

Ms. Gina and Lily-Butterfly hung up the telephone. Lily-Butterfly tried her best to not ramble in her thoughts about Gina's arrival at her home and living with her, Henry, and Dean.

Saturday November 18, 1989 came. Lily-Butterfly left her two children with Mrs. Beech. She arrived at her new address in New Jersey to get the keys from the Realtor. The Realtor was waiting for her at the main entrance of the building.

"Here you are Lily-Butterfly two keys. One key for the front and basement door, and one for the apartment door. Congratulations and welcome to the neighborhood. Do you have any question?"

"No, I do not have any question about the apartment. Where is the nearest furniture store?"

"The nearest furniture store at the mall on route four in Paramus. The same highway where you got off the bus. Go back to the bus stop you came off the bus. Take any bus passing the Bergen and Garden State Mall on route four. You will see the stores. Get off the bus at a stop by the mall. You will figure things out from there. To go back to New York, take the bus on the opposite side of where you got off the bus. Ask the bus driver to make sure that the bus is going to the bus terminal you want to go to. Take this bus over the George Washington Bridge to the bus terminal. You will figure things out. Do not worry. When in doubt ask questions. Okay."

"Okay. Thank you for all your help."

"You are welcome. I gave you all the contact information and the address to mail your rent check. Here is a copy of the lease. Welcome to New Jersey, the Garden State. I think that you will like living here. How many children do you have?"

"I have two daughters, Rebornstar and Holly. Yes, I think we are going to like living here; and in this Garden State."

"Good luck to you and your children. Bye."

"I cannot thank you enough for giving me this opportunity to rent this apartment. It is very nice and peaceful here. I think this is a great environment for my children and I. Bye."

"Good, enjoy. Bye Lily-Butterfly."

The Realtor left. Lily-Butterfly went inside the building to look at the apartment. She left the apartment after twenty minutes. Lily-Butterfly walked back to the bus stop. She got on the correct bus that was going down route four and passing the Bergen and Garden State Malls. When the bus got to the first mall which was the Bergen Mall Lily-Butterfly rang the bus bell and got off the bus. She went into a furniture store and bought a queen size sleeper couch, three book shelves, and a love seat couch. Lily-Butterfly gave the store clerk the address and date to deliver the furniture. When Lily-Butterfly was finished buying the furniture, she went back to the bus stop to take the bus back to New York. The sleeping arrangement Lily-Butterfly planned for the Ms. Gina's situation was, Ms. Gina could sleep on the current couch. Henry and Dean could sleep on the queen size couch that she had just bought.

Lily-Butterfly arrived at Mrs. Beech's home to get her children at 4:35 PM. She told Mrs. Beech and Rebornstar about all her experience for the day journeying to New Jersey. She also showed them the keys to her new apartment. That night Lily-Butterfly felt assured of her new home and moving to New Jersey. The coming week was Lily-Butterfly, Rebornstar, and Holly's last week living in New York. Rebornstar spent the week saying good bye to all her friends and teachers.

By Thursday of the following week Lily-Butterfly was completely ready with everything that was needed to move. Friday night Lily-Butterfly picked up Rebornstar from Mrs. Beech. She said her final goodbye to Mrs. Beech, her husband, and her son. The present moment of the next step had arrived for Lily-Butterfly, Rebornstar, and Holly. Together they step into the un-known, and unpredictable pathway of the next part of their lives.

42

On Saturday November 25, 1989 at 10:00 AM the moving service truck arrived with two men. They were very helpful and polite. After everything was loaded in the truck Lily-Butterfly thanked the apartment environment for keeping her and her children safe. When the prayer of gratitude to the apartment was completed, Lily-Butterfly locked the door and left. She had planned to mail the apartment key to the New York landlord, and give him her new address to mail her security deposit to her. The moving truck had two sections for passengers. Lily-Butterfly and her children got into the second passenger section of the moving truck and the driver drove off.

As the moving truck approached the George Washington Bridge, Lily-Butterfly thanked and blessed the city of New York that had been her home, and where she met Croco to receive the Croco karma repayment of the priceless gift; Holly. As the moving truck entered New Jersey Lily-Butterfly said a prayer to embrace her new life living in New Jersey with her children. After the prayer she took deep breathes and sighed. Unbeknownst to Lily-Butterfly she had entered the State that she would completely awaken all the talents needed to create her life's purpose career and fulfill her chosen destiny. Lily-Butterfly had just entered another rest, simmering, rebalancing, re-alignment, processing, digest, and awakening her talent vortex. After about five years in this vortex another very active and difficult phase began. At the end of this phase someone very important to her will die. She will re-marry and enter the final stage of giving complete birth to her complete chosen destiny and life purpose career. Yes, imagine picky, energy sensitive, aware, and mindful Lily-Butterfly choosing to marry again. Climbing Mount Everest is not an easy journey. As the story continues to unfold you will see the revelations and situations. Moving to the State of New Jersey a new section of Lily-Butterfly's life's experience had begun.

Anyway, the moving truck arrived at Lily-Butterfly's new home. The very helpful movers brought everything inside the apartment. They set up Rebornstar and Lily-Butterfly's bed in the bedroom.

Holly's crib that was still in the box was placed in the spot where Lily-Butterfly would construct the crib. When the moving men were finished, Lily-Butterfly thanked them, and paid the bill. She gave each one a tip. The moving men left.

Lily-Butterfly smudged the apartment and everything in it with sacred herbs. She said prayers and blessings to create a sacred space environment inside the apartment. Next Rebornstar helped Lily-Butterfly to set up and organize the kitchen. When the kitchen was completely set up Lily-Butterfly took the children outside to show them the park. They spent about an hour at the park and returned to the apartment. Lily-Butterfly and Rebornstar put sheets on their bed and prepared Holly's bassinet. Lily-Butterfly wrote a note to remember to call the cable and phone company to turn on the service. The gas and electric company had already transferred the service into her name. At 6:30 PM Lily-Butterfly made dinner for the children and herself. On Sunday morning after breakfast, Lily-Butterfly and Rebornstar finished setting up the apartment and prepared for school and work on Monday. The other things that needed to be done were completed gradually as the week went by.

Sunday afternoon Lily-Butterfly and the children walked to the supermarket about half a mile away from the apartment. She did a major grocery shopping and took a taxi home. On Sunday night when everything was completed and the children had gone to sleep, Lily-Butterfly sat reflecting on the experiences in New York and moving. The reality of being in her new home with her children was gradually sinking into her reality. Monday morning Lily-Butterfly arrived at work at 10:30 AM because she had requested two hours to register Rebornstar for her new school. Lily-Butterfly also registered Rebornstar for after school program. The after school program at Rebornstar's new school was over at 6:00 PM. At 6:00 PM Rebornstar would walk home with the other children from the apartment complex. By the time Rebornstar got home Lily-Butterfly and Holly had gotten home from work, or they would get home at the same time. Rebornstar also had a house key. If she got home before Lily-Butterfly she could open the apartment door and go inside. Rebornstar sometimes arrived home fifteen minutes before her mother. Moving to New Jersey, Rebornstar practiced being a latchkey child. Her next birthday December 15th Rebornstar would be eleven years old. In the state of New Jersey eleven years old child could be a latchkey child.

When Tuesday arrived Lily-Butterfly had digested the reality of living in New Jersey and a new home environment. She got up at 6:00 AM, and looked at her children and smiled.

"I am happy to be here. Living here is the answer to every prayer that I have had about moving. Winter and snow season is here. I do not have to travel in this season from New York carrying, hustling, and bustling with Holly in her sling laying on my chest. Thanks to the Creator, myself, everyone, and everything that has come together to make all of this possible. Amin," whispered Lily-Butterfly.

She got up and prepared breakfast for the children and herself. After breakfast they all got dressed. Rebornstar walked to school with the children from the apartment complex. Currently Lily-Butterfly and Holly walked to work. The furniture Lily-Butterfly had purchased arrived and she set them up in the living room and created a place for Ms. Gina, Henry and Dean in her living room.

For the first two years after Lily-Butterfly moved from New York she stayed in touch with Mrs. Beech by telephone. Mrs. Beech told Lily-Butterfly that Croco stayed in a coma for nine months. It took him three more months to stabilize his coma recovery. After twelve months Croco's medical evaluation showed that he had lost his short-term memory and his long-term memory was unstable, he was paralyzed from his neck down to his feet, and all his bones were still not healed. With the many surgeries on Croco's face and head he looked different. Croco left the hospital after seventeen months. His medical and physical therapy bills were over one million dollars. All his properties, businesses, business assets, and savings were used to pay his lawyers, medical, physical therapy, and other bills. His mother took what she wanted. At the end of two years after Croco had his accident he had nothing left. His mother Ms. Gene put him in a Medicaid nursing home; where the government paid his bills. Croco spent the rest of his life immobile and in this nursing home. He remained lost within himself and his life. This was a sad situation about Mr. Croco and his life. When Holly was at an age of maturity Lily-Butterfly told Holly about her father when she first met him, what happened when they got to know each other, the accident, and about him being in the nursing home. Lily-Butterfly heard through the grape vine that at fifty-five years old the original Croco and the paralyzed Croco died. He was sent back to the island of Kawomaya to find a burial resting place.

Let us go back to the current time of the story. Lily-Butterfly and her children continued on with their life. Rebornstar and Holly thrived and was content and happy within the cocoon of their mother's unconditional love and understanding. By not having to travel back and forth to New York for work, Lily-Butterfly saved over four hours of travel time to and from work. Now she got home from work by walking twenty minutes or less and by 6:00 PM she was home. At twelve years old Rebornstar stopped going to after school program. She walked home with her friends and the other children who lived in the apartment complex. Rebornstar in her teenager years evolved into a person who was self-reliant, independent, strong minded, stubborn, and liked to be with her friends. I guess like a typical teenager. Friends and being a social butterfly became a significant part of Rebornstar's life and social support system. It was like discovering things with her friends that she never knew existed, and wanting more and more of the experiences that they had to offer. Rebornstar grew as a teenager evolving away from her mother's simple spiritual philosophies and teachings, to a more exciting and normal human world view. Lily-Butterfly thought, that maybe this was Rebornstar's chosen destiny and life's path, but she never gave up being the best parent for Rebornstar. Lily-Butterfly's belief was that Rebornstar would have her own chosen path with guidance, and also her mother's parental teachings, disciplines, and spiritual philosophies. Lily-Butterfly got to practice infinite unconditional love, compassion, peace, patience, and diligence, plus more inner talents, with Rebornstar. Lily-Butterfly became aware that practicing these talents with Rebornstar was some of the reasons that Rebornstar was born to her as her child. These talents became very important when Lily-Butterfly got to the destination of discovering her destiny and life's purpose career. A human cannot give what they do not have. Plus, you have to have the talents cultivated within to share it with other humans.

Lily-Butterfly's plan was to have Rebornstar become a child sitter for Holly so that she could venture into her University Career Training. As the children grew and the economy situations changed, Lily-Butterfly needed more financial income and the security of health insurance; just in case they needed medical treatments.

Rebornstar's choice of taking care of Holly when Lily-Butterfly ventured off into her renewed professional career, was not as Lily-Butterfly wanted it to be, or imagined it would be. But she accepted this, and their life went on as best as possible.

Rebornstar's talents were shown to be more on the creative side. Science and mathematics were her weaker academic subjects. Rebornstar showed no interest on improving these subjects and she was still in special education extra help classes. In fifth grade there was another advanced evaluation of Rebornstar's learning situation. The evaluation test showed that in addition to Rebornstar's choices of the creative arts, she had some spectrum of dyslexia. This was affecting her reading, comprehension, and mathematics; but did not affect her general intelligence. Lily-Butterfly attended a parent teacher evaluation for Rebornstar and the evaluator explained to Lily-Butterfly exactly how the brain processed in this dyslexia situation. Lily-Butterfly took all the awareness and information that she was shown about spectrum of dyslexia Rebornstar had. With the awareness she created a cognitive cognition system of treatments and worked with Rebornstar daily until this spectrum of dyslexia improved. With this improvement, it was easier for Rebornstar to learn and read normally, but she still favored the creative arts. Lily-Butterfly used this treatment process to help Rebornstar with an awareness it was from the Creator. She did not think that the process she used was hers to own. Lily-Butterfly was grateful that Rebornstar's learning situation improved and this was her primary focus.

Lily-Butterfly did not have time for normal human friendships. She focused on having great relationships with all the people she met. But did not have time for the entertainment side of social life friendships and so forth. When she was not at work, she was busy as a parent, spending time with Holly, being home and doing things within the home, reading, writing in her journal, praying, meditating, planning, spending time in nature, doing house chores, pondering, and personal studies and reflections, about how her children and her life was doing. Lily-Butterfly felt and acted like being a single parent was one of the most time consuming, responsible, and consequential human activity. She promised herself and was committed to performing to the best of her abilities the responsibility of parenthood. Telephoning Manana Leila and them writing to each other was a constant part of Lily-Butterfly's life. They remained like two peas in a pod and had great respect, unconditional love, compassion, and generosity towards each other until Manana Leila died, and beyond death. Even to this day Lily-Butterfly can hear from within herself some of the ancient teachings that Manana Leila told her and taught her. It is as if everything was recorded with Lily-Butterfly like a library, and gets replayed, refreshed as needed, and when needed.

Anyway, let us get back on track with Lily-Butterfly's current life's experiences. December 1989 Rebornstar became eleven years old and Lily-Butterfly became thirty -two years old. Holly became five months old on December 31st. At thirty-two years old Lily-Butterfly was aware, responsible, and mature far beyond her years. One of the moment Lily-Butterfly waited for with curiosity happened after Holly became five months old. In January of 1990 Lily-Butterfly noticed that Holly was starting to grow hair. Holly's hair growth was a mixture of copper and bronze, and her skin color was still a golden tone. At five months old Holly first two teeth had begun to peek out from her gum line. Plus, she was crawling, creeping, and trying to hold on to furniture and pull herself up. Reading, playing, and talking to Holly was some of Lily-Butterfly's favorite things to do with her. At work, since Holly became more mobile, Lily-Butterfly kept her in Ana's play pen when she was not able to immediately supervise her mobility. At home there was no play pen so Lily-Butterfly put away all the things Holly could break or hurt herself with.

To help with the safety of Holly's advancement in growth, development, safety, and mobile adventures Lily-Butterfly decided to stop using the bassinet and construct the crib that Croco had bought. The crib was great. It was large like a twin bed with rails on three sides like a crib. Attached to the fourth end of the crib was a chest of drawers. There was two drawers on the bottom as well. At six months Holly had mastered pulling herself up and holding on to furniture to walk. At seven months Lily-Butterfly bought Holly a walker with a play mobile in the front. At this time Holly was scooting around in the walker following her mother around the apartment as well. At nine months Lily-Butterfly stopped carrying Holly in the over the shoulder baby holder. She had gotten heavy although still long, slender, and strong. Lily-Butterfly started to use the stroller that Croco had bought. At ten months Holly was walking and at twelve months Holly was running. She grew fast independent and grounded. After five months as Holly grew her hair grew and remained a curly copper and bronze color. By twelve months old the blue birth mark map was no longer visible. It was now covered with copper and bronze curls.

At thirty-two years old Lily-Butterfly still chose not to get a driver's license and buy a car. With Lily-Butterfly's current salary and monthly financial budget she decided to not buy a car. Instead of buying a car she planned to use the money towards other essential expenses for the children and herself. She was the only parent, financial resource provider, and she had decided to not apply for any free public government financial support. Manana Leila would give Lily-Butterfly money if she asked. At this time Lily-Butterfly did not have or use credit cards and she had no debt. Medical and dental checkups were paid for from her budget income and savings. Although Lily-Butterfly was always on a budget her children had everything they needed, and most things they wanted. One of the important things to Lily-Butterfly was that the children were content, happy, healthy in her nurturing care and unconditional love, had food, shelter, clothing, and a nurturing environment to live in. Plus, Rebornstar and Holly had an over abundant of children where they lived to play, grow, and be friends with.

When Ms. Gina, Henry, and Dean arrived to the United States the complete dynamics of Lily-Butterfly's life changed. Not in a dysfunctional way but she had increased situations to deal with and more people to manage and direct. Lily-Butterfly still made sure that her life's balance was not destabilized and thrown into imbalance. This was not easy for her. As usual Lily-Butterfly really did her best. Keep reading and you will see what I mean. In three weeks, Ms. Gina, Henry, and Dean would arrive in the United States of America, New Jersey, and in Lily-Butterfly's home. If you had read book one of Lily-Butterfly – And The Path Of Life's Experiences part one, you will really get the complete view of the dynamics of Ms. Gina, Lily-Butterfly, Henry, and Dean. Except for talking to Ms. Gina on the telephone the other day, they had not seen or talked to Lily-Butterfly since she left the island of Kawomaya. This was in the summer of 1982, six and a half years ago.

If you think I as the story teller is sometimes being repetitive I have a reason for this style of storytelling and writing. Take what you live, love, and find useful. Please leave the rest undisturbed and without criticism. Thank you. And this journey continues onward.

43

On New Year's Day January 1, 1990 Lily-Butterfly got the internal guidance to learn more about the current human scientific views on how the human mind, emotion, and body function work together or not. She already knew how the spirit and soul was supposed to work with the mind, emotions, and body. By now, Lily-Butterfly came to realize that normal people she encountered, did not believe or know that there were spirits and also ghosts. Plus, the emotions of people seem frozen and non-existent. People seemed to mostly function from a mind and body perception, was afraid and uncomfortable showing emotions and feelings, plus value material thing and money the most. Another reason for Lily-Butterfly's intention to learn more about the scientific views about the mind, emotions, and body was, because she wanted to work on any and all resentments, hate, improve forgiveness, and negative energy emotions that she might still have left towards Ms. Gina, Croco, the other people she have met so far, and her life's experiences. One day while processing this intention Lily-Butterfly was passing a book store at the shopping plaza close to her house. She was guided to go into the book store, and she did. Her intuition and inner guidance guided her to go to the section of the book store that had books on psychology and psychiatry. This is the first day she learned that there was such words psychology and psychiatry. The books that she wanted to buy was in this section of the book store. This day she learned that psychology and psychiatry had to do with the scientific study of the human mind and its other functions in relationship to the human biological system. This day Lily-Butterfly thought the word and meaning psychology and psychiatry were interesting.

For Lily-Butterfly this day began a deeper study in the human views on psychology and psychiatry. Lily-Butterfly found the human created study and views on Psychology, psychiatry, and how it relates to her ancient views and awareness about spirit, soul, mind, emotions, fear, love, trauma, child abuse, suffering, death, life, body, and the material and physical human perceptive realm very interesting. She bought five books that day and left the book store. Lily-Butterfly current constant companion Holly was with her at the book store.

Until Lily-Butterfly moved from this town this book store became the best place and resource of learning for her. Lily-Butterfly studies really helped her to understand how humans' function outside the spiritual and soul awareness, universal wisdom, unconditional love, and compassion. This new awareness and studying improved Lily-Butterfly's communication style. To her what she learned from reading the books was like speaking another language, and learning about the mind, emotion, and body function of other humans. Lily-Butterfly learned the distinct difference between normal people rational wisdom views language, and authentic ancient spirit, soul, wisdom, and Universal intelligence, wisdom language. She had grown up in a village where everything was oral tradition, and not even spiritual and soul wisdom information was written down on paper. Her ancestors beyond her, as a young child, even Manana Leila, might never had read English words or any other language written on paper. The authentic oral tradition was learnt and shared from heart to heart, and mouth to mouth, by word of mouth, and sacred rite of passages. Now Lily-Butterfly was increasing her knowledge on the modern human learning, knowledge, and awareness. She found everything about what she was learning very interesting for her curious spirit, soul, mind, and body. To this day Lily-Butterfly's modern human created views learning, has not stopped. This learning and many others helped Lily-Butterfly to fulfill her chosen destiny and life's purpose.

At work, everything for Lily-Butterfly continued to work like a well-oiled machine. Mrs. Diana and her husband were pleased with the quality of work Lily-Butterfly did. Their only major concern was that Ana was two months and one week younger than Holly but was not showing improved signs of using her motor and developmental skills. For example, if Ana was placed on her back she would stay in the spot where she was placed and did not naturally move. They would compare Ana with how Holly was doing. Lily-Butterfly explained repeatedly that different children developed differently. When this issue was presented by Mrs. Diana as a concern, Lily-Butterfly guided her to talk to her Pediatrician about her concerns. Also, Lily-Butterfly started to consider leaving Holly at home during the day with Dean, when he arrived from Kawomaya. Dean could go to work when she arrived home from work. This could maybe give her the opportunity to give Ana some more undivided attention. This was the only thing that Lily-Butterfly saw that she could do to improve the Ana mobility and developmental situation. Holly was at work with Ana, and normally younger children can choose to mimic and copy older children and what they did. At this time Ana was not choosing to copy and mimic what Holly did. Lily-Butterfly felt that with time Ana would naturally improve when it was time for her to do so. Lily-Butterfly noticed that other aspects of the borderline down syndrome spectrum had improved for Ana.

Lily-Butterfly thought, everything is connected. Ana's mobile skills might be the last thing to improve while other things were improving. In time everything will come together in complete improved function for Ana. Her growth and development will take its natural course, until then things are the way they are.

Saturday January 20, 1990 came. Lily-Butterfly had the large living room area set up as a bedroom and living accommodation for Ms. Gina, Henry, and Dean. She cooked different kinds of food for when they arrived at her home. Rebornstar was at the park playing with her friends. There was a knock on the door at 2:00 PM. Lily-Butterfly opened the door. The spicy aroma of the food penetrated out into the hallway. Lily-Butterfly saw Ms. Gina, Henry, and Dean standing by the door with their suitcases.

"Hi everyone, welcome. Henry here is the money for the taxi. Go pay him and come back."

Henry took the money and went down stairs.

"Hello Lily-Butterfly. It was easy for the taxi driver to find your apartment. You live at a nice place. Ha," said Ms. Gina.

"Yes. Come in. Bring in all the suitcases and put them over by the window. This is my small and simple home that I will be sharing with all of you," said Lily-Butterfly.

"Okay thank you. I am very hungry. I am glad that you cooked. The food smells delicious. The food on the plane was like bird food. The food was light as a feather, taste like paper, and had no smell. Oh my. Here we are. I am so hungry," said Ms. Gina.

"You should be thankful that you had some kind of food," replied Lily-Butterfly.

Dean smiled. Henry returned from paying the taxi driver.

"Hi Lily-Butterfly," said Henry.

"Hi come in. All of you please take off your shoes and put on the shoe shelf by the front door. We do not wear shoes inside the house," said Lily-Butterfly.

They all removed their shoes and put their suitcases over by the window in the corner.

"You can all sit down on the couch. Would you all like some tea?" asked Lily-Butterfly.

"Yes. Sure. Tea is good, to start," replied Ms. Gina.

"Okay. Come over here I will show you the bathroom. Wash your hands," said Lily-Butterfly.

They all washed their hands. Lily-Butterfly walked back to the kitchen. As usual, Holly was by her side.

"I am not going to hug them and have a transferal of their negative energy, stress, and toxic emotions go inside me. Sorry. I have to stay healthy to take care of the children, my life, myself, and go to work. Plus, I do not feel like it. I am not going to be fake," mumbled Lily-Butterfly.

Gina came to the kitchen door.

"Are you talking to me? I heard you say something," said Ms. Gina.

"I am talking to myself," replied Lily-Butterfly.

"Oh. Okay. Where is the tea? We are ready for your delicious food," said Ms. Gina.

Henry and Dean smiled.

"Mama you are something else," said Henry.

"Everyone come to the kitchen. There is food in bowls on the cupboard. Plates and utensils are set on the table. There is a mug of tea for each person, sugar, and milk are on the table. Help yourself to how much food you like. Sit, eat, and drink your tea. The children and I will eat later. Later for dinner you will eat some of the same food. There are restaurants on the main road up the street. Later if you like, you can go to one of these restaurants or eat more of the same food. Your choice. I am going to the park with Holly to look for Rebornstar. I will be back by the time you are finished eating," said Lily-Butterfly.

"Okay," replied Ms. Gina.

Lily-Butterfly went to the park and returned. Holly was with her and Rebornstar chose to play some more with her friends.

"Good now that your bellies are full, let us sit, and have a meeting. I need to let you all know of my intentions, guidance, how I choose to share my apartment, and help all of you. Again, welcome to the United States of America and my home. You will learn very quick that things are not like you might have imagined it in this country. All of you might be stressed from having to leave your life behind on the island of Kawomaya. Are there any questions?" said Lily-Butterfly.

"My brain is frozen. It is as if I am still on the island," said Dean.

"Me too. It is as if this has not happened," said Henry.

"For me it is hard. To me it is as if I left over fifty five years of my life behind. I feel more stuck. Moving here was not easy. I came only because I received the opportunity. If I stay in this country it is as if I have to start over. My plan is to go back to the island after six months. Maybe live in both countries. We will see. Lily-Butterfly, why did you have us come live with you instead of us going to mama?" said Ms. Gina.

"I chose to have all of you come to temporarily stay with me because I wanted to help Manana Leila. Her apartment situation might not be convenient to have all of you live there. She would have to be the one helping to manage and direct all of you. I am helping her to not have to stress about all your relocation situations. Plus, I wanted to help all of you to have the best opportunity to restart your lives. Anyway, here we are," said Lily-Butterfly.

"I see. You are right. Maybe we would stress mama out, and she would stress me out. Mama is simple thinking and very country and old fashion. Lily-Butterfly you are tougher in the stressing out department. It takes a lot to rock your ship. Plus, you are acclimated in the ancient ways and the modern human ways. So, what do you have planned for us? Miss manager, organizer, and director. Ha?" said Ms. Gina.

"Ms. Gina I am happy that you know that my ship is hard to rock and become unstable. My offer to stay in my home is six months to maximum one years. I am strongly recommending six months. If you are undecided whether you want to live in the United States permanent or temporarily, please decide what your choice will be, from your own rented apartment. My home will not be the foundation from where you wait to make this decision. I want all of you to make having your own apartment your first priority. After this is achieved you will move to your own apartment and do whatever you like. I hope that I was clear enough with this view and situation. As you can see this is a small place for six people to live in permanent and long term. I am inconveniencing my life, my children, and myself with this generous assistant and help. None of you will take advantage of me. I am being so specific, because I know, and have experienced all of you," said Lily-Butterfly.

"Oh, by the way. Sorry to interrupt your meeting and

announcements. Is this your baby daughter Hol? Where is Rebornstar?" said Ms. Gina.

"Her name is not Hol, it is Holly. Rebornstar is at the park behind the building. Let us get back to the focus of this meeting. As I was saying. I will help all of you find jobs. I will financially give all of you money for winter coats, hats, gloves, clothes, and shoes. You can also live here without paying for rent and food. When you all have jobs, save up the money to move within six months, maximum one year. If the food I can afford and provide is not up to your standard, please feel free to provide yourselves with additional food to your preference. Use the kitchen how and when you like. Just clean the kitchen and things that is used after every use. I do not want dirty dishes in the kitchen over-night. This can help minimize rodents and insects. All of you use your suitcases as drawers and closets. The children and I are already using the two closets we have. Ms. Gina here is the telephone numbers for employment agencies for child care and home health aide. If you find a job that you can live at, this would be great. You have twenty-five years of nursing aid care experience. It should be easy for you to find a job like this. All of you keep me informed of your job search success when you find one. The large couch is a pull out queen size bed, the smaller couch is a full size bed, and the smallest couch which is called a love seat is a seat for two people. Ms. Gina you can sleep on the full size pull out couch bed, and Henry and Dean can sleep on the queen sized pull out couch bed. Henry and Dean buy the newspaper tomorrow at the store on the corner up the street. Look in the classified section of this newspaper for jobs you might choose to work in. Sometimes there are lots of restaurant jobs advertised. Welcome to the United States of America the land of opportunities. But you have to take action to find the opportunity that you like or not. Get with the program. Take time to learn about your new home location. Get to know your environment. With three of you working as soon as possible you should have money to rent an apartment in six months. I am generous. Do not take my generosity for stupidity. I am very far from being stupid. Please do not try to test my boundaries. I have also a no nonsense focus and attitude. I am able to stay un-corrupt and productive by my choices, responsibilities, actions, and practices. Do you all understand me?" said Lily-Butterfly.

"Oh wow. Girl I feel more like you should say 'welcome to the army', instead of welcome to the United States of America. You are so direct in your communication style. No beating around the bush.

You waste no time in giving us the right view of our choices and situations," said Ms. Gina.

"Good that you understand me Ms. Gina. I am not available for anyone to abuse or create suffering situations for me to live with or in. I am not perfect, but I make conscious positive choices. I am happy that I was clear enough for you to understand the picture of my intention and how I would like to assist and help all of you. Ms. Gina make sure that you call the two employment agencies on Monday. Today is Saturday. Welcome to my home. I will help, assist, and treat all of you with respect, unconditional love, and care. Please be mindful of doing the same for me. Ms. Gina be mindful of your entitlement attitude, stubbornness, un-mindfulness, and the abusive ways you use to abuse me, and the negative servant program that you used to want me to live. Inside and outside me this program is all abolished, deleted, and nonexistent. I worked very hard to be the person I am today. Curb your crappy attitudes. Henry and Dean, I will not accept no shitty attitudes from any of you. The abuse program that you used to see your mother use on me has been dissolved and transformed. Do you have questions or concerns?"

"No, I do not have any question. Do you have more commands to tell us? Go right ahead with your demands, announcements, and speech," said Ms. Gina.

"Okay. My telephone can only make calls in the state of New Jersey. So, you will not be able to telephone people on the island of Kawomaya or outside the state of New Jersey. Do all of you have money to pay for public transportation, taxi, and other personal things that you need?"

"Yes, we have some money," replied Ms. Gina.

"Good. Make sure that all of you find a job before the money you have is finished. Creator I know that you are listening, and you know everything already. Please help Ms. Gina, Henry, and Dean to find jobs as soon as possible. Creator I am very grateful for everything. Amin," said Lily-Butterfly

"Ha. You are still very spiritual Lily-Butterfly. Good for you," said Ms. Gina.

"Yes Ms. Gina to me, without my spirituality and the Creator, my life would be useless. Amin," said Lily-Butterfly.

"You basically cannot wait for us to leave. We will find jobs and we will leave as soon as possible. We do not need to feel like we are living in a half-way house, prison, and jail. As you say we will have everything we choose to do when we have our own apartment.

I will make sure that I get a job as soon as possible. We will rent an apartment as soon as we save up the money, and we will leave your sacred sanctuary, nest, and cave. Amin," said Ms. Gina.

"Ms. Gina, instead of saying thank you, this is what you have to say. Blessings to you. Thank you for coming here. I will get another precious opportunity to practice unconditional love, deep understanding, diligence, morality, generosity, patience, and everything else. I really appreciate you and your children being here. I get to see myself, who, and what I am, very clearly. To me humans are very interesting. I think that my chosen destiny and life's purpose career is going to be about assisting and helping the Creator with its wonderful and interesting humans. Everything I experience so far in my life is preparing me for doing this, and using my spirit and soul talents. We will see when the time comes. The way will show the way. Thanks to all of you for your participation in my life's practices, transformation, evolution, and so forth. Amin,"

said Lily-Butterfly.

"Lily-Butterfly you are so deep. We will see. Right now, for us, the farthest we can see is; Monday I will look for a job. All of us need to find a job as soon as possible. We have to move out of your spiritual nest and church. I do not need to listen to this holy talking every day. Ha. I have thrown the ways of the Creator and the ancestors away from the day I choose to leave the forest valley and village of Yaj that I was born in, and grew up in. Now in reality I have chosen the path of the lost souls. This is my choice for now. Until I choose to leave where I choose to be stuck, I am where I am. Do you understand?" said Ms. Gina."

"Sure, I understand you. You are lucky that you got to choose the path of the ancestors. But you choose to waste all the positive opportunities of this path. Your choices and actions are between the Creator, yourself, and karma. I can promise you that you will not escape karma. On your death bed and in your after life, karma will be in front, behind, and around you. Plus, your karma will be your transportation to the afterlife. There is no escaping your actions and karma. Ms. Gina karma means, actions in thoughts, speech, and physical actions. Karma can be positive or negative. Whether you believe in karma or not; karma is real. Anyway, enough of my kind of spiritual talking. Enjoy the rest of your evening. More food is on the stove and in the oven for dinner. You can organize your thoughts and process your experiences so far. For all of you there is an empty book shelf in the corner that can be used. I am going to get

Rebornstar from the park. Later, the children and I will eat. After all of you have eaten go outside and tour the apartment complex. Make yourselves feel at home as best as you can. I am going outside now. Bye," said Lily-Butterfly.

"Okay Lily-Butterfly we will do everything that you guided us to do," said Ms. Gina.

"Yes, we will," said Henry and Dean.

Lily-Butterfly got Rebornstar and returned to have dinner with her children. Rebornstar greeted Ms. Gina, Henry and Dean. After dinner Lily-Butterfly washed the dishes and cleaned up the kitchen, put all the leftover food in the refrigerator, gave Holly and herself a bath. Rebornstar took a shower and watched television. Lily-Butterfly went to her bedroom with Holly. She read Holly a story and put her in her crib to play with some toys. When Holly was ready, she laid down and went to sleep for the night. At 10:00 PM Rebornstar came to bed. Lily-Butterfly came out of her room at 10:00 PM to remind Ms. Gina, Henry and Dean to wash their dirty dishes and clean up the kitchen when they were finished eating. Lily-Butterfly returned to her room for the complete rest of the night. She wrote in her journal and prayed before she went to sleep.

On this day an amplified new vortex of life's experiences had begun for Lily-Butterfly.

44

On Sunday afternoon after the six of them had eaten lunch Lily-Butterfly gave Ms. Gina, Henry, and Dean, detailed instructions on how to take the public transportation. She gave each of them two keys, one for the entrance door to the building, and one to unlock and lock the apartment door. Lily-Butterfly showed them the laundry room in the basement of the apartment. She told them where to take a taxi if they did not want to take public transportation. Guided them where to get the bus to take them to different places on the highway route four, the mall locations, and where the supermarket was located. She also walked with them to the supermarket, and showed them the shopping plaza across the street from the supermarket, as well as where the bank was in this shopping plaza. On the way walking back to the apartment Lily-Butterfly walked with them along the main road to the apartment to see the restaurants and shops that were close to the apartment. Lily-Butterfly felt like a tour guide, group home manager, and director. At the end of the day she felt drained and tired. It was not easy being around people whose perception seemed to be just taking, more taking, and draining everything. After the tour guidance experiences Lily-Butterfly went home and made the third meal of the day; dinner. She reminded Ms. Gina, Henry, and Dean about the basic house rules. Lily-Butterfly finished her daily chores and preparation for work, Rebornstar for school, and Holly. When the children and herself were showered and bathe, they went to their bedroom to complete their activities for the day. As usual at the end of every day Lily-Butterfly processed her day by writing in her journal and praying. The children and Lily-Butterfly were so drained and tired that when their bodies touched the bed within five minutes, they were asleep. Asleep and in dream-land.

The week went by very quickly for Lily-Butterfly having to wake up at 6:00 AM, make breakfast, work from 8:30 AM to 5:30 PM, getting home by 6:00 PM, cooking dinner, and everything else. Ms. Gina, Henry, and Dean were on their own figuring out and making breakfast and lunch for themselves. It was their responsibility to as well clean up the room they used and the kitchen. Plus take the garbage out when they saw that the garbage can was full. If they did not do something Lily-Butterfly would remind them. At the end of the first week Ms. Gina, Henry, and Dean had not gone on a job interview as yet. They made inquirers about possible work employment, and had appointments scheduled for job interviews. On Saturday morning after breakfast Lily-Butterfly took them to the Garden State Mall. By doing this Gina, Henry, and Dean also learned how to get to the mall by themselves. Going to the mall on the bus was their first public transportation experience. She bought each of them winter coats, clothes, gloves, hats, and shoes. They also purchased from their own money other things that they wanted. After shopping they all had lunch at the mall food court. When they arrived home, it was 3:35 PM. Lily-Butterfly took Holly to the park to play and spend time in nature. Rebornstar came to the park with her mother. She played with her sister and her friends. At 5:49 PM Lily-Butterfly went back to the apartment with Holly. At this time Ms. Gina, Henry, and Dean went downstairs to the laundry room to do their laundry, talk, and go for a walk outside. Lily-Butterfly made dinner for everyone. After setting up the dinner she smudged herself, Holly, and the apartment. This purified and cleansed stressful vibrations from the apartment. This helped to minimize her stress, create peaceful and positive vibes, and rebalance the apartment environment.

On Sunday at breakfast Ms. Gina announced, "I have an appointment for a live-in childcare job interview on Tuesday at 10:00 AM. I need help with directions to take the bus. The job is to take care of a one year old baby girl, and a four year old boy. Maybe I will get lost. Lily-Butterfly I wish that you could come with me."

"I have to go to work. Telephone the bus company give the person who answers the telephone the address, and ask which bus to take. You will be fine; this is part of moving here. All of you have to figure out what to do. I am here to assist and help."

Lily-Butterfly stopped talking. She thought, Ms. Gina will not last one week in a childcare job. Ms. Gina is clueless about taking care of children. She does not have one bone of childcare talent. Creator please find Ms. Gina a live-in job where she can work Monday to Friday, and maybe come here only Saturday and Sunday. They would have worn out Manana's nerves she has left in her old age. Creator although you are very busy, please remember me. My prayers keeps us connected. Amin.

"Hello Lily-Butterfly, I am talking to you. You are on one of your day-dream excursions. What time do you go to work in the morning?"

"I leave here for work at 8:00 AM. I have to be there by 8:30 AM."

"Are you taking your Holly with you?"

"Yes. Why are you asking? I would not leave her with you."

"You think that I cannot take care of children? Ha?"

"You know the parts of yourself that you choose to know, better than anyone else. But I know your complete self and everything else. My daughter is safer with me, than leaving her with you. This is all I choose to say about this issue. I do not want to talk about who and what you are Ms. Gina. This would be a waste of my time."

"Suit yourself. You are the smartest human alive. This is what you think. Ha?"

"I am who and what I am. I do not think I am the smartest human on this planet. I just use my Creator created wisdom that is it. This is my choice. Everyone has choices. You stay here and make the best of my generosity or you leave and figure out your way on your own. This conversation is over. Understand?"

"Okay Lily-Butterfly. I understand."

"Good for you."

Ms. Gina went to the interview on Tuesday. She found the address location. Ms. Gina was given the job opportunity with a one week trial. At the end of the week if the employer did not like her work she would be asked to leave. When Ms. Gina returned from the interview, she packed a small suitcase with clothes and personal items. The job was working from Monday to Friday with the weekend off. Ms. Gina told Lily-Butterfly the news when she came home from work on Monday evening.

"I got the job on a trial basis. To tell you the truth I do not like taking care of children. For many reasons I might get fired in two days. Ha. Mmm. I am taking this job because of what you told us, which is basically work, save, and find our own place to live in six months to one year. I do not think that we are going to enjoy living with you in your sacred space."

"Ms. Gina with your personality and attitude you give yourself the freedom of thinking, doing, and saying anything you like. You give yourself the choice of no responsibility and consequences to your actions. I am the opposite. We are aware of each other's ways. I do not want to consistently bicker or have negative conversations with you. Thank you for everything. Ms. Gina from my birth to today, you help me practice my chosen spiritual path. But, please for both our sake, hurry up and find your own way forward in this country. Okay. I have things to do."

"Why with all your education you choose to work in a childcare job?" said Ms. Gina.

"So, that I am available to take care of my children. To me childcare job is one of the most important human job. When Holly is five years old, Rebornstar will be almost sixteen. Rebornstar can baby sit Holly and I can work in my professional training career and so forth."

"I see. You are strict and specific. Good for you that you have this mindful, aware, love, generosity, peaceful spiritual personality, straight forward attitude, and love taking care of children."

"I am happy that you have grown to see me more clearly. Maybe I spent many lifetimes being a spiritual warrior and no non-sense spirit and soul. I love and like being a spirit, soul and human of the ancient pathways."

"Say what you like. I am leaving in the freezing cold and snow next week Monday at 7:00 AM. Oh, my Lord. I wish that you had a car to take me to work. The cold makes my bones scream. Ha. You are in this country long enough to learn to drive and have a car. Why are you still walking and taking public transportation like a country bumpkin?"

"I use my money for more important things, like getting an improved human knowledge and education, taking care of my children, and being the only financial resource for my children and myself. When it is time to get my driver's license and buy a car, I will. Until then I am where I choose to be. Even if I have a car, I would not take you to work. Ms. Gina you can learn to drive and buy a car if this is your priority. I am busy going to work and taking care of my children to be your chauffeur. Good for you that you have found a job. If you get fired telephone the employment agency again and get another job. Ms. Gina my days of catering to you are over. I am cooking dinner and talking to you. I am finished talking to you. Find some other kind of entertainment. I am busy."

"You are the queen of your castle, yourself, and your children. Good that you have the reigns of your life in harmony and balance. Maybe one day I will choose to straighten out my spirit, soul, mind, and life. Right not I am not feeling like I want to. I am going for a walk."

"Good. Come back in an hour, dinner will be ready. I think that Henry and Dean are at the park, gone for a walk, or at a job interview. See you later. Ms. Gina you are lucky."

After saying this Lily-Butterfly put Holly in her walker to play while she completed the cooking. Rebornstar had arrive home with her homework completed and was at the park playing with her school friends. At 7:00 PM Rebornstar came home and took a shower. 7:15 PM Ms. Gina returned and they had dinner. Henry and Dean were still not home. They had dinner by themselves when they came home. Another day went by for Lily-Butterfly and her children. Lily-Butterfly was getting acclimated to Ms. Gina, Henry, and Dean living with her. Lily-Butterfly's day ended as usual with the same routines of getting Holly and herself ready for bed, journaling, reading her new self-help books, and prayer. Rebornstar was self-reliant and growing more and more into her independence and towards teenager-hood. Henry and Dean continued to look for restaurant jobs and going on interviews. They seem to have learned how to take the bus and accepted their situations.

The following week Monday Ms. Gina left Lily-Butterfly's apartment for her first job. The apartment was quieter and more peaceful without her. Lily-Butterfly got a rest from choosing to consistently redirect Ms. Gina. Lily-Butterfly knew that she could ignore her. But she thinks that ignoring Ms. Gina would be giving her the impression what she is endorsing her crap in every way. Work was the same for Lily-Butterfly and by now she had mastered the art of managing the two children, the house work, laundry, and everything else. Lily-Butterfly thought living in New Jersey and working close to her home was a blessing; and she was very grateful for this.

Friday evening Lily-Butterfly got home from work and as usual the first assignment was to make dinner. At 7:10 PM Gina arrived home. She opened the apartment door and came inside.
"Guess what?" said Ms. Gina.
'You are fired," replied Lily-Butterfly.
"Yes. How do you know?"
"I know, because I know you as well as you know yourself, and ever more than you choose to know yourself."
"The lady told me on Wednesday that I am not a good fit for taking care of children and housekeeping. I knew this as well. At least I tried. Ha. Mmm. She let me work until today. And here I am. Sorry. This woman is worse than me with taking care of her own children. I never took care of my own children when they were young. I really do not think I can take care of other people's children. This is the

truth. I do not feel bad that she fired me. I got one week's pay. Good for me. I am going to look for a job as a Home Health Aid provider, taking care of the elderly. I have done this for twenty five years this is where my professional skills, career experiences, and qualification is most efficient. Oh Lord. The cold really gets to my bones and sends shivers up my body. I do not think that I could travel back and forth in the winter. I have to find a live-in job. Lily-Butterfly are you listening to me?"

"Yes, I am hearing you, maybe not listening, because I do not care too much about what you are saying. I know everything that you are saying already. But out of respect I am letting you talk. Find the kind of work you choose to do. I do not care what you choose. All I know is that you will have to work. Period and end of this work issue. I am busy preparing dinner. The children have to eat and it is getting late."

"I know that your children are your first priority, next yourself, and your life; plus, you choose to share what you can. Good for you."

"Yes, you are right about everything you have said. Dinner is almost ready."

"Where is Henry and Dean?" asked Ms. Gina.

"I do not know. They are grown adults. I came home and did not see them. Maybe they are gone on job interviews."

"Job interviews at night?" asked Ms. Gina.

"Yes, maybe restaurant jobs. This is America things are not like on the island. Things happen when they need to happen. They will be back when they are ready. I usually leave their dinner in the oven on warm temperature."

"Lily-Butterfly at least you are not strict with what time they come home."

"They are grown men."

This was Friday of week two since Ms. Gina and her sons came to live with Lily-Butterfly. That Friday night only Dean came home at 11:00 PM. He ate his dinner and put Henry's portion into the refrigerator. Henry did not come home and Lily-Butterfly was not aware of where he was. Henry had telephoned his mother to say where he was. Dean had gone on an interview during the day on Friday. He got a job working on the night shift at a restaurant. The job was as a cashier and food preparation cook. He started to work the same day. Dean's work schedule was Thursday to Sunday, 5:00 PM to 10:30 PM. To prevent wasting food this day was the last day that Lily-Butterfly left food in the oven for Henry and Dean. After dinner she would put the extra cooked dinner in the refrigerator. If they came home and wanted food, they got it from the refrigerator. Dean was the more reserved and serious of Ms. Gina's two sons. Lucy and Henry was more like Ms. Gina's personality. Dean was a mix of his own personality and a little of Ms. Gina's personality.

At breakfast time on Saturday morning Henry had still not come home.

"Where is Henry?" Lily-Butterfly asked Ms. Gina.

"He telephone me last night to say that he is staying with a girlfriend at a motel down the street."

"What girlfriend? He found girlfriend already and sleeping at a motel? Oh wow. Where did he find this girlfriend so quick?" said Lily-Butterfly.

"Oh. It is someone he knows from high school and the island of Kawomaya. She was living in Florida. They were communicating by letter when Henry was still living in Kawomaya. Now that Henry moved here, she moved from Florida to New Jersey, to be with Henry. She just has to find an apartment to live. Ha. Mmm. This is the story in a nut shell."

"I see. This seems like a very simple and interesting story. Okay Ms. Gina. You are keeping something about this story in disguise. Time will reveal everything."

"What Lily-Butterfly. You are the oracle of perception, intuition, and visions. The story is like I told you."

"So, Ms. Gina, Henry made previous arrangements with her to move to New Jersey? Instead of focusing on a job and getting himself straightened out, he is focused on a girlfriend, and her moving from Florida to New Jersey. And now both of them are at the motel down the street. Interesting."

"Yes. What? Do you have a problem with what Henry chose to do? Like you said he is a grown man."

"I find this story presented in a nut shell interesting. I am sensing that Henry is sneaky like you and his father. All I know is that he is welcome to stay here under the conditions that I proposed to all of you on the first day of arrival. Let me wait and see if he has the audacity to try to bring this girlfriend into my apartment to live. I smell a rat and fox in this situation. Ms. Gina, you are co-dependending your children with the same things, attitude, and personality that you have. Know that I am the opposite and I am not having any crap from any of you. None of you will take advantage of me and my generosity.

Know this. We will see. Usually things hidden in the dark and in disguise becomes exposed."

"Henry and his girlfriend already spent the days here when you are at work. When they know that you are coming home, they leave. I am confessing, because knowing you, sooner or later you would find out what is going on. You are too wise Lily-Butterfly. It is not easy to pull the dark veil over your eyes."

"I knew my senses and instincts were correct. I am not having this situation going on in my home. You encourage Henry's crap after I give all three of you the opportunity to stay in my home and share what I have. Let me be silent and see what is next."

After breakfast Ms. Gina washed the dishes and cleaned up the kitchen. Dean cleaned the room they were living in. Lily-Butterfly cleaned her bedroom and went downstairs with Rebornstar and Holly to do the laundry. Rebornstar was learning how to do her laundry. Holly walked around in her walker and played with her toys on the walker tray. At 11:50 AM Lily-Butterfly and Rebornstar had finished with the laundry. All three of them went upstairs to the apartment. When Lily-Butterfly entered her apartment Ms. Gina and Dean were sitting in the living room on the couch. Henry and his girlfriend were sitting around the dining table eating the food from dinner the night before. Dean got up and went into the bathroom to take a shower. Dean basically removed himself from the confrontation that he perceived would happen. Lily-Butterfly passed the kitchen and went into her bedroom with the children to put the laundry away.

When Lily-Butterfly finished with putting the laundry away she left her bedroom with the intention to talk to Henry.

"Why is there two extra suitcases in my living room? Who is this woman? Why is she here?" asked Lily-Butterfly.

"Give them a break. Let her stay here with Henry. Ha. Be nice for a change. Relax," said Ms. Gina.

"So, Ms. Gina you encouraged them to come here. I was very clear about how much I wanted to give you, Henry, and Dean. Henry is welcome to stay in my apartment until he can get his own apartment. There are six of us living in this space already. This woman cannot live here. She must leave now. Do not wait for me to throw her suitcases outside and call the police. I am as nice as I want and choose to be. I am relaxed. None of you will give me stress, extra suffering, and so forth. Henry is free to choose to leave immediately and permanently with her as well. Ms. Gina if you say one word encouraging this situation, I will ask you to leave permanently with Henry and his girlfriend. You can go with them if you like. The days of all of you not respecting me; is over. Do not test me. Now what will you choice to do Mr. Henry and Ms. Gina?" said Lily-Butterfly.

"Where should we go? We do not have anywhere else to go," grumbled Henry.

"Henry, this issue you are presenting is not my problem. I agreed to help you. This is as far as my generosity can be."

"We sleep at the motel at night. We used to spend our days here. What do you want us to do?"

"Already you violated my generosity and what I offered by having her spend the days I am at work here. Give me my apartment keys. If you do not give them to me, I will take them and call the police if you try to fight with me. Give me my keys."

"Here are your keys. What now? You want us to go live in the motel?"

"After what you have done and are trying to do, I do not care where you go. I do not. Talk to your mother. Hello Miss take your suitcases out of my apartment. Go wait for Henry outside in the parking lot. Go now. Henry and Ms. Gina this situation shows me that none of you care about my well-being and my children. I am not going to wait for more of this sitttyness to happen. Now Henry what are you going to choose to do?"

"I am leaving with her. We will go back to live in the motel. We will find jobs. When we save enough money, I will get an apartment for us. Lily-Butterfly be this way. Damn. Mama give us some money so that we can pay the motel bill and buy food."

"Henry here is $950. This is all I have for now. Good luck. I will be getting a new job soon. Keep in touch. All the best with everything. Telephone a taxi to bring all your things and your girlfriend things to the motel. Both of you find jobs. You will be fine. I am going to find a live-in job, so I will not be here most of the time. If you choose to go with your girlfriend that is your choice."

Lily-Butterfly stood there and heard Ms. Gina talking to Henry. The girlfriend took her suitcases and left the apartment.

"Ms. Gina give me the house keys I gave you. Does this girl have a permanent resident visa?" said Lily-Butterfly.

"Why do you want back the keys? No, she does not have a permanent resident visa," replied Ms. Gina.

"I choose to take them back. You might decide to give Henry the keys, and he still comes here with this girl when I am not here. This is a security issue as well for my children and myself. I usually do not wait for problems to take root in my life. Dean has a key, between you and him decide how you are going to share one set of keys. Or Ms. Gina you can plan to come into my apartment when I am home. This girl wants to use Henry to get her permanent resident visa. He has just come here from the island to live. I do not know her and I have not given permission for her to come into my home. Henry planned to use me as a part of his plans; without asking me, wow. He planned to move his girlfriend into my apartment right before my eyes, without asking my permission. Sometimes relatives can be worse than enemies and strangers. Henry is no longer welcome to come here whether I am here or not. Henry you and your girlfriend figure out your plans without using me. Henry if you are stupid, I am not. I do not encourage people who violate me and do not care about me into my life. I have no space and time for problems. I might seem abrupt and mean to all of you. But this is how I perceive I have to be to protect myself. Ms. Gina please go outside and talk to Henry. I do not want to hear what both of you are saying."

"I will leave with my girlfriend. We will live at the motel until we have money to get an apartment together. We are getting married in two months. When I marry her, I will file for her green card. She will get a work permit and will be able to work," said Henry.

"Henry I can see that you are impulsive and stupid. Ms. Gina you know of Henry's plan and kept it a secret. I change my mind about giving a year, to find your own apartment, because of all these experiences. You have $950 to give Henry now to pay for motel. I think all of you have money to put together to rent an apartment right now. So, I am changing my proposal to maximum six months for you and Dean to rent an apartment and leave my apartment, instead of giving your money to Henry. Know that I will not let any of you create situations that can collapse my life. Go Henry. Use my telephone to call the taxi. Take everything that is yours out of my apartment. Know that all your choices have consequences and you have to take responsibility for your actions. Please do not invite me to this wedding. I do not participate in things that do not make sense. This girl is using you for getting her permanent resident visa. Anyway, this is not my business. Good bye for now. My choices are to protect my children and myself," said Lily-Butterfly.

"Okay Henry go. Call the taxi. Good luck. I will be working soon. I have no time to come visit you at the motel. Find work as soon as possible. This foolish plan of yours has ended up costing you, me, and Dean the original opportunity Lily-Butterfly gave us. Ha. Now Lily-Butterfly is saying I must move in six months. Let me know your address and telephone number when you find an apartment. Now Dean and I have to pay for the consequences of your plans and actions. We will keep in touch. Meet me outside in the park on Sunday afternoons. We can talk, and see each other. Bye. Good luck," said Ms. Gina.

"Good. Now that you are feeling the consequence of Henry's actions, and you are choosing to understand and see what Henry is choosing to do," said Lily-Butterfly.

"Mama I am almost twenty one. Sooner than later I have to go and figure out my life," grumbled Henry.

"Good. Henry instead of planning to take advantage of me and being selfish go create and figure out your way at your own expense. Goodbye. I wish you all the best with everything," said Lily-Butterfly.

Henry telephoned the taxi and pulled his suitcases and bags out into the hallway.

"Good bye mama. I will see you at the park in the back of the apartment tomorrow Sunday afternoon, next week Sunday, and so forth."

"Okay Henry. I will walk with you downstairs and help you carry these bags," said Ms. Gina.

Lily-Butterfly went to the kitchen to give her children and herself late lunch. Dean was silent, watching, and listening to everything. He came into the kitchen to make lunch for himself.

This is draining, thought Lily-Butterfly. This was another day in the Ms. Gina, Henry, and Dean invitation to come live in Lily-Butterfly's home. Now after only two weeks it was Ms. Gina and Dean. Plus, the plan was firmly decreased to maximum six months proposal and opportunity for Ms. Gina and Dean to live in Lily-Butterfly's home.

45

On Monday when Lily-Butterfly went to work during her lunch break she telephoned Manana Leila to tell her how everything was going in her personal life and the Ms. Gina, Henry, and Dean situations living in her home. Manana Leila thanked Lily-Butterfly again for deciding to help her by hosting Ms. Gina, Henry, and Dean in her home. Time went by and Holly became nine months old. The first week in May 1990 Lily-Butterfly told Mrs. Diana that she had relatives temporarily living with her. She was going to ask her half-brother to take care of Holly on Tuesdays and Wednesdays. On these days she would not bring Holly to work with her. At this time Holly was more mobile and active. At work Lily-Butterfly felt sad keeping Holly most times in the play pen to manage her activities. Mrs. Diana understood what Lily-Butterfly was saying about Holly. It was now over three months since Ms. Gina, Henry, and Dean had moved to the United States. Lily-Butterfly asked Dean to take care of Holly on Tuesdays and Wednesdays from 8:00 AM to 6:00 PM until she came home from work. Dean agreed to take care of Holly on these days. He perceived it as a contribution and exchange for all that Lily-Butterfly had done and was still currently doing to help him. Dean and Ms. Gina had settled into their new jobs and was saving. In three more months, they would be moving out of Lily-Butterfly's home. Lily-Butterfly was clueless about what was going on with Henry. He seemed to have gone forward in his life how he chose. Ms. Gina got a job as a Home Health Aid provider. She worked Monday to Friday live-in, and came to Lily-Butterfly's home Saturday morning to Monday morning. Monday morning Ms. Gina left for work again. Her salary was $700 per week. When she came home on the weekends Lily-Butterfly was busy with the things she had to do, and kept the conversations with Ms. Gina to a minimum.

With the best intention from Dean, the agreement Lily-Butterfly made with him to take care of Holly on Tuesday and Wednesday only lasted two days. Lily-Butterfly would have brought the arrangement to an end on the first day, but she decided to give Dean a chance to improve. Dean promised that he would improve taking care of Holly. On Wednesday when she returned home from work, she was very sure that the agreement was not going to work at the expense of Holly suffering. Holly went from having her mother's undivided attention and care, to minimal care, neglect, and danger. The situation with Holly was, Dean would get up and out of bed before Lily-Butterfly leave for work. When Lily-Butterfly left home, he went back to sleep. Holly was free to wander around the apartment all day without supervision. Dean did not give her lunch or change her diapers for the whole day. Holly would help herself to what she wanted to eat from the refrigerator and her premade bottles of milk. Holly would drink the milk from her bottles and throw the bottles where ever she liked. The food and left overs that Holly took from the refrigerator to eat was left on the floor. One thing Holly did was close back the refrigerator every time she took something out to eat. Littered around the apartment mixed in with her toys were cookies, bread, crackers, cereal, and other foods. While this was going on Dean was sleeping with the television on. To Lily-Butterfly this meant that Dean had a lackadaisical and do not care attitude. Lily-Butterfly's big question was how could Dean spend the day in the apartment and not see what was happening with Holly? Each day Holly was naked except for her diaper. The diaper was so full it sagged almost down to Holly's knees. Each day Holly had taken off her clothes. Lily-Butterfly tried to find something positive in the negative situation. So, she was grateful that Holly was not hungry, she was not physically hurt, she did not open the door and leave the apartment, did not turn on the stove, and other dangerous things that could have happened. Holly figured out how to help herself to abundant food. Lily-Butterfly thanked the Creator and angels for helping with Holly's safety.

When Lily-Butterfly talked to Dean about the situation he was very apologetic. He said that he was supervising Holly and playing with her. At about 11:15 AM he seem to have fallen back to sleep until Lily-Butterfly came home and wake him up. Thursday morning Holly went with her mother to work. Lily-Butterfly was more convinced that Holly being in the play pen when she needed to was better than Dean's childcare. Lily-Butterfly put the play pen in the living room of Mrs. Diana's home. From this location she could see and supervise at all times busy little bee Holly. Ana at seven months was learning to turn over. Ms. Gina and Dean had saved up more than enough money to get their own apartment. Lily-Butterfly helped them to find a two bedroom house in Lodi, New Jersey. On July 1, 1990 before the six months deadline agreement proposal came to an end, Ms. Gina and Dean moved from Lily-Butterfly's home. Lodi, New Jersey was the town Dean worked in. They both took the bus to and from work. Before Ms. Gina moved, she had told Lily-Butterfly that Henry had gotten married to his girlfriend. They had gotten their own apartment and was living in Ridgefield Park, New Jersey. Henry and Dean work for the same restaurant company, in different locations. Ms. Gina, Henry, and Dean went on to creating their lives and decided to live full time in the United States.

Lily-Butterfly reorganized her apartment to fit her current lifestyle of living with her two children. She purified her complete apartment with sacred herbs and did a renewed house blessing. Lily-Butterfly moved out of the bedroom she was sharing with her two children. She used half of the living room to create a bedroom for herself. The other half of the room was used for a living room. Lily-Butterfly's home had a lighter feeling and she welcomed the renewed stress free home environment. Now she was totally back on track with her life, positive balance, and effortless well-being.

By the time Holly was twelve months old she had mastered walking and was running. Lily-Butterfly seemed to have a technical creative brain so she bought her puzzles and puzzle oriented toys and games to do. Holly loved putting puzzles together. At twelve months old Holly could put together puzzles meant for three years old. Holly did not have a birthday party to celebrate her first birthday. Lily-Butterfly choose to buy her a birthday cake and ice cream. They celebrated just the three of them. At fourteen months old Lily-Butterfly started Holly's potty training. By nineteen months old Holly was potty trained. She still wore a diaper at night until she was twenty five months old.

Christmas of 1990 Lily-Butterfly decided invite Ms. Gina, Henry, his wife, and Dean to a Christmas day dinner. They all accepted the invitation. When Henry's wife attended Lily-Butterfly's Christmas dinner she was seven months pregnant and still not working. At the Christmas dinner Lily-Butterfly kept her interaction with Ms. Gina drama free, by not encouraging her negative speech and actions. At the end of 1990 Lily-Butterfly was thirty three years old, Rebornstar was a pre-teenager twelve years old, and Holly seventeen months old.

Spring May 1, 1991 Lily-Butterfly enrolled Holly into full time day care and nursery school program. This place was within fifteen minutes walking distance from her work. Holly's day care program was Monday to Friday, 8:00 AM to 6:00 PM. Holly was twenty-one months old. She was now grown, athletic, strong, and was now repeatedly climbing out of the play pen. Lily-Butterfly saw that for Holly's development and learning she needed more than the attention that her mother could give her at work. Plus, another opinion of Lily-Butterfly was Holly needed to be with other children to develop her communication skills. Holly was happy going to the day care nursery school. She liked going there very much. At this time Lily-Butterfly left home at 7:30 AM to get Holly to day care by 8:00 AM and walk fifteen minutes to work.

Ana missed Holly as a playmate. Ana was currently almost nineteen months old. Lily-Butterfly created a physical therapy program to assist Ana in improving her motor skills. This was not a part of Lily-Butterfly's work responsibility, but she still helped in this way. Gradually Ana's crawling and learning to walk improved. Lily-Butterfly still took her to the park and library where she played with other children in her age group. At twenty-seven months Ana walked on her own. Lily-Butterfly used Ana's stroller less and less to give her more practice with walking. When Holly became two years old, she had a simple cupcake birthday party at the day care nursery with her friends, teachers, and all the other children. Holly continued to thrive and she seemed to like learning. Her love for puzzles and putting things together grew. Lily-Butterfly encouraged this talent by buying Holly puzzles, building block toys, connect the dots coloring books, games, putty, paper to draw and color, and other toys that she worked with her hands to create something. Rebornstar was growing healthy and strong. She was more into her normal teenager interests with her friends. With Rebornstar and Holly's eight years old difference they hardly had anything in common. Lily-Butterfly found as many ways as possible to keep the close sister and parent bond connected, by spending time with both children together when she was not at work. And at the same time give each child the space they need to independently develop in their age group.

Manana Leila and Lily-Butterfly talked by telephone at least once per week. Manana Leila told Lily-Butterfly that she had the beginning stage of a cataract. This made her have blurred vision in one of her eyes. Her brother's wife who was a nurse recommended that she have surgery, before the condition got worse. Manana had decided to get the surgery done. She would stay at this brother's home after the surgery until her eye was healed. Unbeknownst to Lily-Butterfly and maybe everyone else awareness Manana Leila was ninety-two years old and close to her ninety third birthday. She was strong, completely healthy – except for the eye issue, still working, taking the train and bus, to and from work. Manana Leila never complained about herself, never asked for help with anything, never asked for anything, was always generous, self-reliant; and shared abundant unconditional love, understanding, and care with everyone. Sometimes Lily-Butterfly thought that Manana might not even know how to ask for help and assistance, because she never did and was always so giving. Manana Leila views was that the Creator gave her many opportunities to receive, and she should share the blessings and abundance of herself and life with others. And so, she did. This way she kept a consistent in and out flow cycle of balance. Unbeknownst to everyone including Manana Leila, one of the prescribed medicated eyes drop that she was using for her after surgery, eye care, healing, and recovery; side effect was loss of memory. Gradually Manana was losing her memory and still taking the public transportation, train, and bus from Newton to Somerville, in Massachusetts, to her apartment. She never chose to stop working. Lily-Butterfly thought about this situation sometimes and said something to Manana. Manana Leila's reply was that she was fine and wanted to continue to work. Lily-Butterfly's personal opinion was that people should know their strengths, weaknesses, ask for help and assistance when needed, know when to fold, bring things to completion, and that some people's strengths can be their weaknesses.

Any way Christmas holiday of 1991 Lily-Butterfly had another buffet feast of different foods and invited Ms. Gina, Henry – his wife – daughter, and Dean. They accepted the invitation. That same December Lily-Butterfly became thirty-four and Rebornstar thirteen, years old. Every year since Rebornstar came to live in New Jersey Lily-Butterfly had a birthday party for Rebornstar at home and invited all of her friends.

Manana Leila never visited Lily-Butterfly in her home. When Lily-Butterfly invited her, she would say no. She was not comfortable taking the plane or public transportation to travel so far away from her home. Manana seemed most comfortable staying in her familiar environment. Lily-Butterfly speculated that this decision might have something to do with Manana Leila's eye sight and age. Unbeknownst to Lily-Butterfly she was right about her speculation. Plus, the situation was worse; Manana was currently almost ninety-three years old and losing her memory as well. After having Holly, financial expenses as a single parent, work, and all the responsibility of having two children, Lily-Butterfly never visited Manana Leila in Somerville, Massachusetts.

Ms. Gina had come to the United States of America when she got her visa in January 20, 1990 and in 1992, she still have not chosen to visit her mother Manana Leila. Ms. Gina telephoned her mother a few times. Manana Leila telephoned Ms. Gina to see how she was doing. Lucy, Lily-Butterfly's half-sister telephoned her after not speaking to her for ten years. Gina gave Lucy Lily-Butterfly's telephone number. The first think Lily-Butterfly thought when Lucy telephone her was, what does Lucy want, now. Lucy seems to come into their lives conveniently when she wants or needed something. When Lily-Butterfly spoke to Lucy she told Lily-Butterfly that she had a temporary visa to visit the United, States and was coming to New Jersey to visit Ms. Gina. Lily-Butterfly spoke to Lucy and hung up the telephone.

"That was awkward. I have not spoken to Lucy for over ten years and now she is telephoning me. She always avoided talking to me for her reasons. I respected her choices and stayed away from her and her life. Like I was thinking, she is getting in touch with me for some selfish reason to be revealed. I have not time for Lucy's pretentious, aristocratic, opportunistic, and self-serving ways. Good that Lucy is going to stay at Ms. Gina's home. I will just mind my own business. As a single parent I know that I have a no-nonsense attitude. This is what I think I have to do to be a success with everything I have to do and be. We will see the real roots of Lucy's intention to visit as time goes on. I like helping people, but I am not going to volunteer to be taken advantage of. Oh well. Hu. Mmm. Oh, my Creator you and Manana are my constant support and help. Manana Leila is getting older and older. After she dies, you, myself, and my efforts are all I have to depend on for help and support. Thank you for everything. My life must go on as positive and balanced as possible. Currently, I have to make it in this life with two children. I do not know exactly what the future holds for me. All I know is the present moment and all my karma, creates the future. I will do my best in each present moment and see how the future unfolds itself. Amin," whispered Lily-Butterfly.

46

Lucy came and visited Ms. Gina the first week in February 1992. Lily-Butterfly talked to Lucy once on the telephone. They made arrangements to have lunch at the Garden State Mall food court, on the last Saturday of her visit. Lucy was only visiting Ms. Gina for ten days. Lily-Butterfly brought her children with her. They both did not have access to cars and this kept their visiting each other to only the minimum one lunch outing. Lily-Butterfly thought, maybe this is how it was meant to be. She was satisfied with seeing Lucy only one time during her visit to Ms. Gina.

When Ana was two and a half years old Mrs. Diana took her to a private school. The classes were from 9:00 AM to 11:30 AM. Ana came back home for lunch. Mrs. Diana would eat lunch and then go to work. It was now spring, March 1992. At this time Lily-Butterfly was thinking of getting her driver's license. But financially she needed more income to pay for a driving instructor, a monthly car payment, and car insurance. Paying for Holly's day care and nursery school program, rent, utilities, food, clothing, other children's expenses, and general expenses used up most of her pay check each month. Lily-Butterfly was able to save a little, but needed to create more income to pay for the extra expenses of having a car. She could choose to work at a second job at night to make extra money, but Holly was still too young to leave at home in the care of Rebornstar for over two hours. Lily-Butterfly kept focus on this intention, prayed for help from the Creator, and waited for the best opportunity to reveal itself; for her to take action.

Two months after Lily-Butterfly deep desires to learn to drive, get her driver's license, and buy a car; an opportunity to make this possible arrived. May 1992 Mrs. Diana asked Lily-Butterfly if she wanted to baby sit Ana for three hours every Saturday from 7:00 PM to 10:30 PM. She could bring Holly and Rebornstar with her to work. Mrs. Diana and her husband would go out for dinner and a date night at this time. Lily-Butterfly told her yes. They paid Lily-Butterfly a generous one hundred dollars for the three and a half and sometimes four hour babysitting service. Lily-Butterfly saved this money. The first thing she used this money to pay for was for a driving instructor to teacher her how to drive. Lily-Butterfly studied for her written motor vehicle test. Saturday August 1, 1992 at 9:00 AM Lily-Butterfly started her one hour driving classes. Rebornstar baby sat Holly for ninety minutes while Lily-Butterfly was at driving classes. Holly had just turned three years old on July 31st. Thursday October 1, 1992 at 9:00 AM the driving instructor took Lily-Butterfly to the motor vehicle office in Lodi, New Jersey for her written test. She passed the test. On Wednesday October 21, 1992 the driving instructor took Lily-Butterfly to the motor vehicle office in Lodi, New Jersey for the road driving test. She passed this test as well. On this day Lily-Butterfly was certified to drive and got her driver's license.

On the way home from the driving road test, Lily-Butterfly thanked the driving instructor for everything. He was a very good driving instructor and she was a very good student. Lily-Butterfly's attitude was that she did not have money to waste so she had better get the driver's license with one test. Lily-Butterfly arrived home from the driving test. She stayed home because she had requested off from work for the day. The children were very happy that their mother was a certified driver and would soon buy a car. When Lily-Butterfly went to work on Thursday she told Mrs. Diana that she had passed the motor vehicle certification driving test. Mrs. Diana was very happy for Lily-Butterfly and congratulated her.

During work that day Lily-Butterfly mumbled, "The island of Kawomaya and the valley village of Yaj is getting further and further in my past life's experiences. But everything is within me."

Lily-Butterfly continued to baby sit Ana on Saturday evenings and brought her two children with her. In March 1993 Lily-Butterfly used the money she saved from this baby sitting job as a deposit for buying a very cheap new car. The monthly payment for this very cheap new car was eighty dollars and the insurance per month was twenty dollars. From the baby sitting money Lily-Butterfly would save about $250 per month. She saved this money along with all the saving from her regular weeks' pay, for dentist and medical payments, unexpected things, Rebornstar's school trips, and any emergencies. Lily-Butterfly's prayers to the Creator for help and assistance along with her choices, action, and responsibility; always manifested with success beyond her imagination. Now that Lily-Butterfly had a car her life and transportation situation became much easier. She saved more time not having to walk everywhere and take public transportation.

Ana grew and thrived. After three years old the down syndrome complex was transformed. When Lily-Butterfly bought her car in 1993, she took Ana to preschool three mornings per week from 9:00 AM to 11:00 AM. After Lily-Butterfly bought her car she was comfortable driving around town and the local roads more than on the highways and turnpikes. During the night or very early in the mornings Lily-Butterfly would go out to practice drive on the highways and turnpikes close to her home. At this time there were less traffic. This helped Lily-Butterfly to acclimate herself to driving on these roads until she felt comfortable. Currently Lily-Butterfly was very appreciative for where she was in her life, all the things she had accomplished, positive health and well-being of her children and herself, her job and the family that she worked for, and her continued choice of learning and improving. Every money she received was treated as sacred resource. Lily-Butterfly continued to read and learn from the books she had bought; and she had bought more books.

Lily-Butterfly started to contemplate her next career choice. She strongly thought of opening a day care nursery. She knew that she was good with children and loved them. Lily-Butterfly also thought about her half-sister Lucy and how she could improve some more the resentment that she had for her from a young child. This resentment was created from experiencing how Ms. Gina spoiled Lucy to the point of helplessness. At the same time made Lily-Butterfly into the servant and parent to do everything. Read part one of Lily-Butterfly – And The Path Of Life's Experiences, and you will see and understand more of these situations. Lily-Butterfly had healed the resentment imprints within herself, but wanted to take some physical action to improve the inner work. From Lucy's perception she was busy being the same old Lucy in every way she chose to be and do. Currently Lucy was a Sales Representative for a Chemical Company. Lucy sold varnish, dyes, polish, lubricants. paint, and other industrial chemicals to companies. Lucy and Lily-Butterfly never had a sister bonding, friendship, and any relationship except maybe care giver and parent. When Lily-Butterfly was about four years old she met Lucy for the first time. Lucy was about two years old, and so on and so forth. Lily-Butterfly with generosity, sisterhood creation, friendship, and family creation decided that maybe Lucy and her could work together to create, manage, and direct, a day care nursery on the island of Kawomaya. So, Lily-Butterfly wrote down all her ideas, map, and plans in detail to create this day care nursery. Her intention was that Lucy's father-in-law was a pastor and they had a church building with vacant space to create the day care nursery in. This church location and address was Lily-Butterfly's idea of the day care nursery. In the plan that she intend for Lucy to read, Lily-Butterfly told Lucy to ask her father-in-law how much he would rent the space upstairs from the church. Another option was if the church had a separate building for rent. Presenting this complete day care nursery idea, plan, map, and proposal was also Lily-Butterfly's way of practicing trust with Lucy. At this time in 1992 Lucy was a Christian for over seventeen years.

Christmas 1992 Lily-Butterfly had another dinner and she invited Ms. Gina, Henry-his wife- daughter, and Dean. Again, they accepted the invitation. To Lily-Butterfly she was creating an opportunity for them to be together as a so-called-family. The dinner was a great success. Except to Lily-Butterfly's awareness she wondered if they really appreciated the event. Or where they just choosing to come, because she offered, and the occasion was a free one? Why? They never brought anything to contribute to the dinner celebration and never brought a gift not even for the children. They just showed up, eat, drink, express their negativity, soak up the positive experience, and left. After creating this dinner opportunity for the past three Christmas, Lily-Butterfly gave some thought to maybe not inviting them again to the dinner to see what would happen. During this Christmas dinner at Lily-Butterfly's house she told Ms. Gina about the day care nursery creation idea and how she wanted to include Lucy in this creation. Ms. Gina told Lily-Butterfly that in April 1993 the following year, she was going back to her home on the island of Kawomaya to visit Winston. Within a large brown envelop, Lily-Butterfly gave Ms. Gina the original complete twelve page copies of the day care nursery idea, plan, map, and proposal with a letter attached, to give to Lucy. Lily-Butterfly never kept a copy of the proposal for herself, because she already had the information within her. She leaped with complete trust with the intention of trusting Lucy. At the end of December 1992 Lily-Butterfly became thirty-five years old, Rebornstar became fourteen years old, and Holly was three years and five months old. There was approximately one year and seven months left for Lily-Butterfly to end her employment at Mrs. Diana's home, and find a job in her certified professional training career. July

31, 1994 Holly would be five years old. September of 1994, Holly would be going to kindergarten. With being a successful and busy single parent, the days, months, years had gone by quick for Lily-Butterfly. Her consistent talking to the Creator in prayers, writing in her journal, reading, and practicing all her spiritual practices, was also an infinite and consistent daily experience for Lily-Butterfly.

Since leaving the island of Kawomaya Saturday January 20, 1990 this was Ms. Gina's first visit back to her island home and to visit Winston. April 1993 Gina visited her home on the island of Kawomaya. Her visit was a surprise to Winston. Lucy picked up Ms. Gina at the airport. Lucy and her mother Ms. Gina contacted each other on a need to do so basis by telephone. Ms. Gina gave the envelope with the day care nursery proposal to Lucy. Lucy took the envelope and told Ms. Gina that she would read the proposal. At Ms. Gina's next birthday in 1993 she would be fifty nine years old. Lucy dropped Ms. Gina off at her home. Ms. Gina had a key for the house. She unlocked the door and entered the home. Inside the home was a young girl about nineteen years old with two children. One child was two years old and the other one a new born baby. Ms. Gina recognized the young girl, she lived next door with her parents, brothers and sisters. Ms. Gina asked the girl what she was doing in her house? The girl told Ms. Gina that she lived there with Winston's two children. Ms. Gina collapsed as if she had fainted. The girl caught Ms. Gina and helped her to sit on the couch. Winston her partner of over eighteen years was at work. When Ms. Gina recovered, the girl told Ms. Gina everything about her and Winston. One of the things she told Ms. Gina was that the relationship with Winston was going on in secret since she was fifteen years old and when Ms. Gina was living in the house. Her parents did not know about the relationship with Winston until she was pregnant with the first child. After hearing everything that the girl told her she asked the girl to immediately move out of her house and take her children with her. The girl moved back into her parent's house next door. When Winston came home that night, Ms. Gina gave him notice to move out of the house as well. Ms. Gina finally accepted the rat Winston for whom he really was. Ms. Gina ended her Winston charade and denial of how dishonest and corrupt he was. Winston moved to the other house that they owned together. They agreed to sign over the title of the house as owned by only Winston. The house that Winston moved out of was solely Ms. Gina's, and the title was only in her name. Ms. Gina stayed in Kawomaya for six months until she sold this house and closed the chapter of her life on the island.

While this Ms. Gina transformation of her life was going on, Lucy read the complete day care nursery proposal and letter that Lily-Butterfly had sent her. Unbeknownst to Lily-Butterfly, dishonest Lucy started the day care nursery school creation with Ms. Gina's financial help and a loan from a bank. Ms. Gina gave Lucy ninety five percent of the money from the sale of her house to create the day care nursery school at the same location that Lily-Butterfly recommended. Lucy stole the complete idea, plan, proposal and everything outlined in the information Lily-Butterfly sent her. Lucy quit her Sales Representative job and was now the creator, manager, and director of this day care nursery school. Lucy did not acknowledge receipt of the proposal Ms. Gina had given her from Lily-Butterfly. When Lily-Butterfly accidentally found out about the day care nursery school, and asked Lucy about it, she denied ever receiving any letter and proposal from Ms. Gina. Ms. Gina pretend she knew nothing about the day care nursery creation. Anyway, as you read you will see how simple this stolen business idea came to Lily-Butterfly's awareness.

During the time Gina was on the island, Lily-Butterfly was wondering what Lucy had said about the proposal she sent her. Lily-Butterfly also thought there was a possibility that Lucy would steal the business idea. Lily-Butterfly knew Lucy and that her personality was self-serving, greedy, creepy, opportunistic, and sneaky. But at least she tried to share with her and improved their relationship. Other awareness that came to Lily-Butterfly as she processed the unknown outcome of the business proposal was, if Lucy stole the idea, maybe this was not meant to be her life's purpose destiny career; and it would confirm Lucy's true nature. Ms. Gina returned to her home in the United States. Lily-Butterfly telephoned her to hear how her trip to Kawomaya went. To confirm all the things her intuition was telling her about Lucy, the letter, and the day care nursery business proposal. Ms. Gina told Lily-Butterfly everything she wanted to about the Winston situation, selling the house, and that she had chosen to make the United States of America her permanent home. Ms. Gina did not volunteer any information about the money from the sales of her house, the day care nursery business proposal, and letter that she asked her to give to Lucy. Lily-Butterfly listened and heard everything that Ms. Gina was saying and picked up intuitively what she was not saying. Lily-Butterfly asked Ms. Gina questions to get the views and answers that she was obviously avoiding.

"Okay. Ms. Gina, I hear everything you have said. You had a great and eye opening visit into your past life. You have decided to end the denial about Winston. Good for you. Congratulations. I do not have anything further to say about your Winston situation and experiences. Anyway, did you give Lucy the envelope I asked you to give her?" said Lily-Butterfly.

"Yes, I gave her the envelope. She told me that she would read it."

"So, did she?"

"Yes. I think so."

"What did she say to you about the day care nursery business idea and letter?"

"I do not know."

"What do you mean, by saying you do not know what she said to you?"

"I do not remember what Lucy said about the information you sent her in the envelope."

"What did you do with the money from the sale of the house?"

"I gave ninety five percent to Lucy?"

"Why? What did she need this money for?"

"Lucy told me she wants to start a business. I gave her the money to help with the business. Plus, she plans to get an additional loan from the bank. This is all I know."

"Ms. Gina you are lying. You gave Lucy the money to start the day care nursery school. You can confess to this. If you avoid telling me, eventually I am going to find out."

"So what? If you find out Lucy took your business plan. What can you do? Even if Lucy is creating your idea it was an idea, she did not do anything wrong. Anyway, I do not know for sure what she did. It is my choice to do what I want with my money. Ha. Mmm."

"Integrity is a big deal. I decided to trust Lucy with my daycare nursery school plan and ideas. The problem is Lucy stole my plans and ideas. Hello Ms. Gina you seem to think that it was okay for Lucy to do what she did. Yes, it is your choice to do what you choose to with your money. But you have four birth children and you choose to give one child everything. The one child that gives and does the least for you. This is interesting. The fair thing to have done is divide the money into equal parts and give each of your children a portion."

"I can do anything I choose."

"Okay Ms. Gina you are right. I am going to go now. Thank you for this conversation. All the best with everything. Bye."

"Bye."

Lily-Butterfly never heard back from Lucy about the business proposal. Lily-Butterfly knew that when Lucy wanted something, she will show her appearance. So, Lily-Butterfly decided that she would wait and let the future and time reveal Lucy's karma. Lily-Butterfly shifted her views to maybe creating a day care nursery school by herself in the United States of America; or continue on as the Creator would guide her. Lily-Butterfly continued to investigate, research, and gather information on her choices of career options. For Lily-Butterfly's children's benefit, her financial situation, and the economy at the time; she decided to choose to work in the Food Service Industry. This was a secure industry to work in and she had the qualifications to do so. Other things Lily-Butterfly discovered from her research on the Managerial Food Service Industry professional career were, it seems to be a man's world, hard work, long work hours of minimum ten hours, heavy lifting, can be stressful, lots of responsibilities, and to be successful being good with multitasking was essential. Some positives of this kind of professional career was, there is a lot of opportunities to find a managerial job, good pay, and benefits. The facts and current situation in Lily-Butterfly's life was, the children were growing, she needed more financial resource than her current pay and job could support, and she might need medical insurance; although none of them ever got sick. As the children grew food, shelter, clothing and other expenses increased, and so forth. Lily-Butterfly firmly decided that her next professional career choice was working as a Manager in the Food Service Restaurant Business Industry. Working in New Jersey and as close to her home as possible was her chosen option. Lily-Butterfly had to wait until closer to the end of the five years commitment she had promised Mrs. Diana. She was sure from many internal and the Creator's guidance, and her perception and intuition, that working as a Restaurant Manager was the direction and path, she should peruse next as her professional career. She also decided to start at the lowest Managerial level to learn as much as she could, and work her way from the bottom up. Lily-Butterfly waited to take further action on this decision.

November 1993 Lucy visited the United States. She stayed at Ms. Gina's house. Ms. Gina in her few telephone conversations with

Lily-Butterfly never told Lily-Butterfly that Lucy was visiting. One night Lucy telephoned Lily-Butterfly. The telephone rang. Lily-Butterfly answered the telephone.

"Hi, this is Lily-Butterfly, may I help you?"

"Hello Lily-Butterfly, it is me, Lucy."

"Oh, hi. I did not know that you were visiting Ms. Gina."

"Yes, I am here. I am leaving next week Friday. I was wondering if you wanted to come pick me up at mama's home. I am here to buy things for my new business. We can go shopping and have lunch."

"Oh yeah? What are you here to buy? What business?"

"I am not working as a Sales Representative anymore. I created a new day care nursery and pre-kindergarten. My father in law rented me the complete upstairs of the church and half of the community center building. This is so great."

"I gave Ms. Gina an envelope with a letter and a twelve page business plan, ideas, proposal, and so forth to give you. My intention was that we could create the business together as partners. Did you get the envelope with this information from Ms. Gina?"

"No. Mama did not give me any envelope."

"So, where did you get the money to create this business?"

"Mama gave me the money from the sale of her house and my husband and I got a loan from our bank."

By now Lily-Butterfly had an irritated expression on her face.

"Amazing. Interesting. Really. Lucy you did not receive an envelope with this same business idea at the same location, from Ms. Gina; your mother? This business creation was all your own idea?"

"Yes. Everything about this business was all my idea. This was always a dream of mine. Now it is a reality. For a long time, I had always wanted to create this day care nursery pre-kindergarten. Now this desire and dream is a reality. Do you want to come and pick me up? We can go shopping and you can help me pick out things for this business. We can also have lunch. Bring your children with you. Can you?"

"Listen Lucy. You stole my business idea. Now you want me to come with you to help pick out thing that you want to purchase for this stolen business idea. You had the nerves to be gravalicious and take all the money Ms. Gina gave you from the sale of her house. You are bold face with your corrupt conscience and action. Remember karma is sure. No one escapes karma. I am busy. At this time, I am choosing to say no to your disguised invitation. Your real intention is to use me again. Get a taxi or limonene to take you on your shopping adventure. Maybe we will see each other next time you visit. All the best with everything. Bye."

Lily-Butterfly did not wait for Lucy to reply. She hung up the telephone.

In a nutshell I will tell you how this situation for Lucy unfolded. Lucy bought all the things she needed and shipped them in barrels to the island of Kawomaya. Lucy got the renovation of the building, set up of the furniture, and everything else, Lucy's day care nursery and pre-kindergarten was opened in the spring of 1994. Regarding Lucy and this business situation; this information is basic and is going into the future. As the years unfold, this business never made a profit. In 2000 this business closed down. This business drained all Lucy financial resources. Lucy and her husband took another loan from the bank in the form of a second mortgage on their house. After the business was in operation for two years the staff were not getting paid regularly. Most of the staff quit. Lucy could not repay the loan at the bank. Lucy and her husband's house went into foreclosure. Lucy and her husband filed bankruptcy. By this time Ms. Gina was a United States of America citizen. During the time of this business disaster, Lucy asked Ms. Gina to file for permanent resident visa application for her and her family to move to the United States of America. Ms. Gina fulfill Lucy's request for filing a permanent resident visa for Lucy, her husband, and two children to come live in the United States of America. In 2002 the permanent resident visa for Lucy and her family was approved. Opportunistic Lucy used Ms. Gina as a stepping stone to restart her life living in the United States. Lucy lived with her mother for seven months. Lucy and her family moved to a faraway state from New Jersey to live with her husband's relative. From this relative's home they recreated their fantasy reinvented life.

During Lucy's day care business operation Lily-Butterfly had forgiven Lucy's actions about the stolen day care creation. Lucy came to Lily-Butterfly and asked that they create a business together. Lucy also asked Lily-Butterfly to choose the business creation and tell her how it would work. At the time Lily-Butterfly did not know that the day care business was being a failure. She decided to give Lucy another change, and also to test Lucy to see what she would do with the new business idea. Lily-Butterfly chose to give Lucy the ideas about both of them creating a retail clothing business. After Lucy got all the ideas and plans from Lily-Butterfly she told her she needed time to process the plans. Lucy took all the ideas and plan and secretly created the business on her own inside the day care business operation. Maybe this was one of Lucy's attempt to save the day care business. As you might have guessed; this retail clothing business failed as well. Human nature is very interesting. Energy never lie.

In between 1993 and 2003 Lucy and Lily-Butterfly had other interesting encounters. Stay tuned. Anyway, let us go back to 1993 of this story, the events of Lily-Butterfly, and the things that are next in her life. One road leads to another. The way will show the way. Karma is sure.

47

December 1993 Lily-Butterfly decided that this Christmas holiday and all the others she would only celebrate with her children. She never invited Ms. Gina and her children and they never said anything to her about her decision. At the end of this December Lily-Butterfly became thirty-six years old, Rebornstar fifteen years old, and Holly was four years and five months old. September of 1993 Rebornstar was in middle school.

January 1, 1994 Lily-Butterfly's neighbor invited her to a New Year's Day celebration party. She accepted the invitation. The party was being held at the park where she lived. Lily-Butterfly met a man at the party. His name was Racoon. Lily-Butterfly with her cautious personality was not really interested in Racoon's attention. By the time the party ended Lily-Butterfly and Racoon exchanged telephone numbers. Racoon telephoned Lily-Butterfly and they talked. Racoon was a District Manager for a famous baby formula company. After the experiences with Croco, Lily-Butterfly was skeptical, mindful, and decided to manage the friendship with only dating casually; and with no physical intimacy. Racoon and Lily-Butterfly talked on the telephone, meeting at the park with the children, went for walks, or had Racoon come to her home for dinner. Lily-Butterfly avoided dates where physical intimacy could be convenient. She also told Racoon that they should take the friendship slow and get to know each other. Racoon agreed. On the surface Racoon seemed like a good person to Lily-Butterfly. At the same time, she knew that people were not perfect, things are not like they seem, people can wear many masks, and have shadow sides. Lily-Butterfly wanted to take some time to see if they were naturally compatible.

Holly's pre-kindergarten teacher scheduled a meeting with Lily-Butterfly. She noticed a learning issue with Holly. The teacher could not figure out the root of the issue. The teacher told Lily-Butterfly of her observation. The observation was that Holly seemed to completely learn and understand things taught to her, and then at some point was clueless about the same things. They both decided to work on seeing if they could solve the mystery of Holly's learning issue. Lily-Butterfly seek Holly's Pediatrician's help. The Pediatrician gave Holly an eye exam and told Lily-Butterfly that she did not see a medical issue. Lily-Butterfly continued to observe Holly. She worked with Holly with reading, writing, putting puzzles together, coloring, drawing, and other art projects; Holly did great. Rebornstar had chicken pox when Holly was four years and seven months. Holly got the chicken pox from Rebornstar. Next Lily-Butterfly got the chicken pox. They all had chicken pox around the same time and stayed home for three weeks. Mrs. Diana took vacation days off from work to take care of Ana.

The year 1994 was another time of great change and transformation for Lily-Butterfly. Up to this time her personal studies and reading had helped her to improve her understanding of people, feel sincere forgiveness towards Ms. Gina, Croco and other people. With this expansion of forgiveness Lily-Butterfly became more compassionate, silent, self -reflective, observant, focused, mindful, and aware of her perception in relationship to others perception. Basically, people perceived differently and to not get caught up in people's psycho-drama. May of 1994 Lily-Butterfly observed that Mrs. Diana might be pregnant. She perceived that Mrs. Diana might ask her to keep working for her beyond the five years agreement. Lily-Butterfly was sure that she wanted to leave to pursue her certified professional training career. She waited to see if Mrs. Diana would ask her to stay. One day she processed the awareness of continuing to work for Mrs. Diana.

"I cannot stay with Mrs. Diana to take care of another child. Five years was my commitment. My intuition and internal guidance is telling me that it is time to go on to what is next for me. My children are growing, we need more financial income, and health care benefits. I would also like to move to a bigger apartment, so I can have my own room. This job is not my chosen destiny and life's purpose career. I am ready to say no when Mrs. Diana asks me," mumbled Lily-Butterfly.

At this time Lily-Butterfly was driving Ana to half a day private school pre-kindergarten classes Monday to Friday. The second Monday in July 1994 Lily-Butterfly registered Holly for kindergarten. September 2, 1994 Holly graduated her day care and pre-kindergarten school program. Holly was mature and ready for kindergarten. Lily-Butterfly's second baby had grown up and will be going to kindergarten. Her first baby was an independent teenager in middle school. As a diligent single parent this was a great accomplishment for

Lily-Butterfly. As a parent and human Lily-Butterfly had also grown up, evolved, improve her healing and transformation, and ready for the next part of her life. One strong intuition that repeatedly came to Lily-Butterfly's awareness and instincts was that she should not have any more children. She agreed very strongly with this insight. It was again time to climb the mountainous pathways to discovering her chosen destiny and life's purpose career.

For Holly's fifty birthday on Saturday July 30, 1994 Lily-Butterfly had a birthday party at a restaurant for her. Lily-Butterfly invited Ana, Holly's friends from day care nursery school and the apartment complex, Rebornstar's close friends, and Racoon. Lily-Butterfly invited Ms. Gina, Henry, and Dean. They did not accept the invitation, because they told Lily-Butterfly that they had to go to work. A total of twenty-five people attended Holly's fifth birthday party. To Lily-Butterfly this birthday celebration symbolized completion and new beginnings of her interesting life. Her senses told her that she was three quarters of the way through the momentum tunnel that would lead her directly to her chosen destiny and life's purpose career. The destination to this place was calling Lily-Butterfly. She had to listen to the calling and follow the path to this un-known destination.

August 8, 1994 when Lily-Butterfly arrived at work Mrs. Diana told Lily-Butterfly that she wanted to have a short meeting with her. They sat at the dining table to talk.

"Lily-Butterfly I have very good news to tell you," said Mrs. Diana.

"Yes. What is the news?"

"I am pregnant. It is a girl."

"Congratulations. Good for you and your family. Now Ana will become a big sister and have a play mate."

"I would like for you to stay and take care of this baby as well. Ana will be going to full time all day pre-kindergarten in September. You are the best nanny and housekeeper in the world. Will you? Please we would really appreciate if you could stay and continue to work for us."

"Mrs. Diana, I thank you very much for your complements and everything else. You and your husband have been generous with me over the years. No, sorry, I cannot stay to take care of this baby. My children have grown. Rebornstar is fifteen and Holly is five years old. I need more income, health benefits, and other benefits than the value of this job. I am great with children, but this is not my chosen life's purpose career. I am very sorry. The best I can do is wait until you find a suitable nanny."

"We will pay you more money."

"I am guided to find a job in my certified professional career training. It is time for this. I love you, Ana, and your husband, but I cannot stay. I have to follow how I am being guided. It is time for me to go on to what is really next for me. Sorry."

"Okay I hear you and understand. I am lucky that you came and stayed for the five years until Ana is ready for kindergarten. How long can you stay? I have to find another nanny and housekeeper. It is not easy to find someone to replace you."

"Start now to interview people. I can stay until maximum November 11th. I came here to work October 30, 1989. October 30th of this year is five years since I have been working here. You have about three months to find someone."

"Three months is enough time. Lily-Butterfly how do you know that you will find the job you want?"

"I follow how I am being guided, trust my instincts, take action and responsibility, and usually what is supposed to happen come into manifestation. This is my way and opinion. Mrs. Diana, I have lived a very interesting unnatural life's journey. I have faith, and trust the Creator and myself. I have no choice but to leave here and choose what is next for me and my life. Staying here is not my life's purpose career. Is there anything else?"

"No. Thank you for everything. I will start looking for someone. We will miss you very much."

"I will miss you and Ana as well. You are welcome. Thanks again for everything."

"Okay. Best regards with everything."

Mrs. Diana interviewed many applicants and found someone. The person worked with Lily-Butterfly for one week. Lily-Butterfly left Mrs. Diana on November 11, 1994. Since October 1, 1994 Lily-Butterfly focus was on finding her next job. When Lily-Butterfly signed Holly up for kindergarten she also registered her for after school program. Holly seemed to be doing well in kindergarten with the help of her teacher. Holly's kindergarten teacher had detected that there was an issue with her learning, but could not figure out exactly what the problem was. Lily-Butterfly thought that maybe when the problem is ready it will reveal itself.

48

On Sundays Lily-Butterfly looked through the classified section of the newspaper for an Assistant Manager restaurant job. She had planned to start from the lowest managerial job in the restaurant industry. Sunday November 13, 1994, Lily-Butterfly found an advertisement for an Assistant Manager job working for a famous restaurant corporation. On Monday November 14, 1994 she telephoned the company to schedule an interview. The interview was scheduled for 9:00 AM Wednesday November 16, 1994 at one of their restaurants at a mall in Paramus, New Jersey. Things were moving along at a fast pace. Lily-Butterfly arrived on time at the restaurant for the interview. The Training Manager greeted her.

"Hello Ms. Lily-Butterfly. It is good to see you. Welcome," said Mr. Scott.

"Hi Mr. Scott. Good morning. I am happy to be here. Thank you for giving me this interview, opportunity, and possibly working for your company."

"Okay. Please sit here and fill out this application form and read the job description. Let me know when you are finished."

Close to the restaurant, Lily-Butterfly sat in the food court at one of the dining tables.

When she was finished, she called Mr. Scott. He took the application and read it.

"Mmm. I see, you have no Restaurant Manager experience."

"No, but I have hotel and office management experience. I have a Bachelors in Business Management and a Master in Hospitality and Tourism Management. All that is missing is the industrial handling of food. The quality of my work speaks for itself and I am self-motivated. I am good at people management skills and teamwork. For the past five years I have been working in childcare because I had a baby. Now my daughter is in elementary school. As far as qualification goes, I am over qualified for working as an entry level restaurant Assistant Manager. Working as an Assistant Manager is my choice so that I can learn from the bottom up. If you accept me as an Assistant Manager in training, you will see the proof and quality of my work."

"Ms. Lily-Butterfly I see that you are confident about presenting yourself without hesitation."

"Yes sir. I really would like to have this job opportunity. I know myself and do not want to waste our time focusing only on my weakness; which is no restaurant work experience. I am more than qualified for this job. If you choose to give me this job I will work to the best of my abilities. I am even qualified to be General Manager. But I have consciously chosen to enter this corporate restaurant job structure at the lowest management level. Hire me and you will not regret doing so. Okay. I have said enough. Mr. Scott what would you like to do?"

"I see. Lily-Butterfly you have said everything you could say to represent yourself. Only time and your work will prove all that you have said. I am going to hire you. You will have three month probation period. At the end of the training you will have a three hundred question written test on everything you have learned. On a weekly basis you will be tested on hands on food preparation and many other things. Your people and team work skills will be supervised on a daily basis. The minimum score you can get on everything is eighty nine percent. Do you understand?"

"Yes, I understand."

"Your first day of hire and training is next Monday November 21st. Every work shift is minimum ten hours. This is minimum fifty hours work per week. You will be paid a salary and not by the hour. Your training work schedule is Monday to Friday 9:00 AM to 7:00 PM. This work will require nine to ten hours standing and walking. There will be heavy lifting, being responsible for products, employees, money, customers, plus other things. Working as an Assistant Manager will require you being available for a flexible schedule. Sometimes you will work days, nights, and weekends. Do you understand me so far?"

"Yes, Mr. Scott. I understand."

"Okay. You seem to be listening very well, focused, no-nonsense attitude, and realistic. You are not talking very much, replied Mr. Scott."

"Yes, I am listening. When I talk less, I can hear, and listen more."

"Yes. Energy and time equals money and productivity. So, the less time and food wasted, can create maximum success and profits, within the restaurant industry."

"This is true for life in general and not only in the restaurant industry," replied Lily-Butterfly.

"Okay. You will wear a clean uniform to work every day. The company will supply the uniform shirt and tie at no cost to you. You will supply the black loosely fitted uniform pants, black socks, and comfortable walking sturdy black shoes. For health and sanitation there are rules and guidelines. You can wear a wedding ring and a watch, but no other jewelry. You cannot wear nail polish. Your nails have to be clean and cut as short as possible. All employees including yourself must wash hands for at least thirty seconds if the food preparation station was left to do anything else; as well as, before food preparation. Every employee's hair must be tied back or wear a hair net. Your clothes should be loosely fitted because there is a lot of bending and lifting. The maximum weight that you might have to lift is fifty to sixty pounds. Every sack of potatoes weigh fifty pounds. Depending on the sales in a restaurant, sometimes in a food order deliver there are fifteen to fifty sacks of potatoes. Every food delivery on the shift that you work must be verified, checked, and counted, by one of the Managers on duty. Food and paper product deliveries are Monday, Wednesday, and Friday. If there is no regular employee to put away the delivery, one of the Managers on duty has to do this job or sometimes help. The Manager on duty must be responsible for the food, paper products, money, employees, customers, and everything in the building. Do you still want this job? This job is a lot of, hard and smart work, plus a lot of responsibility."

"Yes, I would still like to have this job. The job seems very interesting. I think that my whole life has prepared me for this job. This job seems to be the training I need for something in my chosen destiny and future."

"Lily-Butterfly this is a man's job. Restaurant Manager work is a multi-talented responsible and consequential career. It requires lots of focus, team work, and decision making skills. It is up to you. I am taking time to explain everything to you because training managers is expensive. If a Manager quits during or right after training, it is money wasted. The regular employees will be as productive and efficient as your management guidance, leadership skills, and you have to help with their training. You will be assigned a restaurant to work in when your training is complete. You could be transferred from one restaurant to another without any advance notice. Ms. Lily-Butterfly do you have any questions?"

"What are the health care and other benefits? What is my starting salary?"

"I will tell you this information. Please fill out this personal assessment questionnaire. I am going to get you five work shirts and two ties. What size shirt do you wear?"

"I wear a medium but for loose fitting purposes, I would like size large."

"Okay. Here. Please answer these questions. I will be back. Would you like something to drink?"

"Please bring me some water. Thank you."

Lily-Butterfly answered all the questions on the two page form. Mr. Scott returned. He read the information that Lily-Butterfly wrote.

"I see that your natural personality is diligent, focused, honorable, steady, team player, and also work well independently, self-motivated, process things slowly, does not like confrontation, good listener, cautious, and direct communication style. Good. We will see how you do. Are you interested in being a Manager or General Manager?"

"Maybe in the future I will be interested in becoming a Manager or General Manager. Currently I would like to work as an Assistant Manager. This way I can learn and improve gradually with support. Assistant Managers usually work with a Manager or General Manager of each shift. You can tell these things about me from these personal assessment questions? Oh wow. Interesting. Modern human creation can be interesting. I also have a curious and inquisitive personality. I love to learn the modern ways, and combine the modern things I learn with the ancient ways I already know. This job is not going to be easy and requires a lot of stamina. But it will help me to improve who and what I am, and awaken more of my talents. My performance, time, the present, and the future, will decide my faith and my chosen destiny forward into the un-known. Anyway Mr. Scott what is next?" said Lily-Butterfly smiling.

"Yes. Good. We will see how you cope with action and practice. Here are your shirts and ties. Fill out these tax forms. Can I have your identification card, college, and university certification? I will make copies and give the original back to you. For identification you can use your driver's license or passport?"

"Okay. Here is my driver's license."

Mr. Scott took the documents and went to make copies inside the office. He returned.

"Here Ms. Lily-Butterfly."

Mr. Scott returned the original copies of Lily-Butterfly's documents.

"Thank you. Here are the tax information forms," said Lily-Butterfly.

"Okay. Now we will talk about the payment information. Your starting salary is $36,000 per year. If and when you are promoted you will be paid salaries within these salary scales. If you stay an Assistant Manager for a year, at the end of one year you will get a three percent raise on the salary that you currently make. You will receive complete health insurance, paid medical prescription, dental, and eye care for you and your dependents. After one year you will receive two week vacation, ten sick, and five personal days off with pay. You can choose to join our 401K profit sharing plan by choosing how much you would like to contribute from your pay. You can read more about the 401K plan inside the employee information folder I gave you. Uniform shirts and ties are given as needed. There are many other things to learn and get to know as time goes on. If you have questions or concerns you can telephone me or the personnel department. Here is my business card. The telephone number for the corporate office and departments are in the folder I gave you. Welcome Ms. Lily-Butterfly. I hope that you enjoy your training and working for our company."

"Yes, thank you very much Mr. Scott. I really appreciate this opportunity. My work performance and time will tell the reality of the quality of my work. Sir, I will try my very best."

"I will telephone your references today. If there is a problem, I will telephone you. If you do not receive a call from me, know that all is well. I will see you on Monday morning at 9:00 AM. Plan to be here until at least 7:00 PM. After three months training you will be assigned to a restaurant. On Monday we will go over the training plan and manuals together. There are two training manuals, you will work from and study these manuals. Every information for the complete training and tests will be in these manuals. Thank you for coming and I will see you on Monday. Ms. Lily-Butterfly welcome to our team of managers."

"Thank you, Mr. Scott. Have a great day. I will see you on Monday. Bye."

Lily-Butterfly bought lunch from the restaurant she was going to work for. She sat and ate. While eating she observed what was happening with all the employees working on the front service section of the restaurant. After eating lunch Lily-Butterfly went to buy three pairs of black pants and a pair of strong, sturdy, comfortable black walking work shoes. When this was completed Lily-Butterfly drove home.

Lily-Butterfly prayed, "dear Creator thank you for everything. You already know about my experience today. Keep guiding me and send all the help and assistance I need. The next pathway and continued training for my chosen destiny and life's purpose professional career has begun. I do not think that this job is my chosen destiny and life's purpose career. I think that it is the way to the way, and un-known destination. Please continue to help me with my health, strength, safety, patience, and everything I need to continue on this interesting adventure called human life. Also continue in every way to help with my children as we continue forward. Amin."

49

Lily-Butterfly got home at 3:30 PM. Holly was at the after school program until 6:00 PM. At 6:00 PM Holly will walk home with her friend's mother who lives in the same building. She took off her clothes and got dressed in her regular clothes. She laid down to relax and process all the events of the long interview. She set a kitchen timer for one hour. During Lily-Butterfly review and processing of her day she fell into dream land.

Lily-Butterfly dreamed: - She was sitting under a holly tree reading a sacred book of instructions. A large white puffy cloud with two large wings came towards her face. She stood up and moved sideways from the cloud. A voice came from the cloud.

The voice said, "wait, do not leave. Do not be afraid. Fear not. The cloud, rain, and thunderstorms can be useful transmutation tools. You have entered the last pathway to awaken all your spirit and soul's talents, Universal wisdom, and completely discovering your chosen destiny and life's purpose. You are never alone. Your guardian angels, spirit guides, and the Creator are always assisting you. The next part of your journey will seem difficult and you will meet challenging people. You will have great losses and great successes. Positive balance, optimism, unconditional love, understanding, simplicity, and choosing to protect yourself is the key here. To stay on the razor's edge of the next sets of pathways, always come back to peace, faith, positive frequencies, diligence, and morality. There will be a steep climb, far leaps, rocky roads, and many cliffs, twist, and turns. Learn and master these ancient pathways. To completely develop and awaken your spirit and soul talents you must grow your human body through six cycles of seven. At the age of forty two years old you will be very ready for your chosen destiny and life's purpose. You would have created the vortex within that you will use as a tool to express outside and beyond yourself. Remember that you cannot give what you do not have. Positive and negative people, places, and things will appear to help you with the next part of your journey. Make the positive choices and take the right action from everything that shows up. Keep on trusting your senses and instincts. So far, they have never been wrong. Even the most bitter and difficult parts of

333

this part of your journey, are here to help and assist you. To climb the next mountain, to get to the end of this pathway, and the next destination, stay mindful, aware, and use everything that you have learned so far. At the end of this pathway you will completely find yourself and what your spirit, soul, and the Creator's will. Never fear. We are here."

At the end of the large white puffy cloud's word, suddenly and mysteriously, the cloud transformed into heavy rain and wind; followed by much thunder and lightning. Hearing the thunder and lightning in her dream, suddenly Lily-Butterfly woke up. She was in a daze and her eyes were not focused in the physical realm.

Lily-Butterfly turned and sat up. Holly was standing by her bed.

"Hi mama it is me, Holly. I am home."

Lily-Butterfly had been sleeping for over two hours. The kitchen timer had gone off. It was 6:16 PM. After greeting Holly, Lily-Butterfly took her dream journal and wrote down the complete dream.

"Here we go again. The infinite revolving doors and wheels have shifted and I am now on another level to climb. Before I go to sleep tonight, I will read this dream message from the cloud wings oracle. My human life is a mythic adventure. Maybe I am crazy. Mmm. Oh, my Creator. What now? More wonderment, I guess?" mumbled Lily-Butterfly.

Lily-Butterfly went to prepare dinner for the children and herself. During dinner she told Rebornstar and Holly about her new job starting on Monday. Lily-Butterfly told Rebornstar that she had to supervise Holly until she gets home from work. Rebornstar did not like her new Holly assignment. This assignment would prevent her from spending more time with her friends.

"Mama, Holly can continue to walk home from after school program with her friend's mother. I will go to her house and get Holly by 6:30 to 7:00 PM. We will eat dinner together and take our shower until you get home. This way I can still be with my friends like I am now. Why do I have to be supervising Holly? She is smart and can be in the house by herself until you get home. Is this okay?"

"I will ask Holly's friend mother if she could keep her until 6:30 to 7:00 PM, and that you will come to get her. Holly is not a problem. Holly is content playing by herself with her puzzles, toys, drawing, coloring book, and so forth. I just need you to be here with her and maybe give her dinner, until I get home. Maybe after three months I will have to work on the night shift. You would have to get Holly at the same time, give her dinner, and stay in the apartment with her. This is what usually happens when I am home. You would come home and stay home. Rebornstar do you understand? Next month you will be sixteen years old. It is time that you contribute something towards helping me. I need more money as a single parent to take care of us. Plus, I want to move to a bigger apartment where I can have my own bedroom. Right now, my bedroom is in the living room. Selfishness can be a limiting place to be. Holly is easy, all you have to do is be here to supervise her and provide company. There is a lot more I can say about your attitude and this situation; but I am not. Rebornstar all you have to do is listen and hear me. Do what I am telling you to do. Okay. When my schedule and situation change, I will let you know. End of story. You are lucky and spoiled."

"Oh, come on. Soon you will start working at night and weekends. I want freedom to be with my friends. Holly is smart enough to supervise herself and follow how you guide her. It is not cool and it is corny to take Holly with me when I am with my teenage friends chilling. My life is going to be ruined, with this new job schedule."

"Rebornstar, first of all you must be in the house no later than 7:00 PM every night; no exceptions. End of story. THIS CONVERSATION IS OVER! You are not the parent. You listen, hear me, and also take responsibility for the consequences of not doing this. It seems as if people's normal tendency is to take advantage of niceness. I have been here at home with both of you all this time. Now things are going to change and that is it. I am the one taking the very best care of both of you; doing everything I can to accomplish being the best parent, and am not complaining about what I have to do to accomplish my responsibility as a parent. Now it is time for you to give me a little help by supervising your sister. That is, it. Go get prepared for bed. Go. Okay."

"Whatever. I guess, I will have to do as you say. You are the boss. Now even on week-ends I have to have a tag-along-sister. This is definitely not cool."

"Holly is not going to be any tag-along-sister to go with you anywhere. When I am not home after 7:00 PM both of you MUST BE INSIDE THE APARTMENT! Do not take advantage of my absence and be outside of this apartment beyond 7:00 PM. I am still the captain of your teenager-ship. Remember this, Miss. Rebornstar."

"Okay I will go get Holly between 6:30 and 7:00 PM at her friend's home on the first floor. I will be home at the time you command me to be here."

"I will prepare dinner every morning for every night. All you have to do is reheat the food. I will cook for two days each time. Food and dinner will always be here. Supervise your sister when I am not home, and continue to help me with house chores. Let me see how you do and I will pay you an allowance of twenty five dollars per week."

"Mama, twenty five dollars allowance? That is, it."

"Rebornstar do not be ridiculous. Who pays me? Do you pay me for being your parents? Ha?"

"Mama, you are the parents. It is your job and responsibility to take care of us in every way. Children does not pay parents. Everything that you do is part of your responsibility as a parent. Mama, you know this."

"Okay Rebornstar, enough. This is our most negative rebellion conversation. You started to show your selfishness and not liking being told what to do since before thirteen years old. I think that I might have spoiled you. Now I really need your help and you are going to help me; like it or not. I am finished with this conversation. Go prepare for bed and school tomorrow. Good night."

"All right mama. You are the boss of me, I guess. I will supervise Holly, and you pay me the twenty five dollars allowance per week," said Rebornstar, with a smirk.

Lily-Butterfly did not answer Rebornstar. To her the conversation was over. Lily-Butterfly had tears in her eyes and her heart felt heavy. She stared into the space beyond the room.

"Mama do not worry. I will be fine. The Creator, myself, and angels will supervise me. If Rebornstar leaves me alone, I will make sure that I am safe, stay inside the apartment, keep the door lock, be safe, and I can give myself a shower and go to sleep. Do not worry. You are the best mama to me before I was born, now, and into the future. You are good to Rebornstar as well. She is acting mean. Mama remember that I am never alone. Sometimes I see the angels. I love you mama. We will be fine."

"I know my child. We will be fine. Thank you for coming to be my child. Thank you for your help and good intentions. I love both of you very much. Both of you are here because of me. I am here because of Nana Gina, especially Manana Leila, and all the other ancestors in the past. You are right my child. Plus, with the Creator's help and assistance we will be fine. Amin," responded Lily-Butterfly.

"Amin mama. Amin," said Holly.

Dinner was completed and Lily-Butterfly had cleaned up the kitchen. The children had showered and gone to sleep. Lily-Butterfly had prepared for bed, wrote in her journal, and prayed. At 9:30 PM the telephone rang; it was Racoon. Lily-Butterfly told Racoon about her interview and new job. Thursday morning Lily-Butterfly went downstairs to tell Holly's friend mother about her new job, work schedule, to give her additional awareness about Holly if Rebornstar does not come to get her by 7:00 PM. Holly's friend mother agreed to help in any way she could. At the end of the week Lily-Butterfly had everything arranged for her new job, journey, and for the children's health and well-being. On Sunday night Lily-Butterfly the last sentence she wrote in her journal was, the experience in the dream and the next part of my life's mysterious adventure has begun, with Rebornstar's amplified rebellion and Racoon's telephone call.

Monday November 21, 1994 the first day of Lily-Butterfly's new job Mr. Scott told her everything she needed to know about the Assistant Manager restaurant training program. He also gave her two manuals to read, study, and learn from. The first day of training was stressful and demanding. Lily-Butterfly did great, but she was tired at the end of the day. When she got home at 7:30 PM Rebornstar and Holly was inside the apartment. They had eaten dinner, showered, and dressed for bed. Lily-Butterfly checked Holly's homework, talked to the children, eat, showered, wrote in her journal, prayed and went to sleep. Tuesday was another accomplished day at work for Lily-Butterfly. When she got home before she went to sleep, she filled her tub with warm water, added three pounds of sea salt, and soaked for one hour. Her body had felt like a truck ran over it. She felt like every muscle and bone in her body hurt. This job training seemed to make her use every muscle and bone in her body that she had never used before. This Managerial training involved every work and duties a regular employee and a manager would perform; from lifting fifty pound sack of potatoes, washing dishes, cleaning the floors, scrubbing the grills, fryers, and stoves; filtering cooking oil in fryers, prepping food, repeatedly lifting fifty pound sack of potatoes for chopping to create French fries, cleaning sandwich stations, knowing food temperatures for cooked, frozen, and refrigerated foods, learning how to use the computer for sales, employee work hours, food orders, and deliveries, learning every office procedures, and everything else. Lily-Butterfly got the complete awareness that a Restaurant System and Managerial Process is very complex and multitasking tasks. Being a General Manager meant that the person has mastered the complete system and process.

   This training went on until February 28, 1995. Lily-Butterfly kept up with managing, directing, and organizing the children, her home life, and work. Her journal writing to process every day and prayer to the Creator was always up-to-date. Lily-Butterfly tired body nestled itself into the embrace of the sleep realm every night.

50

Thursday November 24th was Thanksgiving day. Lily-Butterfly was off from work. She enjoyed the break and rest from work. As usual Lily-Butterfly, Rebornstar, and Holly had a great day celebrating Thanksgiving. Lily-Butterfly made an extensive menu of foods. Cooking was a form of art to Lily-Butterfly, and she loved to cook. Racoon was invited to the Thanksgiving dinner and he accepted the invitation. The dinner was in between regular lunch and dinner time. It started at 3:30 PM and ended at 6:00 PM. This gave Lily-Butterfly enough time for everyone to help with cleaning up everything and prepare for work the next morning. Thanksgiving day dinner Racoon arrived thirty minutes early for dinner. He brought a gift for the children and Lily-Butterfly. Racoon seemed happy to be with them.

The relationship with Lily-Butterfly and Racoon was friendly, simple, easy, and unconditional. Currently a long distance relationship with mostly talking on the telephone at least once per week, because of their work schedules. They spend time together mostly with the girls at holiday celebrations, and so forth. Racoon's job as a District Manager for a major baby formula corporation required him to travel frequently to other States. Racoon lived about thirty minutes from Lily-Butterfly's home. Lily-Butterfly did not have an intention to make Racoon into an intimate life partner. So, she accepted him for what he presented, who, and what he showed. She adored and valued him as a pleasant genuine man friend. Her main focus was still her children, new job, her health, well- being, and where everything was going to evolve to her spirit and soul life's purpose career. Lily-Butterfly knew that the restaurant job was a tool and not her life's purpose.

Racoon enjoyed the dinner celebration. He invited Lily-Butterfly to his home for lunch on New Year's Day Sunday January 1, 1995 at 12:00 PM. Lily-Butterfly accepted the lunch invitation. Rebornstar would have lunch with Holly and supervise her until Lily-Butterfly returned home. Lily-Butterfly planned to be home by 5:30 PM to have dinner with her children. Sunday January 1, 1995 would be the one year anniversary of the first time they met, Racoon's birthday, and the first time Lily-Butterfly had been to Racoon's home. Racoon would be away spending time with relatives this Christmas season. He would not be attending Lily-Butterfly's Christmas day dinner.

The day after Thanksgiving was Friday and the children were off from school. Rebornstar was supposed to be in charge of supervising Holly when Lily-Butterfly was not at home. Only the children and the Creator know what really happens when Lily-Butterfly was not at home. When she got home thing seemed fine, except sometimes Holly was at her friend's house, or inside the apartment alone; and Rebornstar was at the park with her friends or where ever her friends were. Most times Rebornstar made it home and was inside the apartment with Holly before Lily-Butterfly got home. Holly never complained about Rebornstar's childcare supervision. Holly seemed to accept the best her sister could and would choose to do for her and with her.

December came and Lily-Butterfly Managerial training was still going great. The holiday season in the mall was very busy and so was the restaurants in the food court. Lily-Butterfly lived in Bergen County where the malls were closed every Sunday. Lily-Butterfly prepared at home for the Christmas holidays by buying a Christmas tree, decorating the tree with the children, buying presents for Christmas and Rebornstar's birthday, grocery shopping, Christmas decorations for the house and so forth. This Christmas Lily-Butterfly will be celebrating with only the children. Racoon would be away celebrating the holidays with his relatives in another State. Lily-Butterfly was not aware of what Ms. Gina, Henry, and Dean chose to do for the holiday. And they never had an event they invited Lily-Butterfly and the children. After Lily-Butterfly stopped inviting them to her Christmas day dinner they quietly moved on without saying a word to her during the holiday season. Lily-Butterfly and her children kept to themselves. When she felt like telephoning Ms. Gina she did, and Ms. Gina did the same. When Ms. Gina needed a car ride somewhere she would ask Lily-Butterfly and if she could take Ms. Gina, she would, or told her no, if she could not. Manana Leila as usual stayed in Somerville, Massachusetts and celebrated with her half-brother and his family. They lived about a mile and a half from one another. Lily-Butterfly would write or telephone Manana. They kept in constant contact. They were out of physical sight but not out of spirit, soul, heart, and mind. This December Lily-Butterfly became thirty-seven years old. Rebornstar celebrated her sixteenth birthday.

Sunday January 1, 1995 came. Lily-Butterfly ate breakfast with her children and prepared sandwiches for their lunch. The children ate lunch together. Lily-Butterfly got dressed and drove to Racoon's house. Racoon had made a lunch of rice and beans, barbeque lamb chops, vegetables, and different choices of things to drink. They ate while having conversations about the holidays, his visit with his family during the Christmas celebration, Lily-Butterfly talked about work, and other things that came up naturally. They were very much at ease in the friendship with each other. Desert was a surprise. Racoon brought out from the refrigerator a birthday cake for Lily-Butterfly. He placed three candles on the cake and lit them. Lily-Butterfly blew out the candle and made a wish.

"Lily-Butterfly, would you like some wine or Champagne?" asked Racoon.

"I never drink alcohol. I would like some calming tea. Here I brought a box with me. I will put some water on the stove to boil. You can drink what you choose."

"A little wine or Champagne does not hurt anyone. Today is a New Year celebration for us."

"We can celebrate without me choosing to drink alcohol. I choose to not drink alcohol. Maybe at some point in my life I will. I never have alcohol in my home, and my children has never seen me drink alcohol. Maybe this is my way of not contributing to any unbalanced states regarding myself, or to teach my children to drink alcohol. When they are of the drinking age, they can independently make this alcohol drinking choice for themselves. I would like to keep this alcohol experience as it is. Thank you for your offer. Okay."

"Okay. I hear you. I will have some wine."

"I think the water is boiling. I am going to make a pot of tea."

Lily-Butterfly made the tea and brought back the pot of tea to the dining table. They had dessert, drank, and continued their conversations.

"I think I am ready to settle down," said Racoon.

"Oh yes. With who?"

"With you. Would you like to be my girlfriend?"

"I do not know. What does be a girlfriend mean to you? I thought that we were friends already."

"I mean make a commitment to continue from today dating exclusively. This means physical intimacy and sex."

"Is this an engagement proposal?"

"No. It is a promise to date only each other."

"So, before you were open to dating other people? Now I am the chosen one?"

"Sort of, yes. I guess so. You are a great woman."

"Well thank you for making me your chosen selection. My focus at this time is my children, work, and discovering how I am going to use my spirit and soul's talents to perform my chosen destiny and life purpose career practice. This is my current truth and priorities. I am comfortable being the current girlfriend that I am."

"We would continue as we are, make the promise to date exclusively, continue to get to know each other more, start to spend more time together, and add physically intimacy and sex."

"Do you have a promise ring to symbolize what you are asking?"

"Yes. Here. Happy birthday, Merry Christmas, and Happy New Year."

"Interesting you are prepared. Okay. But understand I can only give the amount of extra time I have. I cannot cancel out time from my children to come to your house. Since I am the one with children you would have to fit inside my life's map. Therefore, know that in the present and future you cannot complain that I do not spend as much time as you would like with you. Sorry. Plus, we would have to have similar visions about the present and future. I love to dream, but I love reality as well. Happy birthday to you as well. I did not bring you a Christmas or birthday gift. Sorry. Also know that if we proceed with this girlfriend relationship and it does not work out this complete friendship stuff is over. I do not keep or make friends with my ex-husband or ex-boyfriend. I like to keep clear corners and boundaries. This I find is helpful for my mental health, well-being, and life. This is my personal choice and opinion. Are you willing to risk losing what we currently have for an intimate boyfriend friendship and relationship?"

"No. But I want both. I think that this can work positively for both of us. When you discover your chosen destiny and life's purpose career practice, maybe we can work together in this career."

"This will be a spiritual practice. This is not a materialistic and ideology practice. To me this is serious personal life purpose practice. It is not a choice like choosing a house or a car to buy. Do you really think and feel that you are ready to commit to a long term monogamous intimate spiritual relationship which includes children? I have two children already and they would be a ready-made part of the package. Plus, I could get pregnant again. Sometimes becoming a father can be scary for some men. Where sex is involved spirits and souls are lined up trying to be conceived. For me, I do not choose to have another child, and end up having to be a single parent. I also do not want to have an abortion. Currently if I had to choose between an abortion and having another child as a single parent, I would choose an abortion. I am very serious. Having another child as a single parent is not an option for me. The Creator God would have to forgive me for my abortion choice. I am very serious about this opinion. So, this is why I choose to not have sex with you before. Where there is sex there is always a possibility of pregnancy. This is a reality. The best birth control method for me is no sex. I get pregnant very easily. Spirit and souls are always waiting on my conception line to get an opportunity to jump into the orgasm gap of my sexual experiences. I have multiple orgasms during sexual intercourse. This gives multiple options for conception and pregnancy. From experiences I get to realize I am very fertile. Are you ready and willing to be a father, husband, and so forth? I will not live with a man, unless I decide to marry him. So, asking me to be your girlfriend it also means that you are also open to marrying me. I will not just become a sex pot hole. I use direct communication style. This is another thing most men and people are not comfortable with. I am a soul on a spiritual mission this is my priority. If you disrespect me, treat me negative, and add any negative treatment, I will not choose to stay with you. The Divine Creator God would not like any form of negative treatment towards me. Asking me to be your girlfriend is a very serious request."

"I would like to take the chance to try this kind of relationship with you. This I know for sure. I would like us to try and see what happens. Can we try? Give me and us a chance. You are a strong and independent woman. You know how to make a decision and compromise. A relationship cannot be only from your perception, hearts desires, and intentions. Give some room for you and I to create an intimate relationship and partnership. Can you?"

"Yes, I can. But I am being honest. I cannot be on a shit-ship disguised as a relationship and partnership. Hello Mr. Racoon. If you made a decision that I perceive will damage me and my life; I will choose to leave the so-called-ship. I was not born for normal human entertainment, hostage taking disguised as marriage or relationship, and normal people life's choice perceptions. I am great at patience, sharing, caring, unconditional love, and understanding. But if I had to choose in a situation; I will choose to save myself, my chosen destiny life's purpose, and the health and well-being of my children and I. If this is okay with you, then we can try. I have to be direct and honest with the things I think, say, and do."

"Okay. I am ready and I understand your opinion and choices. I cannot see any disadvantage to this relationship. I love a woman who loves herself. Put the ring on. Okay."

"Okay. Let us cheer to our decision. Good Mr. Racoon. Now we will see what is behind your Racoon mask. Let your shadows come forth out of your personal pandora box, closet, and trunk. Happy New Year, blessings, health, and best regards for 1995."

"To us. Happy New Year and lots of success to us. To seal this commitment today will be our first day of sexual adventure. Is this okay with you?"

"Sure. Do you have a condom?"

"Yes, I have condoms. But, I do not like using condoms."

"If you were me, would you want me to use one?"

"Yes, sure, if I do not want to possibly become pregnant and have a sexual transmitted disease; I would want you to wear a condom. I think pregnancy, being a mother and father, is one of the most responsible human responsibility. Okay, I understand. I will wear a condom. Lily-Butterfly do you always think so responsibly?"

"Yes, I try my best to make the best choice, trust people for whom and what they are, make the best decision, and take responsibility for the consequences of my choices and actions. My opinion is, with two children I do not have the option of thinking only about myself or being selfish."

"I understand. This is why I like and love you so much. You are a great mother and will make a great wife."

"If you say so. Racoon, be ready for what you desire and wish for."

They continue to drink and talk. After leaving the dining room Racoon and Lily-Butterfly went to the bedroom. They made overdue intimate passionate love and sex. Racoon used a condom. Lily-Butterfly checked the condom's expiration date. The condom's expiration date was good. Their romantic and sexual experiences commemorates the one year anniversary of the first time they met. Everything about the sex, romance, and love making was great. When it was all over immediately Lily-Butterfly got up to pee. She sat on the toilet and peed. She felt a strange feeling and something fell out of her into the toilet. When she looked into the toilet bowl it was a piece of the condom; the bottom half. During the sexual experience the condom had ripped completely. She ran into the bedroom.

"Oh, my we have a big problem. The bottom part of the condom ripped off inside me. I think that I am pregnant. Holy Creator, what now? I do not need this. I do not believe in accidents. What could be the reason for this happening?"

"Wait, calm down. I saw that it broke when you went into the bathroom. Let us hope for the best and pray that you do not get pregnant."

"Racoon, for me, pregnancy does not work as an after effect. I get pregnant immediately. I am very fertile. Fertility could have been my name. It is too late to pray that I do not get pregnant. Hello sir? We both decided to do this sex stuff. We are equally responsible. I think I am pregnant. Why do you buy shi**y cheap condoms? Ha. Mmm? What now?"

"Let us hope for the best. You were right the quality of the condom, the expiration date, and how long I have these condom matters. I really hope that you do not get pregnant. The real truth is that I am not ready at this time so prematurely to have children and become a father. At this time sharing your children with you is enough for me. I feel nervous already at the thought of knowing that you might be pregnant. Seriously. Let us hope for the best and keep our fingers crossed that you are not pregnant. Currently we both do not need a pregnancy situation. You just started a new job about six weeks ago. Oh wow."

"Interesting. You do not get it. As spiritual, optimistic, and positive as I am, hoping for the best, and keeping fingers crossed will not help this situation. I have a great instinct, intuition, and sense that I am pregnant. If I am wrong this would be the miracle. So far my instincts are always right."

"Calm down. I have a headache. Let us wait and see if you are really pregnant, before you become hysterical and panic sets in. Okay? Let me know as soon as possible if you have confirmed with a pregnancy test that you are really pregnant. Then we will make a decision on what we will do. I am sorry that the condom broke. No matter what happens I want you to know that I like and love you. Have I really practiced with a woman the reality of love and like? No not really. It, sure sounds reassuring when I say to you that, I love and like you. Saying this seems to be one thing, but I guess actions speaks louder than words. I guess, I need a lot of practice healing my past life's experiences, and practicing loving myself. All of this seem scary to me. I never told you this before, I spent time in foster homes. I am an adopted child. My mother was a drug addict, alcoholic, and she dropped dead in front of me when I was five years old. I guess this is what you mean by my pandora box, shadow closet, and trunk opening. Oh my. Already I feel shaky, nervous, and other stuff about becoming a parent."

"What? You spend time in foster homes, was adopted, and your mother dropped dead in front of you when you were five years old? You never said one thing about this before. Talk about secrets, ha?"

"Yes, I have lots of secrets. I thought that we would have more time to get to know each other before you got pregnant, and so on and so forth. Sorry. When will you be taking a pregnancy test?"

"My menstrual cycle is supposed to come by January 14th. I have to go. I cannot process any more negative news or announcements. I am getting dressed and going home. The pregnancy confirmation, reasons, and consequences for all of this situation, will be revealed very soon. Sometimes good experiences can lead to perceived negative consequences. Negative consequences can also lead to the right pathway. All energies can be useful. I will keep you informed. It is 5:00 PM. I am going home."

"I understand. Telephone me. I will call you as well. Try not to worry and hope for the best. We will wait and see. Sorry."

"We will see."

"Let me know when you are ready to leave. I am getting dressed and will clean up the dining room and kitchen. This is an interesting New Year's Day. What a difference sex can make in human life."

"I know. Really I know for sure."

Lily-Butterfly took a quick shower and got dressed.
"Racoon, I am leaving now. Bye."
"Good bye Lily-Butterfly. I will telephone you. Take care."
"Yes. Bye. I will talk to you soon."

Lily-Butterfly left Racoon's home. She got in her car and drove home. As she drove home, she thought about and processed all her day's experiences.

51

Lily-Butterfly got home and made dinner for her children. They ate. She tried to not think about her possible pregnancy situation. At the end of the night she wrote everything about the day and her thoughts into her journal. She processed the complete situation and her possible decisions, options, and choices. The last thing Lily-Butterfly did before she went to sleep was prayed.

"Dear most Divine Creator of everything. You know everything already. But I am still telling you my situation. My intuition tells me that I am pregnant. Although I chose to have sex with Racoon, I do not want to be a parent for the third time. I am finished giving spirits an opportunity to be born here for their own mission. I choose instead to accomplish my chosen destiny and life's purpose mission. It is very difficult as a human single parent. I do not need any more single parent training. There must be hidden secrets within this pregnancy situation. Creator what are the hidden secrets and reasons for this situation? Maybe the hidden secrets are within my choices; and will be revealed. Please let this pregnancy situation evolve in the most beneficial way for my health and well-being. Amin."

Monday night Racoon telephoned Lily-Butterfly. She answered the telephone.

"Hi Racoon. How are you?" said Lily-Butterfly.

"I am concerned about you and the possibility of you being pregnant. I am not ready to have children. I do not think that I would ever be a father, because I do not want to pass to my children my parent's addiction issues. I struggle with alcohol addiction. No human has a perfect life. There is always something to work out in this human experience of living life."

"Racoon there is an old fashion saying, that to see someone is one thing. To live with the same person is a whole different experience. We got along with no problems before yesterday. Now that we crossed the boundary of our regular friendship and added this extra girlfriend intimacy experiences, look at how you are acting. When you asked me to be your girlfriend, add the physical intimacy and sex stuff; you never thought that there would be a possibility that I could get pregnant? Ha. You knew your past life experiences and secrets.

Maybe you have a lot more secrets in your pandora boxes that you even keep from yourself. A person's name can say a lot about them."

"Do you have a problem with my name, Miss Philosopher? What do you think my name means?"

"Your name could mean that you like to wear masks, keep things in disguise, secretive, have identity disorders, avoid reality, scared of real relationships, intimacy, and commitment, have a cavalier attitude, and many more things. Unstable and shaky people cannot have and support a stable, nurturing, and grounded relationship. Before I was aware of all of these things, but I decided to give you the benefit of my doubt. You cannot give what you do not have. I might be the mother and parent you wished you had. But I will let you know right now; I do not want to be any man's mother or parent. Anyway, I have to go to sleep. Tomorrow I have work and children to parent."

"Yes, I admire your parental skills very much. You are a perfect mother. I guess a complete parent. Lily-Butterfly you seem great at parenting. I wish that I had a mother and parent like you. Seriously."

"Oh yeah? If I am pregnant and choose to have this child, we would have to get married and do this parent stuff together. I will not choose to be a single parent for three children. In a perfect world and life, children need two good parents. Being a successful and effective single parent is the hardest responsibility on this planet."

"I know. This is why I do not have children or gotten married again."

"You were married before?"

"Yes once. It never work out. I was married once and divorced. This I never told you as well. Marriage is scary to me. By the way I will be away traveling for work Wednesday to Friday. I will telephone you. Sorry about my secrets. There is more to be revealed as time goes on."

"Mr. Racoon I have no time to spend being your therapist, mother, and parent. Have you ever seen a Psychotherapist to help you with your mental and emotional trauma issues?"

"No not really. I used to visit a Social Worker when I was a child to teenager. After that I buried all my trauma, suffering, mental health issues, and negative emotions. I drink alcohol to relieve stress. Drinking is my current therapy. That is, it in a nut shell. If you are pregnant, I do not want you to have the baby. This baby stress will blow all my secrets wide open, denial, avoidance, and trauma issues. I am not ready to be a father. You have to have an abortion. I will pay for it. Anyway, we will talk more. Good night. Sweet dreams."

"Seriously. This is interesting. I have enough to digest and process. I choose to be a part of this situation. I have to take responsibility for the outcome and consequences. It is good to know these things about you sooner than later. I have to go. Good night."

Lily-Butterfly hung up the telephone without waiting to hear if Racoon had anything more to say.

"I am speechless. Humans are interesting. This includes myself. I do not seem to have what it takes to co-dependent people's lack of interest in improving themselves and their life's situations. Look how hard I have to work on my life's experiences. I thought that this was a normal thing to do. I am getting more and more surprise that self-improvement is a rare quality in human. I still have a lot to learn about myself and relationships with other people. Now I have this new pregnancy situation that I chose to be a part of; and have to take care of. Creator I know that you are always by my side. Thank you for everything. Amin," mumbled Lily-Butterfly.

Lily-Butterfly wrote in her journal and went to sleep.

The training at work was still going great for Lily-Butterfly. The General Manager of the restaurant she was being trained in seemed to be the only negative cloud. In everything there seems to be some kind of negative experience to balance out the positive. The General Manager Mr. Sunnil's personality was like a ruler, grandiose, dark, damp, and sad. When he was working and managing the employees the restaurant environment felt hostile. All the employees seemed like they were walking on egg-shells. Mr. Sunnil's managerial skills, style, and performance seemed different from what she was being taught in training by Mr. Scott and the company's policies. Lily-Butterfly focused on Mr. Scotts training and avoided having anything to do with Mr. Sunnil. One thing that crossed Lily-Butterfly was that Mr. Sunnil was like his name, Sun-nil; meant that he had no sun inside him and a negative energy person.

One day Lily-Butterfly spoke to Mr. Scott about her perception of Mr. Sunnil.

"Mr. Scott after my training is complete, I do not want to work in this restaurant with this General Manager Mr. Sunnil."

"Why?"

"I will be distracted by his management style and negative personality. This would not be an environment for me to practice what you are teaching me. I would not get the opportunity to grow and improve the training that you have given me. Mr. Sunnil does the opposite of everything that you are teaching. I would not be able to practice the right way and we have opposite personalities. The training manual says that in creating a successful management team to work successfully together their personality must complement one another. The manual refers to this as "putting the aces in the right places." Mr. Sunnil has an abusive domineering style. It is as if he does not want to give the employees the freedom to grown. He also does the wrong procedures. I think that you see and know this already. I am just telling you what I see and my opinion."

"Yes, I see and know. This conversation is between us. We are trying to find someone to replace Mr. Sunnil. This restaurant is the company's training restaurant. His performance does not give a positive reputation to the company. When I train Manager's, they always point out the same things that you say about Mr. Sunnil. It is not easy to find the right Managers for every restaurant. Good insight and awareness. I hope that as a Manager you continue to do as good as you are doing in training. You have natural talents for this job. After training I plan to send you to a restaurant at a mall in Livingston, New Jersey for one month. After one month the District Manager of the New Jersey company restaurant will assign you to one of his restaurants. The name of the Livingston restaurant is Mr. Miller. I think that you will like him. He is from the same island you were born. Go meet him on a Saturday and let him show you around his restaurant. The District Manager is new. He started to work for the company five months ago. He supervises all the New Jersey company restaurants and two restaurants in New York. We are working very diligently to improve our Managerial staff. Okay?"

"Yes, thank you Mr. Scott. I will go visit Mr. Miller and his restaurant in Livingston. You are an efficient Training Manager. Thank you for everything."

"You are welcome Lily-Butterfly."

It was now Saturday January 14, 1995. The end of two weeks since the day Lily-Butterfly thought that she was pregnant. She proved herself to be right, by doing a pregnancy test on this Saturday morning. The start of her menstrual cycle for the month was three days late. Lily-Butterfly telephoned her Gynecologist and made an appointment for the following week Saturday January 21st. Next she telephoned Racoon. Lily-Butterfly's attitude was calm. Her thoughts were, what is done, is done. There is no blaming or anger. Only sadness. Racoon answered the telephone.

"Hello Lily-Butterfly. How are you doing?"

"I am doing fine, except for being pregnant."

"WHAT PREGNANT!"

"Yes Racoon, pregnant. You act so surprised. I made a doctor's appointment for Saturday January 21st at 10:00 AM. I am not going to wait for this baby to take root within me, if you are not going to support us one hundred percent and be a complete father. To me this is very serious. I am not going to take complete responsibility, act cavalier, be a saint, have this child so that you can be a hands-off father at my expense. The sooner I take care of this situation the better for me. Racoon what would you like to do?"

"I am dizzy. Oh wow. Big decisions. Are you sure?"

"Yes. I am sure. I did a test and it was positive."

"Oh wow. The sex was great. But this outcome is not great for me and my emotional state. Let me be very direct. I cannot be a father or husband at this time. I am already having a panic attack just thinking about being a father. My parent's issues have been totally triggered. Not even drinking alcohol is helping to calm my nerves and anxiety. I have been drinking much more than before. I cannot process being a good father or co-parent. I want you to have an abortion. I will pay for the abortion. If you choose to have this baby you are totally on your own. Lily-Butterfly your two options are have an abortion, or taking complete responsibility for having this baby. Also take all the consequences from choosing to have this child. If you have this child do not blame me for not being able to be a good father to this child. I am being honest, sorry."

"Oh wow. This is straight forward enough. I hear you loud and clear. Your decision sounds un-mindful and fear filled. How about you going to see a doctor for your mental and emotional trauma issues?"

"Listen and hear me. I am not going to see a mental health doctor. I am not crazy. All you have to do is, do not have this baby and my nerves and panic attack will stop. I did not tell you that I am a recovering alcoholic. I used to go to alcohol anonymous. Plus, the way you seem so spiritual and take things seriously; you are not my type. Or maybe I might need more time to get to know you. I am not sure if I want you to be my girlfriend any more. Let us just be friends, like we used to be? I know another girl that may be would make a better match for me. She is like me. We can co-dependent each other. Being with this other girl, I am guilt free. You are a good woman. I feel guilty about telling you to have an abortion. Now on top of everything else, I feel so corrupt and stupid. What are you going to do?"

"Mr. Racoon I am speechless. Saying that I am not your type is your way of making yourself feel good. Interesting. I am sitting here listening to you and feel like becoming pregnant is a blessing in disguise. It is a good thing that this happened now, and not after wasting more time, energy, and everything else; being your supposedly girlfriend and sex toy. I have to take responsibility for my actions. I am having an abortion when I go to the doctor next Saturday January 21st. I will only be one to two weeks pregnant. The doctor will just wash out my womb and clear the fertilized eggs. This is the last thing I want to do; but I have to do this. This is my choice."

"Good. Thank you. I will pay for the complete procedure. I am coming with you to the doctor to make sure that you do the procedure. It is not that I do not trust you do the procedure. I need to make sure that my mind and emotions can calm down. Going with you can be very helpful to my shakiness and instability. How much will the procedure cost?"

"The cost is $1,200."

"Yes, I will pay the complete thing to make sure that you get this procedure done."

"You are interesting. Thank you for being direct and telling me your honest decision. In difficult situations the real core and truth of someone's shadow, spirit, soul, and roots can become exposed. Racoon, your name fits you very well. I prayed to the Creator about this situation. My insight into the Creator's reply to this situation is that the secret reasons for being pregnant is within the situation. After experiencing more of the real you, I can see for one thing that this pregnancy situation is a mirror. This mirror is showing me sooner than later the deeper levels of who and what you are. I think that this experience is also helping me to decide if I want to get permanent birth control of tying my fallopian tubes. I was thinking about doing this after I had Holly. After experiencing you; now I am sure. I am now certain that I do not want to bring any more spirits and souls into this realm as babies. Having abortions is not the solution to this decision. But the way will show the mirror of the way. It is not in my chosen destiny to have any more children. The Creator works in mysterious ways. I am sure at the doctor's office or after, more will be confirmed and revealed. My next focus after this pregnancy situation is my life's purpose career practice. I was not born to create repeated problems for myself, or any other human. Today my chosen destiny and life's purpose is much clearer to me. The dream oracle told me that at forty two years old I will be ready to perform my life's purpose. Until then I will continue to; get to know human-nature, improving my learning, heal, transform, awaken my talents, and grow. I think that my life's purpose is to help humans. Currently it is un-known to me exactly how I will choose to use my spirit and soul's talent to help humans who choose to be helped. I can assist humans with their positive transformation and improvements. Helping humans who choose to be helped; helps the Creator and everything else. All healing comes from the Creator God. I will be the healing tool. Humans seem to need help. When I need help; help – in people, places, and things - shows up, and I choose to receive the help. Now I know my life's purpose stronger than before after experiencing your reaction to me being pregnant. One of my perception is, when seemingly negative things happen to me, I look for the hidden messages. When there is a negative situation, positive messages can be found within the negative situation. I cannot damage myself. A damage human cannot really help a damage human. A human cannot give what they do not have. Anyway, you do not seem to like my rambling, spiritual talk, and philosophy. Let me stop talking about my spiritual stuff. Meet me at my home, outside in the parking lot on Saturday morning at 9:30 AM. The doctor's office is about fifteen minutes away from my home. After this conversation I do not feel comfortable driving in your car. I will drive myself. You can drive your own car. Drive behind my car so that you can see where I am going. I am healthy and strong enough to drive myself home after the procedure. Give me the money in cash when I get to the doctor's office parking lot. Remember, make sure that you have $1,200 in cash. Cash makes it real conscious that you are paying. I do not want your check or credit card to be used to pay for this procedure. Racoon thank you for this telephone conversation and everything else. All energies can be useful, depending on the experiencer. I will see you on Saturday morning. Okay? Bye."

"Okay bye. Good night Lily-Butterfly."

Lily-Butterfly hung up the telephone without saying another word. She felt more at peace with all her decisions about the pregnancy situation that she was in. After writing in her journal and praying she went to sleep. Sleep arrived suddenly and took Lily-Butterfly to one of her favorite place of rest and peace.

52

Saturday January 21st came. Lily-Butterfly met Racoon outside in the front of her apartment building. Racoon decided not to wait until he got to the doctor's office to give Lily-Butterfly the $1,200 in cash. He gave her an envelope with $1,200 cash.

"Thank you. Let us go. I will go get my car. Follow me.," said Lily-Butterfly.

"Okay," said Racoon.

They arrived at the Doctor's office, parked their cars, entered the building, and took the elevator to the doctor's office on the third floor. They entered the office. Lily-Butterfly signed in. They sat down. The Receptionist gave Lily-Butterfly a form to fill out. She filled out the form.

"Racoon I will go in to talk to the doctor by myself. You can stay here in the receptionist area."

"Okay. I will wait here."

Within ten minutes the Nurse called Lily-Butterfly to come to the Doctor's office. Lily-Butterfly followed behind the Nurse. The Nurse asked Lily-Butterfly to have a seat in the Doctor's office. The Doctor was busy with another patient.

"The energy revolving door of this situation seems to be moving fast. I feel like I am entering another realm of life changing experience. Lily-Butterfly your life is never boring. Sometimes going down the seemingly wrong path can lead to the right path. I hope so. I have chosen to do a negative thing sooner than later. My instinct tells me that for some unknown reason I am meant to be here today. Creator I trust you and myself. Guide this process in the most positive direction. Show me if there are any more secrets to be revealed in this pregnancy situation. Please sanctify, bless, purify, and cleanse my spirit, soul, mind, emotions, and body regarding choosing to do this abortion termination procedure. Sorry about not giving a spirit an opportunity to be created and born as a human. Creator, honestly, I feel that I have to do this. Amin," whispered Lily-Butterfly.

The Doctor came into his office and he sat down. Lily-Butterfly told the Doctor the complete story of her pregnancy situation. She requested the easiest procedure of an abortion termination that would wash out the fertilized eggs. Lily-Butterfly's opinion was that she was less than two weeks pregnant. Lily-Butterfly requested permanent birth control of having her fallopian tubes cut and tied. They talked in depth about this procedure as well. The Doctor told Lily-Butterfly that the tubal ligation fallopian tube sterilization surgery had to be done in a hospital. After the conversation between Lily-Butterfly and the Doctor. The Nurse came into the Doctor's office and guided her to an examination room.

"Lily-Butterfly, please go to the restroom and pee in this cup. The restroom is behind the closed door over there. After peeing leave the pee on the counter in the rest room. Next put on this hospital gown, and lay on the examination table. I am going to use the pee to do a pregnancy test. The Doctor will be with you in a few minutes," said the Nurse.

The Nurse came back and got the pee. The Doctor knocked and entered the room with another Nurse.

"Lily-Butterfly first I am going to do an ultra sound to see what is happening. The nurse is also doing a pregnancy test," said the Doctor.

The Doctor did the ultra sound examination. He kept looking and looking at the ultra sound screen. The Nurse that did the pregnancy test returned to the room.

"Yes, Doctor the pregnancy test came out as positive. Ms. Lily-Butterfly is pregnant," said the Nurse.

"I do not see where the fertilized egg is. Your womb is empty. No sign of a fertilized egg or baby. Interesting. I will do a physical examination or use an advance ultra sound machine. This is interesting. Where is the fertilized egg?" mumbled the Doctor, like he was talking to himself.

"Interesting can be used to describe me and my life's experiences. I am not surprised. I think that I am here for an interesting reason. Leave no stone unturned to locate the fertilized egg," replied Lily-Butterfly.

The Nurse that brought in the pregnancy test information left the room.

"Lily-Butterfly, you are not surprised about my discovery. I cannot see the egg anywhere and I do not feel a mass inside your womb. Let me look someplace else to see where the fertilized egg is. Mmm," said the Doctor.

"Doctor at this stage of my life nothing surprises me anymore. Even when I seem to have made a wrong decision it turns out to be the right decision. My opinion is that in my life the Creator God works in mysterious ways. I usually take action to follow my instincts, and let the Creator God handle the details. This is how I perceive my life. Amin. Now where is this egg infusion? Doctor an insight just came to me. Look very deeply into one of my fallopian tubes. My intuition tells me that this is where the egg is hiding. You might not be able to see the eggs clearly because it is at a very early stage of infusion. I need to get this egg infusion out of me as soon as possible. Okay. Let me stop talking so as to not distract you," said Lily-Butterfly.

"Okay Lily-Butterfly. Thank you for your help. I will check out your guidance. I was looking in the tubes but I did not see anything. Let me take a deeper look. Interesting," replied the Doctor.

The Doctor brought into the room another ultra sound machine. He used the machine to check Lily-Butterfly's fallopian tubes.

"Oh yes. I found the egg infusion fertilization. The egg infusion is in one of your fallopian tubes. You cannot have this issue fixed today. This is a surgery that must be done in a hospital. My office is not equipped for this surgery. Even if you wanted to have this baby you could not. I have to schedule a surgery for you at the hospital about five minutes away in this same town. Good job Lily-Butterfly, by coming here today you have prevented a much bigger problem and maybe saved your own life. This can be a delicate surgery. I will have to cut the tube the egg infusion is in, and remove this section of the fallopian tube. You requested your fallopian tubes cut and tied, this situation has already confirmed your sterilization decision and intention. Interesting. If you did not come in for an abortion termination of this fertilized egg, the baby would have grown in this tube, and caused a rupture of the fallopian tube. This would create hemorrhage and a life threatening situation. This is called an ectopic pregnancy. This surgery must be done as soon as possible. Thank you for your insight in looking deeper into solving this pregnancy mystery. Lily-Butterfly get dress and come to my office," said the Doctor.

The Doctor and the Nurse left the room. Lily-Butterfly got dressed and went back to the Doctor's office.

Lily-Butterfly sat down in the chair and sighed.

"I have made an appointment at the hospital for the surgery to remove the section of the tube the eggs have fertilized in and close this tube. I will also cut and tie the other tube. The appointment is for next week Wednesday January 25th at 10:00 AM. Be at the hospital surgical Receptionist area at 8:30 AM. After the surgery you will be taken to a recovery room. You can leave the hospital at 5:00 PM. Here is all the information that you need to read about the ectopic pregnancy and tubal ligation surgery for birth control. Lily-Butterfly be mindful that no birth control method works one hundred percent. Read the information it will tell you everything. Okay. Thank you for coming," said the Doctor.

"How much will this surgery cost?" asked Lily-Butterfly.

"For the hospital fee, my fee, and the surgical procedure room, the cost will be about $35,000. Do you have insurance?" said the Doctor.

"Wow, $35,000. I might have insurance. I just started a new job that has medical health care benefits. Doctor I will be at the hospital for my appointment. My health is most important. One way or the other the surgery and hospital bills will get paid."

"Yes Lily-Butterfly your health is most important. I will do the surgery as scheduled whether you have insurance or not. It is important that we get this done as soon as possible. I will see you next week Wednesday. Bye."

"Oh, Doctor what is the cost for today's visit?"

"Nothing. I will add the cost to the surgery bill. If you have medical health insurance bring the insurance information with you next week Wednesday. Have a nice day. Bye."

"Good bye Doctor. Thank you."

Lily-Butterfly left the Doctor's office. She thanked the Nurses as well and walked out to the receptionist area where Racoon was sitting.

"Hello Lily-Butterfly. How are you doing?"

"I am fine let us go outside. We can talk when we get outside," replied Lily-Butterfly.

They walked outside to the parking lot. Standing by Racoon's car, Lily-Butterfly talked to him.

"That was quick you were gone for only ninety minutes," said Racoon.

"The Doctor did not do the termination of the pregnancy. I actually need surgery for ......" said Lily-Butterfly.

Racoon interrupted.

"What? Why not?" said Racoon.

"There is a bigger problem," said Lily-Butterfly.

Racoon interrupted again.

"What now?"

"For me this complete situation is very negative and draining. I am the one with the problem within me. It is easy for you to just talk. Please wait and listen to what I am saying. Your questions will be answered by listening and hearing what I have to say. Okay? The egg fertilized inside one of my fallopian tubes. This is dangerous, because as the egg infusion grown into a baby, the fallopian tube would have exploded, and create a hemorrhage. The grown fetus would spill out inside me, and might have killed me. I have to have this surgery inside a hospital. The appointment for this surgery is next week Wednesday January 25th at 10:00 AM. The surgery will remove the egg fertilized fetus and the section of the fallopian tube that it is in. This will make this tube not work anymore. I have decided to cut the other tube as well. This complete surgery will turn into a sterilization surgery called a tubal ligation. This tubal ligation surgery was something I thought of doing before this pregnancy situation. So, now your idea of intimate girlfriend and sex have brought me to this surgery situation. This to me is a very loud and clear message. This intimate sex girlfriend relationship, that you requested, I choose agreed to, and pregnancy; is not meant to be. If I had not followed my instincts and gone to the Doctor at this early stage, I would have ended up in a dangerous situation. The cost to do the complete surgery, Doctor's fee, and hospital is estimated at $35,000. Would you like to pay half of the cost?"

"Wow. What? Now you will be sterilized. Wow. No, I do not want to pay half. I do not have over $17,000 to pay for resolving this problem. I am only contributing the $1,200 I gave you already. That is, it. Sorry. Do you have medical health insurance?"

"I do not know if my work health insurance is in effect as yet. I have to ask. Your reaction and how willing you are to help pay for this surgery is another signal of how this supposedly relationship would have been. Thank you and thanks to this pregnancy situation I am being stopped from proceeding any further with you being in my life. I am a human who will not get away with going down the wrong negative path. Here is your friendship ring. This friendship is over on all levels. Do not telephone me anymore. I do not want to waste any more energy and time on talking with you about this situation and friendship. If I was to say more, it would be spiritual, and you would not understand. I have to take complete responsibility and consequence for my choice in this situation. Good bye Mr. Racoon. Thank you for everything."

"Why end the friendship? We could go back to being regular

friends like we were before. No one is perfect. No situation is perfect. Ha. Why? You are great for me even as a regular friend. I like your peaceful and positive energy. Plus, I enjoy you being in my life. Lily-Butterfly reconsider your decision."

"No. If I do not listen to the symbology of this experience one or both of us will have more disaster. Go in peace, unconditional love, and understanding. Best regards with your life and everything. Ending this friendship relationship on every level is what is best for both of us. Good bye Racoon."

"Wait. Listen."

Lily-Butterfly got in her car and drove away. Racoon stood by his car for a while. Finally, he got in his car and drove away.

"What a waste of humanity? Sometimes I seem to meet the wrong people for the right reasons of awareness and waking up. When I realize this I have to take action," mumbled Lily-Butterfly.

This was the last time Lily-Butterfly saw or spoke to Racoon. Racoon telephone Lily-Butterfly. She did not talk to him. That night Lily-Butterfly prayer to the Creator was three sentences.

"Dear Creator everything in my current situation and experiences have spoken very clearly to me. I see all the secrets and hidden messages within my current situation. Thank you for everything Amin."

53

Monday when Lily-Butterfly went to work she requested Wednesday and Thursday off from work.

"Mr. Scott, I have a medical emergency. I need Wednesday and Thursday off to go to the hospital for a surgery. I know that at this time I do not have any paid day off. I will take the days off with no pay. I will be here on Friday. Is this okay?"

"Medical emergency days off are allowed. Bring me a Doctor's note and I will choose to pay you for the day. You are doing excellent with your training. I can make these days off an exception to the rules."

"Thank you very much."

"You are welcome. Are you ready for your test on Friday?"

"Yes, I will be ready. I study on a daily basis. So far, I think that I remember everything. I really appreciate all you do to make my training a success."

"You are welcome Lily-Butterfly. I try my best to do my job the best way."

"Is my medical health care insurance currently effective?"

"Telephone the Personnel Department and ask the department Manager."

"Okay. I will."

Lily-Butterfly telephone the Personnel Manager at the corporate head office. She promised to research Lily-Butterfly's insurance availability and let her know.

Lily-Butterfly did not tell the children about her medical, surgery, and pregnancy situation. She never burdened her children with negative news and situations. This was one of her ways of letting the children be children. Her intention was not to traumatize the children with needless worry, suffering, negative information, stress, sadness, and disconcertment to their minds and life. Wednesday morning came, Lily-Butterfly helped the children prepare for school. When Rebornstar and Holly left home for school Lily-Butterfly went to the hospital. While driving to the hospital she prayed again.

"Dear Creator you know everything already. I am still choosing to ask for your support in guiding everything about this surgery in the positive right direction. Help me stay strong and peaceful throughout the surgery, recovery, and healing process. I know that healing happens in stillness. I must stay alive to take care of my children, fulfill my life's purpose destiny, and be at work on Friday morning. My human life is like a puzzle, adventure, obstacle course, revolving door, speechlessness, and many unbeknown situations to resolve and make the correct decisions on. Continue to be my support system on this journey. The great way and pathways have no price tag. They are priceless and speechless. Into stillness and peace, I embrace myself. Thank you for everything. Amin."

Lily-Butterfly arrived at the hospital in a cocoon of peace, surrender, and acceptance. She went upstairs in the elevator to the hospital's surgical center floor. After filling out the forms the Nurse guided Lily-Butterfly into the Doctor's office.

"Hi. Good morning Doctor," said Lily-Butterfly as she sat down.

"Good morning Lily-Butterfly. I am going to go over with you some important information before we do the surgery. If you need blood because of a medical emergency, can I give you blood?"

"No. I cannot accept any other human's blood but my own. It would create many more problems. If you give me saline my body will recreate my own blood. This is what I am used to and want. This is what will work best for me. I do not think that we will have any problems during the surgery. I do not want to explain this blood transfusion suggestion any further. For every known and unknown reasons this is my decision. Thank you for respecting my decision."

"Okay. I understand. Please sign this paper consenting to not wanting a blood transfusion."

"Okay Doctor. Everything about the surgery will go positively. Based on my experiences with you and my instinct, you are a great Doctor. I positively trust you completely. Plus, the greatest Universal Physician, the Creator is directing and managing this complete surgery process. We will be fine. Thank you in advance for everything."

"Okay Lily-Butterfly you are strong in your faith and spirituality. I understand. Go to the Nurse and she will guide you about preparing you for the surgery. Come to my office in two weeks, on Saturday February 11th for a checkup. Here is a business card with this appointment information. I will see you in the surgical room."

"Okay Doctor. Thank you."

Lily-Butterfly left the Doctor's office. She went to the Nurse, who guided her to change into a hospital gown and where to put her clothes and any other personal items. She had left her pocket book inside her car trunk. Lily-Butterfly did not have the medical health insurance information with her to give the Doctor and hospital. She would resolve this insurance situation after the surgery. The Doctor told her this was okay. When Lily-Butterfly was ready the Nurse instructed her to lay on a hospital surgical bed. She was taken to the surgical room. Lily-Butterfly closed her eyes and entered completely within herself and her prayer field. One thought Lily-Butterfly had while lying on the bed was, spirits and souls who are lined up to come into my womb and body, please leave this line. Today I am closing the pathways to my womb, oven, and cradle of life. I am not open for this spirit, soul, and human experience any more. For my greater good the Creator and myself, wills this decision. Amin.

Lily-Butterfly arrived at the surgical room. She opened her eyes. The bed was put in its proper location. Lily-Butterfly saw three Nurses, the Doctor, and the Anesthesiologist Doctor. They were all doing their part in the surgery operation procedure. When everything and everyone was ready the Anesthesiologist spoke first.

"Ms. Lily-Butterfly, now I am going to give you the anesthesia and you will fall into a deep sleep. After the surgery you will be taken to the intensive care recovery room. When the anesthesia wears off you will wake up. A Nurse will attend to you and guide you to want is next. Okay."

"Yes. Okay. I thank everyone for everything. Bye," replied Lily-Butterfly.

"See you later. Find a place that you would like to go within you and go there," said one of the Nurse.

"I will. I am already there. Bye," said Lily-Butterfly.

After Lily-Butterfly said this, she could feel herself quickly drifting off, and then she felt no longer alive, and no physical life; only a spiritual energy essence and presence. Lily-Butterfly's last conscious thought was, this is cool and interesting.

The surgery was completed at 1:30 PM. Everything went well. At 3:24 PM Lily-Butterfly woke up from the anesthesia. The Nurse guided her to stay laying down and to continue to recover and awaken. At 4:32 PM the Nurse guided Lily-Butterfly to get up slowly and go to the restroom to pee. Being able to pee was a positive sign that her body functions were working as they should. At 5:20 PM the Doctor came and approved that everything was fine with Lily-Butterfly and she could go home. The Doctor gave her prescription for pain medication and antibiotic. She took the prescription just in case she needed the medications. Usually Lily-Butterfly did not need pain medication and antibiotic. She thanked the Doctor and Nurses, got dressed, went outside, got in her car and drove home. In fifteen minutes, Lily-Butterfly arrived home. When she got home, Holly was at her friend's home and Rebornstar was at the park playing with her friends.

Lily-Butterfly stopped to pick up Holly from her friend's home. They went upstairs. Lily-Butterfly made dinner. She and the children ate dinner together. She was very hungry because she had not eaten after dinner the night before, because of the surgery. The children never found out about their mother's surgical situation. Lily-Butterfly followed the usual routine in ending the day. When the children were in bed, Lily-Butterfly wrote in her journal about her day's experiences, prayed, and went to sleep. She would have some more needed rest on Thursday when the children were in school. As she laid in bed, she talked to herself.

"My life is a revolving door and cycle of evolving events. Where exactly will all these life's experiences take me? I do not know. Only the Creator and the way knows for sure. What does not kill me surely makes me stronger and awakens my talents. Plus, I learn more about myself and other people, growth – transformation – change happens, and I improve my Universal wisdom; plus, other things. Amin," whispered Lily-Butterfly.

Thursday morning Lily-Butterfly made breakfast, ate with Rebornstar and Holly. The children left for school. Lily-Butterfly cleaned up the kitchen, drank two more cups of calming tea, and went back into her bed to sleep. At 1:00 PM Lily-Butterfly woke up and ate some crackers, fruit, and drank three more cups of calming tea. She went back to sleep; and slept until 5:30 PM. Lily-Butterfly prepared dinner and all her things to go to work on Friday morning. After eating dinner, the children did their nightly routine and went to sleep. Lily-Butterfly took a shower, wrote in her journal, prayed, and went to sleep. Her healing and recovery was improving at a fast rate. Lily-Butterfly felt normal, except for a little sensitivity where she was cut in two places on each side of her lower stomach, below her belly button.

Friday morning Lily-Butterfly was back at work. She worked mindfully and the day was an easy one filled with training tests.

Her over all test scores were 99%. The rest of her training involved office management procedures. This part of Lily-Butterfly training continued until Tuesday February 28, 1995. Lily-Butterfly returned to the Gynecologist Doctor on February 11ᵗʰ for a checkup. The Personnel Manager had informed Lily-Butterfly that her medical health insurance was in effect from January 21ˢᵗ. The medical health insurance paid the Doctor and hospital all their fees, except for the co-pay. The $1,200 that Racoon had given her was used to help with paying the co-pay. The Doctor told Lily-Butterfly that she was healing very rapidly. Lily-Butterfly never had to take the pain and antibiotic medication. Everything regarding Lily-Butterfly's health, well-being, and healing was great on that day; and into the future.

On Monday March 6ᵗʰ Lily-Butterfly went to Mr. Miller's restaurant and worked until Friday March 31ˢᵗ. For all this time Lily-Butterfly was working in the training restaurant with Mr. Scott she ignored Mr. Sunnil. When Mr. Sunnil tried to engage her into any negative situations she would walk away and work around the situations. Mr. Sunnil was unaware that he was trying to have a confrontation with the wrong person. This avoidance of Mr. Sunnil was not long term. Lily-Butterfly was unaware of the plans Mr. Scott the Training Manager was making with the new District Manager Mr. Watson. They were deciding and planning to promote Lily-Butterfly. They thought that she had too much talent to ignore, and waste such an opportunity on her being and Assistant Manager. They were planning to promote her to Restaurant Manager or General Manager and give her a restaurant to operate.

Lily-Butterfly surgical procedure healing continued successfully. With processing all the experiences about Racoon, pregnancy, surgery, recovery, work tests, and work training by the time March came, most of these experience had made their way into her past. The present was clear, peaceful, and stable. While working with Mr. Miller the General Manager of the Livingston restaurant, she worked the 7:00 AM to 5:00 PM shift; Monday to Friday. She performed all the functions of operating the restaurant with and without Mr. Miller. Her review for working in this restaurant was great. On Friday March 31ˢᵗ Mr. Miller told Lily-Butterfly that on Monday April 3ʳᵈ at 9:00 AM, she should report to the training restaurant where she was trained. Lily-Butterfly was scheduled to have a meeting with Mr. Scott the Training Manager and Mr. Watson the District Manager.

On Monday April 3rd Lily-Butterfly arrived at 9:00 AM for the meeting at the Paramus Training restaurant. Mr. Scott and Mr. Watson was already seated at a table in the food court close to the restaurant's operation door entrance. Lily-Butterfly walked over to the table.

"Lily-Butterfly have a seat. How are you doing?" said Mr. Scott.

"I am doing great."

"Meet Mr. Watson your new supervisor. He is the District Manager," said Mr. Scott.

"Hi Mr. Watson. Now I get to meet the man behind the name Mr. Watson. Okay."

"The reason for this meeting is to inform you that we have decided to promote you to General Manager of this Paramus mall restaurant. If you could manage the Livingston restaurant which is three times this restaurant size, then you could manage being General Manager for this restaurant. Mr. Watson would become your supervisor if you choose to accept. If you do not choose to accept, then Mr. Sunnil will become your supervisor. We would still place you in this restaurant and promote you to Manager and you would not be an Assistant Manager any more. If you say yes to the General Manager promotion, we have planned to transfer Sunnil out of the restaurant to another restaurant. We do not want to immediately fire him. We could use him in another restaurant, until maybe he decides to quit. This meeting conversation is confidential and between the three of us. Which promotion would you like to accept?" said Mr. Scott.

Mr. Watson sat quiet and listened.

"I know for sure that working with Mr. Sunnil would be an obstacle course, and I would end up quitting. You already know how he is. My opinion, perception, college, and university training tells me that professional job is not personal. The facts are available from my experience and your experience is that Mr. Sunnil is arrogant, rude, dominating, egotistic, and chauvinistic. He does not follow any of the company managerial, product preparations, and customer service policies and procedures. I cannot work with this person as my supervisor. Working with him will make it a battle to provide the quality of work and service that I would like to practice for my career success and improvements. I am not going to choose a suffering and abusive work environment. This is what I have to say about being promoted to Manager and Sunnil being my supervisor. I do not know Mr. Watson. He will become my supervisor if I accept the promotion as a General Manager. In the future if my experience with Mr. Watson turn out to be a negative one, I will resign from this company and go work for another company, or we will see what happens then. I know the quality of my work is positive. I might look simply, and act quiet, but things about me is not like they seem. Anyway, I will take the promotion as General Manager. Thank you for listening to my expression as I process your offer. What is next?" said Lily-Butterfly.

"Okay you will have to work with Mr. Sunnil for this week. He will be transferred effective April 10th. On this date we will officially promote you with the salary of $49,400. All your benefits will stay the same, except your 401K profit sharing benefits will increase. The current Manager has been transferred to another restaurant. When you become General Manager, you can decide if you would like to train and promote the current Assistant Manager to Manager, and choose one of the other crew employees to shift supervisor or Assistant Manager. Basically, the restaurant will become totally your responsibility to operate as you choose to use the corporation's policies and procedures. Is this okay with you," said Mr. Scott.

"Yes. What is my schedule for this week? Did you tell Mr. Sunnil that I will be working here this week?" said Lily-Butterfly.

"No, we have not told him, because we did not know if you were going to accept what we have to offer you. You know that you have very marketable skills. We do not think that we can push you around to do things that you would not accept. We do not want you to quit. This is the truth. We are going to talk to Mr. Sunnil after your meeting. He will tell you the schedule for this week. Next week you can decide on your schedule. We recommend that you work Monday to Saturday with a day off during the week, and maybe one midshift. This way you are here when the restaurant is most busy. The one midshift can give you an idea of what is happening in the restaurant during lunch and dinner. The mall is closed on Sundays, so you will be off every Sunday. The end of week financial, production, and employee payment reports must be done Saturday nights after the restaurant closes, or early Monday mornings before the restaurant opens. It is up to you to decide which day is best to do these reports. We are going to inform Mr. Sunnil now about what we have planned for him. He will try to give you a hard time this week. Stay professional, calm, and patient. Lily-Butterfly do you have any questions?" said Mr. Scott.

"Not at this time. Mr. Watson I will let you know if I have questions and concerns. It is good to meet you."

"Okay Lily-Butterfly. Welcome to being a General Manager. We will work together as a team," said Mr. Watson.

"Welcome Mr. Watson to being my supervisor. We will see from experience how we work together as a team. Humans can be interesting, strange, and over time they will show their many different faces. As time goes by, we will see how we work together. I will make no assumptions and judgements about you. My experiences with you is what I will trust as to who and what you are. My work will always speak for itself. Friendship is not a qualification and replacement for professionalism and unconditional teamwork. We will see Mr. Watson. Thank you, Mr. Scott and Mr. Watson. Can I go now?" said Lily-Butterfly.

"Yes, you can go. Please go inside and ask Mr. Sunnil to come out to speak to us. Today you will work until 5:00 PM. I am not sure that you would have plan to work until 7:00 PM. I hear that you have two children and might have to go home before 7:00 PM," said Mr. Watson.

"Thank you, sir. I will leave at 5:00 PM. Thank you for the opportunity to leave early. I will tell Mr. Sunnil to come see you for a meeting. Bye. Thank both of you for everything."

"You are welcome," said Mr. Scott and Mr. Watson.

Lily-Butterfly told Mr. Sunnil to go outside the restaurant to the food court for a meeting with Mr. Scott and Mr. Watson. After the meeting Mr. Sunnil came back into the restaurant. He was very upset and angry. Mr. Sunnil scheduled Lily-Butterfly to work 12:00 PM to 10:00 PM close. He scheduled her off the next day which was Tuesday. She worked this schedule Wednesday to Saturday. This meant that she had to prepare Rebornstar and Holly for her absence from home for dinner and everything else from Wednesday to Saturday. Lily-Butterfly took Monday evening and Tuesday to organize the children and her life for the current work week's schedule. All week Mr. Sunnil tried to bully and antagonize Lily-Butterfly. She stayed professional and calm. This did not mean that she acted submissive. She redirected Mr. Sunnil every time he tried to create a confrontation with her. Lily-Butterfly felt that she had to get used to different personalities, negativity, bruteness, and other negative experiences working in such a tough and difficult professional working environment. This started with Mr. Sunnil. For example, Lily-Butterfly arrived at work on Friday at 12:00 PM. She was standing in the kitchen by the prep table, Mr. Sunil walked over to her.

"Lily-Butterfly, open the cabinet under the soda machine it is very dirty, clean inside, you did not get this done last night when the restaurant was cleaned," said Mr. Sunnil.

"Was everything else clean? Is there anything else I did not do?" asked Lily-Butterfly.

"Everything else was done," replied Mr. Sunnil.

Lily-Butterfly walked away. She went to the kitchen sink which was about three feet away from where they were standing. Lily-Butterfly filled a cleaning bucket with soapy water and got a clean dish towel. She walked back over to where Mr. Sunil was standing.

"Mr. Sunnil, here is a bucket of soapy water and a clean towel. You can go open the cabinet, bend down, and clean out all the dirt and soda syrup build up inside. You have been the General Manager in this restaurant for seven years. During these seven years I do not think that you have ever cleaned one thing. I saw inside the soda cabinet. It does not look like it was cleaned since the restaurant opened seven years ago. I personally helped with all the cleaning last night. This restaurant needed a lot of deep cleaning. I was planning to clean this cabinet at a later date. Since you have a complaint about it, you can go clean it now. Tomorrow is our last day working together in this restaurant. Please do not try to exercise your demons on me. Excuse me. I have to go prepare for helping with lunch. Huff and puff your negative energy on your own face, and not me."

Lily-Butterfly walked away and went to the front counter of the restaurant to help with lunch service. Saturday was Lily-Butterfly's last day working with Mr. Sunnil. But in the future, he would return a couple of times to the restaurant to be nosy.

54

Monday evening after the promotional interview Lily-Butterfly went home and created plans to organize the children and her life around her new work schedule for the week. At home Lily-Butterfly became even more organized. Grocery shopping, meal planning, meal preparations, Holly getting to and from school, home chores, laundry, mindfulness about disciplining the girls, managing her stress level, prayer, journal writing, and every spiritual practice learning had been arranged. Rebornstar was the only moving part to the current arrangements. Rebornstar was getting more and more into her focus choice and priority of friendship management and maintenance. If Lily-Butterfly told Rebornstar to do A, she would try to see how she could do Z. Rebornstar tested the boundaries a lot and the house rules her mother created. When Rebornstar went too far over the boundary with her friendship map, Lily-Butterfly would become firm and at times seem abrupt. It seems as if Rebornstar was taking advantage of her mother's unconditional love, understanding, care, and kindness. Holly tried to help herself and her mother by hearing and listening as guided. When Lily-Butterfly was not at work she was with Holly, at home, and busy with home maintenance. Outside of everything one of Lily-Butterfly's main focus and priority was taking care of her health and well-being.

April 10th came and Lily-Butterfly was officially the General Manager for the restaurant. She scheduled herself to work Monday mornings at 5:00 AM to 3:00 PM to get all the payroll and the other financial reports completed, help manage the restaurant, and help with the busy lunch service. Tuesdays she scheduled herself off. Wednesday, Friday and Saturday she worked 7:00 AM to 5:00 PM. On Thursday she scheduled herself to work mid shift 10:00 AM to 8:00 PM. Talia the Assistant Manager was born on the island of Kawomaya. She was a productive Assistant Manager, followed instructions, and eager to learn. Immediately Lily-Butterfly got the vision to promote her to Restaurant Manager with an increase in pay. But she choose to bring the restaurant up to code in every way first. Lily-Butterfly got clutter cleaned from the restaurant, and reorganized the complete restaurant; including the stock room, walk in refrigerator, and freezer. She fixed all the information in the computer to be as it was supposed to be. Fixed the regular employee schedule to match the sales and the budget. Retrain all regular employees, Assistant Manager, and shift supervisor. Created a build to order list for the dry paper goods and all food items. Lily-Butterfly planned, instructed, and organized a five hour Sunday cleaning operation. The Assistant Manager, shift supervisor, and six regular employees to come into the restaurant when it was closed, to clean every inch of the restaurant. In addition, she ordered new uniforms for the Assistant Manager, shift supervisor, and regular employees. Lily-Butterfly gave out the required amount of new uniforms to all the employees. Lily-Butterfly did employee reviews and wage increases to every regular employee. Everything Lily-Butterfly did were things Mr. Sunnil had neglected to do for the seven years he was General Manager. All of this production took Lily-Butterfly three months to complete. By July 10th everything in the restaurant was functioning up to the required level and quality. The employee's moral and motivation improved. Customer satisfaction increased. The employees gave improved speed and efficiency of customer service. The restaurant sales improved by 34%. It was a very magical experience for Lily-Butterfly, and mostly Mr. Watson. Mr. Watson was amazed and felt great that all of Lily-Butterfly's work was making him and his district look productive and efficient. A 34% increase in money and increase in profits was every company's dream. For the first time since the restaurant was opened seven years ago the computer and the financial report reflected the truth. When Lily-Butterfly was fixing all the computer financial reports she saw that Mr. Sunnil was giving fake figures. All the financial records was showing the opposite of what was going on. The restaurant was operating at a 28% loss and Mr. Sunnil reported a steady 7% to 5% weekly loss. Mr. Sunnil did not want anyone to discover his bogus figures, so he did all the General Manager financial reports himself. He never trained any of the other manager to do his job. This way he could restrict their progress and limit their professional destiny, and hide the truth of the restaurant's financial records.

On Monday July 17th Lily-Butterfly promoted Talia from Assistant Manager to Restaurant Manager and gave her a large salary increase based on the Management salary scale. This was the day Lily-Butterfly started to teach Talia everything she did not know and refined what she did know. Lily-Butterfly also taught Talia everything the General

Manager did as far as all computer work, all reports, and employee payroll. Saturday night Talia worked the closing shift. On Monday Mornings she would work with Lily-Butterfly on the same schedule at 5:00 AM to 3:00 PM. In another three months Talia knew everything Lily-Butterfly knew about being a General Manager and Manager. Talia was a high school graduate and started in the restaurant business as a cashier. Talia was a hard worker, patient, and great at following guidance and instructions. This was some of her best assets. During Talia's promotion and training she helped Lily-Butterfly train Peter the shirt supervisor become an Assistant Manager. After Lily-Butterfly's training Peter was certified by Mr. Scott as an Assistant Manager. Lily-Butterfly also took the best regular employee and trained him to be a shift supervisor. Lily-Butterfly had great people relationship skills. This was an asset in doing everything she did with all the employees. The employees followed her training and guidance with ease and self-motivation. By September 30th the restaurant was running like a well-oiled machine. Lily-Butterfly felt at ease and her job responsibility became stress free. She could now manage the restaurant store operation in every way so effortless that she could do it with her eyes closed if she needed to.

Mr. Watson would arrive every Monday Morning at 9:00 AM with enthusiasm to get all the reports from Lily-Butterfly. Although Mr. Watson was the biggest benefactor of everything Lily-Butterfly produced, he had become silently jealous of all Lily-Butterfly's success and abundance with the restaurant's success. He was planning unbeknownst to Lily-Butterfly how he could use Lily-Butterfly to maximize all his success, affluence, and abundance in as many of his failing restaurants; for his benefit. If the restaurants in Mr. Watson's district increased their capacities in function, budget, and profits he would look great, get salary increases, and possibly get promoted to a Vice President level. He watched, waited, and schemed how to take advantage of Lily-Butterfly and her talents. From lifting heavy fifty pound sacks of potatoes and other heavy things, Lily-Butterfly noticed that she had torn the ligament under her skin below her left wrist. Fluid was leaking under her skin and the injury was getting worse. Sometimes she would bandage her wrist for extra support. Lily-Butterfly often thought of taking sick days off from work to get the injury surgically repaired; but never did.

Mr. Sunnil was doing poorly at the store he was transferred to in

New York. He came into the restaurant Lily-Butterfly was currently in charge of two times. He looked around and left quietly. Mr. Sunil saw without a doubt that the restaurant was doing excellent. He also saw from the company's financial reports that the profits were consistently improved. Mr. Sunil never returned after his second visit. He gave notice and left the company in September of 1995; the same year. He went to work as General Manager for a major chicken restaurant.

September 18th Mr. Watson started his disguised plans to use Lily-Butterfly to upgrade two of his worse failing restaurants that he was supervising as District Manager. Mr. Watson told Lily-Butterfly that she should go to each restaurant until everything was improved. When she was finished, she would go to the next restaurant and do the same thing. Mr. Watson told Lily-Butterfly of his plans for her to go to the restaurants, teach the Generals Managers how to operate their restaurants like her restaurant, do audits on everything, and fix all the information in their computers, like she did for her restaurant. At the same time, she was to be General Manager for her own restaurant. He told Lily-Butterfly that she had no choice but to do as he asked. Mr. Watson told Lily-Butterfly that if she did not follow his instructions this would be negative for her annual employee review and salary increase.

The first restaurant Mr. Watson had Lily-Butterfly scheduled to go was in Upstate New York. Lily-Butterfly let Mr. Watson know that this was his job, she was not getting paid to do his job, and that he was sending her to do his job, because he did not know how to do what he was asking her to do. Mr. Watson was not happy that Lily-Butterfly was direct at telling him the truth. Mr. Watson was firm with Lily-Butterfly, but was also cautious of not pushing her to the point of her quitting. Mr. Watson played the negative mean District Manager and seemingly positive kind District Manager. Most times Mr. Watson showered Lily-Butterfly with praises, compliments, and congratulations. If she seemed hesitant in following his instructions to do work in his other restaurants, he would threaten her with a negative annual review and no salary increase, for not doing as he asked.

Lily-Butterfly was not being sucked in by anything Mr. Watson did or said. She was choosing to do as she was guided and her instincts told her. Plus, her other thoughts were, if she act smart, she gets more work to do. If she acts dumb, she messes up herself. Human created knowledge is power in the human material realm, so she could choose to see the things Mr. Watson was telling her to do as opportunities. If she does not do as Mr. Watson instruct her to do then she cancels out all her positive work efforts, and does not get a positive annual work review and salary increase. The bottom line is Mr. Watson was blackmailing Lily-Butterfly into doing his job, and improving the restaurants that he was in charge of improving and supervising.

Lily-Butterfly could see right through Mr. Watson charades, games, masks, and shadow. She comforted herself by surrendering to Mr. Watson's instructions with the most pleasant self-motivational internal awareness. Lily-Butterfly told herself that the benefits she would get from doing what Mr. Watson instructed her to do was, learning how and having the courage to drive in New York, more experience, growth, personal development, and improvement of her talents. So, she went and helped the General Managers of the two restaurant to improve their restaurants. Both restaurants Lily-Butterfly went to do audits, fix their computer financial information, inventory, and product mix, had the same issue of fake financial figures, like the way Mr. Sunnil operated his restaurant. The work Lily-Butterfly did revealed all the lies, fakeness, and bogus information and reports. How these restaurants were really doing was brought to light. The General Managers got a renewed opportunity to operate their restaurant from the true reality. The General Managers of these restaurant were not happy with the reality of their situation. Now they also had to do the necessary work to really improve the restaurant in every way, or get fired. By December 15th Lily-Butterfly had completed the assignment Mr. Watson had given her to do. The greater work Lily-Butterfly did the more Mr. Watson rewarded her with more work to help him with the failing restaurants. She knew that she could have left the job, but her instincts were telling her to stay, for reasons currently unknown. The reasons will reveal itself later. The Creator and Universe works in mysterious ways.

55

In Lily-Butterfly's personal life, things were progressing as well. She had decided that maybe it was time to rent a two bed room apartment. She would have her own room and the two girls could still share the other bedroom. Other beliefs and opinions of Lily-Butterfly was that she should not waste her resources. At the same time, she knew that she was prosperous, and can buy anything she wanted and needed. Lily-Butterfly had simple and elegant taste in everything. The philosophy of simplicity was used to balance these beliefs, perceptions, and opinions; plus kept the idea of lack and greed nonexistent. Lily-Butterfly liked the idea of renting a place to live and not owning house or property. She grew up with the ancient village belief that she could not in reality own the earth and property. Her ancestors were keepers and stewards of the earth, mother-nature, and property. Even if they had titles to property it still meant the same thing. Lily-Butterfly's opinion and perception was that owning the earth and property was a modern way of possession, thinking, and belief. The idea and plan of moving stayed simmering within Lily-Butterfly.

July 31, 1995 Holly became six years old. For summer holiday, Lily-Butterfly registered her for summer camp at her elementary school. She attended this camp with her friends from the building where they lived. Rebornstar had the option of choosing what she wanted to do with guidance. Lily-Butterfly registered Holly for martial arts classes on Tuesday evenings 5:00 to 6:00 PM. At this time Lily-Butterfly felt that she needed to do a social and entertainment activity. She decided to join the gym. It was five minute drive from her home. Lily-Butterfly bought a life time membership to this fitness gym. She went to this gym for aerobic classes, jogging, speed walking, live cycle exercise training, sauna, steam room, and meeting all kinds of people. Currently these were the new addition to Lily-Butterfly's life.

September of 1995 Holly went to first grade. In first grade Holly disguised learning problem seemed to increase. The special education department of the board of education could not figure out what the problem was. During Holly's well child visits at the Pediatrician, the doctor could not figure out what the problem was. When Lily-Butterfly worked at home with Holly she seemed fine. Not even Holly knew what her learning problem was. Currently Lily-Butterfly surrendered to this Holly mysterious learning problem. The child development and special education department at the Board of Education in this town, decided to classify Holly as special education. Holly was transferred from a regular grade one class to all special education grade one classes. Lily-Butterfly kept her awareness on this Holly learning situation. Lily-Butterfly always attended every parent teacher's conference review meetings for both Rebornstar and Holly. For Lily-Butterfly the thought of moving from the current apartment and this town became stronger. On visiting the elementary, middle, and high school in this town she did not perceive that they were providing nurturing and caring environment for children to learn in. The mystery of Holly's so called learning disability and special education classes, continued with disconcertment to Holly and Lily-Butterfly. Currently every night Lily-Butterfly would ask the Creator for insight and help with this Holly learning situation. As usual the Creator answered Lily-Butterfly's prayer about resolving Holly's learning issue. Unbeknownst to Lily-Butterfly, the Holly's learning issue was resolved in a mysterious, instinctive, by her taking actions to naturally follow as she was guided. With trust in herself and her inner guidance, Lily-Butterfly naturally followed her instincts. One pathway lead to another. The way will show the way. Stay tuned.

On Wednesday October 4, 1995 Ms. Gina telephoned Lily-Butterfly at 8:30 PM. Lily-Butterfly answered the telephone.

"Hi this is Lily-Butterfly. May I help you?"

"Oh, my Lord, you answer your phone so professional."

"Who is this?" said Lily-Butterfly.

"You do not know my voice? Wow. It is me, Gina. You forgot my voice?"

"Yes, you sound different. Maybe it is because I have not spoken to you in a while. What now? Ms. Mama Gina you can be interesting and entertaining with your attitudes. Plus, I smell trouble."

"Well, yes, you are right. Like you say, there is a problem. Mama and your wonderful Manana Leila's employer telephoned me yesterday. She told me that I must come and take care of mama. Mama seems to be forgetting her way home taking public transportation. She got lost two times by not getting off the train at the right stop.

Mama ended up being helped by the police. The police helped her get to her home. Her employer say it was time for her to retire. I am not going to change my life to move to Boston to go take care of mama, and live in her life. Do you want to go? I am just saying."

"Mmm. Well, well. Ms. Mama Gina you always show your true colors. This is one positive thing about you. Plus, your so-called free will to choose amazes me. There actually is no free will because it is mirrored by karma. For every thought, speech, and action the karma bank returns everything to you. You have not physically seen your mother in twenty two years. She filed for your permanent resident visa. You came to this country and I offered to host you until you could create your own life. It is almost five years since you have been living in New Jersey since you moved from Kawomaya. You have not gone to visit your wonderful mother not even once. The mother who took care of the first two children you give birth to. You gave me to her before I was born. At two years old you brought Lucy to her to take care of. I took care of Lucy, Henry, and Dean when Manana left your home. I think Manana Leila spoiled you. We have done so much for you. I think it is time you take some responsibility to show some respect and care for your mother. You are the only one she gave birth to. She is my precious Manana Leila, but if I continue to take away the opportunities for you to give her back some unconditional love, compassion, kindness, care, and so forth, I would be standing in both of your paths, and preventing this exchange. Ms. Gina your un-mindful selfishness is going to get the best of you. Thanks be to the Creator I have repaid you a million fold for conceiving me. The rest was up to me and Manana Leila to stay alive, be born, and not end up dying. Your mother and I have taken care of your children. I have been your slave until I left your home after graduating college. It is obvious that it is time you do something for your mother to repay her for everything she has done for you. You must respectfully do something honorable for your mother before she dies. I will not stand in the way of your karma repayment to your mother. Your attitude about this situation is going to stir up old negative vibes between the three of us. I am rambling and repeating myself. I have said enough already."

"Yes, for sure. You always talk and talk. Let the stirring begin. You talk too much spiritual philosophy. She mothered you too. Ha. Mmm. Why me? Why?"

"To pay her respect and act honorable for once. This can give you some positive karma to counter balance all your negative karma. She is your mother, father, and parent. The Creator wills you to do this." This is for your karma repayment. If I take away your opportunity to make things right with your mother, father, and parent, this is not positive for me."

"I am not going to change my life to move to Boston," said Ms. Gina.

"Ms. Gina for once choose to stop rebelling. Manana Leila is the reason why you are here. She told me that when she gets old, she would like you to move to Boston to take care of her. This is one of the reasons she spends two years paying a lawyer to file for you and your two sons to get a permanent resident visa. Manana Leila does not want to move in her old age and have to get used to another environment. She bought a burial plot in Boston, she has her church community there, and her half-brother and his family where she goes all the time, is there. She would have to give up everything to move here to live with you."

"Too bad for her. Mama is old already. She is going to die soon. I have more life to live."

"Yes, you have more life to live. You can go make a life in Boston. You have no young children to relocate or anything to prevent you from going. Try to think and perceive unselfishly. I understand that maybe you need practice to become unselfish. This is a great opportunity to start with."

"No, I do not agree with anything you have said."

"Ms. Gina I am begging you, go live in Boston, please. I have two children to take care of. You have no dependent children to relocate. You can move to Boston much easier than I can. It is time for you to do something for your mother. My instinct tells me that I should not come between your destinies regarding doing something honorable for your mother to show her respect. It is time to repay your mother for everything that she has done for you. All the unconditional love, care, kindness, understanding she has given you seems to have made you selfish and spoiled. You going to Manana's environment, helps her. By going, it helps Manana to stay in her familiar support system and what is familiar to her. How old is Manana?"

"Age is something that we do not focus on. For all I know, mama could be one hundred years old. Her mother my grandmother lived until she was one hundred and five. She was never sick, not even one day. She died looking brand new and healthy. One day she just laid in the bed and never got back up. She died slow smooth and healthy, like a ship sailing off into the infinite unknown. Anyway, back to the subject at hand. I am letting you know right now that I will not go to live in Boston. Mama must come live with me in my life, here in New Jersey. We can share the same bedroom. So much for the luxury of her staying in her familiar environment. Mama is lucky I choose to do this. I will telephone mama and her employer tomorrow, to tell them that I will come and move her into my home in New Jersey. This is my final decision and offer to helping mama. I will tell her 'welcome to my world.' Mama will not be the boss of her life anymore. I will be her boss. Now she has to listen to me."

"Ms. Gina be aware of karma. I will help you with the paper work of Social Security, Medicare, insurance, and moving arrangements. Telephone me after you talk to Manana. I will telephone her as well. Let me know your complete plan and the date that you plan to go move her. I can request time off from work to come with you to Boston. I talk to Manana on the telephone and she never mentioned having issues with her memory. Anyway, this is her nature to never complain or ask for help with anything. She is always helping us. It is interesting how I just see her as a vision of the never ending Universe. I just realize very consciously that she is human as well. I will come with you. Let me know when you plan to go. Give me enough time to request the time off from work. Okay."

"You can say anything you like Lily-Butterfly. I am going to go get mama and bring her to my house. It is her choice to come or not. Dean and Henry will help me, by driving the moving truck. They have their driver's license. I will telephone you after I am finished making all the plans. I have to go. Bye."

"Good night Ms. Gina. My experience is that so far in life you have lived for what you want and choose for yourself. Like I say remember karma. Your karma will show up on your death bed and even after death. Everything comes to an end at some point. The human body does not last forever in its current state. Spirit, soul, and karma energy never dies. This is an opportunity for you to right your own wrongs. No one can do this for you. Okay. Ms. Gina remember this."

"Lily-Butterfly whatever. You should be a philosopher, pastor, healer, or all three in one. Do not practice your spiritual mumbo-jumbo with or on me. I am not on the path of the ancestor's ancient ways. Good night. Bye."

"Bye. Call me so that I can come with you."

They both hung up the telephone. Lily-Butterfly thought, what now? Here come more rivers of stuff. Talking to Gina is like talking to a steel post.

Friday night October 6ᵗʰ Ms. Gina telephoned Lily-Butterfly to tell her the moving plans she had made for Manana Leila. The telephone rang and Lily-Butterfly answered it.

"Hi Ms. Gina. How are you?"

"I am doing great. I am calling to tell you that Henry, Dean, and I are leaving at 4:30 AM in the morning, Saturday to go get mama and move her to my home. Are you coming?"

"What? Tomorrow morning? I asked you to give me some time to arrange some days off from work to come with you. Plus, I have to make arrangements for Rebornstar and Holly to be taken care of. They have to go to school and so forth. Wow. I think you arrange to go this day, because you do not want me to come with you."

"You are right. I do not want you to come. This way it is easier for me to do exactly what I want to do. This is the truth. Your philosophy and kindness irritates me. You will not be telling me how to handle mama like a saint. You have to stay home to manage and direct your precious children. I do not see who you would leave your precious children with. You have a very responsible job. You would not want to get fired if things at work gets messed up. No problem the three of us can manage mama and moving by ourselves. We will return on Monday afternoon. Henry and Dean have to go to work on Thursday. They will help me set up mama's things when we return. I will telephone you when we return. Bye."

"Ms. Gina. Wait. I talked to Manana yesterday. She told me that she does not want to move. Can you reconsider and move to her home?"

"No. No. No. I am not moving to Boston. When I get there, she will just have to come with me. She does not have a choice. This is why I am not interested in you coming with us. You are agreeing with what she wants to do. Now I am the boss. Mama gave birth to me. I am her daughter, more than you. Stop. You are not the boss of me. I can do whatever I want. Mama is lucky. Bye."

"Ms. Gina, wait. Listen............"

Click. Ms. Gina hung up the telephone on Lily-Butterfly. Lily-Butterfly had a sad feeling inside herself. She hung up the telephone.

Lily-Butterfly prayed, "Creator you know everything already. Manana's current situation is tough for me. I know that everything is for a reason. There are no accidents. I get the message and guidance for me to stay out of the way and give Ms. Gina the opportunity to practice unconditional love, compassion, care, and kindness; through her actions and choices, towards her mother. This is Ms. Gina's last opportunity to act positive to her mother. Manana is the sacrificial lamb for Ms. Gina to repent her ways. I am not supposed to take over and fix the situation between Ms. Gina and Manana. I am supposed to be neutral. It seems like I am judging Ms. Gina and the treatment that she will give Manana. But, I know Ms. Gina from experience. I also know deep in my heart that this will not be a positive journey for Manana or I. Ms. Gina will exercise her shadow side and entitlement attitude, and Manana is going to suffer. My instincts tells me this. So, far my instincts have proven itself to be right. I can see that it is time for Ms. Gina and her mother to work on the karma between them. I understand. I will wait to see how I can help in this situation without taking over the complete situation. This is going to be difficult for me. I do not think that I can experience Manana suffer and be abused. I will help Manana how I can. I will consult with you in my prayers. This is a delicate and tricky situation. I feel that it is time again for me to go through another tough cycle. I think that it is time for Manana to die. I do not think I am ready for Manana to die. But at some point, I have to work on letting her go. For whatever the reasons, Manana's experience with Ms. Gina is the last thing for her to experience before she dies. Creator I am getting the strong feeling that it is time for me to move from this town. I do not like the atmosphere and environment in the school. Holly's mysterious learning problem needs to be solved. Maybe going to another school will bring light to her learning problem. I like this town, but not the public school system, teacher's attitude, and teaching style. I want a bedroom for myself, and more room for the children to grown in. Thanks for all your help in helping me to create the material resources for me to afford a bigger home and other material things. Please continue to help me through all my interesting human adventures and experiences. Thank you for everything. Your spirit and soul Lily-Butterfly. Amin."

At the end of the prayer Lily-Butterfly continued with her night's activities. She wrote in her journal before she went to sleep. Rebornstar and Holly had prepared themselves for bed and were sleeping.

56

Lily-Butterfly told Rebornstar and Holly that she will be moving from the town they lived in. Rebornstar told her mother that she did not want to move and that she was not going with her if she moved. At this current time Rebornstar's stubbornness was increasing. Lily-Butterfly chose to perceive Rebornstar's stubbornness as growing pains, her personality, and gave her to an extent, freedom of expression. Lily-Butterfly knew in her heart that Rebornstar would have no other option but to move with her when the time came. When Rebornstar tried to get on the negative path Lily-Butterfly made a commitment to bring her awareness and herself back to the positive path. She felt that this was one of her responsibilities as a parent. When Lily-Butterfly became a General Manager working ten hour shifts, mid shifts, closing shifts, and having more responsibilities; she wished she could be home more. When she worked the mid and closing shifts, she would get home at about 8:00 PM or 11:00 PM. Although she was off from work two complete days, and on three days, she was home by 6:00 PM to 7:00 PM it was still a lot different from working at Mrs. Diana. Lily-Butterfly comforted herself with the thought that there was no perfect situation and that she was making the best decisions possible. To provide more income for the children and herself things are going to be the way they are. She could not be in two places at once.

Every decision Lily-Butterfly made was for the greater good of the children and herself. Now she was planning to move to a different town and school for the children, for the greater good of everything. On Sundays Lily-Butterfly started to look in the classified section of the newspaper. On Monday Ms. Gina returned from Boston with her mother Manana Leila. Lily-Butterfly did not wait for Ms. Gina to telephone her. On Tuesday after work at 6:00 PM Lily-Butterfly went to Ms. Gina's house to see Manana Leila and the current situation. Ms. Gina was surprised to see Lily-Butterfly. Lily-Butterfly entered the home. Ms. Gina and Manana Leila was sitting in the living room. Dean was in his bedroom.

"Hi ladies. How are you doing?" said Lily-Butterfly.

No one answered. Ms. Gina looked serious. Manana looked sad.

"Mmm. What is going on? Why are you ladies silent? I am here. What is the problem?" said Lily-Butterfly.

"What? Are you the problem solver of the Universe?" replied Ms. Gina

"Ms. Gina sometimes your non-sense is so ridiculous that I find what you say and do funny? What is currently happening? I am not leaving until someone answers my questions. Ms. Gina you already know that I am fearless of your crap. You know that you do not love or like me being around. You do not like my spiritual talking. I love you Ms. Gina. I will also remind you that I do not like your attitude and style of action. The faster you tell me what is going on, the quicker I will give an idea about resolving the problem. So, Ms. Gina how are things going?"

"Your wonderful Manana is not happy about coming to live with me in New Jersey. She was crying about leaving her previous environment and Boston," replied Ms. Gina.

"I told you Manana does not want to move."

"Mama is lucky that at least I came to get her. Yes, it is obvious that she will feel out of control with this new arrangement. She has been the only manager and director of her life forever. Mama will just have to get used to this new arrangement. She will because she does not have any other option. Really. I am not going to quit my job, give up my life here, and move to her home. Mama is old and her life is over. I have more time to live. I have to do what I think I need to do to support my life and well-being. There you have the issue in a nut shell. What are you going to do?"

"Gina will be Gina. This is nothing new. Ms. Gina you are always selling fish, lots of selfishness. Unless you choose to stop selling fish, transform your selfishness imprints and ways, there can be no change in your personality and attitude. Your mother Manana Leila was always very unselfish maybe this is part of why you ended up being so selfish. She spoiled you and co-dependent all your negative spirit and soul shadow styles and vibrations. Ms. Gina and Manana you know this and if you do not know; you know now. Okay. This is part of the problem that both of you must choose to work out. Both of you choose how you would like to resolve your issues. I will choose to be the neutral mediator. Okay. Now, Ms. Gina where is all of Manana's things? Where is her furniture and everything else? I do not see them here."

"All we took is her bed, dresser, some clothes, a few kitchen items that I like, one chest of drawer, and all her documents. I do not have room here for anything else. I am not moving from this home."

"What did you do with the other things?" asked Lily-Butterfly.

Manana Leila sat listening to the conversation.

"Henry, Dean, and I put them on the side walk and in the garbage. I put a sign that says FREE. Why was I going to bring them? I am happy that you did not come with us. You would be wasting our time doing the so-called right thing. Oh, my Lord. Stop. Do not say anything to me about karma. Lily-Butterfly I am tired of hearing about karma from you. What is done is done. It is mama's choice to accept what I choose to do or not."

"Ms. Gina your last sentence is an issue for both of you. Manana has accepted all her life too much of the crap that you chose to do. She helped you to carry your crap; while she does things to counter balance all your negative choices. My opinion is that she choose too late to teach you the consequences of your actions. Personally, I think that it was a bad idea to file for your permanent resident visa. I respected Manana's choice and did not interfere with her decision. Everything is for a reason. Now it is time for both of you to resolve your karma issues. Manana Leila is never ending with her unconditional love, compassion, care, generosity, diligence, patience, and so forth. Manana need to stand up to you and your crap. Now she is old and still has not chosen to give you a taste of your own medicine. I think that she is playing the wisdom sword and leaving you to your own karma. This is good but, still. Ms. Gina I can see now that your choice to move Manana here, instead of you moving to her house, is another blessing in disguise. Why? So, that I can see what you are doing Ms. Gina. Thank you. Your selfishness and shadow actions in this case is not an accident. Here I am. Ms. Gina, as usual I have my eyes on you. I call you Ms. Gina because no matter what, I have made a commitment to myself to respect and love you without conditions. But, know that I am one spirit and soul that you will no longer take advantage of. I ended your victimization towards me a long time ago. Ms. Gina, you were one of my best teachers of the shadow realm. Thank you very much for this training. You did a great job. Throwing away Manana's life in front of her eyes like it is useless, is mean, traumatizing, and bad karma. You threw away Manana's things with un-mindfulness and negative attitude. Know that your karma will be returned to you. Remember my words. You will not escape your karma actions. Anyway, I am getting too emotional. Let me calm down."

"Yes, you had better calm down. You are already shredding my nerves. I feel hot. Your energy is making me feel hot," said Gina.

"Good Ms. Gina you need the heat of positive Universal Life Force Energy. Selfish people like to take advantage of unselfish people. This is so sad. Where are all of Manana's documents? Manana cheer up. Do not be so sad. Do not let your sadness take you down into depression. Manana how old are you?" said Lily-Butterfly.

"I do not remember. I stopped counting my age after applying for social security and Medicare. Come I will show you all my documents."

"Okay. Come show them to me," responded Lily-Butterfly.

Manana Leila went into the bed room. Lily-Butterfly followed her. Manana gave a box with documents to Lily-Butterfly. Lily-Butterfly took the box and look through them. She found a copy of Manana's birth certificate, her passport, bank account savings book, Medicare card, and social security information. Lily-Butterfly talked to Manana.

"Manana you are here with Ms. Gina your daughter. Cheer up. We both know Ms. Gina. She will not change unless she chooses to. So, we have to work with managing her actions. I did not get to come to Boston, because Ms. Gina told me the night before she left. I could not get to schedule time off from work. Plus, I have to take care of my two children. I will help with your care, and supervise Ms. Gina's choices and actions regarding your care, health, and well-being. I will visit as often as I can. I will get your bank to transfer your account to a new account that you will open in New Jersey. If I put the money in Ms. Gina's name, she might use it all, as soon as possible. After your money is finished who knows what Ms. Gina will do next with you. I will put your name as the main signer on the account and my name as a co-signer. This means you would have to approve every money taken from this bank account. Ms. Gina will telephone social security administration and Medicare to change your address and give them the new bank account number to deposit your social security payments. Is all that I have said okay with you? Do not worry. I will come here as often as possible to see how you are doing."

"Yes Lily-Butterfly, all that you have said is okay with me. I surrender to my current destiny. I turn everything over to the Creator, and I turn within. I am sad, but such is life. Soon I will die and leave everything behind. The most important thing for me now is peace, surrender to my current passage out of this planet, and prepare to die. Thank you and the Creator for everything," said Manana Leila.

"I understand. You are right. If Ms. Gina does anything negative to you, in the end she will not get away with it. You have to also let her know the things you do not like. You have to take action to save yourself. I guess your action is peace to prevent negative karma. I understand this is your way. My way is peace, plus shining a mirror in Ms. Gina's face so that she can see her negative actions, give her an opportunity to take responsibility for her actions, and show her the consequences of her actions. I am strong and flexible. Ms. Gina will not get away with every negative things she does. Be strong. I will return whenever I can. You know how to pray and heal. I think that the medication you were taking after your eye surgery's side effect was deterioration of your memory. Anyway, what is done is done. Okay."

Ms. Gina came into the bedroom.

"Ha. I hear my name. What are you guys talking about me behind my back? Both of you are talking for a long time. Ha. Mmm. You are both alike, except Lily-Butterfly is more out ward expressive. She talks too much. Ha," said Ms. Gina.

"We are talking about everything. I do not care if I talk in front of your face or behind your back. You know already that I was never scared of you no matter what you do. I am not scared of your demons and shadow side. All we do is give you unconditional love and understanding. You take all our positive energy and use it in negative ways. Anyway, you can only give what you have and what you choose to give. Ms. Gina please take care of your mother."

"Oh yeah. Lily-Butterfly I do not need to be told what to do. How am I going to get money to pay for some of the house rent, utilities, pay me to help with her care, and buy food for mama? I do not see the sense of her living with me and I do not have access to her bank account. This is not a free nursing home with a free Home Health Aide situation. Mama has money in the bank and she gets monthly social security payments."

"Listen and hear me Ms. Gina. Abuse can awaken someone's spirit and soul, or break their spirit and soul, and put them to sleep. I choose to be awakened. Thank you very much. Now, be careful. I will come here as often as possible to visit Manana. You will cook for her, do her laundry, take her for walks, help with her baths, and so forth. Her bank account is still in the town she lived in….."

Gina interrupted.

"Sorry your highness to interrupt. If mama's bank account is still in Boston, why did I bring her here? The account needs to be transferred into a bank account with my name."

"So, you are saying one of your decisions to choose to bring her here is to have complete access to her money?"

"Yes. What do you think? Nothing is free. Where do you think the money is going to come from to take care of mama? Ha. I am being honest and realistic. Money makes this modern world go around and around. I need mama's money to take care of her."

"Ms. Gina, do you know that every human is born for a reason?"

"What does your question have to do with what I had to say?"

"Ms. Gina I was wondering if you have ever thought about your purpose to be born; except for conceiving me. Anyway, I am going to open a bank account and get the money transferred to the new bank account in New Jersey. But the account will be in Manana's name and I am a co-signer on the account. You need her approval and both of our signatures to get money from the account. I will give you monthly money to pay for one third of this rent, utilities, and food. In addition, if you need money for other things let me know. Here is the information for social security and Medicare. Telephone them when I get the new bank account and give them the account number and change of address, and so forth."

"You think that I am going to spend mama's money on things for myself? She is my mother I can do what I want with her money."

"Yes, I know everything that you are saying. You will spend all her money in one month and then throw her in a free nursing home. I might be prejudging you in this situation, but I am also speaking from my own experiences with you. Let us see how you take care of Manana, then we can decide if the bank account gets transferred into your name. Your mother is much nicer than me. The things I have told you will be the current money management situation. I will also buy groceries from my own money and bring it to your house. You can buy groceries from the supermarket across the street from your home."

"Okay Lily-Butterfly. I am mama's real birth daughter the bank account should be in my name."

"Ms. Gina when it is time, I will put the bank account in your name. Okay. I am tired. It is very tiring managing you and your energies. I am going to schedule an appointment for a general Doctor's checkup for Manana. Manana I can take you to this Doctor's appointment when I take you to the bank to open the new bank account."

"Why are you taking mama to the Doctor? She looks fine. This is a waste of money."

"Ms. Gina Medicare pays for the doctor's visit."

"Oh, I forgot."

"I think it is important to see if Manana has any other medical issues. I found Manana's birth certificate. It says that she was born May 5, 1898. This means that Manana is now ninety-seven years old. She was still working and taking public transportation at this age. She still looks strong for her age. Except for the memory issues she seems to be in good health. Her memory loss could also be, because of her age and in addition the side effect of the eye surgery medication."

"I knew that she was old, but I did not know her real age. Our ancestors are strong and live a long time, with no memory loss. Mama is the first one with memory lost. Good that mama stayed healthy. She had better stay healthy, because I am going to work. I work in my live in Home Health Aide job Monday to Friday. I come home Friday night by 7:00 PM. She has to baby sit herself and do not leave the house unless I am home. This way she does not get lost. Really. I am still going to work. I am not going to sit here every day and look into mama's face. She can take care of herself until I get home. Okay."

"I hear you Ms. Gina. I am tired. I have to go home now. I left dinner and so forth for my children, but I have to go home now. It is 8:15 PM. I will let you know Manana's Doctor appointment and when I will be coming to get her. Take care of your mother. I will be back."

"Or what?" replied Ms. Gina.

"Or you will have to hear my speech. By the way, I will be moving as soon as I find a place to rent. I am going to look for an apartment close to where you live. So that it is easier for me to visit and help with Manana's care."

"Good. Bye. Tell your Manana Leila to cheer up and to listen to me. She is not as easy as you might think; or a saint. It is a good thing that she is ninety-seven years old. She is not as strong as in her younger years. I can manage her if she rebels against me."

"Be very careful Ms. Gina. If you abuse Manana know that I will call the police on you. Manana cheer up. I will return soon. Bye Manana and Ms. Gina."

"Good bye Lily-Butterfly. Thank you for everything," replied Manana Leila.

"Manana you are very welcome. Know that I am your biggest advocate and supported. Come give me a hug, my golden girl."

Lily-Butterfly hugged and kissed Manana Leila.

"Good night Lily-Butterfly. You are strong."

"Thank you, Ms. Gina. Take care of your mother and your mental health. I will be back soon. Thank you for everything. Bye."

Lily-Butterfly left Ms. Gina's home. She drove home with a lot to think about, process, and digest.

"Life on this planet is more than an adventure. I think that more interesting everts are coming up ahead on my journey and pathway. Creator strengthen and make flexible my pillars and nerves. You know everything already. Amin," mumbled Lily-Butterfly.

Lily-Butterfly visited Manana Leila at Ms. Gina's home, supervised, and helped with Manana's care. Lily-Butterfly took Manana Leila to her Doctor's appointment. The Doctor scanned Manana's brain and told her that he did not see any damage of her brain cells connected to her memory. Her brain seems fine. There were no Alzheimer's symptoms or brain deterioration. Over all Manana's health was good, no disease of any kind. Just regular old age deterioration. After the Doctor's appointment they went to the bank to open a new savings account for Manana Leila and transferred the money in her account in Boston to the new account. Next they went for lunch. When lunch was completed Lily-Butterfly took Manana back to Ms. Gina's home. Thanksgiving day Ms. Gina stayed at work, and Lily-Butterfly made dinner by 12:00 PM. She ate this food with her children at lunch time. After Thanksgiving lunch Rebornstar and Holly helped Lily-Butterfly to clean up. At 5:00 PM Lily-Butterfly took some of the Thanksgiving food to eat with Manana Leila for her dinner. There was extra food that was left in the fridge for Manana for another day. Lily-Butterfly did not take Manana Leila back and forth from Gina' home to her home. She thought that this would confuse Manana and create some kind of confusion, instability, and unbalance in her mind and emotion; especially because she was already having memory issues. Lily-Butterfly had to stretch her time, energy, and herself more and more to get everything accomplished.

The year 1995 seemed like a very long year for Lily-Butterfly. Professionally and personally she had grown and accomplished a lot. Now there was a very new and big situation with Manana Leila and Ms. Gina, for Lily-Butterfly to help manage and direct. This year's Christmas celebration was one of mixed and complex experience.

As usual Lily-Butterfly made a large menu of cooked food. She took Christmas dinner to Ms. Gina's home for Manana Leila and visited with her. After she went home to have Christmas celebration with Rebornstar and Holly. The Christmas celebration usually included the celebration of Lily-Butterfly's birthday. Rebornstar usually has a birthday party with her friends. Lily-Butterfly never had a separate birthday celebration for her birthday. At the end of 1995 Rebornstar was seventeen years old and in high school. Lily-Butterfly was thirty-eight years old. 1995 ended on a sweet, sour, and bitter vibration. More interesting news was about to reveal itself to Lily-Butterfly at the start of 1996. For Lily-Butterfly the years 1995 to the end of 1997 were times of great challenges to manage, decisions to make, transformation to surrender to, and direct her life without becoming unbalanced and destabilized. These years was as if all the other years came colliding together to create one spirit and soul cocoon. Lily-Butterfly was getting closer to forty two years old, around the time when her spirit, soul, mind, emotions, body, and life was completely mature to know and choose the tools to express her talents and life's purpose.

57

Ms. Gina continued to work her live in job. She comes home on Friday nights and goes back to work Sunday night at 7:00 PM. Dean was home sometimes with Manana Leila. When Lily-Butterfly visited Manana most times Dean was not at home. Manana takes the very best care of herself, cook, do laundry, take showers, read, clean the house, and wash dishes. Tuesdays on her day off Lily-Butterfly spent half the day with Manana. On Thursday evenings after work she went to visit Manana as well. On these visits Lily-Butterfly brings her groceries, cook for her, brings cooked food from her home, does Manana's laundry, takes her for walks, and have conversations with her. Manana Leila would also tell Lily-Butterfly stories about her ancestors, her younger years, and life in the village she grew up in before Lily-Butterfly was born. Curious Lily-Butterfly would ask questions and Manana would answer. This conversations and the questions would give Lily-Butterfly awareness on how Manana's mind was functioning. Conversations can assist an older person to keep their mind in tune.

Into the future and over time Manana Leila seemed to regress within herself in a positive way. She prayed more, became even more peaceful, recapped some stories of her life with Lily-Butterfly, did her own life review and reflections, read the Bible, and sat in silence. Manana never complained or said anything negative about Ms. Gina to Lily-Butterfly. If Lily-Butterfly asked Manana specific questions about how Ms. Gina treated her, she would tell Lily-Butterfly the truth. Then end the conversations with 'the Creator knows best.'

January 2, 1996 Mr. Watson the District Manager and Lily-Butterfly's supervisor came to the restaurant at 8:30 AM and told her that he wanted to meet with her. She went to sit with Mr. Watson for his unscheduled meeting. By now Lily-Butterfly can smell the energy of problem, negativity, disguise, fear, and lies. She paid attention to what Mr. Watson said and what he is not saying.

"Lily-Butterfly your review will be done on February 27th. You are a very smart person. Happy New Year. How are you doing?"

"I am also wise. I know that you are here to send me to work in another restaurant. You know that I do not like to do this, so you are going to say passive and aggressive things to me. What is it that you want me to do? I am sure that it is not anything happy."

"Is Talia able to operate this restaurant completely by herself? Did you teach her everything that she needs to perform the General Manager's job?" said Mr. Watson.

"Yes. Why?"

"I need your help. I need you to go on Friday January 5th to the restaurant in Yonkers, New York to work as General Manager for the day. You have to be there by 6:00 AM. The restaurant opens 7:00 AM for breakfast. Work 6:00 AM to 4:30 PM."

"What does working one day in this restaurant have to do with Talia knowing all the General Manager work? This restaurant in Yonkers is the restaurant that no other Manager wants to work in. I hear that it is like a beast, haunted, and a dungeon. It opens every day of the year including Thanksgiving, Christmas day, and New Year's Day. The operating hours of this restaurant is 7:00 AM to 2:00 AM the next morning. This restaurant never gets time to rest. Oh my. Wow. This is also a union employee restaurant with very difficult employees. It is the company's second oldest restaurant. It loses over two million dollars per year. Very crazy. Why me?"

"I think that you have the skills and talent to work in this restaurant. For now, it is one day. This will help me and the company a lot. Remember your performance review and salary increase is coming soon. Ha. You should want to keep listening to me and do your best work."

"Are you using this performance review and salary increase strategy, again to intimidate me to do as you say? What do you mean by for now it is one day? This restaurant is about one hour or more drive from my home. The traffic coming home on the Cross Bronx Express road is a night mare at 5:00 PM and 6:00 PM. It seems like Managers who do good work in your district gets punished with more work. I hope that you are not thinking of transferring me permanently to this haunted dungeon restaurant, with negative energies, and curses. My senses tells me that this is what you have planned for me. Going on Friday is warming me up to this transferal idea."

"Follow my instructions. I am your supervisor. You do not get to tell me what to do and what you want to do. Change the schedule for this Friday. Schedule Talia to work the day shift, put the shift supervisor to work mid shift, and the Assistant Manager to close.

This should work great. When you go to the restaurant in Yonkers the Assistant Manager in that restaurant will show you everything for the day. She has the key to open the door. I suggest you leave your home no later than 4:30 AM to get there on time. Okay. Is there anything else?"

"I do not have a choice. So, I will have to go, or quit. If you transfer me to this restaurant permanently this will be the biggest disaster for my life at this time."

"Or it could be the biggest opportunity that you will ever have to grow some more. It is the most messed up and difficult restaurant. When I enter this place, it is hard for me to breathe. Everything is screwed up in this complete restaurant. Everything. It is unimaginable. The General Manager for this restaurant is under investigation for financial fraud and he quit. Go for one day. Thank you for your help. We will see how you do. Thanks again."

"Bye. I am lost for words. This is another opportunity to promote yourself as a District Manager using me and my work. I do not think this is how my talents are meant to be used. I will go this one day."

"Okay. I will see you here next Monday when I come to collect the reports. You are doing a great job in this restaurant and with everything else. Bye Lily-Butterfly. Have a great day and New Year."

Mr. Watson got up and left the food court. Lily-Butterfly went back into the restaurant. Lily-Butterfly went back to work. She told Talia about the schedule change and why.

As if Lily-Butterfly did not have enough responsibility and issues to resolve. On Wednesday night January 3rd Ms. Gina telephoned Lily-Butterfly from her home. Ms. Gina had come home because there was an emergency with Manana Leila. Ms. Gina had gotten someone to work for her on Wednesday afternoon and for the rest of the week. Lily-Butterfly answered the telephone. Ms. Gina was the first one that spoke.

"Hello Ms. Organizer. Your Manana Leila almost burned down the house. I came home because mama went for a walk and forgot where the house is. She got lost and a neighbor called the police. The police helped her to figure out where she lived. Manana gave the police my work telephone number. The police telephoned me to talk to me. One of the things that the police told me is that I should come home to check on mama, and that she seemed to need direct daily supervision. I am not quitting my job to stay home with mama all day. No. No way. I am going to put mama in a nursing home. This way she is safe, gets all the consistent care and supervision she needs. I am not going to go to jail for neglect and abuse of the elderly. Mama does not want to go to live in a nursing home. She told me that it would be like being thrown in the garbage. Mama also told me that after everything she had done for me and my children, if I put her in a nursing home; this would be bad karma. You see that when mama want to talk she does talk. Her talking is like fire coming out of her mouth. Mama reminds me of you. She is too wise for her own good. Back to the story, when I got home the house was full of smoke. The smoke was coming out of the kitchen. I ran to the kitchen there was three pots on the stove. Mama was cooking dinner, maybe forgot that the pots were on the stove, and she fell asleep. Mama would be the first one of our ancestors that went to a nursing home. In the village all my ancestors died at home. Of course, where else are they going to die? I never heard of nursing home to put old people until I came to live in a more modern Mansa Town. I ended up working in this nursing home until I left the island. Mama needs to adapt to what is happening now in modern times. Ha. Manana does not want to go to the nursing home, but I do not care. There is a first time for everything. I am just letting you know. You are the only one right now that is going to agree with mama. Dean is ready right now to help me take mama to the nursing home, because he does not want to be responsible for her care. Okay," said Ms. Gina.

"Ms. Gina I sit here and listen to you in silence and amazement. Oh wow. Your brain, spirit, soul, heart, and body is following the ways of your shadow side. You see Manana's situation cut and dry, restricted, and like steel. It is so hard for you to stay around your mother because of your own shame to be in her presence. This is the root of your antics. We are here because of Manana and all the ancestors behind her in the past. You might think that the purpose of life is useless. We really understand the wisdom, function, and purpose of being born to help the Creator God. You can tell yourself that things you do has no responsibility and consequence, because to you it seems like you are getting away with all the negative things that you do to yourself, me, Manana, and everyone else. I will tell you again that you will pay the consequences of all your actions, before you die, and after you die. The spirit and soul does not die. You take all the records of everything you do where ever you go. Instead of cursing negative curse words to you, this is what I choose to say to you about everything that you just told me. Now for your own benefit listen and hear me….."

Ms. Gina interrupted Lily-Butterfly.

"I know that I interrupted your talking. Lily-Butterfly you think that you are a pastor preaching to me every time you talk to me. I am telling you right now that if you mention the word karma, I am going to hang up the telephone. After I hang up the telephone, I am putting mama in a nursing home. I do not need your permission to do this. I am her next of kin. I have full authority to put her where I perceive is the best place for her. Watch your mouth and what you say. I am warning you. Okay?"

"Mama Gina let me finish talking before you comment. I listen when you talk without interrupting you. Okay. Thank you. Now, how about you stay home every day with your mother that never abandoned you one second in her life, and spoiled you as an only child. I will pay all the bills from my money and her social security payments. Or, quit the live in job and work part time from 9:00 AM to 3:00 PM. This way Manana is not home alone day and night. Although Dean lives in the house with her he totally ignores her and minds his own business. If you work these hours Manana does not have to cook and go for walks alone. Loving kindness, understanding, care, and positive mindfulness can go a long way in helping you and Manana. If you work part time I will still contribute to giving you money to help with Manana's living expenses. If I give you money and the social security money you would be getting paid to take care of your own mother. Plus, this way you get to keep the money you get paid for working. Dean pays twenty five percent of the home expenses, I pay twenty five percent, Manana's social security payment pays the other fifty percent, and pays you as well. You will get everything for free and get some financial compensation for each day that you take care of your own mother. This way you win all the way and everything benefits you. I would still come twice per week to visit, help with grocery shopping from my own money, cooking, laundry, and taking Manana for walks. By me giving you all these ideas and options to help with this situation, you are being spoiled again. These are all the things I have to say regarding helping you and Manana. I have two children I have to take care of and manage, plus a job with many responsibilities. I am willing to take money from my life to give you to help with the care of Manana. All you have to do is be here part time with Manana. You can choose one of the options I suggested. Mama Gina what would you like to do?"

"What you said about working part time, not using any of my money for the home expenses, and you coming here to help with cooking, bringing groceries, laundry, taking mama for walks sounds excellent. I will give the agency I work for notice about quitting my live in job and request a part time live out job. Most important one more thing for me to commit completely to this arrangement you Ms. Lily-Butterfly and mama must sign over complete her bank account to only my name. That means close her current bank account and transfer all her money into my bank account. Hello. Now the deal is complete. Remember she is not really your mother. She did not give birth to you, I did. Mama gave birth to me, this makes me her real next of kin, and real legal authority to manage her assets. After all I am going to be the one that is with her on a daily basis. Why should your name be on the account and mama cannot go to the bank? Do this and the deal is sealed. Ha. Money and power sweetens motivation, responsibility, and action."

"Mama Gina I will not fight with you. Do you know that Manana has a will? The will is in the box with her documents. The money she has saved up is only $35,000. It is not a million dollars. To honor Manana's will, $25,000 of this money cannot be used. This money is sacred. In her will she divide up this money and request it be given to the people whose names are in her will. This money is all she has left after giving most of her money away, mostly to you to pay all your living expenses when your four children were younger. Manana was paying your living expenses until I was about seventeen years old. She did this even when you were living with a so called common law husband, Mr. Winston."

"My dear Lily-Butterfly this will no longer exist. I burned it. Why am I going to sit here as her daughter and get less money while she gives the money to other people, including you. Ha. Wake up Lily-Butterfly and smell the real situation."

"You are very interesting. I thank the Creator God every minute for choosing Manana Leila to be my mother, father, teacher, healer, and guide of my destiny and life's purpose journey. If you did not give me to Manana before I was born and after birth I would maybe not be the person I am today. Thank you for not wanting me. This was your best decision in your life so far. Ms. Gina thank you for everything. Really. After you get a part time day live out job, and you prove that you are comfortable and taking care of your mother, I will remove my name from the account, and put your name on the account. The social security payments must be deposited in an account with Manana's name on the account, so the account cannot be in your name only. In addition to everything else this is what I promise I will do. Knowing you I do not think putting the account in your name is a positive idea. But, I will give you the benefit of the doubt, if this will motivate you to take care of your mother. I am very intuitive and I can see what you are going to do when you have access to Manana's money. The same thing you did to me when I gave you access to my bank account when I moved from the island. You went to the account and took out all the money and only left twenty dollars. You get away with a lot of crap. The Creator is giving you lots of chances. One day even before you die all these chances are going to come to an end. I am tired and feel drain from this conversation. Talking to you is like a wrestling competition. For now, I have nothing more to say. Please let me know when you have the part time job. Get one as soon as possible. Good night Ms. Gina."

"Wait one minute. I will give two week notice for this current job. At the end of two weeks I should have a part time job. So, you can add my name to the bank account and remove your name within five more weeks. Okay. This arrangements sounds like it is worth my time and energy. Good night Ms. Lily-Butterfly," said Ms. Gina.

"When I visit I will see how everything is going and then I will decide when to remove my name from the account. I know that this does not give any guaranteed about your actions after you have access to Manana's bank account. I can already see what you might do. But I am willing to give you a chance to prove me wrong. Good night. Bye," said Lily-Butterfly.

"Bye. Good night Lily-Butterfly."

They both hung up the telephone.

Life went on and Lily-Butterfly flowed with the consistent exuberant evolution of her life. Next she had to go to work for supposedly one day in the Yonkers, New York restaurant on Friday January 5, 1996.

58

At work and home Lily-Butterfly organized everything to go work in the Yonkers, New York restaurant on Friday January 5, 1996. She woke up at 3:00 AM and got dressed and put on her winter coat. It was cold outside. It is good that it did not snow last night, thought Lily-Butterfly. At 4:30 AM she was in her car and driving towards the main road. Driving over the George Washington Bridge and the Cross Bronx at 4:45 AM; there were a few cars. Following the written directions Lily-Butterfly arrived at the restaurant location. It was 5:46 AM. She parked her car about a quarter mile from the restaurant. Away from a possible heavy parking lot traffic during business hours. Five employees were sitting on the ground by the door. The Assistant Manager on duty who had the key to open the door, had not arrive. Lily-Butterfly sat in her car observing the restaurant building and parking lot.

"This restaurant building looks like a deserted castle at a dead end cliff. There are other buildings nearby but for some reason I get an eerie and haunted vibe about this restaurant building. Anyway Mr. Watson told me to come here for one day. I think that he is lying. I will wait and see what happens," mumbled Lily-Butterfly.

At 6:05 AM a taxi car came into the parking lot and stopped by the restaurant door. The employees sitting on the ground got up. A woman got out of the car walked up to the restaurant door and opened it. The Assistant Manager and the employees went inside. The Assistant Manager's husband dropped her off. He was a taxi driver. Lily-Butterfly got out of her car, picked up her briefcase, locked the car door, and walked towards the restaurant door. She entered the restaurant and walked up to the counter. The Assistant Manager was busy setting up the coffee and tea machines.

"Good morning Ms. Ema," said Lily-Butterfly.

"Good morning Ms. Lily," replied Ema.

"I would like to be called my full name. It is Lily-Butterfly. Thank you. Is your name Ema?"

"Yes, my name is Ema. Okay Ms. Lily-Butterfly. Mr. Watson told us that you were coming today."

"You do not have to say the Ms. when you say my name. Okay."

"Same here ma'am. You do not have to say Ms. with my name either. It is refreshing to see a new face. Are you from the island of Kawomaya?"

"Yes. I was born in deep country. A small remote village in the valley of Yaj. I am the first one of my ancestors that evolve in such a modern human way. So, I am a country bumpkin at spirit, soul, and heart."

"I know what you mean, country bumpkins stays connected to the ancient ways. My twin sister Edna and I were born on the same island. We are more Capital City people. My twin sister is also an Assistant Manager here. She works only the night closing shift. She comes to work at 3:00 PM and works until 3:00 AM. We work on the clock and get paid overtime. I work 6:00 AM to 6:00 PM. We are working here since we were sixteen years old. We both worked here for seventeen years. We both know this restaurant from inside to outside, and upside down; if you know what I mean. We have seen many Manager and employees come and go during these seventeen years. Please let me know if you need help with anything."

"Yes, thank you. Ema where is the office? The energy vibes here is draining like thick dark smoke."

"I understand ma'am. Welcome to beast of the company's restaurants. You have to be strong in every way to work here. The office is at the end of this counter. Turn left, go through the door, and turn right. The office door is on your right side. Here is the key to unlock the door."

"Thank you Ema. Mr. Watson told me that I was only here for one day. But my instinct tells me otherwise."

"I think your instincts are right. The last long-term General Manager quit during an investigation on the financial operation of the restaurant. They have been trying to find another General Manager for over six months. No General Manager wants to come here and work. A few General Managers came for a day and never returned. I do not blame them. You will see why as the day goes on. Welcome. Let me go finish preparing the restaurant and get the cash drawers. It is almost opening time."

"Okay. Thank you Ema."

By now all the employees had come to work and punched in. They all work together as a team to prepare the restaurant for breakfast. Lily-Butterfly went to the office. She put down her briefcase under the desk. Next she looked through the financial and inventory files on the computer. In the office in front of the desk there was a large clear glass wall from ceiling to below the front of the desk. This glass provided a complete view of the front line counter and most of the dining room. Lily-Butterfly saw Ema walking towards the office.

"Hi ma'am I came to get six cash drawers. I am going to put them into the register, sign in the cashiers and come back to talk to you. It is now 6:50 AM almost time to open all the doors. Sorry that I cannot give you a personal tour at this time. But, you can look around on your own."

"Okay Ema."

Ema took the six cash drawers and left the office. Lily-Butterfly continued to look through the computer files. All the financial figures and reports Lily-Butterfly looked at seems bogus. The financial reports did not match the system she learned and knew. It was the same situation like the restaurants she received from Mr. Sunnil, and all the other restaurant that Mr. Watson had sent her to fix. Lily-Butterfly thought, this is another nightmare situation.

Ema returned to the office.

"Yes ma'am. Do you need help with anything?" said Ema.

"Ema you do all the things you are used to doing including all the money transactions. I will help with everything else. If I need help with something I will let you know, and you do the same. I like simple and I have a down to earth personality. No fuss, no problem. My ancestors were peasant farmers. All this country bumpkin-ness, peasantry, close to the earth, and mother and father-nature is still deep inside me. This is part of who and what I am. I am good at this restaurant management stuff. Ema you are a master of this interesting restaurant operation. Your help will be priceless for me. Thank you."

"I understand ma'am. Take a tour of the restaurant if you like. I am going back to the front line operation. Let me know if you need help with anything."

"Okay Ema."

Lily-Butterfly left the office and went to the kitchen. She introduced herself to five employees. One looked like he was in his mid-fifties and the other four looked like they were in their early twenties. They were all male. Lily-Butterfly walked over to the older man and introduced herself.

"Hi good morning. How are you? My name is Lily-Butterfly. I

am working here today. I am the General Manager of a restaurant in New Jersey."

"Hi, it is nice to meet you. My name is Juan. I work mostly in the kitchen and sometimes help when it is necessary with cooking in the front. I have no special job title. I can do everything in this restaurant except for the cashier and manager job. Every day especially when it is busy non-stop I do the work of twenty people. I started to work here when I was sixteen years old. I have worked her for forty one years. Maybe before you were even born. Please let me know if you need help with anything."

"Oh wow. Yes, I was not born when you started to work here. I am only thirty eight years old. You look young for your age, athletic, quick, and strong. Good for you."

"Yes, thank you ma'am. This job keeps me young and as fit as a fiddle."

"Juan you are the pillars of this restaurant and building."

"If you say so ma'am. This restaurant is one of the main focal points of this town. It is like a carnival, circus, and casino. We serve breakfast, lunch, dinner, and very late dinner. There is a game arcade on the left side of the dining room. This restaurant parking lot is also a rest stop for trucks and cross country bus tours. Sometimes all at once six buses of people come into the dining room at one time to be served, plus regular customers. You will get a sample and real view of what I am talking about today. Friday is one of our busy days. Welcome. I have to go help with breakfast. It was nice meeting you ma'am."

"Thank you Juan. It was nice meeting and talking to you as well."

Lily-Butterfly went to look inside the two large walk-in refrigerator and one large freezer. She also toured the complete kitchen. The kitchen was disorganized, had clutter everywhere, and many flies buzzed around the kitchen environment; like busy bees. The kitchen of this restaurant was 3,500 square feet. The complete restaurant including the basement was 10,000 square feet. This was the company's largest restaurant. It was supposed to be making the most money. Instead it was losing the most money. The restaurant made a lot of money. But, the money seems to be leaking out through many dark holes. Lily-Butterfly finished touring the complete kitchen. She went down the two flight of stairs to tour the basement. Downstairs the first thing Lily-Butterfly noticed was that the complete floor in the basement was wet, muddy, and smelled like poop and pee. There were two large freezers and one large walk-in refrigerator. The basement was empty except for some old and unused restaurant machines, and equipment on top of seven large metal tables.

Lily-Butterfly left the basement and went back to the kitchen. In the kitchen there was a large notice board. She looked at the employee schedule on the notice board. Next she went back to the office to look at the management schedule. On the management schedule there was two names, Ema and Edna. Ema worked the day shift and Edna worked the night shift. Lily-Butterfly went to the computer and looked at the inventory, food and paper orders, weekly and monthly financial records, daily and hourly restaurant sales, and regular employee total wages. The whole system was incorrect. Everything seems fictitious. The inventory, recorded purchases, money income from sales, and all records seems false. Currently all the restaurant business sales were done in cash. At this point Lily-Butterfly took many deep breaths and sighed repeatedly.

"My head is spinning and I feel dizzy. This is a total nightmare and disaster. Ema and Edna makes a lot of money from working so many over time. Many of the employees also work many overtime. The energy in this place is stagnant, stale, tired, negative, doom, the basement have a nasty stinking dungeon energy vibes, and this place seems very haunted. There is a lot of negative history vibrations here in this building. Why would people be dying in here? This is a restaurant. I think Juan has all the answers to the secrets of this haunted house restaurant. I am thirsty. I will drink some water. If I get transferred to this restaurant it will be one of the most difficult things I will ever do in this life time. To work in this restaurant, get all the issues resolved, and keep it successful would take every fragment of my spirit, soul, mind, emotions, body, and talents. Plus awaken all my other currently un-known talents. Oh, my Creator why am I here? To prevent the experience and journey from being premature, as usual, I will be the last to know the answer to this question. It is a good thing that I have a strong spirit and soul to protect my mind and body from breaking. Focusing on the awareness that everything is for a reason, might help to comfort me with all my current experiences. Amin."

It was now 9:15 AM. Lily-Butterfly went to the front line counter operation. She helped with the last part of serving breakfast. Breakfast service was over at 10: 00 AM. Ema was one of the full time cashiers during the breakfast service. This was wrong. One of the company's policy, for many reasons, is Managers do not work as cashiers. After breakfast service was over and the breakfast production line was transferred to lunch service production. All the employees took turns taking a break and getting something to eat. Each time an employee got something to eat, they went and prepared their own food, and then walked out to the dining room to eat. This was wrong as well. Each employee should punch their time card out for every break and completion of shift, go to the cashier, order their food, and pay for the food. After break every employee should wash their hands and punch their time card in before going to work. Lily-Butterfly went to look at the time cards for the employees that went on break. For their breaks they did not punch out their time card.

Lily-Butterfly ordered something to eat from a cashier and had the cashier ring up her food as a Manager's meal. Managers eat at no cost. She sat down to eat. During eating she processed and digested all her experiences and observation so far.

"I am so tired and drained already and it is only 11:00 AM. Creator thank you for this food and everything else. I know that you know everything already. My true feelings is that I do not want to be here today. I do not want to be transferred here to work as General Manager. Between my personal life, my children, helping with Manana's current life situation, and this current career work situation; I am stretched to the maximum. I guess it is time to move out of my comfort zone and expand some more. When are these difficult expansion exercises going to come to an end? I know that the way will show the way. But, currently, as a spirit and soul on a human journey of finding my chosen destiny and life's purpose, I am tired. This is my true feelings at this time. Keep helping me with my children and our health, well-being, safety, protection, and everything else. Also help me to find the next home for my children and I. Show me the solution to Holly's disguised learning problem. Amin."

Lily-Butterfly continued to digest, process, and observe.

59

Ema came out to the restaurant dining room at 11:15 AM to eat. Lily-Butterfly called her to come sit at her table. Ema sat down.

"Ema where are the cashiers? Why are you a cashier for the complete breakfast shift?"

"I was supposed to have six cashiers, only two showed up for work."

"I see. Who usually does the hiring of employees?"

"The General Manager does all the hiring. We are currently working with the employees we have. My sister and I are working as Assistant Managers. We were never trained and certified as Assistant Managers. We work with what we were shown to do. So, we might never be doing proper company procedures. We were never trained the correct procedures."

"I see. How many cashiers are coming to work for the lunch and dinner shift?"

"The employee crew schedule is on the notice board in the kitchen."

"I see. I looked on the schedule and saw a skeleton crew. From the schedule I cannot tell who worked which position. You know everything that goes on here. How many cashiers are coming for lunch and dinner shifts?"

"We need minimum six cashiers per shift. Only two are scheduled for lunch and dinner. They might show up. To work each work station correctly I think this restaurant needs to have about one hundred employees for a three shift rotation. We only have ten consistent employees schedule for each shift. Most times seven or eight show up consistently. Each employee works many hours over time to make up for the shortage of employees. We need maybe nine or ten Managers. Currently we only have my sister and myself; and no General Manager. Ma'am do you have a clearer picture of things."

"Yes, thank you Ema. Why do the employees make their food, do not get their food rang up by the cashier, and do not pay for their food?"

"I think because this is what they are used to. No one corrects them, because we do not want them to get upset and quit. We basically manage the employees the best way we can taking everything into consideration. This is the truth. Sorry."

"I understand. Are there any employees here at work now that can work on the register as a cashier?"

"Carlos knows a little cash register operation; he speaks mostly Spanish. He works mostly on the grills, sandwich station, and French fryer. Three employees works the grill, deli slicer, drinks machines, and sandwich station. One cleans the dining room and restrooms. Juan works every station in the kitchen and empties the trash in the dining room, front line, and kitchen. Plus, he helps to cook on the front line if we need extra help."

"These employees are all men. If there is a male employee cleaning and attending to the dining room and both male and female restrooms, who takes care of the ladies rest room?"

"I would go attend to the restroom, or send one of the female cashiers as soon as possible. When customer complain about toilet paper or a clogged toilet in the lady's room I go or send a female cashier to attend to the situation. We do the best we can."

"Well, Ema I am not touching any money and working as a cashier today. The last thing I need is to become involved with money inaccuracy and shortages. Managers are not supposed to work as cashiers or employee station for many reasons. Managers do not do the best managerial duties doing regular employee work. Take Carlos as a cashier. You are currently the best cashier, because you are used to doing this as a part of your Assistant Manager job. Use the other two cashiers you used for breakfast, and let us see if the two that are scheduled shows up for work. I will work the stations that Carlos was scheduled to work on. The fry person can fill the ice bins and help with drinks, Juan can come up front and help out where necessary. Does the person that works in the deli takes care of everything in the deli section including slicing the meats and making all the sandwiches?"

"Yes, ma'am."

"Ema there will be nine of us for lunch. We need about twenty one employees. Alright Ema; I will do my best. We will work together as a team. You are more used to this situation more than me. Let us go make sure that everything is ready for lunch."

"Okay ma'am. I am used to the disaster."

"Ema, hopefully I can provide some much needed help to make things easier for all of us."

"Okay. Today you are the boss. Let me know if you need my help with something. Guide me what to do if I need to change something."

"Ema, I understand. The crew is used to taking instructions and guidance from you. I am not going to change this too much. I will manage the restaurant and do Carlos's work responsibilities. Please go in and instruct all the employees to work as we both discussed. Give Carlos a register and tell him that I will be doing all his usual work assignments. We will work together as a team. You are a good and productive employee. Let us go prepare."

"Okay Ms. Lily-Butterfly. I mean yes ma'am. Thank you."

Lunch service was very busy. The two other cashiers had shown up for work. There were totally six cashiers. At 2:30 PM the lunch crowd decreased. Gradually everyone including Lily-Butterfly cleaned up the dining room, all the front line stations, kitchen, walk-in freezer and refrigerator, floors, garbage cans, restrooms, refill ice bins, and prepped everything that was needed for dinner and the night shift. At 3:00 PM Ema was responsible for counting, verifying, and depositing in the safe, all the money collected from breakfast and lunch. Every employee had their break, and those whose shift ended at 3:00 PM left. Edna the Assistant Manager who work on the night shift came to work at 3:00 PM. Edna introduced herself to Lily-Butterfly.

"Hello Ms. Lily-Butterfly. I hear through the grape vine that you are a trooper. Welcome."

"Yes. Thank you Edna. Thanks to the Creator I am built for many situations. It was very interesting being here today. I hope that I do not have to return here. Not even for one day. Call me Lily-Butterfly, the Ms. is not necessary."

"Okay. You look tired. But you can do this kind of dungeon work. Hahaha. It is a lot of exercise working here."

"I see. Everything in the restaurant is ready for dinner. The prep for dinner and breakfast tomorrow morning is also ready. Yes, I am very tired. I am currently the General Manager for a restaurant that is about eight hundred square feet. This restaurant is ten thousand square feet. Plus, everything else. Look around and let me know if there is anything else you need for dinner that we have not prepared. Your sister is counting the breakfast and lunch sales."

"Okay. I will let you know about the food prep," said Edna.

"I will stay at the front counter supervise and help to serve the customers. When you are ready to come to the front line counter I will go home. I am supposed to leave at 4:30 PM before the Cross Bronx traffic gets heavy."

Edna went to the office. She got the shift plan ready for dinner, check if she had enough food prepped, brought out new registers, and at 4:26 PM Edna and Ema came to the front counter. Ema took a break and had something to eat. Lily-Butterfly got a sandwich and some water to eat and drink in the car.

"Good bye Edna. It was nice to meet you, and an interesting experience working here."

"I will see you soon," replied Edna.

"What? I do not want to return here, but a feeling tells me that Mr. Watson is going to transfer me to work here. If he does, I can accept the transfer or quit. He is not going to let me stay where I am currently working without harassing me if I say no to the transfer. We will see what destiny has in store for me. This restaurant needs a lot of transformation. Everything needs improving. This restaurant is very busy, money seems to come in, and go out through many holes, like water being poured into a container with multiple holes. This restaurant reports minus two million dollars loss every year. This is unbelievable. Anyway good bye for now."

"I hear you. See you soon."

Lily-Butterfly put on her winter coat and went to the dining room to say good bye to Ema and left the restaurant. She got in her car and drove out of the parking lot. Lily-Butterfly ate the sandwich and drank the water as she drove. The traffic driving back to New Jersey was already a snail's crawl at 5:15 PM. When Lily-Butterfly got home it was 7:20 PM. When she arrived inside her home she felt like a truck had run over her. The children had eaten. Holly was ready for bed. Rebornstar was down stairs in the front of the building sitting outside with her friends. She came inside the apartment at 9:00 PM. Lily-Butterfly ate her dinner and took a shower. Before going to sleep she wrote in her journal and prayed.

"Dear Creator you know everything before me. I see stormy seas ahead for me. Many oceans merging together creating unpredictable waves and strong currents. Everything happens for a reason. I hope the different ocean waves and strong current brings me to my chosen destiny and life's purpose. I am tired. This part of my journey is going to be like towards the end of giving birth to a baby, when the pain is most unbearable, and the baby is being born. Remember to help me manifest our new home. You know everything best. I thank you for everything. Good night. Amin," whispered Lily-Butterfly.

After the prayer within three minutes Lily-Butterfly drifted off to sleep like a soggy wet leaf, laying completely saturated on a stormy ocean.

60

Saturday morning after working in the Yonkers, New York restaurant Lily-Butterfly woke up with pain where the ligament had torn by her left wrist. More fluid had gathered in the area. She put a bandage on the area and her wrist to support the injury. She made breakfast and lunch for the children. Ate breakfast and got dressed for work. In snail pace Lily-Butterfly walked out the door and to her car. After arriving at work Lily-Butterfly did a restaurant tour and checked out everything. Talia and all the employees seem to have done a complete job. Everything was great including the sales. Talia would be at work at 12:00 PM for the closing shift.

As usual Monday Mr. Watson came to pick up the end of week reports. He came to the office and spoke to Lily-Butterfly.

"Lily-Butterfly come let us go outside to the food court and have a thirty minutes meeting."

"Okay. Here is the file with all the reports. I am coming."

Lily-Butterfly got some tea and went outside to sit with Mr. Watson.

"How was your day working in Yonkers?"

"It was interesting."

"That is all you have to say?"

"You know the situation already. Telling you my experience and complaining is a waste of our time."

Lily-Butterfly was now silent. She stared at Mr. Watson. Mr. Watson stared at Lily-Butterfly. Mr. Watson was the first one to speak.

"I was in Livingston, New Jersey on Saturday. I suspend the General Manager, Mr. Miller. His restaurant is a mess. When he returns in two weeks he is going to have to fix the issues in his restaurant, or I am going to fire him."

"Mr. Watson, why are you telling me this? It is part of your job responsibilities as the District Manager supervising the restaurants in your district to help the General Managers fix their restaurants."

"Yes, I know. I do not have to directly do the work. I am busy delegating people to fix the problems. You are very direct in your talking Lily-Butterfly."

"Yes sir, I am. Look at your job situation you are getting more pay than a General Manager to be District Manager. Take me for example, you send me to do your work and at the same time be General Manager for this restaurant. I am doing your job for free. The General Managers need help to get their restaurant up to the correct procedures. It shows that for a long time the correct things has not been happening. This situation is like the blind leading the blind. The General Managers do not seem to know how to fix their restaurants, and you do not seem to know how to help them improve the problems. All the work I do to help you with your job responsibilities you take all the credit for. You do not even say thank you to me. Your actions towards me is; do as I say or you will have a difficult time. For example, I am perceiving that you are telling me that you suspend Mr. Miller as a warning and threat to me. I am not afraid of your psycho-manipulations. Everything you tell me to do I have done, because I choose to. I know that I can leave. I can work with any restaurant company I choose. I have the qualifications, experience, and my quality of work speaks for itself. Trying to intimidate me is useless. I am allergic to abuse. There is not one fragment of myself that thinks that I have to settle for your crap. Now, please be straightforward. Why are we really having this meeting?"

"How did Talia handle the restaurant for the day?"

"Good like she always does. She is a very good employee and I gave her the best training I could. She appreciates all the opportunities I give her. She shows this by doing a complete and excellent job. Plus, everything in this restaurant, I fixed to operate according to the company's policies. The employees are respected and motivated to succeed. The employees are a large part of the restaurant's success. Complete team work and everything else makes this restaurant simple and easy to manage. You are even receiving more profits than what was estimated. You know that everything in this restaurant is working well."

"Yes, I know. I wish every restaurant could be like this one. Your annual review is coming up next month. The maximum salary increase you can get is three percent. Although you do very good work I cannot give you more than three percent. Maybe I give you less depending on how you consistently following my instructions."

"Is there anything else? It is getting late. I have to go open the restaurant. What are you really here to say? Sir."

"One last thing. Do not get upset about what I have to say. I have transferred you to the Yonkers, New York restaurant as General

Manager, effective next week Monday January 15th. I would like you to fix everything to work according to the company's policies and procedures, like you did in this restaurant. If you decide to not go, then you had better quit. If you decide to go, at your next annual review in February you will get the review that I think and perceive you deserve. So, watch your step. Also, because you have been working already as a General Manager your next review will be considered in the same salary category of General Manager. You will not be getting a promotion to the salary scale of the General Manager of the Yonkers, New York restaurant. Unless I decide to upgrade your General Manager category you will stay in the current category. Let me see how you do with all the improvements that is needed in Yonkers. We will see how you do. Maybe in 1997 review you might get promoted to the category salary for the Yonkers restaurant. We will see. Do you have any question?"

"Thank you for rewarding my good work with only more work. I accept the transfer. I will go do the job that you are not capable of doing. I will work here for this week and write all the schedules before I leave on Saturday. I am off on Sunday and I go to work in Yonkers on Monday morning. You are responsible for all the end of week paper work. Are you promoting Talia to General Manager of this restaurant?"

"Yes, I am promoting Talia to General Manager. Starting this weekend, she will do all the end of week reports like you trained her. Tell her to come to me now. I would like to have a meeting with her. Lily-Butterfly is there anything else?"

"Okay Mr. Watson. Have a great day. Thank you for everything."

Talia went to talk to Mr. Watson. She did not want to be promoted to the responsibility of General Manager. Talia was not ready for all the responsibility. Mr. Watson did not give her a choice. Talia accepted the job. She got a salary increase to General Manager pay. Lily-Butterfly talked to Talia about the transfer, her promotion, and things that she could help her with before she left.

When Lily-Butterfly went home from work on Monday January 8th after the meeting with Mr. Watson she told Rebornstar and Holly about being transferred to work in a much larger restaurant in Yonkers, New York and all the new changes this was going to bring to their lives. She also told the children to prepare themselves mentally and emotionally to move as soon as she found a good location for their new home. To Lily-Butterfly and the children some important changes would be: - having dinner with the children only two times per week. Being home for breakfast only two times per week. Holly would have to stop going to martial arts classes. It would take Lily-Butterfly longer to get home. Lily-Butterfly would leave for work at 3:30 AM on Monday mornings and 4:30 AM on the other mornings. Much more work for Lily-Butterfly. At this time the benefits that Lily-Butterfly could perceive were; improving her professional management experience and skills, awakening more of her spirit and soul talents, keeping the job that she had invested so much energy and time in. All of this was positive for the greater good of the children's and her financial security, life, and well-being. She could find the same job with more pay and same benefits. But since she was already at this company she decided to try working in Yonkers, New York. If things did not work out she would leave and find another job. Or maybe her chosen destiny and life purpose would find her.

Before Lily-Butterfly went to sleep that Monday night she prayed. "Creator you know everything already. This is my perception; I feel like I just got on an infinite roller coaster. It is not in my direct control where and when I get off this roller coaster. I feel like I cannot go backwards or sideways. The only way to go is forward. So, I am already going forward. I am now sure that another difficult pathway has arrived again. The path ahead on this roller coaster is going to be technical and difficult. If all of this does not kill me, it will make me stronger, more improved, awake, transform, and transcend me to what is next. I have chosen to support and manage Ms. Gina with the care of Manana Leila, Holly's learning problem is still in disguise, I have to work so much more in my current job, I have to spend more time away from home and the children, I am already stretched to the maximum, and I accept everything else that will happen on this current part of my life's journey. Please continue to help, assist, and support me. Only you know exactly what this pathway will be. Into the unknown I go. I have surrendered to what is next for me. Thank you for everything. Amin," prayed Lily-Butterfly.

On the last day of working in this restaurant Lily-Butterfly helped Talia by making the schedule for the following week. At the end of her shift on Saturday January 13, 1996, Lily-Butterfly left this restaurant for the last time. It had been approximately one year and eight weeks since she started her training and working for this company on November 21, 1994.

Ms. Gina had left her living in job. She was currently working in a part time live out job 9:00 AM to 3:00 PM. Since Lily-Butterfly was going to work in Yonkers, New York she decided that now was the time to add Ms. Gina to Manana's pass book saving bank account as a cosigner; and remove her name from the account. Thursday January 11th Lily-Butterfly took a personal day off from work. She took Ms. Gina and Manana to the bank to do this transaction. Ms. Gina was smiling from ear to ear. Lily-Butterfly did not have a positive vibes about the decision. But she felt it was something that she had to try to motivate Ms. Gina to take care of her mother. This was one of the times Lily-Butterfly went against what her instincts were telling her. During the complete journey to the bank Manana looked sad. Lily-Butterfly had to compromise the money for the possibility of Manana's greater good and well-being. Plus, support Ms. Gina doing some positive act of kindness even when it was under the hidden veil of Ms. Gina's selfish demand and controlling compromise. After the bank Lily-Butterfly treated everyone to lunch. During lunch Lily-Butterfly told Manana and Ms. Gina about being transferred to go work in Yonkers, New York and planning to move in the summer of this year. When lunch was completed Lily-Butterfly took Manana Leila and Ms. Gina home. On the way to her home Ms. Gina she looked very happy. Manana still looked sad. For most of the trip Manana was silent.

"Ms. Gina I trust that you will do as you promised," said Lily-Butterfly.

"Yes. Sure. You can count on me. I will do my best. Mama is my new client to take care of. Thank you Lily-Butterfly for respecting my request. After all I am mama's only real child and daughter. Now I can live a life of leisure. Thank you."

"We will see Ms. Gina. I notice that it is the first time I hear you say thank you. Interesting."

"I guess you will see. Actions speak louder than words. Plus, money speaks very loud as well."

"Ms. Gina I leave you to karma and the Creator."

"Okay. Stop at the supermarket across the street from my home. I need to do grocery shopping. Are you giving me some money to help with the food shopping today; or on Sunday?"

"I will pay the complete grocery shopping bill today."

"Now Lily-Butterfly you are being so nice," said Ms. Gina.

"Ms. Gina you cannot fool me. I am watching you."

"You can watch me all you like. Know that some time the fox is faster than a running chicken," said Ms. Gina with a smirk.

After leaving Ms. Gina's home Lily-Butterfly went home to work on her daily chores. Stay tuned you will see what happens.

61

Trust people for who they really are and not what you want them to be. The people closest to you have the most opportunity to hurt you. Give people time and they will show more of their hidden human nature. Not because you are kind, caring, and share unconditional love and compassion with someone means that they will do the same for you. Some people will use you as much as you will let them.

Remember that on Thursday January 11th Lily-Butterfly transferred Manana Leila's bank account into Manana Leila and Ms. Gina's name; and removed her name. Lily-Butterfly returned to Ms. Gina's home on Sunday January 15th at 10:30 AM to visit Manana. She knocked on the door. No one came to open the door. Lily-Butterfly looked through the window and saw Manana Leila sitting on a chair by the dining table. She wondered why Manana was not coming to unlock the door. Lily-Butterfly knocked on the door louder and longer. Still Manana Leila sat and looked at Lily-Butterfly with a sad look on her face.

"I cannot get up. I am tied to the chair across my legs and my left hand is tied to the chair," said Manana Leila.

Lily-Butterfly heard Manana grumbling through the three inches open window.

"What? Tied up. Stand up with the chair. You can move. Come. Get up slowly with the chair. You can move. Try. You will see, try. Come and unlock the door," said Lily-Butterfly.

"Okay I will try. I feel very sad. Look what I have come to. I feel so disappointed in Gina. I could not imagine that she would do this to me," grumbled Manana Leila.

Manana was able to sort of walk with the chair she was tied up in.

"Yes, good job. Walk slow and come unlock the door. Ms. Gina is something else out of a horror show. I do not feel like calling her Ms. Gina. Right now, I feel like saying very negative curse words. What the hell is she thinking?" said Lily-Butterfly.

Manana Leila got to the front door and unlocked it. Lily-Butterfly opened the door and went inside.

"What is going on? Where is Ms. Gina and Dean?" said Lily-Butterfly.

"They went to work," replied Manana.

"Who tied you to the chair?"

"Gina."

"Why did Ms. Gina tie you to the chair?"

Lily-Butterfly took a knife and cut the cord that Ms. Gina used to tie her mother to the chair. Manana Leila stood up. Lily-Butterfly carried the chair. They walk back to the kitchen and dining room area. Lily-Butterfly put the chair down by the dining table. Manana sat down. Lily-Butterfly sat beside her. They continued to talk.

"Gina tied me to the chair so I would not leave the house and go for a walk. I thought that I could not get up or move. She left my lunch beside me on the dining table. Gina told me that I could use the hand that was not tied to eat my lunch."

"Ms. Gina told me that she does not work on Sundays. How do you get to use the restroom and eat?" said Lily-Butterfly.

Lily-Butterfly sat and listened to Manana Leila talk. Manana did not talk, complain, or explain anything too much. Today she was in a rare talking mood. Lily-Butterfly stayed silent, listened, and heard all that Manana wanted to say.

"Gina put a diaper on me. Oh, my Creator is this my final test of unconditional love and understanding? I never dreamt that I would come to this. My daughter has lost her conscience a long time ago. She will not respect, listen, or hear me. I think that she spent all the money in the bank within the last two days. Thursday when we returned from the bank, Ms. Gina told me to sigh a withdrawal slip for $34,800 to transfer the money into her checking account. She said this would be easier for her to get access to the money. In cases of emergencies she would not have to go to the bank. Gina left only $200 in the saving pass book account with both our names on it. I see Dean with a car. Henry came here one day. Gina went with him to buy a different car from the car he had. I think that Gina used the money to buy them two used cars of their choice. Oh, my. What is going to happen to me now? After I signed over the $34,800 to her the tying up began. I heard Gina and Dean talking about putting me in a government subsidized nursing home, and that the social security payments would be paid to the nursing home. This is a nightmare. It is a good thing that I took care of myself and live ninety-seven years already. Soon, on May 5th of this year I will be ninety-eight years old. Thanks to the ancestors and the Creator I stayed healthy and strong up to now. Oh, my Creator, it is time for Gina to show some kind of unconditional love, compassion, care, and respect. I think in some way I am responsible for Gina's selfishness. I helped her too much. I did not teach her to give to me. I gave Gina everything I could, and every help and assistance she needed. I spoiled her. It is not an accident that I am in her care. This is our karma to work out before I die. Karma is something else. I over give to Gina, and she under gave to me. Our relationship is very much one sided and out of balance. On my side the positive giving is over dose. On Gina's side the positive giving is under dose. Human life is a consistent balancing act. Within two more years I will die. I will die before my one hundredth birthday. My child soon I will be going home to the other side of this realm. I have already began to prepare to die. I am almost finished repeatedly recapitulating my complete life. Everyone automatically conscious or unconsciously goes through a life review before they die. My path is clear and I am ready to die. I do not fear death. The angels of death will come when it is time for me to die and cross over to the realm of my destination. After death I will return sooner than you think. Keep your eyes and heart in-tune and you will recognize me when I return. Anyway, I have surrendered to everything Gina might do to me. I am here as a sacrificial lamb to give her an opportunity to repent her ways. I will not fight with Gina, complain, or let my spirit and soul become corrupt against Gina's actions. Gina's actions will be her own responsibility and karma. Acceptance and surrender dilutes suffering and pain. Positive thoughts and actions will accompany me on the pathway of death. My only issues at this time is, I have some short term memory loss. Lily-Butterfly know that I am meant to be here. Let Gina and I work out our karma. I am not expecting you to remove me from Gina's care. This is between Gina's spirit and soul; and my spirit and soul. This will be tough karma medicine for me. Lily-Butterfly thank you for everything you do," said Manana Leila.

Manana Leila stopped talking. She took a diamond ring she always wore on her finger and gave it to Lily-Butterfly.

"Here Lily-Butterfly take this ring. Gina seems to have taken all the money in the bank. She has burned my will and threw all my other things in the garbage. Take this ring. This is all I have left to give to you before I die. Take it."

"I will get it after you die. This is all you have left of your things. Put it back on your finger. I will get it later. Thank you. Put the ring back on. Okay."

"Alright. I think that Gina will want to take this ring from me as well. She tried before and I told her no. Thank you for everything."

"You are welcome. Do not worry. I will help you manage Ms. Gina. Where is your lunch?"

"In the thermos on the table. Gina told me when I am ready I can eat."

"Does Gina expect you to sit here tied to the chair from she left 8:30 AM until she return from work 4:00 PM, she leaves work at 3:00 PM?"

"Gina told me if I wanted to sleep to put my head down on the table. Sometimes my legs and arm get cramped, being in one position for a long time. Gina gave me breakfast before she went to work."

"Okay, drink some water, eat your lunch, and after eating I will take you outside for some fresh air and a walk. When we return you can lay down and take a nap. I will stay here with you until Ms. Gina returns from so called work."

"Okay blessed child. Thank you. How are your children doing?"

"They are as fine as possible. Rebornstar is seventeen and Holly will be seven at the end of July. They are happy, content, and healthy. The only negative things is my life are Holly has a learning issue that so far we have not been able to figure out, I am not at home as much as I used to be, Rebornstar is exercising her teenager-ship, and currently I have a much more difficult job. Thanks be to the Creator we are healthy and I have money to pay the bills. Manana I thank you for everything. Do your best with Ms. Gina's treatment. When Ms. Gina come home I will tell her what I have to say. Finish eating, after I will take you for a walk, and when you return you lay down and sleep."

"Okay. Thank you."

Manana Leila went for a walk with Lily-Butterfly. When they returned Manana laid down and took a nap. Ms. Gina returned home at 3:30 PM. Manana was still sleeping. Gina entered the home. She put her bag on the couch. Lily-Butterfly was sitting on the other end of the couch reading. Lily-Butterfly closed the book.

"Hi Ms. Gina. How are you doing?"

"Hi Lily-Butterfly. I am doing great. Where is mama?"

"Manana had lunch, we went for a walk, and now she is taking a nap. I would like to talk to you."

"Okay. What now?"

"Let us go talk in the kitchen where we are less likely to wake up Manana."

"Your Manana is lucky. All she does is eat, sleep, and stay quiet."

"Manana worked hard enough already. Now at almost ninety-eight years old she can eat and sleep. How about the negative treatment that you give her?"

"What negative treatment? Hurry up and say what you want to. I am tired and hungry."

"Why do you tie up your mother? Would you like me to tie you up? How about one day I come here and tie you up from 9:00 AM to 4:00 PM?"

"To keep her safe. I do not need to be tied up. Tying her will prevent her from leaving the house, getting lost, walking out into traffic, and everything else. In nursing homes, the staff does whatever is needed to manage the old people. Me tying mama to the chair is like being put in a wheel chair. Wheel chair is modern confinement. Being tied up is primitive confinement. Me tying her hand is like if she had injured her hand and only had one hand to use. I tie her hand so that she does not untie the cord I use to tie her in the chair. This makes sense to me. This might not make sense to you, because of how you are and your perception. Do not judge me in a negative way. You are not the one being here with mama. I have to live my life. I need and choose to go to work. Mmm. The things I do helps me to manage her health, well-being, and safety. Get with the program. That is, it. Is there anything else? You have to go to your house and take care of your children and your own business."

"Ms. Gina your thinking process and perception is interesting. After all the money arrangements you agreed and promised to stay home and take care of your mother. Manana does not like being tied up. This is abuse and wrong. I do not like this care provider program that you are talking about and performing. You made a promise to take care of Manana in a positive way. It seems that after you got control of the money she have you are back to your real self. If I come here and she is tied up in any way, I am going to call the police to write a police report and charge you with elderly abuse. You will go to jail. The evidence will be what the police see when they arrive here."

"I am going to put mama in the government free nursing home. The government will pay for all the expenses. Her social security payment and Medicare will go directly to the nursing home administration. I checked this out and she qualifies. I found a nursing home that I can put her in."

"Manana does not want to go to a nursing home. She is sad enough already. Stop working and take care of her. You will receive her social security and I will help to pay all the expenses like we agreed to previously."

"Oh yeah. Since you love and care about mama so much quit your job, move into a larger apartment, and you take care of her. Or leave me alone and let me do as I choose."

"I cannot quit my job. I have two young children to take care of. You have her money; plus, social security sends her payment to her account every month. Plus, you need to do something positive for your mother before she dies. It is almost time for Manana to die."

"What money in her bank account? Most of that money is finished already. This is why it is a great time to put her in the nursing home. I need more than her monthly social security payments and the money you contribute to pay all our expenses. Lily-Butterfly get with the reality of this situation and the things I choose to do."

"Give me the bank book let me see how much is in the account?"

"Go ahead. Look in the bedroom on the dresser; the bank book is there."

Lily-Butterfly walked to the bedroom and got the bank pass book. She looked inside.

"What is this? Are you serious? There is only $239 left in the bank. What did you do with the money?"

"Why are you questioning me Lily-Dragonfly? Mama is my real and legal mother. She did not adopt me. I can do as I choose with her money. Mama signed the withdrawal slip for me to transfer the money to my checking account. I am her legal guardian by law in every way. I came out of her. Do you understand? If I want to use mama's money I can. Every month Social Security deposits more money into her bank account. Stop telling me what I cannot do, can do, to and for mama, and her money. Okay. Stop. Calm down. Understand?"

"No, no. I do not understand your negative ways of thinking. Do not call me Lily-Dragonfly. This is not my name. I am not afraid of you and all your negative defenses. What did you do with the money? I do not think it is in your checking account."

"Well, well do you really want to know? I really do not think that you want to know."

"Yes, I want to know. What did you do with the money?"

"I bought Dean a used car so that he could go to work easily. If and when I am ready to put mama in the nursing home Dean promised to help me take her there. I bought Henry a used car so that he could have transportation to go to work, for his family, pick me up and take me to and from work. Henry's old car was breaking down a lot. Lucy is having financial problems and I gave her $12,000. I use some of the money to pay off some bills. I have about $3,000 left. This I have for emergencies and so forth. Now with the money spend I have to go to work. Do you understand Ms. Lily-Butterfly? You might be upset because I did not give you any of the money. Such is life. You win some and you lose some. I did not think that you really wanted to hear this answer. But you asked for it. Are you happy now? Anyway, I am the one that should inherit all the money. See what I did as pre-inheritance. Plus, mama does not need a bank account in a nursing home. Now hear me. This is Gina saying 'mind your own business.' You are tired and busy enough with your own career, children, and life. Take care of your life and business. Leave my mother's business to me. Do not say anything about karma to me. Karma is between me and karma."

"Ms. Gina if you put mama in a nursing home after using all her money. I am going to report you to the police for stealing all her money. Stealing Manana's money is against the law."

"No it is not. Mama signed the withdrawal slip. She is not going to tell the police anything for them to lock me up in jail. Mama is too nice and positive. She would not want me to go to jail."

"I see you are taking advantage of your mother's unconditional love and compassion."

"Call it what you like. If mama wants to use her unconditional love and compassion on me; this is her choice. Do you see what I mean? Quit bugging me. I am tired Lily-Butterfly. Please go home. Stop harassing me. Accept that you are powerless in this situation."

"I am leaving. Make sure that you do not abuse Manana. If I ever see one scratch on her I am calling the police. The diamond ring Manana is wearing she gave it to me. I told her to wear it until she dies. After she dies I will take it. I want you to know this. The next thing is we talked about her body after death. She does not want to be buried anymore because the funeral plot she had bought is in Boston. She has decided to be cremated. I promised her that she will be cremated, and I will spread her ashes in the ocean of my choice. Remember to put this ring she give me in a safe place and give to me. Ms. Gina be mindful of your choices and actions. I will return next week Tuesday."

"Go home to your children and life. It is 5:20 PM. I am going to cook dinner. Bye. You are not my parent or boss. Leave. Good bye."

"Good bye Ms. Gina. I will leave after I say good bye to Manana."

Lily-Butterfly went into the bedroom. Manana Leila was awake.

"Good bye Manana. I will be back in one day; on Tuesday. Bye. Like you always say 'the Creator knows best, and is always watching you.' You are to take responsibility the best way you can to manage your situation here with Ms. Gina. Humans come into this planet as a baby, and they leave, before and after death, as a baby. I am learning so much from you and Ms. Gina's current situation. Ms. Gina might not be conscious that her days of death will come. Once someone is born, when the time come, their journey of death is for sure. I know that one way or the other you will make yourself fine; if not in the physical, you will make up for your experiences within and from your spirit and soul. You know your way home after death, and birthing yourself to the other side. I feel sad. I have to work on accepting this Ms. Gina's treatment, and my spirit, soul, mind, emotion, and physical experiences, from the awareness of your death's journey. Death and the angels of death are coming within the next two years to take you home to the other side. Bye, see you soon. I always keep you in my prayers and thoughts. Bye."

"Thank you Lily-Butterfly for everything. I am almost out of this planet. Try not to worry. I will make myself manage. My instincts tell me that no matter what you say Gina is going to eventually put me in the nursing home. I am going to improve my acceptance of this. When the time comes I will be as ready as possible. Gina will be Gina. See you next week Tuesday. Take care of yourself and the children. Bye."

Lily-Butterfly gave Manana Leila a hug and two kisses. Manana Leila walked with Lily-Butterfly to the living room and sat on the couch. Lily-Butterfly turned on the television so that Manana could watch her program.

"Good by Ms. Gina. Take care of yourself and your mother. I will return next Tuesday."

"Bye Lily-Butterfly. Go take care of your children."

"Bye Ms. Gina."

Lily-Butterfly drove home processing all her thoughts. She had already prepare Sunday dinner. The children had the lunch she had left for them. Lily-Butterfly had also organize everything for work and school for the children. When she arrived home, she had dinner with her children. After dinner they all took showers and prepare for bed. Breakfast was set up for the children on Monday morning. Lily-Butterfly was leaving for work on Monday morning at 4:30 AM.

Before going to sleep on Sunday night Lily-Butterfly wrote her days events in her journal. She did a very short prayer.

"Dear Creator of everything. You know everything already. Thank you for everything. Tonight, I feel very tired. Tomorrow morning my next adventure and journey in this human life begins. Good night. Amin."

62

All planted seeds must go within to access its complete potential to grow and become its full potential. Humans are supposed to be the same.

Monday morning January 15, 1996 Lily-Butterfly woke up at 3:00 AM when the alarm came on. She set up breakfast for the children and ate her early breakfast. The next time she might eat would be 11:00 AM. At 4:30 AM Lily-Butterfly left home and drove to the restaurant In Yonkers, New York. She arrived at 6:00 AM and went inside. Ema and the employees were already inside.

"Good morning everyone. Surprise. Here I am."

"Oh wow. Good morning Ms. Lily-Butterfly. I had a strong feeling that you would return. Welcome we are happy to see you," said Ema.

"Ema I am happy that you are here. But, I am not happy to be here. This is the worse news to me. Anyway, I will make the best of this situation. When you have to put in the help to improve this restaurant I hope that you will still be happy that I am here. I will not be running this restaurant the same way. The restaurant procedures and operation used here is totally incorrect. I am going to the office to start my audit and assessment of everything. I will see you later."

"Okay ma'am. My sister is the one that does the reports on Sunday night before she goes home. They are on the desk in the office."

"Thank you. I will see you later," said Lily-Butterfly.

Lily-Butterfly sat at the desk in the office. She looked at all the reports that Edna completed. The reports seem bogus. When she reviewed some of the ending inventory written on the paper and check the physical inventory in the restaurant, they did not match. It seems as if Edna sat down and created all the figures to match with the money collected from the sales. Lily-Butterfly sighed. After all bills were paid the money that was left was minus a large amount. This was what Edna's bogus reports were showing. The bogus reports were covering and disguising the even worse facts of the situation. Lily-Butterfly took deep breaths and sighed again, and again. She calmed her nerves with positive affirmations.

"I will take things one slow step at a time. This is a big mess. Today I will create a list of all the things I see that are incorrect and correct. Make lists of everything that needs to improve, transform, and change. I cannot come here and continue the cycle of incorrect restaurant procedures. This will transform me into a rotten and corrupt General Manager. My positive reputation, quality of work and service, ethics, and honesty is the most valuable asset in my professional career. I will not dismember this for anything or anyone. I will try working here, if this does not work out, I will resign, and go work somewhere else. Oh, Creator help me and stay in touch with me through my prayers."

Lily-Butterfly put in a file all the reports Edna had completed. These reports she would give to Mr. Watson when he arrive. Lily-Butterfly checked in the Monday food and paper delivery. Next she took out of her work brief case a large note book. In this book she planned to write everything that needed to be transformed, changed, added, subtracted, purchased, thrown away, action plans, and everything to do. The first thing Lily-Butterfly wrote was her action plan. The action plan she wrote included; observe, listen, hear, find the problems, create a list of the problems, create a list of the solutions, investigate to find the root of each problem, create long-term solutions to the problems, make a list of everything needed for the restaurant operations to function according to company policies, get to know the current employees and Managers, read the guidelines about working with union employees, see how many more regular employees needed to be hired, check how much overtime is being used for all employees, make a list of equipment – pots – pans-utensils, and other production and kitchen tools that is needed, list of equipment and other things to be repaired, list of things to be improved – repair – and fix - including walk-in refrigerators and freezers, list of new uniforms needed for employees and Managers, list of all employees to be trained; including Managers, create a functioning employees and Manager's schedule, action plan to stop all overtime, investigate and find the root of the annual minus two million dollars, schedule and have meetings with Managers every Friday, get to memorize all menu items and ingredients, and read order deliveries. On computer - audit all food and paper order entries – audit all cash sales, audit all employee and Managers weekly hours and overtime, spot check most recent time punch in cards. Read all financial statements and reports. Write down all the other things that needs improving as the days goes by. When Lily-Butterfly was finished using this book it became like a restaurant operation's bible. This book had everything that was need to improve the restaurant, how she improves the restaurant, and how to keep the restaurant successful. In the future Mr. Watson tried to get Lily-Butterfly to write him a restaurant procedure manual on everything she did to improve the restaurant and keep it successful. She told him no about giving him such a book. Mr. Watson did not know that Lily-Butterfly had already written everything in the restaurant operations bible that she created.

The first thing that Lily-Butterfly did from her to-do list was write a Manager schedule for Ema, Edna, and herself. For now, she left the regular employee schedule as it was. She schedule herself to be off from work Tuesdays and Sundays. Currently these were the least busy days and sales, based on the sales report. She must be at work on Monday, Wednesdays, Fridays, and Saturdays. These were the busiest sales days, food, paper, and cleaning products orders to be done, and deliveries arrive. At 9:30 AM Mr. Watson arrived at the Yonkers restaurant. He came into the office to speak to Lily-Butterfly.

"Good morning Lily-Butterfly," said Mr. Watson.

"Good Morning Mr. Watson."

"How is everything doing?"

"Like it is used to do. I am investigating and making lists of things to work on. Here are the reports that Edna did. This weekend I will see how I can change the reports to reflect the real picture of the restaurant operation and financial reports. Everything needs to be redone."

"Do we need to have a meeting today?" asked Mr. Watson.

"No. I do not have anything new to report. Can I have the restaurant keys, the sequence of numbers to open all the safes that the money is deposited in, and the restaurant personal safe. And I need the current security code for the alarm? Is there armored deposit money pick up. If yes, on what days do they come to pick up the money?"

"Here is a set of keys to open the restaurant doors and the security code for the alarm. The safe combination numbers, and the days the armored truck come to pick up the money, is on this paper in the envelope. Memorize the alarm code and safe combination and shred the paper. For today is there anything else that you need from me?" said Mr. Watson.

"No. Thank you for everything. Have a nice day. Bye."

"Wow. Lily-Butterfly you seem precise with your conversation."

"My head is almost frozen with trying to figure out the entangled web of this restaurant. The only other thing you can be aware of is that I will not work here and pretend that there is no problem. I will not continue with preparing bogus reports. If I am going to be the General Manager here I have chosen to fix the issues. I will not lie for you or anyone else. My reputation and quality of work is the most valuable thing for success in my professional career. If things get fixed they have to be for real. Remember this."

"Yes, I understand this is the main reason for transferring you here. When you are ready let me know what you need from me to create and transform the situations here. Okay. I am leaving."

"Okay. Bye. Maybe next week Monday I will have more new information for you."

"Bye. Yes, keep me informed."

Mr. Watson took the files and left the restaurant. For the whole day Lily-Butterfly performed an audit on the computer, count the physical food and paper goods, toured the upstairs of the restaurant, did food and paper orders, telephoned the orders to the wholesalers, checked employees schedule and time cards, cleaned out the desk drawers, cleared clutter, and anything else she could do for the day. At 11:00 AM Lily-Butterfly had something to eat and drink. Lily-Butterfly did not go to help Ema with the restaurant sales and operation. She rarely talked to Ema and the employees. Edna came to work at 3:00 PM. She came into the office. Lily-Butterfly was checking the reports on the computer.

"Hi Edna. Thank you for completing the usual reports last night before you left."

"You are welcome ma'am."

"Soon everything is going to change to reflect the reality of everything that goes on in this restaurant. I know that on Sunday nights you do not count the inventory for real. You sit at the computer and make up the numbers based on the sales. I recounted the food and paper inventory to check the amounts you put into the computer and none of the actual physical count I saw match what you said the ending inventory was. Right now, you do not have to explain, defend, or justify the reports you do. Know that this will all change. I cannot work in this current corrupt situation. Everything here is wrong and corrupt. Over time I will teach you and Ema the correct report practices and procedure. We will work together as a team. I will teach and guide you how to do things correctly. This corruption and fake reports will not continue as long as I am here. Do you understand?"

"Yes, ma'am. I understand. We basically just try to keep the restaurant in operation. It is not our fault things are this way. We just try the best way we know how, and how the previous General Managers taught us to work. I understand that wrong is wrong, and we went with the flow. Let me know what you want me to do and change. Okay. You are strong to even want to change the things here. This is going to be very hard work for you. This restaurant is like a beast, black hole, demon haunted building. This place is haunted on top of everything else. In time you will see what I am talking about."

"Edna, I understand. I see and sense everything you are saying. If I cannot help with fixing the issues, I will resign and find another job in New Jersey. Until this happens I will be here. We will all work together with the regular employees as a team to transform and improve things. I cannot fix all these numerous problems by myself. It is going to take team work efforts. Okay. At 4:30 PM I am leaving. I am very tired. I will be back on Wednesday morning. I did the inventory and food order for today. The new Manager schedule is on the clip board, right here, over the desk. For now, you and Ema have the same schedule. As time goes on all the overtime will come to an end. We will talk more about everything as time goes on. Every Friday starting this week we will have a Managers' meeting in the dining room. The meeting information is in the Manager's communication note book. Okay. Do you have any questions?"

"No, not at this time. Please let me know when you need my help with something. Let me go prepare for the dinner shift. Good night."

"Good night Edna. Thank you."

"You are welcome ma'am."

Edna put down her pocket book in the desk drawer and left the office.

Lily-Butterfly continued with her office work. At 4:30 PM she told Ema goodbye and left the restaurant.

"I am very tired. I hope that I do not fall asleep driving home. At 4:30 PM the traffic is not yet bumper to bumper. Fixing this restaurant is a lot of work. I keep repeating this, because it is over whelming and true. This is sad and a shame. What does not kill me can create improvements," whispered Lily-Butterfly.

For Lily-Butterfly her first day was completed in this Yonkers,

New York restaurant building that was built in 1863. When Lily-Butterfly got home it was 6:15 PM. She got to eat dinner with the children and checked Holly's homework.

"Mama I do not want to go to school tomorrow morning. I feel sick, my stomach hurts in class, and sometimes I vomit. I do not want to go," said Holly.

"What? You feel sick, stomach ache, and vomit? Why? What is going on in class?"

"Every day in class the Teacher acts mean. She shouts in my face, grabs me, pushes me, slap and punches me if I cannot read or answer a question correctly. I am nervous. Can I change my class?"

"Holly are you sure that the Teacher does these things?"

"Yes mama. I am not making up this story. Come with me to school, you will see what I am talking about. Really. I am nervous. I cannot do any better with my school work. I am not going back to school. I can no longer take the treatment of this Teacher."

"I hear you Holly. I am coming to school with you in the morning. I will ask the Principal permission to sit in your class to observe what is going on. You cannot stop going to school."

"Yes, thank you mama. Come with me to school, you will see. Maybe you can ask to change my class."

"I will come and we will see how I can improve your class learning experience. When we move maybe we will figure out your learning issues. Sometimes when one thing does not work, other things might. We cannot give up."

"Okay mama."

After helping Holly, Lily-Butterfly took a soak in a tub of salt water to help detox her stress. Sleep that night for Lily-Butterfly was a very welcoming experience.

Tuesday January 16th at 7:30 AM Lily-Butterfly went to school with Holly. She went to the Principal to tell him about what Holly had told her. The Principal gave her permission to go sit in Holly's class. He telephoned upstairs to tell the Teacher that Lily-Butterfly would be in the class with Holly. The Teacher Holly was talking about was her first grade Special Education Teacher. She was the first class for the day. Lily-Butterfly entered the class room and introduced herself. The Teacher instructed her to sit in the last row. Holly went to sit in her seat. There were a total of seven students in the class room. The Teacher used the black board to teach. After she called each student to her desk to elaborate on what she had just finished teaching on the black board. When it was Holly's turn to go to the Teacher's desk she did not want to go. She seemed afraid. Lily-Butterfly did not interfere. The Teacher insisted that Holly come to her desk. Eventually Holly did as the Teacher had ask. The Special Education Teacher used the same mean, shouting in the child's face, slapping the child and the book page, pushing, punching, grabbing, and intimidating teaching style with every child. So, Lily-Butterfly saw that the Teacher was not singling out Holly. When the Teacher interacts with Holly in this negative way she cried and tried to leave the Teacher's desk.

"I am sitting here and this Teacher is doing all these things to the children as if I am not in the room. She must think that this teaching style is acceptable. This is amazing. How could this be a normal way to teach? This is abuse, and actually can create trauma for these children. I am going to stop her from doing this to Holly. I am taking Holly and go back to the Principal's office. This is Holly's last day in this class," mumbled Lily-Butterfly.

Lily-Butterfly got up and walked up to the Teacher's desk.

"Enough. Come Holly. Teacher stop. I am taking my child out of this class. You are not allowed to teach Holly anymore. I will make sure of this. You seem to need retraining and have some kind of mental health issue. I am sitting here in this class and your behavior is worse than Holly told me. Shame on you. These are children who come here to learn; not be abused by you. I am going back to the Principal's office to file a report, have Holly transferred to another class, and I am going to the Board of Education in this town to file a report about you and my observation. I will also make sure that the other children do not have to suffer anymore from your negative teaching style. Do you really think that the children can improve their learning with your teaching treatments? Shame on you. I cannot imagine what you would do if I was not in the room. Come Holly we are leaving this room."

Holly got her book bag. She left the classroom with her mother. The Teacher and the other children were silent.

Lily-Butterfly went back downstairs to the Principal's office. She told the Principal her experience. He tried to defend the teacher. Lily-Butterfly was not accepting his excuses and defense. She insisted on writing a report immediately. The Principal gave her a form to fill out. Lily-Butterfly requested a copy of the report. The Principal gave her a copy of the report. Lily-Butterfly requested that Holly be transferred to another Special Education Teacher's class and that another Teacher should replace this current Teacher, for the sake of all the other students. The Principal promised that he would fix the problem and he immediately transferred Holly to another class. Lily-Butterfly also told the Principal that she was going over to the Board of Education to file a formal complaint about her complete experience. The Principal apologized to Lily-Butterfly and Holly. Lily-Butterfly left Holly in the Principal's office.

"Goodbye Holly. Never be afraid to speak to me about any perceived problem you have; trust your instinct. Good. The Principal will put you in another class with another Teacher. If you have a problem in school come to the office and tell the Principal and tell me as well. Do not accept abuse and any negative behavior from anyone. Do you understand?"

"I understand mama. I will see you later. I love you mama. Thank you. Bye."

"Okay. Mama loves you. I will see you at home later. Mr. Principal thank you for everything. I am going to the Board of Education right now. Have a nice day. Bye."

"Good bye Ms. Lily-Butterfly. I will place Holly in another class. Thank you for coming."

Lily-Butterfly left Holly's school and drove to the Board of Education. She told the Teaching Supervisor of the Special Education Program about her experience and wrote a formal report. Lily-Butterfly requested a copy of the report. The Teaching Supervisor gave her a copy of the report and promised to resolve the situation. Lily-Butterfly thanked the Teaching Supervisor and left the building. After this situation in school was resolved with Holly, she was okay with going to school. Between going to Holly's school and the Board of Education, Lily-Butterfly had drank three cups of water. She returned home to eat lunch. After eating lunch and setting up dinner for the day, the next plan on Lily-Butterfly's agenda was to go visit Manana Leila. She was bringing Manana some cooked food that she had put in her freezer from Sunday night's dinner. Lily-Butterfly left her home and drove to Ms. Gina's home. She continued to process all her experiences from work the day before and at Holly's school.

"There are times when nothing can be done to transform and change a system. If I do not like an unchangeable system, the only thing I can do is transform and change my relationship within the system, transform and change me, or leave the system. Whichever choice is the best is each situation is the wisest choice. This can be the same awareness for people, places, and things. Human life is an interesting adventure. I wonder what is going on at Ms. Gina's house with Manana? Ms. Gina never ceases to amaze me. Tomorrow is another day at work in this challenging restaurant situation. I think that this restaurant experience is going to awaken all my talents. I am not going to choose to have a nervous breakdown and get sick from working in this place. Mr. Watson thinks that he is smart. We will see who is smart and wise. The way will show me the way. I will trust my instincts, spirit, soul, and how I am being guided. Amin," mumbled Lily-Butterfly.

The driving journey to Ms. Gina's home continues.

63

Lily-Butterfly arrived at Ms. Gina's home at 2:00 PM. The door was wide open. She entered the home. Ms. Gina and Manana Leila were sitting in the living room.

"Hi Ms. Gina and Manana. How are you both doing?"

"I was doing as fine as possible. Now that you are here to give me a hard time. I do not know how I am going to do," replied Ms. Gina.

Manana did not reply.

"Manana let us go for a walk. Ms. Gina, would you like to come with us?"

"No, I need a break. Mama and I need a break from each other. Mama might seem quiet to you. To me she is not easy to handle. Take mama and go. I will stay home. I go for a walk by myself when I like," said Ms. Gina.

"Do you need groceries at the supermarket? When I return from the walk I could go buy groceries."

"No Lily-Butterfly I do not need groceries at this time. But, you can give me some money and later on in the week I could go to the supermarket by myself."

"Okay Ms. Gina. It seems that when you moved from the valley and village of Yaj you discovered modern money and fell in love with it. Money is not a life preserver. Your spirit and soul is your real life preserver. You need to work on your personal wounds and help yourself to transform and improve your shadow sides. Anyway, here is $250. When you are ready you can buy groceries."

"Lily-Butterfly now you are singing my song. Money is the song of this modern civilization. It is the most useful tool in this country. Without money you will end up flat on your face. Hahaha."

"Gina to me money is an important resource. The Creator, unconditional love, compassion, my spirit, and soul are some of the most important things in every civilization; ancient, new, and modern. I accept you as you are Ms. Gina. But I will not make you run me into the ground. I have my eyes on you."

"Thank you for the money. I will put it in a warm place in my bosom."

"Ms. Gina I find you very interesting. You just said thank you to me. This is the second time I hear you say thank you; and it was from receiving money. Interesting. This is one of the rare occasion that you have said thank you. Ms. Gina you must have been born between the new moon and full moon."

"She was," said Manana Leila.

"What does between new and full moon mean and have to do with my birth?" asked Ms. Gina.

"Figure it out Ms. Gina. To start it means that your personality is neither here nor there. A contrary personality. Just like water your personality is inconsistent and vibes with everything it encounters. Ms. Gina you are a lucky spirit and soul. Every other generation the ancestors give a first born; spirit and soul that would not necessarily get an opportunity to be born in this ancestral lineage a chance to be born. This is why the talents of the ancestors skip a generation. Ms. Gina you are the child, spirit, and soul of the 'every other generation'; a spirit and soul lotto winner. Here you are like a spirit and soul who has won the lotto of a spirit and soul journey, and you are wasting the opportunity. Even at your age of sixty two years old you have not chosen to use the opportunity to transform your spirit, soul, mind, body, and life, negative imprints, triggers, and shadow sides. Ms. Gina I recommend that you do not keep wasting time, taking things for granted, and showing no value for the opportunities of the ancestors and ancient pathways. Remember karma, nothing is free, and that karma manages free will. Free will, is not free. You will get returned to you all the energies of your thoughts, speech, and actions. What you do not know is older than you. Anyway, Manana let me help you put on your shoes. Your daughter is very interesting. Today seems good, who knows what I will experience the next time I come here. I give thanks for today. Ms. Gina we will be back. Enjoy your time alone."

"Lily-Butterfly oracle of the ancient pathways; you talk too much. Leave me be. Go. Bye."

"I am going. One day before you die you will remember all my unused words. All human's spirit and soul have all their life's experiences replay before their eyes, heart, and senses before they die. It is called a life review or recapitulation. It is never too late to choose the positive energy pathways. I will see you when I return. When I return I will be leaving to go home to take care of my life and the two spirits and souls that the Creator gave me to practice unconditional love and compassion with."

"Good for you, your children, and the Creator. Keep minding your own business. I welcome you leaving when you return. Manana will miss you; not me. You get on my nerves. I find you exhausting. Bye."

"Alright I am going. I love you Ms. Gina. I wish for you all the best of things. All I can do is wish and send you positive vibes no matter what you do. I know karma. I am not going to have negative karma from giving you negative, thoughts, speech, and actions. Take care. See you. Come Manana."

"Good go. Maybe the Creator sent you to haunt me."

Manana Leila and Lily-Butterfly went for a good walk around the neighborhood and to the park. As usual they talked about ancient times, Manana told Lily-Butterfly stories about life in the valley village of Yaj before she was born, and Lily-Butterfly asked Manana questions. Manana gave Lily-Butterfly many links to the missing chain of the past ancestors. Manana Leila helped to confirm to Lily-Butterfly that the real human treasures were not in the physical and could only be seen with through and with the eyes of the purified spirit and soul's heart. The humans with a positive spirit, soul, and heart can stay connected to the positive channels of Universal Intelligence.

When Lily-Butterfly took Manana back home to Ms. Gina's house, she helped Manana to sit on the couch and took off her shoes. She hugged and kissed Manana good bye.

"Goodbye my mama Gina. Thank you for everything; the varied amount of abuse, suffering, and trauma. Giving me the opportunity to choose to transform all the negative things you did to me, to be born here in this realm to find my Manana Leila oracle and spirit's guide, being my shadow arts sink or swim teacher, improve unconditional love and compassion, and helping me to awaken fearlessness. These are priceless spirit and soul treasurers. You were a very great dark arts teacher. It is past time to transform all your shame, negative experiences, trauma, and suffering. I will see you again. Take care of your mother. I will be back soon."

"Lily-Butterfly, I am happy to see you go. Bye. My biggest wish is that some day or lifetime I can be like you. I think one of the purpose is you are in my life is to be a mirror and reminder. But, sorry I am not ready to get on this path. I am in control of my choices, karma, and destiny. Good bye."

"Some of your issues are you do not like to be told what to do, stubbornness, shameful, do not like the present, and the truth. Ms. Gina you cannot hide forever. Keep up your act. Soon Manana will die and I will be gone from your life. Nothing lasts forever. Goodnight."

Manana Leila was quiet. Ms. Gina did not reply to the last things Lily-Butterfly said. Lily-Butterfly left Ms. Gina's home. She returned to her own life. Holly was currently okay in school. As long as Rebornstar and Holly were doing well and healthy, Lily-Butterfly spirit, soul, heart, mind, and body was at ease, peace, and contentment. Rebornstar was in high school, having fun with friends, making the best of school how she choose, and trying to outsmart her mother like a fox. With falcon eyes Lily-Butterfly counter managed Rebornstar when she goes too far in the negative energy directions. Lily-Butterfly accepted her responsibilities as a part of being a functionable single parent.

Wednesday Lily-Butterfly went back to work. She checked and verified the food and paper delivery. Next she entered the correct amounts into the computer. Lily-Butterfly picked up her large created book of things to accomplish. From this book she wrote down all the things to accomplish for the day, a list of things for Mr. Watson to do for the restaurant, things to delegate to Ema, Edna, and other employees to do. The first thing on the to-do list was to make a list of broken machines, equipment, and which machine and equipment needed to be replaced, and repaired. Juan who worked in the kitchen for over forty one years was this restaurants encyclopedia. He helped Lily-Butterfly make the lists. Lily-Butterfly perceived Juan as the priceless help she needed and also as part of the problem of the missing money. From her investigation she was aware that Juan was taking food and everything he needed from the restaurant. The restaurant was like his personal supermarket. Over time she planned to skillfully address this situation as much as she could. Lily-Butterfly wrote in her large book everything from every list that she made. At the top of each day's entry was the date. The written entries in this large book was like a video recording of everything she planned to do and did for this condemned restaurant situation. Lily-Butterfly's first major intention was to investigate and get to the root of all the situations in the restaurant. Wednesday to Saturday Lily-Butterfly's discreet investigation continued and she seek help from many different employees when she needed to. She knew that the transformation of things in the restaurant was going to take the help of every employee.

Friday January 19, 1996 at 3:30 PM was the first Manager's meeting with Ema and Edna. They sat down in the dining room where they could observe the customer service. Lily-Butterfly's direct communication works well in professional situations. This communication style is going to be an essential tool in transforming everything in this restaurant situation. The aura of this style of communication is no-nonsense, does not take things personal, saves time, gives the real impression and picture, trust worthy, and straight forward. Ema and Edna did not know what to expect. They were worried about Lily-Butterfly finding out their participation in the mystery of the yearly missing financial resource of this restaurant.

The meeting began with Lily-Butterfly talking.

"Hi Ema and Edna thank you for being present at our first meeting. We will have a meeting every Friday at 3:30 PM. Do you have any question?"

"Ma'am, how long will you work as General Manager in this restaurant?" asked Ema.

"For as long as I choose to work here based on my complete experience."

"I see and understand. I admire your courage coming to fix an unfixable situation. No one in the history of this restaurant have been able to fix the problems. The issues of this restaurant goes back to the beginning maybe fifty years ago. Good luck. I do not recommend that you die or have a nervous breakdown trying to fix the problems. A dead hero does not make sense to me," said Edna.

"Edna, have faith. Be aware that I will not choose to die or have a nervous breakdown fixing the issues here. I need to have myself in positive health and well-being for my life and my two children's benefit. Okay. Sometimes miracles can happen. We will be working together as a team. I have the technical skills and I guide and coach everyone how to help. If we fail after trying our best then so be it. I really think that both of you have some of the solution to fixing the missing money problems of this restaurant. I am here as the General Manager to provide the skills to improve things. Today I will give both of you some of the awareness I discovered since Monday."

Ema and Edna glanced at each other.

"Yes ma'am. We are here to help. This restaurant mysteries seem interesting. We would like to help you. Tell us your discoveries so far," said Ema.

"Great. The first thing is rest assured that I will discover the many ways Managers and regular employees are stealing money and food. If both of you are guilty of stealing money, food, and anything else, work on breaking the habit. I can promise both of you that I will figure out how the money and food is mysteriously disappearing."

When Lily-Butterfly was talking Ema and Edna simultaneously looked at each other and down to the table. They were silent. Lily-Butterfly continued to talk.

"Starting next week Monday January 22[nd,] I will make a management schedule where each of you will have one day off per week. No more working seven days per week, plus overtime. Sorry that you will be making one day less pay. For work productivity, efficiency, health, and well-being both of you need at least one day rest away from work. Currently both of you work daily thirteen to eighteen hour shifts, seven days per week, overtime pay after eight hours, and double time on holidays. I am planning to hire six more Assistant Managers. When the management staff increases I will train both of you to become Certified Managers. After promotion you will receive a salary. This salary increase will compensate for the overtime pay. Both of you will have two days off per week and other benefits."

"Oh my. You will train, promote, and certify us as Restaurant Managers? Give us a salary increase. We will work only ten hour shifts and get benefits?" said Edna.

"Not only this. I would like the restaurant to make a profit each day, instead of losing money every day. If we can work together to make this happen we will make bonus. This means get a percentage of the profits."

"Wow. I did not know that a profit and bonus is possible in this restaurant," said Ema.

"I think the bonus can be possible if the food, supplies, and money is not mysteriously disappearing out the doors, and in employee's pockets and pocket books. Ha. Mmm. Money and food is being stolen like hot cakes from the registers, deposit, in employee's bags, pockets, and pocket books. The restaurant is like the employee's supermarket. The food, paper products, and cash from sales comes in and seems to disappear. If I sound like I am repeating some of the things I say, it is, because sometimes people might need to hear something more than once for the brains and senses to register what is being said. Do you understand?"

Ema and Edna looked at each other. Lily-Butterfly looked at their reaction.

"Ma'am you are straight forward and no-nonsense."

"Yes, this style of communication works best for me. Always ask questions if you do not understand something I say. I like to do a complete job. I am not perfect. I will do everything positive and possible to accomplish the complete and correct results. I like to sleep peaceful at night, have positive dreams, feel less stress, and not having to look over my shoulders. To me honesty is the easiest path. The quality of my work and reputation are two of the most valuable things that I have for my professional career and life. Do you have any special request regarding your work schedule? I will make the new schedule tomorrow."

"Keep my schedule the same as it is currently for the next three weeks. I have to prepare for any schedule changes," said Edna.

"The same for me ma'am. Please let us know how we can help you to fix the restaurant's problems," said Ema.

"Okay thank you. I will keep both of you schedules the same for the next three weeks. The on-going main focus is team-work, no stealing, and improvement of everything, and everyone," said Lily-Butterfly.

"Okay ma'am. Lead with motivation, inspiration, positivity, and care for us, and we will help in every way that we can," said Ema.

"I am naturally like this. We will help one another," replied Lily-Butterfly.

"Okay," replied Ema and Edna in unison.

"Edna you will continue to do the weekend inventory, financial reports, regular employee payroll reports. You must count all the food everywhere and the paper products, for real. No more bogus and guessing games with the reports. Monday mornings I will come in and redo the reports again, by rechecking everything that you did. This means recheck all your inventory counts. This way I am verifying that everything you did was correct. So, do all the reports once, make all of them real, you do not have to double check anything, and do not close out any of the reports. I will come in on Monday morning and recheck everything, verify, approve all the reports, close them out in the computer, and print every report. Sometimes it takes two people doing the same thing to confirm that it is correct. I will be at work every Monday morning by 4:30 AM. Starting this Monday, we will be using only the real and correct counted inventory of everything. I do not take things for granted and I trust what I experience and see. I do not give blind trust. I trust everyone and everything to be as they show up. At work I do not play, do personal entertainment, and make employees my friends. My perception and intention is, business is business. Do you understand me?"

"Are you serious ma'am about everything you have said?" asked Edna.

"Yes, Edna I am very serious. Would you like me to repeat the things I said?"

"No ma'am. You are serious and no-nonsense."

"Yes Edna. Call my style what you like. Okay. This Sunday report will reset everything as it really is. I will ask Carlos and Eddie to come to work on Sundays 6:00 PM to 10:00 PM. They will help you with the organization of all the inventory and the restaurant operation while you count the inventory. Start counting the paper products first. I will train them how to organize the inventory for easy counting. Start counting all the inventory count at 7:00 PM. You should be finished with the inventory count and most of the paper work by 10:00 PM. If you need Carlos and Eddie to stay longer, let them know. After the restaurant is closed you can complete the other reports. This weekend with putting in all the correct inventory, all the percentages will increase. This is what is needed to have the real view of what is really happening. I will not work here continuing the cycle of incorrect non-sense, and end up being charged with fraud. Mr. Watson is in for a surprise on Monday morning. He likes the fake figures, because they help him to cover is ego and not look terrible to his supervisors. Mr. Watson told me he sent me here to fix the problems. I will do this for real. I think that Mr. Watson thinks that I will fail. He might also have transferred me here to teach me a lesson. I will give him a big surprise. He is going to be the one to learn a lesson from this experience. This will be a surprisingly long journey for Mr. Watson and I. We will all learn from this journey and experiences. I will use this experience to awaken more of my talents and master them. The end result is that I will be improved for my spirit and soul's chosen destiny and life's purpose mission. Edna as an added bonus I will give you $180 cash Monday when you come to work; if you do the most correct work possible. Okay?"

"Yes, thank you Ms. Lily-Butterfly this extra bonus money is motivational. I hear everything you say, loud and clear. Say no more. I will do my very best work. I understand. Thank you as well for giving me Carlos and Eddie as extra help. This is great," said Edna.

"Thank you Ms. Lily-Butterfly. Since you have been here I feel less stressed. Take care of yourself. You might seem tough, but we know that you are doing the right things. Let me know how I can be of more help to you. I am ready to be trained, promoted, receive a salary increase as a Certified Manager. Start my training whenever you are ready. I would be going from a crappy un-certified Assistant Manager to a real certified Restaurant Manager. This is great. I am very thankful that you will give me this opportunity. This would be a real professional career asset. Oh wow," said Ema.

"Yes, Ema I will let you know when I am ready to start your training. First I will improve the restaurant operations, profits, and functions. This meeting is over for today. I am going home. See both of you tomorrow. Come prepared to participate in every meeting. Good night. Thank both of you for everything. Step by step we will arrive at the intended destination."

"Yes ma'am," said Ema and Edna.

The meeting was over and Lily-Butterfly left the restaurant. She arrived home and into the realm of her personal life. Saturday at work was another adventure, learning, and improvement opportunity for Lily-Butterfly.

64

Sunday morning came and Lily-Butterfly was off from work. She got up made breakfast and ate breakfast with her children. Lily-Butterfly felt confined, restricted within and outside herself, and felt like she had no more space to expand or move. She had many thoughts about her current work situations, challenges, and experiences. On this Sunday other thoughts that Lily-Butterfly processed were her children and their well-being, her personal life, looking for a place to move, Manana Leila's situations with Ms. Gina, Manana's possible dying, and wondering if she should continue to work in the Yonkers restaurant and transforming it. Lily-Butterfly also consider different options to create the perception of more space within and outside herself. Finally, she decided on doing one unselfish act of letting go, renewal, and paying the act forward to benefit someone else.

After cleaning the complete home Lily-Butterfly told Rebornstar and Holly that she was going somewhere in the next town over.

"Okay mama," said Holly.

"Where are you going?" said Rebornstar.

"When I return you will see. After I am finished with what I have to do in this town I am going to go visit Manana. I will be back home by 4:30 PM. Girls there are sandwiches in the fridge for lunch. Dinner is set up. Rebornstar supervise your sister. The furthest you are permitted to go is at the park in the back yard of the apartment building. I will return to cook dinner. Okay."

"Okay mama," replied Rebornstar and Holly.

Lily-Butterfly left home. She went to the hairdresser for an unscheduled appointment. She spoke to the hair dresser of her choice.

"I would like to cut all my hair off. Leave only a quarter inch, all around. Donate the hair to a cancer organization to make a wig for a child with cancer. Thank you," said Lily-Butterfly.

"Are you sure that you want me to leave only quarter inch. People wish that they have such great hair, and you want to cut it all off. You have beautiful hair with nice texture and everything else. Are you sure? Do you want time to reconsider?" said the Hairdresser.

"Yes, I am very sure. I thought a lot about this decision before I arrived here. Please listen and hear me. Do as I ask. Cut all my hair off. Leave only quarter inch all around. Donate all the cut hair to charity, as I request. I do not want to talk about this anymore. Thank you very much."

"Okay. Sit in the chair. I will do as you request."

Lily-Butterfly sat in the hairdresser's chair, relaxed, closed her eyes, took deep breaths, and meditated. When the complete hair cutting process was over the hairdresser let Lily-Butterfly know. She opened her eyes and looked in the mirror. All she saw was her complete face.

"Wow this is great. Thank you. I feel lighter, untangled, renewed, freer, and spacious. Thanks."

"You are welcome. Is there anything else?"

"No thanks. Now it will take me five minutes per day to do my hair. This haircut will save me time getting dressed on a daily basis and when I wash my hair. This is great."

"Okay. You are welcome."

Lily-Butterfly paid for her hair cut and gave the hairdresser a tip before leaving the hair studio. She got in her car and drove to Ms. Gina's home.

"I can see more clearly my face, head, and my authentic spirit and soul. I have a beautiful shaped oval face and perfectly sculptured head. Thanks to my Manana. Today I have chosen to shed my hair after thirty eight years. I am a renewed lily plant seed and caterpillar. It is time to rebirth, grow, bloom, flower, evolve, and uncover more of my talents. Lily-Butterfly buckle down and turn more within. Everything I want and need is within me. It is time for what is currently needed to come forth. This is good. Now, let me see what happens. People will now see me for me. My opinion is that previously people become distracted with the admiration of my hair. I see myself completely with new eyes. Let me see which man is going to think that I am beautiful with a quarter inch hair and say 'hi beautiful.' A renewed pathway is ahead for me. I have moved beyond the current crossroad. I will keep my hair this short beyond the discovery of the exact nature of expressing and practicing my chosen destiny and life's purpose. Good. Amin," whispered Lily-Butterfly.

Lily-Butterfly arrived at Ms. Gina's home. Ms. Gina was home. Lily-Butterfly walked into the house.

"Oh wow. Lily-Butterfly what happen to your hair? Before you acted over bearing, now this is the icing on the cake. You have no hair. You cut off all your great quality hair," said Ms. Gina.

"Ms. Gina time for everything. This is my new look, for a long time. This is my new no non-sense haircut. Now my head and hair cut matches my no non-sense and direct personality and attitude. People and I can see me more clearly. Now my face is like the full moon and mother-nature combined. Ms. Gina be aware, mindful, and wake up. One day you are going to want to hear my sweet voice and see my beautiful self, and you cannot. Anyway Manana, come let us go for a walk. I have to go home cook dinner and prepare for next week; for the children and myself. I have to be at work tomorrow morning at 4:30 AM. How I can do so many things is amazing. Come Manana. Ms. Gina we will be back in about ninety minutes. Enjoy your alone time. Come Manana I will help you put on your shoes before you get up from the couch."

"Okay Lily-Butterfly. You look interesting and unique with no hair," said Manana.

"Thank you Manana for your complements. Bye Ms. Gina."

"Okay miss know it all," replied Ms. Gina.

Manana Leila and Lily-Butterfly went for a long walk and to the nature park. When they arrived back at Ms. Gina's home, Lily-Butterfly went home. As usual on the way home Lily-Butterfly processed her experiences and thoughts.

"This day was the easiest day ever going to Ms. Gina's home to spend time with Manana Leila. Today Ms. Gina's vibes seem discreet. I think she is hiding something. Maybe it is the calm before a storm. My attitude is much lighter, and I seem to experience and process with less personal perception. My hair cut is working for me already. This is exactly the attitude, views, and perception awareness I currently need for my health and well-being. This current experience at work is going to be an intense and difficult journey. Oh well. Daily, I will make sure that I do not bite off more than I can chew. When the children see me when I get home they are going to be surprised. Human life can be interesting," mumbled Lily-Butterfly.

When Lily-Butterfly got home the children were at the park. She went into the bath room to wash her hair and take a shower. After washing, conditioning, and adding a few drops of coconut oil to her hair; her head was enveloped in beautiful small succulent curls. She looked at her head and smiled.

"I feel light, free, and renewed. What is next? I just have to wait and see. I am ready," said Lily-Butterfly.

Lily-Butterfly went to the kitchen to cook the Sunday dinner and organize all the meals that she plan on cooking for the week. At 5:30 PM, Rebornstar and Holly came home. They looked at their mother with surprise and an open mouth.

"Oh my, mama what happen to all your hair? You look like a monk. Are you okay? Have you gone crazy?" said Rebornstar.

Rebornstar walked over to her mother and rubbed her head.

"Mama, we love you. Are you sad? What happen? Why did you cut off your hair?" said Holly.

"Girls I am doing great. It is time for me to change something about me. This helps me to see myself differently. I cut all my hair off and donated it to charity. I felt too restricted and full with all the responsibilities I have to take care of. Now I feel freer and at ease. Plus, daily, this no hair saves me daily thirty minutes, and two hours when I wash my hair. Now I have one less important thing to do. After I wash my hair I am good to go. A trouble free and worry free hair style. Girls do you like my beautiful curls?"

"Yes, mama I love your curls," said Holly.

"Yes, mama they look cute and strange at the same time, because before you had so much hair. It is a good thing that you have a beautiful shaped face and head. Strange, but okay. I am going to telephone my friend and tell them. Oh my, mama, wait until the people at work see your hair. This is surely a drastic and strange appearance. I will be back. I have to call my friends," said Rebornstar.

"Girls this is the new Lily-Butterfly. Get used to my new look. In ten minutes, both of you wash your hands and come to the table for dinner. I have to get up tomorrow morning at 2:30 AM for work. By 4:30 AM I have to be at work. This time is my new every Monday morning work schedule. The other work mornings I get up at 4:30 AM and be at work by 6:00 AM. Take care of each other in the morning. Okay."

"Yes, mama. Okay. We understand. I will take care of myself," replied Holly.

"Yes mama. I hear and understand you. I am on the telephone. I will come to eat dinner in five minutes," replied Rebornstar.

Lily-Butterfly speculated that she would go through what people had to say the first time they saw her hair. From a lot of long hair, to no hair, was very obvious and strange. Monday morning, she arrived at work at 4:30 AM the restaurant was quiet except for the machines, equipment making their normal noises. The restaurant itself felt its normal creepiness vibes. Lily-Butterfly ignored the creepiness, turned off the alarm, and ventured into the restaurant. The lights she had turned on, suddenly they all shut off on their own.

"Hello spirit ghosts, calm down, and relax. I am not afraid. Leave the lights on. Do you hear me? At this time, I have enough things to be concerned about. Stop," announced Lily-Butterfly.

All the lights that she needed, she turned back on. The lights stayed on.

"Thank you very much," again announced Lily-Butterfly.

Lily-Butterfly went into the office and turned on the light. Next she turned on the computer and picked up the files with all the reports that Edna had prepared. She proceeded to check, recount, and process in the computer all the work that Edna had done. By 6:00 AM when Ema and the regular employees arrived at work Lily-Butterfly had almost completed all the reports. Ema came into the office, and yes she expressed her amazement at Lily-Butterfly no hair situation.

"Ms. Lily-Butterfly, are you okay? What happened to your hair? Why did you cut off all your hair?" said Ema.

Ema walked over to Lily-Butterfly and touched her head and laughed.

"Ema I am fine, except for my head being cold. It is time for a change. I felt like I needed some space, time, and many other emotional feelings. So, I figured out that this is one thing that I could do to help me feel better. I have to tell you that this hair cut did exactly as I wanted, intended, and much more. Currently the most annoying thing is having to answer to people's surprise about my hair and head. This is understandable. In a couple of days people's amazement and comments will diminish. One less time consuming thing for me to do. Before I felt stretched to beyond the maximum. Now I feel improved. I love and like my new hair length. My hair is now simple and easy. One less thing to consume my time and energy is positive for me; less stress. Ema, how are you doing?"

"Ma'am, I am doing great. I feel reassured now that I know that you are here to teach and guide us, plus take care of this place. Take care of yourself ma'am."

"Rest assured Ema that I will do everything it takes to stay positively balanced, not be overly stressed, take care of my health, and well-being. You can count on this. My self-preservation and self-care is part of my secret in arriving where I am currently in my life. My life's experiences and journey is a very interesting adventure. Anyway, enjoy your day. I am going to get back to completing these reports. Your sister Edna did an accurate as possible job with all the reports. I guess she takes me seriously."

"Yes, ma'am, she does. We are all happy that you are here. This place needs lots of care and work. Okay let me go to work. I will see you later," said Ema.

"Yes, Ema I will see you later."

Lily-Butterfly went back to completing the reports, using the correct inventory to prepare the food and paper order, and check in the food and paper delivery. At 8:00 AM she telephoned the food and paper order to the wholesaler. These orders were to be delivered on Wednesday morning. All the end of week reports were completed. But the percentages were very high compared to the percentage budgeted.

"Mr. Watson is not going to like the reality of these reports. He has to eventually accept them. They reflect the current truth of this restaurant operation. I have about thirty minutes before Mr. Watson arrives for the reports. I will use this real inventory to create a build-to for the food orders," said Lily-Butterfly.

At 8:55 Lily-Butterfly was sitting in the dining room eating breakfast and drinking tea.

"This is the calm before the storm. Soon Mr. Watson will arrive and he will not like the reality of the reports. Next it will be the busyness of the lunch crowd. After lunch the restaurant will look like a tornado had visited. All the employees will work together to prepare and clean everything for dinner. I will return after Mr. Watson leave to more transformational preparation, fixing information in the computer, and investigating what can be done to create improvements. The day will end with me leaving here and driving home in the busy traffic. Tomorrow is my day off. Wednesday I return to work and repeat the cycle again. Working as a General Manager in this restaurant takes technical, smart, wise, and hard work. The bigger the restaurant concept the more moving parts to manage. A dysfunctional restaurant operation like this one is like a long distance voyage ship without a captain and insufficient crew. Imagine what can happen on such a long distance voyage. Oh well, I will do my best work in every way. If things do not improve and Mr. Watson tries to treat me like crap, I am leaving," mumbled Lily-Butterfly.

"Good morning Lily-Butterfly. Are you talking to yourself?" said Mr. Watson.

"Yes, I am talking to myself. Talking to myself is good for my spirit and soul. Good morning."

"Are you ready for the meeting?" said Mr. Watson.

"I am as ready as I will ever be. Here are all the reports."

"Alright let me look at them."

"I will be back in five minutes," said Lily-Butterfly.

Lily-Butterfly went to use the rest room. When she returned Mr. Watson, face was pinkish. This usually happens when he is upset and overwhelmed. It is as if extra blood runs to Mr. Watson's face. Lily-Butterfly sat to his left side in silence and waited for him to speak. Mr. Watson looked up from reading the reports.

"Oh, my Lord. What the hell is this," said Mr. Watson.

"Sir Watson, the Lord and hell is not here. We are in one of your district's restaurant and you are reading the reports. I agree that this restaurant seems like hell. But what are you trying to say? What do you mean?"

"The cost of everything is such a high percentage. The food cost is 190%, paper cost is 80%, and labor cost is 185%. Is this correct?"

"Yes, everything is very correct. I suggest that you buckle up your seat belt to embracing the reality of this restaurant's situations. I cannot operate the restaurant with fake figures. You told me to come here and fix the problems. The budget percentage for this restaurant is food 30%, labor 25%, and paper products 5%. This means the budget says for this restaurant only maximum 60% of the weekly sales should use to pay all weekly bill expenses; including management salaries. Look at the fakeness that you have been supporting. Now you can see the approximate current reality of the restaurant you give me to fix. I have to bring the corruption and fake figures from where it is currently food 190%, labor 185%, and paper 80% to the correct budgeted percentage. It is going to take a lot of positive spiritual energy to perform the miracle of transforming this complete mess into improvements. Starting this week real ending inventory was used in relationship to everything. So, after the real inventory and total sales were put into the computer this is what the computer calculated everything to be. As the weeks go by everything should balance out to reflect the current true state of this restaurant's operation. This

447

week is like zeroing out the past and resetting everything. Let us hope that with time I can resolve where the food, paper products, and money from the sales of the food is going. Every employee that works here works forty regular hours and then sixty hours over time. This is why the labor percent is so high. In the past and up to today it seems as if everything comes in and just disappears, zip, zip, and zip. This is very dysfunctional. Sometimes I feel like I want to vomit, seeing and experiencing the reality of what you are asking me to fix. Know that first I will have to peel away everything that is not correct and establish the correct things. I am not going to create improvements on top of all this corruption. This restaurant operation needs about one hundred regular employees there are only eighteen sometimes twenty. The skeleton crew of regular employees are keeping the restaurant in operation, this is one reason for so many overtime. Starting this weekend, I guided Edna to do real physical count of all the food and paper inventory. Before the General Manager, Edna, and whomever else was putting fake amounts into the computer to get the percentage of everything they wanted to present. Everything was fake. I will not be a part of this fakeness. It will ruin my professional career and reputation. Write up all the past losses as you like. I kept a copy of every report I gave you for myself. This way, if you change the reports I gave you, I have proof of the real reports I gave you. I understand that it is hard for you to face your supervisors with this reality, but you have no choice. Tell them to financially write off the past figures and get ready to work with the reality of the restaurant. If you or anyone else want me to lie and present bogus financial reports, I will not do this, and I will leave. Plain and simple. I work very hard, intelligent, wise, and smart to be me; and to be able to do the quality work I can perform. I am not going to sell my soul. Sorry. Face the facts of this horrible situation. Tell your supervisors and the President of this company the truth. Do you want me to tell them for you?"

"Seriously, this is it? This is what I have to present to my supervisors and the President of the company? Ha," said Mr. Watson.

"Yes sir. This is the true reality. Plus, it is wise for me to show the real picture of this corrupt restaurant operation now. If I wait then it seems as if as a General Manager I help to create these horrible situations. This would not be positive for my professional career and reputation. I also made sure that I have a witness to all the reports and to also prevent conflict of interest. Edna is my witness and I am Edna's witness. First I made Edna do all the inventory and all the reports for real, before she left on Sunday night. This will happen every weekend on a Sunday night as long as I am the General Manager here. This morning I came to work at 4:30 AM. I double checked all the inventory and everything Edna did, then rechecked all the reports, approved everything, and closed out the computer for the week. I did all of this before the restaurant opened at 7:00 AM to begin the new weekly cycle. I am for real, and the reports are for real as well. I have earned being whom and what I am. Plus know that everything could get worse before they get better. Buckle up your pants belt to face the reality of the journey to fix this horrible place. Be ready for what you wished for and what you ask me to do. Be serious about doing your job correctly, and chose not to support corruption and lies."

"Lily-Butterfly how worse could things get? Ha. Mmm."

"Well sir, know that I will always do the greatest job. This week the percentage came out like it did. As the weeks goes on we will get a clearer and clearer picture of the financial situation here. I do not know for sure how the percentage will come out until I do the reports. Every restaurant has a natural rhythm. In reality I have to discover what this restaurant's natural rhythm is going to be. Since this restaurant was created in 1945, I do not think that any supervisor in the history of this restaurant knows the natural rhythm of this restaurant's performance. I might be exaggerating; a little. The employees in the past and present are stealing everything to the point of the restaurant annual reports year after years says minus two million dollars. I have to find and fix this minus two million dollars problem. Food, money, and paper does not have legs to walk or run out of this restaurant. All the employees, in the past and present, including regular employees, General Managers, Managers, Assistant Managers, District Managers, and all the employees of this company above the District Manager help to support and create what is currently going on here. I have a very good idea how the money is disappearing. It is going to take time for me to fix the issues. Every mal practice of restaurant operation was happening here. The reports I will do will always be real even if I look bad. Everything added up over the endless lying and corrupt years. I could write a book about everything. As time goes on I will give you list of things you are responsible to do to help me with the improvements here. Negativity and shi**yness sucks away positive energy. If these problems are not fixed, I cannot work, and become a part of this corrupt mess. My professional reputation is very important to me, it is priceless. I might sound repetitive and dramatic but my expression is really giving the real picture of this situation. You already know or speculate that I could choose to quit and find a General Manager job with less crap and get more pay. So please be mindful of my well-being and do not try to stress me out. Know that I am not a fool. Do not take my choice to be here as being afraid of losing this job. I am here because currently my instincts tell me that choosing to be here is the best thing. Why? I guess I will figure this out as the time unfolds itself. I sound like a broken record to myself. I have talked enough for this meeting. I think that you get the picture that I am trying to paint."

"Lily-Butterfly what do you need from me to improve everything? What makes you so strong and at the same time so feminine?"

"Thank you for your complements. Thank you for asking about helping. Who and what I am is a spiritual mystery? I am speculating you will not be able to understand; even if I explain this to you. So, I am not going to try to answer the question about my strength and femininity. Here is a list I was preparing to give you. It is not complete, but since you ask I am going to give the list to you. As time goes on I will give you an additional list. The list has one hundred things I need your help with. I have a list of one hundred and fifty three things that I have to do. We do not have time to go through the list together. The list is self-explanatory. Your list is made in the order of priority starting with the first thing on the list. I see that you are looking at my head. I cut off all my hair to match my focus, create ease, lightness, one less thing to consume time and energy, and to mirror my no-nonsense personality. No hair more ease and one less thing to take care of."

"Okay. I will take care of the things on this list. If I have questions or comments I will telephone you. I like your head with hair and without hair. Now, your face looks more outstanding. You have a perfectly shaped oval sculptured head and face. Your haircut looks nice, cute, and attractive. What else do we need to talk about for today?"

"Thank you for your complements. Look at the list I just gave you. This is at the top of the list; today I would like for you to approve that all regular employees eat one meal per eight hour shift for free. The total cost of this free meal will be $10 each. They punch out, go to the register, order their meal, the cashier rings up the mean, and the Manager cashes out the meal at no cost. These meal receipts are collected by the cashier and put into their registers. At the end of the cashiers shift the receipts are collected and added up. The computer will give a report of every free meal per shift and the food will be calculated on the computer. Right now, from my observation all employee steals food to eat and no food gets accounted for when this happens. With approval of free meals, this can raise the employee's morals and show them respect. Without the employee's cooperation and team work the issues here cannot get fixed. The stealing of food to eat has been going on for too long. It is easier to give them the food for free than to now force them to pay for the food. This is too big a restaurant operation to think that every employees is going to be honest and pay for their food. This will help us to account for some of the missing food and help the food cost percentage."

"Okay I agree. What else?"

"Put an advertisement in the local newspaper advertising for Managers and regular employees. I need six more Managers and eighty more regular employees. This will stop the over time that drains out the money and create high labor cost. I would like to buy new uniforms for every employees. Currently their uniforms look very old, dirty, and shabby. Each employee needs at least three uniform shirts. This is a restaurant and employee's clothes should be clean."

"Yes, I agree to all you just said. I will put the advertisement for hiring employees in the local and state newspapers, and get a banner to put in the restaurant window. You can buy all the uniforms and ties you need."

"Next."

"Fix the sewer plumbing leak in the basement. The sewer pipe from all the restrooms is broken in the basement. When there is a lot of usage of the restroom the sewer leaks out through the over loaded broken PVC sewer pipes. When this happens, the basement gets filled up with sewage and water of 3.5 feet or more. Go look, right now this is the situation. The sewage and water level in the basement sometimes come up about twelve inches from entering the main junction electrical box. This electrical junction box has uncovered wires. This could cause an electrical fire and other dangerous issues. Water takes a long time to drain out through the clogged floor drains. So therefore, I also need all the floor drains in the restaurant to be cleaned and cleared. This also helps with the washing of the floors at night. Currently the floors are draining so slow that they have to be mopped after washing. This takes additional labor. We need a new potato chopper. The current one is missing parts, chops slowly, blades are very dull, and the potatoes for fries are being chopped and produced at a slow rate. Juan currently has the potato chopper held together with wires that sometimes break. I need the company's handy man to come tune-up and fix the grills, fryers, walk-in refrigerators and freezer, and install a plastic curtain at all the doors of the walk-in refrigerators and freezer. This helps them to keep the correct temperature and assist with food preservation and the electric bill. Please pay for all these things from the company's maintenance and repair budget; not from this restaurant personal expense. Do not add these expenses to this restaurant non-existent financial cost. These things are first on the list I gave you. Everything on the list is important, but these are a priority I need done by next week. Thank you very much for your co-operation."

"Okay Lily-Butterfly. I understand. I am going to check the water in the basement before I leave."

"Okay sir. You look overwhelmed."

"Yes, I am overwhelmed. When I told you to come here and fix the restaurant I was intending and meant, I want the store to make more money and profit. I did not mean to really fix what was wrong and a problem."

"Mr. Watson this restaurant already makes a lot of money. It is going in the wrong pockets. My intention is to get the money we currently make in the right bank account and also make even more money. In the end you will be very happy with the results. My professional opinion is the problems must be fixed to long term improve sales and profits. Everything is connected. I think that you will even get promoted from the work that I will perform here. Really. Try to support and follow the architectural map I am creating for improving this hell hole, demon's lair, haunted, and dungeon restaurant. Trust my talents and skills. Another thing is, this restaurant is also haunted; especially in the basement. This is another whole level of issues that I do not think you want to know about. The restaurant needs an exorcism. Mmm. Ha-ha. Anyway, I took a picture of the sewage water filled basement and the water level close to entering the electrical junction box with the raw wires. The picture is at my home. I told my children that if the restaurant catches on fire and I am dead or injured this is what happen. This is for insurances and legal purposes. Fix this problem by next week. Juan told me that this issues is like this for ten years. Be smart and fix this issue; it is dangerous."

"I understand. I will ask my supervisor to approve money to pay for fixing everything that you request. I am afraid to ask if there is anything else. But, for today is there anything else I need to be aware of."

"The last General Manager that was working here, I heard that he is your friend. There was an investigation into him allegedly stealing money and food from here. I heard that he opened his own restaurant when he was hired as a General Manager for this restaurant. He orders all the food, paper, and everything else he needs for his personal restaurant operation on this restaurant's expense and then transport these things to his restaurant. All these expenses are added to this restaurant's weekly expenses. In creative and skillful ways, he also steals the deposits from this restaurant. He got caught and he quit. This General Manager's salary was $65,728 per year. My current salary is $49,400 for operating the mall restaurant that is 10% the size of this hell hole, makes per week in sales what this restaurant make in a day, and does not have any of these problems. All the problems in the previous restaurant I fixed. My annual review comes up next month, February. I need to be promoted to the category of General Manager to operate this restaurant. This is a sincere request. I would like to get at least the correct salary to work here. This would not even begin to pay me for all the work I have to do to fix and improve all the past created problems. Thank you for listening today to my immediate requests. Have a great day. I am finished for today."

"This is more than enough for today's meeting. I cannot discuss with you the legal issues of the previous General Manager. Your salary increase is maximum 3% based on an excellent review. I will read your complete list and do all the things I can. You have my approval for the things we talked about. I will get the handy man schedule to come here and work to fix everything on this list, I will look at the basement and attend to getting a plumber to come in and fix the PVC pipe, the floor drains, and any other plumbing work that is needed, and I will speak to my supervisors and the President of the Company about the percentages and everything else. At our next meeting on Monday I will let you know the results of the other things on this list."

"I am requesting more than a 3% salary increase. As long as I am working here I will do a complete job, this is my style and quality of work, and my quality of work will not decrease based on a salary increase. I could quit and go to another company and get more money than I am requesting here. If you insist on not doing what is right regarding my salary; I will leave you to karma. I will see you on Monday. Have a nice day. Bye."

Lily-Butterfly did not wait for Mr. Watson to reply; she got up and walked to the office. Mr. Watson got up and went to look in the basement and then left the restaurant. Lily-Butterfly put the files in the filing cabinet and used the restroom. After she went to help Ema serve the endless lines of customers, clean up after lunch, and prepare things for the dinner shift. At 3:00 PM Edna came to work. She commented on Lily-Butterfly's haircut.

"Why did you cut off all your hair?" said Edna.

"Edna I am so tired. I need to go home I have been here since 4:30 AM this morning. I cut off my hair to make it easier and save me daily time in combing, styling, and washing. Plus, I felt restricted and needed to make something lighter. Now I feel freer and my hairstyle reflects my no non-sense attitude and personality. To work as a General Manager is this store I have to be focused. Here is the $180 I promised you. Thank you very much for all your help. The reports and every inventory was complete and correct. Keep up the accurate work. I appreciate all your positive help very much. Every week you will do the same things with the reports and inventory every Sunday night before you go home. Good job."

"You are welcome. Thank you very much ma'am. You are welcome I will try to do my best. Please let me know if there is anything else I can do to help with the improvements here," said Edna.

"Okay Edna. I am going home soon. I am off from work tomorrow. I will see you on Wednesday."

"Okay ma'am. Good night. Relax and enjoy your day off. I will see you on Wednesday. Bye."

Lily-Butterfly said good bye to Ema and left the restaurant at 4:30 PM. This was another day in the journey of improving this restaurant. Lily-Butterfly- drove home.

"There has to be a very priceless reason that I was transferred to this restaurant. I think that it is to master my spirit and soul talents, plus other things that will reveal itself when it is time. It is going to take everything I can do to improve this place. When it is time to leave this restaurant, I will know. Until then I am here. Patiently I wait for the signal to leave to reveal itself. One pathway leads to another. The way will show me the way. Now I return to my life at home. I wonder how Manana is doing in the management of Ms. Gina? I guess I have to wait and see when I visit. Dear Creator thank you for everything. Amin," whispered Lily-Butterfly.

When Lily-Butterfly got home, everything was fine. The day ended with the usual activities.

65

Tuesday after grocery shopping, chores, laundry, preparing dinner, and eating lunch, Lily-Butterfly went to Ms. Gina's home to visit Manana. She arrive at 2:36 PM. Lily-Butterfly knocked on the door and Ms. Gina came to open the door.

"Hello Lily-Butterfly. How are you doing?" said Ms. Gina.

"I am doing fine. How are you doing? I telephoned you last night. You did not answer the telephone," replied Lily-Butterfly.

"We are fine. We were sleeping when you called."

"How is Manana doing. Where is she?"

"Mama is sleeping in the bed."

"Okay, interesting."

"Day, afternoon, and night when I need to; I start to give mama over the counter sleeping pills. She started to not sleep at nights and gives trouble day and night. The sleeping pills keeps her subdue and easy to manage. After mama's breakfast, I give her sleeping pills, and I put the pills in her lunch as well, so that she sleeps when I am not home. Before she goes to sleep at night I give her these pills. You told me not to tie her in the chair. The sleeping pill is the only other choice. This prevents her from going for a walk and forgetting where she lives. Safety first; right. But also, I think that the sleeping pills have screwed up her normal sleep cycle. Plus, at night mama walk around the house talking to an invisible presence. I need to sleep. I have to deal with these old people stuff at work and at home. I need a break. Enough is enough."

"Ms. Gina you have a lot to learn and wake up to realize. Do you know that when a human is preparing to die angels of death, and maybe a relative that has already died, come to accompany the person beyond this realm, and so on and so forth? Sleeping pills is not the solution to showing your mother unconditional love, care, and compassion. You are messing with her sleep cycle, spirit, soul, mind, emotions, body, and well-being by giving her sleeping pills. You have the patience to work with elderly strangers for money, but not your mother? Ha. You took all Manana's money. So, do you realize that you have paid yourself to take care of your own mother? Ms. Gina I find you incredible. Look at the complete picture of how you care for your mother since you choose to bring her to come live with you;

and took all her money. If this is how you care for your own mother I cannot imagine the things you do professionally when you are not being supervised. I think that you would treat your mother worse if I were not coming to supervise what is going on here. Really. I choose to love you without conditions, but I do not like a lot of things about you, for example your personality, and attitude. Honestly, this is the truth. You know how you are and you refuse to transform your negative ways. I am not going to accept you abusing Manana. I leave you to the Creator and karma. Ms. Gina I am watching you."

"You can talk and watch me all you want. I am going to put mama in a nursing home. Anytime you come here and she is not here know that this is what happen. I have already researched doing this. Okay. Seriously, this is the complete solution to mama, my care, your supervision, and telling me things I do not want to hear and listen to."

"Seriously, if Manana does not want to go to a nursing home; see this as the only things she has ever asked of you; all your life. Ms. Gina this is your mother's one dying request to you. Reflect on how much Manana has unselfishly done to help you; and make your life easy and effortless. Re-open your heart and conscience; choose to see the truth. You seem to refuse to see the mirror of your actions. I am telling you for the last time if you put Manana in a nursing home your actions will travel beyond the veil of this realm to the spirit and soul of the ancestors; plus, the Creator knows everything already. There are no secrets in this complete Universe. The karma vortex is always managing and supervising everything. The karma for this action you will surely reap before you die and leave this lifetime; and it will follow you beyond this lifetime. This is how serious this action will be. Mark my words Ms. Gina. My words are a cautionary awareness for you as well. Be careful with your selfishness. The mirror of your selfishness where Manana is concerned will be a boomerang effect. Be very mindful and careful, Ms. Gina. Give respect, love, and compassion to just this one view. It seems as if your perception of your personal life's experiences have blurred your spirit and soul vision, heart, mind, emotions, body, and life. It is as if you have de-sensitize yourself. Please choose to wake up. Stop giving Manana all these sleeping pills morning, noon, and night. You could cause an overdose and murder your own mother. Hello Ms. Gina. If Manana dies suspiciously, I am going to know that it could be a sleeping pill overdose. Be very careful."

"Ha. Lily-Butterfly shut up. You and your mumbo-jumbo talking. You are accusing me of overdosing my own mother. You are not my parent. Shut up. Go. Get out of my home. Do not talk to me. What happens to me when I get old and on my death bed is my own business. Get out of here."

"Why are you being so upset, angry, and defensive? You know that I am bringing to light things you are pretending to be unconscious of. Ms. Gina before birth, at birth, during my life, and now; I am not afraid of you. I am not leaving. My talking is not only to protect Manana but also to protect you. Maybe the ancestors and the Creator is talking to you through me; hear and listen. Do not poison the roots of your spirit and soul's pathway with your thoughts and actions. Wise words can be positive medicine for you. Ms. Gina choose to wake up and change your course of actions. Like you want, maybe these are my last words to you, because I could die at any time. Today or tomorrow is not promised to any human. Ms. Gina remember that you are here because of your mother, father, and the other ancestors before you. You choose to be born through them. They gave you the opportunity to be here for a reason. You choose to be born for a reason and purpose. This is the truth; even if you have changed your mind. You have a choice to change your mind; this life is your choice and journey. I think that after this lifetime you are going to end up being a more lost spirit and soul than you were born. It is never too late to choose to improve, take action, and practice the positive things you choose to transform, and change. I am speaking for you, myself, the ancestors, and the Creator. I am trying to help you to realize your ways. Maybe one day you might choose to transform them. Ms. Gina try to understand."

"I say shut up and get out of my home. You talk too much. You are wasting your time talking to me. Mama is almost 98 years old. She is lucky she lived so long with no problem, suffering, and health issues. It is time for her to die. Stop. Go."

"Ms. Mama Gina I am not leaving until I want to. Another thing, when does Manana eat if she is always sleeping from taking sleeping pills. Do you really realize what you are doing? Right now, the ancestors, angels, and Creator are seeing everything you are doing and being. They are giving you an opportunity to show respect, care, unconditional love, and compassion for the first and last time; to, and for, your mother. This will give you a priceless opportunity to repent and grow as a spirit and soul. Ha. Maybe this is a part of the reason and purpose that you choose to be born. This is a priceless opportunity I am intervening and giving you. Stop giving Manana sleeping pills morning, noon, and night. Stay home and take care of her. Now you made things worse by screwing up Manana's natural sleep cycle. If her sleep cycle goes back to normal, maybe you can go to work 9:00 AM to 12:00 PM and be back home for lunch. If Manana dies from a sleeping pill overdose this will be a crime. I will not lie for you. Re-think your actions, you will be responsible for the consequences of your actions. You should think about how your choices and actions affect your well-being as well. Anyway, if I talk more I would be repeating my words."

"Nothing is wrong with me. I am not doing anything wrong. Mama eats whenever she wakes up from sleeping. I spoon feed her in a sleepy state. This is okay. This is done in the nursing homes as well. This is okay. You are being overly dramatic and sensitive. Mama is almost 98 years old. She is acting 98 years old. I have no time and patience for her 98 years old crap. Simple. You are right mama has never asked me for anything. She has given me a lot of help with many things, unconditional love, care, patience, and so forth. This was her personal choice. If this was unconditional it means that I do not obligated to pay her back for anything. Everything is my choice as well. This is how I choose to be as well. Lily-Butterfly leave me along and let me be. Leave. Go home, your children are waiting for their dinner. Go now."

"Okay Ms. Gina, I am leaving. I love you. We know that you have your so-called free will to do what you choose. Remember free will is managed and supervised by karma. You will reap what you plant. When the karma of your actions come to the door of your spirit and soul I hope that you can remember this conversation today, and all the other conversations that we have had. We love you. We wish the best for you. Now I am going to talk to Manana and go home. Ms. Gina thank you for hearing my words."

"Good. Thank you for leaving me alone. You are not my boss."

Lily-Butterfly went to talk to Manana. She was still sleeping. Lily-Butterfly talked to her anyway. She knew that Manana could still hear what she was saying in her spirit and soul. Lily-Butterfly also trusted and felt that the Creator and angels were present. After talking to Manana Lily-Butterfly went to the kitchen to say one last conversation to Ms. Gina.

"Ms. Gina I am leaving. Make sure that Manana eats three meals per day. Stop giving her sleeping pills. Manana can choose not to eat, but you cannot choose not to feed her or give her food. Sleeping pills are not an alternative to not tie her to a chair or the bed. Sleeping pills is not a solution to care, attention, and managing the elderly and your mother. Choose to stop your nonsense actions. If Manana dies from an overdose of sleeping pills, I am going to report you to the police as the person who gave her the pills. Take care of yourself. We love and care about you. I am being warned to trust this process and not get in-between you and your mother's karma. I can help, but I cannot take your karma's energy actions towards your mother by getting in-between both of you, to prevent giving you the opportunity to show unconditional love, care, and compassion for your mother. This is one of the opportunities and reasons you were born to Manana. It is your choice to take this leap or not. All your life and currently the things that are going on between you and Manana and even me; are not an accident. This is real deep stuff. I could solve this issue immediately, but I am being warned to not do this. This is deeper than you think. Do the right thing or not. Know that this is your opportunity, spirit, and soul karma improvement test. Choose to let my words and awareness from the ancestors, angels, and the Creator be sacred messages and testaments. I sound like a broken record; but that is okay. Good night. Bye Ms. Gina. Amin."

Ms. Gina did not reply to Lily-Butterfly. She kept preparing dinner. Lily-Butterfly picked up her car keys walked out of the home and locked the door. It was 6:20 PM. She got home at 6:45 PM, had dinner with her children, and continued on with the things she needed to do before going to sleep.

Wednesday morning Lily-Butterfly went to work. The first thing she did was check the food and paper delivery. Next she entered the amounts into the computer. During lunch Lily-Butterfly helped Ema with the food preparations stations so Carlos could be a cashier. After helping with lunch and preparation for dinner, Lily-Butterfly returned to the office to continue with administrative paper work. She created a notice for all the employees and Assistant Managers. The notice said, "Every employee must use the time punch in and out machine at start of work, breaks, and on completion of work. Remember to punch back in after breaks. Effective immediately you will only be paid for the time recorded on your time punch in card. One FREE meal valued at $10.00 per five to eight hour shifts. If the meal costs more than $10.00 you must pay the additional amount. To receive employee meals please join the line and order like a customer. Write your name on the receipt and give it back to the cashier. YOU CARE - PLUS WE CARE -EQUALS TEAM CARE," Sign Management.

Lily-Butterfly put one of the notices on the employees notice board by the schedule, one on the wall beside the punch in and out time clock machine, one on the outside of the walk-in refrigerators and freezer, and one on a clip board in the Manager's office. Two extra copies of the notice were left on the desk for Ema and Edna to sign. These signed copies will go in each of their personal file. At 3:00 PM Edna came to work and she went into the office.

"Hi Edna. How are you doing?" said Lily-Butterfly.

"Hi ma'am. I am tired but otherwise I am doing okay."

"Okay. Please call Ema and come back to the office with her."

"Okay, I will be right back."

Edna returned to the office with Ema.

"Yes ma'am. What did we do now?" said Ema, laughing.

"Nothing negative. I would like to show both of you this notice. Read it and sign. This way you cannot tell me that you have never seen this notice. I will put the signed copies of each in your file."

"Sure. You are not easy ma'am. You leave no stone unturned; you trust what you see and experience, and you do not take anything for granted," said Ema.

Lily-Butterfly stayed silent. She watched them as they read the notice and listened to their comments.

"Oh wow, official permission for free food. You are smart Lily-Butterfly. Before the company's rules were every employee must pay for their food. No employee ever paid for their food, and we did not enforce this rule. It was easier to just let the employees steal the food whichever way they could. This way you are treating them with respect, they might care more about their job, and there is a more accurate accountability regarding the food and paper. Good," said Edna.

"Punching in and out each time ensures the accuracy of the time each employee worked. This way they are not telling us later that they forgot to punch in or out, and asking us to write in the hours that they are scheduled to work whether they work these hours or not. Less work for us. Now they must take more responsibility for their time worked or take responsibility for the consequences. Amin," said Ema.

"Good, everything both of you said are great reasons, please sign. Plus, employees stealing food to eat after they work so hard can create low motivation and morals, and low work self-value. If someone works in such a busy environment to make the place a success, having an approved meal says we value, care, and respect you. There will be a more accurate accountability of the food and paper products. Employees who do not care about the place they work can end up ruining the company. At the end of each shift when the registers are counted, staple the employee meal receipts to the cashier's register count report sheet. Each receipt must have the name of the employee written on the receipt. The cahier is going to need a Manager's key to ring up the employee meals. Do not give a cashier your key. You approve the employee meal transaction and write the employee's name on the receipt. This is a part of managing your shift. Effective immediately I will be check every cashier's register count report sheet and reference it with the employees on the schedule for each shift. This means there cannot be an employee meal receipt for an employee that did not work for the shift or for the day. Also check the employees and time cards per shifts. Make sure that the employees on your shift is punching in and out. You can no longer just write in a time someone leaves without getting my approval. Regarding this issues if there is an emergency and you have to write in the time, leave the card for me to check and approve. We can no longer operate this restaurant without accountability. At the end of every shift print the time clock report from the computer. This report will give you the hours used and the dollar amount for these hours. From this report write on your written report beside the total amount of money made, how many hours were used, and the cost of the hours used. We will now be able to easily identify which shift and Assistant Manager or Manager is wasting employee hours and money. For each shift the amount of money used to pay all the employees from the total cash made is maximum 25%. I will be checking that everything is being done correctly. This is a part of my job responsibility. At Friday's meeting we will talk about more new and interesting things. Do you understand?" said Lily-Butterfly.

"Yes ma'am. I understand. You do not miss anything. You have many ways to fix and check everything," said Ema.

"Yes Ema. I am just doing my General Manager job. A clear conscience helps me to be stress free, clear minded, and sleep well at night. Do you know how to ring up the employee's meal?" replied Lily-Butterfly.

"Yes ma'am, we do," replied Edna.

"Okay ladies, I am leaving for today. It is time to go home to my next job, which is taking care of my children and home. I will see you tomorrow. Take care of yourselves, the employees, and the restaurant. The transformation of this restaurant mess will take all our efforts. I cannot fix this mess by myself. Okay? Know that my journey of investigating the mysteries of the missing money, food, paper products, cleaning products, and the escalation of the employee hours, and pay check is an ongoing important project. Ema tomorrow morning you are going to help me go through every time card, for me to see if they are any fake employee or ghost employee; time cards. If you know of any fake time cards take them out right now, rip them up, and throw them in the garbage. No more checks are going to be submitted for fake or ghost employees. This is the time for both of you to come clean. Choose to transform all your negative ways and patterns or go to jail. The inside job of robbing this restaurant is over for as long as I am the General Manager here. I do not take professional stuff personal. I do what has to be done to get my job completed in the most efficient manner. Do you understand?"

"No ma'am. I do not understand fake and ghost employees getting a pay check," said Ema.

"I mean employees that used to work here, fake employees that have a punch card that never worked here, and employees that Assistant Manager or Manager created and punch them in and out. These time card hours are submitted for payment on the pay roll. When the payroll checks are delivered to the restaurant, an employee, General Manager, Managers, or Assistant Managers take the check and cash it in one of the cashier's register. The amount of ways employees steal in this restaurant is very creative and interesting. I am investigating; and I have a list that I will be correcting. Stay tuned. Another thing in two weeks no more employee checks can be cashed in this restaurant. This will come to a complete end. This is the way the fake employee and ghost employee checks are cashed. In this very restaurant. Oh yes. Right out in the open these fake checks are cashed. I am giving both of you the heads up signal that I know these things. If both of you are involved; choose to stop. I am giving everything and everyone a grace period to end the corruption. I am giving you the awareness that I know. We wise and end any and all corruption and stealing that you might be involved in regarding this restaurant. There is so much to transform in this place; that I could write two books. But I will not, because I would be showing people how they can be corrupt in a restaurant operation. That is all I have to say for now. More things to be said at our next meeting. Good job so far with all your efforts. There is room for much more improvements. Thank you for everything. Good night. I am tired. Bye."

"Okay. Now I understand very clearly. Oh wow. The entertainment party of corruption; is over. I see and understand. Good bye ma'am. You are interesting," said Ema.

"Good night ma'am. Thank you. Bye. Take care of yourself," said Edna.

"Thank you for your wishes. You can know for sure that I will always make sure I take care of my health and well-being. If I get sick or die, my children have no one else to count on. So, I have to make sure that I am okay."

Ema and Edna went back to work. Lily-Butterfly picked up her brief case and left the office at 5:30 PM. She arrived home at 7:30 PM. Rebornstar and Holly had already eaten dinner. Lily-Butterfly ate dinner and took a shower. The children had already prepared for bed and were in their room. Before Lily-Butterfly went to sleep she telephoned Ms. Gina's home. Ms. Gina did not answer the telephone. As usual before Lily-Butterfly went to sleep she wrote in her journal and prayed. Every day during the day she prayed as well. Lily-Butterfly prayer was no longer done mostly before going to sleep.

As the days and time went by Lily-Butterfly felt more and more improved in the expansion of her talents.

66

Thursday morning came. At 2:45 AM Lily-Butterfly laid in bed reflecting on her current personal and professional career life's experiences. At 3:00 AM she had to get out of bed and start the process of preparing to go to work.

"Life can be simple or complicated. Life is what I choose to make it. My perception is how I see things. Choice, action, responsibility, practice, repeat practice, transformation, and change can assist me in maintaining a positive energy vibration in my life. All energies need to be maintained. It is difficult for the human mind and body to value free things. The things I work to achieve I will naturally value more. I will reap what I sow. Oh well it is time for me to prepare for work. Lily-Butterfly, girl you are lucky. I have a lot to be grateful for. Thank you Creator for everything. Amin," whispered Lily-Butterfly.

Lily-Butterfly got out of bed and began the process of setting up the children's breakfast and getting dressed to go to work. The children were still asleep. She checked to make sure that the alarm for them to wake up was on. Next she looked at the two children laying in their beds and whispered in their ears.

"Remember to get up when the alarm goes off. Mama loves you. Take care of yourself. Mama will see you later. Bye."

There were no replies from the girls, but Lily-Butterfly felt that they heard her in spirit. It was 4:30 AM she left her home and walked to her car. Lily-Butterfly thoughts returned to her self-awareness, mindfulness, and self-motivated reflections.

"If I fail these children will also fail. Let me go on to work. Like Manana would say 'the Creator knows best.' Sometimes part of my life's destiny is like being a sacrificial alter for awakening my talents, growing, sharing with other humans, and learning many things that are known and unknown. Sometimes I am the last to know the meanings of the present experiences. Oh, my Creator keep giving me the wisdom awareness I need to perform my daily tasks, the courage to not collapse in difficult times, and taking care of my children and myself. Human life is a big responsibility. Creator I always try my best to stay close to your connection. Whether you are real or not, I think this is the most positive thing I can do. It is natural to believe in a higher power. In my spirit, soul, heart, mind, body, and life you are very real to me. To me you are the realest thing known and unknown. If I am wrong about these opinion and perception I have nothing to lose. If I am right this is very positive for me. My church is within and around me. Creator remember me in your daily to-do list. Here we go into another daily performance. People might think I am crazy for talking to you and myself, but that is okay," mumbled Lily-Butterfly.

It was now 5:30 AM and Lily-Butterfly was almost at work. The car's two head lights stared through the darkness of the morning, like two bright eyes helping the car and Lily-Butterfly journey safely to work. A work that seems to be one of the biggest challenges of her life's experience and journey. Lily-Butterfly arrived at work. Ema and all the employees were inside the restaurant. It was 5:55 AM. She entered the restaurant and went to talk to Ema.

"Hi Ema. Good morning. How are you?" said Lily-Butterfly.

"Good. I am doing well."

"How are the employees doing with punching in and out for work, breaks, and going home, officially eating at no cost instead of thinking they are stealing food, and ringing up their food like a customer?" asked Lily-Butterfly.

"Well, they like the eating for free, and being acknowledged by being treated like a customer. But as you might already suspect, they do not like to punch out for breaks, and loose an hour pay. Before they would never punch out for breaks."

"Ema money is a great tool and resource, but it is not everything, and the most important thing in human life. This is my perception and opinion. The employees need a break. This is good for productivity. Punching out helps the labor cost and the company to have money to have a business. This is a business. A part of a positive balanced team work is a win, win relationship. Quality of life, well-being, enjoying work life, is important as well. I wonder what is going to happen when I stop all the employee working overtime. Sorry that you and Edna have to do your job more efficiently, and work harder, by making sure that the employees, and yourself follow the correct company business procedures."

"I know that you are right and doing your job. But the employees seem to focus on their priority of making as much money as possible. They might quit when you stop the overtime. To them money, the overtime, and taking all the advantage of this restaurant, is their priority and focus."

"If they choose to quit after I stop the over time; this is their choice. This is why I will be hiring about eight more employees and six more Managers or Assistant Managers, as soon as possible. If they choose to quit I will have more than enough employees. These current eighteen to twenty regular employees will not hold me and this restaurant hostage. After I have increased the amount of regular employees the overtime will be over. The overtime money goes to paying the new regular employees. More employees give the opportunity of making more money. The customer service and speed of service is very slow. This is about ten percent, because of lack of training and not enough staff. I think that about forty five percent of the customers leave per day, because of the slow service and long lines. Ema do you know that this restaurant loses two million dollars every year? Food, money, paper and cleaning products come in and immediately goes out. There are many negative holes in this restaurant operation and we all are going to work together as a team to fix them. Okay."

"Okay ma'am. If you say so. I am happy to be a part of the solution. Come. I am going to the office to get the registers."

"Yes, I will walk alongside you. Things will not be perfect. There is a lot of room for improvements. I give thanks every day for you and your sister. I think it is a blessing to have the both of you to help me with all the negative situations that are happening here. I really appreciate all that both of you do. The only thing that might be difficult for both of you is to transform your negative habits. As soon as I can, I will be training you to be a certified Manager and promote you to a Manager's salary. When this is done you will not punch in on the clock any more. I will pay you more than the current pay working so much overtime, and you will get at least one day off to rest. This way you become more improved, productive, and experience less stress. Anyway, I have talked enough for now. Have a positive day."

"Yes, thank you for everything ma'am. I am going to put in these registers and open the door."

"I will come out to help you with lunch service. During lunch give Carlos a register as a cashier and I will do his work."

"Okay. Thank you."

Ema picked up the registers from the safe and left the office. Lily-Butterfly took all the reports from the previous day and studied them. She looked at the reports in the computer, checked the employee meal receipts, time cards, and labor report. Next Lily-Butterfly ordered uniforms for Assistant Managers, Managers, and regular employees.

After ordering the uniforms and ties Lily-Butterfly took the large book from her brief case and opened it. In this large book the next thing on her to-do list was to telephone the locksmith. She requested an appointment to put locks on all the walk-in refrigerator and freezer, change the locks on all the doors, including the emergency exit, and to fix the alarm on the emergency exit door. Lily-Butterfly discovered in her on-going investigation that this would help to decrease the activities of the stolen food, paper, and cleaning supplies. Lily-Butterfly did not plan to arrest, or directly confront and accuse any employee about stealing. All she had to do was find the root of the stealing problems, perform preventative stealing methods, and close the stealing opportunities, holes, and pathways. Plus, hold Managers, and Assistant Managers accountable to performing their jobs. After scheduling the lock smith Lily-Butterfly worked on updating the employee's files. Lily-Butterfly was finished with updating the employee files. She wrote herself a new to-do list from her large note book.

The to-do list said, "Friday talk to and confirm certified Management Training for Ema and Edna. Promote and train Carlos to be a Certified Assistant Manager. Invite regular employee Eddie to be promoted to Shift Supervisor. Investigate and find out how Ema, Edna, and employees steal money from cash register after it is collected. Observe cashier's system of operating the cash register, and retrain them. Tour kitchen to review issues for improvement. Find the root and source of all the flies in the kitchen."

Lily-Butterfly put the large book back into her brief case, put the new to-do list on a clip board, and walked to the kitchen. Breakfast time was over. It was currently 10:37 AM. One of Lily-Butterfly's intentions about the stealing problem was to tell the employees that she was investigating the many roots of the yearly missing two million dollars. This way they were aware and would choose to stop before they were caught.

Lily-Butterfly knew that Juan was also responsible for the missing money. But she was not going to confront him. Daily, at the end of Juan's work shift when he took out the garbage, he would take to his car the food and supplies he gathered from the restaurant. Lily-Butterfly felt that although Juan might deserve all he stole for his many years of service; stealing was not the way to go about compensating an employee for many diligent years of service. Lily-Butterfly was considering continuing Juan's overtime. She was not going to make it so easy for him to grocery shop in abundant supply in the restaurant; by stealing. She was going to promote him, so that he can make an increased pay. With this increased pay and overtime Juan could buy food at the supermarket; and so forth. Lily-Butterfly took the water boots from the office, went to tour the kitchen, and took notes. She needed the water boots to go into the basement. The basement still had some sewage water and it was muddy. Juan watched Lily-Butterfly as she walked around to inspect the kitchen. When she was ready, she talked to Juan.

"Hi Juan. Good morning. How are you today?" said Lily-Butterfly.

"I am fine. How about you?"

"I am going well. I need your help. You are the dictionary of this restaurant. Walk with me. Let us start in the basement. I will put on my water boots. Get your water boots. Go tell Ema to instruct Eddie to take over your duties until you return."

"Okay. I will."

Juan went to talk to Ema and Eddie. He returned to help Lily-Butterfly. Juan's water boots were close to the basement steps. Juan put on his water boots. They went downstairs into the basement.

"Juan what was the basement used for?"

"It was a place where extra food and other inventory was stored. Meat was cut up for the deli section of the restaurant upstairs, and other food preparations were done down here. Minimum two very mean supervisors worked down here with the employees. The walk-in freezer and refrigerator worked and were used as well. It was where they chopped potatoes in addition to the potato chopping station upstairs. Fresh hand cut fries is one of the signature food items on our menu. Previously, up to fifteen years ago, the restaurant was three times as busy as it is currently. It was the only restaurant in this area with the menu we serve. Every day the inside of the restaurant was like an indoor carnival. The company used to operate the game arcade. Now the game arcade is rented to a private contractor. Ma'am what else would you like to know?"

"Juan the things I am about to say could seem strange."

"Ma'am, and maybe not. What? Go ahead. Talk."

"The other day I came down here by myself. I saw two spirits. You know, I am talking about ghosts. Plus, I sense a very negative energy force. When I talked to these spirit ghosts, the light went on and off by itself. I sensed a lot of suffering negative energy imprints down here. The spirit ghosts look like they suffered a lot. I asked the spirit ghosts why they are here. The answer was a moaning and many snapping sound. It sounded like a belt or stick hitting an object or against something. I was wondering if I was hallucinating. I wondered if the work in this pit of hell restaurant had capsized my mind. Juan, what do you think, or know about this supposedly spirit ghosts, and negative imprint energy situation?"

"You are right ma'am. The restaurant is haunted. I see these spirit ghosts myself. This is a part of the negative disturbances and the curse of the restaurant not making any profit. Regarding this restaurant there are many negative financial problems and stealing. It is as if the employees are acting out the curses. Also, my opinion is the black hole, negative energy, and curses are part of the issue of the flooding of the basement, employees not staying, and so forth. All these things and more are a part of the restaurant's negative issues. I am surprised that you can sense all that you have said. I am the only one left here that knows of the past suffering and abuse of the employees. The employees were treated like slaves, especially the ones that worked in this basement. I was working here when two employees at different times, were beaten to death. I heard that before these two employees, another one died from a heart attack from abuse and over work. I used to be abused as well. The abused employees cursed the restaurant. This is why the union was brought in to help protect the employees. You are not imagining things. Your spirit, soul, and mind is actually brilliant. Ms. Lily-Butterfly I do not know if you realize that sometimes you glow. You are surrounded by light and negativity is scared of you. But do not stay here, try to reverse the curses, and end up sick, have a nervous breakdown, or heart failure. To hurt yourself to work here is not worth the effort. I often wonder why you chose to come do this work. My experience is, this company will suck the last bit of life force out of you to make money, and still want more and more. Their money greed is infinite. I do not think that you will be recognized for all the positive work you will be doing to improve this restaurant. My father used to work here as well. Working here he received a lot of abuse and suffering. God rest his soul; he is dead now. Ha. Mmm. What is next?"

"Thank you Juan for this history. This story is important and interesting. I am discovering the roots of all the corrupt, dark, and haunting energy I sense. Go on. What else do you know?"

"Sometimes the spirit ghosts come upstairs. I send them back down stairs. The root of all the bitterness and negativity of this restaurant is in this basement. Also, the land that the restaurant is built on was a cemetery. Before this restaurant was created in this building it was a failing casino. Can you imagine the extended roots of this restaurant situation? You are trying to fix an infinite black hole of negative horror energy. Be careful of your health. I would not like something negative to happen to you. You cannot completely fix this restaurant's problems. One spirit ghost is a young man, about twenty-three years old. He is shy and stays mostly hidden in the walk-in refrigerator. The other two spirit ghosts are angry and mean. I am not afraid of spirit ghost. Are you afraid? Be careful. What will you do?"

"No, I am not afraid of spirit ghost. Juan I understand everything you are saying. I do. I will think about this conversation and get back to you. Thank you for all the information. Do you know of a place in New York that I can buy sacred purification herbs of sage white incense leaves, frankincense, myrrh, juniper berries, rosemary, lavender, and sweet grass?"

"Yes ma'am. You know about this stuff? You are a woman of many talents."

"Yes Juan. This stuff is natural to me. Purification, healing arts, and so on, is in my spirit, soul, blood, and ancestral linage. To me a ghost is the spirit energy system of a person whose body has stopped functioning. Upon death this spirit energy system is supposed to cross over to the place beyond this veil. This place is sometimes called 'the other side.' Sometimes for many reasons this spirit energy system does not cross over to the other side. All energies positive and negative deserve respect. This is true for a positive or negative spirit energy system, called ghost. This is how I perceive and understand spirit ghosts. I am not afraid of them. I understand what is going on, and spirit ghosts can see that I understand. Fear is the biggest subtractor of everything. It is only up to the Creator God to judge or condemn. I will process this conversation, and see how I can and choose to help this situation, and the spirit ghosts. Maybe they will choose to cross over. This seems like a horrible situation."

"Yes ma'am. It is. What now?"

Lily-Butterfly took one hundred dollars from her pant pocket. She wrote a list of the herbs that she wanted to buy.

"Juan here is one hundred dollars. Please buy three portions of all these herbs on this paper. Keep the change. Bring me a receipt. Until I improve this negative vortex and spirit ghosts situations, I would like you to keep this conversation between the both of us. Bring me the sacred purifying herbs by Saturday morning. Let us go back upstairs.

This basement is the root of the negative energy hell hole infestation. Come. Let us go. Okay?"

"Yes ma'am. You are an interesting person."

"Juan I agree. I am beyond interesting. Thank you so much. I appreciate all your help. Juan you are a good spirit and soul. The Creator put you here to help me with this situation. We were meant to meet. I am going to need some help from you regarding improving all this negativity and curses."

"Okay. Let me know what I can do to help you. You are welcome. Let us go."

Juan and Lily-Butterfly went back upstairs to the kitchen.

"Juan another thing. Why is there so much flies in the kitchen? Where do you think they are coming from? Flies are a manifestation of negative energy, entities, and spirit ghosts. But there is also a root of the manifestation. I will find the root of these flies. It is in this kitchen."

"Daily I ask myself, where is the root creating these flies? I search and investigate. So far I have no luck in finding the source of these flies. Way back in the past, flies are usually a part of this restaurant's kitchen environment. I have gotten used to them," said Juan.

"Juan this is a restaurant, it is not supposed to have flies, much less this many. This is not a positive sign of food sanitation. I am going to find the root."

"How?"

"I am going to use my instincts."

"Wow. Can you. This would be great. All these years I wished that I could solve this problem."

"Juan can you show me the spot or room in this kitchen where the most negative actions to employee and suffering happened?"

"Come, over here in this room is one spot. The room is empty except for this long metal table against the wall. This room is also where I keep the collection of garbage to go outside to the dumpster. Another place is over in the main kitchen by where the employee notice board is. Currently there is a long metal table against the wall. Before the metal table there was another double sink to wash dishes. If the employee washing dishes did not hurry they would get abused. They took out the sink because of plumbing issues, and created another triple sink where the current one is now."

"What is this long metal table used for? It is currently clean."

"This table is used for food prep."

"Okay let me track this fly situation. These flies seem sneaky. You would have no idea where they are really coming from. They seem to be just here. Okay flies the party is over. It is time to go. Juan give me a screw driver. I think I have an idea where the root and source of these flies are hiding. The flies themselves are protecting the source of their creation."

"So quick. You have located the source?"

"Yes, I added up all the information you gave me, tracked the situation, and found the possible source. Flies are intelligent creatures. If you notice they are not gathered around the source. Go get me the screw driver. I will show you."

Juan got the screw driver and returned.

"Here is the screw driver. What are you going to do?"

"Juan take screw driver, unscrew both ends of this table where the sink used to be, and lift up both ends of the metal table top."

"Okay."

Juan unscrewed both ends of the top of the metal table. The top of the table was shiny and clean. There was no swarm of flies in the area. Juan lift up the unscrewed end of the table top.

"Oh wow. You are right ma'am. Look. This is incredible."

Lily-Butterfly looked.

"Oh wow. There is about one inch thick swarm of maggots under the table top. Unscrew the complete table top. Pour as much bleach as possible on top of the maggots. This is the beginning of lightening up and improving this negative energy haunted black hole. Pour the bleach on the complete infestation, leave the bleach to soak in, after lunch you can clean it. From now on every Monday, Wednesday, and Saturday morning unscrew this table top and clean it with bleach. Okay?" said Lily-Butterfly.

"Yes, under the top of this complete twenty four feet metal table top is covered with maggots. It looks like crumbled flour. Unbelievable. All these years this remains unsolved. It was so simple a discovery. Hidden right out in the open. The top of the table was always kept so clean. Things are sometimes not like they seem. Good job Ms. Lily-Butterfly. I will take care of this. Go rest. Drink some water. Go sit down. It is almost lunch time. You have out done yourself already. You must feel drained."

"Yes, Juan I feel tired. I am going to wash my hands and face, and sit for a little before I go help Ema with serving the lunch crowd. Thank you. Remember to bring the sacred purification herbs by Saturday morning."

"Yes sure. I will."

Lily-Butterfly returned to the office. She sat down, drank some water, and rested her head on the desk. It was 11:45 AM and she was already tired. Soon she was going to help Ema with lunch. To Lily-Butterfly this Thursday seem like one of the longest day in this restaurant.

67

At 12:00 PM Lily-Butterfly went to the front service line to help with lunch and have a short conversation with Ema, Carlos, and Eddie about her intention of training and promoting them.

"Ema, Carlos, and Eddie each of you come to the office for about five minutes. Starting with Ema."

"Okay," replied Ema.

Lily-Butterfly and Ema walked back to the office.

"Ema starting today I would like to start your training to be promoted to a certified Restaurant Manager. Here is the training manual; study it. I will do some training with you each day when we work on the same shift. When I am finished with your training I will get the corporation Training Manager to come here test and certify you. With this certification you can work any restaurant of your choice. Currently I need your help in improving this restaurant."

"Oh wow. Improving all my restaurant skills is a great priceless opportunity. Thank you ma'am."

"I am going to train Carlos to be a certified Assistant Manager. For his training he will work mostly with me. You will continue to be the opening Assistant Manager and work by yourself when I am off on Tuesday and Sunday. Carlos will start to attend the Managers meeting on Fridays."

"Good, Carlos is very sharp. Good that you recognize this. He will be a great help to all of us."

"Yes, Carlos seems sharp, focused, and attentive. I can use all the help I can get. Today I am tired and drained already and it is only lunch time. Put the Manager's training manual in your bag. Go back to the front. Please send me Carlos. Do you have any question?"

"No questions at this time. Thank you. I will send Carlos."

Carlos came to the office.

"Hi Carlos I have been watching you work. You seem like a good employee."

"Yes, ma'am, I try my best."

"I would like to train and promote you to a certified Assistant Manager. When I have completed your training, I will schedule the cooperation Training Manager to come here test and certify you. You will work with me five days per week on my schedule. The other two days you will work with Ema and Edna on a mid-shift. Would you like to do this?"

"Yes. Yes, ma'am. Me. This is amazing. I do not speak too much English. Is this okay ma'am?"

"Yes, this is okay. I recommend that if you choose to improve your English Language you can go to school. I have been observing you as you work. I notice you help with every station, and can do everything well in the restaurant operation. You seem self-motivated, pleasant, a team worker, work with speed and efficiency, and seem to have a lot of common sense."

"I try my best with everything I do. I am grateful for everything. If you think that I can become an Assistant Manager, I will do my best. I wish to improve my life in the United States of America. I never dreamed that I could be given this opportunity. Thank you."

"Okay, sometimes wishes can become dreams. Dreams can be created by strong wishes. Do you have a car?"

"No ma'am, I do not have a car or driver's license. I take the bus every day."

"I recommend that you learn to drive and get your driver's license. If you have a car to transport you to and from work, this can be positive for a more flexible schedule. If taking the bus can work for every work schedule, this is okay as well."

"I will learn to drive and get a driver's license. After the driver's license, I will consider if I need to buy a car, based on my work schedule. I will also go to classes to improve my English Language skills. As an Assistant Manager I would have to communicate more with customers and employees. Improving myself is good. Thank you for the opportunities and encouragement to improve myself and my life. When does training start?"

"Training starts immediately. Here is an Assistant Manager training manual; read it. I will use this manual to train you. Everything is in this manual that you need to learn. If you need help with anything inside the manual let me know. When the Manager's uniform come in, I will give you three sets of Manager shirt and ties. You will need at least three pairs of loose fitting pants, black shoes, and black socks. Buy the pants, shoes, and socks as soon as possible. After your promotion you will no longer be a union member. Is this okay?"

"Okay about everything you have said. Thank you."

"Okay Carlos. Read the manual, study, observe me as I work, listen, hear, ask questions, be attentive, focus, learn from the information in the manual, do everything correctly following the company's policies and procedures, and follow as I guide you. I will teach you how to be my Assistant and Manager. You can learn a lot from me. You seem to have a natural instinct and use your senses very well. When I am finished with your training, if you leave this restaurant you can work in any other restaurant as an Assistant Manager or Manager. You will start attending our Manager's meeting in the dining room every Friday at 3:00 PM. Okay?"

"Yes Ms. Lily-Butterfly, okay. This is an opportunity of a lifetime for me. Guide and teach me and you will never regret it. I will study every free time that I have. Thanks again. Oh wow."

"Okay. Thank you Carlos. Go put the manual in your work backpack and go back to the front to work. Please send me Eddie."

"Yes ma'am."

Carlos left the office and Eddie came to speak to Lily-Butterfly.

Eddie came to the office. Lily-Butterfly from observing Eddie she can see that he could be a trouble maker when, and if he wanted to. He was also friendly with Carlos. She also observed that he was an efficient employee.

"Mr. Eddie welcome. Would you like to be trained as a Shift Supervisor?"

"Yes, ma'am. Wow. Thank you. Most times the Assistant Manager and General Manager used to see me as a trouble maker. Thank you. What do I have to do?"

"Well sometimes the best trouble maker can become the best employee. I notice your attitude and personality. One of the intentions of a trouble maker is seeking attention. So, when I train, promote you, and give you a salary increase as a shift supervisor, you will get attention from positive action and behavior. Choose how you want to transform your negative actions. I need positive actions to help me with the transformation and improvement of this restaurant. I need your help to accomplish my job. Plus, now you have to learn to set an example for the other employees, because you will become their supervisor. You will still be in the union. Do you understand?"

"Yes, I understand everything you have said. When does my training begin?"

"Your training begins immediately. Start with you choosing how you would like to transform your negative employee ways, listen, hear, and follow guidance without giving trouble, and set an example as a leader employee. Buy three new loose fitting black pants. You must wear black shoes and black socks. Come to work clean every day and act like a supervisor. Help the other employees to improve. As soon as the new uniforms arrive, I will give you three new employee uniform shirts. Do you know how to work in every station?"

"Yes. I know how to work in every station. I can use some improvements in some of them."

"Okay. When I work on the front customer assembly line, I will correct you when I see you do something wrong. Follow my guidance. This can help you improve everything you know already. There is not test, just keep improving everything I will show and teach you. You can go back to your assigned work station. Do you have any questions?"

"Yes, thank you for the opportunity. I have no question at this time. If I have questions I will let you know."

"Okay. Good."

Eddie left the office with a wide smile on his face.

At 12:45 PM Lily-Butterfly told Ema that she was going to work in the deli and seafood section of the restaurant. She felt that she needed more practice in this department. Juan saw Lily-Butterfly working in this department.

"Ms. Lily-Butterfly be careful when using the deli meat slicer. Remember to watch your left hand that it is not too close to the blade when you hold the meat to slice it. It takes a lot of practice to work safely with the meat slicer. People have sliced off their hands. Be very careful. Okay," said Juan.

"Yes, I will. I need practice. Today is a good day to start. Come and help me if I get busy."

"Okay, I will. Be careful."

Juan left the deli area and returned to the kitchen. There was a large order for pastrami, turkey, roast beef, and cow tongue sandwiches. Lily-Butterfly was doing great slicing these meat. A sandwich maker made the sandwiches. The last meat Lily-Butterfly had to slice was the pastrami. All of a sudden Lily-Butterfly felt a stinging sensation on the upper fleshy part of her left hand close to her thumb. When she looked the slicer and the counter was covered with blood. She stopped slicing the meat and looked at her hand. The fleshy mound on her left hand was sliced off and hanging at the top close to her thumb. Lily-Butterfly lifted up the flesh that was hanging and placed it back in the correct place. Blood was flowing down her hand to her elbow. She recovered from her surprise of cut flesh and blood and ran into the kitchen. The door to the kitchen was very close by. Blood was now dripping on the ground, her shirt, and pants. Juan saw the blood and ran towards Lily-Butterfly. By now the sandwich maker had told Ema what had happen.

"I told you. This slicer is sharp. It takes a lot of practice to manage the slicer. During lunch time when it is busy is not the best time for you to learn."

"Okay. I understand. Go to the first aid kit. Get me hydrogen peroxide, three of the largest band aid, and sanitized bandage. Use hot water from the coffee machine to sanitize a container. Put some hot water in the sanitized container and bring it to me. Wash two lemons with hot water, cut them with a sanitized knife, and bring me an unopened box of salt. Hurry," said Lily-Butterfly.

Juan rushed around gathering all the things Lily-Butterfly had requested. He placed them on a table beside Lily-Butterfly. She stood by the employee's hand washing sink. First she washed her right hand. After, she poured some hydrogen peroxide on the cut area of her left hand. It stung very much. Next she opened one of the large sanitized gauze bandage, placed it on the area, and put some pressure to stop the bleeding. Juan returned with the hot water, salt, knife, and lemon.

"Do you want me to telephone 911 for the ambulance? I think you need stitches," said Juan.

"No, I do not want the ambulance, stitches, or go to a hospital. Squeeze the lemons into the sanitized pan. Add one table spoon of salt. Add one cup of hot water. Mix this all together."

"Okay. I am mixing the things you requested," replied Juan.

"Oh wow. Ms. Lily-Butterfly are you okay. I cut the pastrami using a knife and completed the order for the customer. Juan here is the slicer. Use bleach to wash and sanitize the slicer, clean the blood off the counter, and the floor in the deli station. My Lord. Ma'am how much of your hand did you slice off? Let me see your hand," said Ema.

"Look. I slice off three quarter of the fleshy part of my palm towards my thumb. The bleeding is slowing down. Let me finish fixing my hand."

Juan and Ema watched as Lily-Butterfly worked in silent prayer. She slowly poured the mixture of hot water lemon juice, and salt into and over the cut. Next she use sanitized gauze to dry the excess mixture from her hand. Lily-Butterfly placed two of the extra-large band aid over the cut, and wrapped the hand in sanitized gauze. In-between the cut was the salt, hydrogen peroxide, water, and lemon mixture. The area stung as the lemon and salt soaked into the cut. The blood had clot, and the bleeding had stopped. Juan added another packet of sanitized gauze to wrap around Lily-Butterfly's hand and tied the gauze together.

"Amin," said Lily-Butterfly when the hand repairing process was completed.

"Ma'am are you sure you do not want to go to the hospital to stitch your hand?"

"Yes, I am sure. My body will stitch the two parts of my hand back together. I will be fine. I am used to the natural way of healing. I was born in a valley village name Yaj on the island of Kawomaya. There was never doctors and hospitals. We use the natural Creators way of healing. My body is used to the Creator, my spirit, and soul ways of healing. If I thought that I had to go to the hospital I would go. If my way does not work I will seek modern medicine help. I have nothing against modern medicine. I would like to try the ancient ways first. Okay. No worries. I heal fast. My hand will be healed as soon as possible. I thank you very much for your help. Can you get me a cup of tea and put about two table spoons of sugar in it, and stir? The sweet tea will help to balance the trauma and stress inside my blood and nervous system. I do not usually drink sugar, but now it is necessary. Thanks."

"Alright. I see many employee get cut from this slicer. One time an employee cut off his complete left thumb. He went to the hospital to get it stitched back on. Wow. Wow. I am going to get the tea."

Juan got the tea and returned.

"Juan thank you for the tea. Please remember to bring me the sacred herbs tomorrow, Friday morning. Plus, I am going to give you an extra $200 to buy me nine bottles of vodka. Bring me a receipt."

"What? Ma'am, are you going to drink all this vodka tomorrow morning before work?"

"Bahahaha. Hmm. I guess I needed to laugh. Hahaha. No Juan, I do not drink alcohol. I am going to give the vodka spirit as an offering to the restaurant and the spirit ghosts. I feel that the spirit ghosts want an offering. The energy in this building is dry, dense, and negative. A respectful offering is needed. I came here transforming a lot of negative energies they used to feed off. They seem to want an offering in exchange. They are not going to get any more of my

479

blood; or anyone else's blood. I am going to use all the vodka as a spirit offering. No more blood. Blood offerings conjure up more blood thirsty entities. Alcohol spirit offering calls in positive energy forces to counter balance the negative forces. Today is the last day for them to take blood and exercise their negative forces. Hello, entities and spirit ghosts of this restaurant no more blood spilling. Stop. Be calm. I come in peace."

After Lily-Butterfly said this the kitchen light turned off and back on, by itself.

"Ma'am, they seem to hear you. Oh wow. Did you see the lights went off and back on?"

"Yes. Spirit ghost can hear and understand."

"The spirit ghosts might not like all the positive energy vibrations that you bring. Today you took their platform of maggots and so forth. Do you notice that the kitchen does not even have one fly? I cleared, cleaned, and cured the maggots under the complete table top. After that all the flies left, zip, disappeared. Hu. Mmm. Unbelievable. Be careful ma'am," said Juan.

"Yes, I notice. After I got the bright idea to go work in deli on the slicer. My blood was an exchange for all they have to give up. This is the first and last blood shedding contribution. Mmm. I will give spirit alcohol offerings maybe once per month. Juan bring the sage, frankincense, myrrh, juniper berries, dried lavender, sweet grass herbs, and all the vodkas, tomorrow morning. Can you come to work at 4:30 AM instead of 6:00 AM?"

"Yes, I can be here tomorrow morning at 4:30 AM. What are you going to do?"

"You will see. I will give these suffering spirit ghosts entities an opportunity to leave and cross over to the other side, like they were supposed to do upon death. They need to choose to leave the building or stay in peace. I am not here to hurt anyone. I come in peace, care, and loving kindness. If they choose to stay. We will come to an understanding that as long as I am here they will be peaceful, and not disruptive and destructive. During the time of the restaurant operation they will stay quiet, out of the way, and be peaceful. When the restaurant is closed, they will have the freedom to wander around. Hello spirit ghosts. Do you hear me?"

Suddenly, the complete restaurant lights, even in the dining room, went off and came back on.

"Hello Ms. Lily-Butterfly they are listening and communicating with you. Oh wow. Are you afraid?"

"No, I am not afraid. Spirit ghost to me are just spirits and souls without a physical body. I respect them and they will learn to respect me. After a while they will get to see that I come in peace, care, and love. Thank you spirit ghosts for hearing me. Tomorrow morning you all will have an opportunity to cross over to the other side; or stay in peace and respect. Okay."

"Ms. Lily-Butterfly I think that you are working in the wrong career with your spiritual talents and gifts. Ma'am, do you know this?"

"Yes, Juan I know this. My ancient ancestors from my grandmother had positive energy healing talents. When it is time, I will leave this restaurant and discover how exactly to use my talents. I feel that I am getting closer and closer to arriving at this reality and destination. Daily I hear making money for people is not my destination for using my talents. Time and the Creator has the last word. Everything happens at the right time, and for a positive or negative reason. I am here until I am supposed to leave. Thank you so much for these conversations and for everything else. I will be fine. I am a spirit and soul survivor. Prayer, relaxation, and positive life force energy will assist me with the healing of my hand. Already I feel my hand getting connected back together. Beliefs can cure or destroy. I believe and know that my hand will heal. Do not worry. I will be fine. I am going home right now to rest, relax, and sleep. Juan I will see you tomorrow morning at 4:30 AM. Thanks."

"Okay Ms. Lily-Butterfly. It was interesting talking to you. Bye. Drive safely home with one hand. Rest your hand. Okay?"

"Okay. Juan you are a kind and good man. Thanks."

"You are welcome. Bye."

Lily-Butterfly went to the front line customer service counter to talk to Ema.

"Hi Ema I am going home to rest, relax, and sleep. I will see you in the morning. Take care of yourself, the employees, customers, and the restaurant. Time for me to rest and regroup. Bye. Say hi to Edna for me. Today was another great day in this interesting place. See you."

"Yes. Good night. Feel better. Take care of yourself. I will see you tomorrow morning bright and early. Bye."

Lily-Butterfly went to the office to get her brief case. She walked outside to her car, got inside, and drove home. At 5:00 PM she was home. The children were not home from school as yet. She took a shower with one hand, made some lavender and chamomile tea and drank three cups. As she drank her tea she reflected on all her day's experiences. After drinking the tea, she took a nap for one hour. The children came home and she prepared dinner. During dinner Lily-Butterfly told Rebornstar and Holly the story of her sliced hand.

Before going to sleep that night Lily-Butterfly wrote the stories of her day's experiences, and the insights she received during the day, in her journal. With more appreciation for her two hands Lily-Butterfly went to sleep.

The way is showing the way.

68

Sometimes the weirdest things are more-true; than not true. The truth of a fictitious story is much- stranger than the fictitious story. A story can tell infinite pictures. A picture can say many words.

Friday morning at 4:35 AM Lily-Butterfly arrived at the restaurant. Juan was waiting. She walked inside and turned off the security alarm. Juan came inside after she turned off the alarm. He carried in his arms a box with the nine bottles of vodka and sacred purifying herbs. Juan turned on all the lights in the kitchen and dining room. He walked to the kitchen with the box. Lily-Butterfly brought her brief case to the office. She put on her water boots and went to the kitchen to speak to Juan.

"Juan please unlock all the doors and open them wide. Use the metal knob at the bottom of the door to keep them open. I will get two old pots with handles. Come down stairs to the basement. Bring three bottles of the vodka with you. We have about one hour and fifteen minutes to complete the process I will be doing. We have heat detector alarms, so the purifying holy smokes will not set off the alarms."

"Yes, ma'am I will be right back."

Lily-Butterfly was mindful of not reinjuring her sliced hand. She found two pots, took the sacred herbs from the box, and divided all the dried sage leaves, frankincense, myrrh, juniper berries, lavender, sweet grass, and rosemary equally into each pot. She got the matches, picked up the two pots, walked towards the basement stairs, turned on the basement lights, and walked down the two flights of steps to the basement. Juan put on his water boots by the steps and caught up to Lily-Butterfly with the three bottles of vodka in his arms. Lily-Butterfly put the pots with the herbs on a table. With each hand over one of the pot she said prayers of protection to the Creator and the positive angels. Next she said the sacred prayer ritual to open and call the entrance side of the ascension portal, and guardian angels of the portal, for the spirit ghosts to cross over to the other side. Juan stood behind Lily-Butterfly with his eyes closed for the duration of all the prayers.

When the prayer rituals were complete they both said, "Amin."

"Ma'am. What is next? This place needs cleaning. Good. This is long overdue. Be careful with your hand."

"Yes, Juan I am being careful with my hand. I need my hand to improve sooner than later. I need to do this purification now, before there are more accidents."

"Yes, sure. This is interesting a General Manager with many spiritual talents, and material world talents. Hu. Hmm," said Juan.

"Thanks be to the Creator for creating me with these talents and abilities. I am only the care taker of all that I am."

The lights went off, and then it came back on.

"Oh wow, ma'am. The spirit ghosts are aware of what you are doing. Are you afraid?" said Juan.

"Good. No, I am not afraid. I am used to doing this and all the other spiritual things. The spiritual world is more real to me than the material physical world. The spirit ghosts might be concerned about what I am doing. I just have to present the energy of peace and positive energy, and they might understand that I wish them no harm. I am going to do these purification rituals, and then wait and see what happens. I cannot predict what will happen. We will see," replied Lily-Butterfly.

"Okay. What is next?" said Juan.

Again, the lights went off and then back on. Juan and Lily-Butterfly looked at each other. They looked at the light switch it was still in the on mode. An object crashed down inside the walk-in refrigerator. Juan laughed.

"Hahaha. Hahaha. Ma'am, I guess they know that you mean business."

"Oh yes. They know. They also sense no fear from me so trying to scare me is useless. I am not afraid. Fear attracts negativity. Love attracts peace. Peace creates calm and stillness. Turn off the light switch wait thirty seconds and turn the light back on. So, that they can see that I can do the same thing that they are trying to do to scare us. After you turn back on the lights bring me one of the broom at the bottom of the stairs by the door entrance."

"Yes. Okay. This is very interesting. Some things in life are only experienced once. For me, today is the day for such experiences."

Juan did as Lily-Butterfly instructed him. He brought the broom. Lily-Butterfly took the broom from Juan and turned it upside down. She held the stick part of the broom on to the floor. Juan watched her intensely. Lily-Butterfly banged the broom stick on the concrete floor nine times. After she put the broom down on the top of the metal table. She said another prayer and used both arms in a sweeping motion up to the ceiling of the room, to open a nine sided exit side of the ascension portal in the middle of the room.

"Juan stand behind me with both hands out to your side and with your palms turned towards me. Stand like this until I say I am finished. Okay."

"Okay. Oh yes. I will. Oh, wow, ma'am. I feel all the positive energies of your prayers. You should be a priest."

"Maybe later on in life. Are you ready?"

"Yes, I am more than ready."

Lily-Butterfly started to speak in a loud, firm, commanding, and reassuring voice.

"Hi spirit ghosts of people who have died here in this room and building. I understand your situation. Hear me now. I am here to work. I did not harm any of you. I am here to help all of you. Your participation is your choice. You have died a long time ago. You are now spirit ghosts. You have no physical body. Your physical body is gone. You do not belong in this realm anymore. Right now, I am here to give all of you the opportunity to cross over to the other side. The positive angels will show you the way. Go now if you choose to. I have opened a sacred portal of ascension in the middle of this room. Cross over to the other side where spirits of the dead should go. I will leave this portal open until 3:00 PM. At this time, I will close sacred space and the ascension portal. Choose to go through the portal today. If you choose to stay, do not do, even one thing to harm me or anyone else. Do not get in my way of success with the operation and improvements of this restaurant. I will treat all of you with respect, and do no harm to you. All of you will do the same for me. I come in peace, love, and spiritual help. You will not have any more of my blood or anyone else's; as an offering. No blood offering. No blood. I will give this building and your spirit ghost presence the respect of an offering of clear spirits in the form of vodka. Accept these offering of spirit vodka as a sanctifying baptism. Be sanctified in the blessings and purification of the Creator. Choose to cross over through the portal. Next, I will lighten this darkness and negative energy in this environment with sacred purifying herbs. Be blessed, baptized, cleansed, and choose to cross over. If any of you choose to stay in this building and basement, do so in blessings, love, and peace. All praises to the Creator. I am the facilitator. Amin," announced Lily-Butterfly.

485

After saying these words there was silence. Lily-Butterfly used the broom stick to bang eighteen more times on the concrete floor of the basement. Next she took the three bottles of vodka and sprinkled them around the complete basement, and inside the walk-in refrigerator and freezers. Next she lit the herbs in one of the pot. As she did this the lights went off and on twice. She stayed focused in the sacredness of the performance. When the herbs were lit enough she covered the pot and the flames went out. She uncovered the pot. Strong smoke poured out of the pot. Lily-Butterfly picked up the pot by the handle, using her right hand. She walked to the entrance door to the basement room. From this door she walked counterclockwise around the complete basement in a spiral formation until she reached the center of the room. As she did this she silently said cleansing and purification prayers. Next she went back to the same door and walked in a clockwise spiral formation around the complete basement until she arrived back at the center of the room. As Lily-Butterfly did the clockwise spiral she said prayers of blessings, success, and positive affirmations. During all of this the walk-in refrigerator and freezer doors were wide open. This way inside them could be purified and cleansed as well. Lily-Butterfly worked steadily, focused, and quickly.

"Okay Juan we are finished down here. Let us go upstairs. I will do the same thing I just did, in the complete upstairs section of the building. You will sprinkle the remaining six bottles of vodka in all the rooms upstairs. Use three bottles for the dining room, restrooms, and at the doors of every entrance and exit doors. Use two bottles for every room in the kitchen, walk-in refrigerator, and freezer, and the stairs. Use one bottle in the hallway to the office, office, and front service line counter section."

"Yes, I understand. I will."

When Lily-Butterfly was finished with the purification, cleansing, and blessing in the basement, she took the broom, pot with herbs, matches, and went upstairs. Juan took the empty vodka bottles and the pot that were used downstairs to the kitchen. She used the other pot of herbs to cleanse, purify, and bless all the rooms in the kitchen, dining room, office, and restrooms. Upstairs the broom stick helped Lily-Butterfly to make her announcements and prayers to the environments and spirits ghosts. While Lily-Butterfly worked with the herbs holy smoke; Juan took the remaining six bottles of vodka and sprinkle around every room in the kitchen, dining room, office, restrooms, walk-in refrigerator, freezer, hallway to the basement stairs, the stairs leading down into the basement, and outside every entrance and exit doors. Smoke was pouring out every door of the building and soaked outside into the darkness, around the building, and the parking lot. Even the neighborhood was getting cleansed and purified with the sacred, holy spoke from the herbs.

"Great job you did Ms. Lily-Butterfly. This is amazing. Go make some tea and sit down. You must be drained and tired. I will take the empty bottles to the dumpster and wash the pots."

"Yes, you are right Juan. I feel tired and drained. I will set up the tea and go change into my work shoes. Thank you so much for everything. I really appreciate your help. Really. Today I needed your help and company. Juan, you are a blessing."

"Yes ma'am. You are welcome. I had a fun and interesting learning experience. Thank you as well."

Lily-Butterfly set up the tea and went to the office to change the water boots to her work shoes. She wrote herself a note to go downstairs at 3:00 PM, before the meeting, to close the sacred portal of ascension, and the sacred work space, in the basement. She drank sixteen ounces of purified water, and went to pour a cup of tea to drink. Lily-Butterfly walked into the dining room. She sat around a table close to an open door. She drank the tea and intermittently rested her head on the table. It was currently 6:12 AM. Lily-Butterfly looked at her injured left hand it felt okay. She was very mindful about using her left hand during the complete process. Juan made a pot of coffee, poured himself a cup, and went into the kitchen to drink it. All the restaurant doors were still open. Ema came into the restaurant with the employees.

"Good morning, Ms. Lily-Butterfly," said Ema.

"Good morning Ema. Did you smell the sacred purifying herbs from outside?"

"Yes. I could smell it before I got to the building. I smell sage, frankincense, myrrh, and so on. I did not know that you were a priestess. Hahaha. Ma'am, you are full of surprises."

"I think in many ways I am a priestess. This is so normal I do not think of it as anything unusual. I did a sacred cleansing, purification, and blessing ceremony of the complete building and spirit ghosts. This can improve all the toxic vibration and help the spirit ghosts to cross over to the other side. It was a deep and complex process that I do not have the energy to explain. I hope the spirit ghosts cross over, or at least find some peace for their own greater good. No more blood is getting drawn in here. I am tired already. Negative and toxic energies can be draining."

"Oh yes ma'am, very draining. Be careful with your hand. Good that you found out about the ghosts."

"Yes, I found out about spirit ghosts. How come you did not tell me about them?"

"Hahaha. Ma'am I did not know that you believe in these stuff. Hu. Okay I have to go. We can talk later. Oh wow, purification ceremony this is a big surprise. I will talk to you later it is getting late."

"Okay Ema."

At 7:30 AM Lily-Butterfly closed all the doors in the restaurant and went to the office to continue on with her work schedule. She checked the food, paper, and cleaning delivery and entered the amounts into the computer. Next she did an inventory of food and paper products and wrote an order to be delivered on Monday morning. She called the wholesaler to place the food and paper products order. After she made a Manager and regular employee schedule for the following week. Lily-Butterfly observed that the cashiers and Assistant Managers needed a refresher's training on how to operate the cash register and take customer's orders. She made twenty four copies from the company's training manual about the correct cashier's operation procedures. Lily-Butterfly took ten of these copies out to the front counter to give to Ema to distribute to all the cashiers and herself.

"Ema you, Edna, and all the cashier must start today to practice the correct cashier procedures. You learn and teach all the cahiers. This is part of your job. The correct cashier's process helps to improve service, the line moves faster, and helps with professional customer service. Do you understand?"

"Yes, I understand. You are right. Currently every cashier makes up their own process. I will start today. Thank you."

"Okay, you are welcome. I am going to get something to eat and during lunch I will help with everything. My hand is injured, but I can help to make drinks, French fries, put the orders on the trays, and so forth. Still put Carlos on the register as a cashier. Give him a copy of the correct cashier's procedure."

"Yes, I will. Thank you."

Lunch went as smooth as possible. Lily-Butterfly helped with the cleanup and dinner preparations. At 3:00 PM Lily-Butterfly went downstairs to the basement by herself. She closed the sacred portal of ascension, and the sacred work space. The basement and the complete restaurant environment felt improved in many ways. Most of all the environment felt peaceful with less toxic energies. Lily-Butterfly did not notice any of the spirit ghosts. They had either crossed over to the other side, left the building, or hiding somewhere. Lily-Butterfly went back upstairs. Edna had arrived at work. Ema had told Edna about the sacred purification and blessing ceremony that Lily-Butterfly had done. This was the most recent gossip of the day. As the day went on the story took on many different forms. Edna was finalizing the preparation of the restaurant for the dinner shift. Lily-Butterfly went to the office to get her notebook for the Manager's meeting. She went to the dining room and choose a table away from the customers and sat down. It was 3:45 PM. Ema, Edna, and Carlos came to sit at the table with Lily-Butterfly for the meeting.

"Welcome everyone to our second meeting. Let us start with any questions, concerns, and comments," said Lily-Butterfly.

"Ms. Lily-Butterfly I heard about your ghosts paranormal cleansing, purification, and blessing ceremony. I did not know that you were a priest? You came so early in the morning and did this stuff. You are not afraid? Anyway, the place feels lighter and smells good," said Edna.

"No Edna I am not afraid. Sacred and spiritual things are normal to me. News seems to travel fast in this place. Something needed to be done. Every help can be useful. Positive vibrations can help with success and improvements. Edna and Ema, how come you did not tell me about the stories about the spirit ghosts and paranormal activities?"

"Well ma'am I did not know that you believed in these things. When I am in here late at night and I feel the ghost's presence I use pepper spray to spray where I think they are; especially in the hallway by the office. The lights go off and on repeatedly, things sometimes fly across the room, and pots and pans fall off the shelves in the kitchen. This is creepy, but over the many years I got used to the situation. None of us talk about it. This is why you see cans of pepper sprays in the office. I do not go in the basement. No way. Sometimes I feel invisible forces in the office with me. The pepper spray seem to help. Thank you for what you did this morning. I have heard many stories of what happened here in the past. Take care of yourself ma'am. You do not want to have a heart attack and die here from over work. Look, you sliced off a piece of your hand. What is next? Be careful. I hope that these ghosts are gone, and do not try to create any more blood shedding accidents," said Edna.

"I think things will be improved where the spirit ghosts are concerned. So, now our biggest problem is everything else that is incorrect. Is there anyone else that would like to say something?" said Lily-Butterfly.

"No," said everyone.

"Ema agreed to be trained and certified as a Manager. She will be promoted with a salary increase and no longer will be punching in as an employee. Edna have you decided to be promoted?"

"No. I would like to remain as an Assistant Manager on the clock, get paid overtime, and only work my current night shift; 3:00 PM to close. I will continue to do all the reports and inventory on Sunday nights before I go home. During the day I have to take care of my children and Ema's children as well. My niece comes home from school to babysit them and then I come to work. This is why I have to keep working my current schedule. Plus, I do not have a brain for complicated studies. No promotion for me. If you take me off the clock make sure that I get the same salary as I do currently on the clock. Okay. This is what I would like for me. Thank you very much."

"I see. I understand. Okay. I am going to train Carlos and get him certified as an Assistant Manager replied Lily-Butterfly. He will work my schedule so that I can train him. When he is certified he will work with me three days Monday, Wednesday, and Fridays, and the rest of his schedule he will work mid shift. I am going to promote Eddie to shift supervisor. He has already agreed to this promotion. Eddie will still punch in for work. Ema and Carlos I will train both of you to do the food and paper order the correct way. Soon I will start to interview applicants for regular employees, Assistant Managers, and Managers. The no cost employee meal program seems to be working well. Thank you for your co-operation in making sure that meals are rang up and employees use the time clock machine to punch in and out at the appropriate times. New uniforms for everyone should arrive next week. As soon as they arrive we can distribute them. Each full time employee will receive three new shirts. Part time employees will receive two shirts. All of you will receive three shirts and two ties. Please instruct all the employees to wear clean work uniforms. Make sure they are wearing black shoes at all times. Edna you need to buy new black pants for work. The pants I see you wear are worn out and shabby looking. Last but most important, you are aware that the food, paper, and labor percentage costs are very high. They must go down, or this restaurant will close down, and everyone would have to find new jobs. Be very aware of this. I am sent here to improve all the infinite problems in this restaurant. All the employees that work under this roof are the biggest creators of the problems. The cost percentage of food, paper, and labor must go down. To me this is a simple perception; for the restaurant to make a profit after paying all the bills all the many ways the money, food, and paper leaves this building must stop. Plus stop the wasting of food. Ema and Edna I have already made a list of the many ways the money comes in and seem to disappear on both of your shifts. These money disappearing acts must stop, or Mr. Watson will call the police to arrest the thieves, and the restaurant will have to close. Currently I have not shared with Mr. Watson the results of my discoveries about how two million dollars disappear from this restaurant operation annually. If the money disappearing act does not stop, I will give Mr. Watson the list of the things I know and observe. If I do, he will call a detective to come in here and investigate. The company board members and owners must have a good reason for keeping this restaurant open with this much annual money loss. Be warned. If any of you are participating in stealing, start to make yourself stop the habit. Do you understand?"

Ema and Edna turned and looked at each other. Lily-Butterfly continued to talk.

"I sometimes talk a lot, and repeatedly say the same things. When I stop talking that means action has taken over. If I seem caring, kind, considerate, and everything else you perceive; know that I am only doing my job as General Manager. I do a complete job and I do not take professional business matters personally. This means I will do what I must, to hold you and all employees responsible for their actions. When I graduated from high school, I also graduated from focusing on people as friends; and the word friend. I do not seek friendship in my professional career business. I am not getting paid to be any employees' friend. Currently, I do not like the word friend. Why? I perceive the word as fri and end, or fry and end. Genuine, loyal, and authentic adult friends are a rare thing. Know that I will not set myself up for someone to have negative corruption about me, to use it to fry my end. My opinion is friendship and business do not mix well. It took all the past General Managers, Managers, Assistant Managers, and most employees working here under the negative charade of being friends, to create the deep corruption, embezzlement, and disaster that was created here. As a General Manager of this place and making employees my friend can be a great disaster, end to my professional career and positive reputation, and create conflict of interest. The word friend can be used for many different charade and disguises. Without hesitation I will hold myself and every employee accountable for their actions. I am making my intentions as clear as possible. Know this about me. Ema and Edna, why when I talk about embezzlement, stolen food, paper, and money, both of you look at each other with surprise?"

"Nothing," replied Ema.

Edna was silent. Lily-Butterfly really knew the deeper meaning of her words.

"Effective immediately you cannot operate the register as a cashier unless it is absolutely necessary. I check every report daily. Every cashier is short ten to fifty dollars per shift. At the end of each week this adds up to approximately $2,100 or more. At the end of each year the minimum reported cashier shortage is $125,200. It is as if someone is choosing to take money from the cash registers, and this money is being reported as cashier's shortage. If this is real cashier's shortage, this would mean none of the cashiers can count; and they should not be cashiers. This irresponsibility in handling customer's orders and cash is not a part of being a cashier. These shortages are going to stop. First we will retrain the cashiers. This can help with making less mistakes with money, and taking the orders correctly. No cashier can have the Manager's key. You have to use your keys to make the corrections and not give the cashiers the key to make their own corrections. Starting tonight every cashier count their drawers before they start to work, and at the end of their shift. At the end of every shift if each cashier's resister is short or over two dollars they get written up. After three times they are fired. At the end of the shift the Manager does not touch the cashier's register unless the cashier counts and verifies the money first. The cahier must always count their register in the presence of a Manager at the start and end of their shift. Every cashier must use their own assigned register and not someone else's. A Manager cannot use a cashier's register. When the cashier goes on break, the Manager locks their drawer. When the cashier returns, the Manager unlock their drawer. This is the correct company's policy and procedure. All I am going to do is follow the company's policy and procedures for their restaurant operation. Know that this is what I am doing. I am not making up my own policies and procedures. Edna here is a company manual of all the company's policies and procedures. Read this manual completely and make sure that I see you following all these rules, operation procedures, and guidelines. You cannot be an Assistant Manager if you do not know your job responsibilities. Edna I am giving you the opportunity of not being certified and taking tests. As an Assistant Manager I will give you enough time to study, learn, and change your incorrect work practices. You must learn to perform your job responsibilities correctly. Edna please let me know if you need my help with your reading, studying, and transforming your incorrect habits. Do you understand? Is there any questions?"

"Take it easy Ms. Lily-Butterfly. You cannot kill yourself to fix this place. There is a lot of crap to change in this place. I do not want you go get sick. You are tough, strong, and I know that you are doing your job. Thank you for not confusing our mind by being our friend. This would give us mixed messages and confusion. I like that you are here. I will try my best to improve. Thank you for the manual. Please let me know if and when I do the incorrect thing. I understand everything you have said. Thank you for everything," said Edna.

"I understand. I know that you are doing your job. I will do my best with everything," said Ema.

"Carlos do you have something to say?" asked Lily-Butterfly with a sigh.

"No, I have nothing to say at this time. I am observing, hearing, and listening," replied Carlos.

"Carlos are you sure that you want to be an Assistant Manager? This job is a lot of responsibility," said Edna.

"Yes, I am sure. My opinion is doing the correct thing is easier than being uncertain and worried about doing the wrong thing. Being promoted and certified as an Assistant Manager is good for me and my life. It is like free college certification and professional career improvements. I am ready. Ms. Lily-Butterfly I understand that you are just doing your job. Thank you for everything," replied Carlos.

"Carlos you are welcome. Is there any other business or comment?" said Lily-Butterfly.

"No," replied everyone.

"Okay thank you for coming to this meeting and all your help. We will meet again next Friday at the same time and place. I am going home now. I am super tired and drained," said Lily-Butterfly.

"You are welcome," said everyone.

When the meeting was over it was 5:55 PM. Lily-Butterfly left the restaurant and drove home. She arrived home at 7:30 PM. The children had already eaten their dinner. Lily-Butterfly ate, took a shower, wrote in her journal, prayed, and went to sleep. Saturday morning was another day of waking up at 3:00 AM and arriving at work by 6:00 AM.

Currently the pathway of Lily-Butterfly's life's journey and experiences seem to be tiring, complicated, interesting, time consuming, and difficult.

69

In life one thing leads to another like chain links connecting to create a chain. This can happen with improved mindfulness if the person can let go their personal mind and physical limited control. Becoming unstuck can improve connection to the internal guidance system. To let go and go within can take many attempts, choices, responsibility, trust, action practices, transformation, and a non-judgmental attitude. When the internal guidance system can be followed, it can feel like a train ride on a train track taking you into the unknown. The unknown can seem scary. This unknown journey can also seem like being blindfolded. Trust and letting go can support an improved effortless journey. Resistance can make this train and train track journey much more difficult and longer. If the person gets out of the train, leaves the train, and train tracks; their chosen destiny might still find them on the new path they decide to take. Sometimes there are random and collateral events that can positively or negatively affect the journey. This can sometimes be experienced as driving on a highway and suddenly reaching a traffic jam, or being stuck in a very slow moving traffic. The best things on a human's journey is to learn to love yourself without conditions and to accept who and what you are. Try.

On Saturday the cashier's shortage decreased by twenty one dollars. Lily-Butterfly changed the music playing in the background of the restaurant environment to a more upbeat vibes, put flowers and plants in the dining room, and put a large vase with flowers on an empty part of the counter. She also decided that once per month she would ask Juan to purchase the nine bottles of vodka and sprinkle the vodka around the entire restaurant as an offering. Lily-Butterfly's cut hand was healing at a fast rate. She took off the gauze bandage, and only had a large band aid on the cut. This she changed at the end of each day. At the end of each day before applying a new band aid, Lily-Butterfly washed the cut with hydrogen peroxide, salt, and lemon mixed with boiled water. On this Saturday after Edna came to work at 3:00 PM and made sure she had all the things prepared for the dinner shift; Lily-Butterfly left the restaurant at 4:10 PM to go home. She decided that she needed to really rest, step back, and regroup.

Saturday night she also went to sleep at 9:00 PM. The children were still awake and playing in their bedroom.

Sunday morning Lily-Butterfly slept late and woke up at 9:30 AM. She made breakfast and ate with the children. For the first time Lily-Butterfly decided that she was not going to visit Manana Leila and Ms. Gina. Instead she was going to spend some time resting more, taking a salt soak, and give herself a massage. After breakfast Lily-Butterfly telephoned Ms. Gina to tell her that she would not be visiting for the day. Lily-Butterfly took the children to the supermarket with her to do the food shopping for the week. She returned and they put the groceries away. Lily-Butterfly set up the dinner for the day. They had a light lunch at 1:00 PM. At 1:35 PM Lily-Butterfly spent two hours taking a salt soak and massaging her complete body as she soaked in the salt water. After the salt soak and massage, Lily-Butterfly went back to sleep from 3:50 PM to 5:45 PM. She got up and made dinner. While making dinner she organized and set up the food and meal plan for the week. This Sunday night Lily-Butterfly completed all her day's activities and was asleep by 9:00 PM.

Monday morning Lily-Butterfly was at work at 4:30 AM. She entered the restaurant and turned off the security alarm. Walking to the office the restaurant environment felt improved to her. She entered the office, checked all the reports and inventory that Edna had done, and completed all the reports. Next she prepared the food, paper, and cleaning products order; to be delivered on Wednesday. At 6:00 AM Ema and the employees entered the restaurant. They set up everything for breakfast. Ema came to the office to get the cash register at 6:50 AM and saw Lily-Butterfly.

"Good morning Ema. How are you doing?"

"I am doing great. As long as you are here I feel more relaxed, and less stressed. Before you came ma'am I was responsible for everything, even when I did not really know what I was doing. You are tough on us, but you are right, and your presence makes me less stressed. Thank you. I have to go it is almost 7:00 AM. Time to open the doors. I will talk to you later."

"Okay Ema. Remember the rules. Are you reading the restaurant operation manual that I gave you?"

"Yes. I am."

"Okay, practice what you read."

"Yes. I will do my best."

"Okay."

Ema left the office with the registers. Lily-Butterfly continued with her office administration work and completing the payroll. The armored truck security men arrived at 8:15 AM to pick up the cash deposits like they always do every Monday, Wednesday, and Friday. When Lily-Butterfly was finished with opening the safe with the security men, giving them all the deposits in the safe; she went to wash her hands, went back to the office to get the file folder with all the reports for Mr. Watson, got something to eat, and made herself some calming tea. She sat in the dining room eating, drinking, and waiting for Mr. Watson.

"I still feel tired. Not stressed, but tired in my complete body," mumbled Lily-Butterfly.

At 9:02 AM Mr. Watson the District Manager arrived. He toured the restaurant and inspected everything on his own. He came over to sit at the table with Lily-Butterfly.

"Good morning Mr. Watson."

"Good morning Lily-Butterfly. The restaurant looks good. I like the plants, flowers, and all the improvements that you have done. What happen to your hand?"

"I was using the slicer in the deli department and it sliced my hand. An accident that I learned a lot from."

"Be careful. Deli meat slicers are very sharp and can be dangerous. It takes lots of practice to use one."

"Yes, I know. Practices always begins somewhere and takes repeat practices. Everyone says be careful. I was being careful. Thank you for your concerns. Anyway, what else? Here are your reports."

"Last week I put the advertisement for employees and Managers in the local and state newspapers. I just put up two large signs in the parking lot by the highway and at the back entrance door; on the glass. This week you should start getting people for interviews," said Mr. Watson.

"Thank you. I will direct any Managers who telephone me to the co-operate office for their interview. The company's management training depart and you, are responsible for giving me Trained and Certified Managers and Assistant Managers to interview. I am only responsible for interviewing, selecting, and training regular crew employees. I will do the company a favor and train only Ema, Edna, and Carlos.

When I am finished with Ema and Carlos's training I will schedule an appointment for the Training Manager to come here test and certify them. Edna is not interested in becoming a certified Assistant Manager or changing her schedule. My plan is to get a Trained Certified Manager to work with Edna on the night shift. Ema and Edna has been over worked like a tractor on a farm," said Lily-Butterfly.

"I know everything you have said. What else?"

"Please remember to purchase three plastic curtains for the walk-in refrigerator and freezer. The refrigerator needs two and the freezer needs one. As you know they help to keep the foods at the correct temperature and with the electric bill."

"Okay. You are right. Everything adds up to create the negative financial situation we have here. How was the percentage of everything in the reports?"

"Look at the reports and you will see for yourself. I am going to use the restroom and get some more tea. Would you like some coffee? I will be back soon."

"Okay. Bring me some black coffee."

Lily-Butterfly got up and walked away from the table.

"Thanks to Ms. Gina for all her dark arts and shadow boxing training. If I could handle the negative experiences from Ms. Gina as a child, and even now, and not lose my positive energy, spirit, soul, wisdom, Universal intelligence, and capsize down into hell; I feel I can handle negative situations and people. Things that do not kill me, I can choose to make me stronger. Creator keep helping me. Thank you for everything. Amin," grumbled Lily-Butterfly as she walked to the restroom.

Lily-Butterfly got her tea, the black coffee for Mr. Watson, and returned to sit at the table.

"Lily-Butterfly, these percentages are still very high. Food cost is 90%, labor 85%, paper cost 50 %. Where is everything going?"

"The last time they were food 190%, labor 185%, and paper 80%. This week these percentage have improved a lot. Instead of showing some appreciation for the improvement you seem to be complaining. I know that you know that the financial problems here are going to take some time to improve. If you, or any other General Manager can come and immediately fix the financial problems; for real, I will resign and find another job. As I increase the regular employees and stop the over time, improve the food waste, stop the stealing of food and paper, close the holes where the food and money are disappearing, and increase the sales; the financial problems will improve. Until then, I will be giving you the real figures every, and all times. I will not give you bogus reports. Remember, I keep a copy of every report I give you in this office, Edna is my witness to every report, and I have a copy in my brief case for my own personal protection of not being involved and implicated in a fraud. I am not afraid of doing the right thing. Doing the right thing is a longer path. But in the end it can give the best long term results. Know that complaining to me about the percentages every Monday morning is a waste of your time. Know that if I cannot improve these problems by August of this year; I am leaving. I do not want to be a part of an unfixable corrupt work situation. This can ruin my reputation and professional career. Look at the previous General Manager, he is being sued by the company, and investigated for being a part of creating these problems. Please ask the Personnel Director and Training Manager to send me as soon as possible certified Managers and Assistant Managers for me to interview. Thank you for listening," said Lily-Butterfly.

"I hear you. By the way I fired Mr. Miller the General Manager for the Livingston, New Jersey restaurant. I promoted Moneyca to General Manager of this restaurant," said Mr. Watson.

"Seriously Mr. Watson you promote Moneyca to General Manager. You do not notice that every restaurant she works in even for one day at least one deposit is missing? Plus, when I used to visit the restaurant to help improve them, I hear stories about Moneyca and incorrect cash procedures and cashing nonexistent employee's checks. I viewed the conversations as gossip so I never repeated the stories. Where there is smoke there has to be fire. There cannot be smoke without fire. Moneyca seems nimble with her fingers in the money missing department. From working in Mr. Miller's restaurant, my observations are, I think some of Mr. Miller's issue are being lazy, nice, laid back, friendly, casual personality, and trust people without them earning his trust. It is funny that the very person he trusted the most to operate the restaurant, being his confidant, and friend; told you negative things about Mr. Miller, ran the restaurant into the ground, stole the deposits and employee checks, gets promoted, and a salary increase from Manager to General Manager, to continue her negative ways. And Mr. Miller ends up being fired for not doing his job correctly. This is very interesting. This is why I will never be a friend to anyone where I work. I can only be a professional colleague to you, and every employee of this company. Mr. Watson please do not try to be my friend. Friendship in business and me do not work well together. I am not friendship material. Know that you will not get to fire me, because I will not accept friendship from you. I will just plain and simple do my job responsibility, and follow all the company's policies and rules. I notice when you feel threatened by my strengths you tell me about Mr. Miller, suspending, or firing him. I know my worth, the quality of my work, and I work to maintain the quality of my reputation. Know all of these things about me, and that I will not become corrupt to please your spoken or unspoken desires."

"Lily-Butterfly what do you mean?" replied Mr. Watson.

"After saying all I did, this is what you have to say. Mr. Watson you will find out what I mean soon enough; if you choose to. As long as I am the General Manager in this restaurant, just keep Mrs. Moneyca away from me and this restaurant. If she comes here to work the first rule is; she will not touch one penny of any money here. I also hear that she is your friend and creme-de-la-creme. I wonder why? In this company the news and grape vine is very active. I try to mind my own business; until someone tries to throw corruption in my lap. Learn that I will not play any games with my supervisors. Sir Watson please understand this."

"Lily-Butterfly I do not know what you are talking about."

"We will see, if you want to know and see. Time will tell. I just want you to know where I stand. One thing I know for sure is at the time when you sent me to Mr. Miller's restaurant to help fix the many problems in that restaurant, I saw many current checks for employees that no longer work there. The checks were requested on the weekly payroll. The checks disappear after a few days and they are cashed in the restaurant's cashier drawers. Moneyca was in charge of the payroll and doing all the reports. The checks were cashed on her shift. I worked on the same shift she worked. I did not see employees come to get those checks. Deposits show up missing in Mr. Miller's restaurant. My questions were how often does this happen, and for how long this is happening? Frequently deposits show up missing in the restaurant her bother is General Manager. Interesting. Okay, I have said enough. I do not think that Mr. Miller knows half the things that happen in his restaurant. You just promoted the culprit. All the proof is in the account department of this company. If you want to find out stuff, you will, if you do your job, and not be like Mr. Miller. Would you like to know the roots of why this restaurant is so dysfunctional, corrupt, and financially loosing so much money? Try, not to be threaten me in any way. I can hear the things that you are not choosing to speak. Please understand this. I do not like negative people, places, and things. I have enough things to improve here. The best thing for us is, we both do our jobs appropriately. Please help me with the list I have given you. Thank you very much. If you thought that I was going to come here, and continue with the corruption, you have proven your thoughts wrong."

"I do not want to know the root of the problems; just fix them. I will attend to the list you gave me. What makes you so strong, fearless, and tough?" said Mr. Watson.

"People like you. From a young age, I had a great negative dark arts human teacher, my spirit and soul, other unmentionable things, and so on and so forth. Today is the last time that I am giving you notice to not try to break me down and cross my boundaries. This would be a waste of your time, health, and well-being. Do not use stories of Managers you suspend or fire to subliminally threaten me. I did not think that you wanted to know all the issues in the restaurant that is under your supervision, that you sent me to fix, transform, and improve. Remember I know all the corruption that is going on in all the restaurants you supervise. It takes a network of friends to cover up such corruption. I will not be a part of this friendship charade gang. Okay."

"Okay. Say what you like. As you promise and intend to do; bring down the food, labor, and paper cost. Increase money sales and customer count. Stop the stealing of money and food. Improve customer service, cleanliness of employees and the restaurant. Train and promote employees and hire new employees. These are your stated priorities. Good. Do not hurt yourself. I need you healthy, alive, and functioning. So far I see all your efforts and improvements. Keep up the good and productive work. Hurry with all your improvements. I will attend to the list you gave me. Is there anything else you would like to say?" said Mr. Watson.

"No. I do not have anything else to say. In the future I will talk less and less. Have a great day."

"Lily-Butterfly you are interesting. See you next Monday. Do not get hurt. Bye."

"Bye," replied Lily-Butterfly.

The rest of the week Lily-Butterfly spent doing the same repeated work and improvement processes. In addition, for no extra pay, she decided to come to work an extra half day on Tuesday 6:00 AM to 12:00 PM to train Ema and Carlos. This meant that the time she used to spend visiting Manana Leila on Tuesdays became less. On

Sundays Lily-Butterfly still visited Manana. The experiences with managing Ms. Gina in relationship to her mother was a continuous and consistent management routine.

Lily-Butterfly continued to make the best choices out of the worst options. Her thoughts about moving her home stayed in the front of her heart, mind, and focus.

70

The weekend went by with the same routines for Lily-Butterfly and her children. Monday had arrived again. Lily-Butterfly got to work at 4:35 AM. She checked Edna's work and completed the reports. The sales and customer count have improved. The food cost was 70% and not 90% like the previous week. The paper cost was 40% and not 50% like the previous week. The labor cost had improved as well. It was currently 65% and not 85%. Ema came into the office to get the registers and Lily-Butterfly told her the good news about the financial improvements.

"Ema tell Carlos to come to the office and you come back with him as well."

"Okay ma`am."

Ema got Carlos and they both came to the office.

"Ema and Carlos your training will increase. The training is similar to what you currently do. But you will be learning to do the same things correctly, and following the company's policies and procedures. In addition to your daily training and studying the manuals, starting tomorrow, Tuesday and every Tuesday, I will be here from 6:00 AM to 12 PM to increase progress with your training. In six months, both of you should be ready for certification. Every Friday morning after breakfast shift, I will give both of you a mini test on everything you have learned for the week. The company's Training Manager will come here to give both of you a test, certify you, and give you a certificate. Do you have any questions?"

"No, I have no questions. I am studying, going to school to improve my English language skills, and learning to drive," replied Carlos.

"Good for your Carlos. Self-motivation and taking action can be very productive for your improvements and success," replied Lily-Butterfly.

"I am beyond ready to be certified. It is beyond the time for me to do my job correctly. I am studying and I observe what you do when you work with us," said Ema.

"Good for both of you. If the problems in this restaurant is not improved by August 30th of this year, I am leaving. The good thing for both of you is, if I leave in August and both of you are certified

Managers, and you would not like to work here anymore, you can go work as Managers at another restaurant company of your choice," said Lily-Butterfly.

"Good. Thank you ma'am. You are not easy, but you are an efficient General Manager as well. I really appreciate your respect, kindness, and everything that you do for us," replied Ema.

"Yes, I really appreciate everything you do for me. Just let me know what you need me to do. I will do my best," replied Carlos.

"You are welcome. Doing your best and making your best, better, is all I ask. We need all the help we can get to create transformation and improvements for the restaurant and yourselves."

"Yes, ma'am. Please let me know when and if you need my help with something," said Carlos.

"Ema you can go back to managing the shift. I would like Carlos to do something."

"Okay," replied Edna.

Ema left the office.

"Carlos I am going to teach you how to assist me with some of my work. This way you can learn more than the Assistant Managers training program, help me, Ema, Edna, and the restaurant. Ema already knows how to do the thing I will teach you. Today I am going to teach you how to do the food, paper, and cleaning supply order. Would you like to do this?"

"Yes ma'am."

"First thing is, go to all the stock rooms, walk-in refrigerators, and freezer and organize everything in individual categories. This makes it easy for you to see everything and count them. Everything has to be counted before you can make an order. I have the count of everything already from the weekend paper work, but I want you to do the count and start from the beginning. When you are finished let me know. I will come and check everything you did. Work as quickly as you can. Productivity means, how long it takes to efficiently and completely accomplish an assignment."

"Okay."

Carlos left the office to accomplish the assignment Lily-Butterfly had given him to do.

At 8:00 AM Carlos had completed the assignment. He called Lily-Butterfly to check his work. She did and gave him recommendations and corrections.

"Carlos next we will do one page of the food order together.

After you will complete the food order and do the paper and cleaning supply order by yourself. Ask me questions if you need to. I have made the orders easy by creating a build-to system. This means, I have used the information in the computer to tell me how much of everything the restaurant uses in-between orders. These orders are done every Monday, Wednesday, and Friday. Monday's order gets delivered on Wednesday. Wednesday's order gets delivered on Friday. Friday's order gets delivered on Monday."

"Are you sure that I can do this? What if I mess the orders up?"

"If you make mistakes I will show you how to fix them. In learning people can make mistakes. Every item you see, you count how much it is, write this amount down, and minus it from the amount the build-to says is needed. On every order sheet there are three sections. They are, build-to amount, inventory count available, and amounts to be ordered. I will show you for example, the build-to says I need to have one case of cheese. If you see half a case, you write down half a case under the section that says inventory count available, you write one case under the section that says amount to be ordered, because they do not sell half a case. If you do not order any, then we will run out and this would be a problem. The restaurant must have all the items on the menu, to be sold at all times. This restaurant has a large menu. Most of our sandwiches customers request cheese. There are solutions to running out of products. These solutions cost more money and more time. For example, if we run out of cheese we can go to the nearest company restaurant to transfer some to our restaurant. But they might not have enough to give us what we need. We can go buy a similar cheese in the supermarket. But this is much more expensive than the wholesaler. If we do not have cheese, we lose money, because we cannot sell the cheese the customer requests. So, a part of operating an efficient restaurant is to have in the restaurant everything that is need. The wholesaler that supplies the restaurant is the best place to buy everything that is needed. The wholesaler does not do a few items and emergency deliveries. Do you understand?"

"Yes."

"If the build-to says two cases of something is needed, and you have available a quarter of a case you write this down under inventory count available, and write down two cases under the section that says amount to be ordered. At all times It is best to have more than less. For fifty pound sacks of potato, if there is twenty bags in stock and the build-to says one hundred sack is needed order eighty sacks. You minus the twenty sacks in stock from one hundred. If I am doing the order to make sure I have enough I would order ten extra sacks, and make the order ninety sacks. This depends on if it is a holiday and so forth. One thing to pay attention to is, using the correct day build-to, each time you do the orders. For each order day the build-to is different. We will do one sheet together and you will do the rest by yourself. Okay."

"Yes."

"Here take the clipboard and order sheets. You write and I will confirm what you think each order should be."

"Okay. Yes ma'am. We do one page together. After, I will do the rest by myself. If I have questions I will as you. Okay?"

"Yes. No problem. Try not to worry. The first time with doing something might be the hardest. I am here if you need help. I am going to a meeting at 9:00 AM. If I am at the meeting and you have a question you can come and ask me. If you have completed the orders and I am at the meeting, leave the clipboard with the order on the desk in the office. I think that you will do well. You are smarter than you realize. Do not look so worried."

"Okay ma'am. I understand. Thank you for teaching me. I really appreciate all the things you do for me. I will do my best."

"Okay Carlos."

Lily-Butterfly did the first sheet of the food order with Carlos. Next she took the folder with all the reports for Mr. Watson and went to order some breakfast to eat. She sat in the dining room to eat and wait for Mr. Watson. Mr. Watson came.

"Good morning Mr. Watson, here are your reports. While you read them, I will go get some more tea and check on something in the office. Would you like some coffee?"

"Good morning. Yes, I would like some black coffee."

"Okay. I will be back in ten minutes."

Lily-Butterfly went to see if Carlos had finished with the orders. She checked the orders and they were correct. She called Carlos to show him how to call the wholesaler to give them the completed orders. Lily-Butterfly stayed a few minutes with Carlos to make sure that he was doing it correctly. After she went to get tea for herself and black coffee for Mr. Watson.

"At these Monday meetings I am no longer encouraging too much talking with Mr. Watson," mumbled Lily-Butterfly.

Lily-Butterfly returned to sit at the table with Mr. Watson.

"Hi. I am back. Mr. Watson do you have any question or comments. Everything has improved and the percentages have really improved. I do not have anything to say to you if you think that the financial reports I have presented is not good enough."

"I understand. On Thursday the Personnel Director is sending one Manager and one Assistant Manager here to you. Work with them and see how they do. Soon you should start to get people to interview for the regular crew employees. Here are some application forms that you might need. What else?"

"Please telephone the security alarm company and change the security alarm code. Every past General Manager and Managers have this security alarm code. The lock smith is coming on Friday to change all the locks on every door; including the emergency exit, and fix the alarm section of the door. Also, the locksmith will put locks on all walk-in refrigerators and freezer. Changing the security alarm code and locks, will help with securing everything within the restaurant, regular employee will have less access to all the inventory, and Managers can be more accountable. Retraining and training for Ema, Edna, and Carlos has begun. I will put one of the new Managers to work with Edna at night 3:00 PM to close."

"I will call the security alarm company before I leave and change the security alarm code. Good idea about changing the alarm code and locks. You are right every Manager in the past has the security alarm code and maybe keys to the locks. I have not changed the security alarm code since I became the District Manager for this company. I forgot to do this in this restaurant and all the others. I will get this done today. I am going to the office to telephone the security alarm company about this restaurant's alarm code."

"Okay sir."

Mr. Watson got up and went to the office. Lily-Butterfly went to speak to Carlos about the orders. Carlos had completed the process of calling in the orders and was currently working at the front counter.

"Carlos is the order process completed?"

"Yes. The person who took the order, read back the order to me, and everything was fine. Next time this process will feel more comfortable to me. You make the training process simple and easy. Thank you."

"Good, you find my teaching simple, and easy. Thank you. We will do this again on Wednesday and Friday by next week Monday you should feel more comfortable. I am responsible for doing the orders. Ema knows how to do these orders her way. Soon I will teach her the correct way. When you help me, I have more time available to do other things. Soon I have to interview people for regular employee jobs, and training them. My current job situation is an endless responsible job. I choose to come here and stay in this job because my instincts tells me that it will help me to awaken more of my talents, practice them, and refine and master my talents. This is one of the benefits I perceive I am here to achieve. At all times in life I perceive that I am a student. To be a productive teacher I have to also remain a productive student. This helps me to lead and at the same time follow. This keeps me teachable and open to being told what to do. One of human's negative mental deficiency is not liking to be told what to do. If a human does not like to be told what to do, it can limit their wisdom, intelligence, learning, and can create stuckness and many other limitations. Carlos, do you understand these spiritual ideas?"

"Yes, I agree with everything you say. I understand. I was born in the mountains of Peru, South America. I grow up in a very spiritual village of the ancient ways. Thank you for recognizing my true nature, spirit, and soul," replied Carlos.

"Okay, good. Yes, I see your complete potential, heart, spirit, and soul. All of this shows in your eyes. The human eyes are a mirror of the spirit and soul. Anyway, I have to go back to the meeting."

"Okay ma'am. I see you completely as well. Thank you," replied Carlos.

Mr. Watson returned to the table to continue the meeting. Lily-Butterfly went back to sit at the table.

"Here is the new security alarm code. I just reset the alarm. Only give the code to the opening and closing Assist Managers Ema and Edna; and not any new Managers. I did a quick tour. The restaurant environment feels much more stable and peaceful. The customer count, sales, all the percentages of food, paper, and labor have improved. Good job. Keep the improvements going in the right direction. Is there anything else you need today?"

"I did a sacred purification and blessing of the complete restaurant environment. This has created an improved stable and peaceful environment. The receipts for the items I needed for this process is in the petty cash. The vodka I used as a sacred spirit offering. The herbs were for the purification and cleansing ceremony. I gave Edna and extra $180 on the first week I came here. This was an extra bonus for car service to go home and to motivate doing the reports and inventory correctly. Doing all the reports correctly takes more time. These receipts are also in the petty cash reimbursement report. Currently Edna arranges her own car ride to go home. These receipts might look strange and out of the ordinary. Please remember to send the plumber to fix the PVC sewage pipe in the basement and the other plumbing improvements, and remember to send the handy man."

"Okay. I understand. Is that it?"

"Yes. I have nothing else to say."

"Okay. Have a nice day Lily-Butterfly. I am leaving."

"Thank you sir. Have a nice day."

Mr. Watson got up and left.

The breakfast shift was over and preparations were being made for lunch. Lily-Butterfly called Ema to come to the office. Ema came into the office.

"Ema I requested the security alarm code to be changed. Mr. Watson did the change. Here is the new code number. I have ordered clear garbage can bags. We will no longer use black garbage can bags. With clear garbage can bags we can see if employees are stealing the inventory by taking them out in the garbage cans. Every lock will be changed on all doors by Friday. Plus, locks will be placed on the refrigerators and freezer. The Manager in charge of the shift must make sure the walk-in refrigerator and freezer are locked at all times. From these refrigerator and freezer Managers will supervise the stocking up of the smaller refrigerator and freezers in the front and in the kitchen. The Manager in charge of the shift will only put in these refrigerator and freezers the items needed for the shift and relock these doors. This stock can be replenished as needed. Juan and every employee taking out the garbage will need you or another Manager with a key to unlock the emergency exit door and turn off the alarm. The Manager opening the door must check every garbage bag to ensure that stolen items are not in the garbage bags, wait by the door for the person taking out the garbage to return, and relock this door. All employees must leave work through the front. The back door will no longer be able to be open without the keys. All of these changes will improve the current and future employees and Manager's accountability. If a Manager or regular employee is caught stealing the police must be called and the person will be arrested. This is the company's policy."

"Wow, ma'am you do not miss anything. Good that the security alarm code is changed. It has not been changed since the last General Manager and even before he came. This place was really like an open flee unaccountable reckless market. There was no management and accountability. Wow. I will try my best to do my job."

"I am only doing my job. I will give Edna the new code when she comes at 3:00 PM. I am leaving work on time today. On Mondays I am supposed to work until 2:30 PM, but I never do, and today I am leaving by 3:30 PM. I still feel tired. Remember that I am coming here on my day off tomorrow 6:00 to 12:00 PM to train you and Carlos. Remember to use the new code in the morning. If employees choose to not stop stealing, soon they will be caught with the evidence. I already know what is going on with this stealing situations. I am giving every one the opportunity to stop the stealing. Okay."

"Okay. I understand everything that you have said."

"Okay I am finished talking to you, go finish preparing for lunch, and get something to eat. I am going to the kitchen to check in the Monday food, paper, and cleaning products delivery, and talk to Juan. I will come to help you with lunch when I am finished."

"Yes okay Ms. Lily-Butterfly."

Lily-Butterfly checked the delivery. After she talked to Juan.

"Juan I am going to officially promote you to shift supervisor. There is no test for this promotion and salary increase. You will still work the same schedule and overtime. You have been working in a shift supervisor capacity already. With the new promotion you will earn more money. This salary increase will be on your next pay check. Is this okay with you?"

"Yes, thank you ma'am. This is great and long overdue."

"I know. Next I have a few changes to tell you about the restaurant operation. The company has been losing two million dollars annually from employees stealing. The things stolen are money, cooked and raw food, paper, cleaning products, and food waste. There are some changes to help stop these issues and practice the company's rules and policies. The changes are, by Friday every lock will be changed; including the emergency exit that you take the garbage out of. This door alarm will be fixed. After Friday if you or another employee open the emergency exit without the Manager coming to unlock the door and turn off the alarm; the alarm will go off. So as of Friday, you will need one of the Manager to come unlock the door, turn off the alarm, check the garbage bags before you take them outside, and wait for you to come back in and lock the door. This is the correct company policy. Managers cannot give employees their keys to use. Starting on Friday we no longer use black garbage bags. We will use clear garbage bags. The walk-in refrigerator and freezers will have locks on them. Only the Manager will have access to these refrigerator and freezer. The manager will supervise and monitor the stocking of the refrigerators and freezers in the front and kitchen with what is needed for each shift. Managers must start doing their job correctly. You cannot leave work anymore through the back door emergency exit. You and all employees must leave work through the front section and door of the restaurant. If an employee is caught stealing the Manager is going to call the police. The person will be arrested. A plumber will come soon to fix the PVC sewage pipe in the basement, clean all the drains, and fix the plumbing issues. The handy man is also coming to make repairs. You are a great employee. Keep up the great work. This restaurant would be lost without you. Okay. Do you have any questions about the new changes?"

"Wow you are doing a great job with transforming the incorrect things here. I appreciate the promotion and the raise. Thank you. I understand."

"Okay thank you for everything. I am going to help with lunch."

Lily-Butterfly went to the office to put the items delivered in the computer, put down the clipboard with the delivery invoice, and went to help with lunch. She chose to make drinks, get French fries, sandwiches, and other things for the customer's orders. Plus, train the cashiers to take the orders and give the change correctly. At 3:00 PM Edna came to work and Lily-Butterfly had to tell her personally about the new changes and give her the new security alarm code.

"Edna I requested the security alarm code to be changed. Mr. Watson did the change. Here is the new code number. I have ordered clear garbage can bags. We will no longer use black garbage can bags. With clear garbage can bags, we can see if employees are stealing the inventory by taking them out in the garbage cans. Every lock will be changed on all doors by Friday. Plus, locks will be placed on the refrigerators and freezer. The Manager in charge of the shift must make sure the walk-in refrigerator and freezer are locked at all times. From this refrigerator and freezer, Managers will supervise and monitor the stocking up of the smaller refrigerator and freezers in the front and in the kitchen. The Manager in charge of the shift will only put in these refrigerator and freezers, the items needed for the shift and relock the large walk-in refrigerators and freezer doors. This stock can be replenished as needed. Every employee taking out the garbage will need you to unlock the emergency exit door and turn off the alarm. The Manager opening the door must check every garbage bag to ensure that stolen items are not in the garbage bags, wait by the door for the person taking out the garbage to return, and relock this door. All employees must leave work through the front. The back door will no longer be able to be open without the keys. All of these changes will improve the current and future employees and Manager's accountability. If a Manager or regular employee is caught stealing, the police must be called, and the person will be arrested. This is the company's policy. Remember to use the new security alarm code tonight. The old one will not work and might set off the alarm. Do you have any questions?"

"I hear and understand you. These company policies are great. But with so little employees at night I cannot be in ten places at one time supervising everything. This is more responsibility and work for me. These improvements are easier said than done. You have Ema, Carlos, Eddie, Juan, and more sensible employees working during the day than I have. Who do I have? A skeleton crew with half a brain. Hah. Following all these right procedures is impossible. This is the truth. You like directness, honesty, and truth. This is what I have to say. Ha. Mmm."

"Edna I understand how you feel. You are right about the amount and quality of employees you have. This is why starting on Thursday I am giving you a new Manager to work at night with you from 3:00 PM to close, and one Assistant Manager will work mid shift and leave at 10:00 PM. So now there will be you, a new Manager, and an Assistant Manager. Soon Carlos will work two mid shifts as well. He will be helping you until 10:00 PM. See, I got help on the way for you starting this Thursday. You will be the one with the keys and the security alarm code. You will be the one in charge of everything. Plus, soon I will hire new regular employees for cashiers and so forth. Is this good?"

"Hahahahaha. Wow. Hahaha. New Manager and Assistant Manager; thanks a lot. This will be a nightmare. These Managers will be clueless, brainless, and more work for me to manage them. This will be a big headache for me. After all the negative experiences I have had with General Managers and other Managers in the past, my optimism has died. They have all come and gone. Soon you will be gone as well. I do not recommend that you waste all your wonderful talents in this hell hole of a place. You should be a priest or something along these vibes. Try to leave here in one piece. How is your hand doing?"

"Edna you make me laugh as well. Thank you for asking about my hand. My hand is healing very rapidly. It is almost completely healed. I understand about the new Managers. Use them as best as possible. Do not let them touch any cash or do the register. Make sure that you are aware of security when new Managers come here to work. You are the only one that will have management keys. Remember these Managers are trained, certified, and the company has done background checks on them. But, I am still not ready to give them keys and security code. Maybe they will quit after experiencing the business and situations here. As a Manager working in a restaurant like this one, they have to have great multitasking skills, focus, and concentration. Let us wait and see how they work. Keep me informed of their work performance. Leave me written notes in the Manager's log book. Do your best job possible. During the day shift we will train the new regular employees before I schedule them on the night shift. This way they are trained when they work with you. I am the one who has the responsibility of everyone and everything in this restaurant to account for. We will see how they work, and how long these new people last. Edna cheer up, so called help is on its way. Hahaha. Oh wow."

"Hahaha. We will see. Training the new regular employees during the day is great, thanks. Maybe after working with me on Thursday night, the Managers will both quit. I have no time to baby sit Managers, and show them how to do their job here. Plus, they make more money than me and have all the company's benefits. Let me go get the shift prepared for dinner. This place is very interesting. God help us all. Oh, by the way, I had forgotten to say thank you for solving the fly and maggot mystery, in the kitchen. It is great that we have no more flies like confetti parading and flying around in the kitchen. Thanks."

"You are welcome. Edna you are funny. Yes, maybe these Managers will quit even before the shift is over. Let me know at Friday's meeting how they worked. Please do not purposely give them a hard time. I am leaving, going home, now. I am tired. Every day I work extra hours that I do not get paid for. Anyway, good night. Do your best. Okay."

"Okay. Bye. Good night. Have a safe drive home. The roads are a little slushy from the snow yesterday."

"Okay I am not worried about the snow or slushy roads. Normally I drive slowly; snow, or no snow. Good night. Thank you for everything."

Edna left the office. Lily-Butterfly left work for the day. She arrived home at 5:56 PM. She had dinner with the children. They cleaned up the kitchen, dishes, pots, pans, and so on. Lily-Butterfly was the first one to take a shower that night. Before going to bed she wrote in her journal, and prayed. She prayed every day for most of the day. At night her prayers became shorter and shorter because of her everyday all day praying.

This night her only prayer was, "thank you Creator for everything. You know everything best. Continue to help me with my health, strength, courage, flexibility, understanding, and my ability to love unconditionally. Give me the signal when it is time to leave this current job. Until then I will continue to do my best with everything. Amin," prayed Lily-Butterfly.

71

Saying thank you, acknowledges you have received something of perceived value.

Tuesday afternoon Lily-Butterfly returned from work and training Ema and Carlos. When she got home at 2:00 PM she telephoned Ms. Gina to check how everything was going with her and Manana Leila. Ms. Gina answered the telephone.

"Hi Ms. Gina. How are you doing?"

"I am fine."

"Let me speak to Manana."

"She is sleeping."

"Is she eating at least three meals per day, snacks, and drinking water?"

"Yes. Yes, and yes."

"Are you giving Manana sleeping pills?"

"No. No and no. Are you my supervisor? I have been taking care of the elderly for over twenty five years; as my career. The things I do with my mother are things done in nursing homes. They might not seem humane to you, but this is the elderly and nursing home reality. When I put her in a nursing home things could get worse for her."

"Hello, Ms. Gina, maybe this is why she does not want to go to a nursing home. I can see that you are giving her the nursing home treatment and not a daughter's personal unconditional love and compassionate treatment. This is what you are supposed to do for your karma's sake."

"Lily-Butterfly please do not say anything to me about karma. I do not like when you say karma to me. I would like to get some money from you to help with the bills."

"You use all of Manana's money and now you have eyes on my money. You are interesting. To me your behavior is sad. How much money do you need?"

"I need $900 or more. I have to buy groceries, pay bills, and so forth."

"I am coming over there now to see what is going on. I am going to hang up the telephone now. I will hurry to the bank to get some cash before it closes."

515

"Okay. Yes sure. Now you are talking my language. I will see you soon. Bye."

Lily-Butterfly went to the bank and got $1,200 cash. She drove to Ms. Gina's home. Arriving there she knocked on the door and Ms. Gina opened the door.

"Hello Lily-Butterfly you got here so fast. Mama is still sleeping. Come in."

"How long is Manana sleeping?"

"About two hours she went to sleep after lunch. Since the sleeping pills she mostly sleep. Maybe to avoid me. Although I still give her two sleeping pills after every meal. The pills keep her calm and easy to manage. Plus, sometimes I need a break from her falcon eyes. Do not say one word to me about karma. You and mama think the same. We will see where these nice and positive thoughts get both of you in these modern times. In this country money and material things seems to be the most important thing. All the other nice stuff is secondary. Wake up to the reality of modern people and ways. This is not the valley and village of Yaj on the island of Kawomaya, where we did not use money; except outside the village. I need to go back to watching my television program. Did you bring the money?"

"Yes, I brought the money. You ask for $900. I am giving you $1,200. Go to the supermarket across the street, now. I will wait here until you return. Take the basket with wheels like you usually do. I will stay here with Manana until you return."

"One thing I know about you is that you are kind and wise. Good that you bring even more than I ask for. Okay, I will go food shopping to the supermarket across the street. Good."

"Hurry. I would like to see what you buy. I will talk to Manana until you return."

"It is interesting that you talk to Manana when she is sleeping. You are weird. Both of you are a chip of the ancient Universal block. Oh well, I am an ignorant spirit and soul with a lot to learn."

"Okay. Ms. Gina. I know that you are aware of everything that you choose to do. The one person you cannot fool is me. I will be here when you return?"

"Whatever queen of the Universe. I will be back."

Ms. Gina separated the money she plan to use at the supermarket, and put the balance in the bottom of her hand bag. She left the house pulling her cart on wheels. Lily-Butterfly went into the bedroom to talk to Manana and pray. She also looked around the home. There was food in the cupboards and refrigerator. The place was clean, Manana was clean, and her hair was combed. In ninety minutes, Ms. Gina had return with a cart full of groceries. Lily-Butterfly helped Ms. Gina unload all the groceries on to the dining table. From the table Ms. Gina put the food in the refrigerator and cupboards. When this was completed, Lily-Butterfly said goodbye to sleeping Manana Leila.

"Goodbye Mama Gina. Take care of your mother. I have accepted that you will be whom you choose to be, no matter what I say and do. I leave everything about you, between us, and between you and your mother to the Creator. After today I have put everything about this situation and us in the Creators hands. Ms. Gina everything about you is your responsibility. Regardless of who and what you are, we respect and love you without conditions. This is the foundation, awareness, and mindfulness of my actions towards you. We are giving you limitless hope, space, and time to, forgive yourself, choose to step outside the box of your shame and pandora box, repent, ask for forgiveness, and choose to transform your demons and negative ways. Until then I understand that you will be whom you choose to be. I wish for you all the best of everything. You are creating your own negative karma. I am leaving. Brightest blessings to you Ms. Gina. I am going home to continue on with my situations and life. Take care of yourself and your mother. I will see you again. Bye."

"Bye. The money you gave me was very generous of you. See you when you return. I am going to make dinner now while I watch my television program."

Lily-Butterfly left Ms. Gina's home and drove to the supermarket close to her home. She did some grocery shopping and went home. It was 6:53 PM when Lily-Butterfly got home. She parked her car and went to the park to get the children. They helped her carry all the groceries into the house. Lily-Butterfly finished preparing their dinner; and they ate. They carried out their usual end of day routine and went to sleep.

Wednesday at work was another of the same activities. Lily-Butterfly supervised Carlos with the counting of the inventory, creating the orders, and calling in the order to the wholesaler. Next she taught Carlos how to count the orders that were delivered and enter the amounts into the computer. Lily-Butterfly helped with lunch service and did some training and corrections during lunch service. Wednesday went by with many improvement and success. Thursday's work experience came with a new spin on things.

Thursday morning when Lily-Butterfly, Ema, Carlos and the other regular employees arrived at work. The new Manager and Assistant Manager were also waiting in their cars. They came inside when the door was unlocked and the alarm was turned off.

"We were assigned to come here to work. Good morning. Who is the General Manager?" said the Manager.

"I am the General Manager. My name is Lily-Butterfly. Good morning to both of you."

"Good morning. Hi," said the Assistant Manager.

"Today I will give both of you a tour of the restaurant. When this is completed you will go to Ema and help her prepare for breakfast and help with breakfast service. Lunch time you will help with the lunch service. After lunch, both of you will help with cleaning up and preparing everything for dinner. This way you will get even more practice and familiarize your selves with the food, station set up, and everything else. I will not give both of you a shift to Manage by yourself until you become familiar with everything and everyone. Okay. Is there any question?"

"No, I have no question," said Mr. Assistant Manager.

"Where is the men's room?" said Mr. Manager.

"The restrooms are to the left of the door you came in. First let me introduce you to Ema."

"Okay," replied Mr. Manager.

"Come with me. Hi Ema come and meet our two new Managers."

"Yes ma'am. Good morning. It is nice to meet both of you. Welcome. I have to go do somethings. I will see you later," said Ema.

"Okay Mr. Manager you can go to the restroom. Please come and see me in the office when you are finished. The office is at the end of the counter and to the right; behind the wall of glass."

"Okay Ms. Lily-Butterfly," said Mr. Manager.

"Mr. Assistant Manager please come with me to the office."

"Okay Ms. Lily-Butterfly."

They went to the office.

"Mr. Assistant Manager today you will work 6:00 AM to 5:00 PM. I will schedule you tomorrow Friday, Saturday, and Sunday on the mid shift which is 12 PM to 11 PM. You will have one hour unpaid break. Be at work fifteen minutes before your scheduled time to work. The closing Assistant Manager in charge will be Edna. You will work a minimum of ten hour shifts. Working mid shift, you will learn everything about the lunch and dinner service and everything else. This is the busiest time in the restaurant. Is this okay with you?"

"Yes, this is okay."

"I will give Tuesday and Thursdays off. Your regular work schedule is Monday, Wednesday, Friday, Saturday, Sunday 12:00 to 11:00 PM. Is this okay with you?"

"Yes, these days off are okay with me."

"Great. Welcome to the companies busiest and second oldest restaurant. You will learn a lot from working here. Have you completed all your training and certification?"

"Yes, I have completed all my training and certification."

"Please let me know if you every have a question or need my help with something. Ema, the Assistant Manager, is in charge of the day shift. Edna is available to help you as well. When Mr. Manager returns we will go on a tour of the restaurant."

"Yes."

Mr. Manager had gone for thirty minutes and still had not returned from the men's room.

"Please go tell the Manager that I am waiting on him," said Lily-Butterfly to Mr. Assistant Manager.

"Okay."

They both returned. Lily-Butterfly took them on a tour of the restaurant. When the tour was completed they returned to the office.

"Mr. Assistant Manager go to Ema. Ask her to come to the office."

"Yes, I will."

"Mr. Manager please wait here. I would like to talk to you."

"Okay."

Ema came to the office with Mr. Assistant Manager.

"Ema please use Mr. Assistant Manager to help with everything. That means all the things you would physically do, tell him to do it, and supervise that he does everything correctly. Do you understand? This means you are going to perform more of a supervisor role and let him perform the physical roles. This way he gets practice to get into the flow of service and everything that goes on here. We have no time for babysitting as Edna would say. Any Manager who does not want to get their hands dirty is in the wrong restaurant. Okay. Mr. Assistant Manager go with Ema."

"Okay."

Ema and Mr. Assistant Manager left the office.

"Okay Mr. Manager today you will work 6:00 AM to 5:00 PM. Every schedule, you will have one hour break. Your schedule for the rest of this week Friday, Saturday, and Sunday is 10:00 AM to 9:00 PM. On these shifts Ema, Edna, and I are your supervisors. Please arrive fifteen minutes before the time to work. Next week and in the future your schedule is off on Tuesday and Sunday. On Monday, Wednesday, Friday and Saturday you will work 6:00 AM to 5:00 PM. On any day you have to stay long than 5:00 PM you must do this. The Manager's schedule is minimum ten hours. This means it does not have to be exactly ten hour work day. You will work on my shift, so that I can continue your training. Is this schedule okay with you? Any time you need to request a different day off or schedule let me know. Is your management training and certification completed?"

"Yes, this schedule is great. My training and management certification is complete."

"Good. Welcome. Please let me know if you ever have questions or concerns. Today you will be assigned to assembly the customer's orders on the trays, including getting the drinks ordered. This will help you to become familiar with the menu items. During lunch for one hour, you will be the second sandwich maker at the sandwich station. One hour you will do the grill, and one hour you will do the fry station. I will let you know when to change work assignments. Do you have an apron?"

"No, I do not have an apron. Yes, I understand your instructions."

"Here is a new apron. To work with food, you have to wear a clean apron. You are going to need to bring an apron to work every work day. I notice that you keep your cell phone in your pocket. You cannot talk on your phone during working hours. Your cell phone must be off during the time you work. You have one hour break per shift. I suggest you leave your cell phone in your car when you come to work. Do you understand?"

"Yes, I understand. I will keep my cell phone off and leave it in my pocket. This is my choice."

"Okay. I am giving you a probationary period of six weeks. After six week, I will decide if you are a good fit for working in this restaurant. This is my choice. If you do not like working here you can let me know. I will get you transferred to another company restaurant. This restaurant is very busy. Okay go work with Ema. Tell Ema to come and see me in the office."

"Okay Ms. Lily-Butterfly."

Ema came to speak to Lily-Butterfly.

"Ema on this paper are the things that I would like Mr. Manager to do on the shift and the time duration for each assignment. Please let me know if there is an issue with his work performance. My instinct tells me that he will not be a good fit for this restaurant. I think he is an office professional type of a person. Someone who works best sitting at a desk with a computer and paper. As you know this restaurant is no joke. I am going to give him a chance to perform as a Manager. I will not judge him based on what I sense. I will give Mr. Manager a chance to prove my instinct wrong. If he cannot or does not want to do the work, he will be transferred back to the Personnel Department, or he will quit. As for the Assistant Manager, we will monitor his work performance as well. Okay?"

"I understand. I get a little irritated when new Managers come here to work, because it is always extra work for us to help them earn their paycheck, and they always make more money than us. Plus, they want to just sit and drink coffee, and keep their hands clean. This is not fair. I understand that you believe in team work. So, I will do as you request. Thank you for everything."

"Okay. I will be out to help with everything. Do not worry. I am the one supervising everyone. I am just letting you know what my plans are for them, so that we can be on the same awareness vibes. I do not want to confuse your rhythm and work performance. I will be out shortly."

"Okay. I am going back to manage the shift."

"Alright."

Ema left the office.

At 9:00 AM Lily-Butterfly went to the front service counter she did not see Mr. Manager. She went to talk to Ema.

"Ema have you seen Mr. Manager?"

"He keeps leaving. I do not know where he is. I do not have time to manage this so called certified Manager."

Lily-Butterfly went to look for the Manager. She looked in the complete restaurant upstairs and downstairs; and she asked the Assistant Manager to see if he was in the men's room. He was not in the men's room and no one had seen him. At 10:15 AM Mr. Manager did not return to where he was supposed to be working. This means he was missing for another one hour and fifteen minutes. Lily-Butterfly thought of the places she did not look for him.

"I did not look for Mr. Manager in the walk-in refrigerator and freezer. Seriously, could he be inside these places. Why?" grumbled Lily-Butterfly.

She went to look first in the walk-in refrigerator and then the walk-in freezer. Inside the walk-in freezer was Mr. Manager in his winter coat, talking on his cell phone. Lily-Butterfly thought, oh my Creator your humans are very interesting. Seriously, he is hiding in the freezer. Mr. Manager was standing with his back towards the door. Lily-Butterfly went into the freezer and stood in front of Mr. Manager.

"Hi Mr. Manager seriously. Are you okay? You were gone for more than ninety minutes. What is so important that you keep disappearing and talking on your cell phone? I told you that there is no cell phone talking and private calls during work hours. I recommended that you leave your cell phone in your car. If you choose to bring it inside the restaurant you must have it turned off. Let us get out of this freezer."

"Sorry. Excuse me."

"Please come with me to the office."

They walked to the office.

"Mr. Manager where did you work before coming to this company?"

"I worked as a Telemarketer."

"Do you have any Restaurant Manager experience? Have you worked in a restaurant before?"

"No and no."

"Well, I think that you are going to find working here very difficult. This is a complex, no non-sense, and busy restaurant. You cannot go away to talk on your cell phone. Or if you get overwhelmed, you leave your work station. We cannot work to pay you for not working, do minimum work, and hide. This is not a hide and go seek job, where you go hide and I go look for you. This is not my job. Here it can get busy that for hours all you see in front of the counter is endless lines and a crowds of people like a wall. This restaurant is at a rest stop and it can sometimes get very crowded without notice. This restaurant might not be a good fit for you. By Monday, please let me know if you choose to stay here. I will let you know if I would like you to stay here. Why do you leave for long periods to talk on your phone?"

"I am still doing my Telemarketing job; part-time."

"Seriously. Doing telemarketing job while I pay you to do Manager job? This will not work for me. Leave your telephone in your car. You cannot work your telemarketing job while you are supposed to be doing your Managerial job here. You get a salary to work here as a Manager. A restaurant Manager here is responsible for taking care of the complete restaurant and employees. If you are performing on the first day in this manner, I cannot trust that you will do your job with supervision and without supervision. I do not want to have to explain your job to you anymore. I have said enough already. I am really surprised by your actions. Do you understand?"

"Does this mean that you are going to fire me? My uncle is the Director of Franchise Operations for this company in the cooperate office. I am going to tell him that you are giving me a hard time."

"Please, let me be clear. I do not care who you are related to. If the President of this company was your father and he came here and told me to treat you special, let you do your telemarketing job, not work, and not following the company's rules and policy; I would tell him to give you my job as General Manager and I would leave. This is how serious I am about what I am saying to you. Maybe your uncle should hire you as his assistant and pay you to talk on the phone and look in his face. I am not going to work to pay you, while you talk on the phone, and perform a telemarketing job. I do not want to spend any more time and energy talking to you about this situation. This is ridiculous."

"Are you firing me?"

"No, I am not firing you. Today through Sunday will be a probationary period. If you do not and cannot perform your duties as a Manager, I will transfer you back to the Personnel Director's office. My responsibility is that while you are here you perform your job as a Manager. The money that pays you comes from this restaurant. This is not a dainty fool around work environment. So, you have today to Sunday as a test. On Monday I will give you my decision if you stay here or not. I have changed my decision about your work schedule for today. I have decided that for today I would like you to leave and come back to work 3:00 PM to close. Edna will be the closing Assistant Manager and your supervisor for the night shift. You can go use your cell phone until it is time to work. You can telephone your uncle or whomever to report what I have said. You can come back at 3:00 PM or leave permanently. If I do not see you return to work at 3:00 PM, this means you quit. This is your choice. Know that I am refine, I am also jungle, and unafraid. What would you like to do?"

"I will leave and come back at 3:00 PM. Bye."

"Okay. I have to go help with lunch and so forth. I will see you at 3:00 PM. Arrive fifteen minutes before the time." Bye.""

Mr. Manager left the office and the restaurant. He got in his car and drove off. The new Assistant Manager was working in the front doing what Ema assigned him to do. The Assistant Manager's right hand was normal. His left hand seemed to have a birth defect. His left hand was half the length of his right and did not function completely. Even with this handicap the Assistant Manager tried his best, seemed eager to learn, and functioned as efficiently as possible. Lunch service was over and Lily-Butterfly helped with the preparations for dinner. At 2:30 PM she gave the Assistant Manager a break until 3:30 PM. At 2:40 PM she ate a chicken sandwich and some tea for late lunch. While Lily-Butterfly ate, Mr. Manager returned to work. He came to ask her where he should work.

"Hi Ms. Lily-Butterfly I am back. Where should I work?"

"Welcome back. Go work at the front counter helping the cashiers by putting the orders on the trays. This helps you become familiar with the menu item and service in this restaurant. Ask questions if you need help with something. Edna the closing Assistant Manager is in the office. She will give you further instructions when she comes to set up the shift plan for the night shift. Edna is called an Assistant Manager, because this is the job title; but in her own way she knows how to do everything in this restaurant, and works like a horse. She is not going to have any foolishness from you."

"Okay."

Lily-Butterfly finished eating and went to the office to talk to Edna.

"Edna the new Manager and Assistant Manager are here. Put them in your shift plan to help with customer service, working in the sandwich station with an experienced sandwich maker, on the fry station, and the grills. This helps them become familiar with the menu items, how to prepare the foods in this restaurant, and to get used to the restaurant customer service. The Assistant Manager tried his very best. The Manager seems lazy, slick, he leaves to talk on his phone, thinks he does not have to work, and acts very interesting. You will see what I am talking about when you work with him. Like right now I sent him to go work to help the cashiers put the orders on the tray; and I do not see him. I will be back."

"Okay. Hurry. I have a lot to do."

Lily-Butterfly went to go look for Mr. Manager. She found him outside the emergency exit door smoking and talking on his cell phone. She opened the door looked at him. He looked at her. She walked away and went back to the office to finish talking to Edna.

"Edna is there anything you need from me before I leave? I added the two new Managers to the schedule. Today the Assistant Manager leaves at 5:00 PM. The Manager works today 3:00 PM to close with you. Look on the schedule you will see the rest of their schedule. Give the Manager specific duties that keeps him busy. Supervise him, or he is going to disappear to be wherever he wants."

"Thanks a lot. I see I have them every day."

"Ema and I have them as well. Starting next week, I have the Manager scheduled on my shift until 5:00 PM and he is off when I am off. The Assistant Manager works mid shift and he is working lunch and dinner. He works more conscientious and efficient than the Manager. You know that in the beginning new employees and Managers are going to make us work harder. This is the nature of this job. Thank you for all your work."

"I know the reality of this managerial situation. I have been working here for over eighteen years. I see your so called Assistant Manager and Manager. The Assistant Manager has one arm. The Manager seems like an office clerk, sit down type. Whose bright idea to put them in here to work? They will not last one week. I am letting you know right now that I am not babysitting them. They are so called certified Managers and get paid a salary with benefits. I am only a so called uncertified person who works like ten horses. If they choose not to work I am not going to make them work. So, you will be paying them for doing no work. You work so hard to create all the improvements here. I am telling you that from my experience you are wasting your good talents, energy, and time working here. Take care of yourself. Do not work yourself to death in this place. The owners will just come call an ambulance to take you out of here and find some fake General Manager. For example, my experience is that this current new Manager, is the type that they would send here to be General Manager. This is one of the reasons this restaurant was in such a shitty place."

"Edna, I understand. You are right about everything you have said. I will take care of myself. I will not ruin my health and well-being. Thank you for your concerns. Do your best. I will take care of the rest. As long as I am General Manager here I will continue to do my best job. This is my chosen work performance standard. Trust that I will know when to resign this job. Write me a review in the Manager's log book every night about their work performance. Your main priority and focus is to manage the restaurant as efficiently as you are used to doing. Okay. I appreciate everything you do."

"I understand. I am going to prepare for the long night shift. Every morning I get home from this place at 3:00 AM. Go home, I would not want your job even if I was paid six figures. Take care of yourself. Bye."

"Bye. Try to take care of yourself as well. I will see you tomorrow. I am going to finish the regular employee's schedule and go home. Have a good night."

"Okay."

Lily-Butterfly was finished with her day's work. She said goodbye to Ema, Edna, Carlos, and the two new Managers and left the restaurant. It was 5:30 PM and the Assistant Manager left work as well. Lily-Butterfly took the long drive home in the snail pace traffic.

72

How the Universe functions and how humans think it functions are two different views.

Everything at Lily-Butterfly's home was working as best as possible. At work the restaurant was on an upward climb. The spirit ghosts in the restaurant basement did not give any more trouble. Whether they had crossed over to the other side or not Lily-Butterfly did not investigate if they did. She thought, as long as there were no paranormal activities, no accidents, and things were peaceful, things were more positive. The PVC sewage pipe still needs to be repaired. She still gave the vodka spirit offering to the complete building. Lily-Butterfly's hand had healed about 80%. She still continued to wash the part of her hand that was cut with warm sanitized water mixed with lemon juice and real salt.

Friday was another day in Lily-Butterfly's current training and development. She drove to work in the dark of the morning. On her way she contemplated certain aspects of the current work experiences.
"Every day, I see much more reasons for this restaurant experience. I develop, transform, and improve. Now I know for sure the talents of unconditional love, compassion, and the golden touch of positive life force energy. Creator you are very funny. The way you teach and guide me is mysterious, elegant, surprising, and interesting. I can only wonder what is next. But I will not know prematurely, so as to keep things authentic. Creator please assist me with hiring and training all the new employees. Please give the signal when it is time to leave this restaurant. Creator in my dreams at night I hear the messages that tells me this restaurant professional career is not my chosen destiny, and life's purpose destination. Creator thank you for all the people in this restaurant that have helped me. I bless them for their help and kindness. I am grateful for everything. You know everything about Manana Leila and Ms. Gina. I surrender to your will about this situation. You know everything about everything. Thank you for everything. Amin," whispered Lily-Butterfly.

Lily-Butterfly arrived at work and got out of her car. She unlocked the door, entered, and turned off the security alarm. Ema was not at work as yet. She walked in a slow stride towards the office. Getting to the office door she unlocked the door, turned the door knob, and entered. She read the note that Edna had written in the Manager's log notebook. Lily-Butterfly smiled and sighed. She looked up and through the one way mirror and wall of glass. Ema had arrived with the employees. With focused intentions they walked into the kitchen to wash their hands and began the repetitious task of preparing for breakfast service. Lily-Butterfly sat down in the chair, turned on the computer and read through all the financial and labor reports from the previous day. In the computer she saw one of the things she was investigating. The last cash register on the front counter was not closed out like all the others in the computer. The information left unattended to. She walked over to the front counter and unlocked the cash register slot. The slot was empty. She closed the cash register slot. Lily-Butterfly checked the wire connection to the cash register from the computer in the office the connection was disconnected. She reconnected the wires and walked back to the office. Arriving at the office she sat down and retrieved from the computer, the information for that same cash register slot. The information for this unaccounted for and unverified cash register read $953. Lily-Butterfly checked the total deposit of sales for yesterday. This register's cash was not included in the report.

"This is very interesting. I will continue to investigate this situation and keep watching to see who is working on this particular register. They must stop this stealing. They have cut back the stealing very much. This is one way they steal from the sales. This is the cash register that Ema and Edna use in the day and at night. Or they could be disconnecting this slot at the end of their shift. It does not matter if they directly use the cash register to take customers. I will find a way to stop this stealing. I have been watching this from the first week I came to work here. Now I am sure of what is going on. Soon I will call the company's computer system technicians to verify my discovery. Based on my investigation on just this one register if they steal minimum one thousand dollars per day, at the end of the week this would total up to about $7,000. For the year this would be minimum $364,000 stolen from just this one register. They will be very surprised of my discovery. Finding the missing two million dollars mystery investigation is being solved. Wow. This stealing is all happening fearlessly right out in the open. I will keep looking for these unverified, unlogged, and open cash register slots in the computer system," mumbled Lily-Butterfly.

Ema came into the office to get the cash registers.

"Hi Ema good morning. Please send Carlos to me. I need him for about ninety minutes. This morning I will come over and help you with breakfast service. Okay."

"Okay ma'am. Good morning. Your hair is growing into beautiful curls."

"Yes. I wash my hair when I take a shower and put in some leave in conditioner and coconut oil; and the curls just form by themselves. I am grateful for this simple and carefree hair and style. Thanks be to all my ancestors for this quality hair. I think I need another haircut. I will go soon. Our wonderful new Managers will arrive at 10:00 AM and 12:00 PM. Oh well, it is one of the nature of my job responsibilities. Please send Carlos to me. I will be there to help you soon."

"Okay."

Carlos came and Lily-Butterfly helped him with organizing and counting the inventory and doing the food order. Carlos telephoned the wholesaler to give the order, checked the delivery, and entered the amounts into the computer. The clear garbage bags came in this Friday delivery. After this, Carlos went back to help Ema with the breakfast service.

The locksmith came to change the locks on the doors and put locks on the walk-in refrigerators and freezer. Lily-Butterfly showed the locksmith all the things she wanted him to do. Lily-Butterfly requested that first the locksmith fix the alarm on the back door emergency exit and change the lock. Next the locksmith put locks on the walk-in refrigerator and freezer. Last he changed the lock on every door including the office door. After communicating with the locksmith Lily-Butterfly went to the front to help with serving the customers. At 9:50 AM Mr. Manager arrived at work. He came to speak to Lily-Butterfly.

"Good morning Ms. Lily-Butterfly. What are my duties for today?"

"Breakfast is over at 10:00 AM. Help to put away the breakfast menu items and set up for lunch. I will get Carlos to guide you in want to do next."

"Okay."

Lily-Butterfly got Carlos to work with Mr. Manager to show him how to remove every breakfast item for the sandwich station, grills, and fryers, how to wrap them, and where to put the items in the walk-in refrigerator. Next Carlos showed Mr. Manager how to set up the sandwich station, grills, and front service station for lunch. Lily-Butterfly talked to Ema about the lunch shift plan and work stations that Mr. Manager and herself were going to work. She took over managing the shift and Ema went on break. When Ema returned from break at 11:10 AM, Carlos went on break. Lily-Butterfly went to talk to Mr. Manager.

"Mr. Manager for your awareness the emergency alarm on the back door is fixed and the lock was changed. If you open this door the alarm will go off. This morning locks were put on the walk-in refrigerators and freezer. The only Managers that will have keys for these locks are Ema, Edna, and myself. If you need to use one of these places let us know. We will unlock them for you. During lunch today I will be working on the front service counter. Between 12:00 and 2:00 PM your work station is the grill next to the sandwich station. Eddie will be the sandwich maker. Your secondary station will be watching Eddie make the different sandwiches. This way you can learn about the sandwiches we have on this menu. If you need to use the men's room, let me know. I will come over and work your station until you return. If you leave your station to use the men's room, you have maximum ten minutes, and wash your hands very well before you return to your work station. Every time you leave your work station you remove your gloves. When you return you put on a new pair of gloves. Gloves are on the sandwich station. If you do not see the gloves ask Eddie to show you where the box of gloves are located on the sandwich station. Never touch raw or cooked meat and touch anything on the sandwich station. We cannot have cross contamination of cooked or raw meat, and other food products. I will be working on the French fryer making fries. The French fryer station is the busiest station. For every order a French fry is ordered. Carlos will be working in the deli. If I have to work your station for whatever reason, Carlos will work on my station until you return. If you do not return within ten minutes I am coming to find you. After lunch you will clean the grill, help with cleaning up, and preparing every station for dinner. Always find something to do. If you have questions and want guidance on what to do ask Ema, Edna, Carlos, or myself. Do you understand? Do you have any question?"

"I understand. When is my break time?"

"After you work six or seven hours. If you are hungry now, I will give you fifteen minutes to have something to eat. At 5:00 PM you can have one hour break. Would you like to go eat something now?"

"Yes, and at 5:00 PM I will take my one hour break."

"Okay. All employees join the line and order their food from the cashier. All Managers eat at no cost, a maximum $15 order per shift. Today if you need to eat two complete meals, I will do you the curtesy of having two complete meals at no cost. The cashier will ring up your food as Manager's meal. Please write your name on each receipt after you have placed your order. Okay. Please hurry, it is close to lunch time."

"Okay. Thank you."

Ema returned from break and Lily-Butterfly told her of the shift plan and that she will help her to manage the lunch shift.

"Are you sure you want to work on the French fryer. It is hot and it is the busiest station. Plus, your left hand is still not completely healed," said Ema.

"Thank you Ema for your concerns. If I need help, I will ask Carlos to help me. He is working in the deli station close to the French fry station. I will manage Mr. New Manager. You manage the Cashiers and help to get the orders on the trays. Mr. Assistant Manager will make all drinks and help you with putting them on the trays. You manage Mr. Assistant Manager and I will manage Mr. Manager. Plus Mr. Assistant Manager is close to where I am going to work. We are going to have a great day. I am going to eat a sandwich in the kitchen. Please watch the French fry station I will be back in ten minutes."

Lily-Butterfly went to order a chicken sandwich. She ate, drank some water, and returned in ten minutes. Mr. Manager had put on his apron and was working on the grill. Mr. Assistant Manager arrived on the front customer service counter wearing his apron. Ema guided him on his work responsibilities during the lunch service.

At 12:15 PM there were six long lines of customers to be served. At 1:15 PM Lily-Butterfly looked over to the grill station Mr. Manager was not there working.

"Carlos please make fries for me. I will be back. I am going to go see where Mr. Manager went."

"Okay."

Lily-Butterfly went to the sandwich station to ask Eddie where Mr. Manager went.

"Eddie where is Mr. Manager?"

"He told me he would be right back. I do not know exactly where he went," replied Eddie.

"Okay."

Lily-Butterfly went to look for Mr. Manager. She found him outside in the parking lot close to the restaurant smoking. She went to talk to him.

"I told you to let me know if you had to leave your work station to use the restroom. Now I am going to say as well if you need to smoke. You cannot just leave without someone working at your work station. Eddie cannot touch meat and at the same time make sandwiches. Why did you not tell me you needed to go smoke?"

"I did not want to bother you," replied Mr. Manager.

"Well, it is not bother to me to use the men's room. I could choose to see the men's room and smoking in the same category. The issue would be how often you need to go smoke. You have to manage your smoking urges and so forth. You are not getting paid to smoke, but I can be reasonable if you have to leave your station once during lunch service. What else? I need you to return to your work station you left this station about twenty minutes now. Please I cannot encourage your kind of management style, and then expect all the other Managers and employees to work responsibly, professionally, and do their jobs efficiently. I need you to return to your station now. Do not leave again during the lunch time service."

"I get panic attacks when it is so crowded, busy, and I have to work so fast. This is another issue."

"I see. I was sensing this. Okay. I will put someone else on the grill and you make sandwiches with Eddie. If you need help with how to make a sandwich ask Eddie. Is this okay with you?"

"Yes. I think so."

"I do not think that this restaurant is a good fit for you. Work until Sunday. I will pay your for Thursday to Sunday. Come to work on Monday and I will tell you my decision. If you work here you have to be able to really work, and you have to be good at multitasking. You cannot even work one station without having a panic attack; which then can trigger the urge to want to smoke. Oh my. Come back inside. To get paid you have to be able to do some kind of work for today, and the next two days. Okay. Come inside wash your hand. Go to the sandwich station to work."

Mr. Manager and Lily-Butterfly went back inside. He went to wash his hands at the employee's hand washing sink. Lily-Butterfly told Ema to put another employee on the grill, and that Mr. Manager was going to help make sandwiches with Eddie on the sandwich station. Lily-Butterfly went back to the French fry station. Carlos moved back to the deli station. Mr. Manager stayed on the sandwich station with Eddie for the complete lunch service. At 2:45 PM Mr. Manager worked with Eddie to prepare the sandwich station for dinner, clean up, stock stations, and other jobs. At 3:00 PM in-between doing these jobs Mr. Manager left to go use the men's room and smoke. Lily-Butterfly did not say anything to Mr. Manager. She had arrived at accepting the situation with Mr. Manager. She had also decided that next week Monday she was going to speak to Mr. Watson about Mr. Manager, and send him back to the Personnel Director for reassessment, and putting him in another restaurant.

At 3:00 PM Edna arrived at work. Lily-Butterfly looked at her and laughed. Edna laughed back.

"We will talk at the Manager's meeting. I have an idea about what you would like to say about Mr. Manager. Hurry and make sure that everything is prepared for dinner. Give assignments to Mr. Manager, the Assistant Manager, and the employees if you need additional things done to prepare for the night shift. Come to the dining room for the meeting at 3:30 PM. Okay Ema?"

"Okay. Hehehehehe," replied Edna.

Lily-Butterfly ordered tea and a small salad and went to the dining room to sit at the meeting table and eat. She also observed the employees working behind the counter.

At 3:40 PM Ema, Edna, and Carlos came to sit with Lily-Butterfly for the meeting.

"We have one hour for this meeting. So, Edna what is your report on the new Managers?"

"Hahahaha. This is a funny situation. I do not think that they are Managers for this place. Maybe they will be okay for a very slow mall food court restaurant. Saying this I am being nice. My real view is the Manager seems to have an entitlement attitude, overwhelmed, lazy, scammer attitude, and he keeps disappearing. After a while I stop giving him any attention and let him do as he wants to. I have to work hard as it is. I do not need this kind of harassment situation. The Assistant Manager tries very hard, but he needs consistent redirection, and he cannot work as fast as he should, because one of his hands maybe work ten percent. So, it is as if he is working with one hand. This is a big problem."

"I understand. We will keep the Assistant Manager and see how he does with more practice. Starting next week, you will have him for five nights; you need the help. The night is a slower pace and no multitude of people from bus tours and rest stop to serve. The night shift can be a productive environment for the Assistant Manager to get practice, grow, and learn in."

"Thanks a lot. If you say so."

They all laughed.

"Now, look at Mr. Manager. He is drinking something in front of the customer by the cashier. A total no, no. Give him five more minutes and he is gone to smoke, hide, eat, and talk on his cell phone. He talks on his cell phone for two hours sitting in the dining room last night. I did not stop him. I am not his real supervisor. Plus, I have a lot to do already. This guy is a total loser," said Edna.

"Edna I know. Do your best. Keep me informed."

"Yes. I understand. I will leave you notes in the Manager's notebook."

"Monday when Mr. Watson comes for the meeting Mr. Manager is going back to the office with him. I have done so much already in such a short time. Know that if and when the time for me come to leave here, I will leave. I do not think I will be working here for years and years. All of you would have gotten some benefits from me being here, when it is time for me to leave. Know that I will not damage my health and well-being from working here."

"Ms. Lily-Butterfly I totally understand. If this restaurant work does not kill you, ruin your health, it can make your stronger, more improved in many ways, and, or turn you into a thief to compensate for all the hard unrewarded work performance. My new mantra is we will see. Ms. Lily-Butterfly I like you a lot, but we will see. Look I told you the Manager is going to be missing in action. He is nowhere to be seen. Maybe he is in the office talking on the telephone, or outside smoking. Oh, my God give me strength and nerves to work with this Manager tonight. Seriously," said Edna. She sighed and grunted.

"I really like these meetings. It gives us an opportunity to come together as a team and express our thoughts. Ms. Lily-Butterfly we are better off without these two so called Managers," said Ema.

Carlos was silent except for when he laughed.

"Alright everyone let me continue with some announcements. The alarm on the back door works. The locks on every door front and back has been changed, including the office. The walk-in refrigerators and freezer now have locks. Ema and Edna here is a master key for every lock. The same key works in every lock. Very simple one key works in every lock. Take care of this key. It is for the Managers use only. Designate an employee to supervise the front if you have to go to the back for any reason. Here, add this key to the other Manager keys you have. Throw away the old door keys. Next the clear garbage bags have arrived. Use all the black garbage bags we currently have and start using the clear garbage bags when the black one are used up."

"Thank you. More new changes to digest and get us out of our comfort zone. What else?" replied Edna.

"Instruct the employees to use the service cart to load the items on to be restocked in the front; this saves time. You must manage the employees, the service, the food, paper products, cleaning supplies, the opening and closing of every door, and everything else. Effective today the Manager's office is locked unless there is a Manager using the office. Managers are not cashiers, taking customer's orders with their backs to the employees and everything else. Starting Saturday there is a waste bucket on every shift. The food in this waste bucket must be counted at the end of every shift. The items must be written on the waste sheet and added to the computer reports at the end of every shift. Leave the waste sheet on the clip board with the daily reports. I will look at them before I file them. This is part of your job, and is called responsibility, accountability, and managing. Do you know what waste is?"

"I think so, waste is wrong sandwich, food returned by customer, food that falls on the floor, broken food, and so on and so forth," said Ema.

"At the start of the shift the cashier counts their drawers and at the end of their shift they count their drawers. During this counting the Manager is always supervising. Two dollars or more shortages the employee gets written up. At the third time the employee's drawer is short these amounts they are fired. I have said this before and I am saying this again. Do you understand?"

"Yes, we understand. You are closing all the possible holes and opportunities used for stealing money, food, paper, cleaning products, and everything else," replied Ema.

"Yes, and I am doing my job. These things that are stolen prevents the business from staying open. The business needs money and profits so that everyone can have a job. The money must go into the bank to pay the bills. The food must stay here to be sold. The paper products to use for the food selling, and the cleaning products to keep the place clean. The overtime must end so that the overtime money can pay for more employees. Efficient and fast customer service we can have more opportunity to make more money. More money can create more profits and employee benefits. This is a very simple awareness and philosophy. The last announcement today is, the employee new uniforms have arrived. They are in the uniform cabinet in the Manager's office. Each of you take only three shirts and two ties. Give to each full time employee three new shirts. Part time employees gets two shirts. Make sure everyone gets the correct size. Encourage the employees to buy new work pants and wear black shoes. Starting Monday every employee and Manager must be clean and dressed appropriately. I am finished speaking. Do you have questions or concerns?"

"No questions or concerns from me. Thank you for the new uniforms," said Ema.

"Look the Manager is still missing. Oh, my Lord please help my nerves tonight. Ma'am thank you for everything," said Edna.

"Thank you for everything. Go home now and rest. We will see you tomorrow," said Carlos.

"You are all welcome. It is 5:15 PM. I told the Manager that at 5:00 PM he can have an hour break. Maybe in addition to his previous disappearance he is now gone on his break. Anyway, Edna do your best. I will be going home after this meeting. At this time the traffic is very busy. Good night," said Lily-Butterfly.

"Good night. I am going to count the rest of the cash registers for the day shift and go home," said Ema.

"Edna do you need me for anything?" asked Carlos.

"No Carlos you can go home," said Edna.

"Okay thank you. I will see all of you tomorrow. Bye."

Carlos got up and left. Ema and Edna went back to work. The Assistant Manager went on break. Mr. Manager is still missing. Maybe he went somewhere on his break. At 5:43 PM Lily-Butterfly was in her car and driving home. Lily-Butterfly looked to the right side of the sky at the setting sun. She smiled.

"Thank you Creator for everything," whispered Lily-Butterfly.

She drank some water as she continued to drive, reflect, and focus on the traffic.

For Lily-Butterfly on a daily basis the restaurant experiences continue to reveal its purpose. At this point you might be wondering where this is all going, and what is the purpose of a detailed restaurant experience in this story? All I can say is 'the belief that everything is for a reason' also applies to this restaurant story experiences. In spirit and soul talent discovery and awakening it is wise that the person follows the designated pathways, follow the way, and be mindful of each step. Plus, remember Lily-Butterfly has to evolve through six cycles of seven years to be completely ready for her chosen destiny and life's purpose career. Right now, Lily-Butterfly is still in the evolution, growth, discovery, and preparation stages.

73

Saturday at work was a usual busy day for Lily-Butterfly. The day at work came and went like sunrise and sunset. Sunday off from work was the same activities of spending time with the children, cleaning, laundry, grocery shopping, visiting Manana Leila and Ms. Gina, cooking, going to bed early and preparing for the following week. Visiting Manana Leila, and experiencing the events between her and Ms. Gina was the same sad events for Lily-Butterfly. In one day, Lily-Butterfly had to do many things.

Monday morning Lily-Butterfly arrived at work. She unlocked the door, entered the restaurant, and turned off the security alarm. The smell of bleach and disinfectant was her first significant greeting. Lily-Butterfly turned on the light and walked to the office. It was now 4:45 AM. She checked all the reports Edna had done and completed all the report process. The food cost was 51%, paper was 25%, and labor was 50%. The sales and customer count had increased.

"No profit yet, but we will get there. Yes, we will. The off line and open cash register is unaccounted for again. I am convinced that Ema and Edna are responsible for this situation. I will telephone the computer company to fix this issue. I am going to secure the connections myself with tape until the computer company can come to permanently repair the wires. This morning I will give Mr. Watson every uncollected employee check to return to the accounts department. This money will get deposited in this restaurant's financial budget. Things are improving with everyone's assistance," mumbled Lily-Butterfly.

Lily-Butterfly looked through the one way wall of glass and saw Ema and the employees at the front counter. She looked up at the clock over the door, it was 6:10 AM. Mr. Manager came into the office.

"Good morning Ms. Lily-Butterfly."

"Good morning. What have you decided? Do you volunteer to return to the Personnel Director and Training department? I have decided to send you back to them. The truth is for many reasons you are not a good fit for this restaurant environment."

"I choose to go. You are right. I am not a good fit for this restaurant. It is too fast pace, consistently busy, too big to manage, too many moving parts, and everything is too maximum. I could not imagine being scheduled to manage this place on a shift by myself. This is too much."

"Okay. I agree with you. There is no need for me to add anything else to what you have said. Why tell a snail that it is a snail, when it already knows that it is a snail? Go help Ema with breakfast. Wait until Mr. Watson comes in at 9:00 AM. I will tell him of our decision, and you can return to the office with him when he leaves. Do you have any question?"

"No. I have no question."

"Alright you can go to help Ema. Please tell Carlos to come seem me in the office."

"Okay. I will."

Carlos came to the office.

"Good morning Carlos your uniform looks great. How are you doing?"

"I am doing great."

"Okay. Now that you have improved with the inventory and ordering on Mondays you do not have to go physically count the inventory. This is done every Sunday night by Edna and I recheck everything she counted. Take this inventory count sheet, use it to subtract from the Monday build to amounts, and complete all the orders. Afterwards count and recheck the food, paper, and cleaning supply delivery, and enter the amounts for everything into the computer. The last thing to do is telephone the wholesale company to give them the order. When you are finished, return to help Ema with breakfast service."

"Would you like to check the order before I telephone the wholesaler?"

"No. From experience I trust the quality of your work. Let me know if you need help with anything."

"Okay. I will."

Carlos took the clipboard and all the forms he needed and went to sit in the dining room to create all the orders.

"Let me complete this payroll." Lily-Butterfly sighed. "In this place work is never complete. My choices to be here is my own decision. I have thirty percent grey hair already. I hope that these grey hair symbolize improve wisdom and not old age, because I am only thirty eight years old. I have to work hard and smart to earn my life; and being me. Oh, my Creator remember me in your busy schedule. I still have so far to go within and outside me on this path of human life." She sighed again. "Human life is an infinite highway of possibilities. If my children only knew all the things I have to perform to keep our life as a single parent in harmony, success, health, and well-being. When Holly gets summer holiday off from school; sometimes I will take her to work with me. I hope Rebornstar keeps herself safe. My choice is, failure is not a choice for me in this life. I will live life and not let life live me. Reflecting, processing, and talking to myself is good for my spirit and soul," whispered Lily-Butterfly.

The time was 8:55 AM. Mr. Watson would arrive soon. Lily-Butterfly placed all the reports for Mr. Watson in the folder, locked the office door, and went to sit in the dining room. Ten minutes went by Mr. Watson did not arrive. Lily-Butterfly went to order some breakfast from the cashier. With her breakfast she ordered coffee. This was the first time she drank coffee. After this day coffee became a chosen breakfast drink. In the future the restaurant got busier and busier, and Lily-Butterfly drank more and more coffee. When Lily-Butterfly discontinued the restaurant career she weaned herself off drinking coffee, and returned to drinking decaffeinated teas. She ate and continued to wait for Mr. Watson.

Mr. Watson arrived when Lily-Butterfly finished her breakfast.
"Hi, how are you said Mr. Watson?"
"I am alive. I feel tired. I am thankful for everything."
"Any good news?"
"What do you mean? If you mean money, look at the reports. I will be back. It is your choice if you feel the reports are good news or not. I have done beyond my best."
Lily-Butterfly got up and left the table. Mr. Watson read the reports. Lily-Butterfly returned to sit with Mr. Watson.
"Good job. One more step to go. Ha. Make sure that you get the budgeted percentage this week. I do not know exactly how you are able to do these improvements, but keep it going. I like the results."
"I see. I cannot put the process into words to tell you, because I do not think that you believe in Divine Interventions and positive life

force energy stuff. Getting the physical results is what you believe in, no matter how the results happen, even if it is to lie."

"When you hire regular employees and end the over time, have quicker service, completely end the stealing of money, food, paper and cleaning products, and so forth the reports will be the correct percentages. The financial situation will be great, the company makes profit, and you, and the Managers can get a bonus," replied Mr. Watson.

"All you have just said cannot happen in one step. Oh wow. When am I going to get the pay to reflect all the great improvements? As you know the salary I currently receive is to be General Manager for a restaurant with less work and responsibilities. You can do one step and make this happen. If you do not, it is more to your benefit. You keep the labor percentage in your district under the budget, and get rewarded for a great job. Plus, when I am finished fixing this restaurant you will take the credit as well."

"You know that if you do not like what I am doing you can quit. If you choose to stay you know that you would have to fix the problems. Like you said before, you will not stay on a sinking ship. Is there anything else?"

"The Manager you sent me is not a good fit for this restaurant. He is doing a telemarketing job while he is supposed to be working. He gets overwhelmed with the consistent busyness, customers, and lots of work. He has to leave his work station frequently to smoke. He has decided to leave. I have not fired him. I am sending him back to the corporate office and the Personnel Director. He will drive his car to the office when you leave. Plus, I found out this morning that his salary is $10,000 per year more than my salary. My salary is another story that I have said enough about. After today I will not complain anymore about my salary. When I am ready to leave I will."

"Okay. Tell the Manager to leave and go to the office. He does not need to follow me in his car. He knows his way to the office."

"The basement is flooded again. Please send the plumber. I have placed all the old uncollected employee checks in an envelope inside the file. Ask the accounts department to, add these check amounts back to the labor financial cost, and check the deposits at the bank to see if they match the reports. I think that maybe in the past some of the deposits were being stolen. This would make the actual money deposited less than what was reported. The deposits are one amount and the computer reports are another amount. I think this was a part of the previous issues of the missing two million dollars. People in the accounts department seems not to be doing a complete job. My observation is, some people will basically try to get away with what they can. There is another incident that I am investigating. I am going to stop cashing employee checks in the cashier's registers. This is one of the ways Managers cash checks for previous employees that does not return for their pay check. Another awareness is when employees quit the termination forms must be filled out, and a copy sent to the accounts department. This way Managers are not sending in hours for employees that no longer work in the restaurant; and then cashing the check in the restaurant's cash registers. Can I call the computer technicians to come here to permanently connect the cable wires to each cash register? This is an extra necessary repair cost."

"Wow. Stolen deposits, actual deposits, versus computer reports, Managers cashing employee's checks. These are great awareness. Good job. I will talk to the Senior Accountant and my supervisor about these things. Yes, stop cashing the employee's checks in the restaurant. This started as a courtesy to the employees. But it has become a major issue in all the restaurants I supervise. I will investigate everything that you just told me. I will send the plumber as soon as I can. Yes, you can arrange for the computer technician to come here and do the computer cable repairs," said Mr. Watson.

"Thank you. In this situation getting the right results and success takes team work. I almost forgot, here is your master key for the restaurant. I changed all the locks. Fix the emergency exit alarm, and put locks on the walk-in refrigerators and freezer. This key opens every door and lock in the restaurant. Last but not least, I will let you know when I will be taking ten sick days off from work. I need to fix the torn ligament at my left wrist that was damaged in the Paramus food court restaurant. Maybe you or another General Manager would need to come here and work for two weeks. I have to repair my wrist. This surgery is long overdue. When I schedule the surgery, I will let you know the days I have to be off. I came to this company with no damage to my hands. I at least need to repair this damaged left wrist."

"Okay let me know when you are ready to take the sick days off from work," said Mr. Watson.

"Great. Thank you for transferring me to this restaurant. I have had lots of priceless experiences, transformation, confirmation of my talents, recognized more of my value, I have grown, matured, and improved greatly. I will take these improvements within me, wherever I go in life. I have nothing more to say for this meeting," said Lily-Butterfly.

"Okay. Good bye. See you on Monday."

"Okay bye."

Lily-Butterfly told the Manager that he could leave and go to the corporate office. The Manager left. Wednesday morning of this week the plumber came to fix the PVC sewage pipe in the basement, clear all the drains, and did all the plumbing repairs. This was another accomplishment for this restaurant situation. The week went on and Lily-Butterfly continued to do her job while motivating, guiding, teaching, and inspiring the other employees to do their best. Lily-Butterfly kept her investigation about the missing cash register money to herself. She wanted to be sure about what was actually happening.

Thursday morning at work while doing some computer work Lily-Butterfly's thoughts drifted to some major personal concern that she had forgotten about. She thought, I must find a different place to live by July 1st of this year. This current school district is supposed to be number one in the state of New Jersey. I do not agree. Where we live, I like the park, recreation area, the neighbors, my landlord, and the community. I will miss all of this, but not the school system and environment at the schools. Next September Rebornstar will have one more year in high school. Holly will be going to second grade. She will be seven years old on July 31st. Book knowledge is important, but so is care, and nourishing environment and people. I have had enough of Holly's mysterious supposedly learning disabilities. My instincts tell me that if I move the mystery will be solved. Only the Creator knows how this is going to happen. The idea seems far fetch and ridiculous. But so far my instincts and the Creator have not proven itself wrong. Maybe it is time for the disguise to be unmasked about Holly's situation. As Manana Leila would say the Creator knows best. I will give more attention to this personal situation. It is time for this improvement in my life.

Lily-Butterfly was brought back to the awareness of the restaurant. She continued on with all her Thursday work responsibility.

74

If someone is using a hammer and it hits their finger, it is not the hammer's fault. The person using the hammer is responsible.

Currently it is the third Friday in April 1996. The day and restaurant carried on with its usual activities. With all the improvements at work the restaurant was operating in a more improved and efficient way. The employees had adjusted to all the new changes. As time goes on with consistent and continuous practice, and repetitive practice the new improvements became normal. Lily-Butterfly had interviewed and trained seventy new regular employees. The restaurant got busier and busier, and made more, and more money. As soon as Lily-Butterfly recovered from the tiredness of the day the next day's events brought back the feelings of tiredness. Sometimes she felt the tiredness in her heart and chest like a slow burning flame. As she achieved more and more awakened mastery of her talents and improvements in every area of the restaurant, her curly hair looked like it was uniquely dusted with white powder. The new addition to Lily-Butterfly's features was, her hair became whiter.

At 3:40 PM Lily-Butterfly sat in the dining room waiting for Ema, Edna, and Carlos. The new Assistant Manager was still working at the restaurant and he took care of managing the service and employees during the meeting. Edna arrived at the meeting with a smile on her face.

"I am so grateful that the new Manager left. I am thankful for this. He was distracting and irritating to work with. You are one brave woman with a lot of directness, no nonsense, and fearless courage. Hahaha. Thank you for everything. I am less stressed since you came here to work. I see that your hair is becoming whiter as the weeks go by. Let us see how long this so called Assistant Manager is going to last," said Edna.

"Edna thank you for your compliments. Hope after today's meeting you feel the same way about me."

"Oh, my Lord. What now? What is next?" said Edna.

"Everyone listen and hear. Ask questions if you do not understand," said Lily-Butterfly.

"Yes ma`am," said Carlos.

"Money most times is the resource, root, and bitter vine that people use to create their biggest downward fall. My opinion is money is a great tool in these so called modern time. Money is never the problem. People in relationship to money is the problem and gives money the power it ends up creating. Money cannot do anything, or have power and value, unless people spend it or do something with it. Money does not have hands, legs, and feet. Money cannot run out of the cash registers, safe, and restaurant; and disappear. Do you understand me so far?" said Lily-Butterfly.

"Yes," they all replied.

Ema and Edna repeatedly glanced at each other.

"Good. Okay. Today I will present to you some money issues I am investigating. They are going to have to come to an end, or I will turn over my investigations to Mr. Watson. He will send in a private investigating company to research about these issues and find out who is responsible for the issues. I am counting on all of you to follow the company's cash handling policies. These policies are in the training manuals I gave you."

"Okay," they all replied.

"Great all of you are doing great so far regarding the general improvements of the employees and restaurant. The cash handling policies, money disappearing acts, and cashing checks of non-existing and invisible employees; this still needs improving. This restaurant operation is infested with malpractice and stealing. These past and present issues need major improvements," said Lily-Butterfly. She continued, "the total list of things from the past and present that still need improving and are being investigated are: - *when employees quit some do not return for their last pay check. A Manager cashes the check in the cashier's cash register. No termination of employee form is filled out for employees that quit or are fired. The Manager that does the payroll keeps submitting work hours for this employee to be paid, and continues to cash these checks. I have put an end to this, but if there is any attempt to continue this action, the Manager will be caught, and be charged with forging checks. On Monday I returned to the Accounts Department all previously employed employee checks. When Managers work as a cashier they do not ring up some of the orders. They know the prices of a certain combination of meals and tell the customer the cost. At the same time, they ring up the next customer's order, takes the money and cashes the next order out for the cash register to open and gives change back to both customers.*

Or the Manager does not ring up the order and uses their cash register key to open the drawer to give the customer their change. The extra money is taken from the cash register by the Manager when they count the cash register at the end of the shift. The total cash sales at the end of the day does not match the deposits for the same day. On some days deposits are missing. For the armored security cash pick-up; all the cash is collected from the master safe, and is placed in one secure locked bag. The General Manager has one key and the armored pick up security has the other key to this bag. The next key to open this bag is at the bank. So, it cannot be said that the armored security took deposits from the bag. Also, once the deposit is dropped into the master safe the deposit cannot be taken back out. There is two sets of combinations to the master safe. The General Manager has one set and the armored security has the other set of safe combination. It so happens that Ema has all of these safe combination and one key. I am going to request that these safe combinations and keys be changed. Currently I am here at work on the armored security money pick up which is Monday, Wednesday, and Fridays. Therefore, Ema you no longer have to be involved with this safe and armored pickup. If I am not here on any of these day I will give you my safe combination numbers and key to use; when I return I will change them again. This is how things are supposed to be. This will improve the situation of Managers doing the complete computer reports, not dropping the cash deposits in the safe, and floating deposits. Floating deposits is using the current day's deposit to cover the previous day. Managers deliberately take money from each cashier's register and report these amounts as short or missing. This should have stopped with the new cash enforcement policy of writing up shortages of two dollars or more. One biggest genius money stealing scheme I have ever encountered is a Manager totally disconnecting individual cash register cable from the master computer cable system. They take the money from the register or registers and do not account for this money. They let the cash register information float in empty space. They know that after a day or two the information totally disappears and the information can never be found again for this particular register or registers. The person gets away with this thievery; so, they think. I am thinking this is why in the past and present not all cash register drawers are used daily. This way there are cash registers that are not used every day to perform this floating cash register thievery system. I am letting you know that I know that this malpractice is happening. I see it all, and I know who is doing all this stuff; and when. The computer has all the information. You just have to know where to look to find every information. I have been printing the missing floating cash register information in the office. I have also telephoned the company that manages and maintain the company's computer system. They have helped me to track exactly what is happening. They have send me all the missing information over the past five years that no longer show up on the office computer. Hello? Know that the information does not show up in the office computer, but the technicians at the company can retrieve the information. Based on the Management schedule and who is physically managing each shift I know who is doing everything date, schedule, and time. Please stop these activities. I have schedule an appointment for the computer management company's technicians to come here and permanently attach the cash registers to one another, and to the main cable that is connected to the office computer. This morning I have temporarily reconnected all the cash register cables, and the main computer cable, and taped them in place. Ema and Edna you are both the only Managers from the past team that are here, have Manager's keys, and perform all the money counting transactions. My latest experience of this cash register thievery transaction was on both shifts; yesterday. Since I have been General Manager here I have not taken a customer's order, worked as a cashier, count cash registers, and make deposits. Why did I choose not to do these work activities? It would be conflict of interest. The company's policies says the Management staff must not work as cashiers for conflict of interest reasons. All I have done so far is retrieve the deposits from the master safe in the presence of the two armored security guard pick up crew. There is always two armored security guard pick up crew; one supervisor and one regular. I guess they supervise each other. Next, Managers and regular employees do their grocery shopping in the restaurant. Know, if this activity continues I know that it is mostly going to be done directly by Managers and, or Managers are responsible, because currently there are locks on the stock rooms, walk-in refrigerators, and freezers. I do not think that I can completely end all stealing in such a large restaurant operation. All I can do is my best job managing all the things, and people that work in this restaurant. This is my job responsibility as General Manager. There are some other things I am investigating and observing. I will let you know what they are, if these things do not stop. Now all of you be wise. Stop all these activities. Mr. Watson and the company's accounts department have become aware of some of these activities. If you get caught you are going to jail. This is written in the company's policy manual. These illegal stealing activities have been happening for years. This is not an alleged situation. There is a long trail of physical information proof of everything is in this management computer, and the company's accounts department. All they would have to do is connect all the dots. As long as I am the General Manager here I will perform my job responsibilities. If I do not do my job responsibilities and Managers are stealing I will be going to jail as well, because it is part of my job responsibilities to prevent all of these things from happening. This is why I am so interested in not continuing all this stealing situations, and bringing them to an end. Going to jail for me is never an option. You know that the previous General Manager was in jail for all the missing annual two million dollars. He has been bailed out of jail and currently there is a court trial. I have no time for any of this negative energy things. We will work together to operate this restaurant following all the correct procedures, including the handling of the company's cash money, food, paper, cleaning products, employee's payrolls, checks, and everything in this complete building. All that I have said here today is the last part of the things that still needs to completely improve. Hear my words very clearly and listen. Also know that I am not saying that everything must be perfect. I am saying we must do our jobs as complete as possible. When this is done the chips will fall where they may, and in the most complete manner possible. When all of these things are improved, things will come into balance, money will be available to pay all the bills, the restaurant will make a profit, and we can have the opportunity to make a bonus. Stop yourself and every employee on your shift from stealing the company's property. This is part of your job. If you do not want to do your job the correct way and you choose to quit, please do so. As long as you work in the role of a Manager you are responsible for the consequences of all your actions. I will not go to jail because of your actions. I know that I personally will not do something to go to jail. Do you understand?"

There was silence for the complete duration of Lily-Butterfly's eye opening speech. They were very surprised that she knew so much and said nothing about some of the things until at this meeting. Ema and Edna seem embarrassed, they were looking down on the table, and they looked and acted obviously guilty. Carlos looked surprised and uncomfortable. In Lily-Butterfly's investigation she knew that

Carlos was not responsible for any of the illegal things and stealing. This is one of the reasons Lily-Butterfly chose Carlos as her personal assistant and an Assistant Manager.

"Hello everyone. Did you hear me? Is there any question, comments, or concerns?" said Lily-Butterfly.

"I understand everything you told us. Now everything about this place makes more sense to me. The bottom line is, if we do not want to go to jail, immediately stop every, and all stealing. This is a simple request. But for the stealers, it might not be an easy act to stop. Mmm. Hmm," said Carlos.

"Carlos, exactly. Ema and Edna, what would you like to say?" said Lily-Butterfly.

"I hear and understand everything you have said. I will take responsibility to do my part to correct these situations," said Edna.

"Wow. I am speechless. I am nervous. These situations are getting more serious. I feel hot. You have known all these thing since you came here, treated us with respect anyway, help us to improve our work skills, training us and getting us certified, promoting us, giving us salary increases, give us new uniforms, and everything else that you have done, knowing everything that you knew. Wow. I find this interesting. I feel speechless. Really. Thank you for everything. I hear, listen, and understand. I will do my part and my job in the continuation of the transformation, improvements, changes, and so forth. Thanks for giving us a change to change our action," said Ema.

"You are welcome. This is giving all of you a change to reset, renewal, a second chance, and an opportunity to not go to jail. Mr. Watson is aware of the issues here. All he wants is for me to fix the problems. My presentations of these issues and situation here today is my last step to ending the corruption of the present and past, and you being a part of the problem. Ema and Edna after today if I observe any stealing of the past form any of you I will report the incidents with proof to Mr. Watson. It will be up to Mr. Watson to take action. Just like the previous General Manager went to jail both of you will be going to jail as well. Do not take for granted this opportunity I am giving you to transform your ways and actions. At all times your management keys must be used by only you. When the garbage needs to go out to the garbage dumpster outside, you observe through every clear plastic bag that there is no stolen items inside the bags, go to the back door turn off the alarm, unlock the door, wait by the door, when the person returns you lock back the door, and turn back on the alarm. Do your jobs as Managers. Soon Ema and Carlos will become certified Manager and Assistant Manager. Edna you must study the manual and I will guide you about the proper procedures. You will be uncertified but you must still perform all the work responsibilities as an Assistant Manager. You will continue to work overtime punching in on the time clock. You already make great salary working on the time clock. I am finished talking for this meeting. I am going home when this meeting is over. I am tired. I will see you all tomorrow."

"Alright. Have a safe journey home. You are something else. You should choose another career to use all your talents, intuition, perception, and sacred spiritual insights. Bye. I will see you tomorrow," said Ema.

"You are right about my talents and life purpose career. This will happen in the future. Currently I am preparing and practicing. Thank you all for everything you have done for us, and this restaurant operation to improve so far. I really appreciate your team work, help, and assistance. My opinion and perception is, in this situation I could never achieve success and improvements all by myself. There is no 'I' in the word teamwork. There is 'I' in the word win. In this teamwork situation and environment there can be no one winner. Thanks again."

The meeting was over and Lily-Butterfly left work. In the parking lot she sat in her car for ten minutes reflecting on everything she said at the meeting, grounding herself, and prayed.

"Dear Creator thank you for everything. You know everything already. Help me to get home safely. I am tired. Help me with my next focused intention, which is to find the town and best place to move to. I think that this will help Holly's learning situation. Rebornstar has only one more year in high school starting in September. I am grateful for the place we lived for the last almost seven years. My instincts tells me it is time to move. If my instincts are right and positive, please help me to find the place for our next home. I want you to know that I keep hearing from within me that this restaurant job is not my destination, and life's purpose career. Keep guiding me on the journey to this destination. Creator as you see and know that this human life's experiences and journey is not an easy path. I will continue to do thy will, and my best with everything. You know everything best. I appreciate all the help and assistance I receive. Thanks again for everything. Amin," whispered Lily-Butterfly.

Lily-Butterfly started the car ride home. As she drove, she opened one of the car window to let in some cool breeze. The cool air came in and washed over her body. After the experience of the management meeting Lily-Butterfly felt hot. She needed this cold air to cool her down and refresh herself. In another ten minutes she closed the car window and simmered into the current warmth of the car's heated environment.

Lily-Butterfly arrived home. She unlocked and opened her apartment door. Holly was sitting on the floor doing a puzzle. Rebornstar was not at home.

"Hi mama," said Holly.

"Hi Holly. How was school? Where is your sister? Did you eat dinner? Have you done your homework? I am tired. Oh, I forgot that today was Friday. You have the weekend to do your homework. Thanks to the Creator for helping me to get home safely."

"School was good. Rebornstar is at her friend's apartment in the next apartment complex up the street. We ate dinner already. I did my homework although there is no school until Monday. You can check my homework. It is in my book bag. Can I have some money for the book fare on Monday? I am asking you now, because I might forget," said Holly.

"How much money do you need for the book fair?"

"Ten dollars is enough. Thank you," replied Holly.

"Take ten dollars from my purse. Do this now because, I might forget to give it to you."

"Okay. I will."

"Holly prepare your mind for moving during this summer holiday. I think that we will be moving by July 1st Remember to say goodbye to your teachers and friends before school breaks for the summer holiday."

"Yes, mama. Where are we moving to?"

"Holly we are moving to the place that the Creator guides us to go for our greater good. It is time to go to what is next. Rebornstar is not going to like to move. But we must move. I would like to try a different public school system and teachers. We will see where I am guided to go. I came a far distance from where I was born on the island of Kawomaya. It has been a very long journey of positive and negative experiences. Maybe one day you will get to hear the wonderful and interesting parts of my life's story and experiences. My life's experiences and story can be used as positive transformational medicine. Where I was born and the place of my ancestor's storytelling and dreams were used as medicine. This is part of the ancient ways. We dream asleep and awake. Anyway, before I take off on a long journey of talking let me contain my talking expressions. I would like to move to a middle income village vibes community. My opinion and perception is that this village community vibes can be positive to support care, unconditional love, and togetherness. Maybe this is only true for me, but still this is what I think will work best for us. It is a village community vibes living at this place. I love and like it here. But it is time to move. Let me go take a shower and eat. A warm shower cleanses the day's events from my body, and helps me feel more relaxed. After eating I am going to write in my journal, pray, and go to sleep. Mama is very tired. When I am finished with the bathroom you can take a shower and prepare for bed. I hope that your sister comes home soon. If she does not come home soon I will call her friend's home before I go to sheep. Sunday I will start looking in the newspaper for our next home. Sigh. My Holly thank you for taking care of yourself. Life can be very interesting."

"Yes mama. I know. We will see where we go next. Hahaha."

"Yes, my child, we will see. The way will show us the way."

Saturday at work was the same usual events for Lily-Butterfly. Sunday was another situation. You will see what the situation is when Lily-Butterfly gets to work on Monday morning. Anyway Lily-Butterfly was off from work on Sunday. She looked in the apartment for rent section of the newspaper. She could not believe her eyes when she saw an advertisement for a two bedroom apartment. The town was Elmwood Park, New Jersey. As you know from reading this book Lily-Butterfly saw things with some kind of symbology and beyond the surface. Lily-Butterfly read the advertisement repeatedly. She pondered and processed the address information and advertisement.

"I think, this is the place. I like the name of the town, Elmwood Park. Elm like the elm tree. I also like woods and parks. There is a lot of positive mother-nature vibes in this name. Wow. I never thought that the place was going to show up so soon. The Creator works in mysterious and immediate ways. It is really time to move. I am going today to check out this address, the community vibes, and public school location. I will do this before I go to Ms. Gina's home to visit Manana. Holly is at the park. I will go tell her that I am going somewhere. I will not tell Holly and Rebornstar about this place until I am sure. When it is time for something it happens, whether people are aware or not," mumbled Lily-Butterfly.

She left home and found the address of the village of apartments in Elmwood Park, New Jersey. She arrived at the address. It was the office of a community of two story brownstone garden apartments. The name of the community was another pleasant surprise for her. There was a large blue and red sign that says 'Welcome to Our Village of Apartments'. All the symbols of this place were positive to her. Another one of her favorite words was village. She was born in a village. These symbolic associations were positive and pleasant to Lily-Butterfly. She felt as if she was about to close another chapter in her life's experiences and enter a new pathway. She parked her car by the office and got out to tour the apartment village complex. Each apartment section had a courtyard in the middle and front. The place was clean and quiet. In a court yard some children played and rode their bikes. The village of apartments were away from the busy street. Close to the village of apartment complexes were supermarkets, restaurants, banks, a shopping plaza, a large and popular department store, about two miles away was route four, and two malls. The only negative thing about this place's location was, it was about an additional thirty minutes away from her current job. She left the apartment complex and drove to the public elementary school which was about a quarter mile away; and on the back street where motor vehicle traffic was not busy. Next she drove to the high school that was less than half a mile away, on a quiet street across from a river and a small park. There was also another park, library and post office about a half mile from the apartment complex. This place was in a location with easy access to most of the major highways in this part of New Jersey. After the tour and visit Lily-Butterfly was convinced that this was the place. Everything felt positive, balanced, and right for her intended move.

"Monday I will telephone this village of apartment's office in Elmwood Park, New Jersey and schedule an interview for Tuesday at 3:00 PM. I will fill out the application and give a check deposit. If it is meant to be for me to have this apartment; it will be. So far so good. Now I will go visit Ms. Gina and Manana Leila. Human life is a consistent and contentious management and maintenance practice. It seems it is time for me to take another leap forward. I choose to take this leap. Amin. I am thankful for everything," whispered Lily-Butterfly.

75

Lies and secrets are a great disguise and mask. The solutions are hidden within the problems.

When Lily-Butterfly returned home on Sunday she did not say anything about the apartment to the children. Monday at 4:36 AM Lily-Butterfly arrived at work. She read the messages in the Manager's note book from Ema and Edna. There was a note from Edna that said, 'the new Assistant Manager took all the money from a cash register and left'. One of the work responsibilities Edna decided to give the Assistant Manager was counting with the cashiers their cash register drawer. After the Assistant Manager counted the first drawer with the cashier and the cashier left the office. He put all the money in the cash register in his work backpack and left work. Edna did not see when he left. The amount he stole was $1,206.29. Edna said that she called the police and they wrote a report.

"Nothing is perfect. There is always something that can disturb harmony, peace, and positive energy balance," grumbled Lily-Butterfly. She sighed.

Lily-Butterfly continued on with her work responsibilities and to-do list. First she checked all Edna's reports and inventories. After she completed all the reports. The food cost was 41%, the labor cost was 39%, and the paper cost was 15%. Every percentage has improved again. But still not where it should be.

"I hope that by the end of June these percentages get to the correct budget of food cost 30%, labor cost 25%, and paper cost 5%," grumbled Lily-Butterfly.

Ema, Carlos and the other employees arrived at work at 6:01 AM. Lily-Butterfly showed her Edna's note about the Assistant Manager and told her about the report percentages.

"Ema did Edna tell you about the Assistant Manager stealing $1,206.29? The food, labor, and paper cost has improved again, but still is not where it should be," said Lily-Butterfly.

"Yes, Edna told me. I plan on not saying anything to you about this stolen money situation. This can be discouraging. You work so hard to improve everything. This guy comes here not even six months and he feels brave enough to do this. Shame on him. He was waiting on the perfect opportunity to steal. No wonder he was born with one of his hands deformed. Maybe part of this is karma in his spirit and soul. I cannot imagine what he could have done this. It could be worse. Good that he left now. He could have set up an armed robbery at the end of a shift and my sister gets hurt or killed. I see more clearly why the security guidelines you give us is so important. Plus, immediately giving new Managers keys and safe combination is not the best idea. After you choose to hire this guy with one arm, this is how he repays you. Sad. I am telling you something will always go wrong in this place. The foundation of this restaurant and the restaurant is a black negative energy hole. Do not let this place destroy you. Do not kill yourself trying to fix this place. This is all I have to say. I am going to work," said Ema.

"I hear and understand. I will choose to do my best as long as I choose to be here. Okay. If and when it is time for me to leave I will. I will schedule your certification test for July 10th. Be prepared. After your certification I will schedule Carlos in August. Nothing will kill me before the time for me to die. I am not scared of death. Know this. Set up Carlos with managing the breakfast shift and return to me. This morning I am going to show you how to do the food order using the build to system I created. After doing the order you will telephone the wholesaler to give them the order. Next you will check in all the Monday delivery and enter the amounts in the computer. You know how to do these things already. The difference is doing them correctly. I am going to finish the payroll and print all the reports for Mr. Watson."

"Okay. I will return after setting Carlos up with the things he needs to get done."

Lily-Butterfly taught Ema to do the inventory and ordering process correctly. At 8:30 AM Lily-Butterfly took all the reports in a file and went to the dining room. She had breakfast while she waited for Mr. Watson. He came at 9:05 AM. She put down the file folder in front of where Mr. Watson was sitting.

"Here, read these reports before you say anything. There is a police report regarding the Assistant Manager stealing last night $1,206.29. Now we are back to only Ema, Edna, Carlos, and I. I will be back."

Lily-Butterfly got up to use the rest room. She returned.

"Here is your annual review. I gave you 2.5% raise and not the maximum 3%. There is always room for improvement. I have not decided to give you a salary increase to the General Manager's salary for working in a restaurant with this responsibility and revenue. Maybe next year I will do so. I did your work review in March and was waiting to give it to you to read and sign. Here, read the review and sign that you agree with what is written. So, the percentage in the restaurant has improved a lot. But......,"

Lily-Butterfly was sitting there in silence listening to Mr. Watson and observing him. She interrupted what he was saying.

"But nothing. My perception is learn to say thank you. Sometimes thank you is all that there is to say, especially when you have never said thank you to me for anything. When you say thank you it means that you are acknowledging something of value you receive. You might think that I get paid to do my work responsibility, but you benefit as well from all the work I perform. It seems as if you get pleasure from causing suffering, and the perception of pain and domination. Please do not try to push me around like a race horse. I am doing more than my best, and without the correct salary. Look at how far I have improved everything. I no longer want to hear... but anything, and that I need to do better. The quality of the work I do speaks for itself. If things can improve more I will make sure it does. The report for the stolen money please take it and do as you choose. I am going to the office to read the review and make a copy. You can continue to read all the reports. When I come back let me know if you have any questions?"

Lily-Butterfly got up and left the table without waiting for Mr. Watson to reply.

Mr. Watson read the reports. Lily-Butterfly went to the office read the review and made a copy. She returned to sit at the table with Mr. Watson.

"Here is your copy of the review," said Lily-Butterfly.

"Did you sign the review?" Asked Mr. Watson.

"No. I did not sign it. I do not agree with your decision of 2.5% salary increase. I should be receiving the correct salary for working in this restaurant. Usually people endorse and sign a document they agree with or to. You can do as you wish with this review. My views about my work performance is not depended on your endorsement and views. The quality of my work performance speaks for itself. My work performance comes from within me. I do not want to talk about my review any further. Thank you. The plumber came to fix all the plumbing issues and the PVC sewage pipe. This is great, thank you for sending him. There is nothing else I would like to say."

"Okay write a manual or book on everything you did to fix this restaurant, and what the issues were. I will give it to the President of the company. We can use this manual to fix every restaurant and also every franchise restaurants. If we do this, the company will make a lot of money and profit. This would be great. Ha. Mmm."

"No, I will not. The authentic nature of my talents, positive life force energy, and techniques are beyond words, and cannot be written down. I carry them within my spirit, soul, and heart. I was not born to use these talents to make money for people's greed and perception of material wealth and richness. Currently I can see the true nature of your heartless-ness. If you keep showing your direct true colors, I will be leaving this place sooner than I am meant to leave. I am here, because I feel guided from within to be here. Know this. I will see you on Monday. Do not try to push me any further to the edge of this negative restaurant cliff situation, because I will leap. I am used to leaping. I am not afraid of leaps. I will see you on Monday. For today I do not want to talk to you anymore. Bye."

"Okay. Bye."

Lily-Butterfly got up and walked to the office. She put the copy of the review in her brief case, and telephoned the village of apartment's office, in Elmwood Park, New Jersey to schedule an appointment for 3:00 PM on Tuesday. Next she went to help Ema with the service and preparing for lunch. Ema took a break and ate breakfast. During lunch Lily-Butterfly took care of the service and managed the shift. Ema worked in the deli section of the restaurant. At 3:00 PM everything in the restaurant was prepared for the dinner shift. Lily-Butterfly was in a no-nonsense but pleasant mood for the rest of the day at work. She spoke to Edna about the stolen money and a few other things. At 4:30 PM she left work.

Tuesday at 3:00 PM Lily-Butterfly arrived at the village of apartment, Elmwood Park, New Jersey rental office for her interview and tour. The Rental Manager greeted her.

"Hi Ms. Lily-Butterfly. Welcome. Have a seat. My name is Matthew. I am the Manager."

"Thank you Matthew. I would like to rent the two bedroom

apartment at 105B Boulevard, as advertised in the Sunday's newspaper. Here is the advertisement."

"Okay sure. Let me go get the key. Let us visit the apartment to see if you like it before you fill out the application," said Matthew.

Matthew got the apartment key and returned.

"Come, we will walk to the apartment. It is across the street in the third court yard," said Matthew.

Matthew and Lily-Butterfly walked to the apartment. They arrived at the address. The apartment was upstairs on the second floor. Matthew guided Lily-Butterfly up one flight of twelve steps. Seven steps straight up and the last five steps turned slightly to the left. At the end of twelve steps they entered the living room. This was a large open room.

"Ms. Lily-Butterfly look around I will wait here by the banister. Please let me know if you have any questions," said Matthew.

"Okay."

They were both silent. Lily-Butterfly looked at the apartment.

The apartment layout was – at the entrance a large open room – the living room. In this room to the left was a large walk-in closet. Continuing to the left was a small dining area with the kitchen in an enclosed room to the right of the dining room. This whole area had six windows and one window in the kitchen. Leaving the kitchen Lily-Butterfly walked to the right of the living room to the bathroom and bathrooms. There was a window in the bathroom over the bath tub. Next to the bathroom was a bedroom with two windows and a closet. To the right of this bedroom was the master bed room with one window and two closets.

"I completely like and love this place," whispered Lily-Butterfly, as she stood in the master bed room looking out the window.

She returned to where Matthew was standing.

"How do you like this place?" asked Matthew.

"I really like it very much. I would love to have it. Can I?"

"Let us go back to the office. You will fill out the application and I will do a credit and background check."

At the office Lily-Butterfly filled out the application and gave it back to Matthew.

"Alright let me see. You have two children, single, and no pets?" said Matthew.

"Yes, two daughters, and one rabbit. I do not know if a rabbit fits into the pet category that the application ask."

"A rabbit is okay. You make more than enough income to qualify. I will telephone your references, and do a credit and background check. Is it okay to telephone you on Friday to confirm that you will receive the apartment?"

"Yes, you can telephone me at work on Friday. Currently I do not use credit cards and have no debts. So, my credit report will reflect this. Is this okay?"

"This will be fine. The background checks will show any warrants, arrest, negative character, bankruptcies, and so forth. I have to check these things; it is the rules. You should be fine."

"When will the apartment be available?"

"July 1st. We have to do some repairs, paint, and get the fire department to inspect it. Is the rental date okay?"

"Yes. This date and month is great. I will appreciate it very much if you choose to rent this apartment to me. My children and I are looking to find a good place to move to. I like everything about inside this apartment, the location, schools, and everything I see so far. We will be so happy to move here."

"Sure, I will give it to you if your references, credit report, and background check is positive. There is no agent fee."

"Okay. I will leave you a check for $3,000. This will be for one and a half month's security and $1,200 for the first month's rent. This payment in advance is to confirm that I would like to get the apartment. If you do not give it to me I could come back and get my check. When you telephone me on Friday let me know when in June to return to get the keys."

"Sounds good Ms. Lily-Butterfly. I will telephone you on Friday."

"Okay thank you for everything."

"Bye. You are welcome. Thank you for coming," said Matthew.

"Good bye Matthew."

Lily-Butterfly left the office. She got in her car and drove towards the route four highway.

"It is really time to move. I feel joyful and content. After Matthew telephone me on Friday I will give my current landlord notice. It is good that currently I had a month to month lease. All is well," whispered Lily-Butterfly.

Lily-Butterfly drove to Ms. Gina's home. She got out of her car and instantly had a sinking feeling in her heart.

"I wonder what this feeling could be about," said Lily-Butterfly.

She walked up to the door and knocked. Ms. Gina did not come to unlock the door. The knocked again repeatedly and louder. All the windows were closed and locked. The home seemed isolated.

"Maybe they went for a walk. I will wait," said Lily-Butterfly.

She waited for thirty seven minutes. Ms. Gina and Manana Leila did not arrive. Lily-Butterfly went back to the door and knocked again repeatedly. Still no one came to the door. She looked through all the windows she did not see anyone inside the home. She got into her car and drove home. On the way home many negative thoughts came to her mind. When she got home she telephoned Ms. Gina's home, no one answered the telephone.

After going to Ms. Gina's home and no one was home Lily-Butterfly went back on Sunday and had the same experience. When she telephoned Ms. Gina's home no one answered the telephone; not Ms. Gina or Dean. Lily-Butterfly returned the following Tuesday and it was the same situation. At one point she thought, maybe Dean is inside and hiding from her in the bathroom, because when she looked through the window she did not see any one. She telephoned Dean's restaurant job; the owner and Manager told Lily-Butterfly that he was not at work. This situation felt very disconcerting and helpless to Lily-Butterfly. There was nothing more she felt that she could do. After this incident regarding Ms. Gina and Manana Leila; Lily-Butterfly felt sad and she talked less. Along with this feeling she also felt empty. Usually with this feeling Lily-Butterfly's senses became more fine-tuned, and amplified, sharp, and clear. She focused these experiences into her life and work performance.

Lily-Butterfly said nothing to the children about Ms. Gina and Manana Leila's disappearance, and finding an apartment. She decided to wait. One of Lily-Butterfly's strongest intuition was that Ms. Gina and Dean were avoiding her, because they are hiding something from her. Her instincts told her that they were hiding the fact that they put Manana Leila into a nursing home. She would not know which nursing home until Ms. Gina's conscience digs her down and she chooses to confess to Lily-Butterfly. Until then she had to wait. Lily-Butterfly prayed to the Creator for help with Ms. Gina telephoning her. Lily-Butterfly had faith that at some point Ms. Gina would telephone. Ms. Gina would tell her which nursing home she had taken Manana Leila in, so that she could go visit her. Lily-Butterfly learned a lot from this disappearance situation.

Friday Matthew telephoned Lily-Butterfly at work.

"Hi Ms. Lily-Butterfly congratulations I have decided to rent you the apartment. All your references were positive and your background check as well. A one year lease will be given and automatically renewed each year. If at any time you do not choose to renew the lease let us know three months before the expiration date which is July 1st. Every year your rent will be increased by 3%. You can come next week Tuesday at 10:00 AM to sign the lease, and return on June 18th to pick up the keys. After picking up the keys you can prepare the apartment for moving in the weekend before July 1st. Do you have any questions?"

"This is great. Thank you so much. I will be there at 10:00 AM next week Tuesday. I have no questions at this time. Have a great day. Bye."

"You are welcome. See you then."

Lily-Butterfly hung up the telephone. She sat at the office desk with her forehead on the edge of the desk. She cried tears of joy and relief about accomplishing the next step in her life for the children and herself. Lily-Butterfly sat like this for ten minutes and then got up and drank some water. She went back to her work duties.

Friday at the meeting Lily-Butterfly choose not to talk too much. The meeting started at 3:45 PM and was over in an hour.

"Hi everyone by now you have heard about the new Assistant Manager stealing the money. The situation speaks for itself. Edna you did the right thing by telephoning the police and filing a report. Continue to keep the office door locked when you are not using it. Practice awareness and security. I gave the police report to Mr. Watson. We are all doing a great job. I really appreciate all your help with the improvements and maintenance of this restaurant operation. The employees look very good and presentable in their new uniforms; and you do as well. Your participation in your training is excellent. Keep up the inspired self-motivation for yourself and all the employees. The percentages for this week have improved. Do you have any comments?"

"You seem to have a sad vibe and not talking too much. Are you okay?" said Edna.

"I am okay. I feel sad about a personal matter. After this matter is completely processed, I will be fine. I choose to talk less. I am choosing to rest in ease and take a break from my normal speed and vibes. Sometimes stepping back and resting, to step forward is wise. I never aim to be perfect."

"Thank you for believing in us and upgrading our awareness and skills. You are not easy, but you take us and everything else where it needs to be. This benefits us personally and professionally," said Ema.

"I agree," said Edna.

"I am happy to have met a woman like you. Thank you for everything. I will be ready for my test in August," said Carlos.

"Yes, Carlos be ready. I will be interviewing more new regular employees next week. Keep giving applications to interested people. We will get the new employees trained. This will decrease the overtime for regular employees. When Ema is certified she will work midshift two times per week by coming to work at 10:00 AM instead of 6:00 AM. Eddie the shift supervisor will start to work all mid shifts. Carlos will be the opening Assistant Manager when Ema takes a day off and works midshift. Edna this way you will have more help at dinner time and so forth. Plus, Ema can get some rest. Carlos will assist me and help Ema. Take care of yourselves and take your vitamins."

"Yes, we will," said Ema.

"One last thing. The computer technician are coming to repair and change all the computer cables next week Wednesday morning. After this if there are any further disconnection with these cables, I will be printing the evidence, give it to Mr. Watson, and he will call the police. Be warned, listen, and hear. It can take time for negative habits to transform. Ema and Edna these negative habit of your past actions in this restaurant needs priority attention to transform and change. I do not think both of you want to go to jail. I usually give more than enough warning, and after I have to take action. Are there any comments?"

"No. We hear you. Thanks."

"Okay I am going home now. When you do not see me, I am gone. Be wise. I will see all of you tomorrow. I am very tired. Goodnight."

"Bye. Go rest. See you," said Edna.

Lily-Butterfly left work for the day. She processed her day's experiences as she drove home.

"The computer cables will be permanently repaired next week. This stealing will come to an end. I hope the stealing of money comes to an end. I think they will stop or decrease the stealing as much as possible. This is the last major step to improve the cash income and overall budget percentage. Enough Lily-Butterfly. I am taking a break from these negative work situations. Creator I am grateful for everything. Get Ms. Gina to telephone me. Amin."

76

Authentic expansion of consciousness does not come in physical sizes. The roses comes after the thorns.

Monday Mr. Watson came for the meeting. Lily-Butterfly gave him the reports. He looked at her she sat in silence. Mr. Watson read the reports.

"Food cost 31%, paper cost 9%, and labor 29%. Good job. One more step to go to food 30%, paper 5%, and labor 25%. Effective Friday May 3rd the company has discontinued cashing every employee's checks in the restaurant cash drawers. Employees must cash their checks at their personal bank or check cashing place. Please let every employee know. You were right about the employees check. We are doing an investigation on this issue and it is a major problem. We are discovering that checks are being requested for employees who no longer work for the company. These checks are being cashed in the company's cash register drawers. Is there anything else?" said Mr. Watson.

"Okay I will let the Managers and employee know about the check cashing situation. The computer company technician is coming this week to repair and permanently connect the cable wires. In the past these cable wires were consistently disconnected as a part of a stealing operation. So, after this is fixed we will see what happens. I perceive this is the last major thing to be done to improve everything financially. I will add the invoice for the computer work to Monday bill report. I have nothing else to say."

"Okay. Bye, have a god day," replied Mr. Watson.

"Bye, same to you."

Tuesday April 23, 1996 Lily-Butterfly retuned to the village of apartment's office, in Elmwood Park, New Jersey to sign the lease. This confirmed her moving plans. After leaving this office she drove to Ms. Gina's home. Lily-Butterfly knocked on the door repeatedly. No one came to the door. She left and drove home. When Lily-Butterfly drove home she told Rebornstar and Holly about finding an apartment.

"Rebornstar and Holly we are moving on Saturday June 29th. I will take the day off from work. Start to put in garbage bags all your

564

clothes and things that you do not want; I will donate them. I will give you boxes to pack all the things that you do not need for the next two months. On Sunday I will take both of you to look at the village of apartment community and schools."

"I am not coming. Why do we have to move? Next year September, I graduate high school."

"Rebornstar you are coming. I have had enough of your rebellion and unmentionable negative actions and attitude. Also, know that after we move you will not take the bus back to this town to visit your gang of friends. It is time to transition on in life and also make new friends. After graduating high school, you can do as you choose. When you graduate high school, you will be close to nineteen years old. Until you graduate high school you will follow this path that we are on. I need to change this school district for you and your sister's benefit. Hear and listen to me without choosing to be stubborn and rebellious. Stop taking advantage of my niceness, unconditional love, and compassion."

"Whatever you say," replied Rebornstar.

"Ms. Rebornstar I know that you will blame me for, not being a productive parent, and what you could have done, but never choose to do. So, I will never stop doing the very best job as a parent whether you like it or not. So, prepare to move and do as I request. I insist that you are coming when we move. You are graduating high school no matter what you say and think; and whether you like school or not. Becoming eighteen is not an age to think that you are an adult and can do only as you choose. Okay, this is all I currently have to say about our moving situation. Sunday after breakfast we will go to visit the place, school, and town we are moving to. Period and end of this announcement."

Rebornstar was silent. She knew how far to push her mother's buttons. When Lily-Butterfly draws the line, Rebornstar knows that the lines are firm. This is part of her mother's parent-ship and style.

"Mama, when do I start to sort out the things I do not want and need?" asked Holly.

"As soon as you are ready. Take garbage bags from the kitchen. Soon I will bring home empty boxes from work. When you see the boxes, you can start packing."

"Okay mama," replied Holly.

"After school closes for the summer holiday, we are moving that weekend. I have to do so many things to take care of this family. A one parent family is one of the most difficult things in human life.

Maybe I make parent-ship look simple and easy, but it is not. Both of you help me with this move by doing your own personal packing and sorting. Resistance, stubbornness, and extra un-necessary problems do not help you or me. Please and thank both of you in advance for your co-operation and help. Helping yourselves helps me. Thank you very much. Enough is enough."

Both Rebornstar and Holly were silent. They sat on the couch looking at their mother. Lily-Butterfly walked away from the children and entered the kitchen.

Lily-Butterfly made dinner. The children took showers one at a time. The children came to the kitchen/dining room for dinner. It was Holly's turn to say the grace to bless the food. They ate dinner mostly in silence. Lily-Butterfly was processing moving, work experiences, and the mysterious disappearance of Ms. Gina and Manana Leila. Lily-Butterfly instincts still told her that Ms. Gina had put Manana in a nursing home. Ms. Gina went back to working in a live-in Home Health Aid job and comes home when she chooses. Lily-Butterfly prayed and waited until Ms. Gina choose to telephone her to confess and say where Manana was. Until then she just had to wait for the Creator assistance with this Manana Leila situation. She did not tell the children about this situation. Rebornstar and Holly looked repeatedly at their mother surrounded by her silence aura. They knew that when their mother was talking less this was when she was most serious and beyond an outward expression.

Conserving time, speech, action, and positive life force energy was Lily-Butterfly's new attitude. She felt like she was at the thresh hold of being burned out, although she had an inner ability to override her very tired feelings. On Wednesday the computer technician came to fix everything that was an issue with the computer. They replaced all the old cables and permanently connected all of them. On Wednesday, Thursday, and Friday Lily-Butterfly had interviewed new potential regular employees and hired eight of them. These new employees were scheduled on the day shift for training. New regular employees were hired until the regular employees totaled one hundred. The previous employees that currently worked in the restaurant were promoted to shift supervisors with a salary increase. These shift supervisors supported the Managerial staff. At this time and in the future no additional new Managers or Assistant Managers were sent to the restaurant from the company's training department, to work in this restaurant. Mr. Watson told Lily-Butterfly that they did not have any new managerial help.

Friday at the meeting Lily-Butterfly's attitude of focus and no nonsense continued.

"Thank you for coming to this meeting. Are there any questions, comments, or concerns?" asked Lily-Butterfly.

"Thank you for all the new employees at night including the two shift supervisors, and the help from Ema and Carlos when they work mid shift. This has helped me tremendously. What a welcoming relief. Now that you come to show us the right way, I am loving these experiences. If you ever leave this restaurant, I am leaving as well. There is no way I am going back to work in the previous hell hole," said Edna.

"Thank you for training me and upgrading my managerial skills. With all these new employees I work less, I am less burned out and stressed, I work smarter, and I now know the right policies and procedures. Now I can work as a certified Manager where ever I choose. I no longer feel stuck to this place and in my life," said Ema.

"Thank you for everything. I do not know how you do all you do. You are like an infinite waterfall and flow of positive energy," said Carlos.

"You are all welcome. In life I have a village perception. It is simple. The perception is; if I help one person from the village, I help the whole village. Humans do not realize that originally humanity was one complete village perception. One of our responsibility as humans is to help one another. Currently one view is that money and material possession replaces everything as the major priority. Anyway, I do not want to get carried away with my philosophical views and talking. The last major changes that goes in effect on Friday May 3rd is no Manager, Assistant Manager, and every regular employee can no longer cash their check in the cash register. I have put a notice about this on the employee's notice board. Please tell every employee on your work shift about this new decision. They are not going to like this, but cashing employees check is not the company's responsibility. The original policy is, no cashing of employee's checks, because of conflict of interest reasons. Someone started this as a courtesy to the employees. This has become a major way to exploit, create conflict of interest, steal, and take advantage of the company financially."

"What about the people who have cashed their checks here for over twenty years. They might not have bank accounts. They are not going to like this," said Edna.

"There is no alternative to reintroducing and reinforcing this no check cashing policy. Tell the employees that the company has discontinued the cashing of employee's checks. Maybe they can go to the check cashing place to cash their check and pay the fees," said Lily-Butterfly.

"Oh wow," said Ema.

"Another thing, starting Monday all the over time is over for 90% of the employees, soon it will be 95%."

"Yes, we saw the schedule. The employees do not like this as well," said Ema.

"Yes, we saw the schedule. The employees do not like the fact they make less money," said Edna.

"Business is about making money and profit. The money that was used to pay overtime went to pay the new employees. With more employees everyone works less and the customer service and speed of service improves. We have a cleaner dining room and restaurant. We have the opportunity to make more money with faster and more accurate service, and so on and so forth. The right view here is that this is a business, and not personal piggy bank, entertainment, and hobby. This restaurant is open 365 days per year, including Thanksgiving, Christmas, and New Year's Day. A revolving door of never ending business, with no profit and minus two million dollars. Soon we will all rotate to work one of these days so that the same Manager is not working on these holidays," said Lily-Butterfly.

"Good. This is music to my ears. Edna and I work in this place every one of these holidays," said Ema.

"Now, I have to face these night employees to tell them about the check cashing situation. I hope that they do not stop working here."

"If they leave, we have enough employees. I doubt that they will leave. Some money is better than no money. They can leave if they choose to. The company will no longer accept employee checks in the restaurant's deposit. Okay. Is there anything else?" said Lily-Butterfly.

"No," said Ema, Edna, and Carlos.

"Alright, I am going home. See you tomorrow. Goodnight. Be safe," responded Lily-Butterfly.

"Bye. Rest up. Be well. Thanks," said Edna.

"Yes. Goodnight. You are not easy. But you are wonderful. Hahaha. Oh wow," said Ema.

"Goodnight ma'am. See you tomorrow. Have a safe ride home," said Carlos.

"Thank each and every one of you. I could not have done all I did without your help, plus all the regular employees. Thank you for helping with the financial situations and budget percentages. I think that next week Monday all the percentages are going to be within the required budget. Let us see what happens. Doing the right things helps me to rest in peace, sleep great at night, and enjoy my dreams. Bye," said Lily-Butterfly.

After the meeting Lily-Butterfly took her briefcase, got in her car, and drove home. Saturday at work was business as usual.

Sunday Lily-Butterfly brought Rebornstar and Holly to visit the village of apartment complex, the apartment complex laundry facilities, and where their schools would be.

"I love this place," said Holly.

"It is nice," said Rebornstar.

"Good for both of you that you love or like this place. This is where our new home will be created for all the known and unknown reasons. Both of you will meet new people and create new friendships and relationships. I really do my best. You will get to see inside the apartment when I get the key, or when we move. Both of you will share the large master bedroom. It has two closets. I will take the small bedroom. Rebornstar I will buy you a new bed. It will fit on one side of the room. You do not have to sleep on the top bed of the bunk bed anymore. Plus, I will divide the room with screens. It will seem like you are in your own private bedroom. After I get the key on Tuesday June 18th we can return to clean on Sunday June 23rd. At this time, you will get to see inside."

"Okay. Thank you," replied Rebornstar.

They had lunch at one of the restaurants in the area and went home.

Rebornstar and Holly seem to like everything they were shown. This was a relief to Lily-Butterfly, one less issues for her to have to be concerned about. They all drive home in silence. On the way home they stopped at the supermarket to do the food shopping for the week. The girls helped their mother with the food shopping, pushing the shopping cart, and carrying the bags into the apartment. On arriving home, they all prepared for the coming week. Later the girls went outside to the park to play with their friends.

Monday came again and as usually Lily-Butterfly was at work on time. It was 4:30 AM when she got out of her car to enter the restaurant and turned off the security alarm system. Reaching the office, she turned on the light and started to review the reports and inventory that Edna had done. She checked the inventory and completed the reports. Finally, all the report percentages were less than the budget. The food cost was 27% - 3% less than it should be. The labor cost was 23% - 2% less than it should be. The paper cost was 4% - 1% less than it should be. The sales had increased by $150,000 for the week. Plus, the fixed computer and cash register's cables prevented Assistant Managers and cashiers from stealing.

"Thank you Creator for all your help and assistance. Thanks to Edna, Ema, and Carlos and all the other employees as well. Now that everything has been accomplished to create all these improvements let me see what Mr. Watson is going to do and say next. For the first time in many years now the restaurant can make a profit. I will wait and see what happens," whispered Lily-Butterfly.

Lily-Butterfly sat and prayed in silence. At 6:00 AM Ema and the opening employees arrived inside the restaurant. They prepared for the breakfast service. Lily-Butterfly drifted out of her prayer mode. She noticed Ema and the employees through the thick one way mirror wall. Through this mirror she could see the complete front service production, service section of the restaurant, and most of the dining room. Lily-Butterfly thought, I hope this complete improvement continues. At 6:35 AM Ema and Carlos came into the office to speak to Lily-Butterfly.

"We did it," announced Lily-Butterfly.

"Really. Hahaha. How much is the percentage?" said Ema.

"Food 27%, labor 23%, and Paper 4%. All less than the required budget. If this becomes consistent over three month periods we get a percentage of the profits as a bonus. Hooray. Good job to us."

"Good job to you Lily-Butterfly. All we did was following your guidance. You are strong, flexible, and tough," said Ema.

"Good. All of this is long overdue," said Carlos.

"Yes, thanks very much for all your help. I could not have done this all by myself. This took team effort. Team effort indeed. Thanks to the Creator as well."

"Oh wow. Later I will telephone Edna and tell her the good news," said Ema.

When Mr. Watson came for the meeting at 9:00 AM Lily-Butterfly gave him the file with all the reports. He read them.

"Good. Finally. I hope this improvement continues. Great plan of action and decision making. My supervisor, the board members, and the President will be happy about achieving this goal. Great job. Do you have anything else to say today?" said Mr. Watson.

Lily-Butterfly was silent for about thirty seconds. She thought, I cannot believe the disappointed look on Mr. Watson's face and his down beat attitude vibes. It is as if he was disappointed now that the negative financial problems were improved. So sad, so sad. Humans are interesting. After these thoughts she replied.

"No. I have nothing else to say for this meeting. I will see you next week Monday. Bye."

She got up from the table and walked away from Mr. Watson before he replied, if he was going to reply. Lily-Butterfly walked to the kitchen to tell Juan about the positive financial budget news and accomplishment.

"Juan we have accomplished getting the financial budget to the required percentage. This week for the first time the percentage came out less that the budget. Thank you Juan for everything you did to help me with every improvement. Juan you are one of the priceless pillars that holds up this restaurant. Thanks."

"Thank you for your recognition. You are welcome. I say the same back to you, good job. Keep up the good work. Take care of yourself, do not let this place ruin your tranquility and peace. Good ma'am."

"Yes, Juan when people really try and perform their best efforts positive things can happen. I am going to get something to eat before breakfast is over. Have a great day."

"You too. I will see you later."

"Okay."

When Edna came to work she shared in the celebration of all the improvements. They reminisce about how horrible things were in the past. Even the spirit ghosts had calmed down or crossed over. Things were in harmony and positive balance.

77

Be aware, this story will start to move faster. The foundation is created for the completion of this story. Lily-Butterfly is almost 90% closer to her chosen destiny and life's purpose. A tree has to mature before it can bring forth blossom, fruit, and food. Lily-Butterfly has to mature and develop as a human through six cycles of seven years. She must get to the age of forty two to bring forth from within her spirit and soul everything that is needed to perform and maintain her chosen destiny and life's purpose career. The deepest levels of unconditional love and compassion is the same towards angels and demons alike.

At work the Manager's meetings continued every Friday. The financial budget percentages continued to be lower than the required budget. Everything that was improved in the restaurant stayed improved. The Managers and employees became self-motivated and happy. Mr. Watson continued to come on Monday mornings to get the reports and meeting with Lily-Butterfly. She chose to make the meetings very short or nonexistent, by just giving Mr. Watson the reports. So far Mr. Watson had still not told Lily-Butterfly 'thank you'. Lily-Butterfly thought that this was strange.

Lily-Butterfly returned to Matthew the Manager for the village of apartment on Tuesday June 18th to get the keys for the apartment. They had almost finish packing. Sunday June 23rd Lily-Butterfly, Rebornstar, and Holly went to the apartment to clean. Rebornstar vacuumed and Holly cleaned sinks, refrigerator, cupboards, and window ledges. Lily-Butterfly did all the other cleaning. The cleaning was completed and they left their new home at 2:00 PM and went to the supermarket before they went home. At this time Ms. Gina still had not contacted Lily-Butterfly to tell her where Manana Leila was. Summer holiday came. Rebornstar and Holly said goodbye to their teachers and friends. On Saturday June 29th Lily-Butterfly had taken a personal day off from work. The moving truck came to her current home and moved them to their new home at the village of apartments, in Elmwood Park. Lily-Butterfly and the girls spent Saturday and Sunday setting up their new home. Unbeknownst to Lily-Butterfly some days during the summer Rebornstar took the bus back to the town they moved from to visit her friends. Holly made new friends with children in the courtyard where they lived and in the adjoining courtyard. Sometimes during the week and on the weekend Lily-Butterfly took Holly to work with her. Holly celebrated her seventh birthday on July 31, 1996.

Lily-Butterfly made plans at the end of summer 1996 to put Holly in summer sleep away camp starting summer 1997 the month she became eight years old. Summer sleep away camp for Holly was the second Saturday in July to the fourth Saturday in August; a total of six weeks. This camp was located in a mountain encampment in upstate New York. Holly would come home at the end of every two weeks to visit and wash her laundry. Lily-Butterfly would go visit Holly on the scheduled parent's visiting days. Holly went to this sleep away camp every summer from eight years old to fifteen years old. From sixteen to seventeen years old Holly became a Consoler-In-Training to help take care of the children and work in the kitchen. At this camp Holly got the opportunity to mature from many different structured activities and disciplined programs. Some of the programs were understanding the river and the many creatures that lived in the river at the camp, boating, swimming lessons and swimming in the river, surviving in the wild, rock climbing, kayaking, nature programs, athletics programs, art, craft, hiking, learn different kinds of native dances, how to build and maintain a camp fire, camping in the wild, meeting new people, making friends, having nourishing relationships, fishing, leisure time, gardening, and other high-quality programs. Holly loved this sleep away camp and looked forward to going every year. At this time Rebornstar was too old for this camp. The maximum age limit was fifteen years old. Rebornstar at this time during the summer went to work, stayed at home spending time in the neighborhood with new friends, traveling back to her old neighborhood to spend time with friends, and going to different places with them. Some of the benefits of this sleep away camp for Holly was that she became more independent, developed confidence and self-worth, improved her relationship skills, learned and improved team work qualities, developed and improved athletic skills and talents, improve her strengths and weaknesses, learned how to swim very well, become a team leader, awaken talents, helping other people, and many other things. This sleep away camp was great for Holly. It provided a safe, supervised, nourishing environment, and a home away from home for Holly during the summer. Plus, it helped Lily-Butterfly to not be concerned about Holly being home and in the neighborhood to figure things out by herself; when she was at work.

Let us go back to the summer of 1996 when Rebornstar, Holly, and Lily-Butterfly moved to their new home. Lily-Butterfly went to Ms. Gina's home and she was not home. She left a piece of paper with her new telephone number and address taped to Ms. Gina's front door. With sadness in her heart she closed the screen door and walked away from Ms. Gina's home. During this summer 1996 Rebornstar worked and she did okay making new friends. She was a social butterfly and had an extroverted personality. Holly was more of an introvert personality and choose friends more mindfully. Plus, Holly was content with being her own friend, and enjoyed doing things alone. Rebornstar and Holly naturally did not choose to watch television or use game devices. Currently most times they love playing outdoors. Lily-Butterfly, Rebornstar, and Holly went to their schools and registered. Holly registered for being in special education for her classes, like in her previous school. The summer came to an ended. Life at work continued to be successful, positive, and time consuming for Lily-Butterfly, Ema, Edna, Carlos and all the employees. Ema was certified as a Manager. Carlos was certified as an Assistant Manager.

The first week of September 1996 school was open. Rebornstar went to twelfth grade. Holly went to second grade. On the first day of school Holly came home with a letter from her homeroom teacher. Lily-Butterfly read the letter out loud so Holly could hear.

The letter said, "Dear Ms. Lily-Butterfly. I think the root of Holly's seeming learning disability is that she cannot see from a distance. She is nearsighted. Today I worked with Holly at my desk and she seemed perfectly fine with the things I was teaching her. I sent her back to her seat and asked her the same information written on the black board. Holly became totally lost as to what I was pointing to, and what I was talking about. I asked Holly to come back to my desk. We went over the same information. Holly knew all the information I was showing her. I tried teaching her from the board again and she was totally unaware of what I was teaching. I brought Holly to the school Nurse. I asked the Nurse to give her a basic visual eye reading test from near and far. Near Holly read the words and alphabet correctly. When the same test was given from a distance she did not say one correct word or any of the alphabet correctly. This confirms my suspicions. Please take Holly to an Optometrist as soon as possible. Below is the phone number and address of an Optometrist across the main road from this school, and two blocks over. To me Holly seems even intellectually smarter than the average main stream student. I hope that you find the information in this letter helpful. We practice a 'no child gets left behind' teaching policy. I will give Holly a seat in the front row of the class to help with her eye sight. All the best with everything." Mrs. March.

"Oh wow. I was right about my instincts to move and choosing this place to live. Holly this is the root of your mysterious supposedly learning disabilities. This is what I am talking about, one day in this school, and the mystery is solved. I could not figure out the problem, because I teach and work with you only from sitting at a table with the learning information maybe twelve inches from her eyes. Oh, my Creator and Mrs. March, thank you very much. Holly I am taking you to the eye doctor next week Tuesday. I will schedule the appointment tomorrow morning from work. I am over joyed about this situation being solved. I will give you a letter to give to Mrs. March tomorrow; thanking her, and letting her know that you will be absent from school next week Tuesday. She seems like a very caring and kind person, and loves her teaching job. This is great Holly."

"Yes mama. Finally, I realize my learning difficulties. Mrs. March explained the situation to me. I feel relieved. I was used to being like this. So, I by myself could not know what my problems were. Mrs. March have positive loving and caring vibes. I like her. Thanks be to my teacher and The Creator, like you said. Human life can be a mystery."

"Holly good people are always around. Based on karma and what is meant to be, when the right time comes, they usually show up. Thanks to Mrs. March your learning can improve. Wow."

"Mama I wonder what it is going to be like being able to see from far away. I can see near. Now I realize that I am supposed to also see from a distance. Before I could not see from a distance and I thought that this was normal. I was blind from far away. Oh wow. This solution to my eye sight and learning will be interesting. It will be like solving a puzzle. Mmm."

"Holly a whole new world will open up to your eye sight, awareness, and mindfulness. Your non-eyesight helped your intuition, perception, spirit, and soul eye to develop and mature. Plus, develop your senses of seeing, smelling, hearing, tasting, and feeling. Now with near and distant eyesight you should be fine learning in school. It will take you some time to get use to improved seeing, and normal learning. The Creator works in mysterious ways; my child. Holly as you grow you will naturally get to know and realize more about the spirit, soul, and the ways of the Creator. Continue to pray every night before you go to sleep. You have a lot to be thankful for. Holly, today is a miraculous and great day in your life. Amin."

"Amin, mama. I cannot wait until I get my glasses. I love school mama even when I had an unbeknownst learning problem. I love to learn new things. Learning is interesting to me. Now I will love school even more. Wait until I tell Rebornstar. Let us see what she says."

"We will see. I wonder where Rebornstar is. She has not come home from school as yet."

By dinner time Rebornstar was home. Holly set the table for dinner. They all took what they needed from the pots on the stove and sat down to eat. Lily-Butterfly said the prayers to bless the food.

"Rebornstar my home room teacher Mrs. March figured out my learning disability issues and mystery. I am so happy. The issue was I could only see near. I could not see from far away. I am nearsighted. I never figured this out by myself, because I was used to seeing this way, and thought this is how I am supposed to see. Life is funny," said Holly.

"Good for you Holly. Now you will be wearing glasses all the time and look like a book-worm and geek."

"Oh well I do not care what I look like with glasses on. Everybody has to look like something. To me it is better to look like a book-worm and geek than to look like crap," replied Holly.

"Hehehe. Bahahaha. Holly I never heard you talk like this before," replied Rebornstar.

"Good for you Holly. The renewed Holly has awakened. Thanks be to Mrs. March, her spirit, soul, and the Creator. Sometimes one positive, loving, compassionate, and caring person can show up in a person's life and help to create a renewed, infinite world of positive improvements, and difference. So, Miss. Rebornstar, how was your first day of new school?"

"My first day was good. I met some new people that I like. The school environment vibes seem homely. The first information I received from my homeroom teacher is a booklet of school rules. One rule is, if I am not coming to school, you the parent must telephone the Principal's Secretary and tell her. If I am not present in class and you did not telephone the Principal Secretary, she will be telephoning you, or sending a letter home to notify you of my absence. You must sign this letter and I bring it to my homeroom teacher before I will be allowed to return to class and school. They are strict. This way they monitor students skipping classes and school without their parents knowing. I guess this school is okay. At my previous school there was no rule like this. I could be absent fifty times, they would seem not to notice, or let you know, and they seem not to care if the student wants to learn or not. I am thankful that I have only one year left in high school."

"Rebornstar so how many times have you skipped school?"

"Mama, do not ask questions that the answer would give you a headache. Some things you better off not knowing. Here I am still in high school and going to graduate. Thanks be to the Creator for everything. Mama you have enough to do. Okay. I am happy we moved here. Look, you thought moving might resolve Holly's learning disability problems; and it did. I am happy for Holly. Okay my eye glasses sister. Now you are going to look wise and smart; and will be wise, smart, Miss Geek, and book-worm."

"Rebornstar leave me alone. I will be fine like I am supposed to be. Okay."

"Good Holly tell her. Miss. Rebornstar make sure you keep your grades at the level that you can graduate. This is your responsibility. Okay?"

"Okay mama. No matter what is going on, you are the boss. I will keep my grades up and graduate high school."

"I am happy you know who the parent is. Your sister is going to get her eyes tested next Tuesday. Soon she will have two extra pair of eyes."

"I know. I cannot wait to see her in glasses. Hahaha. Miss. Studious."

They finished eating and carried on with their evening activities.

The next morning at work Lily-Butterfly made an appointment for Holly to see the Optometrist.

Tuesday came and Lily-Butterfly and Holly went to the Optometrist's office. This Optometrist gave Holly three eye tests and examined her eyes. Lily-Butterfly got to see clearly Holly's eye situation. Holly failed every distant eye test. Holly seemed to only be able to see things from a twelve inches distance. Lily-Butterfly thought during the eye tests, Holly eye situation is sad. How was Holly able to cope having to live like this since she was born? The answer is she learned how to cope and thought her experience was normal. Holly figured how to over compensate to see what others saw or not, in relationship to what she could see. This must have been confusing. Lily-Butterfly was brought out of her thoughts by the Optometrist speaking to her.

"Ms. Lily-Butterfly you have directly seen Holly's eye sight situation. Yes, she is very nearsighted. It seems as if she has no distant vision. As she grows this nearsighted vision could get worse. I am going to refer you to an Ophthalmologist. This Doctor specializes in eye and vision care. He will do an eye exam to diagnose the exact problem and prescribe the appropriate lenses for Holly. Here is his telephone number and address. The office is about a mile down the street going towards route four, and across the street from the donut and coffee shop. I will telephone him now and tell him that you are coming now," said the Optometrist.

"Sure. I will go now. Thank you very much for all your help. Come Holly. Let us go," said Lily-Butterfly.

"Bye. You are welcome. Thanks for coming."

Holly and Lily-Butterfly left the Optometrist's office and went to the Ophthalmologist's office. During the car drive they were both silent. They arrive at the Ophthalmologist's office and glasses show room. The Ophthalmologist examined Holly' eyes. The result of the examination was Holly's vision was 20 over 230. Holly had no distance sight after maximum eighteen inches. The Ophthalmologist prescribed a glasses to correct the vision problem. Lily-Butterfly was very appreciative beyond words for this solution to Holly's learning problems; and the now discovered vision problem. She paid the doctor and bought the glasses immediately. Holly choose the glasses frame she liked. Holly and Lily-Butterfly left the Doctor's office and went to lunch at a restaurant. Lily-Butterfly returned to pick up Holly's glasses the following Monday on her way home from work.

On the way to lunch Holly and Lily-Butterfly talked.

"Holly I feel so sad about your eye situation that you had to live with half of your eye sight missing, even unknown to yourself. Even in day care the teacher thought something was wrong, tried to figure out the issue; and could not. I could not figure out the eye sight issue, because I worked with you up close. The Pediatrician could not figure this out. You never complained. Oh wow. Nothing is perfect. I am just rambling about this situation. I know that when it is time things usually happen. When the person is ready the solution appears. The person has to choose the solution and take action. This wonderful human of a teacher Mrs. March came with the solution. Now Mrs. March discovered the answer to your seeing and learning issue. It is up to you to value this opportunity. You can start with telling Mrs. March thank you; if you have not done so already."

"Yes, mama. I understand everything you have said. I will tell Mrs. March thank you. Now I am going to be more improved with my learning. With all the effort I used to put into learning with the vision I had; the learning process should be easier for me. Mama thank you for all your love, care, kindness, taking me to the eye Doctors, paying for my glasses, and everything else you do. Mama with your unconditional love I feel safe. Amin."

"Yes. Amin and Amin. Would you like to have a computer at home? Maybe it is time I buy a computer for you to use at home. It is 1996 and I still keep things as ancient as possible. Ha. You would have to do what it takes to set up the computer for it to work. The computer comes with a manual that you can use to help you to set it up. I am no good with these computer technology things. I am good with the computer at work. It only has to do with the restaurant financial operating system in the specific restaurant. You love solving puzzles, putting things together, constructing things, and seem technologically gifted. Your sister is one hundred percent creative."

"Yes mama, although I am seven years old. I think I can assembly the computer and get it to work. I will use the computer manual to help me. After eating lunch, we can go to the computer store. Today is a great day in my life. Thanks."

"Yes, today is a fabulous day for both of us. I am going to buy a twenty-four inches colored television. I still have the twelve inches black and white television. We hardly watch television, but still it is time for me to improve with this as well. I can always see things with renewed eyes even when my eye vision is good. I can choose to upgrade my perception vision. Lily-Butterfly welcome to the nineteenth century. Well, well, there is always room for improvements."

"Yes mama, welcome to both of us to the improved vision in many ways. Thank you. I cannot wait for my glasses and to see how I am going to see with them. Now I will get to physically see everything at one time and completely. This is going to be interesting. Oh, wow Holly welcome to more of this human world view," said Holly.

"Yes, Holly welcome to physically seeing more of this human modern world. Before I think you used to use your spirit and soul eye to see. Now let us see what happens in school and in your life. We will see. To me, every day human life gets more and more interesting."

After lunch Holly and Lily-Butterfly went to a large electronic store. They bought a twenty-four inches color television, a desk top computer, and accessories for the computer. The cashier asked Lily-Butterfly if she wanted to apply for a credit card to pay for her purchase instead of using her bank card to pay cash. She told the cashier yes. This store credit card was approved. This was the first credit card for Lily-Butterfly. Holly and Lily-Butterfly brought all the things they purchased to the car. As they drove home they continued to talk.

"It is amazing how one road leads to another in the process of life. My choices creates the actions and steps that interconnects and have an effect on other things. With responsibility I manage myself, the things, and events in my life," said Lily-Butterfly.

"Mama this is great. Now, in addition to my one electronic game, I have a computer at home for additional entertainment, and learning; of course. Rebornstar will love this as well," said Holly.

"Yes. For safety and security, I will parent proof this computer world wide web and so forth. You know me, the caution and safety detective. It is better to be safe than sorry," said Lily-Butterfly.

"Yes mama. You are right. Safety and security is very important."

When Holly and Lily-Butterfly got home Rebornstar was home from school. Rebornstar was happy for Holly regarding her glasses and being able to improve her seeing. The computer and larger color television was another source of happiness to celebrate for the children. Rebornstar removed the television from the box, remove the twelve inches black and white television from the television stand, and replaced it with the new television. She turned on the new television to try it out.

"Mama welcome to the nineteenth century and improved modern life. Hahaha. Cool. Holly you set up the computer. Next week Holly I will see you in your new eye glasses. It is a good thing we moved. Mama you were right. Now I understand what you were talking about. This is great. I still miss my friends and the cool unmentionable things we used to do together. Anyway, I will get used to my new friends. My life is what I choose to make of it. Thank you mama for everything," said Rebornstar.

"Rebornstar good for you that you understand. Life can be a learning and growing journey. I have to make dinner and do other things. You children are lucky."

Holly continued to set up the computer. Rebornstar did her homework. This glorious day ended with their usual routines.

78

Sometimes the most important thing can be a feather, a seed, or a drop of water.

Monday Lily-Butterfly picked up Holly at home and took her to the Ophthalmologist to get her glasses. Holly put on her glasses and the Doctor made sure they fit and worked as they were supposed to. Holly laughed and could not stop laughing for about five minutes. She was over joyed about her improved ability to see. The Doctor, Lily-Butterfly, and the Receptionist were happy for Holly; they laughed too. Holly continued her excitement regarding her glasses until it was time to go to sleep. This night and many nights Holly slept wearing her glasses. She would only take them off to take a shower. By the end of this week the computer was completely set up. Over time Holly taught her mother how to use the computer. Lily-Butterfly learned how to use the email feature of the computer in 2001.

At school Holly's learning improved within two weeks of wearing her glasses. After five months Holly was removed from special education class program. She was transferred to regular classes for all her subjects. An extra help teacher was placed inside the classroom for assistance if Holly needed help. This teacher also help other students.

At work Ema and Carlos had officially received their certificates for Manager and Assistant Manager. They were promoted, given a salary increase, and no longer punched in on the clock. By October 7th the restaurant had accumulated so much profit that that Ema, Edna, Carlos, and Lily-Butterfly received a bonus. Lily-Butterfly received $2,300, Ema and Edna received $1,200, and Carlos received $600. They received this bones with their regular pay check on October 11th. The bonus to Lily-Butterfly symbolized job well done, and arriving at a positive intended destination. She also knew from experience that when a certain destination is accomplished a renewal of the same pathway and journey begins. Lily-Butterfly watched and watched to see how this would manifest. She had an instinct that Mr. Watson would present some kind of challenging assignment for her. Lily-Butterfly observed how Mr. Watson was uncomfortable with her success and accomplishment. She waited to see what Mr. Watson would present for a challenge to her and his benefit of greed, self-serving, and career promotional intentions. Lily-Butterfly had already decided that if she did not like what Mr. Watson did, she was going to resign this current job, and go to work for another company; or maybe it would be time to start her life's purpose career. The dream oracle, the Creator, and Manana Leila told her that she had to wait until six cycles of seven years old grown, and develop solid spirit and soul talents energetically, to perform her chosen destiny and life's purpose career. Currently in December 1996 Lily-Butterfly was going to be thirty nine years old.

Currently Lily-Butterfly was on the brink of burn out. Her hair had turn whiter and she still kept it about half inch short. Lily-Butterfly looked strong and healthy, because she practiced a healthy lifestyle in every way. Currently work and wondering what Ms. Gina had done with Manana Leila was her only two most stressful things. She had faith and with the help of prayer that at some point Ms. Gina will reveal to her where Manana Leila was. October would be another month of two major revelations. Sometimes when it rains, it pours. Stay tuned. Lily-Butterfly's perception of the benefit from this restoration and improvement of the restaurant was growth, practice of her talents, improved communication skills, improved professional career skills, confidence in operating any restaurant concept, confidence in operating her life, knowing that she could operate her own business, improved wisdom and knowledge, and improvement of all that she was and is.

Lily-Butterfly believed in balance and she did not want to expand any further beyond where she was in the same professional restaurant management career. Her College training of Business Management and University training of Hospitality and Tourism Management, and every work experiences had served her well. These certifications and experiences were great tools of transformation, growth, change, improvement, and modern human knowledge. But she felt deep within her heart that this current career was not where she was born to use her spirit and soul's talents. She thought that she was ready to take the leap into the next part of her chosen destiny and life purpose. But she had to wait for the right time and signal. So, she watched and waited like a falcon looking to see the vision of its next flight direction. Unbeknownst to Lily-Butterfly, Mr. Watson was planning exactly what she was thinking about him. Mr. Watson would make an unbelievable presentation to Lily-Butterfly. Mr. Watson was in the final stage of being confident enough to approach Lily-Butterfly.

Monday October 14th Mr. Watson arrived at the restaurant with extra pep in his steps. Lily-Butterfly noticed his vibe as he walked towards her sitting in the dining room waiting to give him the reports. She thought, here it comes. Mr. Watson walked over to the table she was sitting and sat down.

"Here are the reports. I will be back in ten minutes," said Lily-Butterfly.

She got up and walked to the office. She sat down.

"Creator you know everything first. You know that I am tired. I have had enough of this demon realm, people, and places. I know that all energies can be useful, but I am tired. I feel that Mr. Watson has come this morning to create another difficult situation for me. I hope within Mr. Watson's next difficult proposal I will find the needle in this hay stack to finally leave this place. I feel that it is time. I am frustrated as a spirit and soul having these human experiences. This is my honest feelings. Keep helping, supporting, and guiding me. Please help me this morning to not react to the things Mr. Watson is going to tell me. As soon as I see and feel the signal from within me I will leave. Thank you for everything. Amin," whispered Lily-Butterfly.

Lily-Butterfly returned to the table and sat down. In silence she looked at Mr. Watson.

"Lily-Butterfly the reports says everything. These numbers are great and consistent. You should have received the bonus check last Friday. This morning I would like to tell you some good news. Monday October 28th renovations will begin on the interior of this restaurant. I have presented a great plan to my supervisor, the Board of Directors, and the President of this company the plan to turn the interior of this 10,000 square feet restaurant into a mall food court concept. We seem to have the right General Manager to manage this improved restaurant concept and make this restaurant an even bigger success. What do you have to say about this plan?"

"So far I have nothing to say about your plan. You are the boss and my supervisor. I know that I can choose to stay or leave. Nothing is permanent. Plus, I was not born to use my spirit and soul talents to help people make money; and support greedy people's adventures."

"Lily-Butterfly relax."

"Is there anything else?"

"Yes. During the construction we will keep the restaurant open until the counter, front service area, and kitchen needs to be reconstructed. The three days these area are being remodeled are Wednesday, Thursday, and Friday. You will operate the restaurant in the parking lot under tents. All food will be served in to-go containers. During this time, you will offer only basic menu items and only a small amount of the employees will work on these three days. During these three days the menu board will be reconstructed to offer the new food items. The construction supervisor will have plastic sheets put up to contain the dust and debris when the restaurant is open. Do you have any questions?"

"I have no question. Is there anything else? I have some work to finish before lunch time."

"Yes, I have more to say. The renovation and expansion of the restaurant will include a drive thru restaurant section in the kitchen by the large windows. A famous franchise ice cream parlor, a children birthday party room, a children play area with slides, swings, sand box, and jungle gym. The section of the restaurant close to the office will be a famous franchise pizza section. The other thing we will do is add a famous franchise sandwich section in the deli section in addition to our regular deli menu items. In the basement we will repair the walk-in refrigerator and two freezers. We are going to need them for the extra food items. You are going to need to manage an additional three times the food items and paper you currently order, and have on hand for the new concept restaurant. You must learn all the new food items, how to order them, and how much to order for each order delivery. Currently you order everything from one wholesaler. After the renovations you will order from five wholesalers. You have to monitor and manage the orders, sales, deliveries, money, management, and regular employees labor, training, and everything else. The traffic of customers will increase triple fold, with this comes more money, and profits. When the renovation is completed, for two weeks you, the Manager, and Assistant Managers will get some basic training from the company's Training Manager to make and prep all the new menu items. After this you are responsible for making sure that all these Managers, and every food preparation employees know how to make the new menu items, and do them correctly. The renovations will be completed by November 22nd. Which means this renovation, re-assembling the restaurant, getting all the food and paper purchased, and everything else will take approximately four weeks. Everything, should be prepared and ready to open the Wednesday before Thanksgiving Day. Would you like to say something? Do you have questions?"

"Currently I have nothing to say about this restaurant's construction and expansion. Sometimes the wisest thing is silence. Are you finished with this meeting?" replied Lily-Butterfly.

"Yes, I am finished talking for today," said Mr. Watson.

"Okay. I will see you on Monday. Enjoy your week," said Lily-Butterfly.

Lily-Butterfly got up and walked to the office. She did not wait to hear if Mr. Watson had something else to say.

In the office Lily-Butterfly completed some reports on the computer. The armored security came to pick up the deposits. Next she put on her apron and went to the front food service line to help manage the restaurant for lunch. At 2:30 Lily-Butterfly went to office. She telephoned the Surgical Center located about one mile from her home to schedule an appointment for Tuesday October 22nd to have surgery on the back of her left wrist. The wrist where the ligament was ripped under the skin from consistent wear and tear picking up fifty pound sacks of potato and other heavy items. Lily-Butterfly planned to take eight sick days off from work. During the sick time off from work she planned to work Mondays October 21th and 28th; to get the Monday reports and payroll completed. The sick days she would request off was October 23rd to 26th, and October 30th to November 2nd. The Tuesdays and Sundays in-between was her regular days off.

"I will fill out the sick days off request form and give to Mr. Watson on Monday. Friday I will tell Ema, Edna, and Carlos of Mr. Watson's and the company's restaurant renovation and expansion plans. I think that unbeknownst to me I am waiting on one significant thing before I leave this place. When it is time to leave, I am leaving; this I know for sure. I will not take personally the things Mr. Watson tells me; even if I sense his personal intentions towards me. I will start to focus more on Mr. Watson as a teacher. Until it is time to leave, I will continue to use the difficult opportunities he gives me as opportunities to grow, transform, and improve. Human-nature is interesting. Ms. Gina had better at least telephone me to tell me where she put Manana."

This Monday Lily-Butterfly felt sad. Ema, Carlos, and Edna

noticed her melancholy mood and asked her what was wrong. She told them that at the meeting on Friday she will tell them. Right now, she needed to process and digest her recent awareness and news. Lily-Butterfly left work that day and the digesting of her past and current life continued.

Thursday October 17th when Lily-Butterfly went home Holly had important news for her.

"Mama Ms. Gina telephoned. She left a message for you. Here is the paper with the message."

Lily-Butterfly took the paper from Holly and read it.

"Thank you Holly."

The message said, "In April I put mama in a nursing home. The name of the nursing home is Memorial Nursing Home, 25 Stay Street, Memorial Park, New Jersey. I have another live-in Home Health Aid job. I come home when I feel like it. Do not try to bother me about my decision."

Lily-Butterfly went into her bedroom and sat on a chair.

"Good that Ms. Gina telephoned to give me this information. I will go visit Manana on Sunday. Let me go see what is going on with Manana and after maybe I will talk to Ms. Gina. Calm, peace, no-nonsense; protecting myself from human's dark - shadow sides - negativity, work on refining my shadow side, awareness, talking less, listening more, and mindfulness is my current chosen focus. Thank you Creator, guardian angels, spirit guides, and dream guardian oracle for everything. I feel that this week I have entered another new pathway in my revolving door of transformation, growth, change, and awakening my inner talents. Continue to help and assist me. I appreciate everything and thankful for everything. Amin," whispered Lily-Butterfly.

Lily-Butterfly removed her uniform and took a shower to cool off. Next she checked Holly's school work and saw how she was doing at school. After that she prepared dinner, and continued on with the day.

Friday at the management meeting Lily-Butterfly told Ema, Edna, and Carlos about Mr. Watson's plans.

"I have two major announcements. First, is there anything you would like to report?" said Lily-Butterfly.

"No," replied Ema and Carlos.

"The night employees have finally accepted no overtime and check cashing," replied Edna.

"Good for them. Soon things will get more difficult and they will have to work harder," said Lily-Butterfly.

"What is going to happen? There is never a consistent positive balance and calm in this place. As you know by now this place is cursed," said Ema.

"Yes, Ema is right. There is never ever a consistent stability in this place. Since you have come here this is the best it has been. Believe me soon the darkness roots are going to try to take root again. All it takes is one person with the same darkness to revitalize the negative unstable vibes in this place. What now?" said Edna.

"I agree, understand, and hear what you are saying. Know that as long as I choose to be here the demons negative energy curses will chill and be still. Okay. Now listen very carefully, first announcement is I am taking eight sick days off. I will work Monday October 21st and 28th to complete the reports and payroll. I will be away October 22nd to November 3rd. The Tuesdays and Sundays are my regular days off. I am having surgery on Tuesday October 22nd to fix the back of my left wrist. This is over two years overdue. I came to work at this company with no injury and I would like to at least fix this injury. I will schedule Ema to open, Carlos on mid shift, and Edna close as usual. You will have lots of regular employee help. Please maintain the same standard of cash handling policy, and all the other restaurant policy and procedures while I am gone. Thank you very much. As long as I work here I will maintain the correct positive standards, and do my job completely; and so, will all of you, and everyone else. Do you understand me?"

"Yes, I understand. What is happening? I think that you are preparing to leave," said Edna.

"Maybe. If I do leave, now all of you are equipped with options to make a decision to stay or leave. This is your personal choice. In life, spend more time being wise than blaming others. Now what I am about to say, try not to react. Okay."

"Hahaha. What now?" There is never a dull moment in this place. My sister and I have seen it all. Hahaha," said Edna.

"I think that what I am about to say is new, very new, you will be surprised to hear. Okay. The short to the long story is, Mr. Watson told me on Monday that he has presented the ideas and plans to his supervisor, the company's Board of Directors, and the President to renovate inside the restaurant by adding a drive thru in the kitchen over by the two large windows......."

"What are you serious? Hahaha. How is this possible? This will block the street traffic. This building was not constructed for a drive-through restaurant situation," said Ema, interrupting.

"Wait let me finish talking before you speak. Okay, as I was saying. He wants to create a food court presentation inside this restaurant, and expanding the work space at the service counter. The other additions are a famous pizza franchise at the end of the counter by the office, a famous ice cream parlor franchise by where the deli is, move the deli section over to the center of the counter, add another famous sandwich franchise after the deli, keep all the menu items we currently sell, add a children's playground and party area over by the right side of the dining room. Which means he is eliminating all the dining tables on the children party and playground area. He is repairing the walk-in freezers and refrigerator in the basement for the extra food inventory storage. I will order from five wholesalers instead of one. The amount of food I will end up managing and ordering is more than triple. Training Managers will come here for two weeks to give basic training on how to make all the new menu items. I will be responsible for ongoing training of everything, and making sure that all the new products, and everything is done. Mr. Watson's intention is that the customer count and sales will increase. We will all have more work to do and things to manage. The restaurant will stay open during this construction. The construction crew will put up plastic partition to minimize the dust. When it is time to work on the service counter, menu boards, and so forth we will operate the restaurant under tents in the parking lot. At this time, we will cook with propane gas and have a food selling set up like a carnival. We will sell selected food items from the menu, carry out only. These new plans and more will be the next addition to our job responsibility. For your information currently I receive same pay as I was working in the small food court restaurant that I started working in. My review was given to me in April and I receive the same percentage increase like I would working in the other restaurant. I am not receiving the salary of the previous General Manager or the General Manager salary to work in this volume restaurant. I am giving you a view on my salary situation so that you know. Do not think that I get the big bucks to give you more work. The promotion and salary increase that I give all of you is generous, and the correct amount of salary for your work. Salary wise you are all doing better than me. So as long as we are here working please continue to do a complete job. Your salary is reflective of performing all your work responsibilities in a complete and efficient manner. I know that it is just the four of us. Mr. Watson knows this as well. But he is still creating his new plans regardless of not having and not giving the management team to perform all of this managerial work. Mr. Watson told me the construction will begin on Monday October 28th and end by November 20th. The sick days I am taking off is during the first two weeks of this construction. I need a break to step back, fix my hand, completely rest, regroup, refresh, re-cooperate, digest, re-asses, defrost, process, and step into the things that I feel is true and right for me. I give so much to others, places, and things. Now I choose to stop and replenish myself. I will return to work on November 4th. As I proceed after November 4th I will see my path ahead. If and when I am leaving I will let you know. I am strong, wise, flexible, caring, giving, and everything else. But I will not damage my health, well-being, and myself for the sake of anything or anyone. Do your best in this evolving situation. Mr. Watson will not immediately agree to my request for these sick days off. I am not going to give him an option about these days off. He is going to demand that I am here for the complete renovation process. I am going to recommend to Mr. Watson that he be here for the two weeks I will not be here. If another Manager comes here to work while I am gone, do not give them the security alarm code, keys, or combination to the safes; they should not be cashiers, count any money, or make any deposits. All three of you are the only ones I am authorizing to handle and manage the money. I know that it was hard for you to sit there and listen to everything without interruptions. Thank you for hearing and listening to my announcements. So far these are all my announcements for this meeting. These announcements are draining."

Lily-Butterfly drank twelve ounces of water. Ema, Edna, and Carlos were still silent. Their body language reflect the things they were not saying. Edna spoke first.

"I am speechless. Seriously? A drive-thru restaurant service in the kitchen? Hehehe. I cannot even laugh. How is this possible? We do not even have enough Managers for this size operation much less what Mr. Watson is planning to create. Now I have to manage a section of the restaurant in the kitchen, children playground, birthday party, and all these other things, running back and forth. Making pizza seems simple, but it is not; there will be a lot of ingredients to work with and manage. Oh, my lord. Is Mr. Watson trying to kill you, give you a heart attack, and a nervous breakdown? It is very clear to me and my opinion is that this Mr. Watson does not like you. Oh, my

Lord. People? Mr. Watson is clueless. He could not even work one station in this restaurant during a busy period much less to manage a shift here for ten straight hours; and we have to work ten to fifteen hour shifts. Ha. Now everything will get unstable again. I need to drink some water. This is too much," said Edna.

"People and their greed is the root of all evil; not money," said Ema.

"Taking everything into consideration that we know; this idea is crazy. The building structure, plumbing, electricity, gas system, restroom, sewage, and so forth is not built originally for so much additional usage. The restroom situation is already over loaded, breaks, and toilets and sewage lines get clogged from their current use. More customer complaints, craziness, more work, more inventory to manage, more food and paper to order, more over load on the refrigerators and freezers. Oh well. As long as I am here, and I choose to work here, I will do my best," said Carlos.

"Take a ten minutes break. Go use the restroom, get some water to drink. Okay," said Lily-Butterfly. She went to use the restroom.

They all returned to the meeting table.

"No. This is not fair to us. Mr. Watson is a greedy and a selfish self-serving moron. He looks like a coconut tree without leaves and coconut. Mr. Watson is an evil, corrupt, and dark soul. Ms. Lily-Butterfly are you going to fix your hand because you are planning to leave? If you leave I am leaving. No way will I go backwards to how things used to be and negative treatment. Thank you for coming to show use the right path. No way. Let me know when you are leaving. You are more qualified than Mr. Watson and will find another job very quickly. Do not let Mr. Watson work you down to death's door, nervous breakdown, and damnation. I recommend that you leave," said Edna.

"I am lost for words. This is unbelievable," said Ema.

"I am going to fix my hand, because I was negligent in my action to do this. If I choose to leave, I want to leave here with my hand fixed. I know that this is not what I was born to do as my life's purpose career. This career profession has served me well in every way. I am thankful for this job and everything else. I think I was meant to be here for many reasons. I think there is one more reason for being here that has not revealed itself to me as yet. Until it is time to leave I will be here. As long as I choose to be here I will continue to do my best work. This job is a way to the way, and I

591

have to respect it. My attitude, actions, and all my experiences are recorded in my spirit and soul's records. I try to use the opportunity to work here as positive as possible. I have not taken a vacation since I started working at this company. Currently, I have six weeks' vacation days, ten sick days, and ten personal days off to take. In the spring of next year 1997, I will take ten vacation days off. Know that I will not damage my health and well-being from working here. I have two beautiful spirits and souls as my daughters to manage and parent. One daughter is over eighteen years old and one is seven years old. I have to live in positive health and well-being for them and myself. I was born for a purpose; I have to stay alive and well for this purpose; as well. I am passionate about everything I choose to do, even working here. Passion is a centered, balanced, harmonious, and unstuck revolving door. We will keep doing the best complete work possible. I appreciate everything that all of you have done so far. My job would have been harder without all your help and assistance. I hope that all the kindness and care I showed to all of you, help you to do the same for yourselves. In life there are many bridges to grass. I will keep you informed. Amin. I am finished with this meeting. I am going home. I will see all of you tomorrow."

"Okay ma'am. Thanks," said Carlos.

"Yes ma'am I will continue to do my best as long as you are the captain of this ship," said Edna.

"I hope that when you are not here Mr. Watson does not even say one word to me. If he does I will be ignoring him. I am not going back to the corruption of the past. I will do my best as usual," said Ema. She sighed.

The meeting was over. Lily-Butterfly went home.

79

If someone intends to want all. They might eventually lose all. Sometimes one person's greed can provide the thread for the needle of a satisfying, simple, and content person.

Sunday morning came. Lily-Butterfly woke up early and got her chores done and had breakfast with Rebornstar and Holly. When breakfast was over they went to the supermarket. At 10:00 AM Lily-Butterfly left her home to find the nursing home Manana Leila was living in and to visit her. Lily-Butterfly drove for about an hour. She got lost twice. Finally, she found the nursing home on an isolated street, at the end of a dead end location. Lily-Butterfly parked her car in the parking lot and entered the building. She asked the Receptionist for Manana Leila and was directed to where her room was located. The supervisor for the department told Lily-Butterfly that Manana was in the recreation and television room. She went to the room and saw Manana Leila sitting in a wheel chair with an iron bar across her legs. Manana Leila was slumped over to the front sleeping. The iron bar seems to secure Manana Leila and restrict her movement and prevent her from getting up on her own. Sadness washed over Lily-Butterfly from head to toes. She sat down on a chair close to Manana Leila's wheel chair and observed her.

Lily-Butterfly thought, whether or not she should wake up Manana or not. She also reflected on the time when Ms. Gina had tied Manana to the chair. – If a human does not take action, responsibility, and plans on being their best advocate for their older years, this is how they can end up having the experience they do not want or like. - Manana Leila thought that because she was so kind, considerate, helpful, loving, and compassionate to Ms. Gina that she was going to do the same for her. - Lily-Butterfly realized that this was innocently naïve of Manana to think this. Look at what is happening. – Being unconditionally loving, compassionate, kind, caring, and the Creator's gift to humanity and your own children, is no guarantee of what will happen when old age arrives. The guideline of choice, action, responsibility, practice, transformation, and change also applies in this kind of situation. I am learning a lot from Manana's current situation and experiences. I am great with my children, but I will make sure that I do not end up at their mercy in this negative way; if I do not want or choose to have this experience. There is no guarantee on how humans will choose to exercise their karma rights. This is one of the reasons being unconditional is best. Sometimes if someone does not take responsibility they can experience and receive the negative karma choice of someone. Creator to me, these messages and awareness are loud and clear. Amin. As Lily-Butterfly waited to see if Manana would wake up she got deeper and deeper in her inward reflections, processing, and thoughts. As if in a trance and day dream Lily-Butterfly travelled further within her heart; to me other messages and awareness are – even with the greatest positive karma practicing the sacred laws of human living applies – take nothing for granted – nothing is like it seems – take action to create the things I really desire – take responsibility for my actions – pay attention to all the signs of life, people, places, and things – the people whom I help the most could be the people that will help me the least – The people whom I help the most could be the people who can and might hurt me the most – a human is as healed as their shadow and dark side – surrender and accept situations for a path towards a solution to appear – not surrendering can create stuckness and a dead end – learn from my mistakes – when I encounter hardship focus on transforming the situation into positive rebirth, renewal, empowerment, transformation, and change – remember positive balance, too much of any one thing is good for nothing – at the end of a great harvest, comes new beginnings, rest, and renewal – there is a time for planting seeds, taking care of the seeds, and reaping the harvest of the seeds – repeatedly empty to be refilled – understanding, compassion, and forgiveness keeps my spirit and soul's wheel of life and tree of life revolving door in positive motion and turning – I am never alone – there is a positive or negative reason for everything – Manana Leila and I are ancient spirit and soul travelers – we show up for each other time and time again – Manana Leila is an ancient spirit and soul survivor and she will make herself be fine in this and every situation – Manana Leila knows the ancient pathways to birth and to death – do the things I choose to do, can do, and should do to help Manana in this situation – do not rock the cradle of life and death - do not relate to Manana current situation with pity, sadness, and sorrow – respect Manana Leila's pathway towards death and her journey to the other side – respect, care, and kindness is a part of unconditional love – collateral karma can affect me and my life if

I am not protecting myself and setting boundaries between myself, people, places, and things – Amin. Creator these are great reminders. Thanks for everything.

"Hi Lily-Butterfly. You found me," announced Manana Leila.

Lily-Butterfly was awakened from her contemplations and day dream by Manana Leila's very familiar voice.

"Oh yes Manana I found you. I have not seen you in over five months. Two days ago, Ms. Gina telephoned my home to tell me where you were. Here I am. You remember me; your memory is not completely gone. Good. I thought that maybe you had lost all your human memory. Your spirit would never forget me. Manana it is great to see you."

"My child I would never forget you, even after I am dead. Human body memory is one thing and spirit and soul memory is another thing. How are you?"

"The children and I are doing great. As long as we are healthy; have food, shelter, and clothing, we are doing great."

"Do you like living here?"

"I have accepted my situation. So, yes I like being here, because whether I like this place or not, at this time, this is the best place for me. The Creator works in mysterious ways. There is always opportunity to practice. Even journeying towards the path of death I can practice. This was a great opportunity for me to learn deep acceptance, improved and unshakable unconditional love, and compassion. Do you see what I am saying?"

"Yes, I see and understand Manana. I understand the reasons more and more. I am guided not to interfere, jump in, and create a seemingly perfect situation. I am working on accepting your situation and not to feel sad. This is not easy. I will continue to improve this. Have Ms. Gina and Dean come to visit you since they brought you here? Has Henry visited?"

"No none of them visited. Gina and Dean brought me here with a few clothes, underwear, one pair of shoe, and one pair of slippers. They registered me here and walked away. The last thing I remember is they said bye. I have not seen them since. Why would Henry come?"

"How could they do this, walk away, and never return? This is amazing to me. If this was a test for them, they have failed miserably. I see that if this was a test for you; you have gotten over their treatment of you and are practicing the reasons, and mastering the tests. Good for you. Here I am, for whatever this is worth. I am learning a lot from this experience and situation. I have to practice patience, not being angry, non-judgement, and unconditional love towards Ms. Gina. Hate is not great. No matter what Ms. Gina does, I will practice non-hate. In this situation this is difficult. But I will do my best?"

"Lily-Butterfly the Creator knows best. I trust the Creator one hundred percent. I have moved beyond being upset, even with this nursing home situation and the people who work here. They do wrong things to me and the other people, but I try my best to hold on the gates of compassion, unconditional love, peace, kindness, patience, and so forth. Look at me I forgot how to walk. I cannot walk any more without support. From the first day I came here I was placed in this wheel chair with this metal bar across my legs. They told me that this metal bar is to prevent me from walking away from this building, not hurt myself, and so forth. Medicare pays for being here and everything. I never thought this would be happening to me. But I have accepted this reality and using the experiences to improve my spirit and soul's wisdom. Do not mess up your spirit and soul with negative thoughts about Gina. The hard truth to me is, being here is better than being in Gina's care. I trust the Creator. I had to accept that this experience is my fault and responsibility. Things did not work out like I hoped, wished, and thought. Know that every person must take responsibility for the consequences of their actions; including me. I have stopped crying over this spilled milk. I recommend you do the same. Learn from the spilling of the milk. Take caution next time to not spill the milk. Anyway, I am now ready to die. I was ninety eight years old last May. I will be dying after my ninety ninth birthday. Ninety nine is a great age to die. Be aware this is my time to leave this realm. I have moved beyond my daughter Gina and her actions. I leave her to her karma and the Creator. Currently I have no negative energy vibes towards my daughter Gina. My spirit, soul, and heart is purified of Gina's actions. I am good to go into the arms of the Tree of Life and Death, the Universe and the Creator's will. Lily-Butterfly do you understand?"

"Yes, I understand. Thank you for everything you have said. Great positive energy and words are refreshing. Let us go to your room. I will see the clothes you have. I will buy some clothes, and underwear and bring them next time; shoes as well if you need more. You have lost so much weight. Are you eating?"

They continued to talk as Lily-Butterfly pushed Manana to her room.

"Sometimes I eat and sometimes I do not. Eating is for the living. When I am dead weight does not matter."

"Manana Leila, are you eating less as a part of your death strategy? Ha?"

"We will see. Time will tell everything. When someone is going to die, one of the things that happens is that they naturally eat less and less, until the day comes. It is a way of surrendering to death, and being at peace with life and death. My life is coming to an end. The only time I leave this wheel chair is to use the toilet and go in my bed. My knees are locked into sitting position. Sometimes when I lay in my bed I cannot stretch them out. To stretch out my legs is a lot of pain. No Health Aid attendant in this place has time for individual care. I just get the basic attention to keep me alive. I never dreamt that I would come to this, but this is the reality of my situation. I never in all my life complain. I am just saying things as it is. It is my choice to eat or not. At this place I get to have this choice. When they bring me my food if I eat or not; no one cares. The people that work here seems to put themselves in a safe place of no empathy. I understand their situation. Anyway, I still give thanks for everything. It could be worse. Amin."

They arrived at Manana Leila's room. Lily-Butterfly pushed Manana into the room and left her beside her bed. The room had three beds including Manana's bed. Beside each bed was a night stand. Inside the night stand drawer was a Bible. There was a bathroom with a shower, sink, and toilet. She had a dresser for her folded clothes, and a closet for her clothes and shoes. The room and bathroom was clean. Lily-Butterfly looked at the Manana's clothes in the closet and drawers.

"These clothes are all shabby, some are torn, and they are all worn out. I will bring you some clothes the next time I come to visit. I will label your clothes with your name; Leila. Where did these clothes come from? I never saw you with these old clothes before. I will come to visit on Tuesdays. If I cannot come on Tuesdays I will come on Sundays. Next Tuesday I am having surgery on my hand, so I cannot come back to visit until Sunday. Okay?"

"Okay about visiting me. I am thankful whenever you can come. I understand. These are not my clothes. Gina brought about three pieces of my worse clothes. The Health Aid that takes care of the people in this room gave me some used clothes from other people that have died, because I only had three pieces of clothes. These clothes are better than being naked. I overheard Gina telling Dean that she is not bringing more of my clothes here, because the people that work here will steal them. Gina kept my clothes for herself. After today I do not want to talk about Gina and what she did, should have done, and did not do. Do you understand? Gina bringing me here is better than the treatment she gave me at her home. I do not want to sadden your heart or create pain for you by telling you all the things that Gina did and did not do. Be at peace with my situation. I am at peace with my situation. Do the things you choose to do to help me from the kindness of your heart; and leave the rest alone. Do not say Gina's name to me unless I ask you something. Learn from my experience, mistake, and acts of naivety. Make sure that in your last old age days you do not end up with this treatment; if this is not what you want or like. Be wise all the way through this life even after going through death's door. Take nothing for granted. Do you understand?"

"Yes, I understand everything. I will not complain anymore about what Ms. Gina did, or did not do. I will do what I can and choose to do for you. Like you say, your perception and choice is that death's door is near. I will respect this and act accordingly."

"Thank you for everything. Currently I am preparing to die. I am ready. I do not fear death. I can die in peace, awake, conscious, content, and free. Okay."

"Okay Manana. I hear you, and I understand."

The Health Aid came into the room.

"Hi nice to see you. Are you Mrs. Leila's daughter?"

"Yes. I am her daughter and granddaughter. Her only birth child Ms. Gina is my birth mother. Ms. Gina brought my Manana here. I call her Manana because she is my Nana and Mama. Ms. Gina gave me to my Manana from I was born. This is a long complicated story. Please take care of my Manana for me. I will appreciate this very much. The Creator will also give you extra blessings. Thanks."

"I will do my best. Your Manana is hardly eating. Sometimes even when we try to feed her she does not open her mouth. We do the best we can. It is her lunch time. Would you like to bring Mrs. Leila to the dining room and help her to eat?"

"Yes. I will push her to the dining room, sit with her, and help her to eat. Come Manana, it is time to eat. Let today be one of the days you choose to eat. Ha. Mmm. Come."

Manana was silent. The Health Aid led the way and Lily-Butterfly followed her pushing Manana in the wheel chair. They arrived at the dining room and sat down. Manana Leila's food was brought to her. She would not eat on her own. Lily-Butterfly fed Manana. She would eat what she liked; then stopped. Manana would not open her mouth to take more food if she did not want to. Lily-Butterfly did not force her to eat. Manana was finished eating she wiped her mouth. Lily-Butterfly took Manana back to her room and helped her to use the toilet. The Health Aid came to tell Lily-Butterfly to bring Manana to the recreation room when she was ready to leave. At 2:46 PM Lily-Butterfly was ready to leave.

"Manana remember I will return to visit you on Sunday; Tuesday I have a surgery to fix my hand. I am leaving. I will take you to the recreation room before I leave."

"Okay. Do not think I have forgotten you. You are always in my thoughts and prayers. Bye. Take care of yourself and your children. Thank you for coming and finding me. I know that you would show up when you found out what happened. Better late than never. The way will show the way."

Lily-Butterfly started to cry.

"I love you Manana. One thing I know for sure is that the Creator has lent me one of its best angels. When you die, what am I going to do?"

"When I die you will evolve into realizing that you are an angel as well, consciously be your own angel, and be closer to your chosen life's purpose. I can leave you now. You will be more than fine without me. It is almost time for me to go home to the beyond. Go, I will see you on Sunday. Today it was refreshing and comforting to see you. I will be fine, go. Bye."

Lily-Butterfly took Manana Leila back to the recreation room where she found her, and left the nursing home. With tears flowing down her cheeks and a heavy heart Lily-Butterfly drove away from the nursing home.

Lily-Butterfly did not get off the exit to go home. She drove one more exit down the highway and got off at the exit to Ms. Gina's home. She decided to visit Ms. Gina before she went home. Lily-Butterfly arrived at Ms. Gina's home and knocked on her door. She saw Ms. Gina peek through the living room window curtain.

"I see you Ms. Gina. Please unlock the door."

Ms. Gina unlock the door.

"What do you want?"

"Why did you take Manana to the nursing home without her good clothes?"

"Mama does not need good clothes in the nursing home. The people that work there will steal the clothes and give her the same free, dead and left behind, donated clothes she currently has."

"Where are Manana's clothes?"

"I took them for myself."

"Where are all Manana's furniture and other things that you brought from Boston, when she came to live with you?"

"Dean and I threw all mama's things in the garbage dumpster, except Dean took her antique mahogany wood bed. Oh, there is a small box on the dresser with some old Kawomaya coins and other old coins in it. If you want that you can have it. But that is it."

"Please give me the box with the old coins."

Ms. Gina got the box of old coins and gave it to Lily-Butterfly.

"Thank you for the box of old coins. Where is the diamond ring Manana gave me, that she used to wear?"

"I do not know."

"This is a lie. You have it and choosing not to give it to me."

Ms. Gina was silent.

"Have you gone to visit your mother since you put her in the nursing home over five months ago?"

"No, because I do not have anyone to take me there. I do not drive and have a car?"

"You had Dean take you there to drop Manana off in the car that her money bought. You have Henry with a car that Manana's money bought. But you have no one to take you to visit her. Dean and Henry take from Manana and never gave her anything; not even to visit her one time. This is interesting."

"Lily-Butterfly do not say anything more to me. You are not my supervisor. Do not say anything to me about karma. My karma is my business and between me, mama, and the Creator. Okay. Is there anything else?"

"After everything your mother did for you this is how you choose to repay her?"

"Hear and listen to my words. All the things mama did for me she said it was unconditional -love, kindness, and caring. Ha. Mmm. Do you know what unconditional means? Ha. This is unconditionally what I choose to do with her. Mama has her choice and I have mine as well. I have to live my life. Living in New Jersey is not an old fashion village and valley of Yaj situation. It is said when you go to Rome do as the Romans do. A nursing home is where people put their old people in this state, place, and time. Wake up Lily-Butterfly this is one of the ways of modern times and living. Mama is old and on her way to death's door. I do not want to talk about this situation anymore. If you do not like what I did, go take her out of the nursing home, bring her to your home, stop working and give her the beautiful compassionate care that you are expecting from me. Hello. Leave. Stop getting on my nerves. What is done, is done."

"The ancestors and your karma will take care of your actions, thoughts, and speech. You will see. As a spirit and soul, you used your mother and father to be born here in this planet. This alone earns respect. You choose to break your spirit, soul, mind, and body and remain a lost person. Every human born on this planet goes through some kind of tribulation. You should seek help to transform your negative imprints and triggers. I know that this has to be your realization and choice. I love you unconditionally Ms. Gina, but I do not like the things you choose to do. You are here, because of the ancestors, Manana, and your father. I am here because of the ancestors, you, Manana, and my real father; because of this I unconditionally respect you as well. Know that the root of all my talking comes from helping you to be aware and mindful. Ms. Gina if I never see you again best wishes and brightest blessings."

"Your preaching is not working. Use your spiritual preaching and philosophies on someone else other than me. Enough. Go. If and when I choose to transform and change it is between me and the Creator. Now, go. Leave, preach to your children and yourself. Goodbye."

"Okay. Time will tell. We will see. Bye."

Lily-Butterfly turned and walk out of Ms. Gina's home. She got in her car and drove away.

"After today seeing and having anything to do with Ms. Gina is in the hands of the Creator and the Creator's will. Seriously. Amin, so let it be. I learn to never say never, and to not burn my bridges down, after I use them to cross the pathways of this human life and living. I never know for sure if I have to use these bridges again. Wisdom is golden," said Lily-Butterfly.

Lily-Butterfly got home and continued on with the rest of her day and responsibilities. She did not discuss with Rebornstar and Holly the details of her day's events. She only told them that she went to visit Manana in a nursing home. After dinner Rebornstar washed the dishes. This night Lily-Butterfly had a lot to write in her journal. Her prayer this night was a short one. Short focused prayers can be powerful as well.

Like a tired log on the ocean of life Lily-Butterfly fell into a deep sleep. A deep sleep that transported her to the realm beyond the planet's veil. In the dream Lily-Butterfly saw herself sitting on the ground under a birch tree. She was looking up in the star covered sky at a full moon embraced by the darkness of the night. Her dream oracle guardian angel walked up to her blowing a long golden trumpet, Tu-tu-tu-too-too-toom-tu-toom. The dream oracle guardian angel sat down beside Lily-Butterfly. The oracle spoke to her.

"Take a break from your leadership qualities, being tolerant, tough, strong, nurturing, and caring. These qualities are useful but it is time to see in between things. Focus a little more on yourself and your personal needs. Do not get lost in people's perceptions and projections. It is time again to focus on honoring your feminine. Tu-tu-tu-too-too-toom-tu-toom. With balanced ease relax your feminine into your masculine, like the music coming from this trumpet. Keep hearing and listening to your instincts. A spirit and soul in human male form will arrive in your life soon; and when it is time. This will be your personal teammate and life partner support to help and assist you with a very far leap, and a sharp turn, within this leap. From this person you will experience sincere and equal unconditional love, care, compassion, and kindness. He will not be perfect. He will come with the complete support that you need, will choose, and desire. This spirit and soul will seem familiar to you. He is a free spirit and soul like you. Like you; he cannot be owned or taken as a possession. You have to think outside your usual perception to recognize him when he arrives. Do not miss this unusual arrival. He will stay with you for one cycle of maximum seven years. He will arrive at the very end of this cycle, the beginning of the next cycle, when you take the leap to enter the next pathway of your chosen destiny life's purpose career; and he will automatically leave when your chosen destiny life's purpose career has taken strong roots. When it is time he will leave to go take care of his life purpose destiny and karma responsibility. You will continue onward in your life, and on your chosen destiny and life's purpose, doing the same thing. Make no mistake, by choosing to follow him down his destined life's path. Use his appearance and disappearance wisely. Do not take his

appearance for granted. Use his appearance wisely. Pay attention to everything. Do not be distracted by non-sense, people, places, and things. Continue to trust yourself and the way. The way will continue to show you the way. You are never alone. We watch you from behind the veil. Tu-tu-tu-too-too-toom-tu-toom."

The dream oracle guardian angel disappeared.

The dream came to an end. The clock alarm went off. Lily-Butterfly opened her eyes and turned off the alarm clock. It was 3:00 AM on Monday morning. Time for her to get up and get dressed to go to work. Lily-Butterfly got up wrote the dream down, got dressed for work, drank some tea, ate cereal, and left for work. As she drove to work the dream percolated, and digested within her.

80

Words, pictures, actions, thoughts, and nothing; all have value and power.

Lily-Butterfly completed all the reports and payroll by 8:30 AM. Ema did the food, paper, and cleaning supply orders, check in the delivery, telephoned the order to the wholesaler, and entered the items delivered into the computer. Carlos managed the shift, customer service, employees, and everything until Ema returned to the front service counter. Lily-Butterfly got some breakfast to eat and sat in the dining room. She had all the reports in a file and sick days off request form. She ate and waited for Mr. Watson. At 9:15 AM Mr. Watson arrived. He sat at the table. Lily-Butterfly gave him the file with the reports. He read them.

"Good, every financial report is better than the required budget. The restaurant is making more and more money, with the construction we will make even more money. It is a great thing to finally have the right General Manager to make this all happen. Is there anything else or maintenance?"

"Here is the sick leave request off to get my hand fixed. The surgery is tomorrow October 22nd. I will be off from tomorrow October 22th to November 3rd. I will return Monday October 28th to complete the reports and payroll. Four of these days are my regular days off. I have scheduled all the Managers and regular employees to cover all the shifts."

"Wow what is going to happen regarding the construction when it starts on October 28th?"

"I do not have to be here for construction. My job responsibility does not include construction responsibilities. The construction plans and operation is part of your job responsibility as a District Manager. It is your choice to do as you like regarding this construction situation. I have scheduled surgery for my hand. This surgery is over two years delayed. I have taken care of making sure the restaurant operation is a success during my absence. I do not need outside management assistance. I do not need Moneyca to come here to help. If you ask her to come here to work this is your choice. But she will not touch any money or handle any financial transactions in this restaurant. Every restaurant Moneyca works, money disappears."

"Do you have proof about Moneyca and money disappearance? What are you talking about?"

"Yes, I have proof. There is a lot of proof. I could tell you where to look for the proof. You are the District Manager for all the restaurants that she works in your district. You know the restaurants money disappear from. Look at the dates that she goes to these restaurants to work and the dates money disappear from these restaurant. Plus, there is so many proof with her actions. Moneyca is your creme-de-la-creme. Something is fishy. Ema and Edna was a part of the financial money disappearing act in this restaurant. I have brought this to an end. I am not sure if you have corrected Moneyca's money disappearing act situation. So, I do not want her to come here and work, and if she does, she will not touch the money or do financial transactions. As you already know my communication style is direct. Sorry if I am too direct for you. My direct communication style is a part of me being as clear as possible, and no nonsense protection device. I know from experience that people can be very interesting and shady. The face and appearance a human feels comfortable showing is one face, in addition they have many hidden faces. I can see beyond people's surface face. I have a copy of my sick request days off. I always keep a copy of every document I give you. I will be taking these days off no matter what happens. My hand was damaged for over two years from working at this company's restaurant. It is way over due to fix."

"Even if I do not approve the requested days off?" said Mr. Watson.

"Yes. Even if I have to telephone the President of the company to approve my sick days off. Do you realize that since I have been working for this company I have not taken vacation, sick days, and I only took one personal day off?" Even a horse would need rest from this work situation. It is my responsibility to take my days off, and now I am. This sick days off request conversation is over. Why would you not be supportive of me fixing my hand?"

"Let us change the subject. You are very interesting. Do you have any feedback on the restaurant expansion, renovations, and so forth?"

"No. I have nothing to say about this restaurant's renovation and expansion. You can plan the things you like. I am the General Manager of this restaurant. My job responsibility is this restaurant's complete operation. This restaurant is the largest one in the company, and it currently makes the most money. Within months I have brought this restaurant out of the minus two million dollars annual depression. You have never said thank you, and you reward me with more work. When all of this restaurant renovation and expansion is completed, and I receive the things to be General Manager for, these things becomes my responsibility. Until then renovations and restaurant expansion is your business and responsibility. I have gotten to know you professionally and you are aware of me professionally as well. I am not interested in being your so called friend or colleague. You and your job is above my pay grade, so we cannot even be colleagues. Do you understand? I know that you are using my work, me, my work, and talents to climb the ladder of success. I am not dumb, and you know this. I will not give you feed back about this project for you to take the things I say as your own ideas and present them to your supervisor, Board Members, and the President as your ideas. When I receive the additional work and job responsibilities, if I do not like my experience, I will decide what to do. Until then I am here as the General Manager of the complete operations of this restaurant. I know that I can leave if I choose to. While I choose to work here I will do my complete best. My reputation and the quality of my work will always speak for itself. Also know that you cannot crush or punish me with more work responsibility. I will use the things you give me to do as motivation to improve even more. Your karma is your responsibility. The things you do will always come back to you, now, in the future, before you leave this planet, and into where you go after you leave this planet. Once energy is created it cannot be destroyed. You do not know how to do the things I can do, because your success is premature, you did not work for your success, you just use your ego to climb the ladder of professional success. I have made myself, intention, and perception clearer. Is there anything else?"

"No. Have a good time off and rest. You are going to need it during the construction and after with the restaurant expansion. We will see what happens."

Lily-Butterfly got up and walked away from the table. Mr. Watson sat looking straight ahead.

Lily-Butterfly went back to work. She had a great day at work. Lily-Butterfly's day ended with her being in a meditative, content, and contemplative mood.

Tuesday morning October 22nd Lily-Butterfly arrived at the Surgical Center on time. The Surgeon and, other medical staff were pleasant, courteous, and professional. The surgery was a great success. The Surgeon seemed spiritual. He gave Lily-Butterfly spiritual awareness on how to - care for the incision for it to heal as successful as possible, and a treatment process to perform on the incision to prevent scaring tissue. The Surgeon gave Lily-Butterfly an appointment to return the following Wednesday October 30th for the Doctor to remove the bandage, check the incision, and remove the stitches. Lily-Butterfly's hand healed rapidly and the incision healed without any scaring. By the time she returned to work on November 4th, the healing of her hand had achieved great success; and she was still mindful on using her hand for the progress of the healing to continue.

On Friday October 25th Lily-Butterfly went clothes shopping for Manana Leila. She labeled the clothes with Manana Leila's name. On Sunday October 27th she visited Manana Leila and brought her the clothes. Lily-Butterfly arrived at the nursing home at 10:55 AM. Manana was sitting in the wheel chair with the iron bar across her lap. Lily-Butterfly brought the bags with the clothes to Manana Leila's room. She went to get Manana and pushed the wheel chair to her room. Manana woke up when Lily-Butterfly arrived in the room.

"Hi Manana. It is me. What is my name?"

"Hahaha. Do you think I could have forgotten you or your name?"

"No. This is why I ask. If you cannot remember my name or who I am, then I know that your mind is totally beyond gone. So, tell me what my name is?"

"Hahaha. Lily-Butterfly. Do you want me to spell your name as well?"

"No. At least I made you totally laugh. I brought you some new clothes and underwear. They are simple and colorful house dresses, that opens in the front. Wearing them can help to cheer up your mood. Very well. I am going to remove all these old clothes and hang up the new ones. By the way what happened to the diamond ring you gave me?"

"Yes, hang up the new clothes and put the underwear in my dresser drawer. Thank you very much for all the things you do and can do. Gina took the ring off my finger before she took me here."

"Okay regarding the ring. When I was born you were there completely for me. Now that you are journeying towards death I choose to be here for you in every way I can. I will not take you to my home, because I have to go to work and the children are at school. I am very sorry that I cannot be there for you every day and take care of you. Here you have some company, people in this room and the entertainment room to talk to, and daily care. It is not the best place, people, and environment, but thanks be to the Creator it is better than nothing. Like you told me you do not want to talk about Ms. Gina and her actions. So, I will try my best not to talk about her to you. Things are between you and Ms. Gina, and the Creator. Good that you have accepted being here."

"I appreciate everything you do. I understand regarding you taking care of me at this time. I feel that Gina should be helping me with my care. If she chooses to not do this, I have gotten to where I understand and accept her choice. My current focus is preparing to die by processing the recapitulation my life's journey, experiences, and making peace with everything. Next May 5th, I will be ninety nine years old. Sometime after my birthday I will die. Maybe I will see you again as a human; before you die. Human life can be interesting."

"How will I see you again as a human? Ha?"

"The Creator works in mysterious ways. Within time and at the right time things usually reveal themselves."

"I know. We will see. If I see you again as a human child or adult, I will be sure to recognize you. Manana using the funeral plot that you have in Boston is not going to work out. I was thinking that I could make plans with Ms. Gina to cremate you. I will take your ashes and sprinkle it in the ocean or a river to all the directions of the Universe. This way your body becomes a part of the earth and life again. Would you like me to do this?"

"Yes. Mmm. Sure. This cremation and ashes process seems more exciting and infinite. Good. Thank you. Amin."

"I am happy that you like this idea. I will get this done even if I have to wrestle with Ms. Gina. Humans can be interesting."

"Yes, even us."

The Health Aid came into the room.

"Hi ma`am. I have brought my Manana some new clothes. Her name is inside each piece of clothes. They are hanging in the closet."

"Okay. Would you like to give back the other clothes to the nursing home? We can use it for another client," said the Health Aid.

"Yes, sure. Where should I put them?"

"I will go get the clothes donation hamper. Sometimes people come here without clothes. We can give these clothes to them. There are lots of less fortunate people that come to this nursing home. Good thing your Manana has you."

"Yes, we have had each other for over thirty eight years. We are lucky."

"It is lunch time. Bring Mrs. Leila to the dining room. You can help her to eat."

"Okay. I will. Manana it is time to eat. Please eat something. I am not going to force you."

"I will eat as much as possible. Okay. Let us go."

The nurse put the clothes in the hamper.

Lily-Butterfly took Manana to the dining room for her to eat. After lunch they went back to Manana Leila's room. They talked about old times in the village of Yaj. Manana told Lily-Butterfly stories about her life when she was a child. Lily-Butterfly asked her questions and they had a great conversation. Lily-Butterfly massaged Manana Leila's knees and complete legs.

"Manana I am leaving. It is 5:04 PM. I will see you again next week Tuesday. Thank you for your stories."

"You are welcome my child. Thank you for coming. Take care of yourself and your children. You are blessed. Bye."

"I will take you back to the entertainment room. You can talk to the other patients there."

"Okay. Thanks."

Lily-Butterfly completed her visit and left the nursing home at 5:20 PM. She kissed Manana Leila goodbye and took her back to the entertainment room. At the entertainment room Manana smiled at Lily-Butterfly. They hugged each other and Lily-Butterfly left. She felt sad driving away from the nursing home. Lily-Butterfly got home, prepared dinner, and ate dinner with Rebornstar and Holly. After dinner she proceeded to prepare for her work week, meal plans, and so forth. Then she realized something.

"Oh, wow I only need to prepare for going to work on Monday. Except for Monday I have the rest of the week to relax and rest. I am thankful for everything. I am sad I cannot take Manana home with me. I have to accept that this nursing home is the current best thing for her. Creator you know everything best. I thank you for everything. Amin."

Monday October 28th Lily-Butterfly went to work. She ignored the construction progress and went to the office to do the end of week paper work. Ema came to speak to her at 6:30 AM when she came to get the registers.

"Good morning Ms. Lily-Butterfly it is great to see you. How was your surgery?"

"My surgery was great. My hand is healing nicely. How are you doing?"

"I am hanging in there. Your absence makes a big difference. We miss you. As usual the nonsense construction and expansion is in progress. We ignore this situation and just do our work. Sometimes Mr. Watson is here. He does not talk to us and we do not talk to him. I have no time for foolishness. Rest on your sick days off you need it to recuperate and for all the extra work ahead. When the construction is completed we have five different wholesalers food and paper orders to do instead of one. Oh, my Lord, negativity never ends in this place. Let me get the cash registers and go open the doors."

"Okay. I hear you. I am going to take everything with as much ease as possible. I am not worried. If this restaurant or work becomes unbearable for me, I will leave. Very simple solution. Ema I will do all the food, paper, cleaning supply orders today. Plus check the delivery and put the things in the computer."

"I agree with not worrying. I am not worried either. I do my best and that is it. Edna the same. I have to go."

"Okay," replied Lily-Butterfly.

At 9:00 AM when Mr. Watson arrived Lily-Butterfly was not sitting at a table for a meeting. She was checking in the food and paper deliveries and doing the food, paper, and cleaning supply orders. Mr. Watson came to the kitchen and saw her working.

"Good morning Lily-Butterfly," said Mr. Watson.

"Good morning Mr. Watson."

"The reports and payroll are in a file in the office on the desk. Please let me know if you have any questions or concerns. If you need to have a meeting let me know. I do not have anything new to report today."

"Okay."

Lily-Butterfly continued to work on the orders. After Mr. Watson read the reports he came to the kitchen to speak to Lily-Butterfly.

"Everything looks good. Okay. Have a nice day."

"Okay. You too."

Mr. Watson left and went to the dining room to speak to the construction manager. Lily-Butterfly continued with her work. She put the orders in the computer and telephoned in the orders to the wholesalers. Next she had breakfast. After breakfast she helped with customer service, cashier training, lunch service. After lunch service and preparation for the night shift. Lily-Butterfly did some more office work, talked for fifteen minutes with Edna, and went home.

Tuesday Lily-Butterfly went to visit Manana Leila, spent lunch time with her, and left the nursing home at 3:15 PM. Wednesday October 30th she went to the Surgical Center for the Surgeon to remove the stitches. Lily-Butterfly's hand was healing very well. The rest of the week Lily-Butterfly spent going on walks in nature, resting, reading, writing in her journal, meditating, praying, reflecting, and processing her life's experiences. It was the first time in almost two years she had such a long rest.

Sunday night after prayer and before Lily-Butterfly closed her eyes to go to sleep she laid in bed reflecting on the situation at work.

"The calm and break from work is over. Now it is time to face the storm and unstableness at work. Creator give me the signal when it is time to leave this place. Amin."

81

On Monday November 4th Lily-Butterfly went back to work. She entered the restaurant at 4:36 AM and turned off the security alarm. She could see that the construction was in an advanced stage and she smelled the dusty environment. Lily-Butterfly went to the office and completed the reports and payroll. The financial reports were still below the budget requirement. She put all the reports and payroll in a file. Ema came into the office before the restaurant opened at 7:00 AM for breakfast.

"Hi Ms. Lily-Butterfly it is nice to see you. Welcome back."

"Thank you. Keep doing your best. I do not want to talk about what happened when I was not here. I read all the notes in the Manager's note book. I definitely do not want to focus my time and attention on the construction work. I have enough work to do. Enjoy your day."

"I understand. You too."

Again Lily-Butterfly did not go to the dining room to wait for Mr. Watson for a meeting. She checked the information in the computer, attended to giving the armored security the deposits, did the orders, checked in the deliveries, telephoned in the orders, put the orders deliveries into the computer, made Managers and employee schedule. During all this work process Mr. Watson came to the office. They greeted each other. Lily-Butterfly gave Mr. Watson the file with the reports and payroll. He read the information in the file. He said goodbye and left. Lily-Butterfly planned to conserve energy and time by not wasting these things with useless talking and entertaining people's projections. The week went well and at Friday's meeting Lily-Butterfly did not feel like talking too much. She told Ema, Edna, and Carlos that she did not want to gossip about the constructions or entertain expressions of worry and fears. The meeting had a light vibe. Lily-Butterfly had no announcements. She listened to the Managers and responded according to their expressions. The Manager's meeting lasted sixty five minutes only. After the meeting Lily-Butterfly went home.

On Monday November 11th Mr. Watson arrived at 9:10 AM.

Lily-Butterfly was busy with her regular work. On Monday mornings she was not sitting waiting on Mr. Watson for meeting anymore. Mr. Watson came into the office to talk to her.

"Good morning Lily-Butterfly I would like us to have a meeting this morning. I will be sitting in the dining room waiting for you."

"Okay. I will ask Ema to continue the work I was doing. I will be there in five minutes."

"Okay."

Mr. Watson left the office and went to the dining room. Lily-Butterfly asked Ema to continue to do the work she was doing until she was finished with Mr. Watson's meeting. Lily-Butterfly took the files with the reports and payroll with her to give to Mr. Watson. She sat at the table with Mr. Watson. Lily-Butterfly was silent. Mr. Watson talked first.

"I would like to give you an update regarding the construction. As you have seen, the children's play area and birthday party room is complete, but not open for use, so this section is still enclosed with plastic sheets. The drive thru section in the kitchen is almost completed. From Wednesday November 13th to 20th the complete restaurant will be closed to reconstruct the front line service stations. During the time the restaurant is closed we will put in a completely new menu board, the new addition of ice cream parlor, sandwich, and pizza restaurant franchise, and reconstruct our original food counters. A miniature version of the original food stations in the front line will be created by the drive thru service and cashier station. The drive thru will operate with minimum three employees including one cashier. The Manager on duty must also supervise the drive thru operations. For the days the restaurant is completely closed schedule only ten percent of the regular employees to work. Give the other ninety percent unpaid days off. Some employees might have vacation days. They are welcome to take these days off if they want to be paid. Make the regular employee schedule to reflect this situation. Maybe all the night regular employees must be scheduled to be off from work. During this time the restaurant will operate from 7:00 AM to 7:00 PM. A temporary restaurant will be set up under tents in the parking lot. You will use propane gas to cook with. During this time, you will sell basic menu items. Here is the list of the food items you will sell outside in the temporary restaurant. Here is the information on the four new additional wholesalers that you will order food and paper supplies from. Included in the folders are the new order forms. The first order will come automatically. Make preparations where you are going to store the new food items. I recommend that you store the ice cream, pizza, and new sandwich food items in the walk-in refrigerator and freezers downstairs in the basement. Get Juan to go downstairs in the basement to scrub and clean with bleach, the floor and inside the walk-in refrigerator and freezers. The refrigeration technician will be here on Wednesday November 13th to repair the walk-in refrigerator and freezers in the basement. Take the new food order forms and type each item into the product mix and inventory inside the computer. There is information inside the folder that tells you how to do this. Get this computer work done by November 21st. When the new food and paper arrives for the first order put every item you receive into the computer like you do with the current deliveries. Plan and schedule all the employees you would like to receive the two weeks initial training on how to prepare and cook the new food items. Here is the training schedule for each new food item. Plan to be present at every training session. After this two week training session you will be responsible for training everyone else. The computer company will add to the current cash register system all the new food items. They will telephone you to tell you where each new menu item is on the register; and they will mail you different cash register lay-out sheets. By November 21st exchange the current cash register lay out sheets for the new ones. The cashiers must relearn where each item is on the new cash register lay out sheets. This will slow down customer service for maybe three weeks, until they get used to the new formatting. I will bring in a temporary cash register, fryer, grill, small refrigerator that works using a generator, sandwich station, and a soda station, and set them up under the tents. Get the soda syrup set up every morning. At closing bring the boxes of soda inside the restaurant. Your job is to get everything that I have just said organized, processed, and into operation. Tuesday evening, I will get the tents and equipment set up in the parking lot. I will bring take-out boxes and leave them in the office. You have the rest of today to adjust the schedule, inform Ema, Edna, Carlos, and the regular employees of this emergency situation. You are off on Tuesday get Ema, Edna, and Carlos to remove every food items from the front line food service stations and put them in the walk-in refrigerators and freezer. Everything must be removed. The construction people will be taking out everything in the front line food service stations, cash register counter, everything will be remodeled and reconstructed. We will be reopening the restaurant on November 21st. I will give you more information next week Monday when I arrive. Please prepare for a meeting where we can sit down and talk. Okay? Do you have any questions, concerns, or comments?"

"No, I have no questions, concerns, or comments. I understand everything you have told me. Thank you for letting me know this information. We will prepare for everything you have said. Here is the file with the reports and payroll. Is there anything else?"

"Do you remember everything I have just told you from memory? You did not write down anything. No, I have nothing else to say, for today. I will see you on Wednesday morning. I will come to see how things are going with the temporary restaurant in the parking lot and the construction," said Mr. Watson.

"Okay. Yes, I remember everything you have told me. I have a photographic memory for spoken and unspoken words. I am going to get everything you have said arranged for Wednesday. Have a great day."

Lily-Butterfly got up and walked to the office.

At 11:00 AM on this same day Monday 11/11/1996 Lily-Butterfly called Ema, Carlos, Juan into the office to give them the work plan instruction to organize everything as Mr. Watson had instructed and given her the information to do.

"Ema, Carlos, and Juan please focus on the things I will say. I recommend that you stay positive and focus your positive energies on the process I am going to guide you to perform. Okay?"

"Okay ma'am. But I must say that I already know that whatever you say is Mr. Watson egotistic crap. Anyway, let us have it," replied Ema.

"Okay. I will do my best," replied Carlos.

"Do you need to write down the things I will say?"

"Let me hear it first, after I will decide if I have to write the information down," replied Ema.

"Okay Ema during the day shift you are in charge of the restaurant when I am not here. Carlos will assist you. Tomorrow, Tuesday I am off. By Tuesday night when Edna closes the restaurant, food and everything else must be in the kitchen, and walk-in refrigerator and freezer. Mr. Watson told me the restaurant will be temporarily closed from this week Wednesday November 13th to 20th. This temporary restaurant outside will open from 7:00 AM to 7:00 PM. My perception is that the construction will not be completed on November 20th. We will work outside under tents in the parking lot for the duration of the front line food service station construction. Everything that is needed, including food, to operate in the tents outside will be taken through the emergency exit door. Mr. Watson will set up the tents and equipment needed outside, on Tuesday. Before I leave today I will re-do the schedule. Effective Wednesday all the night employees are off from work until the restaurant reopens. Before I leave today I will make a new schedule for this temporary restaurant closure. I will be here Wednesday morning at 5:30 AM. All three of you please come to work on Wednesday morning at 5:30 AM. The four of us will set up the restaurant service and cooking production outside. The other employees can come at the time I will rewrite the schedule. Today, I will put up signs about the temporary restaurant closure in the dining room and on the doors, for the customers. We will use one cash register and one cashier from 7:00 AM to 3:00 PM. At 3:00 PM we will change the cash registers and a different cashier work from 3:00 PM to 7:00 PM. Edna is responsible for the 3:00 PM to 7:00 PM shift, cleaning, closing down everything, and bringing back everything into the restaurant that needs to come in overnight. Try not to worry or stress. I will be here to guide you through the process as the days unfold. Juan between today and November 20th please have the complete basement floor and walk-in refrigerator and freezers scrubbed with bleach and soap. Juan you will do everything that you usually do during your normal work day. Juan if you need to, please ask me questions as the days unfold. Ema and Carlos the Friday meetings are cancelled until the restaurant reopens. We will have daily mini meetings as needed. I will set up the new food and paper orders in the computer, create a paper build-to order system, and teach you how to do these new additional food and paper orders. There will be scheduled new food training program that you must attend. I will let each of you know when to attend these training sessions. I will be attending these training sessions as well. On Wednesday I will let you know the other things I would like you to do. I will talk to Edna when she comes at 3:00 PM. Do you have any questions?"

"Mr. Watson should have closed the restaurant completely until the construction is over. This would be easier and make more sense. Temporary restaurant in the parking lot is a waste of time and labor. Only a few dedicated customers are going to come," said Ema.

"Ema I do not have the answer to this question. I could speculate the answer, but you can too. I do not agree with this construction and restaurant expansion plan. But as long as I choose to be the General Manager I have to follow the orders relating to my job. I would like to use the time and energy to work with all these situations productively. I am trying to use my energy wisely, stay grounded, and maintain my peaceful and positive energy vibes. This is my primary focus. Stress and fear are not my friends. Meditate on positive vibes and peace. Be realistic and also process your negative views and emotions. I understand how you feel. Okay. Let us focus on getting the things that needs to be done and the things Mr. Watson requests from us. Okay. This is positive and wise."

"Okay ma'am I will," replied Carlos.

"Yes ma'am I will do my best as usual," said Juan.

"Okay. Tell all the employees to look at the notice board if they will be working or not. Tell all the employees of these plans. I will be busy in the office today and cannot come to help with lunch service. All the shift supervisors including Juan will work their normal schedule. One cashier, and one sandwich maker from the day shift will be scheduled to work. As requested by Mr. Watson everyone else, will be scheduled off from work; with no pay. The same thing for the night shift. If an employee has vacation days available, they can request these days off, and be paid only for the vacation days available. The vacation days request forms are in the filing cabinet, if you need it for an employee. Okay. As you choose write down the things that you need to remember. Okay go back to your work plan for today. Currently I have nothing more to say."

"Okay ma'am," replied Ema and Carlos.

"Ma'am, do not stress. Like I told you before this place carries the killing, abuse, suffering, dark, toxic, and punishing curses and vibes. This is part of why this restaurant was haunted. Employees die here from being over worked, abused, and from suffering. Be careful ma'am," said Juan.

"Thank you Juan, Ema, and Carlos; Edna too, for all your caring, work performance, concerns, and positive intentions. I could not perform my job and operate this restaurant without you, and all your help and assistance. I really appreciate every single thing that you do. Every financial and production standards remains the same high quality in the temporary restaurant operations procedures, like the permanent restaurant operation procedures. Remember this as well. Thanks," said Lily-Butterfly.

"Yes, we understand," said Ema, Carlos, and Juan.

They left the office. Lily-Butterfly re-did the regular employee schedule, typed the notice to put in the dining room and on the doors.

By 3:00 PM everything that Lily-Butterfly had to do before she went home was done. Edna arrived at work and into the office at 3:15 PM after speaking to her sister Ema about the temporary restaurant closure and everything else.

"Hi Ms. Lily-Butterfly, Ema told me the news. Why did Mr. Watson tell us about the temporary restaurant closure so close to the time they plan to renovate? He is inconsiderate. Ha. Tonight, I have to tell the employees that they are off starting this Wednesday night; without pay? This is not cool," said Edna.

"Yes, you have to tell them. Ask those who have vacation days off if they would like to request vacation days off, so that they can get paid. This is their choice. The vacation days off form is in a file in the filing cabinet. The new schedule is on the employee notice board. You will have a cashier, sandwich maker, one cook, one kitchen person, and one dishwasher from 3:00 PM to close. The official close and stop selling food time is 7:00 PM. After 7:00 PM you clean up and bring the things on this list back into the kitchen. Use the emergency exit to go out and in. Do your best and continue to follow all the rules, financial, and operating procedures. When the restaurant reopens the end of week reports and inventory will be more time consuming, but I will schedule help for you to do your part. Try not to worry. I will continue to do my best to help us be successful with the increase in work. The Friday Manager's meeting is cancelled until the restaurant reopens. I have put up the notice in the dining room regarding the temporary restaurant closure; and that some menu items can be purchased outside between the hours of 7:00 AM to 7:00 PM. Here is a list of the menu items that we will be selling outside. All food orders are to go; in boxes, and so forth. When you arrive at work on Wednesday I will go through the closing operations with you. Tuesday night when you close the restaurant move all the food, paper, and everything else to the tables in the kitchen, walk-in refrigerators, and freezer. Do you have any questions so far?"

"No, so far I have no questions. I am frustrated. Anyway, continue with the guidelines."

Lily-Butterfly told Edna everything she had told Ema, Carlos, and Juan. Edna agreed to perform the instructions given. By 5:00 PM Lily-Butterfly completed everything she had to do for the temporary restaurant closure to be performed. She went home at 5:17 PM.

Lily-Butterfly made sure that she conducted her personal home life in a complete manner. She continued to visit Manana Leila once per week at about 11:00 AM to 3:30 PM. They talked, Manana told Lily-Butterfly stories, Lily-Butterfly combed Manana's hair, massaged her knees and legs, and so forth. Sometimes Lily-Butterfly visited Manana Leila on Sunday and brought Rebornstar and Holly with her. Holly was doing great in school and loving her glasses. At work things were unpredictable and unstable. Lily-Butterfly was in acceptance, focused, peace, listening, hearing, and silent speaking less mode. This helped her to be flexible with her experiences.

On November 22nd the restaurant renovations were not completed. It was not completed until November 29th. With two weeks of training to prepare all the new foods the restaurant was not ready to permanently reopen until Monday December 16th. The pizza operation was the most time consuming production. With so many sensitive moving parts, delicate preparation procedures, ingredient, and other work; the pizza production process was the most difficult addition to the restaurant menu. This was true for Lily-Butterfly, all the Managers, and every current cook employee. From experiencing this complete pizza preparation process Lily-Butterfly's heart felt passion and perception was - the pizza production process was complexed, unique, and simple all in one context – this pizza production was a process and journey to be respected. So, after a lot of retrospect and insight about this pizza production Lily-Butterfly consciously decided that the right thing to do to respect the pizza production process was - hire a new employee that was an expert at preparing pizzas from this particular pizza franchise; and could also supervise the pizza production process, plus teach Managers and all cooks to produce the pizza in the most correct manner. This could consistently create the best pizza product on every shift. Regarding this pizza product Lily-Butterfly followed through with her decision, perception, and intention; without telling Mr. Watson. In really honoring this truth about the pizza production process, stay tuned to see how things transpired. Working with integrity the way usually shows the way. Anyway, let us go back to the current happenings. Thanksgiving Day came and went. Lily-Butterfly had a good Thanksgiving dinner at home with the children.

On Monday November 25th Mr. Watson arrived at 9:12 AM for the meeting he read the reports and payroll. Even with the unstable environment and difficult situations the financial and all the reports were still a success in relationship to everything. Mr. Watson did not comment on this.

"The restaurant construction will be completed on November 29th. I told the President and all the Executives that we can open have the restaurant grand opening on December 2nd at lunch time. Okay?"

"No, it is obvious to you that this date is not okay. This is not possible. Last Friday November 29th the restaurant construction was completed. The restaurant production process needs to be reassembled and the new stations be created. We need to learn how to operate this drive through service station in the kitchen. You offered only two weeks training for the new menu items and franchise quality procedures, and production training. No training has been done. We need at least three weeks minimum for this, plus time for all the other things to be completed. If the grand opening was to happen on December 2nd what would we be presenting for sale? Would we be presenting only the past regular menu items; or the complete menu?"

"We would have to present the complete menu. I told them about December 2nd grand reopening date before the delay of the construction," said Mr. Watson.

"You still choose not to change the grand re-opening date. So, how would this be possible with the current situation and having only Saturday and Sunday? The grand restaurant reopening is not possible on December 2nd. I think that you want me to agree with you about this grand reopening date. Then you blame me for everything that will be presented and happening when the President, Board Executives, and everyone shows up here and a negative grand reopening is presented. Nice try Mr. Watson this covert plan is not going to work in trying to make me look bad. Tell all these people that you would like to impress the truth. Tell them the restaurant reopening can be possible on December 18th. This is my firm estimated date commitment. I would like to remind you that I did not apply for a General Manager job, with this current job responsibilities; and with very limited management help and assistant."

"I cannot change the date to over two weeks delay. This does not look good for me. Let us keep the December 2nd date and you take the blame when it does not work out," said Mr. Watson.

"This, I will not do. To help you, do you want me to tell the President the truth and reality of this situation? You will not put this on me. The construction created some of the delay. Your planning did not work out as you wanted it to. This plan of yours was not given enough time to develop and be created. This is the truth. Plus, my opinion is that your restaurant renovation and expansion vision is not going to work in this restaurant. There is a lot more I could say about this plan, but I am choosing to only say the minimum, and save my energies and views for doing my job. Would you like me to help you tell the President the truth? I understand that sometimes it can be difficult for egotistic people to accept mistakes, failure, disappointment, and defeat. Would you like me to tell the President the truth?" said Lily-Butterfly.

"Okay Lily-Butterfly. Let us go to the office I will telephone the President; you tell him your opinion of the truth and the December 18th date that you are committed to have the restaurant ready. After I will brief him from my perspective. Let us do this."

"Okay good idea, because if you did not agree with me when you leave here today I was going to telephone him myself and tell him the truth. This way you would not totally blame me. I know how to protect myself. I did not get this far in life by being stupid and afraid. Mr. Watson you are something else, plus interesting. Let us go to the office, I will talk first to the President."

"Okay there is no other way. You are right about December 18th," said Mr. Watson.

Lily-Butterfly and Mr. Watson spoke to the company's President about the grand reopening situation and date. Lily-Butterfly stayed in the office and listened to the things Mr. Watson told the President. This way she was sure of what he said. Mr. Watson hung up the telephone.

"I am going to use today to Wednesday to get the restaurant production departments recreated. By Wednesday morning we will move the temporary restaurant out of the parking lot and back into the restaurant. Until we are ready with the complete menu items we will temporarily operate inside with the same selected menu items. You can send the training people here on Thursday December 5th to start the training. The food deliveries will be here on Wednesday December 4th. I will get all the food and paper products organized, and get this complete restaurant cleaned, set up, and ready for operation. I have the booklets with the lay out and instructions. You can have the new menu board installed tomorrow Tuesday; be here to supervise this installation. Make sure that the menu board is exactly how you want it to be. Mr. Watson is there anything else for today?" said Lily-Butterfly.

"No. I will get the menu board done tomorrow and the other

things I need to do. The training people will be here on December 5th. I am leaving. Bye," said Mr. Watson.

"Bye," replied Lily-Butterfly.

The journey and process of reconstructing, organizing, training, and the completely new restaurant operation without more expert professional management help was very difficult for Lily-Butterfly, the other management staff; more than you can imagine. On Wednesday December 18th the restaurant grand reopening was a celebration for Mr. Watson, the company's President, Board Member Executives, other senior corporate office employees, and guests. The President cut the ribbon and they seemed to enjoy the experiences. Not one of these people told Lily-Butterfly 'thank you' for anything. She found this unappreciative gesture surprising, strange, and interesting. As usual she learned from the experiences. Mr. Watson got all the cheers and congratulations. He also did not say one thank you to Lily-Butterfly, the other management staff, and or the employees. It seems as if they were only seen as 'the helpers.'

Time went on and Lily-Butterfly job responsibility became infinitely more time consuming and difficult. Mr. Watson did not send more managerial assistant even when Lily-Butterfly requested this. She had to constantly retrain the employees and management staff when they forgot how to teach or make the new food products. There was no time on Fridays to have management meetings. Meetings were conducted individually when necessary. Since the first bonus there were no further bonus, although the reports still showed that the financial statements were under the current budget. Lily-Butterfly guessed that the extra profits were currently being used for the construction repayment.

Tuesday December 24th Lily-Butterfly was off from work. She prepared a great Christmas day lunch feast. Lily-Butterfly ate with her children until 3:00 PM. They packed a dinner basket with food for Manana Leila. At 5:16 PM Rebornstar, Holly, and Lily-Butterfly went to the nursing home to visit Manana Leila and gave her the food that they had brought for her. At 8:00 PM they arrived back home to open Christmas presents on Christmas eve. Christmas morning Lily-Butterfly woke up early and went to work. She had given Ema the Christmas day off. Carlos and Lily-Butterfly operated the day shift. Edna came to work at 3:30 PM to manage the closing shift. When

Lily-Butterfly got home at 6:30 PM on Christmas day she had dinner with Rebornstar and Holly. Rebornstar celebrated her eighteenth birthday on December 15th and Lily-Butterfly celebrated her thirty ninth birthday on December 27th.

On Monday December 30th while doing the seemingly endless reports Lily-Butterfly stopped to reflect on her previous plan to hire an experienced supervisor from the same pizza franchise to totally manage, train, and take care of the pizza operation. She also reflected on Manana's obvious action plan to die. Manana was eating less and less.

"My stress level is beyond healthy. Again, I feel burned out. With all these new franchise concepts of menu items, the money made is back to the amount we used to make. The customers have more choices, and they are spending the same amount of money. Just like I thought would happen. I will not have a nervous breakdown. I am going to write an advertisement for an experienced pizza restaurant supervisor, and tape it to the dining room glass. My hope and prayer is maybe someone will pass by, see this advertisement, and want the job. Creator I know that you know everything already. This is my current prayer to you. I am serious about this request. I will wait until next year after Mr. Watson do my salary increase review. If he does not compensate me the correct salary for this General Manager responsibility, and give me six more management staff; I am leaving. This is my coping limit. I have already out done myself. I am way across my limit of how much work I should be doing for one General Manager with basic management staff," mumbled Lily-Butterfly.

Lily-Butterfly took a sheet of copy paper and wrote: - "Dear Creator although you know everything already I am grounding my request and prayer into writing. I will be as specific as possible. Today is December 30th; by January 6th I need help and support in the manifestation by January 6th an experience pizza restaurant supervisor, that will take over the pizza operation, training, preparation process, and supervision of this complete pizza process. Also, Creator Manana is going to die in 1997. This is her desire. Maybe it is time that I have a positive spiritual intimate partner. I do not think that I can live through the death of my Manana. Her death is going to leave a very big space within my heart, spirit, and soul. I do not think that I can live through this big heartache of Manana dying. Please send me now, the person in the dream that the *trumpet dream oracle guardian angel told me would arrive*. I think it is time for this. You know everything best. I will also leave this job in March of 1997. By then, please also send me the last piece of the puzzle as to why I came to this restaurant to work. I ask these thing, but I also humbly wait for your decision and will. Thank you for everything. Amin."

Lily-Butterfly folded the piece of paper into nine parts, blow her prayer onto the folded paper, and put it into the bottom of her briefcase. She took a piece of large white construction paper, a red marker, and wrote in bold letters, 'PIZZA SUPERVISOR NEEDED IMMEDIATELY. APPLY INSIDE THIS RESTAURANT.' Lily-Butterfly walked to the dining room and taped this advertisement on the dining room glass; here it could be most visible from the street.

Next Lily-Butterfly put all the reports and payroll in a file, close the office door, and went to get something to eat. She sat waiting in the dining room for Mr. Watson to come. Mr. Watson came he saw the sign taped to the dining room glass. He did not say anything to Lily-Butterfly about the advertisement and she stayed silent about this as well. Mr. Watson read the reports. She stayed silent.

"The sales have gone back to where they were before the renovation and restaurant expansion. Ha. This was supposed to attract more customers and get the customers to spend more money. Why is this not working?" said Mr. Watson.

"Mr. Watson it is simple. This restaurant has very dedicated customers whose income remains the same. So now you give them more variety and options on things to buy. This does not mean that they are going to spend more money they do not have. This is a cash only business. Plus, do you realize that the addition of food items that you added to the restaurant's menu, along this highway there are individual restaurants with the same food concept. These restaurants were established before you added these franchises to this restaurant. These places have their dedicated customers that are not going to come here to eat. If you choose to steal these restaurant's customers, you have to give them an incentive to come here. Maybe coupons can help with this. When saying this, I am not encouraging you to steal other restaurant customers; I am just showing you what is really going on. You have to have a demand for something before you can be successful with the supply. The original customers come here for this restaurant signature items that none of the other restaurant supplies. We were great at giving these signature items supply. Now the current few Managers, myself, and all the employees are tired with all this unnecessary extra work. Plus, the drive thru services block the street traffic and access to the parking lot. How this building was designed, does not support having a drive thru restaurant operation. I am thankful that with all this extra production, issues, problems, and everything else, we can keep our financial budget where it should be. Is there anything else for today's meeting? We are all tired. I need to go help in the pizza section of the restaurant."

"No, I do not have anything else to say," said Mr. Watson.

"Thank you for everything. I have learnt a lot from coming to work in this restaurant and from having you as my supervisor. I really appreciate this journey. But I think I have had enough of these experiences, your management style, and everything else. This is the truth, said in a diplomatic way. Bye and have a great week. Happy New Year 1997. New Year's day is on Wednesday. Did you forget? You look surprised when I said happy New Year."

"Yes, I forgot. Bye," said Mr. Watson.

"I have not forgotten this restaurant is open New Year's Eve and New Year's Day; and every day. Amin," said Lily-Butterfly.

She did not wait for a response from Mr. Watson. She got up and left the table.

Lily-Butterfly went to the office to put on her apron and went to help with the pizza preparation, cooking, sales, and customer service. The end of Lily-Butterfly's work day came at 5:30 PM on this day Monday December 30th. She went home. Tuesday December 31st was her regular day off from work. She went to visit Manana. Wednesday morning New Year's Day Lily-Butterfly got up at 3:00 AM and arrived at work at 5:55 AM. She had given Ema the day off. Carlos came to work the mid shift, and Edna worked the closing shift. This was another day in this interesting restaurant environment.

82

Some people say, "be careful for what you wish for." I say, "be ready for what you wish and pray for."

On Friday January 3rd a man came into the restaurant and requested an application for the job as experienced pizza restaurant supervisor. He filled out the application and gave it to Carlos. Carlos took the application and gave it to Lily-Butterfly. She was working in the office. Carlos entered the office.

"Ms. Lily-Butterfly here is an application for someone interested in the pizza supervisor job. He is waiting in the dining room," said Carlos.

Lily-Butterfly took the application and read it.

"Tell him to wait. I will come to speak to him."

"Alright."

Lily-Butterfly read the application again.

"I think that my wish and prayer has manifested. He is already a pizza supervisor at the same pizza corporate restaurant, two miles up the street. His application says he can start working on Monday January 6th 9:00 AM to 4:00 PM. This is as complete as I wished, prayed, and envisioned. This is scary good, because I did not think the solution to my most immediate need would manifest so quickly. Thank you Creator for everything. Let me finish this computer work before I talk to him," whispered Lily-Butterfly.

Lily-Butterfly went back to the work she was doing on the computer. As time went by and she did not come to speak to the man, Carlos returned to remind her that he was waiting.

"Ms. Lily-Butterfly, did you forget that the man is waiting. It has been over one hour since I brought you the application. If you want to hire this man come now; or I think he is going to leave. Hurry. Come. We need this person. He can help you a lot."

"Yes. Sorry. Carlos you are right. I forgot. Please tell him I am coming now."

"Okay."

Carlos left the office.

"I seem to be acting like this person manifestation is a dream; and

626

this is all a dream. This needs immediate attention. I will go now," said Lily-Butterfly.

Lily-Butterfly put the application and the relevant hiring information into a file folder and left the office. She went to the dining room to interview the man.

"Hi how are you? My name is Lily-Butterfly. I am the General Manager."

"Hi I am doing well. My name is Theo. I work as a supervisor about two miles up the street at the same pizza corporate restaurant."

"Your application says that you have done this job for three years, working in the same pizza restaurant. Are you a supervisor at this restaurant?"

"Yes, I have worked at this restaurant for three years and I am a supervisor."

"Your application says that before this job you worked downtown New York as a chef in a restaurant. Why did you leave this job?"

"I moved to this town three years and three months ago. I live twenty minutes away. I use the bus or taxi for transportation. Regarding transportation working in this town is easier for me. At this pizza restaurant, I make the same salary as a chef working in the other restaurant. Working with food is my passion; it is like a work of art to me."

"Did you attend culinary school? Are you certified as a chef?"

"Yes, and yes. I am a certified Culinary Artist. Plus, this career is in my blood line. I was born in Greece. My ancestors worked in the restaurant business. Currently, my parents own a restaurant in Greece. This restaurant has been in the family for many generations. So, you see it is as if I cannot escape this kind of work. I try; but cooking seems to follow me where ever I go, or maybe I am following cooking where ever I go. It is as if I cannot escape the art of cooking. Anyway, would you like to hire me, or not? I would work here in the day 9:00 AM to 4:00 PM. I go to work in the other pizza restaurant up the street at 5:00 PM."

"Why work as a pizza supervisor and not as a chef?"

"I could not find a chef job in this town. I found the pizza job and the General Manager was willing to pay me the same hourly pay as a chef. So, why not take this pizza job? I am at a place in my life where I am not in the mood to travel far away for the same pay; just to keep a job title of *Chef*. I am confident in my cooking. Maybe one day I will go back to an official chef job, or owning my own restaurant.

I moved to the United States to attend this prestigious Culinary School in Manhattan. I was supposed to go back to Greece after I graduate. I ended up getting married to someone from my school that I fell in love with. I got my permanent resident visa. Now I am divorced. After my divorce I moved to this town. We were two chefs as a married couple; as the saying goes, 'too many cooks can spoil the broth.' I got the pizza supervisor job; and here I am offering my great talents to work here. You will see how I work. Cooking is really an art form for me. My parents want me to return to Greece to take over their restaurant. But I do not want to follow in my parents and other ancestor's foots steps. I would like to create my own footsteps and path. The medicine of my ancestor's traditions are strong. I am trying to run away from my ancestor's restaurant career traditions and my seemingly inherited destiny. That is a part of my history in a nut shell. Is there anything else you would like to know to decide to give me this job?"

"Okay, makes sense. I understand. Thank you for the short story of your life's journey. Can I call your current pizza restaurant job for reference?"

"Yes, you can call them."

"Okay. Fill out all these forms. I will return in fifteen minutes. What size shirt do you wear?"

"Large, if you have extra-large this will work best. More room in my work shirt is more of a relaxed fit to work in. Thank you."

"Okay. I will be back."

Lily-Butterfly went to the office to get three shirts for Theo.

"That was easy. He seems completely like the person I need for this job. Thank you Creator and all the angels. This is an immediate big relief to my work load and stress. Amin," whispered Lily-Butterfly.

Lily-Butterfly took the shirts and returned to speak to Theo.

"Theo here are three work shirts, a hat, and two aprons. You must wear black pants and black shoes and socks. Every day your complete uniform must be clean. Your schedule starts as you requested on Monday. You will work every week Monday to Friday 9:00 AM to 4:00 PM. I will pay you the same sixteen dollars per hour like your other job. With these two jobs you make $1,120 per week without the chef title; this is smart. Here is a paper with information about employee's rules and guidelines. You will use a time clock to punch in and out. You are responsible for having the correct hours on your time card. When you come to work on Monday I will give you a tour of the restaurant and an orientation. Do you have any questions or comment?"

"I have no questions. Every day when I come to work I will do my best work. I am self-motivated. You do not have to train me to do anything about the pizza. I will train and continuously teach every one regarding the pizza section of the restaurant. Every day before I leave work, I will make sure that everything is prepared and available for the night restaurant shift. If you like, I will even help you with the pizza food order. Regarding my pay; now you see what I am talking about regarding job title and salary. My current opinion is, my chef school training and certification was a great experience and journey. But, seemingly important job titles and lots of stressful responsibilities without compatible pay; can be stressful, useless and a waste of talent and time. I will see you on Monday at 8:45 AM. Ms. Lily-Butterfly thank you for everything. Bye."

"Thank you for coming Theo. I will see you on Monday. Bye."

"You are welcome boss. I will see you on Monday," replied Theo.

Theo left. Lily-Butterfly went back to the office to work and continued on with her work and all the other daily responsibilities.

Monday morning Theo arrived on time for work. Lily-Butterfly gave him a tour of the complete restaurant, gave him an employee orientation, and showed him where all the ingredients and everything was kept for the pizza section of the restaurant. The pizza section of the restaurant was the first section close to the office. Lily-Butterfly watched Theo work from inside the office. He was a great worker. He worked with everything to do with the pizza as if he was in meditation and a work of art performance. He kept the pizza section of the restaurant clean and spotless. In this section of the restaurant he worked with one other employee and one cashier. Theo was the complete answer to Lily-Butterfly's prayer and more. She could see the complete restaurant operation through the one way mirror wall of glass. Theo became the director, teacher, and manager for everything that had to do with the pizza restaurant operation. Over time the employees did not call Theo by his real name they called him Hercules. He did look like the ancient mythical Greek god Hercules; and he was born in Greece. Interesting.

Again, starting this Monday morning January 6th Lily-Butterfly did not wait for Mr. Watson in the dining room for meetings. He came to the office and she was working on the computer. She gave him the file with the reports and payroll. He read the reports.

"Mr. Watson I have a lot of work to do in the office, food orders to prepare and call them in, and lots of other work to perform in the restaurant. Plus, I have to help supervise the complete staff and restaurant; including the drive thru section of the restaurant. So, starting today I will not be sitting down in the dining room waiting for you to have a meeting. Please let me know when and if you would like to talk to me, or have a meeting. I have so much to do, I am tired already and it is only 9:30 AM. I am been at work since 4:20 AM. Since the restaurant's expansion I have to work faster to get all the extra work to fit within the same amount of time. Thank you for your consideration and cooperation with this request. Please let me know if you have questions or comments regarding this restaurant. As you can see in the reports all the percentages are under the current budget."

"Okay. Bye," said Mr. Watson.

"Bye," replied Lily-Butterfly.

One day Lily-Butterfly asked a question to the cashier in the pizza section of the restaurant.

"Why do you call Theo by the name Hercules?"

"He looks like Hercules from ancient Greek Mythology. Research on the computer Greek Mythology, you will see for yourself, and the resemblances," replied the cashier.

"Okay I will. All I know is that he is the answer to my prayer, and even better than I could imagine; regarding this pizza operation. Thanks be to the Creator and the angels," replied Lily-Butterfly.

The month of January continued on with everyone getting used to the new and expanded restaurant operations. Everyone including Lily-Butterfly was more stressed and tired from all the additional work. Ema, Edna, and Carlos expressed their gratitude for having Theo working and taking care of all the pizza operation. The Managers did not complain too much. Things at home and with Manana Leila were operating in a fine tuned positive cycle. Maybe it was again the calm, before a storm.

Tuesday February 4th Lily-Butterfly arrived at the nursing home to visit Manana Leila. She did not see Manana in the entertainment room or her room. Lily-Butterfly talked to the Nurse Aid to ask where she was.

"Where is Mrs. Leila?" asked Lily-Butterfly.

"Mrs. Leila is in the hospital since Thursday. She had pneumonia symptoms and the medicine we were giving her did not seem to be working. When she recovers, she will be taken back to the nursing home. You can go to the hospital and visit her. Okay."

"Okay. Thank you."

Lily-Butterfly left the nursing home and drove to the hospital. When she found the ward Manana was in the Nurse told her that Manana was in intensive care, and that she could see her for only ten minutes. When Lily-Butterfly arrived at Manana's bedside she was sleeping. She visited with Manana for ten minutes, talked to her while she was sleeping, and left. Lily-Butterfly left the hospital feeling sad. She decided to drive to Ms. Gina's home. While driving in the car, many reflections swim around in her thoughts.

"My intuition tells me this is Manana's first attempt to transition on her intended journey of death. What am I going to do without Manana? She is my beginning, life, best teacher of unconditional love and compassion, kindness, care, and positive reference point of my human life's journey. I have to improve my acceptance of Manana's death; I must do this. Let me go see if Ms. Gina is at home and tell her," whispered Lily-Butterfly.

Arriving at Ms. Gina's home, Lily-Butterfly knocked on the door and Ms. Gina came to unlock the door.

"Hi Ms. Gina. I am the last person you expect to see, but here I am. I came to let your know that your mother Manana is in the hospital. She has pneumonia. Have you gone to visit here in the nursing home?"

"No, I have not gone to visit mama since I put her in the nursing home."

"Ms. Gina it is eleven months now since you brought her to the nursing home. You still have chosen not to visit her. I know this is your business. But I am just saying."

Ms. Gina looked at Lily-Butterfly in silence.

"I visit Manana once per week. I went to the nursing home this morning and the Health Aid told me she was in the hospital. I went to the hospital to visit her. She is in intensive care. I came to tell you that since Manana cannot use the burial plot she bought in Boston she chooses to be cremated after she dies. I promise her that I will take her ashes and sprinkle it into the ocean or a river. You are registered on her file as her next of kin. So, you will be the one they call when she dies. Choose a funeral home and have her cremated. Cremation is cheaper than a cemetery burial. Okay. Promise me that you will do this one thing both of us are asking you to do."

"Yes, I will have the cremation done. You told me this two times already. This is easier than a cemetery burial. The government gives a certain amount of money to assist with burial. Anything over this amount I would have to pay the balance. So, cremation is good and the expense is even cheaper than the amount given by the government. Cremation is perfect. You do not have to tell me this again. Anything else?"

"Manana told me that you took the diamond ring I asked you about. You told me you do not know where it is. Ha. Give it to me."

"Mama is not your real mother. She is my mother. I can do what I feel with her things. I gave the ring to Lucy. She came to visit to buy things for her business and I gave it to her. The ring is gone, gone, gone. You cannot have it. Now what?" said Ms. Gina.

"Okay Ms. Gina. If and when Manana dies let me know. Please plan the memorial service so that I can attend. For work reasons give me two days advance notice so that I can plan to attend. Goodbye and thank you for everything. Have a great life. I wish for you all the best of everything. Bye."

Lily-Butterfly left Ms. Gina's home and drove home.

"My opinion is Ms. Gina is a perfect gift, reflection, and an example of how not to be. Every human spirit and soul has a shadow side. I will continue to practice and train my shadow side to be as positive, as my light side. I choose the shadow side of my spirit and soul to be my fearless sacred positive strength, and protector. There is no need to take out my sacred swords if I do not have to. All energies can be a useful teacher. I choose to always respect and love Ms. Gina without conditions no matter what she says and does. No matter what the quality of conception and birth journey was, at the time Ms. Gina was the only way to be conceived and be born to get to Manana Leila, my first human spirit guide and teacher. I give many thanks to my ancestors for everything, because of them I got the opportunity to be born here. Ms. Gina gets a lot of second chances, because no matter what she is my birth mother. But I also know that based on the law of karma she will have to reap the consequences of her actions. This is between her, The Creator, and karma. I am born for a chosen destiny life's purpose to use my spiritual talents for something purposeful. Being a steward of the planet, like my other ancestors before me, is my major focus in this human life. I think that I am getting closer and closer to figuring out how to use all my talents for a life purpose career of service to the Creator, humanity, the planet, and the Universal nature of the Cosmos. I give thanks for everything. This is the temple within me that my spirit, soul, heart, mind, emotions, body, life, health, and well-being resides. Everything and everyone I experience and come into contact with, is a part of the steps and ladder of transformation, change, and creation of my chosen destiny and life's purpose journey. It is sometimes difficult to stay attuned to all of this. But I will continue to stay connected to the Creator, unconditional love, compassion, peace, care, kindness, faith, prayer, positive life force energy, respect, and my spirit's mission. No matter what happens this is my main focus. Human life can be interesting. Amin," prayed Lily-Butterfly.

It was as if currently experiencing Ms. Gina and her attitude gave Lily-Butterfly the complete awareness to turn within, remember herself, and her primary focus as a spiritual being, having many human experiences.

Manana Leila's health improved and she was returned to the nursing home. The following Tuesday when Lily-Butterfly went to the nursing home Manana was there, sitting in the wheel chair, in the entertainment room. In the entertainment room Manana can have the opportunity of speaking to other residents.

"Hi Manana. You are alive. Did you do a trial run of your right of passage to the other side? Ha," said Lily-Butterfly.

"Yes. It is not time to go yet. But I am preparing and testing out the journey. You know I have no fear of death. The vehicle of life and death works together like companions. The vehicle of life brings me here, and the vehicle of death takes me to the other side of where I will go after death. On both sides there is life. To me there is life after death. Death is not my end. There is no beginning and there is no end. Everything is a continuation of the other. This is my experience, opinion, and perceptions. If I am wrong about this philosophy I have nothing to lose. Every human believes in one thing or the other. Anyway, here I am again. When the right time comes I will be gone. I know for sure that I will see you to say goodbye on the day when it is time for me to go. I am giving you notice to prepare yourself for this separation of our human life's connection. We will always be connected in spirit, heart, and soul. We are from a spirit lineage of soul survivors, way makers, stewards, and keepers and care takers of the sacred laws of creation. I give thanks for everything. My child prepare yourself for my departure. Amin," said Manana Leila.

"Manana I understand everything. I am preparing, but I do not think I will be totally prepared for your death no matter how much I prepare. So, the natural emotional expression after your death will be what it will be. I know that you told me not to talk about Ms. Gina to you. But I simply want to tell you that I visited her and told her again about the cremation process for your body after you die. She told me she would do this. Come, I am going to take you to your room, comb and brush your hair, and massage your legs. You can tell me some more of your beautiful stories. I love you infinitely Manana. Thank you for everything you did for me. It is almost time for you to depart from this very interesting realm. I can see that you are ready to go and you are just waiting on the right time."

"Yes, my child, the time is close at hand. My body is the temple of my spirit and soul. Thank you for making the preparations with Gina regarding the cremation, and to return the ashes of my body to the Universe, earth, and mother and father-nature. I am ready to go. I am just waiting on the guardian angels of death, the flight plan, and the scheduled time. Let us go to the room."

"I see that you remember me. Some things I guess cannot be forgotten."

"Yes, my child this is so true."

"At 3:00 PM I am leaving to go take care of my life for the girls and myself. I am thankful for these children. They help me with all my spiritual training and practices; and they keep my company and encourage my life's purposes. I am amazed how I am able to handle so many things and responsibilities. The answer is in the Creator's will, help, assistance, and support. Amin."

As usual Lily-Butterfly had a great visit with Manana. They like two owls and falcon meeting in no time. They enjoyed their time together and Lily-Butterfly left the nursing home. The following week Lily-Butterfly visited Manana twice, on Tuesday and Sunday morning. This Sunday morning and as many Sunday mornings as possible Lily-Butterfly took Rebornstar and Holly with her to visit Manana.

Monday February 24th, 1997 came, it was the last Monday in the month of February. It was the month for Lily-Butterfly to have her salary increase and work performance review done, by Mr. Watson.

Mr. Watson arrived at the restaurant at 9:15 AM. He came into the office and requested from Lily-Butterfly that they have a meeting in the dining room. She picked up the file with the reports and payroll and went to the dining room. Lily-Butterfly arrived at the table and sat down.

"How is everything going?" asked Mr. Watson.

"Things are going as good as possible. I have a new employee working in the pizza section."

"What more can you do to increase sales. The sales are like it was before the renovation and expansion," said Mr. Watson.

"I have done everything I can possible do in the restaurant to make the environment positive and pleasant. Sometimes I go to the dining room to talk to the customers, give fast and friendly service, and make customer service a positive experience. The other thing you can do is put coupons in the newspapers and give us coupon to give to the customers. But this will possibly decrease the sales we already have. It is your choice if you want to take the risk of offering coupons. This restaurant has been here for over ninety years. Over these years the reputation of this restaurant might have decreased. But people from near and far knows that it is here. You could put a mascot outside on the highway by the restaurant to attract people's attention to see and remember the restaurant. These are my current ideas."

"I will think about these things and see what the best choices are. I do not want to make a decision that will take away from the current sales. We need more sales to pay for the renovations and construction, the bills of the past losses, pay for the franchises, and other long term expenses."

"All of this new addition call it anything you like, is an added expense on top of the previous yearly expenses and loss in money. The money the restaurant currently makes pays all the current bills, payroll, and gives profit. I do not know what else to say about making more money here. We are already working at maximum capacity without the required amount of Managers."

"I hear you. You have more magical ways to improve the sales even more. Ha?"

"No. Plus, I cannot work any harder, longer, faster, and wiser. I am tired and burnt out. You ask, and want more and more from me. You have not said thank you once, or pay me the correct salary. Do you think that I am a mechanical iron horse? With being over worked on every level, by now even a real horse would have dropped dead, or lay down and refuse to move. My performance review and salary increase is due in February. Today is the last Monday in the month of February. Have you done my review?"

"Yes, I have done it. I was waiting on the best time to present it to you."

"Excellent today is a good day for you to go over my review with me."

"Alright. There is nothing to really go over. I chose not to increase my district financial budget to give you a salary increase compatible to the salary scale of working in this restaurant. All your work speaks for itself. But, I have to write your review to reflect the salary increase I am going to give you. I cannot give you a perfect score which is maximum 3% salary increase. I have to write your performance review to show that you have room for improvement. Here you can read it. After you read the review sign it."

"How much salary increase am I getting?"

"I am giving you twenty five cents per hour salary increase."

"Twenty five cents per hour salary increase? Two dollars and fifty cents per day salary increase if I work ten hours per day. If I work more than ten hours per day the twenty five cent per hour decreases. Are you serious? You also save money in your district by not giving us the five other Managers that is needed for this volume restaurant; while we do all this extra work. You are interesting."

"Yes, I am serious about your maximum twenty five cents per hour or $2.50 per work day. This is the best I can do and choose to do at this time."

"Really. After all I have done you wrote my review to keep me down, while you go up. The rumor through the company's grape vine is that next month you are going to be promoted to Vice President of Franchise Operations; and you have promoted Moneyca to your job as District Manager; with the salary and benefits you used to make. You are not going to give this restaurant to Moneyca to supervise as District Manager. This restaurant and my work is your cash horse, cow, gives you credibility, positive work performance review, and makes it look like you know your job. Plus, Moneyca cannot be my supervisor. This restaurant has become the best one in the company and makes the most money. The roots of every rumor contains some truth. Where there is smoke there has to be fire. Unless there is fake smoke. I do not think this rumor is fake. I will wait and see. Time tells everything. Keep Moneyca out of this restaurant as long as I am General Manager here. Anyway, I am not going to waste your time or my time reading this review, or turn this useless conversation into a complain festival or carnival. What goes up must come down, or will come down. I will be right back."

Lily-Butterfly did not wait for Mr. Watson to reply she got up and walked to the office.

Lily-Butterfly made a copy of the performance review, and filled out a vacation request form for ten vacation days off; from March 10th to 23rd. Lily-Butterfly returned to the dining room to return the original copy of the review and vacation request form to Mr. Watson.

"Mr. Watson here is a copy of the review. Here is a vacation request for ten vacation days off. I have six week vacation days. I have never taken vacation since I came to work for this company. I think it is past time I take some of my vacation days off. During my vacation period I will have Edna prepare the complete weekly reports and payroll. You can pick up the file on the desk in the office on Monday mornings. I will leave the schedules and everything organized for when I am on vacation. Ema will manage the restaurant during the day and Edna will manage the night shift. Carlos will work mid shift. I have taught all of them how to do the complete food ordering process, inventory, and all the basics of everything to be able to operate the restaurant without me. They can do all these things for me for two weeks. Another General Manager coming from another restaurant to work for me is more expensive, and they do not know how to operate this restaurant. I need to rest and recuperate for my health and well-being. Please sign and date my vacation request form. Thank you."

"Okay I will sign it."

Mr. Watson signed and dated the vacation request form.

"I will be right back," said Lily-Butterfly.

She went to the office to make a copy of the vacation request form. She returned and gave the original to Mr. Watson.

"Here please submit this to the payroll department. Thank you."

Mr. Watson face had a constipated appearance. He was silent. Lily-Butterfly was silent as well.

"Is there anything else?" asked Mr. Watson.

"No, I have nothing more to say."

"Okay. Bye. Have a great week," said Mr. Watson.

"You as well," replied Lily-Butterfly.

Lily-Butterfly walked to the office. She continued working on the administrative office procedures. Mr. Watson got up and walk towards the fifty feet menu board. He looked up at the menu board and seem to be reading it. Lily-Butterfly wrote a note in the Manager's note book. The note read, *Ema, Edna, and Carlos - Managers meeting on Friday February 28th at 3:30 PM, in the dining room.*

"Every time I perceive Mr. Watson is trying to use money and salary to control, manipulate, suppress, and diminish his perception of my power and talents; I feel like moving out of his way and attend to my health and well-being. I am not open for his energy of negativity, sour, and sad energy. Creator I think it is time to leave this place. I hope that I have already gotten everything I needed from being here. I have learned a lot. I am not open to become damaged by anyone or anything. I do not want to continue working in this place and with Mr. Watson, where I do not sense safety and feel protected. I am choosing to be finished here. I give thanks for everything about this part of my journey. I am taking two weeks to step back, refresh my health, well-being, and decrease my stress. Plus, seek another job as a bridge to the next part of my chosen destiny and life's purpose. I think I am close to this destination and career. Manana is leaving and I am emotionally preparing for the day she dies. Please continue to guide me and send the help and assistance I need. Let thy will be done. Amin," prayed Lily-Butterfly.

Lily-Butterfly continued on with her work day. Theo was still performing a great job. Since he came Lily-Butterfly has been free to attend to all the other restaurant operation process. Theo calls Lily-Butterfly 'boss', instead of her name or ma'am.

Tuesday Lily-Butterfly went to visit Manana at 10:00 AM. Manana was less talkative. Lily-Butterfly combed her hair, massaged her legs, read to her, asked questions about their lives living in the valley village of Yaj, helped her to use the toilet, and help with eating her lunch. Lily-Butterfly left Manana at 3:20 PM.

Friday at the Manager's meeting Lily-Butterfly told Ema, Edna, and Carlos that she was going on vacation.

"Hi everyone this is an emergency meeting. Thank you for being here. Please do not interrupt me while I am talking. Let me finish and then you can take turns talking. I am going on vacation for two weeks; March 10th to 24th. Edna please do the part of the weekend reports you are used to doing. Complete and print all the reports and payroll in the computer. Also close all the weekly reports in the computer. When I return I will check all the reports you did. I will let you know if you made a mistake. On Sundays, start the inventory and paperwork as early as possible; so that you do not stay later than the 3:00 AM you are used to. We will go over all the report and payroll process before I leave. On Sundays when I am on vacation I will schedule Carlos to work 12:00 PM to close. Edna leave in a file on the desk all the completed reports and payroll for Mr. Watson. He will come on Monday morning to get this file. Ema on Sundays you will work as the Manager. I will schedule enough shift supervisors to help you. Please continue to do all the correct financial procedures and operation policies while I am on vacation. Ema on Monday, Wednesday, and Friday morning you will do all the food orders, check the deliveries, enter the amounts in the computer and telephone in the food, paper, and cleaning supply orders. This ordering process is set up to make things as easy as possible. Ema, Carlos will manage the shift while you do the administrative work. I used to do all the birthday party process. During my absence take birthday party reservations only if you can manage to take time away from the normal restaurant operations to prepare and manage these birthday celebrations. You can choose to say birthday party reservation is not available at this time. If you do the best job on each shift, things should work out okay. Ema I will give you the combination to the master safe, so that you can give the deposits to the security armored pick-up. You know how to do this process already. I am finished speaking. Is there any questions?"

"I think that you are going on vacation to prepare to quit. Are you?" said Ema.

"Maybe. First I have to find another job. I will give you advance notice if I am leaving."

"If you leave I am leaving too," said Carlos.

"I do not like this Mr. Watson. Thank God I work nights where I do not have to see this axs hoxe scammer disguised as District Manager. I hear that our friend the General Manager in Larchmont is leaving in March and moving to Florida. Mr. Watson is going to officially be promoted to Vice President of Franchise Operation to open this company's restaurant, as a franchise all over the world. I hear that he is keeping this restaurant in his supervision. He has promoted his friend Moneyca to take his job as District Manager with free car and all the benefits he had. The Larchmont restaurant will have no General Manager. This is one of the restaurants in Mr. Watson's district that is being given to Moneyca. I think that they are already promoted. But they are not officially putting this information in the company's newsletter, because Mr. Watson and the others, think that you are going to be upset. Why? Ma'am you are the one that is in line to be promoted to District Manager, because of your credentials, being the General Manager of this restaurant that makes more money than all the other company restaurants combined, and your work performance to bring this dungeon haunted failing depression restaurant out of the two million dollars annual loss. They are afraid that you will quit and everything collapses. No one else in the past has ever been able to do what you did in improving this hell hole. I do not have the patience for these supposed officials. I am sorry that I took so much time talking. Enjoy your vacation and do exactly what you think is right for you. You are too good for this place. They do not deserve your beautiful talents and work. You will find a job very easily. Let me know if and when you are leaving. Ma'am do you realize your talents and potential?"

"Yes, I realize my potential. I came and stayed here, because I felt that I was being guided from within to do so. I do not want the job as District Manager. They are wasting their time in fear and useless worry. Eventually the truth always comes out. This restaurant professional career is not my destiny and life's purpose. It is a learning tree to get to the purpose of my birth. The things I did for this place and all of you were unconditional, and was my job responsibility. I did everything willingly, because it was the right thing to do. I always knew that at any time I could leave and find another job. I chose to stay. Maybe it is now time to transition to the things that are next for me in my life's purpose. I do not choose to tell you everything that I perceive Mr. Watson is negatively intending towards me. But one thing I will say is that all of you are being generously respected for your work, by the salary I approve for your work performance and everything else. Mr. Watson does not do the same for me. He actually does the opposite, and takes all the credit for my work efficiency and performance. This is as much as I will say. I think I have had enough. I think maybe it is time to leave. We will see based on the job I can find. I am the only financial support for my two girls and myself. So, I have to make wise choices regarding money income, as well."

"I am a little numb and speechless. I think that you are going to prepare to leave. I understand everything ma'am. Enjoy your vacation. We will miss you. It is good to take a break from this tiring place. If you leave I am leaving too. Finally, I feel confidence and more restaurant management knowledge to leave this place. Do not just disappear. Come back to work, give notice, so we can enjoy the last maybe two weeks of your presence. Okay. Thank you for everything you did for us," said Ema.

"I am speechless about your situation as well. I am happy that I could leave this job and get an even better one, thanks to you ma'am. I am now very confident to seek another management job in another restaurant. Now I even have my driver's license and bought a car. May God keep blessing you Ms. Lily-Butterfly. You are everything," said Carlos.

"Thank you for everything ma'am. Know this right now, if you leave I am leaving too. I came here to work at sixteen years old and I have never left to go work any place else. I am not certified by a paper certificate. But you know that I know how to do everything. I will leave this hell hole and go to work for another restaurant company. For the first time I feel free and confident to leave this place. You have taught me so much more than I ever felt that I could know and be confident about. The acknowledgement, love, respect, guidance, care, patience, generosity, lessons, teachings, and everything else that you gave us was nourishing to our spirit and soul. Currently they do not deserve me staying here after I see how they treat you. If I were you I would leave. This is how I know that you are leaving, and planning to leave. Go with my blessings. You came here with your positive energy and light, and brighten every dark corners of this establishment, and lifted everything upwards. Now take your positive energy and light and leave. They will see what happens. Money is a great tool, but it is not everything. Really, go. We will be fine. Thanks again for everything. Now it is time for this hell hole and cemetery to collapse again. If someone wants everything they will end up losing everything. Thanks," said Edna.

"Thanks to all of you for everything and you are welcome about everything I did. I could not have done the things I was able to do without all of you, Juan, and all the other employees. We were all a great team. I was a productive, experienced, and talented coach, guide, teacher and performer. A coach cannot win a game without all the members of the team working successfully towards the same goals and being a success. I know that I am supposed to use all my talents to help humanity in a spiritual way. I have to seek what this means, discover, and uncover the tools that I choose to share my talents and serve humanity, as a steward and keeper of the sacred laws. Being here I have decided to give up my beautiful hair, I love and like my current very short haircut, and I have achieved many white hairs. It was a blessing working here with all of you and meeting all of you. Here I was a student as well as a teacher. I am leaving with priceless awakened talents, and as an improved student and teacher. I give thanks to Mr. Watson for this as well. If it was not for his intentions I would not have come here; and I would not have met all of you. All energies can be useful depending on the wisdom of the experiencer. Thank you. I am going home now. We have until March 9th to prepare for my two weeks absence. Use the Manager's note book to communicate with one another. Okay?"

"Okay," said Ema, Edna, and Carlos.

The meeting ended with everyone in a sad mood. Lily-Butterfly planned everything for the restaurant and the employees to be a success while she was on vacation. As Lily-Butterfly drove home on the Saturday before the start of her vacation she reflected on her life's journey. On this Saturday night March 8th her intentions were in her last prayer for this day.

"Dear Creator the first focus of this vacation journey is to rest, decompress, and replenish myself. As you know already, I am choosing to leave this current job. I sense it is time to leave. Before I leave this current job please help me to make sure that I get everything that I went there to receive. The second focus is finding another job in New Jersey; closer to my home. I will seek another restaurant job as second in charge like a Co-Manager – second to the General Manager and not a General Manager job. This could give me less responsibility to discover how to use my talents as spiritual tools. I will look in the classified section of the newspaper starting this coming Sunday. Guide me to the next job, direction, and show me the way. I feel as if I am about to give birth to another part of my spirit, soul, and human life; and at the same time transform my past into a complete rebirth, change, and resource. Manana is going to die. When this happens, it will be a symbolic ritual for me to bring forth a renewed life, new beginning, transformation, and change to the life I currently have. Only you know exactly how all of this is going to evolve and manifest. You know everything best. Give me all the resources, tools, and everything I choose, want, and need to create and reap the best success. I have to do the final work and preparation of letting Manana go. The trumpet dream oracle guardian angel told me that when it is time a personal teammate, intimate life partner, and support will arrive. I feel it is time for this courageous man to appear. I think he is coming to be my support for giving birth to my chosen destiny and life's purpose spiritual career. I surrender to what is next for me as spirit and soul traveler of the ancient pathways. Let thy will be done in my human life as it is meant to be for my spirit and soul's purpose and journey. I surrender and leap into the next part of my life's experiences. Creator thank you for everything. Good night. Amin," prayed Lily-Butterfly.

83

As the story continues the events will flow in a more condensed manner, like a river in a mountain valley that turns into a waterfall.

The next Monday March 3rd when Mr. Watson came to get the reports and payroll Lily-Butterfly was doing administrative work. She gave Mr. Watson the file with the reports and payroll. He did not request a meeting. Mr. Watson read the reports, told her bye, and left. During the week Lily-Butterfly trained, showed, instructed Ema, Edna, and Carlos everything they needed to do in her absence She adjusted the employee schedule to create the best restaurant operation. Unbeknownst to Lily-Butterfly, Ema, Edna, and Carlos Mr. Watson had a creepy, underhand, disguised, and spiteful thing he intended to do before Lily-Butterfly returned. Why would Mr. Watson do what he would did? Your guess will be as good as mine. Stay tuned you will see when the time comes.

Lily-Butterfly went on vacation. She rested, visit Manana Leila, read, wrote in her journal, visited a nature center, went to the mall, went to the movies for the first time with Holly, spent time with Rebornstar and Holly, and other activities by herself and with her daughters. Every day she looked in the newspaper for a new job. On Sunday, Lily-Butterfly saw a job advertising for restaurant Co-Manager, to work in New Jersey. On Monday she telephoned the number in the newspaper and scheduled a meeting for an interview. Her interview was Wednesday March 19th. The corporation District Manager did the interview with her. It was a smaller company with one District Manager. This company's managerial structure was General Manager, Co-Manager, and Assistant Manager. This company's restaurants sold a similar menu that was 75% less than the restaurant she was currently working in. She was hired at the interview for a salary $15,000 more per year than her current salary. Her health insurance package was improved. The vacation, sick, and personal days off were the same. The only disadvantage of this new job opportunity was, no 401K plan. Currently, with the company she was working for she had chosen to save a percentage of her salary every week in the 401K plan. At this time, she had $20,367 saved in her 401K plan. When Lily-Butterfly left her current job, she transferred all her savings into an IRA retirement plan at her bank. Lily-Butterfly diplomatically told the interviewing District Manager why she was choosing to leave her current job. She asked him not to telephone the current company for reference. If he needed reference from the current company he could contact them after she left. Instead she gave him the copies of all her three General Manager work performance reviews. These reviews with the District Manager Mr. Watson's signature, her job title, the address of the restaurant location she was working, the things Mr. Watson wrote about her job performance, and the corporation's information at the top of the paper, were proof of the quality of her work; proof of what she was saying, and why she chooses to leave the current job. It is always best and wise to have physical evidence about things; instead of depending on circumstantial views, perception, complaints, and judgements. She also gave the interviewer copies of her college, university certifications, and copies of her work performance reviews from working in the hotel. Lily-Butterfly proved that she was over qualified for this job. Lily-Butterfly was hired to start work on April 7th. The District Manager gave her three uniform shirts and two ties. The color uniform pants and shoes she already had from her current job. She was to report to the training restaurant for three months training. Usually the training program is six months but Lily-Butterfly did not need six months of training, because of her current experiences. At this restaurant training certification, she learned about everything to work as Co-Manager in this restaurant concept. The administrative work was very easy compared to her current administrative responsibility. Everything about this job was a mini version of her current job. The passing grade for each test was 90%. Compared to Lily-Butterfly's current job all of this new job responsibility was very easy. She got an 'A' average for all her test. After training and certification, she was placed in a restaurant that had a drive thru section. Lily-Butterfly was hired as Co-Manager, second in charge to the General Manager. She choose to not be General Manager anymore. So that she can have less work responsibilities to figure out how to use her talents for her chosen destiny and life's purpose career. All of Lily-Butterfly's choices and plans were meant to be, but you will see how things unfold. Let us go back to the current time, job, and situation.

Friday March 21st Mr. Watson had a plan he had put into action.

He really thought that Lily-Butterfly was returning to work and conducting business as usual. So, Mr. Watson thought that his plan would really screw Lily-Butterfly. The plan Mr. Watson put into action unbeknownst to Lily-Butterfly would turn out to his disadvantage. The karma from Mr. Watson's plan was immediate for him.

Monday March 24th Lily-Butterfly arrived at work. It was 4:25 AM when she arrived in the office. She checked all the reports and inventory that Edna had done. They were all correct. She proceeded to complete all the reports and payroll. The percentages were still under budget and the sales and customer count was in the same range as before she left. Lily-Butterfly looked up at the clock it was 6:10 AM. Ema, Carlos and the other regular employees had not arrived. At 6:15 AM Lily-Butterfly got up and walked to the entrance door. She saw Carlos waiting outside with the other employees. She unlocked the door.

"Hi Carlos, where is Ema, what happen, why are you waiting outside? Ha?" said Lily-Butterfly with curiosity.

"Good morning ma'am. I hope that you had a very good vacation. Welcome back there is a big problem. Did you read the notes in the Manager's note book?"

"No, not yet. What is the problem? Is Ema okay? Is she sick?"

"Ema is not sick. Friday morning Mr. Watson came into the restaurant. He told Ema that he is promoting her to General Manager, and transferring her to the Larchmont restaurant. He told me to come and work as the opening Assistant Manager today and forever. No more Ema working here. He told us it was good that you trained Ema and got her certified as a Manager to do everything including the basic General Manager work. Mr. Watson gave Ema to Moneyca as the General Manager for the Larchmont restaurant. The previous General Manager quit. He told Edna to continue to close as an Assistant Manager. Mr. Watson knew that Ema was very useful to you and this restaurant. I think that he is trying to spite you and some kind of creepy revenge for something. Mr. Watson seems to always be playing games with you. He seems to never win these games. He knows we are five Managers short and over worked. This is not good. The General Manager in Larchmont has had enough of Mr. Watson she quit and is moving to Florida. Mr. Watson was officially promoted to Vice President of Franchise when you went on vacation. Moneyca was promoted to Mr. Watson's District Manager job. With the Larchmont General Manager quitting, Mr. Watson and Moneyca had no General Manager for that restaurant. Instead of promoting the Manager in the Larchmont restaurant to General Manager of transfer a new certified Manager to go there and work; he took Ema. Although Mr. Watson is promoted he kept this restaurant in his supervision; and so, he is still your supervisor. He also knows that based on the line of supervision he should have not taken Ema without consulting with you first and so on, and so, forth. Oh my God, what now?"

"Carlos, thank you for your concerns. Focus. Go help the employees finish preparing for breakfast and open the doors. Did Ema leave this restaurant's set of keys here?"

"Yes, Ema's set of keys are in the safe with the cash registers."

"Okay. Come and get her set of keys. Do you know how to use the keys?"

"Yes, I do."

"Okay. Come and get her set of keys. We will bring out the registers." Do you remember how to open and close each register in the system and all the cash register procedures I taught you?"

"Yes ma`am."

"Okay. From now on you supervise the shift and I will help you. Do not panic. It is time to take everything I taught you to the maximum level. Difficult situations can give you opportunities to grown; if you choose this. It is sink or swim, and go with the flow, time. We will work together. It will be much more difficult without Ema, but we can manage. Do you understand?"

"Yes, I understand. I do not know how you stay calm in the worst of situations. I will follow your guidance and lead. Oh wow. Now we are down to you, me, and Edna. Edna is so mad. Maybe she does not come to work today. I hope she does, or we will have a bigger problem. Okay let us go to the office."

"Okay. Stay calm. This is the first rule. Do not suppress your emotions, process the reality of the situation; but remain calm, focus, and positive. Being in negative energy and fear will slow you down and create more difficulties. Come, follow my lead."

"Okay."

Carlos and Lily-Butterfly arrived at the office. She opened the safe and took out eight cash registers and the set of keys Ema left.

"Carlos here are the keys. These keys are for you to use. Only you can use them. You already know the rules about these keys. Here, on this piece of paper are the security alarm code and safe combination for the safe with the cash register drawers."

"Thank you ma'am," replied Carlos.

"Carlos memorize this information as soon as possible, and tear up this paper. Come, today I will put these registers into the cash register slots for you. Follow all the current cash and financial policies, and things should work out well. Tomorrow I will come to work on my day off and we will do this again together. Sunday morning you will open the restaurant and work as the Assistant Manager all by yourself. Sunday is the day with the least customers, so it will not be as crazy and busy. I will take my day off on Sunday. Next Tuesday and Sunday you will open and supervise the shift all by yourself. You are off as usual on Thursdays. Thursday when you are off, I will supervise everything by myself. Is this okay with you? Starting today, as long as I am here I will do all the food orders, check in the deliveries, register them in the computer, and telephone in all the food orders. I will schedule enough employees on your shift. Now for as long as I am here, I have to do my job, the five missing Managers job, and Ema's job. Now it is time to focus inward, use everything I have taught you, use your natural talents and instincts, and common sense. Later I will read all the notes. If you are opening the restaurant by yourself, and you are late to open the doors for breakfast; open the door as soon as possible. Stay calm and do your best."

"Everything you have told me is okay with me. Like this morning we are not going to be ready at 7:00 AM to open for breakfast. What time should I open the doors?"

"You can open as soon as everything is ready. Go make sure that by 8:00 AM everything is ready. Okay. As soon as I am finished with all the administrative office work I will come to help with everything. Do your best, work fast, and still follow all the correct procedures. It is very difficult to transform negative habits. Okay. Here we go."

Carlos and Lily-Butterfly took the registers out to the front counter and put them in the cash register slots. She helped Carlos to make sure everything was ready for breakfast. At 7:46 AM Carlos opened the doors for breakfast service. Lily-Butterfly returned to the office to write her letter of resignation, fill out a vacation day request form, and complete most of the administrative work. She made a copy of the termination letter and vacation days off form. The letter of resignation was short and to the point.

The letter of resignation said, *"Dear Mr. Watson; I have chosen to terminate my job as General Manager and employment working for this company. This letter is to inform you that I am giving you two week notice effective Monday March 24th to April 6th. After April 6th my job as General Manager for this company is over, completed, and terminated. Attached is my four week vacation days request form. I am to be paid for these days with my last pay check. I will telephone the Personnel Director and Accounts Department Manager to follow up with payment for my vacation days, termination of employment, and transferring my 401K plan to an IRA. Thank you for every single thing. Best regards. Sincerely Lily-Butterfly."*

At 9:10 AM Mr. Watson came into the office with a smirk on his face. Lily-Butterfly gave him the file with the reports and payroll. He read them. He was still had a smirking smile on his face. Lily-Butterfly thought, who laugh last, laughs for real.

"Everything looks good as usual. By now you must have figure out that I have promoted and transfer Ema to Larchmont. The General Manager there has quit. I have been promoted to Vice President of Franchise Operations, but I am still your supervisor. Moneyca has been promoted to my job as District Manager. She now manages all the restaurants I used to manage in my district; except for this restaurant. I am still your supervisor. This restaurant is the only one with other restaurant's franchises in it."

"Why did you take out Ema from this restaurant without communicating this intention to me, getting my approval, and knowing that we are very short in management staff? You also knew that I would say no. You transferred Ema to Moneyca's District Management restaurant. So, Moneyca's job is easy with one of the most well trained Manager for a restaurant that makes the least money in the company. This is negative ethics management. I will not call your supervisor or the President of the company to complain about all your behavior towards me. I could, but I have chosen to not complain or explain to them. I will let karma take care of everything."

"Everything I do it is, because I can. I am currently Vice President of Franchise Operation and still your supervisor. This gives me double power over you, automatic permission to do things regardless of rules, and what you want and think. Now let me see what you are going to do. You think that you are the wisest and most talented person. You are not going to choose to walk away from this place, all the work, and everything that you invested in transforming this place into everything it is today. Although Moneyca and I receive all the benefits of all your hard and smart work, you are not going to quit. If you quit you would have left with nothing but burn out. You will never be promoted unless I say so and you choose to be subservient to me. You are all talented, wise, powerful, a great worker, and so on and so forth; but you have to act like you are serving as a means to my benefit, and that you need me. I wish that I could be talented like you. But I am not. You might say that I am jealous; maybe. I am your boss; stop acting and being like you do not need me. Stop being so efficient."

"Mr. Watson I am only performing my job like the company manuals, policies, and procedures instruct that I should. The standard and quality of my work is natural. My actions are unconditional and has nothing to do with being or feeling powerful and power. My perception is that you are saying I should act less than I am, so that you can feel valuable, powerful, talented, confident, wise, and so forth. This is not what I was paid to do as a General Manager for this restaurant. You are my supervisor and the company is my boss. The company pays me to perform my work responsibilities, the money I get paid I earn, the money I get paid does not come from you. Okay this conversation is over. I have a lot of things to do. While I am here I will continue to perform a complete job; this is part of my personality. Sorry if you find me offensive and irritating by me doing all the right things."

"This is all you have to say? You are not angry because I took Ema?"

"No, I am not angry. This is not my business and company. I will not be here when all of this collapses. Here is my two week notice in writing of resigning this job. Now you have to figure out what you are going to do. See if your arrogance, mean, and rude behavior as a supervisor is going to help you. If the President of the company and Personnel Director come and asks me why I am leaving, I will tell them the truth of my experiences. If they do not come, I will leave in peace and grace. You have two weeks to get another General Manager to manage this restaurant. This restaurant is now completely yours. Everything I did was unconditional, so therefore I do not perceive that I have anything to loose. Have a nice day."

Mr. Watson took the letter and read it. Now his face was beet red and the smirk vanished into wrinkled forehead and a frown.

"Are you serious? You are leaving?" said Mr. Watson.

"Yes, as serious, as serious could be. Now you have to explain everything about my resignation to your supervisors, the Company's

Board Members, and the President. Know that if they ask me I am going to say the truth of my experience working with you for the past over two years. I also sense that Moneyca and maybe you are going to go to jail. I could be wrong. I have so much work to do. I am behind already. I have to go back to working. Thank you for every single thing. It was more than an adventure working here. Today is the last day we will have a conversation. After today if you need to speak to me ask my permission. I will leave the report and payroll for next Monday March 31st on the desk. There is nothing more that we have to say to each other. It was a good thing that I could take so much negative experiences and transform them into positive experiences and discovery of my talents. Anyone else would maybe have a nervous breakdown, heart attack, or quit; a long time ago from the treatment you gave me as a so called supervisor and District Manager. Everything you gave me to do you thought that I would fail and set me up to fail, so that you could feel good about yourself; and so forth. You took all the benefits of our success for your own personal gain. All the things you did towards me could be interpreted as a serious case of misogynistic behavior and inferiority complex. You yourself told me that you never thought that I would be able to accomplish all the assignments, difficulties, and never ending tasks, even by not giving me the required amount of Managers I needed to manage the restaurants. On top of all the difficulties I currently have, you took Ema out of this restaurant; creating an even more difficult and challenging situation for me. At the same time everything we did assisted and helped this restaurant become a success and stop the two million dollars annual loss. I could say a lot of negative things about you to your face, but I choose to not do this. I came to this company with grace and I will leave with improved grace. Humility, peace, grace, unconditional love, and compassion is the foundation of authentic fearless power and empowerment. I will stay until the last day of my notice no matter what you try to do. The only other thing I will caution you to do is watch your step, because the power of your karma will be coming back to you sooner than later. All I did I chose to do. I am in no way perceiving myself as a victim of your actions and behavior. Amin. Bye. Please close the office door when you leave."

Lily-Butterfly walked away from Mr. Watson without wait for a response. She went to help Carlos to set up the restaurant to prepare for lunch. At 2:15 PM when the lunch crowd had diminished Lily-Butterfly went back to the office to continue with the administrative work. Edna came at 3:00 PM and she talked endlessly about Ema's promotion to General Manager with the same pay and being transferred out of the restaurant. This was the first time Ema and Edna would be working in a different environment. Lily-Butterfly listened as Edna talked about the last two weeks experiences, Ema leaving, and Mr. Watson. Lily-Butterfly did not tell Edna and Carlos that she had had given Mr. Watson her resignation letter. Lily-Butterfly thought she wanted to give them an opportunity to digest the current situation of Ema leaving and the difficulties that they all would have to experience from her being gone. She planned to tell them at the next and last Manager's meeting on Friday March 28th. Edna talked and left the office to go prepare for the night shift. Lily-Butterfly wrote a note in the Manager's notebook.

The note said, *"Edna and Carlos please attend Manager's meeting on Friday March 28th at 3:30 PM in the dining room."*

At 4:05 PM Lily-Butterfly went to manage the shift, while Edna continued to plan and prepare all the things she needed for the night shift. It was also time for Carlos to start counting the cash registers with the cashiers from the day shift. Lily-Butterfly helped Carlos with the cash verification, computer cash register report closure, preparing the deposits, and dropping every deposit in the master safe. This was the first time Carlos was performing this job. Ema was the one that used to do this. Every day when Lily-Butterfly worked she trained and supervised Carlos when he did this new cash verification and deposit job responsibility. When Lily-Butterfly was not at work Edna helped Carlos and checked to make sure that he was doing the process correctly.

This Monday and every day after Ema left Lily-Butterfly completed her work day at 6:45 PM. She arrived home by 8:30 PM. Every day after Ema left Lily-Butterfly was more and more appreciative of Theo and everything he did. Theo's help was complete in his thoughtfulness and everything he did for the pizza section of the restaurant and the employees that worked in this section of the restaurant. Theo also did not talk unless he had to. He focused his energy in his work and work performances.

Lily-Butterfly would say, "Theo thank you so much for everything you do. I really appreciate everything you do. The work you do with the pizza really helps me, the customers, and everyone else."

Theo reply would be, "Boss you are welcome. I really admire your work performance as a General Manager and how you treat every employee. Thank you for everything as well."

The week continued to unfold with difficulties, more work load, and challenges. Edna, Carlos, the other employees, and Lily-Butterfly did the best they could, and continued to work together as a team. Lily-Butterfly telephoned Ema on Wednesday March 26th in the Larchmont restaurant to see how she was doing, talk about her promotion, transferal, and experiences in that restaurant. Lily-Butterfly did not tell Ema that she had resigned her job. She wanted to tell Edna and Carlos first.

As usual Lily-Butterfly's journal and the Creator was her continued support system.

84

Friday March 28th at 9:30 AM the Director of Corporate Restaurant Operation came to visit Lily-Butterfly to talk about her resignation. He was the first one from the corporate office to visit Lily-Butterfly before she left. They sat in the dining room to talk.

"Hello Lily-Butterfly I am here to see if there is anything I can do for you to stay and cancel your resignation. The President and Personnel Director have decided that I should take over from Mr. Watson and become the supervisor of this restaurant. I will be your supervisor as well. Mr. Watson have agreed with this decision. Tell me what you would like for you to change your mind about leaving."

"At this point there is nothing you are anyone else can do. I have found another job with 75% less work responsibility for more pay. Speaking in general terms, I have been working here very understaffed, with the same salary and salary increase as I was making in the New Jersey mall food court restaurant. Still, I have done everything I could possibly do to improve everything here. The financial reports, the quality of my work, and everything else speaks for itself. When I was transferred here this place was a useless dungeon, hell, and haunted black hole; that sucks away every penny made here; plus, two million dollars annually. Currently it is the restaurant that makes the most money and profits. The reward I got for my excellent work performance is, more work, less help; and not even one thank you from Mr. Watson my supposedly supervisor; or any other corporate executive. I do not choose to spend time telling you or complaining about my negative personal and professional experiences with Mr. Watson as a supervisor. Now, I have decided to professionally and personally transition to the things that are currently right for me. The best thing for you to do at this time is to get someone to perform the job of General Manager here."

"I see. Many years ago, I used to be General Manager here before I was promoted to Director of Corporate Restaurant Operations. Are you leaving because Moneyca was promoted to District Manager instead of you?"

"I never wanted to be promoted to District Manager. My view about Moneyca being promoted to District Manager is, she is not qualified; and she gets rewarded for being an unqualified corrupt person, and restaurant managerial personnel. This is my view in a nutshell about her promotion and work performance."

"I see. We have an ongoing investigation on missing company money and deposits in Mr. Watson's district. Moneyca seems to be the most common theme in this investigation. Plus, we have come to know that Mr. Watson and Moneyca seems to be personally close. Is this what you are talking about?"

"I choose to leave this restaurant and company and go on with my life. I do not want to become a witness in court in relationship to your investigation. I do not want to be specific about what I know. I have done enough for this company already. The last thing I need is to get involved and tangled up in this investigation. If you and everyone else in this corporate head office do your job you will figure everything out. The evidence is hidden right out in the open. I am not sure of the relationship between Mr. Watson and Moneyca. But the evidence is there as proof that she gets rewarded for being corrupt. The biggest problem you have right now is getting a General Manager to work here, that can keep this restaurant successful; this will not be easy."

"I agree and understand that it will not be easy to get the right General Manager to work here. This has always been an issue. Anyway, regarding Moneyca. I am going to tell you some things. This is between you and I. Tell me if the things I say is correct. By just saying yes, or nodding your head. Our conversation is off the record. Anything you say is between us; and can help me as Director of Operations. Just so you know I will not tell Mr. Watson the things you tell me. Mr. Watson and I do not get along. He seems to always be competing with me. I do not like him, and he does not like me. Okay."

"Okay. What do you know so far regarding Moneyca?"

"We are investigating stolen deposits and forging of checks. Every time, and in every restaurant the deposits get stolen or missing Moneyca is the only familiar person in all these situations. In the restaurant she was the General Manager, in the same restaurant when she was a Manager, when she goes to a restaurant to work for another Manager or General Manager; large amounts of money and complete deposits for a shift goes missing and stolen. Even in the restaurant where her brother is the General Manager deposits goes missing/stolen there as well. I think her brother is involved in the same behavior as well. In the restaurant when she was a Manager and even when she was promoted as a General Manager the regular employee payroll checks for employees that no longer work at the restaurant were being signed as the employee and cashed. Employees that no longer worked at this restaurant, payroll checks were being requested for them, gets signed and cashed in the cash register in the restaurant. Now, how we know that Moneyca had something to do with forging and cashing these checks is, because these checks were cashed on her shift, and showed up in her deposits. We have been telephoning these employees and they told us when they have stopped working at this restaurant. There are other things, but these are the major incidents. Thousands and thousands of dollars are stolen in this manner. This is what we found out in a nutshell."

"I could say many things about the financial transactions in all the company's restaurant in Mr. Watson's district; but I am not. I know these things, because Mr. Watson sent me in the past to help the General Managers fix the product mix in their computers, and many other issues. I experience things along the same lines of your investigation and discovery. I think that these illegal financial procedures are going on in all your company's restaurants. I found some of these illegal financial transactions operating here as well when I came here to work. I stopped all of these transactions. I do not want to get involved by telling you the specific things I found out here. My help to you is to tell you that you are on the right track and going in the right direction with your investigation. You are right about everything you have discovered on your own. So, dig deeper, follow the familiarities, follow the path you are on with your investigation, gather all the evidence, add things up, and you will find all the evidence and confirmation hidden wide out in the open. Another thing I will guide you to look at is, General Managers and Managers are floating their deposits; taking one deposit, using another deposit to cover up for the missing deposit, and sometimes not even replacing the deposits. To find this issue, start to add up the actual deposits reported on paper from the restaurant's computer reports that are sent to the accounts department; and the actual and physical deposits of the same restaurant at the bank. The company's bank accounts might not even be set up to check the actual deposits from the individual restaurants. The amount of money they think they have; they might not. The amount of money the accounts department is presenting as bank balance might be fake. Hello. The people in the accounts department are not doing their job correctly. I do not want to continue to work here as General Manager or ever work for this company again; the roots from the foundation and upwards is like rotten infestation. My opinion is that the corporation is floating on dead roots. Check things out in the direction of this conversation you will find the many roots of the real situation. I am choosing to leave as quiet as possible. This conversation is between you and me. Thank you for coming to try and make me an offer to stay. This is not for me. Do you understand?"

"Yes. I understand. Your insights and information is very useful. I wish that you could stay. Would you like to be my assistant; like an Assistant Director of Corporate Restaurant Operations? We would work well together as a team and fix this rotten infestation and mess. Ha? Think about my offer?"

"No, I do not choose to take your offer. This is not what I was born to do for my chosen destiny and life's purpose career. I work with the things I choose to do with heart felt passion and unconditional vibes. This is part of my success with everything I choose to do. But I was not born to use my talents in this kind of career and to help people make money. Spirit, soul, heart, mind, and body; I am not wired for this kind of shark infested human career. No, I know I am not. I would never be fulfilled or feel purposeful working in this kind of business where corruption is always close at hand, with the people, and environment. I found another job already in the same restaurant business. I will use this job to help me transition to find the right life's purpose career, and what is true, and right for me. I am grateful for the opportunity to have worked here. I have grown and learned a lot from being here. I am very grateful for this priceless opportunity. Now it is time to leave. I wish you all the best with finding someone to come replace me."

"Thank you for everything. It is going to be difficult to replace you. I will see if I can. Bye."

"Okay. Best regards with your investigation and everything else. Try to fix the issues and not just end at investigation. As Director of Corporate Restaurant Operation this might be a part of your job. Thanks again for coming. Bye."

The Director of Corporate Restaurant Operations left and Lily-Butterfly returned to the many things she had to do for the day. At 3:30 PM Lily-Butterfly, Edna, and Carlos were in the dining room for the Manager's meeting.

"Hi Edna and Carlos it has been a tough week for us without Ema. I miss her help a lot. I do not choose to use this meeting to complain. I will get to my intention for this meeting. I would like to inform both of you that next week is my last week working here. I have given my two week notice and letter of resignation to Mr. Watson on Monday.

Mr. Watson's action of transferring Ema out of the restaurant, and in the manner he did this was the last straw. I was planning to leave and used the vacation time to find another job. On Monday when I found out he transferred Ema I knew for sure leaving was the right decision for me. Saturday April 5th is my last day. Sorry."

"I had a feeling that you were going to leave. There is only so much any real human can and should take. You do not deserve to get a nervous breakdown in working in this cursed place. I understand you came here and made this place and everyone improved. Mr. Watson worked against you every step of the way to sabotage your success, create difficulties for you, give you more work, not give you the current amount of managerial help, expansion of the restaurant, renovations, like he wants to see you collapse, take credit for all your work, and the current last thing is to take out Ema to help and benefit Moneyca. At the same time, he used the success and improvements of this restaurant to look good and get promoted. My sister is in Larchmont in a new hell of crap and shixtness. Good that you chose to leave. I am not surprised that you are leaving. I will miss you. But I carry within myself and my heart all the respect, love, and compassion that you showed my sister and I. I will not go back to where I was before you came here. After you leave, I am leaving too. I never had the courage or confidence to leave before; now I do. I am going to start looking for another job. When I find one I am leaving. I am not going to give any notice. I am just not going to show up for work on a Monday. Amin so let it be. Enough is enough. Everything will get dumped on me. I have had enough as well. Thank you for everything," said Edna.

Carlos was silent.

"Edna I will not tell you to leave or stay. Do what you feel is right for you. I agree with everything you have said. I already have another job. This is our last meeting. My gratitude to you, Ema, and Carlos is infinite and beyond words. Without all your help, assistance, and support the accomplishments would not have been possible. I will telephone Ema to say goodbye. I could say more about Mr. Watson and my past experiences, but I will not. Today before I leave work I will put a notice on the employee's notice board to say I am leaving. Be good to yourselves. The Director of Corporate Restaurant Operations came to ask me to stay; I told him no. Next week let me see who is going to come next. The reply will still be no."

"I do not like to think or talk about this situation. Ma'am, I thank you for everything. I know that you will be okay where ever you go. I know that I will be leaving the same Saturday you leave. I am going to go work in another restaurant as a Manager; I know the General Manager of this restaurant. This is my choice. Sorry Edna, but you will be here on Monday April 6th by yourself. We all know the situation here and about Mr. Watson. I do not want to spend my time and energy criticizing him. Ms. Lily-Butterfly I wish you all the best of everything. Thank you," said Carlos.

"I wish all of you the best as well. You are welcome," replied Lily-Butterfly.

"This place will crash down again. This I know for sure. I am trying very hard to not say curse words. Really," said Edna.

"Okay. Thanks again. This meeting is over," said Lily-Butterfly.

"Okay. You are welcome," replied Edna and Carlos.

Friday before Lily-Butterfly went home she put a notice on the employee notice board that she was leaving and that Saturday April 5th was her last day.

Monday March 31st Lily-Butterfly was at work at 4:30 AM. She did all the reports, payroll, and all the other administrative responsibilities. At 9:10 AM Mr. Watson came to get the reports and payroll. The President of the company, Director of Corporate Restaurant Operation, and Personnel Director came as well. They called Lily-Butterfly into the dining room for a meeting. They all expressed the reason for their visit was to ask Lily-Butterfly to stay. She graciously said no, and that she had another job with 75% less work responsibility and $15,000 more pay per year. She told them also that their offer was not sincere, they were offering, because they wanted her to stay. When they insist that they would improve their performance, she did not accept any of their offers. Without complaining and blaming Lily-Butterfly told the corporate executives about her experiences with Mr. Watson as her supervisor, and the basic reasons she chose to leave. She did not tell them anything about the investigation conversation with The Director of Operations. Lily-Butterfly told them that Saturday was her last day and to put her last check in the mail. She thanked them for coming and excused herself from the table. Lily-Butterfly left them looking at one another in silence. She went back to work. The corporate executives and Mr. Watson all toured the restaurant and left.

Lily-Butterfly telephoned Ema to tell her that she had resigned the job, thanked her, and wished her all the best with everything.

The news about Lily-Butterfly leaving circulated very quickly. She spoke to Juan personally and thanked his for all his support, help, and assistance. He wished her all the best of everything. On Wednesday the cashier in the pizza section of the restaurant spoke to Lily-Butterfly about her leaving.

"Ms. Lily-Butterfly I am sorry that you are leaving. We will miss you. Thank you for everything. Ma`am another thing is; do you notice how when you walk by Theo, he admires you? I do not think that you ever noticed; but I am just saying," said the Cashier.

"No, I never notice Theo's admiration. I am usually so busy, plus I have a boundary rule that I do not make employees my friend, and this is the company's policy as well; for sexual harassment and conflict of interest reasons. Another thing is, workplace gossip, it can be distracting for everyone. I admire Theo's work all the time, from my office. His work is exceptional."

"I know, he is a good employee. I understand. I am just letting you know that I think he likes you. You never give him a second glance, if you know what I mean. Theo also told me that you are a wonderful lady. He never thought that he would meet such a woman such as you with so much courage, strength, kindness, care, understanding and loving vibes. He talks about how you treat all the employees and Managers with respect. He expressed sadness that you are leaving, and he would never see you again. He wants to buy you a thank you gift for everything you have done for him as an employee. He told me to ask you what you would like," said the Cashier.

"Seriously. This conversation is happening and I had no clue. I do not pay attention this was the last thing on my mind. Why does he not tell me these things himself?" said Lily-Butterfly.

"You are his boss and you have a direct no nonsense way about you. Although he looks like Hercules he might be intimidated by your confidence and beauty. What should I tell him?" said the Cashier.

"Where is Theo now?"

"He is in the kitchen," replied the Cashier.

Theo returned from the kitchen while Lily-Butterfly was talking to the cashier. She turned to talk to Theo.

"Theo is it true what the cashier is telling me about how you admire me and want to give me a goodbye gift of gratitude?"

"Yes boss," replied Theo.

"I am the one that is supposed to be giving you a gift. You have no idea how much your helped my health and well-being by coming here to work in this pizza department. You were the answer to my prayer regarding this pizza department; including training, and everything else. I thank you very much for everything that you did. Buying me a gift is not necessary. Thank you for your kind thought and intention. You might use your money to buy me something that I do not like."

"This is why I would like to know what you would like. After Friday I will never see you again. Remember I do not work here on weekends. I would like to give you a token to express my gratitude," said Theo.

"Theo, I surrender to accepting your kind offer about me and what I want. Let me try to honor and respect your kindness and thoughtfulness. I give kindness, so I have to be open to receiving kindness. Okay. Let me step outside my rules for once. I will compromise, I still do not want you to buy me something. How about we go out to eat? This way you do not have to go buy a material gift. I like seafood and vegetables. Is there a seafood restaurant close to this restaurant? I have to go home to my children and I live in New Jersey. I need to get home as soon as possible. We can go Friday after work. If this is okay with you."

"Yes, Friday is okay. I will request the day off from my night job. About two miles up the street there is a seafood restaurant. What time would you be ready?"

"Wait for me outside by my car at 5:00 PM. I will go after work in my uniform."

"Okay. Thank you. Friday I will wait for you by your car at 5:00 PM," said Theo.

"Okay Theo. Thank you again for everything. I appreciate everything you did."

"See, Theo, that was not as hard as you thought," said the Cashier.

"Thank you for asking her," replied Theo.

We will get back to the Theo and Lily-Butterfly seafood restaurant dinner in the next chapter.

Lily-Butterfly went back to focusing on work and all the things she had to do, without second thoughts to Theo's request and the conversation. When Edna came to work she told Lily-Butterfly how the employees had given her money to buy large bouquet of flowers and a cake for her; as a thank you gift. Saturday Edna arrived at work with a large bouquet of flowers and a cake. Lily-Butterfly thanked all the employees. She left a thank you note on the employee's notice board. Lily-Butterfly shared the cake with every employee at work at this time. She also left some cake for the night employees. Lily-Butterfly took home the flowers. As she drove home she reflected on her past experiences at this restaurant.

"Leaving this restaurant, I have a sad feeling like leaving a funeral. Today is like an end to an unbelievable experience of my past, and a new beginning of my present life. This present life will bring me to the things that are next in this life's journey. Sometimes the most difficult situation can give opportunities for growth, transformation, and improvements. What is next? Amin," whispered Lily-Butterfly.

At this time, I will conclude everything Lily-Butterfly would like you to know about this restaurant experience and corporation situation. Saturday April 5th, was her last day as General Manager at this restaurant. A full time General Manager could not be found to replace her. The Director of Corporate Restaurant Operation scheduled other General Managers from other restaurants to work one day per week; until they found someone permanent. Carlos quit on Sunday April 6th. He got a job as Restaurant Manager at the restaurant he mentioned in the last Friday meeting. Within a month Edna found another job as closing shift Restaurant Manager at a different restaurant concept franchise. Most of the employees at the restaurant went to work at the restaurants that Carlos and Edna went to work. Six months after Lily-Butterfly resigned, Juan got injured at work and went on permanent disability. Theo also left this restaurant. Ema was arrested by police at the restaurant for alleged theft, about three months into her job at the Larchmont restaurant. The story about Ema's arrest was in the newspaper. The newspaper said the reason for the arrest was alleged stolen money deposits. No further information on this case.

After further investigation directed by the Director of Corporate Restaurant Operation, Moneyca and her brother was arrested by the police, for alleged check forgeries, robbery, and theft. No further information on this arrest. Mr. Watson continued to work at this company as the Vice President of Franchise Operations. Until Mr. Watson retired, he worked at this corporation as a sales-man selling franchises of the corporations original restaurant concept.

Within nine months the restaurant Lily-Butterfly worked as General Manager the operating procedures and financial success collapsed. The financial issues were worse than before, because in addition to the old debt money was borrowed for the renovation and expansion. Plus, after the financial investigation and the collapse of this restaurant the corporation realized their real financial situation. The corporation sold all their corporate restaurant, to private individuals as franchises; except for the first three original restaurants. This gave the corporation some cash and business opportunities. One of the restaurants the corporation decided to keep was the one Lily-Butterfly was working in. In 2009 this restaurant was completely demolished. A smaller restaurant with similar menu was built with a modern drive thru. Today this rebuilt restaurant continues to exist on the same sport, at the same location; and have the same negative issues and situations.

Darkness gives more darkness. Light gives more light. Darkness can cancel out light. Light can cancel out darkness. The stronger and the amount of vibration, is the more dominant and powerful one. Everything and all vibrations needs to be maintained to exist in the desired states.

85

Be aware of the signs, resources, things you pray for, and tools for your life. They are usually around you. Be aware that with the right view, sometimes the wrong road and people; can lead you to the right road and people.

On Friday April 4, 1997 at 5:10 PM Theo and Lily-Butterfly were in the car driving to the seafood restaurant. In ten minutes, they arrived at the restaurant. Theo and Lily-Butterfly left the car and entered the restaurant. Theo seemed confident enough to give Lily-Butterfly the first option on everything she pursued. Theo did not try to open her car door for her, he seemed down to earth, unpretentious, letting her make her own decisions, offered ideas and support, sensing things out rather than jumping ahead, friendly, reserved, and relaxed. At this outing Theo gave Lily-Butterfly complete space to be herself. Theo also seemed respectful of the awareness that Lily-Butterfly was his supervisor. At the restaurant he did not call her by name or ma'am. He refers to her as 'Boss.' Lily-Butterfly thought, being called 'Boss' is cute and interesting. No one had ever called me Boss before.

They each ordered food and drink. After they sat in silence, I guess sensing out each other's vibes. Lily-Butterfly was the first one to speak.

"Theo you seem quiet, reserved, and observant. At work you mostly focus on doing your work."

"Yes. You are right. This is my personality. When I talk it is direct, genuine, and considerate."

"These are positive leadership qualities. Good for you."

"Where in New Jersey do you live?"

"Elmwood Park. About ninety minutes from here; depending on the traffic. How far from here do you live?"

"About twenty minutes. I usually use the bus for transportation. If I work later than the last bus, I take a taxi home. The taxi takes about ten minutes. I work at the pizza restaurant at the plaza next door."

The waiter brought the soups, salads, and drinks.

"Theo I would like to say a prayer to bless the food. Is this okay with you?"

"Yes sure."

"Thank you Creator for this food and the money to buy it. We eat this food to nourish ourselves so that we can continue on the journey of this human life. We are also grateful for everything else. Amin."

"Boss, you seem like an interesting person, spiritual, beautiful, strong, flexible, kind, direct, understanding, independent, wise, focused, no nonsense, and so forth. Where were you born?"

"I am an island girl. I was born on the island of Kawomaya; in a remote valley village called Yaj. So, I am currently a naturally refined country bumpkin at heart. I like being country, and at the same time a balanced blended harmony of the ancient and modern ways of humanity. This is wise; it is where the ancient ways is positively woven with the modern ways."

"Oh. I see. Mmm. Good. As I told you before I was born in Greece. Actually, Northern Greece in Kavala. My parents owned a restaurant in a sea port city in Kavala. We lived upstairs the restaurant. I had a very simple life living in the place of Greek Mythology. My ancestors fifteen generations were farmers and had a grape vineyard and restaurant. How about your ancestors?"

They continued to eat. The waiter had brought the rest of their food.

"Your life sounds interesting. My personal life is a very unique adventure. I have two mothers a birth mother, and an earth cradle mother-nature mother, who was my first guide and teacher of the ancient ways and this human life. This is a long story. Anyway, my ancestors were peasant farmers. Farming is one of the most original and ancient human careers. In these modern times this career is seen as inferior, poor, and peasantly. Humans are interesting. I am the first of my ancestors to be as modern and educated as I am; and maybe the last one with all the knowledge of my ancestor's ancient ways and knowledge. The basic philosophy of these ancient ways and pathways is; respecting the sacred process of mother and father-nature. Currently in this so called modern human created world, people seem to respect the most; money and material possessions. I could go on and on with my spiritual and philosophical views. Why did you come to New York to study the culinary arts?"

"I came to learn the modern ways of cooking to add to my culture and ancestor's way. But I am also in conflict with following my ancestor's ways of farming, cooking, restaurant, and to maybe choose to create my own path, and not follow in the footsteps of my parents and ancestors. My parent wants me to take over and operate their restaurant; the vineyard was sold. I am the first born; and a son. I am traditionally expected to take over the family business when my parents retire or dies. After Culinary Arts School I thought I wanted to switch careers and attend law school. After one year of law school I did not like my experience; so, I stopped attending law school. I was married, divorced, and have no children. My ex-wife was American and we were both certified Chefs. We had many personal and cultural conflicts. We got a divorce and I moved from Manhattan to Yonkers. My parents wants me to return home to Greece and operate the family restaurant. I am resisting fitting into an ancestry pattern. I am trying to avoid my pre-created ancestry destiny, and maybe my spirit and soul's destiny. Until I firmly decide what to do, I am here. Did you find another restaurant job?"

"Yes. It is usually easy for me to find the jobs I want and seek. I think the reasons are I have good work experiences, positive references, and many qualifications and certifications. I love to learn and study. I am a single parent with two daughters. I was married and divorced; once so far. I am the only financial support for my children and myself. I treat the things I choose to be a part of my life with completeness, respect, and passion. I have to go in fifteen minutes. Pay the waiter."

"Okay I will pay the waiter."

Theo called the waiter and asked for the check. He paid.

"I would like to keep in touch with you. Can I have your phone number? Sometimes I could telephone you," said Theo.

"No. I do not like talking on telephones. Most times I am at work or out running errands. Most times I just have time to rest. I am not the friend kind of a person and personality. I have no time to wait for your phone calls. I am not interested in having a long distance intimate relationship. I only have time to take care of my daughters, myself, go to work, visit my Manana Leila – who is in a nursing home, and so forth. I am very busy."

"You are so busy that you do not have time to talk on the telephone for ten or fifteen minutes. No one should be that busy. Maybe you are just trying to avoid me. Maybe it is time to explore other things than the responsibilities that you currently have. Take a chance and see what else is waiting for you to discover. Maybe it is time for this. You have nothing to lose by giving me your phone number. When I call, if you have no time to talk to me just ignore the call."

"I have no time and patience for men's games. It is time for me to discover how I choose to use my spirit and soul's talents to create my chosen destiny and life's purpose career. I know that I was not born to seek the normal things of modern human world. For example, the turtle is in the ocean with many other sea creatures, the turtle has a specific purpose, and focuses on performing this purpose. The turtle has no concern about what the octopus does as its purpose. Theo, do you understand?"

"Yes, I understand. I am writing my telephone number on this napkin and I will give it to you. It is your choice to give me your phone number or not. I have a strong feeling that we were destined to meet for a divine reason. It is up to you to give me your telephone number or not. Sometimes a spirit and soul is traveling on an adventure of many important discoveries, and needs to let in help to find their destination. If I telephone and you are not available, I will call again. If you give me your telephone number the opportunity for us to keep in touch is doubled. There are no accidents in this realm and Universe. To accomplish great things, you know that sometimes you might need help. Trust me and trust this chance encounter. If it was not my initiative and your wise choice and participation, we would not be sitting here eating and having this conversation. Okay. Here is my home and work telephone number. I am going to use the men's room. I will be right back," said Theo.

While Theo use the men's room Lily-Butterfly reflected on Theo, the message from the dream oracle guardian angel, and her prayer to the Creator asking to send the person the dream oracle guardian angel told her was coming. Lily-Butterfly was amazed that Theo had even arrived and was around her all this time. She got up to use the lady's restroom; and continued to process her reflections and thoughts.

"I can see that I am hesitant to give Theo my phone number. The truth is, I am used to getting my prayers answered and all my dreams have come true. But it seems scary and unbelievable that Theo is the person that would appear from the trumpet dream. – *Reference the dream towards the end of chapter seventy nine* - In this dream, the dream oracle trumpet guardian angel told me my next personal teammate and life partner support will appear soon to help me to get to my destiny life's purpose career. I am pushing my luck with my resistance. This also means Manana will dies soon. Theo is here to continue on with me in my life for one cycle of seven years like the dream oracle guardian angel told me in the dream. Oh, my Creator you surely work in mysterious ways. Theo was here all this time and in disguise. Hello Lily-Butterfly get out of your own way. Okay I will

667

give Theo my telephone number, surrender, and let the way show the way. Amin," whispered Lily-Butterfly.

Theo was sitting at the table when Lily-Butterfly returned. She took a pen and wrote don her telephone number and gave it to Theo.

"Theo here is my telephone number. I have no time to come to Yonkers regularly to pick you up and so forth. If I seem hesitant and nervous it is, because of my own life's experiences, and wanting to stay in a safe space of my own protection. We will see how things evolve over time."

"Boss thank you for choosing to give me your telephone number. I am lucky that you changed your mind. Time will tell everything. Let us go now. I will telephone you. Come."

"Okay. You are welcome. Thank you for this dinner and giving me your telephone number. I will give you a ride home. We are going in the same direction. I will take you home and get back on the highway."

"Thank you. Ten more minutes more for us to be together. Even one minute with you is a priceless gift. You are a great person; more than you even realize. Thank you for suggesting this dinner opportunity as a gift. It was really a meaningful gift for both of us. Remember we are here, because you choose to receive this dinner as a gift," said Theo.

"Theo you are right. You are welcome."

Theo and Lily-Butterfly got in the car. They were both silent for the drive to Theo's home. They only spoke when it was time for Theo to give directions to get to his home. They arrived at Theo's home in fifteen minutes. Theo opened the car door to get out.

"Goodbye Boss. I will telephone you sometimes at 11:00 PM after I leave work at night. There is a public phone where I wait for the bus. No pressure. When I call, take my telephone call at your own choice when you feel like it. Goodnight. All the best with your new job. Bye."

"Bye Theo. All the best with everything as well. Bye."

Theo got out of the car and closed the door. Lily-Butterfly drove away. As she drove home she continued to process all her experiences with Theo. At the end of the night Lily-Butterfly wrote in her journal. She took from her work briefcase the prayer she had written to the Creator about Manana's death, sending someone to take responsibility for the pizza section of the restaurant, and sending the personal teammate and life partner support. She read the prayer on the paper.

"Manana is going to die this year. It is time for me to completely prepare for her death; and not block her pathway through death's door, by wishing that she will live. Theo seems to be the one to accompany me further up the pathway. Theo and my destiny are aligned for karma reasons. Oh wow. More big life changes are arriving. I will burn this prayer now in my sacred purification incense bowl. Creator you know everything already. Secret Theo has been revealed. Monday April 7, 1997, I start a new job for whatever reason. I will see where this new job take me. I understand that to make my experiences as authentic as possible some things are not revealed to me until it is time. Creator as an ancient spirit and soul sometimes I am even surprised at the miracle of your revelation of events, people, places, and things. You are truly mysterious. The tests you give me are truly profound. I really have to work to earn my 'Way.' Thanks Creator and everything, for everything. Amin," said Lily-Butterfly.

She burned the paper with the written prayer.

That night Lily-Butterfly felt a cool breeze blow consistently over and around her as she lay in bed falling asleep.

"I think the winds of transformation and change are here again. The kaleidoscope and revolving doors of my life is turning again to take me to the next steps of my chosen destiny. Amin," whispered Lily-Butterfly.

The realm of sleep arrived. Lily-Butterfly entered the realm of sleep, rest, and rejuvenation.

86

Daily, take time to breathe. Conscious breathing can be cleansing and relaxing.

Sunday Lily-Butterfly felt like a heavy load was lifted off her body. Monday she went to her new job training. The managerial training was very easy compared to her previous General Manager responsibilities. As time went on the new Co-Manager restaurant training continued to be an excellent alternative to her previous work experience. Lily-Butterfly got an 'A" grade for all her tests. Lily-Butterfly continued to visit Manana Leila. Holly improvement in regular classes at school. She was consistent and conscientious. Holly continued to love and like her glasses experience. Rebornstar had totally settled into her new school and had new friends. She had not totally let go of her old friends. At this time Rebornstar got her driver's license. Lily-Butterfly bought her a used car. The same week Rebornstar got the car she crashed it into a tree, trying to prevent hitting another car. There was only liability insurance on the car. As a teaching lesson about responsibility, Lily-Butterfly told Rebornstar that she would have to wait until she could fix the dent or replace the car herself. Rebornstar became a more mindful driver after this car accident. One day Rebornstar told her mother to not be so concerned about her making mistakes, not seeming to hear or listen, and doing wrong things. Rebornstar reassured her mother that she was a young spirit and soul, who might need to make mistakes, and do trial and errors, to learn on her own to improve her wisdom. After this conversation Lily-Butterfly decreased monitoring Rebornstar's choices, actions, and practices. Rebornstar graduated high school the first week in June. Holly and Lily-Butterfly attended Rebornstar's high school graduation. Rebornstar celebrated her nineteenth birthday on December 15th. Lily-Butterfly assisted Rebornstar in enrolling at the Community College to start a degree as a Registered Nurse. Within two months of starting this course, Rebornstar switched her course of studies to Tourism and Travel. After six months of college Rebornstar stopped going to college. She told her mother that she needed a break from going to school. Rebornstar stopped attending college and went to work at a place of her choice, and creating her own personal life to enjoy.

From the day Theo and Lily-Butterfly exchanged telephone numbers he would telephone her about three times per week. She never had to telephone him; he was the one that usually called. They talked and got to know each other.

Thursday June 19th Lily-Butterfly was at work in the training program. The telephone rang and the General Manager for the restaurant answered the telephone. He told Lily-Butterfly that the call was for her. She went to the office and picked up the telephone.

"Hi. This is Lily-Butterfly, may I help you?"

"Hello Lily-Butterfly, it is me Gina. The nursing home telephoned me to tell me mama is dying and she is in the hospital. Henry, Dean, and I am here to say goodbye to her. If you would like to talk to her before she dies you should come now."

"How did you get this phone number?"

"Holly gave it to me."

"Are you coming? You had better hurry. We said goodbye to mama already," said Ms. Gina.

"Ms. Gina, no I am not coming while you, Henry and Dean are there. I am at work. I started a new job a little over two months ago. At this time, I am in training class. In two and a half hours, after work, I will go visit Manana by myself. I visit Manana every week. I saw her on Tuesday. She is not ready to die as yet. Manana will not die until after I say goodbye to her. So, sorry she is not dying today. Do as you choose. Thank you for letting me know about your perception of this situation. You, Henry, and Dean have not visited Manana since you and Dean put her in the nursing home, over one year ago; last year April. Today you show up to say goodbye to her, because you think she is dying. I guess this is better than nothing. You are there for your chosen reasons. Thanks again for your telephone call. I have to go back to work, bye. I hope that you are available when she is really going to die. Bye."

"As usual, you talk too much," said Ms. Gina, before she hung up the telephone.

Lily-Butterfly put the telephone down and went back to complete the test she was doing. When Lily-Butterfly was finished with the test she asked for permission to leave work. She went to visit Manana Leila at the same hospital she was the last time she was sick with pneumonia. Lily-Butterfly arrived at the hospital at 5:30 PM. Manana Leila was in the Intensive Care section of the hospital. The Nurse told Lily-Butterfly that she had another episode of pneumonia; and was given medicine. Lily-Butterfly went into the room to see Manana. She seemed to be in a very deep sleep. Lily-Butterfly felt her forehead; it was very hot. Lily-Butterfly wet a small towel and put it on Manana's forehead. After she talked to Manana.

"Hi my mother and father-nature. My first healer, teacher, and spirit and soul guide. Today is not the day you go home beyond this veil. Your ninety ninth birthday just went by on May 5th. But, I do not sense the angels of death and the keepers of the ascending portal gateway. This is how I know today is not your day of death. As you know death is a process and a journey. I am here. You will feel better and return to the nursing home. This is another trial run. Maybe in another three months you will be totally ready. I am almost completely ready to let you go."

Lily-Butterfly could see Manana Leila smiling from within her deep sleep. Lily-Butterfly smiled as well; and continued to talk to Manana Leila.

"I see you smiling; I am smiling too. You will feel better and patiently wait for the right time and appointment. Keep focus and steadfast on arriving more and more at peace with this life time and yourself. Keep on recapitulating your life, give thanks for everything, work out your regrets, awareness, and mindfulness. Say I love you to those whom you choose, acknowledge all the positive things that you have done and accomplish, ask the Creator for forgiveness for anything you perceive you did wrong or negative, and so forth. When it is really time, I will be here to help you birth yourself home to the other side; beyond this veil. I will see you at the nursing home on Tuesday. Keep prepping. I will see you again my angel. The Creator, the Universe, and I love you. Rest and prepare. I am going home now and I will see you again. See you soon. Bye."

Lily-Butterfly kissed Manana Leila on the cloth on top of her forehead. Manana Leila smiled a wider smile. Lily-Butterfly smiled. She walked away from her Manana Leila's bed, thanked the Nurse, walked out of the hospital, and got in her car. As Lily-Butterfly drove home, she processed the experience about Manana.

"Manana is not ready to die. It is not her time. I am almost finished emotionally committing to letting her go. I also have a feeling she is waiting on something else. I will try to figure out what this could be," whispered Lily-Butterfly.

Friday June 20th Lily-Butterfly returned to the hospital to visit Manana Leila, instead of waiting until Tuesday. Manana was still in intensive care, sleeping, medicated, and being fed by a feeding tube. Lily-Butterfly sat and talked to Manana for about an hour. Saturday Manana health improved and she was returned to the nursing home. The following week Tuesday morning Lily-Butterfly was off from work. She woke up at 5:00 AM and did all her chores and errands. On her way to visit Manana in the nursing home, Lily-Butterfly stopped at the YMCA to register Holly for six weeks of summer sleep away camp. Holly's first day of camp was July 13th. School would be closed for the summer the following week. Lily-Butterfly arrived at the nursing home. Manana Leila was laying in her bed. Lily-Butterfly walked into the room. Manana looked at her and smiled.

"Manana, what is my name?" asked Lily-Butterfly.

Manana laughed. Lily-Butterfly laughed.

"Journeying to death and after death's door I will not forget you, or your name," replied Manana Leila.

"I know. Anyway. What is my name?"

"Hahaha. Your name is Lily-Butterfly the Creator's messenger and prayer master," replied Manana Leila.

"Ha-ha. Mmm. Good girl. You still have your memory. Your senses and your brain seems to be working; plus, you can talk. This is great. I knew that it was not time for you to die. Keep preparing. The time is up to your appointment with death. Until the time arrives you are here. You know us; we are not scared of life or death. Life and death is just the continuous continuation of the other. How could it be easy to let go an angel such as you. Manana you are so beautiful inside and outside. The ascending realm is so happy to have you return, and you are ready and happy to go. But, you have to wait on your appointment. Your death is not going to be premature. The path of peace is your path and way out of this realm.

"I know. I know and understand, my child. I am thankful for everything. How are you and the children doing?"

"As good as we can be; thanks be to the Creator and everything else. When my girls and myself are healthy and alright; I am content. We are all doing great."

Manana Leila and Lily-Butterfly continued to talk and share past and current stories that day; every time into the future, and until the day she died. At the nursing home Manana stayed laying in her bed after this current hospital experience. In the future Manana Leila was returned to the hospital for the third and last time, for another diagnosed pneumonia illness.

July 13th came, Holly was packed and ready for her adventure and enjoyment at sleep away camp. Lily-Butterfly took her to the YMCA and watched her leave on the bus. Holly was excited to go on her new discovery and adventure. Lily-Butterfly was not as happy as Holly. Lily-Butterfly stood crying with a heavy heart as she watched Holly wave to her from the bus; and the bus drove away. At home it was very noticeable to Lily-Butterfly that Holly was not at home. The home was quiet, and most times Lily-Butterfly was home alone. Rebornstar was away at work, and busy with her own life creation. She promised her mother that she would return to college after her so called indefinite college break. Theo still telephoned Lily-Butterfly three times per week. Theo's telephone calls, visiting Manana Leila, and work kept Lilly-Butterfly's attention away from missing Holly presence at home. After three weeks of Holly being at camp Lily-Butterfly got used to Holly not being home.

Theo telephoned Lily-Butterfly and invited her out to dinner. This was the second time they would be going out to dinner. He suggested that they meet at the same seafood restaurant they went to the first time. Lily-Butterfly surprised herself and Theo by saying yes to the invitation, without some kind of a resistance. She agreed to meet him at the restaurant at 5:30 PM on Friday July 25th. With Holly in sleep away camp and Rebornstar independent, and busy with and in her own life, Lily-Butterfly had more free time. Tuesday July 15th Lily-Butterfly went to visit Manana Leila at the nursing home she was still in bed. She entered Manana's room.
"What is my name?"
"Ha-Ha. Lily-Butterfly."
"Good. The last drop of your memory is still here."
"Yes it is, but I am slowly leaving."
"Okay good for you," replied Lily-Butterfly.
"My child the last important things I will say to you is this: - on your next birthday you will be forty years old. After your forty second years old you would have gone through six cycles of seven years old. Around the age of forty two your spirit and soul talents mind, body, health, well-being, life, and pillars will be solid, strong, and flexible to manage and maintain your chosen destiny and life's purpose career. Always be unconditionally loving, compassionate, caring, kind, patient, and positive for and with yourself. You can never give things that you do not have. Around the time of your forty second birthday you will mysteriously enter the gateway and

path of your chosen destiny and life's purpose career. The tools you choose to express this career is your choice. You will discover how to mix and weave the ancient pathways with the modern pathways; and at the same time keep the original sacred authentic vibrations. You will assist humans with their chosen requests, prayers, and positive rebalancing, by the Creator's guidance and will. Towards the very later part of your life you will transition to the path of Earth Keepers and Steward of the Planet, Universe, and the Sacred Laws of Humanity. All the work you will perform will benefit every living thing. This might seem like a very intense and responsible life's purpose; but you will manage fine. You have been preparing for this destiny and life's purpose before you were born in this life time. You are never alone, when you need help ask in prayer; seek and you will find, knock on doors and you will be helped. You will marry again. Do not get lost in the relationship, companionship, and partnership; and waste time. This will be a holy matrimony of purpose and karma for both of you. This will be a harmonious, unconditional love, understanding, and compatible union. He will arrive to help you to relax your masculine, work less, be supported for the second time in this life time, and practice improved trust of the opposite sex and humans. After this marriage you will discover all the tools you choose to express your chosen destiny and life's purpose career. Stay grounded in integrity, truth, loyalty, gratitude, forgiveness, compassion, love without conditions, peace, and positive Universal life force energy frequencies. Let people earn your trust; and trust your instincts and senses. Plus, see and trust people for who and what they are; and whom they say they are. Faith is an inward creation projected outward. Humans can be interesting, have many hidden faces, and use many masks. Be safe, be aware of protecting yourself. Seek help when you need it. Take nothing for granted; and always be grateful for everything. Stay aware and mindful. Maintain a profound, exquisite, elegant, simple, and humble, well nourished, good fortune, and blessings foundation. Remember to show appreciation for everything. Say thank you to others; this shows a respectful appreciation for receiving something of perceived value. You are here because of the ancestors, so always respect the ancestors. Remember karma. Keep a positive resolved inner and outer reverence regarding your ancestors, birth mother, and birth father; whether they are known or unknown. If there are issues, resentment, and negativity towards the mother that gave you the opportunity to be created and birth you here, it will create a negative separation imprint

675

from your inner personal feminine essence and mother-nature. If there are issues, resentment, and negativity towards your birth father that gave the seed to be created, it will create a negative separation imprint from your inner personal masculine essence, father-nature, and the Creator. This will make you incomplete and unbalanced. I will die before your next birthday. These words are my last gift and rites of passage to you. I am ready to go home. I might be back before you die. When I arrive and you see me, you will know that it is me. Amin," proclaimed Manana Leila.

Lily-Butterfly cried as she soaked in and digested Manana's words.

"Thank you Manana for everything. These words are priceless reminders digested in my spirit, soul, heart, mind, and body. I understand everything that you have said. I will miss you, and can never forget you. With infinite authentic wisdom comes infinite authentic responsibility. Birth mama Ms. Gina was my best teacher of the dark and shadow arts realms and vibrations. After her I can be aware of similar energies and to protect myself. You were my mother and father-nature, and positive Universal love and life force energy vibration teacher. Thanks be to all my ancestors, including my birth father wherever he may be. Amin."

Manana Leila and Lily-Butterfly continued to enjoy their visit, like two wild and wise falcons resting on the tree of the Universe. At 3:00 PM Lily-Butterfly left the nursing home to continue on with her day. Next week Monday July 21st, Lily-Butterfly will be transferred to a restaurant in a mall about forty five minutes from her home. Her new assignment will be Co-Manager for the General Manager of a mall restaurant, in a food court.

When Lily-Butterfly arrived home from visiting Manana Leila the home was very quiet without Holly's presence. Very consciously it came to Lily-Butterfly's mindful awareness that it was the first time in her life without 100% care of her daughters. Holly will be eight years old on July 31st and she will celebrate her birthday at sleep away camp.

Lily-Butterfly sat at her dining table contemplating her life.
"This is the calm before the next storm, transition, and revelation. Let me enjoy this break. Amin," said Lily-Butterfly.

87

Things are meant to be for as long as they are meant to be.

July 25th came and Lily-Butterfly arrived at the restaurant to meet Theo for dinner. Theo was waiting for her inside the restaurant's lobby. They greeted each other, and the waiter showed them to their seat. They looked at the menu, placed their orders, and continued to talk. As Lily-Butterfly participated in the conversation with Theo she was also processing thoughts inside her. Some of Lily-Butterfly's thoughts were, with my personal guardianship and protection shields relaxed, I sense more that Theo is the one the *dream oracle trumpet guardian angel and Manana Leila were talking about.* Currently the connection between us seems in harmony. My natural alpha female resistance and testing Theo's courage, confidence, and strength will still happen automatically. This is the way of an alpha female. An alpha male will automatically understand this. Oh well.

As the conversation between Theo and Lily-Butterfly continued her resistance became more and more relaxed. They finished eating their meal and ordered desert. The conversation became more personal.

"Can I say something deep," asked Theo.

"Yes. Sure. To me everything you say is deep. While you talk, my animal instinct is sensing the things you are saying, and the things you are not saying," replied Lily-Butterfly.

"When I was sixteen years old and living in Greece I had a dream. This same dream I have had repeatedly all my life. In this dream I met a woman. She was like a goddess. When I met you at the interview, I was very amazed. Your spirit seems like the woman in this repetitive dream. The dream told me that I would meet this woman when it was time. When I have met this woman, I should ask her to be my wife," said Theo.

Lily-Butterfly interrupted.

"Nice try Mr. Theo. Stop. Really. Your repeated dream told you to ask me to be your wife. Ha. This is a profound magical synchronicity and coincidence. I am just joking. This is my nervous alpha female resistance. Theo are you serious about having this dream?"

"Yes. Let me finish. In the dream I was directed to ask you to marry me. But, I thought, it was only a dream. As I get to know you, I sense the essence and spirit of the woman in the dream is similar to yours. This feels a little weird. There are no accidents in this realm and Universe. I have been processing everything and conclude that the interpretation of the dream means that through our karma and union we will experience unconditional love, compassion, and trust beyond where we are currently. We need this as medicine for our spirit, soul, and heart's maturity; and for whatever other unknown reasons. Plus, you seem to be conscious, focused, and running willingly towards your chosen destiny and life's purpose career. While I am unfocused and running away from my unconscious chosen destiny and life's purpose career. I am rebelling against my ancestor's path and you are not. Maybe my real forgotten chosen destiny and life's purpose career is within my ancestor's authentic pathways. There is an ancient saying that a person can find their destiny on the path they take to avoid it. This seems to be a perfect example. I will not distract or encourage you to leave your chosen path. I totally understand your intentions. I promise to help you and not hurt you. We can help each other. Maybe we are destined to help each other. Lily-Butterfly will you marry me?"

"I do not know. I do not know you. I do not feel like saying yes. I know you unconditionally at work, but I do not think I know you personally. Marriage is a big deal. I have to be committed to my chosen destiny. I cannot be a regular human created wife role model. My spirit, soul, mind, and body cannot be owned by a human. Marriage and playing the role of a wife is not part of my spirit, soul, and heart's mission. I am never impressed about marriage. My perception is the modern ways of marriage is a modern human created map for many materialistic reasons. I can only be committed to following the guidance and map of the Creator. I cannot and do not serve human. I am committed to serving the Creator. I had a dream that I would meet someone that I am supposed to marry as well. But my spirit and soul's personality is, I have to choose and make sure that this feels right for me as well. I am guided to not share the dream I had with you, because it will prematurely interfere with something that should happen towards the end of a seven year cycle of the marriage; if I choose to marry you. I have to think about your proposal even if it is ordained by the Creator. I have to be honest this is how I personally feel. I thank you for the proposal."

"Lily-Butterfly I am not going to try and convince you to

marry me. You are your own independent woman. Greeks are very spiritually aware people. We come from the mysteries of the ancient pathways as well. The energies I will bring to your life will enhance who and what you are already. You will do the same for me. Maybe I am the one that was chosen by the Creator, gods, and goddesses to help you get to, and through the next part of your life's journey; and you will do the same for me. I understand that the marriage and relationship will last as long as it is meant to last; and our choices. My instincts tell me that based on the gifts that will evolve out of this union, we will both benefit from the marriage and relationship while it lasts, and even after. I know nothing lasts forever, and everything is a continuation of the other. Would you like to say something?"

"Theo I am hearing, listening, and processing the things you are saying. Your words sure sounds true. But still, my natural instincts says we will see."

"Lily-Butterfly, will you marry me?"

"Well I think this is the longest, deepest, unique, and most sensible proposal conversation. Really. How come you are proposing to me and you have not presented a ring" Do you have a ring?"

"Yes, I do. It is in my pocket. I think you should say yes or no from your heart first before a ring is presented. The ring should not motivate you to say yes or no."

"Okay you are right. But, let me see the ring."

Theo reached inside his pocket and took out a small box and opened it.

"Here is the ring. Look. Do you like it?"

"No. Would you like to hear the truth?"

"Yes. What?"

"The ring looks delicate and the diamond is small. I use my hands a lot at work. This ring would become ruined and the diamond might come out and get lost. You work very hard for your money. I would not want to worry about wearing your engagement ring. If I wore this engagement ring it would be broken in one week. This is a mindfulness view and not based on materialism. If you had bought me a strong ring without diamonds it would be okay as well. If I say yes, we could even use the same ring to get married with, instead of buying another wedding band ring."

"Or are you trying to be mean."

"Sorry if I hurt your feelings. I am just being direct and honest. To me it is not about the size of the diamond. It is about being practical. If the ring breaks and the diamond gets lost, I would be concerned.

You would have wasted your hard earned money. You can change the ring by buying a stronger ring that I could wear daily and do not have to be distracted with protecting the ring. I do not have to have two rings to get married. I will continue to process marrying you and will let you know if I want to accept your proposal. In the meantime, it is your choice to listen to my ring suggestion."

"Okay I hear you."

"The next thing is my tubes are tied and I cannot have any more children. I will not live with any man I am not going to marry, or choose to marry. My life's purpose, my children, and I are my primary focus. If we get married I would choose to embrace you in my life within the same sacred space as myself. This would be a big deal to me. I am the serious and deep type. I am not superficial or cavalier about anything. I would have to have the genuine time and space to incorporate you into my life; and you the same with me. You would have to move into my home, because of my daughter and school. I do not want to live in New York. You, the marriage, and the relationship would have to work in harmony with our priorities. I will not live in a relationship that is negative energy for my children, life, spirit, soul, mind, body, health, and well-being. I am a free spirit and I must remain free to be me. I do not have romantic lovie-dovie falling in love feelings towards you. I love you like I love myself. Oh, another very important thing is, do not have anything to do with my daughters. Do not even look at them, and stay away from them. I am their only parent and manager. This can help to prevent sexual attraction towards my daughters, and so on and so forth. I recommend that we live together even for a short time before getting married. From living together before marriage, we can see more clearly if we really want to get married. What else? Mmm. Hmm. I am not easy and can be territorial. That is it for now. I think that you should digest everything I have said and see if you would still like and love to marry me. Sometimes things are not like they seem, or we think. The things I have just said might seem like things are only going to work on my terms; but I do not think so. I am sure there are things about you that I have to consider as well. You can tell me about your primary concerns regarding this marriage. I am direct and considerate for both our greater good."

"I understand. As time goes on, in words and actions, I will let you know my primary focus. I hear everything you have said. I will process this conversation. I will let you know if I have changed my mind about marrying you. This is a lot to think about. Like you have said although this is meant to be we have to consciously decide what is best for our greater good."

"Theo thank you for listening and hearing me. This marriage could be a match made in the ascending realm, but we should make conscious decision and commitment based on the real facts before making a commitment. To me marriage is a serious commitment. Marriage to me is a sacred commitment to uniting our spirit, soul, mind, body, and life. Also, I genuinely care about you and your feelings. I would not want you to get hurt. I want for you the things I want for myself. This relationship and marriage cannot just benefit me. I naturally love you without conditions. To me love is not a special thing reserved for special people, situations, occasions, and circumstances. I have a mindful and cautious personality. This personality works great with helping me to make correct decisions and for safety purposes. Sorry, if I seem too direct, abrupt, mean, honest, and cautious. Theo is there anything else you would like to say?"

"No."

"Theo, I like everything you said during this conversation. This was like a dream proposal. Thank you for showing honor, understanding, respect, and a dream dinner experience. I have to go now. It is way pass my time to go home. The clock on the wall says 10:00 PM. I will not get home until about 11:30 PM; and I have to go to work tomorrow morning. I will take you home, it is on my way home."

"Okay. I will pay the bill."

"I am going to use the ladies' room."

"Sure."

Theo paid the bill, used the men's room, and they left the restaurant. Lily-Butterfly took Theo home. He told Lily-Butterfly goodnight, they hugged, and kissed each other on the cheek. Lily-Butterfly was staying grounded, being cautious, and not choosing to get ungrounded by romantic notions. Lily-Butterfly had her guard up and Theo was not making any attempts to cross her boundaries without permission. When Lily-Butterfly got home she wrote everything about the day's experiences in her journal and prayed before she went to sleep.

Work at the new restaurant location was okay. By the second week of being in this restaurant the General Manager started to give all the end of week reports and payroll to Lily-Butterfly to do, she did this work on Monday mornings at 5:30 AM or Sunday nights after the restaurant close. Although this was the General Manager's job Lily-Butterfly could not say no, because this General Manager was now her supervisor. The reports and payroll was easy compared to her previous work responsibilities. So, she did the work without complaint or resentment. She was currently still off from work Tuesdays and sometimes Sundays.

The following week Theo telephoned Lily-Butterfly. They scheduled another dinner date for the same restaurant at 7:30 PM on Saturday August 9th. Lily-Butterfly was off from work the following day; Sunday August 10th.

88

Genuine, positive, and sincerity of spirit, soul, and heart can work miracles. Remember, karma means every action. Be aware, both positive and negative karma matters.

Saturday August 9th came and Lily-Butterfly arrived at the restaurant. Theo was waiting for her outside.

"Let us go for a short walk," said Theo.

"Okay."

They went for a walk next door at the plaza.

"Lily-Butterfly I would like to give you the engagement ring before dinner."

"Okay. Go ahead."

"Here. Look. See if you like it. I got a ring like you described. A wide wedding band with three very small diamonds in a slant across the front. Please try it on."

Theo put the ring on Lily-Butterfly's finger. It fit.

Lily-Butterfly took the ring off. In silence she looked at the ring, inside and outside, and all around.

"By the way how did you know my ring size?"

"I guessed using my intuition. Do you like it?"

"Yes, I like it. Thank you. Can I have the box?"

"Yes, sure."

Lily-Butterfly put the ring inside the box and closed it. Theo looked at her in silence. Then he spoke.

"What happen? Why did you take the ring off?"

"I still did not say yes to your proposal. I will keep the ring in the box while I continue to process this engagement marriage proposal. If I decide yes, I will put the ring on and wear it. If I decide no, I will return the ring. I would also have to introduce you to my youngest daughter to see if she likes you. If she does not like you, I will choose not to accept this engagement marriage proposal and so forth. My oldest daughter Rebornstar will be nineteen in December. She is not an issue and would not mind if I got married. I think Rebornstar is going to choose to move out of my home soon. She resists following the house rules. Rebornstar thinks she is grown and should not have house rules. I am giving her time to choose to follow the house rules or move out with her boyfriend. My awareness is after graduating high school, Rebornstar spends time with her boyfriend day and night. Plus, unbeknownst to me, most times I do not know where she is. Between us there will be no physical sexual intimacy of any kind, or exchanging of our DNA and bodily fluids such as kissing, until I totally choose to accept your engagement marriage proposal. These things I have said might sound weird. But I think I should be honest and tell you these things in advance, for your decision making process. This is not just about me and what I want."

"I understand. You are doing and saying the right things. Wait I almost forgot. Here?"

"What is this?" asked Lily-Butterfly.

"Open the box and look."

"A watch. Why? The ring is great and enough."

"After I bought this ring there was some money left over from the ring I returned. With this money I bought you a watch. I wanted you to have the complete money benefit of the previous ring. Lily-Butterfly do you like the watch?"

"Yes, I like the watch. Thank you for your care and thoughtfulness. I really appreciate all your kind gestures, attention, and care. Okay let us go to eat. It is 8:00 PM."

They walked back to the restaurant.

"Boss, I am happy that you like everything."

"Why do you call me Boss? I am not your boss."

"At this time, I do not mean like a work boss. Where I grew up in Greece the women is usually considered the boss of the home, family, and relationship. The men are the hunter, gatherer, provider, protector, and so forth. A man will be as successful as the woman in his life. This is the truth. If you are not happy, then I usually am not happy. In the home everything usually functions off the woman's vibes. I live for your happiness and mine as well. My love for you makes you bloom. I am the water to your flowers and rose garden. We help each other like gardeners to take care of our own gardens and each other's garden; and bringing different flavor and essences to each other's garden and life. Boss, do you understand?"

"Yes, I understand perfectly; Mr. Romantic," replied Lily-Butterfly.

They arrived at the restaurant, received their table, and sat down. Immediately the waiter took their orders. The conversation continued through dinner. After dinner was completed Lily-Butterfly took Theo home, and continued on to her home. Lily-Butterfly got home at 12:30

AM. When she got home she put the ring and watch in her treasure trunk. Although it was late Lily-Butterfly wrote in her journal and prayed before she went to sleep.

The next time Rebornstar, Holly, and Lily-Butterfly had dinner together at home, Lily-Butterfly told the girls about Theo, his engagement proposal, possibly getting married, soon introducing Theo to them, and Theo moving into the home. The girls were happy for their mother; and congratulated her. Rebornstar expressed this was great so that her mother would possibly give less attention to what she was doing. Lily-Butterfly did not tell Manana Leila about Theo. Things and time went on with Lily-Butterfly and Theo.

The summer was over. Holly had a great time at sleep away camp. At school Holly went to main stream third grade. At work Lily-Butterfly was sensing that the District Manager and the General Manager of the restaurant she was working, wanted to promote her to General Manager. This General Manager was requesting a transfer to a restaurant closer to his home. He was recommending that Lily-Butterfly be promoted to take his job. Lily-Butterfly did not want to be promoted. At this time, she gave deeper thoughts to opening her own business.

"Doing what?" was Lily-Butterfly's question.

After many days of reflection one night Lily-Butterfly decided to take her conclusion into prayer.

"Creator I am ready for my chosen destiny and life's purpose career lead me in the right direction. I have two years left to get to forty two years old. Maybe it is time to choose and use my talents to create the tools I will use for my life's purpose career. If the District Manager asks me, or tells me I am being promoted; I will not accept the promotion; I will quit. I will totally get off this train I am currently on. I will take some time completely away from work, create an empty space, see the things I will attract, and need to do. I will start out creating a healing arts business practice and go to healing arts school. I will offer the home services of creating purification and sacred space, cleaning clutter, and organizing. I will name this healing arts business practice Creating Sacred Space & Organizing Home Services. I am not sure if I can make an income from providing these services. I will try my best and see what happens. I think this will work. Keep guiding my thoughts, spirit, mind, emotions, body, and life in the right directions. Thank you for everything. Amin," prayed Lily-Butterfly.

Tuesday October 21ˢᵗ Lily-Butterfly went to the nursing home to visit Manana Leila. The Health Aid told Lily-Butterfly that Manana was in the hospital since Sunday. Lily-Butterfly went to the hospital to visit Manana. She was in a room by herself and had an IV with saline solution connected to her left arm. At this visit Lily-Butterfly was now sure that Manana was going to die. She seemed to be in a deep sleep, and she could sense the angels of death in the room. Lily-Butterfly talked to Manana. She told her that she was currently completely prepared for her to die; and that it was okay for her to go. During this conversation Lily-Butterfly became aware that in addition there was something Manana needed to experience before she left. This is when Lily-Butterfly told Manana about Theo, him asking to marry her, the trumpet dream, and the conversation Manana had with her that she would marry again. Lily-Butterfly promised Manana to return with Theo on Thursday so that she could meet him before she died.

When Lily-Butterfly got home she telephoned Theo at work. She asked him to come with her to the hospital to visit her dying grand-mother and mother.

"Theo please take off from your day job on Thursday morning and come with me to visit my Manana Leila. She is really going to die. I think she wants to meet you before she leaves. Do you understand?"

"Yes, I will come. I understand. Yesterday I quit my day job at the restaurant you used to work. It is very crazy there now. About this restaurant is a long story. Where should I met you?"

"Take a taxi and come to my home. You have the address already. Be here at 9:00 AM. From my home we will go together. After the hospital visit, I will take you back to my home. From my home you can take a taxi back to Yonkers."

"Okay. I will see you at your home on Thursday morning at 9:00 AM."

"Thank you Theo."

"You are welcome. Bye."

"Bye."

They hung up the telephone.

Lily-Butterfly went for a walk to process her thoughts and feelings about Manana's death.

"After I introduce Theo to Manana I think she is going to die on Thursday night or early Friday morning. If this happens, then it is the sign and confirmation that I should accept Theo's engagement proposal and choose to marry him. Amin,"

Tuesday night Lily-Butterfly told Rebornstar and Holly that Manana was going to die.

Theo arrived at Lily-Butterfly's home on Thursday October 23rd morning and they went to the hospital together. When they arrived in the room Manana was alone. Manana seemed to be in the second to last stage of death. Her breathing was making the death rattle breathing; a scraping and rattling sound. This happens during the dying process when the heart is closing down its function. Theo sat down. Lily-Butterfly stood by the bed side close to Manana's head. She talked to Manana Leila. Manana was in a very deep death sleep. Lily-Butterfly knew that she heard her. Manana Leila's facial expression changed from a serious appearance to a pleasant light smile as Lily-Butterfly talked to her.

"Theo please come and stand beside me," said Lily-Butterfly.

Theo came. Lily-Butterfly started to talk to Manana again.

"Hi my Manana for ninety nine years you have been on this planet. As I talk to you keep moving forward on your path of your death. Do not turn back. Here is Theo standing here beside me. He came to say hi and bye to you. Theo was born in Greece. He has come to take over from you. Theo has arrived to be my company for the next part of my journey, and as I create my life's purpose. We will get married and take things one day at a time. Do not worry about me. I will be fine. Theo will be with me for as long as the Creator wills it. Okay Theo, say hi to Manana."

"Hi Manana Leila, it is me Theo. It is nice to meet you. Goodbye and have a great journey home to the other side. Lily-Butterfly and I will be companions for as long as it is meant to be. Bye. Keep journeying forward to the other side. Bye, bye," said Theo.

After Theo said this he sat down.

"Hi again my Manana. Keep following the path of light in the ascension portal. The angels of death are with you. You are not alone. I see two purple glowing light angels on either side of your spirit. Plus, there is an angel of death standing in the room on the other side of your body. Manana thank you very much for everything. Thank you for your love, understanding, being my first human teacher, healer, guardian angel, and guide. Thank you for having the courage, care, and kindness to do all the things you did for me. Without you I would not be the lucky person I am today. You helped to birth me here in this realm; and now I am helping to birth you to the other side beyond this veil. Keep going. Keep going. Do not turn back. Bye for now. I love you so graciously. I will see you again. Thanks again for everything bye. Follow the path of death and keep going. By tomorrow you would have transitioned beyond this realm. I will miss you although our memories will always be in my spirit, soul, and heart. Bye, bye, my sweet and kind Manana. Bye. Keep going. Bye. Amin."

After Lily-Butterfly finished talking the Nurse came into the room to check the IV and turn up the drip. The Nurse and Lily-Butterfly talked. Manana had this pleasant, relaxed, peaceful look on her face. The Nurse left the room. Lily-Butterfly kissed Manana Leila goodbye. Next she talked to Theo.

"That is, it, Manana is gone. Everything is complete. By tonight or early tomorrow morning Manana's body will no longer have life. Her spirit will be totally gone. It will take her spirit about three days to reach its destination. If Manana does not die by tomorrow I will come back to the hospital. Thank you for coming. We will leave now and go back to my home. From my home you will take the taxi back to Yonkers. Okay?"

"Okay. You are welcome. Thank you for including me in this very sacred and personal process of your Manana's death."

"Okay Theo."

Theo and Lily-Butterfly left the hospital.

They were silent as they drove in the car. Lily-Butterfly returned to her home with Theo. Lily-Butterfly telephoned the car service to come take Theo to Yonkers. Lily-Butterfly had to be at work at 2:00 PM and Theo had to be at work at 5:00 PM. They talked until the car service arrived.

"Theo I will accept your engagement proposal and start wearing the ring. We will continue to talk and plan the next step. Please let me know if you have any questions or concerns about marrying me and living in my home. Telephone me on Sunday night. Tomorrow night I will be at work until 11:00 PM. Thanks again for coming."

"You are welcome. Thanks for asking me to come with you and accepting my marriage proposal."

The car service came and Theo left. Lily-Butterfly went to work.

89

Trust is an inward and outward creation. Faith is an inward creation.

The next day after Lily-Butterfly visited Manana, Friday morning October 24th, Ms. Gina telephoned Lily-Butterfly at 10:00 AM. Ms. Gina called to tell her Manana Leila died early in the morning. Lily-Butterfly's telephone rang and she answered it.

"Hi Lily-Butterfly. This is Gina."

"Hi, good morning."

"The Doctor at the hospital telephoned me last night to say that mama was dying. If I wanted to see mama before she died I should come. I did not have a car ride, so I did not go. I telephoned the hospital this morning. The Nurse told me that she died. I telephoned the funeral home this morning to pick up her body at the hospital."

"Dean could not give you a ride to the hospital?" asked Lily-Butterfly.

"Yes, he could, but he was sleeping, and I did not feel like going. We said goodbye to her already about three months ago when we thought she would die."

"I see. Thank you for letting me know. Remember she agreed to be cremated. When you receive the ashes, I will come and get it at your home. Please have the funeral on Monday so that I can attend. I will request the day off from work. This is a new job. I have not earned any days off as yet, but I can request a bereavement day off. I have to open the restaurant on Sunday morning, so do not have the funeral on Sunday."

"I will telephone you on Saturday night to tell you when I decide to have the funeral memorial service. Lucy wants to attend. She bought her plane ticket this morning to come here this afternoon from Kawomaya. Lucy's ticket and flight reservation to return home is on Sunday evening. Lucy have to be back at work on Monday morning."

"Ms. Gina please have the cremation three complete days after Manana's death. This way she is totally disconnected from her body before you put her body in the furnace of fire. Again, I am asking you to have the funeral memorial service on Monday so I can attend?"

"Lily-Butterfly you and your usual spiritual views and ideas. The ancient and old fashion days are over. We live in a modern place and time. What I choose to do about this funeral, cremation, and the date; will be what it will be. I will telephone you on Saturday night to tell you my decision. Bye."

Ms. Gina hung up the telephone before Lily-Butterfly could reply. On Saturday, Lily-Butterfly telephoned Ms. Gina three times. She did not answer the telephone. Saturday night at 11:00 PM Ms. Gina telephoned Lily-Butterfly; and she picked up the telephone.

"Hi Ms. Gina. How are you doing?"

"I am fine. Please do not try to preach to me; or I will hang up the telephone. I have made all the funeral and memorial service arrangements so that Lucy can attend and return to Kawomaya. It will be held on Sunday October 26th at 10:00 AM at the funeral home. It is your responsibility if you can attend or not. If you cannot attend, your children can come if they choose to. Your daughter Rebornstar can bring Holly. Sorry is you cannot come. Ha? Mmm,"

"Seriously? Ms. Gina I am not stupid. You plan the funeral memorial service so I cannot attend. I could say a lot of things; but I not going to. If this is your choice karma will take care of you. This is the final disagreement we will ever have."

"Do not say anything to me about karma. You are right. It was a simple choice. My options were, plan this arrange for the convenience of Lucy or you. I choose to plan the arrangements for Lucy to attend. You spend the time with mama from the day of your birth, to the day of her death. You have spent enough time with mama when she was alive. Both of you were like two peas in a pod. This is enough. Mama is dead and gone now. No big deal if you cannot attend her funeral memorial service. The ashes will be ready in two weeks. You can come here and pick it up. Bye. Have a nice day."

Ms. Gina hung up the telephone. Lily-Butterfly did too.

"Dear Creator Ms. Gina is unbelievable. She did not like me, and was mean to me from I was inside her belly. Ms. Gina's perceived shame and secrets inside her will continue to haunt her like an entity and hungry ghost. Until Ms. Gina choose to face her life's experiences and work out her negativity, her attitude towards me will not change. Ms. Gina's bitterness towards me has reached its maximum limit. I do not choose to digest any more of Ms. Gina's negative energy and attitude towards me, and vice versa. For my awakening and transformation, I no longer want or need the energy and attitude Ms. Gina gives me. I am finished working with these kinds of negative energy frequencies. Starting today I am not going to be available for her mean, bitter, and negative expressions. Creator you know everything already. These tests, negativity, and difficult situations are over between Ms. Gina and I. I am going to choose to let Manana's death remain at the gateway of peace, love, and light. I am not going to fight with Ms. Gina about Manana's death situation or anything else. Maybe not going to the funeral is the best way to honor Manana Leila's memory in a positive way. Maybe if I go to the funeral memorial service I will feel so disgusted by my perception and my experiences of the complete situation. I will go to Ms. Gina's home unannounced in two weeks to get Manana's ashes. Who knows what Ms. Gina's next unorthodox plans are, regarding Manana's ashes and I.? Ms. Gina you have outdone the time between us. Creator the karma connection between Ms. Gina and I, is complete and over. Creator if I am to communicate with Gina again it will be from a renewed place and your will. Creator starting tonight everything regarding Ms. Gina is in your hands. Creator as you know it is not easy being a positive human on this planet. Thank you for everything. Amin," prayed Lily-Butterfly.

Lily-Butterfly made arrangements with Rebornstar to take Holly with her to Manana's funeral memorial service. Rebornstar got the address and information about the funeral memorial service from Ms. Gina; and they attended. Lily-Butterfly went to work. All day and into the following week Lily-Butterfly processed her feelings about Ms. Gina, Manana's funeral memorial service, and not being able to attend.

About two weeks after Manana Leila's funeral memorial service on Sunday November 9th Lily-Butterfly telephoned Ms. Gina to see if she was home. She just wanted to confirm that Ms. Gina was at home. Ms. Gina answered and Lily-Butterfly hung up the telephone. Lily-Butterfly drove over to Ms. Gina's home. She arrived and knocked on Ms. Gina's front door. Ms. Gina unlocked the door and opened it.

"Can I come inside?"

"Okay. Yes. What?"

"I am here to get Manana's ashes."

"Henry picked up the ashes and brought it to me yesterday."

"Where is it?"

"On the table beside where you are standing. It is in a container in the white cardboard box. The cremation certificate is inside."

"Okay. Thank you."

Lily-Butterfly picked up the box.

"Wait. Lucy wants half of the ashes. I need to pour out half and mail it to Lucy."

"No, you are not pouring out half. Why would you and Lucy want to do this? Both of you never seem to care about Manana. This was not the arrangement I promised Manana. My agreement with Manana was to pour all her ashes into the ocean. The ocean, the other elements, and the Universe will naturally do what it will with the ashes. With complete honor, love, and respect, I would like to keep the complete agreement I promised Manana. Manana's ashes is not a possession. I will not divide the ashes. She was born as a complete system, and her ashes will be returned to father and mother-nature as one complete system, as she intended and perceived; based on my promise. Ms. Gina I will fulfill my complete promise. Ms. Gina thank you for everything. My perception and experiences with you is that you were a great dark arts and shadow teacher for me. You have performed this function very well. Our karma as it was in the past is completely over. By the way, soon I will be getting married again. Good bye Ms. Gina. I might never see you or talk to you again. I love you and wish you all the best. Maybe one day you will choose to understand the roots of your shame, secrets, resentments, and all your life's experiences. Goodbye."

"Lily-Butterfly I hope that one day you will figure out how to use the talents of your spiritual mumbo jumbo instead of using them on me. Bye."

Without replying Lily-Butterfly turned and walked out of Ms. Gina's home; carrying Manana's ashes.

Lily-Butterfly got home and placed the box with the ashes on a table, by the window, in the east, and the very left of her living room. Every time Lily-Butterfly made an attempt to take the ashes to scatter in the ocean she changed her mind, and told herself not today; another day. When Lily-Butterfly was ready to release Manana's ashes into the ocean, she took Holly with her. They went to a beach in New Jersey. Lily-Butterfly performed her own memorial service with prayers and blessings. She walked out into the ocean, placed the box under the ocean, and opened it. The complete ashes was released into the ocean, like she had promised Manana.

"I am happy that I completed my promise to Manana. Amin," said Lily-Butterfly.

"Amin, mama. This was a very interesting experience. This

memorial service for Manana feels better than the one that I went to with Rebornstar. Here, there is a lot of love energy present. Thank you for taking me with you mama. This was so cool, magical, and mystical. Mama you are a great spiritual prayer person," said Holly.

"Thank you Holly. I try my best. Thanks be to the will of the Creator. Holly let us sit, meditate, and relax for a while before we leave."

"Okay, mama. Good."

They sat in the shade gazing out at the ocean.

Lily-Butterfly invited Theo to come to her home on Sunday November 16th for dinner and to meet Holly. Theo came, he had a great time, and Holly seemed to like him. After dinner Theo took a taxi back to his home. Holly told her mother that she liked Theo and it was okay for her to marry him. The following week Tuesday Lily-Butterfly invited Theo to move into her home. Theo agreed. Theo knew someone that was the General Manager of a full service restaurant in New Jersey about two miles from Lily-Butterfly's home. Theo asked him for a chef job and this General Manager hired him. Things uniting Theo and Lily-Butterfly worked out step by step in synchronicity. Theo moved in with Lily-Butterfly on Sunday November 23rd. They applied for a marriage license and had a very simple marriage ceremony. On Tuesday December 9, 1997 Theo and Lily-Butterfly got married in a civil ceremony performed by the Judge at the courthouse close to their home. Lily-Butterfly bought Theo a wedding band, and they used Lily-Butterfly's engagement ring as her same wedding ring. Rebornstar and Holly attended as the witnesses. They had a professional photographer take pictures and they went out to a restaurant close to their home to celebrate. Theo had written to inform his parents that he was getting married again. His parents were not happy that he was getting married again and they could not attend. Theo's parents gave him their blessings anyway. They told him if that was what he wanted to do; it was his choice.

The marriage vows that Theo and Lily-Butterfly decided on was: - I (Theo or Lily-Butterfly) take thee with guidance and blessings from the Creator, ourselves, and our dreams, to live together in sacred union as spiritual intimate partners; and companions. We will live together sharing unconditional love, compassion, respect, loyalty, trust, care, generosity, harmony, and everything else it will take to have the most successful relationship. May we grow together and individually in this union and relationship, for both our positive greater good, guided by the Divine Creator's will. May this relationship and union work in compatible harmony and balance, nourish our spirit, soul, mind, body, health, well-being, and lives for as long as it is meant to last; and beyond. Amin.

Theo and Lily-Butterfly's integration into each other's life was a simple process. It was like adding earth to earth and water to water. Rebornstar became nineteen years old December 15, 1997. Lily-Butterfly became forty years old December 27, 1997. Theo became thirty eight years old January 5, 1998. Rebornstar moved out of her mother's home to live with her boyfriend January 1998. Theo and Lily-Butterfly agreed to design the relationship map of their life, the best way it would work for both of them; and their design worked. It was a relationship map created with the will, choices, and foundation of agreed commitment, financial responsibilities, partnership, teamwork, love without conditions, expressions of like or not like, loyalty, sharing, generosity, and understanding. At the same time the relationship was not perfect. When there was an issue; together they worked out their differences. Maybe they naturally understood each other as good as they did, because they were the same astrological sign and had similar personalities. Before the marriage Theo and Lily-Butterfly also agreed that if the marriage did not work out for whatever reason, both of them would leave each other without taking any financial and material possessions from each other. They came into each other's life in peace and they would leave each other's live in peace. Theo and Lily-Butterfly main financial arrangement throughout the complete journey of the relationship was - they had a joint account where they put equal percentage of their salary for all home expenses and to pay all bills. The other portion of their salary went into personal individual bank accounts. Their lives were occupied with work, individual activities, together activities, sharing stories from their lives and cultures, social activities together, sharing disagreements, doing grocery shopping and laundry together; and everything else. Holly continued to be the complete responsibility of Lily-Butterfly. Sometimes Theo acted as a mediator between Holly and her mother. If Lily-Butterfly was quiet or silent, Theo would check in with her to see if he could help with any unspoken issues she was having. They were both nourished by each other's sharing of unconditional love, affection, intimacy, generosity, care, understanding, spirit, mind, emotion, body, health, and well-being offerings. Lily-Butterfly did not like negativity and fighting; Theo was the same. This relationship was positive, compatible, spiritual, and mindful for the complete time they lived together. With this relationship they both thrived, had good fortune, and complete blessings. Lily-Butterfly felt more and more relaxed and in harmony inside and outside herself. Her view of her chosen destiny and life's purpose career came closer and closer into her awareness.

Lily-Butterfly often thought, marrying Theo was like a transmission that grounded and supported me more into the planet's physical dimension and out of the perception of past life's experiences. The positive unconditional love and everything else I share with Theo is similar to the relationship I had with Manana, and my children. I am very grateful to Theo for these experiences. I guess it was important for me to receive this positive energy vibration and mirror of my spirit and soul from Theo as a human, man, spirit, soul, and individual. This I see helps me to heal negative relationship experiences within me, my personal masculine is taking a break, my feminine feels supported inside and outside by someone other than myself, my missing birth father vibes have improved, I am experiencing the Universal masculine, and a human masculine. This is a very interesting awareness. I cannot tell Theo about the trumpet dream oracle guardian angel dream. I have to let things evolve naturally. Human life is an oracle on to itself.

Time went on. It was now February 1998. At work Lily-Butterfly had a stronger sense that the District Manager was going to offer her a promotion for General Manager of the restaurant. She also one day over heard the current General Manager speaking to him on the telephone. She prepared herself for the offer and the decision she would make if The District Manager offered her the promotion. Lily-Butterfly's decision was if she was offered a promotion, she was going to quit without notice. It was time to get off the current life's train. She was not going to give notice and have them pester her for the whole time to change her mind. Plus, she had finally decided to stop her current career and create the time and space to manifest and figure out her destiny life's purpose career. Like the dream oracle told Lily-Butterfly; do not bask in the goodness of the relationship with Theo. Use the opportunity for the divine reasons it was meant to serve. Everything is for a positive or negative reason.

On Saturday February 28, 1998 the District Manager telephoned the restaurant. The General Manager answered the telephone. He gave the telephone to Lily-Butterfly, telling her that the District Manager wanted to talk to her. Lily-Butterfly took the telephone.

"Hi. This is Lily-Butterfly."

"Hi Lily-Butterfly. I am calling to tell you that you have been doing a great job at the restaurant. I would like to offer you a promotion to General Manager of the restaurant. You will get a salary increase to a General Manager's pay," said the District Manager.

"No. For personal reasons I am not interested in being hired or promoted to be a General Manager. Although this current General Manager gives me all his reports to do; I do not want to be totally responsible for a restaurant."

"I hear you, but I do not understand why you would not want to be promoted and have an increased salary."

"No. I am not interested. I do not want more money or more responsibilities. Currently my salary is even more than this General Manager. No and no. This is my answer."

"Think about this offer some more. There is no rush to decide. On Monday I will telephone you again. Okay."

"My answer will not change on Monday. I am sure about my decision. On Monday I will tell this General Manager my final answer. Bye."

"Okay. Give the telephone to the General Manager."

Lily-Butterfly gave the telephone to the General Manager.

Lily-Butterfly took a break and went outside the mall for a walk and some fresh air.

"On Monday my answer is still no. I will not stay. He will keep offering me a promotion, and if I do not take the promotion he is going to transfer me to a restaurant that he knows I will not like to passive-aggressively punish me. I am finished playing human's crappy games. I am going to finally tell Theo that I have decided to quit my job, and start my own business using the spiritual talents I have already know I have. It is time to do this. Oh, Creator the path of authentic spiritual transformation, awakening, and practice as a human is not easy. I feel like I am walking on a thin thread in the sky. I feel like quitting right not. Why wait? I am off from work tomorrow, Sunday. Monday is my maximum time to wait to quit," mumbled Lily-Butterfly.

She returned inside to the restaurant.

Saturday night Lily-Butterfly told Theo about the promotion offer, her decision to not accept the offer, and her decision to quit.

"Theo the District Manager offered me a promotion to General Manager today. I told him no. I am going to quit effective Monday. Today was my last day. Tomorrow I am off from work. I am going to create a healing arts practice starting with the things I know that I can do. What do you think?"

"Boss, first thing is, do what you feel is right for you and makes you happy. I do not like when you are sad. Do the job that you are passionate about, that makes you feel content, inspired, and fulfilled. But at the same time, you need money as well. I do not see you as the person waiting for me to completely financially support you. You like to feel independent and have your own money. What about the health and other benefits?"

"I am going to lose all the health care and other benefits. You can get health benefits from your job for me and Holly. You would have to do this. Can you? I have enough money saved for six months without working, plus I have over $20,000 in a retirement IRA. I must stop this restaurant career path. I am tired of perceiving that I am being used to make money for people's profit and egotistic material benefits. Every human needs money. Money is a great resource and tool in these modern times. But I was not born to be a modern day cash cow for others and myself. It is time for me to make money using my spirit and soul talents to help myself, humanity, and the Universe. There is no perfect time to get off this current professional modern train. It is time to get on a new path of my chosen destiny and life's purpose practice. Thank you for being in my life. Currently I feel very loved and supported by someone other than myself. I think that now is the time to do this. Money is not an issue for me. If the things I plan to do does not work, I have professional training experiences and certifications I can use to reenter a modern day regular career. I could get another modern world job very easily. Now it is time for me to seek, find, and start my spiritual destiny and chosen life's purpose career practice. It is your choice to agree and support my decision or not. Whether you agree or not, I am going to do as my instinct tells me. I am quitting this job on Monday. Okay?"

"Okay Boss. When you are happy, I am happy. When I am happy, you are happy. We will work together as a team whether I agree with you 100% or not. Be happy. Do what makes your spirit, soul, and heart sing. I know that you will continue to tell me the daily stories of your new plans, creation, and journey. I am confident that you will be successful with your plans. Making money from your creation, ideas, and plans is another situation. Ha-ha-ha. We will see. Ha-ha."

"Bahahaha. You think I am a dreamer. Ha. Mmm. Hehehe. As usual I will do my best, see what happens, and let the chips fall where they may; and where the Creator wills it. Ha-ha-a. This human life can be an unbeknownst magical adventure. Ha-ha. Amin."

"We will see. As you usually say; the way will show the way. You are a great dreamer. So, let us see how you make your dream into a successful reality. Do you think in this modern area people are going to want, need, and pay for the spiritual services you are going to provide? The people around here do not seem very spiritual to me. They seem to focus on money and the material physical world. But if you say this spiritual career is going to work, I believe you. I always believe in you. Ha-ha-ha. I love you. I never knew that I would find the woman of my dreams. Ha-ha-ha. You are funny as well. Finding you is more than enough for me. So, Boss do as you are dreaming and wish. Let me know if you need help with anything. The Creator will help you as well. Ha-ha-ha."

"Mr. Theo. We will see. The way will show the way. Thank you for hearing and listening to me. I will tell you my daily creation of this idea as the days unfold. Starting Monday, I am a job-less woman floating in the wind, like an unplanted seed. Let us see where the seed of myself is going to take root; and be a success in my renewed growth, transformation, manifestation, and dream creations. Sir Theo, Amin."

"Boss, Amin. I am with you all the way."

Monday morning Lily-Butterfly got dressed in her regular clothes and went to her workplace. She did not go inside. At the customer counter she called the General Manager. He came.

"Did the pay checks arrive?" asked Lily-Butterfly.

"Yes. The checks came early this morning."

"Can I have my check, please?"

"Sure," replied the General Manager.

He went and brought Lily-Butterfly her pay check.

"Thank you. Here are all the keys to the restaurant. I have decided to quit this job, without notice. Tell the District Manager, your friend, that this is my answer to his offer of promoting me to General Manager. Sorry that I am not giving notice. You can find someone else to take your job, so you can eat your pie and have the same pie. I have had enough of the game playing and inconsiderate behavior from people in this modern world career profession. I am convinced that as talented as I seen about doing this job, I was not born for this normal professional career; and therefore, I am not wired for it. This restaurant and normal professional career is not the problem. I am the problem in relationship to this system. At the same time, I have learned so much from this system, people, and the process. Goodbye and thank you for everything."

"Okay. Bye," replied the General Manager.

Lily-Butterfly walked away and to her car.

"I feel light and relieved. Wow. I sense my next step will arrive soon. Creator you know everything already. Please send the next step on my path. I know that I have to take action to create as I am being guided and my instincts tells me. Amin,"

Lily-Butterfly went home. She got her journal and went to the environmental nature center. Lily-Butterfly sat at a picnic table in silence, meditation, and prayer. After thirty minutes she wrote in her journal to process the events of the morning and how she felt. Next she wrote down her vision into an action plan. Create a business name, register the business name, and make business cards and door hangers to advertise the spiritual services she can offer. Put an advertisement in the local parent paper. After writing all her current plans and ideas Lily-Butterfly went home. These plan and ideas continued to evolve as the days unfold.

On the first day when Lily-Butterfly performed the first action to the next part of her life's purpose career, with synchronicity the doors on this path opened effortlessly, and the alignment of coincidence happened consistently.

90

A picture can say many words. Many words can paint infinite pictures. It does not matter how long it takes; a human will reap what they sow. This Universal planet is a work and service station gateway for spirits and souls. This planet is a Universal one of multidimensional opportunities. The most immediate karma is the positive and negative things people do to themselves. Some books and stories can be like Universal drum beats. Thank you for taking this long story telling journey with me.

This last chapter will summarize the future years of Lily-Butterfly life's experiences. Further views into Lily-Butterfly's healing arts life's purpose career can be seen in the next book; UNIVERSAL WELLNESS – A SHAMAN'S VIEW – BY D. O. GRANT.

Okay, we continue on. I will begin this section with a summary of the professional aspects of Lily-Butterfly's chosen destiny and life's purpose professional career; how it simply began, some inner workings, and how it evolved. In this chapter the time, flow, and years overlap and are mixed.

Sitting at the picnic table at the environmental nature center in sacred space awareness Lily-Butterfly decided to create healing arts wellness services for the home environment. She decided on the name *Creating Sacred Space & Organizing Home Services.* These home services include going to people's homes to provide the services of - creating sacred space through purification and cleansing of the home environment's energies, assisting with the cleansing of ghost hauntings - intrusive energies - entities in the home environment, clearing clutter, organizing, consultation on downsizing the material possessions in the home, private at home - after school - child sitting; for children that were handicapped or have special needs. Lily-Butterfly registered the name of the healing arts practice services. Currently she did not plan on having a business office location.

The first thing Lily-Butterfly did was put a business card size advertisement into a very popular community newspaper for the area she lived in. This newspaper published articles and advertisement for parents and children. Next she went to a printing company close to her home, to create business cards, flyers, and door hangers for the healing arts home and services. Then on her own, Lily-Butterfly distributed advertising materials to; libraries, individual people, on community notice boards, distributed at flea markets, hang on the door knobs of homes, and everywhere else she chose. The advertisement information had only a phone number. When interested people telephoned Lily-Butterfly and she was not available they left a messages on her answering machine. She was dedicated to telephoning people to reply to their messages. In many ways when Lily-Butterfly communicated with people her conversations were spiritual, she naturally showed talented awareness, and she had a magnetic personality. Her words would emanate with sincere passion and vibrations of positive life force energy. People could not prove or measure the things Lily-Butterfly said, but to them it sure sounded true, positive, uplifting, inspirational, motivational, and resonated within them. Lily-Butterfly and people noticed that the conversations were usually refreshing, reenergizing, and uplifting.

The first time Lily-Butterfly went to the printing business to create her marketing and advertising materials, she had a conversation with the owner about her plans for the healing arts wellness center services and ideas. After the conversation, she thanked the man and was about to leave, a woman came from a room at the back of the business. This woman was the owner of the printing company's daughter. She strongly recommended to Lily-Butterfly to visit a woman that had a book shop and healing arts center that came to them for creating marketing material. This woman also gave Lily-Butterfly a business card with all the information for this book shop and healing arts center she recommended. This healing arts center was located about ten minutes in the town over from where Lily-Butterfly lived.

The next morning Lily-Butterfly went to visit this book shop and healing arts center. The name of the owner of this center was Oa. Lily-Butterfly entered the center as a customer and looked at all the things Oa was selling. She spoke to Oa about the healing arts services she provided, and her current healing arts wellness services. She also spoke to Oa about maybe unknown reasons she was guided by the daughter of the printing business to visit her. Lily-Butterfly recommended to Oa that she would visit her from time to time. They would randomly and naturally talk, and see where the conversation naturally went, to see what the conversation would reveal; Oa agreed. Lily-Butterfly became a customer of Oa. She bought herbs, books, energy purification tools, and many other things Oa sold. These things she needed for her new healing arts and wellness services career. Lily-Butterfly sounded very spiritual to Oa. On the third visit to Oa, she gave Lily-Butterfly a book from a Theology Institute and recommended that Lily-Butterfly might like to register as a student. Lily-Butterfly took the Theology Institute book and read it. She decided to register for a Doctor of Metaphysics Certification. This was a three years certification course and the program consisted of subjects that Lily-Butterfly was already familiar with. The Theology Institute gave the option of studying at home. Lily-Butterfly liked this convenient option. Every morning for three years, to participate in completing this program, Lily-Butterfly would wake up every morning at 4:30 AM to study, and do tests until 8:30 AM. This was easy for her, because she was already used to waking up early, being dedicated, and used to hard work from her previous careers and life's experiences. The next very important spiritual awareness Oa brought to Lily-Butterfly was her realization that the positive Universal Life Force Energy was tangible. To Lily-Butterfly and her ancestors this energy vibration was a natural part of their everyday life, and an important contribution to their health and wellbeing. They thought this was very normal; so, no big deal. Oa started to learn an ancient Japanese Monastery style about how to use the disciplined art of positive Universal Life Force Energy for her own personal healing, as a healing treatment for others, and teaching the style to people. There was a sacred attunement process which was a part of this learning and teaching program. Oa was learning this energy healing art from levels one to the teaching level. Lily-Butterfly would listen with amazement to Oa's stories about her learning experiences, her teacher, her attunement process experiences, how she used the energies for her own treatment and healing process, and how to tangible use this positive Universal Life Force Energy for assisting other people. These conversations sounded and felt very familiar to Lily-Butterfly.

Lily-Butterfly listened to Oa's stories about her complete learning process and certification from level one to three. After listening to Oa stories Lily-Butterfly bought a book from Oa on how to tangibly use the positive Universal Life Force Energy for personal healing, working on others, and learning how to teach this healing arts. From reading the book Lily-Butterfly saw that it was the same positive Universal Life Force Energy healing she was already attuned and connected to. This was the positive energy she used in everything she did; it was one of the sacred, secret, and tools of her life's performance. Her Manana Leila – her ancestors – and the village of Yaj where she was born, also naturally used this positive energy process for healing and everything else. It was the positive energy found in nature, used by the Creator to create all things; and the vibration of love. Lily-Butterfly decided to learn this tangible and disciplined art form of using Universal Life Force Energy. Lily-Butterfly personally studied the disciplined art of using this energy on herself and studied to beyond the teaching level for over three and a half years. After the teaching level certification, she used the process to give treatments to clients. Lily-Butterfly also taught this energy healing process to clients for their personal treatments and giving treatments to others. Some of these students chose to become teachers.

So, two great things came out of following the guidance to visit Oa. For the first five years after quitting her last restaurant career job, from 1998 to 2002 Lily-Butterfly studied and become certified in the first two main healing arts process. She became certified as a Metaphysician and teacher of the disciplined art of using positive Universal Life Force Energy for self-treatment, working on other people, and teaching. During these five years of studying she worked very successfully in her first created healing arts practice of *Creating Sacred Space & Organizing Home Services.* As the years went on Lily-Butterfly because a grand master of the conscious, tangible, and disciplined art of positive Universal Life Force Energy. Lily-Butterfly studies of how to awaken, expand, and use her spirit and soul talents went from 1998 to 2009.

Lily-Butterfly had many people requesting all the services she advertised as healing arts wellness services for the home, and private after school care for children. The first client came five weeks after putting the advertisement in the popular parent and child community newspaper. This client hired Lily-Butterfly for twelve months, three times per week. The client, Sue, hired Lily-Butterfly to come into her mansion and another summer home; to completely, declutter and organize – all rooms and basements; drawers, closets, cabinets, book shelves, and everything else in these homes. She also create sacred space and purified all rooms in these homes, using sacred herbs prayers and blessings. Sue was the client that let Lily-Butterfly know that what she was doing had a formal name. Sue told Lily-Butterfly that the art form she was performing was called Feng Shui. Sue recommended that Lily-Butterfly attended the Feng Shui Institute she was attending on Long Island, New York. As a part of Lily-Butterfly work contract to work in Sue's homes; Sue gifted Lily-Butterfly with a paid tuition to attend a certified course in Clearing Clutter and Creating Sacred Space with Feng Shui at the Feng Shui Institute she was attending in Long Island, New York. Lily-Butterfly accepted this gift and attended the Institute. From doing this Feng Shui course Lily-Butterfly became more confident in performing her natural talented art form of what she was practicing all along. After the class program Lily-Butterfly gave the art form a name – Feng Shui.

In 2000 Lily-Butterfly decided it was time to create a formal healing arts practice center. She created a new business name, registered the new business name, and used this new name. This new Universal Wellness name was used in practicing and sharing her healing arts talents with individually humans, teach in groups, and perform Feng Shui in people's homes. In 2000 Lily-Butterfly returned to Sue's mansion to perform some maintenance work for the Feng Shui she had done previously. Sue guided Lily-Butterfly and took her to a business complex in an antique center that she could rent space to create a wellness center office. At this location Lily-Butterfly rented a small room. This window-less room was the landlord's closet for his building supplies. At the time it was the only room available. This location was where Lily-Butterfly's first and only healing arts practice center was created. From 2000 to 2017 the size of this very small fifty square feet room closet, healing arts center expanded into one thousand and two hundred square feet. This healing arts center was very successful over the years. Most of the clients that came to Lily-Butterfly's wellness center came through word of mouth, prayers, and Divine intervention. Lily-Butterfly specialized in working with humans who choose to be on a spiritual path. She worked in private or in small groups in a holistic way with her healing arts talents to assist, help, and teach humans of varied ages.

In November 2001, Lily-Butterfly decided to become a semi monk-nun practitioner at a Zen Buddhist Monastery. She would primarily practice meditation and the ways of a Zen Buddhist monk and nun. Lily-Butterfly went to live and practice with these monks and nuns for a month, three times per year, for two years. In 2003 after the Zen Buddhist practice Lily-Butterfly was guided in a dream that there was one more healing arts tool she should use her talent to bring into her spiritual healing arts wellness practice. She was guided to learn the healing art forms of the ancient Inca Shamans. Lily-Butterfly found a school that taught this ancient Inca Shaman's way of healing. She did training programs in the Shaman's Way of healing from 2003 to 2009. These training programs were done at a school in the United States of America, and some was done from journeying to the Sacred Valley of the Incas and the Amazon jungle in Peru, South America. These Shaman's way of healing Lily-Butterfly also found familiar. It was similar to the healing style her Manana Leila used to transform her from death's door back to life, reconnected her spirit and soul to her physical body, and reshaped, resculptured, and repaired her physical body; when she was born.

This ancient Inca Shaman's way and style of using her talents was the last formal tool that Lily-Butterfly learned and studied. At the end of Lily-Butterfly's consciously learning how to use her natural talents as tools, she came to realize that everything she was looking for was within her. They were also her ancestor's ways and practice of living, healing, and well-being. All the styles of physical learning helped her make her natural talents into tangible tools to use in this modern times and environment. Lily-Butterfly also got certified as a Birth Doula to offer the services of assisting women with nurturing care during the birthing process. Lily-Butterfly's last certification was becoming a nondenominational Ordained Minister of the Divine Creator's Ministry. Lily-Butterfly practiced with heartfelt passion for the rest of her life these tangible ways of using her talents. She used these talented tools to help herself, other humans, the environment, the Universe, and everything else; guided by the Creator's will.

In the spring of 2001 Theo and Lily-Butterfly went on vacation to the island of Oahu, Hawaii. They had a great time. On this trip Lily-Butterfly was internally guided that at a time in the future she should move to this island. In 2017 this internal guidance became a reality. Starting the spring of 2001 Lily-Butterfly would visit this island once per year for her personal retreat and resting.

The healing arts talents also evolved into another passion of Lily-Butterfly; writing. She dedicated her passion and love for writing and reading into writing teaching stories. Through her story telling she shares the ancient, entertaining, and elaborate storytelling style of her ancient ancestors. Lily-Butterfly shares these stories with other humans all over this planet. She perceives her writing as Universal Drum-Beats. On December 5, 2017 Lily-Butterfly semi-retired and moved permanently to Oahu, Hawaii. After moving to this island in the Pacific Ocean Lily-Butterfly worked less, and continued all her chosen destiny and life's purpose career.

By now some of you might be wondering what happen to Ms. Gina. After Lily-Butterfly took the box of Manana Leila's ashes from Ms. Gina's home she never saw or talked to her from 1998 to 2001. After Lily-Butterfly created her formal healing arts center she prayed to the Creator one night about her creation and asked a question. The question was, whom should she use the hands on healing arts tools to assist and help? The Creator guided her that the first person and client she should help with these tools was Ms. Gina. The Creator guided Lily-Butterfly with the awareness that if she could practice unconditional love and compassion with Ms. Gina, and help her to transform and improve her chosen negative imprints and triggers, then she would be even more successful with helping and assisting other people. Lily-Butterfly was reluctant and surprised at the Creator's guidance. But she knew that the complete awareness made sense. At this time Lily-Butterfly had improved a lot more of her negative imprints and triggers relating to Ms. Gina and her experiences. Lily-Butterfly had even mostly forgotten about Ms. Gina. Working with Ms. Gina was the Creator's way for Lily-Butterfly to see how she was really doing with her own personal healing, forgiveness, learning, awakening, patience, unconditional love, and compassion.

Lily-Butterfly telephoned Ms. Gina. Lily-Butterfly told Ms. Gina about discovering her chosen destiny and life's purpose career - her healing arts journey and learning – the creation of a healing arts practice center – and that she was calling to offer her healing arts services. Lily-Butterfly told Ms. Gina that the Creator had guided her to telephone her to make the offer. If she was ready, it was her choice to accept the offer or not. Ms. Gina seemed overwhelmed with everything Lily-Butterfly told her. She cried and cried throughout the complete conversation. Ms. Gina told Lily-Butterfly that over the last two most recent years, she would pray for the Creator to help her. The last person she thought the Creator would send to help and assist would be her. Ms. Gina accepted Lily-Butterfly's offer to assist and help her with the current healing arts services she had to offer. *Ms. Gina became Lily-Butterfly's first paying hands-on Universal Life Force Energy healing treatment and Holistic Healthcare Coaching client and student.* Lily-Butterfly worked professionally with Ms. Gina from a renewed, neutral, intense, and passionate place of patience, care, nurturing, unconditional love and compassion. Ms. Gina choose the things she wanted to work on improving, cleansing, transforming, and purifying. Ms. Gina would release an abundance of negative emotional energies, and did a lot of crying through every healing session. Ms. Gina would express to Lily-Butterfly her amazement at how she could help and assist her from such a sacred and neutral place; after how badly she had treated her. At the end of the personal hands on healing sessions, Lily-Butterfly taught Ms. Gina how to use the Universal Life Force Energy in a tangible way to perform her own healing treatment. This would help Ms. Gina to continue her own personal healing with the treatments. Lily-Butterfly taught Ms. Gina this healing art to the third practitioner level, and certified her as a practitioner.

When Lily-Butterfly became trained in the ancient Inca Shaman's way of healing, she worked on Ms. Gina again. This improved the healing that had been performed before. During all these healing sessions Ms. Gina was the one that choose the things in her past and present life's experiences that she wanted to work on improving. People will be as healed as they choose and want to be. Ms. Gina mostly worked on the things she perceived others did to her. She never took responsibility for the things she did to other people. Ms. Gina did not present for healing any of the following things: - not one issue or situation to do with Lily-Butterfly and Manana Leila — secrets — shame — apologies for negative actions — ask for forgiveness — no expression of gratitude, love, and compassion. Directly to Ms. Gina's face, Lily-Butterfly totally forgave her and apologized for anything that she might have negatively done or said to her; knowingly and unknowingly. Again, and again Lily-Butterfly thanked Ms. Gina for everything. To Lily-Butterfly, Ms. Gina was one of the most important, interesting, and amazing humans in her current life's journey.

After the healing treatments and teaching, the last things Lily-Butterfly did for Ms. Gina was, assist her in applying for Social Security benefits, and senior housing. Lily-Butterfly assisted Ms. Gina in being placed in a beautiful senior two story brownstone apartment building. Lily-Butterfly visited Ms. Gina at least once per week, did chores for her, gave her car rides to places, and made sure that she had the groceries and things she needed. She did this even when Lucy her creme-de-la-creme used her to move to the United States; and then moved away to Massachusetts, and mostly ignored her. Lucy visited maybe on a holiday and so forth; and never came around for anything consistent and long term.

Lily-Butterfly completely and totally helped Ms. Gina as much as she chose; with the healings arts and in any other ways she could, and with all the other things she needed and wanted. After these things in January 2006 Lily-Butterfly chose to again move on with her life without Ms. Gina in it. Why? To give Ms. Gina's other three birth children a clear path and opportunity to assist and help her. Another reason; Ms. Gina had the free will to work on whatever she choose; and she did. But, it seems she never chose to work on her perception regarding Lily-Butterfly, improving her communicating style and treatment of Lily-Butterfly, and seeing her with renewed perception and projections. Ms. Gina continued to treat Lily-Butterfly with an entitlement, mean, and dismissive attitude. Lily-Butterfly would consistently accept Ms. Gina as she presented herself. Maybe unbeknownst to Lily-Butterfly, Ms. Gina did her best with these other healings in private between herself and the Creator. But, Ms. Gina's overall negativity, meanness, dismissive behavior, un-mindfulness, negative communication and treatment, and negative actions towards Lily-Butterfly stayed basically the same; plus took on a passive aggressive aura. These continued experiences from Ms. Gina was not supportive and positive for Lily-Butterfly's personal transformation, change, health, well-being, life, and life's purpose practice. It was clear to Lily-Butterfly that Ms. Gina had additional deeper rooted healing, transformation, and change to perform. Lily-Butterfly knew that Ms. Gina had to do this from her own sincere choice, action, and responsibility. Although Lily-Butterfly removed herself from the path of Ms. Gina, from time to time she ask Rebornstar and Holly to visit, check on Ms. Gina, bring groceries, and so forth.

On December 24, 2018 Ms. Gina died at the age of eighty five from cancer that had taken over her body like a vine, from her root to her brain. When Ms. Gina found out that she had cancer, the disease was in a very advanced stage. Ms. Gina chose to not have medical intervention or any treatment for the cancer. Ms. Gina was the first one so far in her past ancestry lineage that ever had the dis-ease of cancer, died from the symptoms of cancer, and died in their eighties. On Ms. Gina's death bed and on the day she died, Lily-Butterfly visited her in spirit form, and gave her a death rite of passage to the other side. Throughout Ms. Gina's life and even at the end of her life her children Lucy, Henry, and Dean treated her like she taught them to. Amin.

Regarding Lucy I could elaborate on the next sentences, but I choose to not do this. In the fall of 2006 Lily-Butterfly created a chance and opportunity to visit Lucy in Boston. Her intention was to create peace with Lucy, apologize for any resentment, express forgiveness, and so forth. Lucy seemed to listen to Lily-Butterfly, but was obviously safely protected within her denial and avoidance cocoon. During this visit Lily-Butterfly told Lucy the ring that belonged to Manana Leila that Ms. Gina gave her, was hers; and was given to her by Manana. Lucy ignored Lily-Butterfly and did not choose to give here the ring. Lily-Butterfly left Boston and Lucy accepting everything as Lucy chose to be and do. Since this visit Lily-Butterfly chose to not see Lucy again; for many reasons. Henry and Dean were in similar category as Lucy where Lily-Butterfly was concerned.

Regarding Rebornstar. She made another attempt to go back to college but stopped again. Rebornstar worked in different main stream jobs. Rebornstar married her boyfriend whom she moved in with after her nineteenth birthday. This relationship lasted seventeen years. Currently she has two children, one girl, and one boy. The girl child was born on December 27, 2005; on Lily-Butterfly's birthday. Even before this child was born she and Lily-Butterfly were like two peas in a pod. When Rebornstar was pregnant this baby would move around and seem to be doing somersaults inside her mother's stomach; when she heard Lily-Butterfly's voice. After birth this very wise and awake child spent lots of time with Lily-Butterfly. Lily-Butterfly was her spirit guide and teacher of the ancient ways and pathways. One day Lily-Butterfly was strongly guided that this child was Manana Leila reincarnated. To Lily-Butterfly's perception this girl child had the aura, spirit, and soul energies, with some personality of Manana Leila. Throughout their life they remained close bosom buddies. In the spring of 2005 when Rebornstar became pregnant with her daughter, she went to school to pursue a passion of hers. She studied massage therapy while she was pregnant with her daughter. The first week of December 2005 Rebornstar became a certified and licensed Massage Therapist. Rebornstar practiced massage therapy as a career practice. Clients often commented to Rebornstar that 'she is an excellent massage therapist, and it is as if God was working through her hands.' Rebornstar's second child a boy, was born July 27, 2015. He also seems to be a talented wise spirit and soul.

Regarding Holly. She naturally achieved excellence in her school work from the day she received her first pair of glasses for her nearsightedness. Holly attended summer sleep away camp until she was seventeen. From sixteen to seventeen years old she became a counselor-in-training. In high school Holly maintained an A and B average on every subject and became a member of the New Jersey National Honor Society. At seventeen years old Holly graduated high school. For four years she chose to attend a Private Computer Technology University to be certified, and graduated with a degree in Computer Management Systems; this was a natural talent of hers. When Lily-Butterfly performed her life's purpose career in the healing arts career of Creating Sacred Space & Organizing Home Services, Holly worked with her as an apprentice practitioner, when she was not in school and away at sleep away camp. During the times Holly was working with Lily-Butterfly as an apprentice she naturally and subliminally learned the healing arts her mother was performing. Holly also assisted Lily-Butterfly in the creation of her first healing arts practice center office. Over time, Holly naturally awakened her spirit and soul talents as well. Holly worked in a main stream computer career as well as Lily-Butterfly's Administrative Assistant. Holly also became an assistant facilitator for many healing arts events at the healing arts center. In 2012 Holly became certified by Lily-Butterfly in the art of teaching the healing arts practice of Universal Life Force Energy; and performing the hands-on healing treatments. In Holly's late twenties she chose to make her full time chosen destiny and life's purpose career in the Holistic Health Care Healing Arts using her spirit, soul, heart, talents, and trained healing arts. In 2015 Holly created her own healing arts practice assisting humans on a spiritual path. Holly is very talented and passionate in performing her chosen destiny life's purpose healing arts career practice. To date Holly remains passionately dedicated to assisting other humans who choose to be on a spiritual path, and improving their spirit, mind, emotions, body, well-being and life. Lily-Butterfly perceives from experiences and guidance in dreams and vision that Holly was one of her guardian angels born as a human to assist her with her life's purpose journey and creation. In exchange in many ways Lily-Butterfly ended up being Holly's spirit guide, teacher of the ancient pathways, and assistance in creating her chosen destiny and life's purpose career practice. Currently in 2020 Holly is single and has no children. Holly still has the blue map on the left side of her head, close to the crown of her head.

Mr. Theo remained Lily-Butterfly constant companion and spiritual intimate partner until 2005. As the years went by the marriage evolved and the relationship blossomed and remained a complete partnership to the end. Unbeknownst to Lily-Butterfly she got pregnant in one of her cut and tied fallopian tubes for Theo in 1999. Even with permanent sterilization and her tubes tied, she became pregnant in one of her tied tubes. The baby grew and the tube ruptured, the fetus fell into the stomach and Lily-Butterfly was hemorrhaging very much. This was a life threatening situation. She went to her Gynecologist Doctor and the reason was the hemorrhaging was discovered. In addition to performing surgery to fix the issue of the ectopic pregnancy and rupture, the Doctor after consulting with Lily-Butterfly decided to completely remove the fallopian tubes to prevent the same thing happening again. This was the only negative thing that happened during the marriage. Theo and Lily-Butterfly were both happy, content, and successful. Lily-Butterfly often wondered what could happen to end the marriage like the trumpet dream oracle guardian angel had predicted, in chapter seventy nine.

In 2005 Theo's father became very ill. Theo's mother wrote to him and asked him to come back to visit his father before he died. This incident reminded Lily-Butterfly of the time when Manana Leila was going to die. She encouraged Theo to go see his father, and mother at this time when they needed him the most. Theo agreed to go and wrote back to his mother to tell her he was on his way to Greece. After Theo arrived back home to see his father, five days later Theo's father died. Theo's father had asked him on his death bed to return permanently to Greece to operate the family's restaurant, and continue the legacy of his ancestors. Theo agreed out of duty as the first child and a son. He also realized that his destiny and life's purpose career had found him on the path he took to avoid it.

Theo returned to Lily-Butterfly to talk to her about making a decision. Theo invited Lily-Butterfly to take Holly and move to Greece with him. She told him that she could not come with him, because where she was performing her life's purpose career practice, was where she needed to be based on her chosen destiny and the Creator's will. Lily-Butterfly gave Theo unwavering support like he did for her regarding her life's purpose career. She encouraged him to fulfill his promise to his dead father. Talking to Lily-Butterfly to work through making the best decision, Theo came to realize that his focus was running away from his spirit and soul's destiny. While Lily-Butterfly's focus was working towards discovering her chosen spirit and soul destiny and life's purpose. Theo told Lily-Butterfly that the most valuable lessons he learned from Lily-Butterfly was to honor, respect, choose, and face his destiny, spirit, and soul's purpose; and that once you love someone unconditionally no matter what happens there will be no loss; or loser.

With these valuable lessons in his awareness and mindfulness Theo sadly returned to Greece without Lily-Butterfly. With heavy hearts they separated; and got a divorce over two years later in 2008. Taking into consideration the story of the first engagement ring Theo gave to Lily-Butterfly; he had created the tradition of giving Lily-Butterfly a beautiful new ring every wedding anniversary date. At the end of the relationship and marriage Lily-Butterfly had a total of eight gold and diamond rings from Theo. To dilute the very strong bond between Theo and herself she sold all the rings, and invested the money into the healing arts center. Another yearly tradition of Theo, that Lily-Butterfly loved and liked was every year on Valentine's Day, Theo would buy her twelve very large and beautiful strawberries covered in dark chocolate. To this day every Valentine's Day Lily-Butterfly remembers this sincere passionate act of gift giving from Theo. Plus, there were other numerous positive acts and enjoyable collection of past memories from Theo that Lily-Butterfly often thinks about. Theo's physical presence was in Greece; but never forgotten by Lily-Butterfly's spirit, soul, and heart. And

Lily-Butterfly's physical presence in the United States of America was never forgotten by Theo.

Theo returned to Greece with lots of experience to operate the family restaurant as his life's purpose; and with great success. Theo choose the moon to represent the mirror image of his first personal unconditional love and dream lover Lily-Butterfly. Every night he would look for the moon in the sky and send his never dying love in prayers and blessings to Lily-Butterfly. In 2011 Theo met a woman in his home town and choose to marry her. They remained married for the rest of his life. During their marriage and relationship, they had three children; one boy and two girls.

Lily-Butterfly often ask herself this question.
"After such a man as Theo could there be another man like him on this planet for me?"
Lily-Butterfly would reply, "maybe and maybe not. So far I have not found another; and another have not found me."

After Theo left and returned to Greece and even at sixty three years old December 27, 2020 Lily-Butterfly remained single, and lives alone without a spiritual intimate partner and companion. She remains passionate, dedicated, content, joyful, at peace, and completely committed to fulfilling her chosen destiny and life's purpose career practice. Within her she carries the pleasant, content, and enjoyable unconditional love memories of her life's experiences with Theo.

Like the sun and the moon circulates and evolve each day the unconditional love, and sacred prayer from Theo to Lily-Butterfly; and from Lily-Butterfly to Theo infinitely continues. A love like this never dies; but is sprinkled out into the Universe like star dust, to nourish those who choose unconditional love.

Amin – Amin – Amin.
Thank You

Thank you to Pia G. Pessoa for the line editing of this manuscript.

Thank you everyone for: - journeying with Lily-Butterfly as she awakens to her spirit, soul, talents, destiny, and life's purpose. Human life, living experiences, talents, love, destiny, and life's purpose, is available for everyone. The truth is a big responsibility; therefore, most people run and hide from it. A person can have many faces and masks. The shadow side of a person can even stay hidden from the person. Every person has a right to what they want to believe. As a part of growing and awakening, people sometimes must leave their comfort zone in people, places, and things. There are infinite, perception, intention, and sides to everything.

Amin.

Reminder take from this story what you like, want, and need. Leave the rest undisturbed without judgement. Thank you.

D. O. Grant – 2020.

The Next Book Is

UNIVERSAL WELLNESS

A SHAMAN'S VIEW
By D. O. GRANT
Coming 2021

FICTION/Spiritual/Classic - This book gives information and awareness on the symbolic spiritual maps of the original ancient pathways of the Universal Healing System. When these healing improvement treatments are being performed they are always facilitated by the Divine Creator Source, and its Divine Guidance. Step by step and drop by drop in this book are sample stories which can give views on how this ancient system works. To get the views in the stories, each person should choose how they interpret and perceive the mysteries and situations in each story. This way this book can become each person's individual and personal journey.

Be aware that people's personal secrets are one of their major imbalances. Fear is the most major negative energy frequency of breaking down people, places, and things.

NOTICE FROM THE AUTHOR

The material contained in this book is **not** intended as medical or mental health advice. Please see a medical and mental health qualified professional for all medical and mental health issues, and illnesses.

This is a work of Fiction. Names, characters, places, and incidents either are the products of the author's imagination or are used fictitiously. Any resemblance to actual persons, living or dead, events, or locales is entirely coincidental.

All and every right reserved. Including the title LILY-BUTTERFLY – And The Path Of Life's Experiences; Parts One and Two. No part of this publication may be reproduced, stored in a retrieval system, or transmitted in any form or by any means, electronic, mechanical, photocopying, recording, verbally, or otherwise. All and every fictional imagination material contained in this book is the original work of the author. All and every fictional imagination material, words, content, fictional imagination suggested healing treatments written in this book are covered by the copyright law. All and every content and fictional imagination material contained in this book **cannot** be professionally or personally used in any lectures, workshops, classes, telephone conversation, in person conversation; **cannot** be created in all and every form, including scientifically, sold as treatments, taken and given to anyone. Absolutely no one and nothing from this book can be used or taken. **In addition,** if a person and or human, chooses to use anything from this book for personal or professional use, or for whatever reason, and in any form whatsoever, the author is **NOT** responsible or liable for the persons' experience or outcome. Absolutely and completely no exception(s).

Author Contact Information: - <u>dogrant108@gmail.com</u>

Thank you. D. O. Grant.
2020

Biography

D. O. Grant is the author of six books and two CDs. D. O. Grant started to write stories at nine years old as a treatment, to process thoughts, feelings, and emotions. The alphabet and the written English language were discovered by D. O. Grant between four and five years old in an environment where the language spoken was learned through oral tradition. D. O. Grant continued from nine years old to write and read with passion, and maybe out of habit. Along with the passion of being a traditional storyteller and author, D. O. Grant life's purpose career is practicing as a Grand Master Teacher and Practitioner of the positive Universal Life Force Energy Healing Arts, Metaphysician, Shaman, Healer, Positive Energy Environment Feng Shui Consultant, Holistic Life Coach Consultant, Birth Doula, and nondenominational Ordained Minister of the Divine Creator's Ministry. She currently lives on one of the Hawaiian Islands.

CPSIA information can be obtained
at www.ICGtesting.com
Printed in the USA
BVHW081230060720
583060BV00001B/2

9 781982 249946